LOST COLONY

A MARTIAN ADVENTURE

by

Michael McMurtrie

Copyright © 1998
Mike McMurtrie

ISBN: 0-9662885-0-5

Merc Frontiers
Hagerstown, MD 21742

Printed in the USA by

3212 East Highway 30 • Kearney, NE 68847 • 1-800-650-7888

Dedicated to my parents, Doris and John, whose unwavering faith in God and devotion to family and friends has been an inspiration to every life they've touched.

"We have the power to begin the world again. A situation similar to the present has not happened since the days of Noah until now. The birth of a new world is at hand."

Thomas Payne
1775

CHAPTER

1

The long, cylindrical leviathan of wire and steel rambled warily over the rock strewn confines of the barren, rust-colored vista. It's deep blue shell, tainted by the weathering effects of wind and dust, still proudly displayed the stars and stripes insignia on each of its massive flanks. Three pairs of wire mesh wheels, each standing six feet in diameter with a four foot width, crunched along the frozen ground towards the northwest as it skirted the rim of one of the many long, narrow, steep-walled canyons that transverses the high-latitude plain of Acidalia Planitia. The wide, squared nose of the beast hovered over the front pair of wheels, receding upward to join large, slanting panels of heavily tinted glass that enclosed much of the forward compartment. Large oval windows with similar protective coating dotted the forty foot long frame. A jet black communications dish sat directly on the center of the flat roof and embedded to its rear was a rotating set of black and silver solar panels. As broad as a two lane highway, this rover was designed to transport a very small party over rough terrain and to provide all necessary life-support for prolonged periods of time. Except for the two-man, short range exploratory rover, this excursion model was the runt of the litter.

Within its protective walls, two explorers sat in awe, gazing out over the red-hued panorama and the strange pinkish skyline that characterized the planet Mars. Well into the morning of their journey's fifth day, the two scientists had recently passed well east of the Marotis and Tempe fossaes and Perepelkin crater and were approaching the great lava plain of Vastitas Borealis. Within the next three days of their northern latitude trek, the men expected to reach the edge of the seasonal polar cap and the coordinates of those unusual electromagnetic and thermal energy readings that the colony instruments had been detecting.

Lee Imamura briefly rose from his seat, rubbing his backside gingerly. "I feel like I've been in a saddle for a week. I'm going to suggest to A and C that they build us an airport out here."

John Osborne snickered as Lee settled back down into the heavily padded chair. "Now, I had always thought of you as one of the last great explorers. Except for the initial survey teams, no one has ventured up this way in the thirty-one years that man has been on this planet."

"Yeah," Lee replied wryly. "Everyone finds Valles Marineris and the Tharsis Bulge much more interesting."

"You mean profitable," John corrected. "With all that ore and precious metals we're mining and those damnable shipping quotas that the NSCA is imposing on us, who has time for a trip to the polar wastelands."

Lee shifted his body weight in the seat, turning towards the driver with a twinkle in his eye. "You know, John, if we could discover a way to harvest water from a fraction of all that ice up there, it would be more valuable than all the minerals we've mined so far."

John nodded emphatically. "We can barely extract enough water now from the permafrost and the air to sustain the colony. It's imperative that we find more water resources before we can expand or even contemplate terraforming some day."

"Speaking of valuable resources," continued Lee with renewed vigor. "What have you heard about the gold deposit discovered by that geological team in Coprates Chasm?"

"Well, a friend of mine with one of the mineral extraction teams said that it could be the richest vein yet discovered."

"If they can get at it," replied Lee dubiously. "That's pretty rough terrain to get in equipment and supplies ."

"And I'll bet you a week's credits that the NSCA is already planning our production quotas and shipping schedules," John added disgustingly. "It just pisses me off that the government, an Earth government, tells us what and how much to ship without so much as one single representative on any governing body."

Lee reached out to place a gentle hand on the shoulder of his comrade. "I know, John. A lot of us are frustrated over the control that Earth imposes on us. But you do realize that it took a lot of government, corporate, and financial market sponsors to get this project off the ground. They have a right to expect a return."

"And we're producing one," John irritably interrupted. "If they would only let us run our own affairs, we could be even more productive. Their financing got us established, but it is our labor and our risk that sustain the colony. I sometimes feel more like an indentured servant than an equal partner."

Lee turned away, staring longingly out the window at the reddish alien landscape. "What does David Hart say about the situation?"

"Dave is as upset over this predicament as anyone. He's been pressing the NSCA for two years to gain us representation on the Governing Council, or so he tells me. But as colony Chief Administrator, he has to remain somewhat diplomatic. I understand that he is already in hot water after insisting that hearings be held on the taxation issue."

A smirk crossed over Lee's face as he shook his head in exasperation. "If he's not careful, a squad of space marines is going to arrive and toss his rebellious butt onto the next transport to Earth."

John's eyes turned from the fretted terrain ahead. "His butt won't be the only one, my friend."

The rover rambled deliberately beyond the fossae, crunching under its weight the many diminutive stones in its path and scrupulously skirting the larger ones. Checker board indentations embedded in the sandy, fine-grained, russet soil in the wake of the immense mesh wheels. The knobby terrain ahead had a distinct mottled appearance, caused by the sharp contrast in albedo between the ejecta around craters, the bright remains of old cratered country, and the much darker surrounding plains. It was studded with steep, oval pits 90 to 150 feet deep and some approaching nearly a mile in diameter.

"Alases," Lee commented as John deftly maneuvered the rover around the rim of one of these great holes. "I've never seen them this big before. They are so much larger than our terran counterparts. It's a definite indication of permafrost. Seasonal freezing and thawing could cause the soil to sink like this."

"Yes, Lee, this place is a geologists dream."

I wonder what we'll find up there." Lee speculated as he twisted to face John, his hands moving aimlessly in conjunction with his mouth. "Maybe it could be some kind of volcanic activity, or the venting of expanding gases from a shallow magma chamber."

"There is no evidence of any volcanoes anywhere near that region," John replied, shaking his head in contention. "In fact, there has never been any sign of any active volcanoes or any plate tectonics for that matter since man has been studying Mars."

Lee looked out over the frozen panorama ahead. "It's probably just some natural phenomenon that we don't yet understand."

"The thing that I find curious," John added, "is how steady and regular those energy indicators were. Almost too regular to be from natural generation. Ah! I wouldn't be surprised if we can't find a thing. This could be just a wild...." John abruptly pushed the large break button on the left side of the padded steering wheel, bringing their massive transport to a rolling stop. "What the devil!"

The rover had just reached the pinnacle of a gentle rise, allowing the two men a clear view of the ridge line to the north. Near its summit the reddish-brown mottling of the plains gave way to a deep bluish-green or black umbrella of something that covered the entire horizon. Even with the light of the midday sun beaming down on the ridge ahead, the color and composition was undetectable. John and Lee rose in unison, pressing against the forward window as they silently stared in awe at the spectacle before them.

"It's like a dark carpet of something that was spread across the crest," Lee observed.

"Yes, but a carpet of what? Lee, hit the magnifier."

Lee pressed a button on the central control console and immediately the view from the forward window panels doubled in size.

"Enlarge to four power," John requested.

The two men lurched backward, startled at the enhanced image. Slowly Lee turned to his companion, hesitant to look away from the scene. "I thought this was supposed to be a dead planet."

"It looks as if something is growing out there," John exclaimed, his eyes focused attentively on the image. "That's impossible!"

"Well, come on," Lee cried out excitedly. "Let's get over there."

"Okay! Okay! But first get on the transmitter. This we've got to phone in."

The brilliant rays of the receding sun glistened off the surface of the choppy blue water as Caroline Hart leaned against the railing of the oak deck of her country abode that sat on a wooded knoll overlooking Bogue Sound in Carteret County, North Carolina. She basked in the soothing sensations of the sizzling beams that permeated her back as the yellow-orange orb fell towards the tree line to the west. The aroma of the sea saturated the air and a refreshingly cool early autumn breeze off the Atlantic brushed against her face. Strands of curly, brunette hair flew about unfettered in the draft. She would have to groom herself once more before his call came through. Yes, this was a much more pleasant environment than the three months that she had recently spent with a project team on the frozen tundra of Antarctica testing various strands of cold-resistant algae. After another six to nine months of stateside research in a cooperative effort between East Carolina University and Biotechnology's, Inc., she could finally devote some thought to the possibilities of joining him on that alien world. Her musings were constantly interrupted by the tumultuous crash of the ocean against the shoreline, the churning and racing motor of a passing recreational speedboat as it skipped and pounded against the water below her, or the occasional squeaking of a flock of seagulls as they flew overhead or puttered along the waterline on their tiny twig-like legs and webbed feet, pecking at the wet sand for specks of nourishment. It would be difficult to leave this place....this planet.

Memories of their togetherness flooded her mind. Perceptions so sharp as if they had been frozen in time. Images of that first kiss, of moonlit walks along the beach, Pirate tailgate parties, that glorious weekend in the Smokies. But he was now far away, very far away, and she longed for his company, his touch. She had seen him for only four weeks in the past two-and-a-half years, ever since he had accepted the position of Chief Administrator of Jamestown, the first and only permanent human colony on the planet Mars, aptly named after its earlier North American counterpart. He had wanted her to join him from the start, relentlessly begging her throughout the first year to jump aboard the next transport, finally resigning to her misgivings. She wanted to finish her research and perhaps, the fruits of her labor would benefit the colony. Her family was here, her friends. Everything she knew and loved was on this tiny blue world....except for her husband. And she was afraid. David Hart was a pioneer, an adventurer, and Caroline's mind constantly recalled that old western saying 'the pioneers were the ones that took the arrows.' There were many dangerous arrows on

Mars. But he was determined to start a new life on that barren, red planet, and she desperately wanted to be with him, not live apart like this. Despite her fears, she decided, she was going to risk all. She would complete the cooperative assignment with the University and take the accumulative research to the frozen planet where she would finally reunite with the man she loved and use her bioengineering skills to serve the colony. She also wanted to start a family.

The maternal instinct was strong in Caroline, and at age 32, she wasn't getting any younger. They had discussed their desire for children in the past, but Dave's most recent assignment postponed indefinitely any further deliberation on the subject. Conflicting and disturbing thoughts of desires and reason engulfed her head. Would he want the momentous responsibility of raising a child beyond the protective confines of the Earth? What kind of life could they provide for their offspring in such a desolate, unyielding place? A place without green grass, flowering meadows, the rustling of a tree in the wind, the fragrance of pine and honeysuckle. A place where a child cannot run outside to play without an environment suit. Where a simple tear in the protective clothing could mean a quick, agonizing death. To be human, but born and raised on a world inhospitable to man. Growing up in an environment so far removed from that of your ancestors, away from the geology and the geography, the biology and the history that every other human being experienced daily since the dawn of civilization. How would it be? Would that child be accepted back on Earth, be able to assimilate into this world's society and culture? Would he or she still be considered part of mankind? Caroline cringed from the ache pounding at her forehead brought about by the heavy mental burdens deluging her. She turned to walk inside. She was jumping ahead of herself. There were many more immediate concerns. But Caroline Hart was a woman of many passions. It wasn't until she strutted over to her mahogany dresser that she realized just how much time had elapsed. Dave's call was late. Curious, she thought, last week's call was also nearly a half-hour late. His calls were historically very punctual. This time she was grateful for the delay. It would give her a chance to put herself back together. Standing in front of a full-length mirror with brush and curler, Caroline fashioned her thick, shoulder length, wavy, dark brown hair into perfect symmetry, every strand neatly patted down, curling smartly inward about her shoulders, insuring its conformity with a generous amount of spray conditioner. Her face was clean and flush, her lipstick and eye shadow frugally applied, just enough to accentuate her sensuous, pouting lips and deep, hazel eyes. She reached for a bottle of perfume before realizing that he wouldn't be able to smell her. She snickered - silly girl. Caroline straightened in front of the mirror, pressing down the sides of her dress with her hands. She had chosen the tight red, satin one that her husband had liked so well, the one that clung firmly to her curves and with a plunging neckline that highlighted the cleavage of her ample breasts. It pleased her to discover that it still fit so well after nearly three years in the closet. proud that she was still able to maintain a trim physique to her five-foot-seven frame. She was still by all accounts an attractive woman, but time was slipping by without her man, a fact made depressingly manifest each evening she retired to an empty bed. Opportunities for an affair occasionally presented themselves in her husband's absence, but Caroline graciously deflected each mating attempt, even a strangely intriguing one from a woman, remaining faithful throughout to her David. But it was difficult. She absorbed herself in her work, read mystery novels, and took trips to area art exhibitions after developing an appreciation for abstract expressionism and impressionistic paintings, especially the revered works of Jackson Pollock and Claude Monet. But at the moment, her life felt terribly unfulfilled.

Satisfied with her appearance, Caroline walked into the spacious family room inundated with the sweet aroma of flowering life, every nook and cranny embellished with dangling. dense, vibrant green foliage or colorful blossoming planters. She stood by the rectangular, black and silver, metal and Formica table on which the vidphone and a computer console were placed, gazing out through the grand picture window at the darkening wooded slope and green valley below as the shadows from the setting sun slowly inched across. Within a few minutes the silence was interrupted by a soft, intermittent beeping sound emanating from speakers mounted on the sides of the vidphone monitor, followed by a sweet, feminine, computerized voice announcing .... "Call waiting for Caroline. Call waiting for Caroline. From Mister David Hart."

Caroline excitedly jumped into the cushioned, rolling swivel chair sitting in front of the vidphone screen. Her hand reached for the gray, square control pad that extended from the base of the monitor and eagerly pressed the large, circular green button that allowed the machine to receive voice input. "Accept!" In a flash, the dark oval screen encased in a light gray shell brightened and the face and chest of David Hart, her husband of six years, radiated into the room.

Hi, Dave!" she exclaimed as waves of unbridled joy swept across her face. "It is so good to see you. I miss you so much."

"How are you, dear?" came his brief time delayed reply, courtesy of a series of newly developed ERW (Enhanced Radio Wave) communication beacons interspersed throughout the inner solar system that increased the speed of transmissions more than tenfold. "You're looking as ravishing as ever."

A huge smile crossed her moistened lips as she stared at the tiny camera eye situated in the middle of the shell below the view screen, its red activation light burning brightly. "Do you remember this dress?" Caroline rose to her feet and provocatively posed in front of the camera. "It still fits."

'You're still a stunner," Dave studiously observed as Caroline settled back in her seat, intentionally leaning forward to afford him the best possible advantage of her deep bodice.

"I was beginning to worry. Your calls are seldom late."

"I'm sorry," Dave apologized with a grimace as he rubbed his forehead. "I've been distracted. Just one problem after another out here."

Caroline began to notice certain things as they engaged in small talk. He was sitting on a padded chair in the dimly lit, spacially challenged living room of his private quarters by the desk from where he had always talked to her from, bit there seemed to be an absence of things in the background. His room always seemed to be cluttered in the distance. Maybe he had finally cleaned it up, she imagined. Ten years her senior, David's closely cropped hair was turning gray around the ears, his normally rugged but clean shaven face now showing the wrinkles and darkened eyes of age or stress, the facial grizzle of irregular maintenance. Life on Mars was tough enough without the weight of administration hanging around one's neck. He really needed her now, she thought, and she wasn't there! At least he was wearing that purple and yellow East Carolina University T-shirt that she had recently sent him. But his voice was somber, his expressions melancholic, not the cavalier, giddy Dave that she knew.

"Did you enjoy those Pirate football disks I sent you?"

His eyes brightened momentarily and a slight grin cracked from his mouth. "Yeah! I can't believe that they finally beat North Carolina after twenty-two years. Thanks, honey, it brings back memories of...." Dave paused in reflection. "....well, of those football weekends during our early years."

"What's the matter, Dave?" Caroline asked with concern. "You don't seem yourself. Are you fighting with the NSCA again?"

She could see the frustration burning on his face.

"I will never understand the mentality of a government bureaucrat," he clamored. "They're like leeches, sucking us dry. Every time that we discover a new vein of mineral ore or precious metals, the NSCA increases our quotas. Oh, they let us keep enough to maintain the colony, but not enough to enable us to grow and prosper. I didn't come here to be the manager of an elaborate resource production factory for Earth. I came here to carve out a new beginning on this desolate ice and rock. There's a lot of grumbling among the people here. Jamestown was to be an autonomous colony, not a territorial possession. I'm afraid we'll never shake this yoke until we are completely self-sufficient."

"How long do you think that will be, Dave? How much can the colony grow without a larger source of water?"

"Water is critical, Caroline, you are right. But that is just one of the many obstacles confronting us. An even bigger one is the NSCA."

"What do you mean, honey?"

"In order to be self-reliant, we have to be able to survive on limited imports. We now have the capability and personnel to produce metals, plastics, paper, cement, glass, and our agronomists are providing more than enough food. What we lack is electronic circuitry and microprocessor production capability. High-tech stuff."

"Surely there are manufacturers and people with those skills who would want to go to Mars," Caroline surmised.

"But the NSCA controls immigration," a perplexed David replied as he restlessly squirmed in his chair. "And despite my requests, they claim that sustenance and mineral production concerns have top priority. They insist on a policy of controlled growth. Controlled is right!"

"Come on, Dave. I'm sure that they have the interests of Jamestown at heart. Maybe it would be wise to go slow on this."

"But that should be our decision, the permanent inhabitants of this colony," Dave bellowed as he leaned forward. "Not theirs."

Caroline could see the anguish in his haunting, dark eyes.

"Caroline," he continued in a suddenly soft, placid tone. "I don't think that they will ever allow us complete autonomy. Keep us dependent on those bimonthly supply shipments. Keep us subject to their designs."

"I know how important this is to you, my love," Caroline compassionately responded as she stared longingly into those deep, brown eyes. "Give it some time. Permanent settlers have been there for only fourteen years. It took over fifteen years for construction engineers to build Jamestown before colonization began. Rome wasn't built in a day, you know."

Dave broke a wry smile. "Now I know why my predecessor cracked up and took a slow boat home."

"Last month you were telling me about your efforts to get the NSCA to conduct hearings on granting the colony representation on the governing council, if not Congress itself." Caroline continued. "Have you heard anything?"

Dave leaned back against the thick black padding of his chair, his hands wearily rubbing his eyes. "Not a peep on the subject." His hands flung down to relax against the armrests. "Frankly, I'd rather have them screaming hell." After a momentary pause, his body abruptly lurched forward to the edge of the seat. "But this taxation issue gives me the red ass!" he roared with rasping voice. "Everyone is up in arms. How can the government levy a flat-rate tax on people living on Mars! We get no benefit from federal funding, no entitlements, no social programs. The investment capital needed to get this project started is being returned with our mineral shipments and research grants. We provide for our own insurance, our own security."

"The government still provides a defense force, the space marines," Caroline pointed out. "They certainly proved valuable during the Lunar Conflict. And it's the government who contracts with private carriers to provide shipping and transport spaceships to and from the colony. And most of you are still United States citizens."

"Yes, yes, I know. But we transportation costs for imported goods and I would rather pay a surcharge on those to pay our share of the space defense costs. Shit! We have to tax ourselves to pay for common services. I think a war was once fought over taxation without representation."

"I sympathize with your feelings, Dave. Having no representation stinks." Caroline straightened as she recalled a sobering thought. "Speaking of space marines, I have some potentially disturbing news for you. There is some talk that a marine detachment may be garrisoned at Jamestown."

Caroline could see Dave's handsome but weary features turn beet red. "I've heard that rumor, but nobody ever asked me!" His hands flew up in exasperation. "We have our own security force. What do we need federal troops for? We're the only people here." His fingers feverishly worked in the air as he spoke. "I'll tell you one thing. The day that federal soldiers land here without our invitation or permission is the day we revolt."

A fleeting smirked escaped from Caroline's lips. "Oh, Dave! Don't let the NSCA here you talking like that. They'll start calling you George Washington."

Finally, Dave was overcome with a genuine snicker of amusement. "Oh, I'm sure they're already calling me many things, but that isn't one of them."

The shared chuckle came as a great relief to Caroline, if for only a special moment, as she fought a foreboding feeling that she was losing her husband to events bigger than the two of them. "I think I get the political picture," she continued, obviously anxious to change the subject. "So, tell me about the colony. Anything interesting been happening?"

Dave slothfully slumped deep into his chair, hands clenched together, shaking his lowered head dejectedly. "You've heard of Murphy's Law? Well, on Mars we're going to start calling it Hart's Law."

Caroline pressed forward with concern. "What's going on?"

With surprising serenity, Dave looked up and with lightning alacrity, began to recite the checklist. "I have a missing survey team, our communications have been on the blink, we're getting peppered with meteorite showers, we lost a rover and a digger trying to get equipment into Coprates Chasm, our solar panels are constantly saturated with blowing dust and the scrubbers can't...."

"Hold on, Dave," Caroline energetically interrupted. "Hold on. You're rambling so fast that I can't understand you. One thing at a time. What about a missing survey team?"

Dave took a deep breath and robustly exhaled before raising his eyes to gaze at the image of his wife. "I sent John Osborne and Lee Imamura to investigate those strange seismic and thermal anomalies our instruments were detecting somewhere north of sixty degrees latitude. Damnedest geological aberrations I ever saw on this planet. They were on the great lava plain of Vastitas Borealis at our last contact. That was six days ago."

Caroline shook her head, frowning in despair.

"We sent out a search and rescue team," Dave unemotionally continued. "But it will be several days before they reach the area. It may be nothing, a broken transmitter, perhaps. We'll just have to wait it out."

Dave's perfunctory demeanor completely puzzled Caroline, especially when it involved the fate of a friend. He was a very emphatic man when it came to the welfare of a colleague, and John was one of his closest friends. A few accidental deaths were expected at any extraterrestrial colony, but nobody had ever simply disappeared. She was gravely troubled that the pressure could be affecting him.

"Our communications with Earth have been experiencing sporadic interruptions," he casually resumed. "I wasn't even sure if this call would get through. Our technicians think it may be some faulty modules in the communications tower, but we won't have any replacement parts until the next supply ship arrives in six weeks. On top of that, Lunae Planum has been getting hit with scattered meteor showers. Most never reach the ground, but a few larger pieces have struck nearby."

"Good grief, Dave!" Caroline exclaimed in exasperation. "Is Jamestown in any danger?"

"Who can say," came his insouciant reply with a shrug of his broad shoulders. "I don't think so, unless a large fragment strikes near a dome or access tunnel. Just another day at the office."

The sudden mood swings of her husband became readily apparent to Caroline. She vacuously stared into the screen as a million disquieting, incongruous thoughts raced through her mind. Could the enormous challenges of survival on that distant world so ossify the emotions of one so fervent towards the ever present dangers threatening his very existence? Why does he become so animated over political concerns, yet sedate over the problems of life? He was always so full of energy and vigor. Could Mars be changing him that much? And if so, was he still the same man that she so dearly adored? Would he still feel the same passion for her after so much time apart?

"Caroline," a gentle but masculine voice shook her out of her stupor. "Caroline, where were you?"

"Oh, I'm sorry," she replied, shaking her head from side to side. "I just wandered off, thinking about what you said." Her eyes intensely refocused on the image beaming from her monitor as her voice became more vigorous. "I'm worried about you, Dave."

"Ah, I'll be all right," he remarked offhandedly as he shifted his weight on the seat. "On a happier note, Sam and Patricia Falanga had a baby girl. You remember, the entrepreneurs I told you about who came here and opened a clothing shop. That makes sixteen births in the last two years. Soon we're going to be needing a high school. That brings our resident population to three hundred and eighty-seven. I wonder if the NSCA will try to control that too!"

Caroline's facial disposition brightened considerably as she pondered the possibilities. "You know, honey," she said in as soft and feminine tone as she could muster, batting her eyelashes enchantingly. "When I join you, we should think about having a child of our own."

Dave grew noticeably uneasy at the thought, his body moving restlessly as he paused in reflection. "I....I don't know. With everything that's going on....who knows what the future holds."

"Men and women have been facing that unknown since time began," Caroline delicately countered.

"But not on Mars!" His fidgety hands and fingers shifted from lap to armrest and back again. "I mean, what kind of life could we provide out here? It may be all right for some, but I'm not sure that I would want to raise a family off the Earth."

"Okay, Dave," Caroline replied with obvious disappointment. "Please, just give it some thought."

Dave solemnly nodded.

"I'd really like to be a mother," she continued with a voice choked in emotion. "Remember, I'm not getting any younger, and by the way, neither are you."

A peculiar hush filled each room, interrupted only by the irregular crackling of the transmission caused by disturbances in the Earth's atmosphere. Slowly David Hart leaned forward, his face engrossing most of Caroline's monitor, his dark brown eyes piercing through her very essence.

"Caroline, I must be honest with you." His deportment was serene, his tone disclosing a tender fervor. "It has been very difficult for me these last two years without you. I needed you to share in the trials and tribulations; to confide in and gain comfort in your arms; for you to help me build this colony, this life." His speech became broken as he struggled to express his pent-up emotions. "I don't know....what the future cards will deal us...., but whatever....happens, I'll always remember the joy....and love....that we shared....together." His head drooped as he leaned back in the padded chair, rubbing his eyes with the forefinger and thumb of his right hand.

Caroline's body trembled, her stomach churning in anxiety in response to the release of suppressed intense feelings of guilt that shook her very soul. She had perfectly rationalized every decision, every procrastination, but had completely quelled the affect that her absence might have on her husband, and her marriage. Now those influences were becoming apparent, and she couldn't control the inauspicious premonition that the man she loved was starting to fade away. Moisture welled-up in her eyes as she frantically clasped both sides of the monitor, pressing herself forward against the screen. "I am so sorry, Dave!" she cried out in despair. "I'll be there in a few months, I promise you. I know I should have been there for you. I'll wrap-up my research, sell the house, and join you as soon as I can. I want you so much." You can speak to the NSCA about expediting my immigration papers." Her half-hearted attempt at a giggle and a smile failed miserably. She bit her lower lip as she wiped away a wayward tear from her rosy cheek. "Everything will work out, I swear it will." Caroline's voice turned more soft and sensuous as she wiggled her shoulders suggestively. "Honey, I'm dying to feel your caress again."

Dave seemed strangely unaffected, avoiding direct eye contact as he soberly responded. "You may be too late. So much has happened over the past two years."

"To late for what, honey? I don't understand. We can still...."

"You're right," interrupted Dave. "You don't understand, how could you? This is a cold, desolate place, untouched by man. We're trying to create something new and vibrant out of this rock in space. A new beginning. I'm just afraid, Caroline, that by the time you get here, wherever I go, you may not be able to follow." His eyes lifted and longingly gazed at her delicate features, sighing in resignation. "If only you had been...."

Suddenly the screen went pitch black in emptiness, not even the snapping sound of atmospheric interference to break the silence.

"Dave! Answer me, Dave!" Caroline vainly screamed into the terminal, her fingers frenetically manipulating the control pad to no avail, finally pressing the voice input button. "Reestablish link, last call."

The few seconds of stillness seemed like an eternity.

"Unable to comply," announced the vidphone's refined, automated voice. Communications interrupted. Communications interrupted."

"Locate source of interruption," Caroline fretfully commanded, barely maintaining some semblance of composure.

"Communications interrupted transmission point."

"Please, I've got to talk to him!" she harrowingly shouted aloud. After a few moments thought, Caroline pressed the input button once more. "Establish link, interplanetary call. Instant link number zero-zero-one. Caller ID Caroline Hart for David Hart."

"Unable to comply. Martian link terminated. Martian link terminated."

"No!!!!" she screamed, pounding the table with her fists. Tears streamed down her cheeks as she glanced over at a framed picture of her husband and herself taken on their wedding day. Caroline turned back to the darkened screen, touching it firmly with both hands where the image of her husband had once been displayed. "Dave!" she wailed in anguish as moisture dripped down the deep neckline of her red satin dress. "Oh, my Dave!" Caroline broke down in turbulent contortions where she sat, crying incessantly as she came to a sudden realization. She had never told her husband just how much she loved him.

CHAPTER

2

The colossal wheels of cream and silver spun serenely above the dreary, gray, freckled world below. Connected to a broad cylinder that stretched 600 feet in length, the entire assembly rotated around a central axis, providing the work and living space with the simulated effects of gravity for the hundreds of inhabitants and visitors. Maintaining a geostationary orbit 575 miles above the southern tip of the Sea of Tranquillity, space station Constitution became operational fourteen years after the United States established a permanent colony on the Moon in the year 2022. Each of its massive disks, measuring 410 feet in diameter, were attached to the central spoke at four equal distant points by 40 foot long access channels. The central disk served as the primary residential, business, and administration area. The function of the wheel attached to the end of the cylinder, whose attitude was away from the Moon, was exclusively for docking, warehousing, and transportation of people and cargo. Because of the enormous demands placed on the services of the station over the succeeding 25 years, especially by the National Space Colony Administration, a third wheel was being built at the end of the cylinder closest to the surface, but only a third of its steel and titanium support structure was complete. Space construction engineers in environment suits and tether lines diligently worked on the project, supported by an army of small, crab-like robotics assembly vehicles. The station had become the center of activity for shuttling people and freight to the colony on the Sea of Serenity or to any of the numerous, remote research or mining camps. It had also become the principle staging area for missions throughout the solar system by government and private interests alike, surpassing its smaller, older, battle-scarred sibling, space station Freedom, still operational in Earth orbit.

Extending from the hull of Constitution Terminal, as the outer wheel was named, were four broad, 30-foot long gantries equipped with multiple docking collars designed to mate with most space vehicles in present service. Ships were locked to three of these docking ports; a freighter offloading supplies for the Plymouth colony below; a small military lunar transport; and an expansive interplanetary space cruiser contracted by the North American Space Agency, which interestingly enough carries the same acronym as its long disbanded predecessor, the National Aeronautics and Space Administration. The new generation NASA was a joint venture cooperative between hundreds of industrial and commercial interests and the governments of the United States, Canada, Mexico, Great Britain, France, and Brazil. The National Space Colony Administration was a major subsidiary and oversaw all affairs concerning the establishment and maintenance of all colonial projects amongst the NASA partners. The cruiser belonged to a fleet of craft owned and operated by Continental American Spaceships, Inc. from whom whose services NASA contracted. This Independence Class model was designed for long range transportation, exploratory missions, and deep space search and rescue operations. These ships were also pressed into service by the military during time of war, to be used as rapid deployment transports or auxiliary support craft, as was the case during the Lunar Conflict.

Within the protective walls of this massive, revolving disk, the docking port was bristling with activity. People were scurrying about like ants on a hill. Automated freight haulers. oversized golf carts with long trailer beds, followed their preprogrammed sensor trails embedded in the floor panels along the left walls. The procession of robotics transports and their platforms of crates grew by the minute as they trudged towards the shipping bay, slowed by the constant obstruction of humans darting in front of their path. Amidst this throng of energy briskly strolled a strikingly handsome yet inconspicuous man of average stature and medium build, carrying a black leather portfolio in his left hand; indiscernible except for his one-piece, zippered, navy blue flight suit with an American flag insignia on the upper right arm and a circular ship patch on the other, the uniform commonly worn by CAS crews. The sight of the uniform was natural enough aboard the Constitution, but this man seemingly drew the attention of all he passed. Waves and shouts of support and good fortune followed him towards Docking Bay 2, as if everyone knew what lay ahead for the Captain and crew of the CAS Guilford Courthouse. He politely acknowledged each well-wisher with a nod of his head or a slight upward flick of his right hand. He had just concluded a brief, private meeting with the Chief of Operations of the NSCA himself, who had come to the Constitution to personally present the mission briefing to the crew the day before. There had been no contact with Jamestown for seventeen days. They were going to Mars with a full compliment of support personnel and a cargo bay packed with supplies. He had been given details of intelligence reports accumulated in the weeks before the loss of communications, but so much was unknown. The mission was to reestablish contact with the colony, restore communications, render all aid and assistance that the colony may require, and to evaluate and rectify all other contingencies. That last instruction amused him, as seemingly all mission profiles ended with that generalized ambiguity. Translation - find it and fix it!

The docking bay was now devoid of freight, all of which had been loaded hours before. Supplies and equipment were now being drawn from ancillary storage sections of the great wheel. Matthew Maitland walked deliberately through the causeway of the docking port, pausing just outside the huge portal that led into the cargo hold of his spacecraft as a parade of mechanical haulers rolled by. As was his custom before entering his ship on the dawn of a new mission, Matt reverently lowered his head and offered a brief prayer for the safe return of himself and his crew. Once inside he was amazed at the amount of wood and plastic containers in countless shapes and sizes that were neatly anchored in holding compartments throughout the spacious bay. Many more were collecting to the right side of the room as the robotics haulers delivered their loads to the predetermined location. Manned wide-wheeled machines with large lifts and clamps ferried these containers to their appropriate storage areas where they were secured by other workers. Sometimes old-fashioned human muscle performed subtle adjustments. A short, stocky, middle-aged Hispanic man stood in the middle of the floor, shouting instructions in all directions in a heavily accented, sonorous voice. Upon noticing the presence of the ship's master, his eyes brightened and a gleeful expression overwhelmed him as he rushed forward with extended hand.

"Captain Matt! Captain Matt! It's so good to see you."

"How are you, Jose," Matt replied as the two men clasped hands energetically. "Oh! For this mission the official title is Commander."

An even wider grin crossed the face of Jose Alvarez as he firmly grasped Matt's upper arm. "Yes, of course, of course. And very well deserved, my friend. Very well deserved."

"So, is the best Dock Manager in the solar system keeping this place in shape?" Matt chortled as they began to walk, placing a friendly arm around Jose's shoulder.

"I don't know about shape, but we keep it moving. I tell you something, Matt. I've never loaded so much tonnage on an outbound ship before. What's going on? We loaded food, medicine, science equipment, building materials, communications gear, electronic components, and who knows what else."

"Too many unknowns," Matt responded with a shrug of his shoulder. "They're just being expedient. We don't know what condition Jamestown may be in."

"In any event, we worked through the night to get your cargo stowed. We should be finished within the next two hours."

"Thanks, Jose. You've got good people."

"I don't want to disappoint my favorite Captain," Jose chuckled boisterously. "I enjoy having the Guilford Courthouse dock at my station. You are very kind to me and my workers. Your entire crew is, even that rambunctious Shoals. Most flight crews won't give us the time of day."

Matt paused and turned to face his friend. "This place couldn't function without the competency and energy of you and your staff and the whole fleet knows it."

With broad grins, the two men slapped each other on the back and continued their inspection of the storage compartments.

"You're hauling enough stuff to start your own colony," Jose observed.

"Don't tell me that," Matt replied with a snicker. "I may reach Mars and keep on going."

"No you don't. I expect to see you and the Courthouse back on my dock within the next two months."

"Good Lord willing," Matt nodded as he glanced down at his watch. "Well, my old friend, I'd best be getting up to C-and-C."

Jose abruptly grabbed Matt by the arm. "Matt, you be careful out there." The look of disconcerting fear was burning through his gaze. "This whole business gives me an uneasy feeling. Don't try to be a hero. My whole family will be praying for you."

"I appreciate that, old friend," Matt replied with a comforting pat to the arm. "Don't worry. I'll try to come back without messing up the job too badly."

Jose was emphatic. "Forget the job, Matt! Just come back."

The access passage from the cargo bay led into the long, hollow main cylinder that surrounded the heavy, forty foot diameter central axle which spun the great vessel while in space. The corridor ahead stretched 100 feet to near the bow of the ship and led to the Command and Control deck, but it was far from symmetric. Occupying the right third of the bottom half of the middle tube, the walkway's upper left ceiling curved inward, conforming to the circumference of the central spoke. Clearance to the far left was less than seven feet but quickly rose as the curvature of the ceiling bent upwards. The right wall, the outer shell of the craft, gradually warped inward from the ceiling until it joined the deck, effectively eliminating about a quarter of the potential walking space. Still, the hallway had about ten feet of passable lateral area. Not far from the cargo hold, the main cylinder passed through the heart of the great centrifuge, a massive disk that provided the living space and all the amenities for the passengers and crew. Located at this juncture along the right wall was the entrance to the steeply graded ramp that spiraled upward to connect to the bulky ring, a climb that seemed to the traveler to be nearly flat due to the clockwise rotation of the ship. As Matt passed by this opening, he became conscious of the unusual quiet and serenity that pervaded over his domain. That was sure to change, he whimsically thought. The walls were a soothing light beige, the ceiling constructed of thick, square panels of illuminated grids, drawing their power primarily from the solar panels deployed outside amidships. To his left he passed by a succession of thirty foot deep rooms of various widths. First was a science lab, followed by equipment storage, the medical bay, a lavatory, and the staff meeting room, until he came upon the captain's stateroom, near the head of the long passageway. He reached out with his free hand and passed it across the round, red electronic sensor embedded shoulder high into the wall to the right of the entrance. With the low, rumbling sound of mechanization, the door immediately swung open to the right, gliding along its grooved tracks into the frame of the wall itself. Matt briskly strode into the darkened room and instantly bumped into something solid but soft.

"Lights!" he hastily called out, jumping back in alarm.

As the voice activated environment system slowly brightened the room, Matt's eyes focused on the beautifully radiant face of his Flight Officer, equally startled from the sudden impact, her hand clutching her chest as she recovered from her yelp of fright.

"Sheri!" he exclaimed, regaining his composure. "What the hell are you doing in my office?"

"Shit! Matt, you scared me." Catching her breath, Sheri approached, reaching out to lightly touch both of his forearms, her infectious smile returning to her expression. "I'm sorry. I just came in to leave the mission staff personnel disks on your desk."

"That's fine, Sheri," Matt replied with a grin as he brushed by, patting her on the shoulder. "Thank you. I'll be up to C-and-C in a minute."

Sheri turned to leave but paused in front of the door, spinning towards Matt who had moved behind his diminutive metal desk. "It looks like we're transporting a full load. I think we'll need to double-up on some rooms."

"Well, Sheri, I guess you had better take care of it."

"I'm already on it. See you soon."

With a broad smirk, Sheri pivoted and walked through the doorway. Matt studied her petite figure closely as he took a seat on the rotating, cushioned chair. He loved her flowing, wavy black hair, how it draped lavishly over her shoulders and ended in thick curls along her upper back. She was short in stature, but trim and very well proportioned. He enjoyed the sight of her tiny, tight rear jostling seductively as she moved. The navy blue flight suit did little to hide her ample feminine charms. She always seemed to be wearing a uniform one size too small. She was considered pretty, certainly not a beauty queen, but she carried an aura of sensuality around her, at least as far as Matt was concerned. They were close friends, serving aboard the same ship for three years, and spent a lot of off duty time together. At age 34, she was just four years his junior. Yes, he was very attracted to Sheri Alderman. But he was the captain of the Guilford Courthouse, and she was his subordinate. A romantic entanglement could involve unimaginable problems concerning ship's operation and morale. A volatile situation. The conflicting sentiments tugged at Matt's soul, a situation made painfully evident by her obvious interest in him. Amorous thoughts of her inevitably led to memories of his failed marriage many years before and shook him back to reality. The pain of that betrayal ran deep, and he could never seem to develop a trust with another woman that would facilitate a serious relationship. He feared it.

Matt tossed aside his portfolio and loaded the mission staff reports into his desk computer. Accommodations were certainly going to be tight. The ship contained twenty living quarters, but eighteen mission staff personnel had been assigned to add to the normal operational crew of eight. Mission specialists included five engineers of various mechanical and systems disciplines, two doctors, two bioengineers, two geologists, two planetary science engineers, and one biologist, agronomist, chemist, astrophysicist, and a communications technician. A few of the names were familiar to Matt as he nearly always had a small science or technical staff assigned by NASA on board. He had rifled through several of the individual files before he noticed the presence of a small package sitting on the corner of his desk. It was neatly wrapped in garnet and gold metallic paper with matching bow and a card attached. It read:

> *"Here's to another successful mission together.*
> *I'm looking forward to your company.*
> *My room is always open for you.*
> *Love, Sheri."*

Matt was engulfed in a warm glow of contentment created by the persistent attention of his colleague. If only she were not his subordinate, he thought. He guessed the contents even before opening the package. She knew of his fondness for the bindery and press over the on-line library systems available or the disk literature. It had become a kind of tradition over the past two years to present him a book on an historical subject, an interest of his. A good luck charm. Over that time every mission had ended with, at worst, modest success. As he unraveled the paper, Matt recalled the last book given to him, an old twentieth century documentary entitled *Apollo 13*. He shook his head in wonder and snickered aloud. The mission was to rescue a disabled exploratory ship in the Jovian system. It had been a difficult assignment that ended magnificently with no loss of life, and served to elevate the exalted reputation of the Guilford Courthouse and her crew. The jacket of the thick book was in burgundy and black and had been published in the last ten years. In burnished gold lettering the title read *'Early English Colonization of the America's'*. How apropos, Matt thought. She had done it again. He would have to be sure to read it during the voyage. What intimations could it convey for this excursion?

Matt's nomadic mind was refocused towards the task at hand. He needed to get to Command and Control to oversee the status of pre-flight preparations. Turning left from his suite. Matt was abruptly confronted by the end of the corridor, terminated by a security door that led into the missile bay. Only himself and the Security Officer had possession of the access code. To his left was an extended hallway that traversed under the great central axle to the elevator and the secondary ladder tube that provided the only means of admittance to the bridge. He strolled down this passageway and, forgoing the comforts of the elevator, decided to manually climb the ladder. The first few steps fed into a half rounded enclosure that used the wall of the elevator shaft as its flat side and, hand-over-hand and 45 rungs later, he emerged onto the small foyer outside the bridge, panting heavily.

Regaining his breath, Matt passed a hand across the face of an electronic sensor, instantly eliciting a metallic swishing sound as the door to the room slid into the framework. Matthew Maitland stepped onto the dimly lit, Cimmerian enclosure of the Command and Control room, the nerve center of his ship. Shaped like half an octagon, it stretched forward 25 feet with a breadth of 40 feet at its widest point. The walls and luminous ceiling grid tile were painted in a deep charcoal, the softer lighting reducing the glare on the numerous digital and schematic displays on the diverse gray and mauve consoles around the bridge. The panels were inundated with illustrious rainbows of colored, glowing buttons and computer screens. An eight foot tall, outward sloping viewing window that encompassed much of the forward wall, the narrowest part of the room, extended from the ceiling across the entire breadth. Dazzling points of light sprinkled across the screen like the glow of a Christmas tree, due to the ship's docking orientation which had its bow arrayed away from the Moon. The engineering station was located directly ahead of Matt, encompassing the left side of C-and-C. From here all ship's internal systems, environment status, and engine parameters could be monitored and minor adjustments made. Ten feet from the forward window, a fifteen foot wide console spread across the floor, behind which two black revolving chairs were situated. The left side of this station contained all the equipment and controls for the navigation and guidance of the spacecraft. To the right was the command station which contained auxiliary controls to many systems, a computer terminal, and to which all weapon systems could be transferred to or overridden from. Along the right wall directly opposite the engineering station was sited the communications and operations post. From here all internal and external communications were controlled and monitored. Additionally, it housed displays and controls for external sensors, several computer terminals, all functions for specific scientific equipment such as deep space or planetary probes, and a tier of monitors focused on various communal areas of the vessel. Adjoining this station sat Sheri Alderman in a comfortably padded swivel chair, assiduously interfacing between an electronic notepad and a computer terminal. She spun around at Matt's approach, her luscious black locks sweeping sensually against her rosy cheeks. He couldn't help but notice her - he was only mortal. How her fluffed bangs sprang from the right part and brushed the top of her soft left eyebrow, that long, thin nose, those bright, baby blue eyes, and that sparkling smile that she always threw his way. His eyes roamed freely, admiring the sight of her ample, rounded breasts as they salaciously protruded outward from under the snug uniform. Even the ship's captain could afford the luxury of looking. Matt hovered over her, delicately touching her leg above the knee. "Thank you for the book. I'm also looking forward to spending some time together. You are very sweet." Matt straightened and proceeded to his seat by the command station. "Besides, I've got some new movies to show you."

Sheri studied him closely as he scanned some current mission data on his computer screen. What intrigued her about this man? His general physique was average in every way, but his facial cast was attractive with thick black hair neatly trimmed above the ears, tapered in back, professional yet non-conforming in its laxity. Only a dark shadow on the chin marked an otherwise clean and pure appearance. And his eyes! She could feel those intense, piercing, deep brown eyes every time he glanced her way. They captivated her. That glint and gaze could induce jolts of passionate electricity that careened throughout her body and thrilled her very soul. She could only dream of the lustful feelings that his caress might elicit. But why his look? Why couldn't she experience a similar feeling with someone who was free to explore their emotions? It must be something she sensed within him. His unbridled self-confidence; his keen intellect; his genuine concern and respect for others; how he invariably makes her feel important. Or something even deeper. Anyone who had served with or befriended Matthew Maitland for any length of time quickly came to an undeniable realization about his character; his staunch, uncompromising devotion to his principles, the truth, and doing what was right. Rare qualities in an age of unabashed self-importance and personal gratification. Unfortunately for her, she realized, those very same qualities that so entranced her were probably keeping them apart. She was determined to help him resolve those conflicts, somehow!

"Where is everyone?" Matt called out from his post, snapping Sheri out of her trance. "Have you seen Jack?"

"I believe that he's still in his quarters," Sheri replied as she turned to concentrate on her work. "With one of the station's secretaries."

"Well," Matt declared with a quick nod and sly grin, "I hope he completes his docking maneuvers before it's time to conclude ours."

Sheri giggled loudly. "Oh, Matt! You know Jackson Shoals. He would have made a perfect sailor; a girl in every port. Reggie and Tracy were having brunch at one of the station's restaurants." Sheri whirled in her seat to face Matt with electronic notepad in hand. "The last decent meal for awhile, he said."

"Is anything going on between those two?" Matt questioned, still scrutinizing the monitor.

"No!" Sheri clamored obstinately, settling the notepad on her lap. "Besides, she's married, and he wouldn't mess with a married woman, I don't think. They're just good friends." Sheri's head lowered lethargically , her inflection turning to somber resignation. "Like us."

Matt spun around, immediately perceiving the dejection in her forlorn face. He desperately wanted to rush over and embrace her, but that could lead to other complications that he was uncertain that he could manage. Besides, that was not a captain's prerogative while on duty station, or so he told himself. He wanted to say something, to tell her what she meant to him, to endeavor to clarify his predicament. But the words eluded him. Fortunately for Matt, Sheri bailed him out with the continuation of her report in a more lissome voice.

"Vijay is in the engine room with the Constitution's reactor maintenance chief conducting a final inspection. I've completed the quarters assignments, awaiting your approval." She rose to her feet and moved lithely to the command station, handing the plastic and metal notepad to Matt. He briefly scanned the report as it advanced on the screen before applying his initials with the attached entry pen.

"Thank you," he said with a grin as he returned the notepad to Sheri. "I noticed that Susan Oliver has been assigned as Chief Medical Specialist. Oh, joy!"

With a wry expression, Sheri pressed close to Matt, holding the notepad tight to her chest as she reached out her right hand to rest it on his shoulder while gazing deeply into his engrossing brown eyes. "Matt, will you do us all a favor and try to contain yourself on this trip. Do you remember the last time we had her aboard? The two of you fought nearly the entire voyage."

"I'm trying to forget it," Matt acknowledged, twisting restlessly in his seat. "But you know how all her liberal gibberish gets me riled up."

Sheri replied with the admonishing glare of a mother who had just caught her son with his hand in the cookie jar.

"Okay! Okay!" Matt consented with a chuckle, tossing his palms into the air. "I will try to be on my best behavior." His right arm crossed his body, its fingers lightly resting on the top of Sheri's hand. His eyes longingly stared into her beauty, resisting the hardy temptation to add a suggestive remark.

Sheri could feel that familiar sensual tingling working through her body, brought about by that hypnotic attraction of his manner. She became dazed, her mind momentarily lost in a flood of amorous sensations. A gentle hand on her hip snapped her back to attention.

"Sheri, it's time to get back to work."

Sheri took a deep breath. "Yes, Matt, of course." Her hand softly brushed against his cheek as she affectionately blew a kiss his way.

As Sheri returned to her console, the door to the elevator slid open with the metallic, whizzing sound of its mechanized drive. From its confines briskly strode a tall, lanky young man with short, curly, golden blond hair. With sparkling bright blue eyes and a long, sleek nose, his baby-face complexion reflected not a hint of facial hair. His thin physique and uncommonly good looks served to substantiate the stereotypical image of this southern California boy from Santa Barbara.

"Well, Jack, I'm glad that you could join us today," Matt sarcastically called out.

"I'm sorry if I'm a little late for duty, sir," Jackson Shoals swiftly remarked as he paused in the middle of the room, still panting from an apparently effervescent walk, before continuing in a slower, more deliberate voice. "I was unavoidably detained."

"Sir?" Matt challenged, rising to his feet as Jack approached the navigation station. "You never call me sir unless you're hiding something."

Jack rolled his shoulders, frowning in resignation.

"Well," Matt continued, "I hope that she was worth it."

A devilish leer overcame Jack as he assumed his post by the console. "Aren't they all," he quietly mumbled.

"Very well." Grinning in amusement, Matt turned towards Sheri. "The mission staff should be reporting at any moment. Perhaps you should meet them in the cargo bay and show them to their quarters."

"All right, Matt," Sheri replied, batting her eyelids tenderly as she gathered her portable terminal.

As Sheri proceeded to leave the deck, Matt turned forward and loomed over the right shoulder of his navigator, pointing to the guidance controls and schematic displays. "Now, Jack. This will not be the normal low consumption trajectory, you understand. We need to get there as fast as possible so we'll be burning the engines longer than usual to pick-up momentum. Program the guidance system for as direct a course as possible, utilizing all available gravitational fields. of course, but time is of the essence."

"I understand, Matt."

Matt slapped him on the shoulder. "That's better. I'll be in my office for the next thirty minutes while you work on the plot."

"I'll have it ready by the time you return."

"Very well."

As Matt sat in his suite studying the mission reports, the support staff was slowly gathering in the cargo area, carrying shoulder packs and personal baggage of various descriptions. Some wandered amongst the boxes and crates, searching for the location of their special equipment. Once Sheri had accounted for everyone on her roster, she quickly guided them into the massive disk, briefly took them on a tour of the dining, recreation, and shower areas, and finally to each of their designated rooms. Observing this parade of humanity from the operations station monitors were Jack and the Ops and Security Officer, Reginald Lewis. A city rat from Patterson, New Jersey, and a two year defensive back from Syracuse University, his six-foot-two frame was complimented with a trim, muscular physique. His closely cropped, thick, fuzzy black hair and dark brown skin highlighted his wide, effulgent eyes. A thin black mustache softened his stern but flawless facial features, giving him an air of amicable self-confidence.

"There's a number of interesting women on this mission, Reg," Jack noted as he delicately maneuvered the monitor controls.

"Is that all you ever think about, man?" Reggie haughtily inquired as he jadedly glanced at him.

"No, of course not," replied Jack objectionably as he remained focused on the screen. "But you must have priorities."

Reggie crossed his arms and backed against the counter. "I've heard about your legend aboard the Saratoga. How you took the panty of one of your conquests and attached it to the outside of the forward gun port. The ship traveled from space station Freedom to the asteroid belt and back again with this bikini flying proudly off the bow."

A broad, nefarious grin crossed Jack's face. "All true....all true."

Reggie shook his head and scoffed. "I don't believe it." He braced his hand against the back of the chair and leaned into Jack. "How did you get it outside....in space?"

Jack turned and somberly looked up. "Sorry, Reg, I never divulge trade secrets."

"Some friend," Reggie snorted as he straightened, turning his attention to the closed-circuit screens. "Woah! Jack, hold it there!" he exhilaratingly shouted. "Stop it there. Stop it!." His hands reached out and brushed Jack's aside, seizing the controls, working the knobs frenetically. His fingers relaxed when the image he desired focused to clarity; that of a young, thin, elegant black woman with long, vibrant dark hair, dressed in conservative shirt and slacks attire. "Hmmm....she's cute. I wonder if there's a chance that she's a teacher?"

Jack looked up in bewilderment. "Why a teacher?"

"I love dating teachers," Reggie explained insipidly, staring enchantingly at the image. "When you do something wrong, they make you do it over again."

"If you think that she is special," Jack remarked as his hands regained the controls, "then you've got to see this." The camera deliberately panned the assembly in the rec room. "Somewhere in the back of....there!"

Jack focused the camera on a tall, voluptuous woman with long, wavy blond hair bustling with large, succulent curls. She possessed the face of a goddess, soft eyelids highlighted with heavy shadow, melodious, rounded cheeks, a small upturned nose, and thin, pouting lips accentuated with a generous dose of rose lipstick. She was enticingly dressed in a tight, short sleeve, leather trimmed, black knit top with plunging neckline that exposed much of her cavernous cleavage, and an equally snug denim mini skirt.

Reggie admiringly whistled. "Look at those long legs, man."

"I haven't gotten down that far," Jack replied as the two men ogled the screen. "If she's advertising, I'm definitely buying."

The young woman moved out of camera range.

"They're leaving the rec room, Jack," Reggie hurriedly clamored. "Quick! Get on the corridor camera."

Jack scrambled to the controls of the appropriate monitor.

"Come on, man," Reggie impatiently urged. "Pan it lower....that's it. Get it focused, you idiot!" Finally the engaging blond came into view as Sheri began to issue quarters assignments.

"How can a woman board a spacecraft wearing a mini skirt?" Reggie mused in bewilderment , shifting his weight anxiously.

"With a body like hers," Jack noted with a fleeting nod of admiration, "she's overdressed." The two men pressed closer to the monitor as the alluring woman approached one of the rooms with her baggage. "No, Sheri!" Jack called out distressfully. "Don't assign her quarters yet!" Jack slammed back into the chair as the woman disappeared, throwing up his hands in exasperation. "Gone."

Reggie turned to move away, giving Jack a brotherly slap to the shoulder blade. "Thanks for the show, man, but it's time to get back to work. I'll be down in my pit." Reggie walked to the forward window where the access hatch to the bow turret was embedded in the floor and turned back to his friend. "Jack, you really need to get a grip."

Jack vacuously stared into the air. "Yeah, a nice, tight grip."

Upon his return to C-and-C, Matt was gratified to find his Chief Engineer and best friend sitting at his customary post conversing with his staff over the communications link on his console in his usual serene, concise but poignant tone.

"Listen to me, Frank. I want those boron rod controls tested again and then be sure to reset the coolant sensors."

Vijay Prophu was a third generation immigrant from Bangalore in southern India. Educated at Georgia Tech, he broke with the family banking tradition and entered the field of aerospace engineering, much to the ire of his father. At age 41, he had spent nearly his entire adult life working with spacecraft nuclear reactors and system designs. His ostracism became complete when he broke with Hindu custom and chose his own wife. He made an imposing sight at a husky six feet with thick, loosely groomed black hair and deep, hawkish eyes, but his polite and gentle mannerisms soon put one at ease. Along with their common interests of chess, sports, and the thirst for adventure, Matt admired his tranquil demeanor and independent spirit.

Matt casually paced to his side, carefully leaning against the console. "My mechanical wizard finally appears! How are my engines?"

Vijay sat forward, raising a finger towards Matt. "Our engines," he quickly corrected.

Matt acknowledged the mistake with a dip of the head. "Sorry."

"Ah! Never better," he answered, settling back in the seat. "Frank and Tracy are running diagnostics on all reactor systems as we speak."

Matt slowly began to move away but paused to rest a hand on Vijay's shoulder. "Good, good. I'll tell you Vij, with all this weight we're packing, I'm not sure that even nuclear engines can move this tub."

Vijay spun around in the chair with a glint in his eyes. "Don't you worry, Matt," he enthusiastically cried. "I'll get us to Mars, even if I have to get out and push. Besides, our cargo is weightless in space."

"Just making conversation," Matt innocently remarked as he returned to the command station and looked inquisitively at his navigator.

"Course plotted and programmed into the guidance computer," Jack proudly announced. "I estimate six-and-a-half days to reach Martian orbit. And Reggie is below deck checking out the weapons systems."

"Very well. Once Sheri has our passengers safely tucked away ...."

At that moment the elevator door glided open and out of its depths gingerly stepped a mature, blond woman of modest proportions, wearing a loose, shoulder-snap, blue floral blouse and denim pants. She nervously stood just inside the doorway, her calculating eyes darting from side to side until they caught sight of Matt sitting at the command station. Her complexion brightened as her lips cracked open. "I hope I'm not interrupting anyone," she apologetically announced.

Matt took a reluctant gulp before rising to his feet. "Why, hello, Susan. How are you?"

"Captain Matthew Maitland!" she cried, swiftly approaching him with outstretched arms. "It's so good to see you again." She briefly embraced him before pulling away, clasping his arms below the elbows. "Forgive the interruption, but I just had to come up and pay my respects. Miss Alderman said that it would be all right for a few minutes. I just wanted to say how nice it is to be aboard the Guilford Courthouse again."

"Well, thank you, Susan," Matt tenuously responded, desperately trying to sound diplomatic. "Allow me to introduce my navigator, Jackson Shoals. Jack, this is Doctor Susan Oliver."

Jack turned his head and nodded courteously. "Ma'am."

"Mister Shoals, a pleasure."

"Doctor Oliver has become an old space veteran," Matt whimsically commented. "We've served together several times in the past."

"Watch that old stuff," she protested, striking his arm playfully.

Matt guided her towards Vijay who was already approaching.

"And this is my Chief Engineer, Vijay Prophu, whom I believe you know."

"Yes, of course," she acknowledged with a smile and an extended right hand. "Nice to see you again as well, Mister Prophu."

Vijay accepted her hand firmly. "The pleasure is all mine, Doctor."

Matt abruptly tossed a strange glance in Vijay's direction before stepping her over to the middle of the room. At 45 years, a few subtle lines across her otherwise comely, slightly freckled face betrayed her age. Her glistening blond hair, without a hint of gray, banged above her right eye and laid meticulously against her ears, ending in lavish, dense, inward curls perched above her shoulders. A pair of thick lens, white gold framed glasses gave her a scholarly appearance. Of average stature, her physique was strong and fleshy, but by no means considered corpulent. Her loose blouse hid her well formed but proportionately modest breasts. A thick gold band and large, extravagant diamond setting adorned her left hand, a reminder of her marriage of more than twenty years. Confident and assertive, Susan had been employed by NASA as a medical mission specialist for nearly fifteen years and was highly regarded within its medical community. Prolonged absences from Earth did not seem to disturb her as she was consumed by her assignments and the adventure it wrought.

"May I offer my congratulations on your commission as Chief Medical Officer for this mission," Matt politely accorded. "As perplexing as it is."

"Thank you, I'm pleased," she replied with satisfaction. "How about all the mystery! What do you make of it?"

Matt nonchalantly shrugged with a twist of his head. "Who can say? A down transmitter, perhaps. It may be nothing. You may have nothing to treat but cuts and frostburn. Not even the common cold."

As they privately conversed, Vijay leaned over Jack's shoulder on his way back to his post and softly whispered. "If you want to be amused, sit those two together at the dinner table."

"Don't be so self-righteous," they overheard her ringing, indignant voice. "He has his life and I have mine. It works fine for us. We don't need to share the same bed every night. And I've never had any desire for kids."

"Okay, Susan, okay," Matt conceded, touching her shoulder. "Whatever makes you happy. It just seems to me that lifestyle defeats the whole purpose of marriage."

"Your idea of marriage," she retorted, "not mine."

Vijay glanced back at Jack with a whimsical sneer.

Matt judiciously maneuvered towards the elevator, compelling Susan to follow. She stopped by Vijay at the engineering station, clasping his upper arm with a suddenly gleaming expression. "Mister Prophu, I do hope that you will find the time to discuss with me some more aspects of your Hindu religion. I find it fascinating!"

Vijay slowly turned and rose to his feet, offering his hand. "I would find that most enjoyable, Doctor," he politely responded with a wily smile.

As Susan neared the elevator, she noticed a picture that Matt had recently purchased on Earth hanging on the wall to the left of the door.

"What is that?" she inquired, inching studiously closer.

It is a representation of the battle of Guilford Courthouse," Matt proudly announced as he moved beside her. "The battle of the Revolution that this ship is named after. I thought it appropriate to display it here."

Double matted and in a broad, gold lacquered frame, the aged Dale Gallon print depicted the 1st Maryland Continental Regiment engaged at close quarters with a British infantry regiment from a vantage point within the British line.

"Hmmm....," she mumbled with a frown. "I thought this ship was named after the location of some great judicial case."

Matt snickered, shaking his head in amusement. "Come on, Susan. You've been around long enough to know that all CAS cruisers are named after events of the American Revolution." His chest pushed forward as his countenance beamed with satisfaction. "I take great pride in the honorable name we carry."

Susan looked around at the walls with open palms and commented somewhat pretentiously. "So this great vessel was named after some big American victory."

"Actually, Susan," Matt authoritatively corrected as he shuffled closer to her, "it was a defeat." Her eyes widened in unexpected surprise. "But the colonials inflicted such heavy casualties on the British and kept their own army intact which ultimately paved the way for the British capitulation at Yorktown seven months later."

Susan's face went blank. "Where?"

With a growing level of impatience, Matt accentuated each syllable. "**YORK....TOWN!**"

Susan grimaced in fatuous indifference, folding her arms in front of her. "Never heard of it."

"Great!" Matt exclaimed as he whirled away, rolling his eyes in bewilderment. "That restores my faith in public education."

"Well, Matt," Susan offhandedly remarked without a hint of shame, backing against the wall beside the picture, "I never cared much for history. I just wish that they would stop naming such magnificent human creations after such stupid, terrible events."

"Such events built our country!" exploded Matt, his face flushed with ardent conviction as he spun to face her, his hands moving emphatically. "The men and women of antiquity laid the foundation of our world with their sweat and blood. None of this would have been possible without their beliefs, their actions, and their sacrifices. By remembering their events, we remember them."

"I don't care to remember war and death," Susan vehemently argued, shifting her weight forward. "All the greed and ambition and thirst for power. Why not celebrate the beautiful things, like love, art and music."

Matt lowered his head dispiritedly and commented in a doleful tone. "I'm sorry that you don't have a better appreciation for history. How can you move forward if you have no understanding of where you've been?"

"Matt," Susan staunchly declared, "history is dead. It's irrelevant. Get into the 21st century, for god's sake. Live for today." With a smirk of compassion, Susan inched close and gave Matt a quick peck on the cheek. "I still love you." She lightly touched the spot with her fingers, then hastily turned and exited into the elevator.

Matt stood motionless for a moment, rubbing his chin. "I'm really not liking her," he ardently announced. "Sheri, you rat! You did that to me on purpose."

On his way back to the command station, Matt abruptly stopped by his seated friend, reflecting on Vijay's amicable interaction with the doctor, resting his arm on the back of the chair. "I have to confess something to you, Vij," he said with some consternation as Vijay looked up in wonderment. "Sometimes you worry me."

Before Matt could even reach his station, his attention was once more directed towards the swishing sound of the elevator door. He thought that it was about time that Sheri returned. "Sheri, we're going to have to have a little...." His speech terminated in delightful surprise. Sheri had, indeed, emerged from the cubicle, accompanied by an extremely attractive, well proportioned woman of average height with luscious brunette hair that fluffed above her brows and curled extravagantly about her shoulders. She was smartly dressed in a casual, thin, tight fitting, mauve knit pullover embellished with tiny patterned cable stitching, and cream colored, pleated, cotton slacks. Her sparkling hazel eyes and pure, rosy complexion accentuated her beauty, but also revealed a weariness and mood of nervous apprehension. Matt was instantly enchanted by her refined presence, his stomach muscles tightening as Sheri led her close.

"Commander Matthew Maitland," Sheri proclaimed with perfect diplomatic protocol, "may I present to you Mrs. Caroline Hart."

Still in a bit of an infatuated daze, he casually offered his hand, though the marriage reference quickly jolted him back to reality. Caroline reached out and clasped it firmly. "Mrs. Hart," he greeted, beaming with joy. "This is a distinct pleasure. A pleasure and an honor, ma'am."

"Thank you, Commander Maitland. I can't tell you what a thrill it is for me to be aboard your wonderful ship."

Caroline's soft, broken voice, watery eyes, and distressful facial contortions all revealed the vehement hoard of emotions that were hammering at her. Feelings of guilt, desperation, despair, anger, sexual frustration, and personal loss merged with those of hope, strained anticipation, and the anxiety of the unknown as she stood on the bridge of this great vessel that would provide the revelation that would finally end her agony. "Sheri was gracious enough to allow me this privilege," she began with some trepidation, her voice cracking with emotion. "I wanted to personally thank you and your crew for all your efforts in the attempt to contact my husband. I appreciate this remarkable undertaking more than you could ever know."

Matt removed a clean handkerchief from his pocket and gently dabbed a single tear that leisurely rolled down her cheek. "Don't worry Mrs. Hart," Matt consoled as he clutched her shoulders, glaring deeply into her moist yet dazzling eyes. "We're going to find him, all of them."

"Please," she said, regaining her composure. "Call me Caroline."

"How have you been? You must be one tough woman to get assigned to this mission."

Caroline snickered briefly as she meekly lowered her head. "I've managed. I'm taking some sedatives to help me sleep. I haven't had much of that lately." Her pretty head lifted as her demeanor became more lively. "Thank you for asking. I sort of coerced the NSCA into appointing me as a bioengineer. After all, my husband is out there. I've been working with arctic environment plant life, trying to engineer strands that could survive in Mars type conditions. I even brought a few specimens with me. I plan to stay with my husband this time, be a part of the colony."

"Well, I certainly wish you much happiness in your new life," Matt replied as he motioned with his left hand, guiding her towards the communications station. "I'm sort of envious of you. That sounds like something I might like to do one day." Stopping near Sheri's chair, Matt supported his weight against the console and spoke in a subdued, solemn tone. "Listen, Caroline, maybe you can help me out. Was there anything in your final conversations with your husband that you think may be of some help in understanding the situation there?"

"Not that I can recall offhand," Caroline responded as her focus sharpened, crossing her arms behind her as she inched closer to Matt. She was charmed by the scanning of his cavernous brown eyes, by the special attention that was bestowed on her. It had been a long time since she had felt the stirring of her awakening passions. "I was fully debriefed by the NSCA," she continued sprightly. "I'm sure that you've received all the reports." Matt silently signaled his confirmation. "I'm not sure what more I can tell you, Commander Maitland."

"I'm not sure either," Matt chuckled, shifting his weight nervously. He couldn't help but notice the alluring femininity of this woman and the disjointed thoughts that his lecherous gaze induced caused him momentary embarrassment and left him feeling a little uncomfortable. "If you can think of anything," he awkwardly continued after clearing his throat, "feel free to tell me, no matter how insignificant." He paused, placing his hands upon her shoulders and whispered softly. "You can call me Matt."

Her elegant face brightened with resplendent radiance. "Okay."

"I don't mean to be brusque, Caroline," Matt remarked, extending his right hand towards the elevator, "but there is much to do before launch."

"Yes, of course," she replied, turning to follow his guidance. Passing Sheri's chair, Caroline stopped and faced the Flight Officer, who had already risen, with outstretched arms. "Thank you, Sheri." Caroline bypassed Sheri's extended hand and smothered her with an affectionate and overzealous embrace. The two women hugged silently for a moment before Caroline inched away, her manner brimming with fervent gratitude. "Thanks for your kindness and understanding." Her hand reached out and lightly brushed against Sheri's cheek before being led away by Matt's gentle but firm hand on the small of her back.

"We'll talk later!" Sheri called out supportively.

Matt's kindly, masculine touch evoked passionate memories within Caroline of life with her husband; how much she missed being wrapped in a man's arms; how she longed for his kiss, his caress; how it felt to be a woman laying beside a man who loved and adored her. She desperately yearned for those feelings again, and the temptation was great to seek those affections with another. But her love for him was greater. She needed her David intensely. But was he alive, or was he dead? How could she cope with that event? Tears welled up within her eyes once more as she gazed upon those daring souls who would finally ascertain his condition, whatever that may be, and deliver her to him. "Thank you, Matt," she fervently said, placing a delicate hand on his chest. Scanning the other members of the crew, she continued with an emotional, broken voice. "Thank you everyone. I'm eternally grateful."

Matt bid her farewell with a consoling pat on her back and slowly moved towards the communications station.

"That is so sad," Sheri remarked with an air of frustration. "I feel so sorry for her. She's such a sweet woman. I hope everything works out."

"So do I," added Matt as he placed an affectionate hand on Sheri's waist, kneading softly with his fingers. "So do I. Get me Constitution Control." Matt pointed towards the command station. "Pipe it down there."

By the time Matt reached his post, a young, feminine, Asian face with long, glistening, coal black hair that flowed behind her ears and down her back appeared on his viewing monitor. "Constitution Control, acknowledge."

"This is CAS cruiser Guilford Courthouse," Matt proudly proclaimed, "requesting preliminary departure clearance."

There was an unusual pause as it appeared that the operator was being distracted by something off screen, finally putting to her ear a small, cylindrical, silver personal receiver. After a few seconds she lowered the device and looked back into the viewer. "Sorry, Guilford Courthouse. Request denied. Departure temporarily delayed."

"Delayed!" Matt exclaimed incredulously. "Why delayed? What's going on?"

There was another brief pause that seemed to last minutes as the operator consulted with someone out of view. Finally her monotone though affable voice broke the confusing silence. "Constitution Control has no further information at this time. Your instructions are to remain at departure stations. Delay is not anticipated to be significant. We will advise you as additional information becomes available. Constitution Control out."

Matt flung himself back into the swivel chair as the monitor went blank, tossing his hands impotently into the air. "How do you like that!" he clamored to Jack.

"With all those women and me on board," Jack casually remarked with a wry grin, "maybe they forgot to pack the contraceptives."

"Would that not be a nightmare for NASA psychologists and sociologists?" chimed Vijay in his customary low, dignified manner. "If we go out with twenty-six and return with thirty, then we'll know that Jack has been a naughty boy."

"Just remember, Jack," Matt lightheartedly advised, "you're flying the ship, not the staff."

Turning to Sheri he flirtingly winked and then instructed. "You had better inform the crew that we're held up for awhile."

With a broad smile, Sheri playfully batted her eyelids and then proceeded to make the proper announcements. Within minutes the hatch to the laser turret could be heard buzzing open followed by the heavy thump of rubber pressing down against metal rungs. Slowly the brown face and muscular shoulders of Reggie Lewis emerged from the floor near the forward window , followed by his trim, sturdy frame. He casually leaned over the front of the navigation console and whimsically asked a rhetorical question. "What have you done now, Jack? Forget to renew your driver's license, man, or is someone about to serve you a paternity suit?"

Jack's expression contorted insouciantly. "Well, I would have a problem with my alibi. But at least I'm in demand."

Matt slumped in his seat with his hands clasped behind his head, silently pondering the endless possibilities that this mission could produce - and trying to relax. Interruptions to departure schedules were rare, and one involving such an important endeavor was downright unnerving. "If they don't soon pull up their pants," he offhandedly remarked as he looked around at the anxious faces on the bridge. "I'm going to let Reg test the new laser gun by...."

"Matt!" Sheri abruptly interrupted with excitement. "The station is hailing us."

"Down here, Sheri," Matt instructed, lurching forward sprightly.

In a moment the enchanting, petite image of the operator filled his communications monitor.

"This is Captain Maitland," he said with some degree of impatience. "What's the score, Constitution Control?"

"Guilford Courthouse," came her passionless, professional riposte, "prepare to receive additional passengers and cargo."

Bewildered faces exchanged skeptical glances around the bridge. Matt hesitated in confusion. Last minute changes were a rarity, and did nothing to alleviate the unsettling churning in his stomach.. "Say again, Constitution Control?"

"Prepare to receive additional personnel, Guilford Courthouse," the operator's unruffled voice replied. "They will be arriving shortly."

Matt became animated, his hands flying aimlessly in the air. "What passengers? How many passengers?"

"Departure time has been delayed two hours Universal time," continued the operator. "Further information will be provided later. Constitution Control out."

Matt slouched back in resignation, his fingers nervously tapping the aluminum shell of the console. "This is going to be one crowded ship."

The extended, cambered corridors of the gigantic outer wheel of Constitution Terminal were buzzing with energy. As word spread of the approaching column from the central cylinder, workers and visitors alike clamored ecstatically into the halls to catch a glimpse of the passing spectacle, as if to preserve for themselves a morsel of memory from the dawn of some grand, climatic event. The hullabaloo of celebration reverberated throughout the enclosed passageway as the parade of flesh and metal ceremoniously entered the great disk. Wild, festive cheers and lauds of support, the cascading resonance of clapping hands, and an occasional tear from a watery eye accompanied the marching troop as it neared the entrance to Docking Port 2, their heavy black boots thumping the metal floor in unison. To the vivacious bystanders, the uniforms were unmistakable. Dark olive jackets with thick chest and pouch pockets, five finely polished brass buttons running down the right side, over a slightly longer, mustard colored, heavy turtleneck knit. The deep gold sleeves of the shirt extended an inch beyond the length of the jacket arm and its thick, rounded collar hugged the neck below the chin. The baggy olive pants had deep side pockets and thinner zipper compartments above the knee, and were held in place by adjustable, elastic snap closures. They were packing brown, bulky, canvas and leather haversacks with olive, steel combat helmets strapped to their tops. Rifles were slung over their right shoulders. Their heads were capped by strange looking, ancient, but distinctive high crowned and wide brimmed black 'Hardee Hats', adorned with black feathers, light blue hat cord, and an upward sloping bugle made of brass pinned to the front. The right side of the brim was bent upward and pressed against the crown. The unusual caps caused a jocular stir, but an astute few recognized their significance. Each had a right shoulder patch of the flag of the United States of America and on the left a triangular regimental patch of a generic planet orbited by a warship. Yes, this was unquestionably a platoon from the First Regiment, United States Space Marines. The soldiers marched into the docking bay singing an old tune that had been a favorite of the military for over 200 years, the refrain resounding throughout the station.

> *Glory, Glory hallelujah!*
> *Glory, Glory hallelujah!*
> *Glory, Glory hallelujah!*
> *His truth goes marching on.*

The column was led by an officer, followed by two rows of men, six deep. The first man on the right carried a large American flag, hanging limply but proudly in the breezeless circulation of the station. It was the traditional Stars and Stripes save for some indistinguishable gold lettering and a large gold tassel at the top of the staff. Alongside the column to the right of the color bearer marched the sergeant of the unit, shouting instructions at each turn. Following this procession of drill and precision rolled a small caravan of robotics haulers loaded with crates of supplies and equipment.

Within the softly illuminated walls of C & C, Sheri Alderman was beginning to pick up the sights and sounds of the excitement on the external docking port monitor. She watched in disbelieving awe as the procession of soldiers advanced towards the ship's cargo bay. Her pretty head quickly snapped around, eyes blazing with astonishment, her luxurious black hair swishing against her cheek. "Guys!" she frantically cried out. "You've got to see this!"

Matt and the others scurried to surround her chair. None could believe the image that beheld them. Some didn't want to believe. All observed with consternation the body of men that sung and marched onto the ship with all the pomp and circumstance of a parade ground review. Sheri promptly switched the picture to the cargo bay camera. Reggie whistled with stupefied regard as the column came to a dashing halt. "Now that's something you don't see every day."

Vijay soberly looked on, calculating its implications, before anxiously glancing across at his friend. "Did you know about this, Matt?"

Matt silently shook his head, unable to look away from the monitor. Even though his thoughts were engulfed with dire apprehensions, Matt couldn't help but crack a smile of admiration for the men and the military protocol. "What is that on top of their heads?" he whimsically questioned, lurching forward and squinting his eyes for a better view.

Vijay winced. "I may be mistaken, Matt," he asserted emotionlessly, "but I believe that they are referred to as hats."

Matt tossed a darting glance of contrived indignation in Vijay's direction that ripped through his heart. "Thank you very much, Vij, for that definitive observation." His intonation became milder as he refocused on the monitor image. "I'll have to take your word for it."

They observed the sergeant bark some orders that resulted in the troop dispersing in all directions; some collecting packs, rifles, and those peculiar headgear, others converging on the haulers and, with the help of Jose Alvarez and a few of the dock workers, maneuvered them towards storage bins. The color bearer reverently furled the flag and carefully encased it in a blue plastic tube. By panning and magnifying the camera, Sheri was able to ascertain some of the wording on the crates; labels such as *Thruster Packs, Missile Defense Grid, ET Environment Suits, LR5 Power Clips, SAR Launchers.*

Sheri's senses were wracked with premonitions of apocalyptic disaster that caused her delicate frame to shudder uncontrollably. She nervously turned to Matt, her expression flushed in stark terror. "What's going on here, Matt?" she cried out despondently. "They didn't say anything about soldiers at our briefing."

"This means, Sheri," Reggie soberly interjected, placing a firm hand on her shoulder before moving away with folded arms, "that we have suddenly stepped into some pretty deep shit."

"No! No!" Jack blurted out, shaking his head emphatically as he slowly backed away from the console. "This can't be happening!"

All eyes astonishingly trained on the normally imperturbable, cocksure navigator who was now visibly agitated and distressed by the turn of events. Within the dark recesses of his mind he was reliving the nightmare. The kind of event that creeps up on an unsuspecting soul and violently explodes in torrents of fear and confusion. Images and perceptions that fiendishly return in dreams, so horrific as to jolt one out of a deep, peaceful sleep. Experiences so traumatic that they leave eternal psychological scars, alter a person's very essence. Macabre mosaic's of dreary gray and jagged rock, of blinding flashes of light, vigorous percussions, flying mountains of dirt and stone, heaps of twisted, smoldering metal, the bloody ripped and torn pressure suits and cracked faceshields of the strewn and mangled bodies, the frantic cries of the frightened and the dying echoing incessantly within his helmet. Those terrible reverberating screams!

"Jack!" Matt called out with concern. "What's wrong?"

"Oh, I'm sorry," he said with renewed serenity as he emerged from his stupor. "I was just remembering the last time I transported space marines. Three years ago during the Lunar Conflict." He gradually strayed towards the navigation post where he gingerly took his seat, pivoting to face the others. Their impatient looks compelled him to continue. "I was a shuttle pilot temporarily assigned to the Saratoga when the war broke out. We were transporting a company of marines to the fight for the Fra Mauro highlands. I was shuttling one platoon at a time down to Copernicus when on my last run the ship took ground fire and I was forced to crash land."

"You were at the Battle of the Crater?" interrupted a surprised Vijay with unusual zeal. Jack solemnly nodded.

Reggie stepped forward. "I heard that fight was rather harry."

"Oh, Jesus," Jack moaned as he wearily rubbed his drooping forehead. "What a mess. I've never seen anything like it. Rockets and tracers zipping across the dark sky like fireflies in the night. Bombs bursting everywhere. The wounded slowly dying from atmosphere loss and decompression. All the panic and confusion, blood and guts everywhere." He reclined back, running his fingers lithely through his thick blond hair. "I was damn lucky to live through it," he continued forcefully. "Half the troops I shuttled didn't." Jack vacuously stared up at the ceiling. "I can still remember some of their faces. All I know is if they are coming, they must be expecting trouble. Those space marines are some tough bad asses, I'm here to tell you."

"Now let's not jump to any rash conclusions," Matt argued, sensing the growing tension on the bridge. "You all are getting too wrapped up in this." Matt turned sharply towards his apprehensive Flight Officer. "Sheri, those boys are going to need quarters. See to it." Calculations quickly raced through his head. "You'll need to double up every room, including mine." Sheri silently nodded her understanding. "Reggie, would you please give her a hand."

As Sheri stood and gathered her electronic notepad, Matt could see the trepidation in her eyes. "Sheri," he warmly said, taking her hand and tenderly massaging its top with his fingers. "It will be all right."

He stood silently within the bounds of the elevator, shrouded with an air of equanimity and self-confidence. Though not physically domineering, he possessed a power within, a driving force that could inspire by his very presence, a composure that could steady the frenzied, an eloquence that projected competency and authority. Tall and lean, he was a living, olive obelisk to the ideals of the Corps. A billed fatigue hat of the same color, adorned with the triangular regimental emblem, covered most of his short, military cut, brown hair. His deep blue eyes radiated a grave sense of purpose as well as a tranquil predilection for compassion. A serpentine scar traversed his left cheek and, along with a double chin and fractured skin, gave him a battle-hardened appearance. A long, thin mustache embellished his upper lip and served to add a stately guise to his rugged though agreeable exterior. His voice was both polished and assertive. "Permission to enter?"

Matt sprang to his feet and stepped towards the impressive man before him. "Permission granted."

"Commander Matthew Maitland?" the man continued, meeting him half way with extended hand. Matt nodded politely. "Lieutenant Thomas Reynolds, First Platoon, B Company, First Regiment, United States Space Marines."

Matt accepted his hand with a long, vigorous shake. "Welcome aboard, Lieutenant."

"Thank you, sir," he cordially replied as a slight smile broke across his mouth. "It's an honor to be aboard the Guilford Courthouse."

Matt stared at the officer suspiciously. "Don't take this the wrong way, Lieutenant," he said apologetically. "but I suppose that you have an explanation as to why you are here?" Reynolds opened the flap to his left chest pocket, reached in, and removed a small data disk. "Here is a copy of my orders and supplementary instructions for yourself."

Matt accepted the disk, idly scanning its smooth surface.

"We are to accompany you to the Martian colony, sir," Reynolds explained. "The NSCA has come to the conclusion that since communications have been terminated. it would be prudent to have a military presence available, just in case."

Matt's brows raised. "In case of what?" he calmly asked.

Reynolds sighed, glancing around uneasily. "Unknown, sir."

Matt inserted the disk into his own chest pocket, noticing Reynolds's rigidity. "Relax, Lieutenant, we're not military here. You do not have to address me as sir. Commander will do in public. Privately, the name is Matt. You'll find that we are rather informal on this ship."

Lieutenant Reynolds breathed easily, allowing himself to slump comfortably. The unusual casualness came as a welcome relief to him, since he was normally interacting with military superiors or with private transport captains who were absorbed with their self-important titles. "You'll retain overall command of the mission," Reynolds continued, "but defer all military matters to me."

"Defer my authority?" Matt challenged incredulously as he hurried to his station and inserted the orders into his computer terminal.

"On military tactical matters only, Commander," Reynolds clarified, feeling sympathetic to Matt's position as he followed him to the command station. "Never mind. We can....cooperate....as they say."

Matt was skeptical after reading the platoon's standing orders and his own instructions. Not of the Lieutenant himself, but of his purpose. There was no indication of any kind as to why it was deemed that a troop of marines might be necessary. Matt stood to confront the officer. "These orders are quite specific on the what and the where, but the why is mysteriously neglected."

"Prudence," Reynolds offered with a shrug.

Matt tilted his head with a gnarled sneer, troubled by the inadequate detail. "That's a little vague, Lieutenant. What does the NSCA suspect could happen to an isolated colony of less than 400 people that would require your services?"

His interrogatives simply met with a silent shake of the head. The few moments of repose allowed Matt's mind to contemplate a disturbing possibility. His eyes bulged with frightful anxiety as his weight lurched forward. "There isn't some sort of insurrection or civil discord going on, is there?"

Again Reynolds quietly shook off the suggestion and calmly replied. "I have received no speculation of any such contingency."

Matt assertively reached out and grabbed the Lieutenant's arm, his face ablaze with earnest trepidation. He had serious misgivings about their presence, realizing that a platoon of space marines was not normally assigned unless trouble was anticipated. "You're not holding out on me, are you Lieutenant?" he said with utmost gravity.

Reynolds looked upon Matt with a glint of compassion. "I assure you, Commander," he replied with sincerity. "I am not aware of any kind of trouble at the Martian colony. But if there is, my platoon is here to protect your people."

Matt studied Lieutenant Reynolds closely. He could usually tell a lot about a person's character through his facial expressions and mannerisms. There were circumstances about this mission that were unsettling to him, but something about the Lieutenant's demeanor and tone told him that this was a man that could be trusted. Matt's apprehensions slowly diminished with this officer's assurances. Sufficiently consoled, at least temporarily. Matt's outlook brightened as he patted Reynolds on the shoulder. "Very well, Lieutenant," he said with a smile. "You may carry on.

My Flight Officer is arranging billets for your men as we speak. I hope that you and your platoon have a pleasant voyage aboard the Guilford Courthouse."

Reynolds nodded cordially as the two men firmly clasped hands. "Thank you, sir."

As Reynolds turned towards the elevator, his progress was abruptly halted by Matt's voice. "Oh, Lieutenant! The name is Matt."

Reynolds chuckled as his head bobbed in acknowledgment. Before entering the lift, he stopped to take notice of the picture hanging on the wall. "Ah! The battle of Guilford Courthouse. What your ship is named after." He pointed at the image and gazed majestically at Matt. "Nathanael Greene was a good general. I respect him very much. That was a helluva fight! The American defeat that helped win the War for Independence."

"You know about that battle?" Matt inquired with surprise as the war in the south was widely ignored in most history classes.

"I'm familiar with hundreds of military encounters. It's my profession and an interest of mine."

"Mine too," Matt enthusiastically replied. "We'll have to talk."

"I would enjoy that, Matt," Reynolds appreciatively beamed. "You and your crew carry a very honorable name."

Jose Alvarez stood contemplatively alone in the center of the massive cargo bay, now teeming with crates and containers of all shapes and sizes. It was hard for him to shake the premonition of calamity that haunted his thoughts as he looked around his favorite vessel. They had stowed a lot of marine equipment and armament, much more than was normal it appeared to him. He fully understood the risky nature of space travel, but it would break his heart if something dreadful happened to his good friend or this wonderful ship that he was so fond of. He sighed reluctantly. He had made sure that every supply container had been accounted for, every bin firmly secured. There was nothing more that he could do to help his friend. It was now up to the men and women aboard, and a higher authority. He devoutly crossed himself before stepping restlessly through the portal and respectfully watched as the heavy clang of thick metal and the swishing sound of compressed air signaled the sealing of the inner and outer doors by the docking crew. "God go with you, my friend." The Guilford Courthouse was now on her own.

It was less than thirty minutes before departure time when Sheri and Reggie finally returned from below, jabbering away like the chirping of sparrows as they emerged from the elevator.

"Well, it's about time that the two of you got back here," Matt called out impatiently as he twitched in his seat.

"Those marines have got everyone on edge, man," Reggie remarked with concern. "Did you find out anything more about our unexpected guests?"

"Yeah," Jack replied derisively, "it's worse than we thought. They don't know anything either. Just like Copernicus."

"I figured as much," Reggie nonchalantly commented as he moved past Jack's station.

"I'll tell you one thing," Sheri bellowed indignantly. "I'm sure that they are all very sweet, but I'll castrate the next humper that makes a suggestive remark about my ass. I had to slap one upside the head."

Reggie burst into raucous laughter. "You should have seen it," he chortled, clutching his stomach. "She cracked him good. Then their sergeant, Douglas I believe his name is, grabbed him and reamed his butt with language that my trashiest high school friends couldn't match, man. That poor guy is going to be cleaning johns with a toothbrush for the rest of his natural life." He activated the floor hatch to the forward turret and began his descent. "Catch you on the flip side, man."

The ship was given preliminary departure clearance and the crew efficiently completed their pre-flight systems checks. Matt had internal ship communications transferred to his station. "This is Captain Matthew Maitland," he formally announced. "Welcome aboard the CAS Guilford Courthouse." His voice strongly resonated off the hull and walls throughout the ship. "Prepare for departure. We will be firing the main engines shortly after leaving the Constitution, so please remain in your rooms and buckled in your seats until further notice. You may experience slight discomfort from the pressure of acceleration, but it will pass in a few minutes. Thank you for your cooperation." After a moment's pause, Matt turned to Sheri. "Verify all hands on station, please."

Sheri leaned towards the embedded microphone intercom on the communications console. "All hands report departure stations."

In rapid succession, like the falling of dominoes, came the masculine and feminine voices over the speaker. "Reactor room checking in. Engineering room checking in. Central disk checking in. Forward turret checking in."

Sheri spun around in her chair. "All stations manned and ready, Matt," she dutifully announced with a definitive bob of her head.

"Very well," Matt replied as he felt the familiar nervous excitement of the dawn of a new mission cartwheeling in his belly. "Sheri, get me Constitution Control. Down here, please."

The pleasant face of the operator popped onto the screen in front of Matt, her long, dark hair framing a pretty picture. He smiled admiringly. "Constitution Control, this is the Continental American Spaceship cruiser Guilford Courthouse," he officially announced with no small measure of pride, "requesting final departure clearance."

The operator's expression radiated warm adoration and Matt could see a reflecting glint of moisture in her eyes. "Permission for final departure clearance granted," she responded with uncharacteristic passion, as if she might know something that he didn't. "Good luck, Guilford Courthouse," she continued, wiping a solitary tear from her cheek. "See you soon. May God bless and protect you."

Matt was genuinely touched by her sentiment and nodded his appreciation with a grateful, glowing gaze, "Thank you, Constitution Control."

After transferring external communication back to Sheri's station, Matt calmly turned to his navigator and extended a hand towards the forward window. "All right, Jack," he said with confidence. "Take us out."

CHAPTER

3

It shot like a raging missile, slashing a deliberate, blazing path through the icy cold of space. A swollen fireball of gas and radiation. A grand testament to the fortitude and insatiable curiosity of mankind. Yet to the cosmic observer, a trifling grain of sand, a glowing speckle in the vast, dark, twinkling canvas of the heavens. The unobscured rays of the burning sun reflected brilliantly off its sleek, light gray hull. Stretching 310 feet in length, the cruiser Guilford Courthouse was an impressive vehicle. The fuselage of the front quarter resembled that of an obese earthbound commercial airline. Its rounded nose encompassed the laser cannon turret and the controls for the missile launch system. The thick black barrel of the gun protruded several feet through its heavily reinforced glass shell, which resembled the nose of the ancient German Heinkel He-111 bomber of the Second World War, and afforded the occupant a clear 180 degree view of the dazzling universe. The cylindrical hull bloated to a thickness of 90 feet directly behind the nose, its expanding symmetrical curvature mitigated by a flatter rising slope on top. This thumbnail indentation provided the overlook for the forward window of Command and Control. The missile bay was situated below C & C and underneath the central spoke. It accommodated two rectangular, retractable platforms each containing three 20-foot long projectiles equipped with low-yield conventional warheads. Once the platforms were deployed on each side of the vessel, the operator in the forward turret could program each missile to home on a target using any number of parameters such as heat, hydrogen gas, radioactive discharge, tracking a radar beam, etc. Thirty feet behind C & C, the corpulent fuselage pierced the heart of the great bowl, the 60-foot disk with flattened ends that housed the living domain for all the inhabitants. This massive saucer dominated the configuration of the ship, looming all around it like a giant inflated balloon, with a circumference of 575 feet and extending 182 feet in diameter. Computer controlled lateral jets helped to maintain the rotation of the entire bowl and cylinder assembly around the central spoke at about three rpm, providing the human passengers a pseudo gravity of .6g, slightly more than what they would experience on the surface of Mars. Emerging from the core of the gigantic disk for ten feet, the main hull coupled to the foyer of the cargo bay. This 50-foot tall, two floor structure reached 60 feet in length and was nearly twice as wide. The lower level harbored the ship's PL, or Planetary Lander. The freight storage area and further aft sections were held in nonrotating space, the designers concluding that heavy, bulky objects could be maneuvered more easily in a weightless environment. 40-foot long tubular channels stretched back from the port and starboard sections of the rear wall of the cargo bay to enter the huge half-hexagon shaped engineering station. These two passageways allowed for human access between the nuclear fission reactor and the rest of the ship as well as the jungle of wire, cabling, and conduits that transferred energy requirements from section to another. The reactor, engines, battery storage cells, and primary monitors and controls for all power systems were contained within the immense 60-foot long engineering section that had a 100-foot width at the top and sloped outwardly downward to a bottom width of 150 feet. The primary propulsion drive came from the gas core fission reactor and was termed the 'Nuclear Light Bulb' engine. The fissioning uranium gas is enclosed in a transparent shell and the propellant hydrogen gas flows around it through seven concentrically arranged cavities. Heat and radiation passes through the shell, is absorbed by the hydrogen gas, and rushes out one of the five, tiered exhaust nozzles. Part of the tremendous temperatures generated are used to provide heat for the vessel, and the reactor design transmits some of the more dangerous radioisotopes, such as plutonium, by neutron induced reactions into less toxic isotopes of stable elements. The reactor also harvested great amounts of battery power, but the primary source of electrical energy came from a large array of black and silver, squared solar panels on the roof of the engineering compartment that absorbed the radiation from the sun and converted it into voltages that are stored in power cells for distribution throughout the ship. A massive, rounded lead shield blanketed the engineering compartment from the rest of the craft, adding an additional measure of protection from any inadvertent radioactive discharge.

The Independence class cruiser was the largest civilian or military space vehicle ever owned and operated by Continental American Spaceships or its two other competitors, but only a part of a much larger fleet leased to private concerns and government agencies. The Guilford Courthouse was commissioned nine years before and was one of the older siblings of this distinguished though diminishing family. Still in service were the Saratoga, Yorktown, Bunker Hill, and the Monmouth. The Trenton and the Lexington were destroyed during the Lunar Conflict, and the Valley Forge was lost in deep space during an exploratory mission to the outer rim of the solar system the previous year. The costs of operating and maintaining these spaceships were enormous and the refitting time between missions usually required several months in dry dock. Consequently it required a joint business and government effort to finance such a mission, and there was a lot at stake. The NSCA had its own jurisdictional and administrative affairs, not to mention the general welfare of the Jamestown inhabitants. Numerous corporate interests including electronic manufacturers, extraterrestrial engineering construction firms, mining, and technological and scientific research companies that had invested heavily in the Martian project were anxious for a quick resolution before the mercantile markets became wary. Therefore, it was no surprise that these organizations conspired together and approached CAS with open wallets. Financial stability and careers supplied the motivational drive; the well-being of the colonists, to many, a distant third.

The blinding, sultry rays of the midday sun glittered brilliantly off the undulating, rolling ocean water, its tropical warmth permeating the comely face of Sheri Alderman. She had never before felt such joy and contentment within her heart. Strolling hand-in-hand through the foaming surf with Matt Maitland, their near naked bodies cooled by the glistening beads of moisture from the soothing spray ejected from the crash of the nearby waves, Sheri was living in her consummate idea of heaven. The sky was a cloudless baby blue and a gentle breeze spread the distinctive, salty fragrance of the sea. And they were alone, not a sign of another human being along the entire length of the white, sandy beach; not even the squawking of a hovering seagull. They playfully romped through the breaking water, jumping and skipping and laughing as in their childhood days. Finally they stopped and tenderly embraced as the sea repeatedly rushed past their calves and receded again. With only a tiny triangle of white to protect her modesty, Sheri's naked breasts brushed salaciously against Matt's chest as their lips pressed together in a long, amorous kiss. She felt his hands running freely through her luscious, wavy black hair as the thunderous smash of an animated wave bolted past their thighs and splashed the temperate sea over their heads, the force of which momentarily jolted them from their passionate embrace. With saline water freely dripping from their faces, Sheri stared wantonly into Matt's deep brown eyes, wrapped her arms around his neck and snuggled tight to his simmering, wet body. "I love you, Matt." she proclaimed with fervor. She felt the powerful squeeze of his arms pressing against her back as their tongues once more explored the deep alcoves of each others mouth. Erotic sensations swept through her body like jolts of electricity, tingling her womanly charms. She moaned in pleasure. Swept up in desire, they raced over the hot, fine-grained sand and fell together on a large, velvety, multicolored beach towel. Sheri stretched out invitingly as Matt rolled on top. His fingers and tongue sought out her most erogenous spots, causing her body to tremble with excitement. She cried out in bliss as his caresses elicited unwavering surges of sensual titillation. Then she heard the scream.

The cry reverberated as if escaping from the deep, dark bowels of some distant, barren corridor. A wail of despair out in the blackness of space and time. The sun and the ocean and Matt were gone, and she found herself aimlessly floating in a vast emptiness, devoid of all light and matter. Her thoughts were disjointed. Where was she? How could she return to that warm beach by the ocean with the man that she loved? Then she heard it again, this time more clearly.

"Dave! Don't leave me, Dave!"

Sheri's eyes gingerly opened to the familiar dimness of the room. "Oh, shit," she quietly murmured, slowly regaining her awareness, still very mindful of her aroused sexual state. Sudden sounds of rustling and swishing drew her attention to her left. Groggily she rolled over on her bed and propped herself up on her forearm. "Environment control," she weakly called out, "night lights." As several panels in the wall and ceiling softly brightened, she noticed her roommate, Caroline Hart, sitting up towards the near side of the bed, her legs still draped by the bed sheet, her face buried in her hands as she sobbed uncontrollably.

"Caroline," she wearily called, rubbing the sleep from her eyes, "are you all right?"

"Bad dream," she muttered softly amidst whimpers of distress.

Sheri leaped from her bed and whisked to Caroline's trembling side, placing a tender arm around her shoulder. Even in the throngs of anxiety in the middle of the sleep period, Sheri was amazed at just how womanly Caroline was able to present herself. Her sleek, shimmering satin chemise in frilly, deep majestic purple clung alluringly to her well proportioned curves, her thick brown curls still laying lavishly about her shoulders. Sitting beside her, Sheri felt the pangs of inadequacy as she contemplated the slovenly state of her own stringy black hair and simple night attire of blue Kansas Jayhawk crop sleep shirt and small white cotton panty. She had no need for fancy, delicate sleepwear aboard a spaceship; no one to wear it for in any event. Caroline laid her head gently above Sheri's breast, an occasional tear rolling down her moistened cheek, and rested a hand atop her firm thigh.

"I'm so sorry for disturbing you," Caroline said somberly before looking down and continuing more spiritedly. "Look at me! I'm still shaking all over. It was just a dream! I feel so stupid."

"It's okay," Sheri comforted as she wrapped her other arm tightly around Caroline, still feeling the tingling from her own excursion into the world of slumber. "I know how vivid they can be."

Caroline's trepidation slowly ebbed away as she gradually returned to reality, sighing in relief as she leisurely reclined against Sheri, her other hand delicately clasping Sheri's forearm. "Dave and I were on the dock of some seaside port waiting to board a luxury liner for some distant Caribbean shore where we were going to start a new life," Caroline calmly explained. "We had our luggage, furniture, everything. It seemed so real! The next thing I knew I was tied to one of our chairs on the dock, our luggage and furniture were gone, and Dave was standing on the deck of the ship looking down at me with some pretty, long-haired red-head clinging to his arm. I couldn't move!" Caroline grew more agitated. "I called out to him, pleaded for him to come back for me, but all he did was put his arm around the girl and smile. I screamed for him as the ship sailed away, but he merely stood against the railing and waved good-bye to me. What a nightmare!"

Sheri cuddled her sympathetically as her torso rhythmically rocked. "Well, this ship is sailing to meet him. You should have been in my dream. You would have enjoyed it."

Caroline noticed the hardness of Sheri's breasts as they pressed against the thin nightshirt. "That must have been some dream!"

Sheri smiled awkwardly and nodded, her face blushing with embarrassment. As Caroline slightly shifted her weight away from Sheri's side, her hand lightly trailed along her panty. Sheri shuddered responsively to the accidental caress. Her reaction briefly startled Caroline who quickly unveiled a playful grin once she realized what she had done. "Anyone special?" she curiously inquired.

Sheri briefly dipped her head before looking back at Caroline. "No, not really," she ambivalently answered. "Well, yes. Someone special. Just not mine." Sheri noticed Caroline staring at her with meddlesome eyes, finally raising her sleek eyebrows in conjunction with a subtle forward jolt of her head, silently pleading with her to elaborate. "I was dreaming that Matt and I were alone together on some tropical paradise," Sheri explained. " It's been over four years since I've had a serious relationship." She lifted her left leg onto the bed and turned to the side to rest on hip and forearm. "This job is not exactly conducive to fostering one. I've dallied with an occasional tryst, two ships that pass in the night sort of thing, but no love or romance." Her inflection and hand motion emphasized her sincerity. "Do you know what I mean?"

Caroline smiled and silently nodded.

"After serving a few months aboard the Guilford Courthouse, I began to feel an attraction for Matt. But he's the captain, and captain's aren't supposed to get involved with another crew member."

"He seems to be an intelligent. compassionate person," Caroline observed. "Not bad looking either. If I didn't love my husband, I could see myself pursuing him. I think that the two of you would be great together. How does he feel about you?"

Sheri's eyes dipped as a broad grin of satisfaction crossed her face. "I know that he likes me, a lot. I can tell by the desirous way he looks at me." Sheri reluctantly shrugged. "We spend some time together, but nothing more intimate than a little light petting. I think that he is inhibited by his position on the ship, fear of how involvement with me would affect its operation, and something about his past bad marriage, but he never talks about it. He's pretty much a private man."

Caroline slid closer, placing a tender hand upon Sheri's knee, glaring affectionately into her bright blue eyes. "You both are professionals. I'm sure the two of you can handle it discreetly." Her fingers gingerly traced small, congenial circles around the joint. Sheri grew uneasy as she noticed Caroline leering at the junction of her open thighs with the salivating hunger of some dark appetite, but a small, licentious part of her was intrigued by the attention. Caroline soughed and rested her hand when she perceived the bewilderment in Sheri's countenance. "You can relax," she said with a snicker. "I'm not into women, at least not yet. I'm just a touchy, feely person, as you can tell. I guess my sexual frustrations and my impending reunion with Dave have awakened some strange, animalistic passions in me." Caroline chuckled in amusement once more, lightly pressing on Sheri's knee as her thigh widened further. "You are an attractive woman. I bet Matt would give his right arm to be in my place right now."

With her anxiety at least partly assuaged, Sheri lecherously grinned, but deep within her soul she was battling a medley of chaotic and contradictory emotions. "I would like to think that was the case." An awkward silence fell upon them, finally broken by Sheri's fatiguing yawn. "I had better get some sleep," she remarked as she swung her left leg away from a disappointed Caroline and sat up on the edge of the bed. "I have a double shift tomorrow."

"Yes, of course," Caroline replied, sliding close to her side. "I'm sorry for waking you." Her hands reached out and lightly stroked Sheri's ribs, eliciting a sudden spasm and soft giggles. "Thank you for talking with me. We're two frustrated women trying to reach the men we love. I think we can help each other."

Sheri quickly rose to her feet and leaned forward to warmly brush her fingertips across Caroline's delicate cheeks before crossing her arms behind her. "You're very sweet, Caroline. I'm sure that we're going to be close friends."

Caroline's licentious and devilish gaze betrayed the torrent of conflicting emotions taunting her psyche, but it no longer seemed to bother Sheri "All right," Caroline called out with an admiring smile, "get back to that tropical paradise of your. We'll continue this another time."

Sheri hurriedly scrambled under her sheet as the room slowly dimmed to total darkness, wondering if she would ever find Matt again on that warm, sandy beach. Caroline's passions were not the only ones being heightened on this journey.

It was deep into the second evening, as measured by Earth time, as the majestic Guilford Courthouse raced uneventfully through the dark, twinkling vacuum of space. The sojourn had been tranquilly routine, with only the inevitable sporadic failures of electronic circuits and lighting grids, and general maintenance duties to keep Vijay Prophu's engineering team actively employed. The ship cut a stealth, curvilinear track away from Earth, propelled by the forward inertia created by her now dormant nuclear engine at 200 miles per second, towards the rendezvous point with the Red Planet, whose orbit around the sun now carried her some 70 degrees behind the Earth on the plane of the ecliptic. Just five months before the two planets were in opposition, only 45 million miles apart, but the tighter orbit of Earth was pulling her further away. Now Mars was nearly 115 million miles from space station Constitution. But the timing for this unfortunate situation could have been much worse for NSCA planners. The distance between the two planets will continue to increase for another 230 days. The return trip would take much longer.

Within the protective walls of the mammoth, revolving bowl, most of the passengers and crew had gathered within 70-foot wide recreation room and the adjoining exerciser chamber. In fact, most of the support personnel practically lived there, as there was little else to occupy their time. Small pockets of animated flesh and bone in numerous forms of casual attire were clustered everywhere. Some were utilizing the exercise and weight machines; others were hibernating within the tall, circular enclosure of the ship's surround theater; a few solitary souls were sitting inside the virtual reality pods; many of the soldiers, still in their olive and mustard uniforms, were hovering around the tennis and billiard tables. A spirited round of poker was being conducted around a large, circular composite polystyrene table that included Caroline Hart, Doctor Susan Oliver, ship's engineer Frank Sharp, robotics engineer Garrett Yamakawa, Reggie, Jack, and Lucinda Desjardin and Nichelle Bennett, the two young ladies that had so wantonly admired from the C & C monitors. Around a smaller table in a reclusive corner of the 40-foot deep room sat Matt and Vijay, engaged in a fierce mental war over a mahogany chess board complete with elegant black and white pewter pieces of medieval design. Jumbled sounds of boisterous voices and laughter permeated every cranny, intermixed with the shuffle of rubber-soled shoes against the small, tight fibers of the bluish-gray carpet. Nearly every person was nursing a synthetic bottle or flask of nonalcoholic beer, fruit drink, or carbonated beverage.

Matt fidgeted restlessly for several minutes, studying the board thoughtfully, before advancing his rook to a threatening position. "Check. This place is turning into a zoo," he observed as his eyes randomly scrutinized the various clumps of humanity. "It's getting difficult to concentrate around here."

"You're a man of aspiration," Vijay noted as he calmly ascertained the situation on the board. "You're easily distracted. You must learn to better discipline your mind." His hand pushed forward a protected pawn in a blocking position.

The quick countermove snapped Matt's wandering attention back to the game. "That may be, my friend, but you're feeling the heat now, I can tell. I've lost to you....what....eight times in a row?"

"Ten times," Vijay proudly corrected. He attentively watched Matt contemplate his forthcoming strategy before interjecting another thought. "You miss Sheri, don't you?"

Matt's head dropped in brief reflection. "Yeah," he scowled dispiritedly before sitting back and glaring at his friend. "I hate it when she pulls night duty. She adds a certain sparkle to this place."

Vijay grinned and casually remarked without emotion. "Have the two of you been intimate?"

Matt leaned forward with the look of astonishment. "Vij!" he exclaimed. "Now what kind of question is that to ask your captain?"

Vijay folded his arms and slumped against his chair. "I'm not asking my captain. I'm asking my friend."

Matt rested an arm on the table as he stared disheartened at the chess board. "You know that I can't do that."

Vijay's face was swept with the air of concern as his broad frame pressed into the table. "Matt, if I may be so bold," he politely said in a deep, gentle voice. "The two of you would make a wonderful couple. Forget about your title and your cheating ex. If you don't soon corral that filly, some other young, handsome cowboy is going to sweep her off her feet and you will be nothing but a memory. It will haunt you for the rest of your life. She won't wait for you forever, you know." He paused to catch a quick breath. "Don't throw away another chance for love."

A hundred incongruous thoughts raced through Matt's mind as he contemplated Vijay's thoughtful and sincere advice. "I hear what you're saying," Matt replied as he looked up. "I've been troubled by the contradictions of my desire for her, duty, the past, and basic morality. To be honest, I don't know what my feelings are. But I must admit that I find her very stimulating."

Vijay broke into a broad smile. "It may interest you to know, Matt, that Sheri has expressed similar sentiments about you in the past."

"Really!" Matt glanced quickly at the board before snickering in amusement. "You know something, Vij. I think that *you* are trying to distract me from my game."

"Sorry."

Over at the poker table, Caroline Hart tumultuously rejoiced in self-satisfaction as she gathered up her winning chips for only the second time. "Finally! I was beginning to think that you boys stacked the deck."

Jack, who had been flirting with Lucinda, the gorgeous blond to his right, turned to Caroline with a crafty grin as he gathered up all the discards from the middle of the table. "Well, we have to let the wife of the head honcho of Jamestown win once in awhile. We only use the stacked deck in mixed company when it's strip poker."

"If that were the case," Caroline whimsically mused, "I'd be looking for a fig leaf."

"We can always change the stakes," Jack cheerfully continued. "Anyone for strip poker?"

Almost in unison all the men and Lucinda voiced their farcical, enthusiastic support.

"In your dreams," remarked Caroline disdainfully.

As Jack reshuffled the deck, Caroline's eyes curiously roamed across the room towards the cluster of soldiers who were having a vociferous time around the gaming tables.

"You know something," she said, still gazing in their direction, "We should start mingling a little with those boys. Most of us have hardly spoken a word to any of them."

"How about it, Jack," Reggie, seated to his left, kiddingly remarked as he grabbed Jack by the arm and the back of his neck, shaking his head playfully. "Would you like to get to know them better, man? Would you like to tell these naive people about your last experience with space marines?"

Jack silently shook his head as he buried it on the table top as Susan Oliver sneered acrimoniously at Caroline. "Speak for yourself. I don't care to be within fifty feet of those Neanderthals."

"Don't be so harsh, Doctor," Lucinda suggested as she turned to admire the group. "I could get interested in four or five of them."

"Lucinda!" Susan gibed impatiently. "You're interested in anything that wears pants, or skirts for that matter, or so I'm told."

Lucinda snickered without a hint of offense, glancing over at Caroline and winking licentiously.

"I hate the military," Susan continued to rant. "We should find more important uses for those people."

"What?" Reggie quipped. "Defending your life and protecting your country's interests isn't important enough for you?"

"If people and nations would just learn to understand and communicate with each other, Mister Lewis," Susan adamantly replied, "if man would stop being so selfish and greedy and become more caring, then we wouldn't need any protection. People everywhere are good and decent if given a chance and a fair shake."

"Where did you learn that crap, Doctor?" Reggie bellowed irritably. "Fantasy Island?"

"No," Jack interrupted as is head slowly rose. "Probably Cal-Berkeley."

"Well, welcome to the discussion, Mister Helper," Susan sarcastically remarked. "So tell me, Mister Shoals, what were your impressions of the experience you had with those marines?"

Jack sighed grudgingly. "It was the worst workings of humanity..."

"See," Susan briskly chortled with a gratified nod of reassurance.

"....and the very best of humanity." Jack concluded.

Susan's demeanor abruptly turned morose as she lazily slumped into her chair.

"What I saw of the human spirit during that terrible inferno around Copernicus was unforgettable. You may loathe them, Doctor, or you may criticize them, but however you feel about their nature and purpose, you have to respect them."

"I'll never respect the taking of life," Susan scoffed. "Life is too precious to be sacrificed for resources, commerce, or petty national pride."

"How about freedom?" Caroline delicately interjected. "Because that's what all those things mean."

Susan stared at her as if she were demented.

"Look, Susan, I detest war as much as you do. If everyone felt about life as you do, we'd have no problems. But if one human or group doesn't value life, then the soldier becomes necessary." Caroline's head twitched towards the uniformed group. "Those people defend your right to openly express your scorn."

"Here! Here!," Reggie cheered as he raised his flask of beer. "I'll drink to that."

Susan immediately perceived his facetiousness. "Be honest with me, Mister Lewis. You've been the security officer aboard this ship for awhile. Have you ever had the desire to kill someone?"

Reggie soberly looked across the table and offhandedly replied. "Not until now."

The air surrounding the mental battlefield of the chess board was sporadically violated by the resonate bantering from the poker table. Matt could delineate most of the conversation that caused him to chuckle in amusement. "The good doctor is at it again," he lightly jested as he leaned towards Vijay. "I'm sure glad it's someone else this time."

In eerie unison, all eyes focused on the entrance as Lieutenant Reynolds leisurely strolled through, followed closely by Sergeant Geroy Douglas, a muscular, barrel-chested black man of average height with a gruff, self-assured manner that seemed to be common among non-commissioned platoon leaders, a veteran of 17 years who twice rejected military promotion to lieutenant. The men moved smartly past the poker crowd as Susan painfully grimaced and approached Matt and Vijay.

Lieutenant Reynolds stopped by the chess players and nodded politely. "Matt, Mister Prophu."

"Lieutenant....Sergeant," they both acknowledged courteously.

Reynolds hawkishly studied the game, evaluating the situation with his keen, tactical intellect, somewhat impressed with the lack of clutter on the board as most of the pieces stood idly along the side after being eliminated, including both queens. "Ahh...reduce and simplify," he surmised with a certain measure of delight. "A very sound strategy for most problems we face....except war."

"So you play chess, Lieutenant?" Matt inquired after advancing a bishop to support his rook.

Reynolds threw out his hands and shrugged. "I've dabbled with it on occasion. Well, if you'll excuse us, gentlemen."

Reynolds took a step away but abruptly turned back to Matt. "I believe that will be mate in three. I'd like to see you extricate yourself out of that one."

Vijay openly chuckled at Matt's puzzled expression that reflected a hint of irritation as the officers made their way towards their men.

As the Lieutenant passed by the billiard table, some of the younger privates snapped to attention.

"Relax, marines," he said in a fatherly tone. "You're off duty now. Tomorrow will be a full day of training so enjoy yourselves this evening."

"Thank you, sir," came some scattered replies as the two men sought refuge at a nearby counter.

The cards and wagers were flying fast and furious around the poker table as the night wore on, but the boisterous discussions issuing from the group of soldiers was drawing increasing auricular attention from the tiring participants. Inquisitive eyes noticed a lean, dapper, six-foot figure with corporal's stripes on his sleeve, leaning into a cur stick while holding court amongst his colleagues. He had the look of the All-American boy with short brown hair and a pure, clean shaven face, save for a thin, meticulously groomed mustache. Though young and robust, he was obviously more mature than the others. He articulated in a gentle, confident fashion, without a hint of rankness that was so common among male dominated military groups. The respect he commanded among the men was apparent.

"If you guys think that these peace time milk-run assignments are exciting," he chiddingly laughed, "being stationed on the moon and flying around in spaceships, then you should have been around during the Lunar Conflict. Romania. The Carpathian Mountains."

"You were at the Carpathian Chaos, Bob?" one private questioned.

"Yeah, I was there. So was the Lieutenant and Sarge," he proudly replied, scanning the face of each man. "I know that most of you weren't in the service three years ago, but I was like you back then; green, gung-ho, and scared." He slyly grinned. "Not the rock of strength and competence that stands before you now."

His statement was met by a tumult of scathing and whimsical jeers. The corporal exchanged some good-natured gibes before resuming his story. "Our battalion was assigned to Earth operations, part of an amphibious fleet that secured the Black Sea. Our quick strike assault force was given the task of neutralizing am ICBM site and satellite control center located in the Carpathians near the Ukrainian border. That was some rough but beautiful country, I'm here to tell you. You guys don't know what fear is until you've been in a fight like that." He paused in somber reflection, conscious of the eager eyes trained on him, before continuing in a more subdued tone. "We achieved our objective, but the casualties were high, very high. One major, four captains, and two senior lieutenants later, Lieutenant Reynolds found himself in command of what was left of the battalion. The LZ was too hot for extraction. We found ourselves relentlessly assaulted on three sides and the noose being drawn tighter by the hour. Air support was not very effective in that terrain. Ground support couldn't reach us in time."

The young soldiers pressed quietly closer, their enthusiastic though untried faces enthralled by the account.

"The nearest secured LZ was twenty miles over rock, crevice and heavy timber. The Lieutenant decided that was our only hope of salvation before we were completely encircled and annihilated. We withdrew under cover of night, forced to leave behind all our wounded unable to walk and one unfortunate company as rear guard to cover our retreat." The corporal lowered his head in painful recollection. "As you all know, rear guard is always on their own, and they sold their lives dearly. They were wiped out to the man. But they bought the rest of us the time to escape. I will never forget it. We went in with over 500 men, we came out with less than 200. I pray that none of you will ever experience anything like that." He paused, delicately propping the cue against the wall and slumping remorsefully into a nearby seat. "The stink of it all comes from the fact that the cease-fire was signed the very next day. If we had held on for a few more hours, some of those men might still be alive today. But who could have known."

It took a few moments for him to realize just how gloomy the mood around the gaming tables had become. "Hey! It don't mean nothing," he clamored in a contrived, upbeat manner, flinging his hand nonchalantly. "It's peace time, right?" Looking around, he noticed the two officers solemnly listening in the distance. "Hey, Sarge!" he energetically called. "How about shooting some pool?"

Geroy Douglas glanced sympathetically at Reynolds and spoke in an unusually soft tone. "If you will excuse me, Tom, it's time for me to teach these young greenhorns another lesson in humility."

The Lieutenant's mouth cracked slightly as he nodded his approval, his mind reliving the tormenting events of those fateful days. The hard decisions on those rugged precipices had forever altered his perceptions of his life's direction. Once news had spread of the Carpathian Chaos, the media had crucified the military and him personally. The attacks were vicious and relentless. Although a military tribunal absolved him of any negligent culpability, the service needed a scapegoat, and he was a convenient candidate. Any aspirations of further promotion were summarily shoved into the distant future where the substance of traumatic events gets eroded and obscured in the ever-widening expanses of time. It was ironic, he thought, that if the truce had been signed just a few days later, hundreds or thousands of additional lives would have been lost, and this personal tragedy would have gone largely unnoticed.

During this span of time the conversation permeating the poker table became noticeably less dynamic. Susan Oliver grew increasingly agitated, her expression simmering with anger. Caroline repeatedly glanced over at the corporal with a curious measure of admiration and empathy, not to mention a certain physical attraction. Jack could feel his stomach acids churning as he was reminded of his own little nightmare.

"Come on, Jack," Lucinda urged as she tugged at his arm. "Are you going to deal or play with yourself for the rest of the night."

"Oh, sorry," he replied, flipping her a card. "The dealer takes two."

When it came to Susan's turn, she aggressively bet five additional credits that were quickly matched by Frank and Lucinda.

"I'll see those credits," Jack assuredly announced, "and I'll raise you another five." The chips rattled into the middle of the growing pile. "Well, Reg, throw it on in, my man."

Reggie sneered suspiciously at Jack. "You're bluffing, man," he declared defiantly as he tossed in his bet.

Jack continued around the table. "Nichelle and Garrett folded their tents long ago. What do you say, Caroline....Oh, Mrs. Hart, hello!"

Caroline slowly snapped out of her dormant trance with a quick smirk and chortle. "My turn again? Please forgive me." She hastily examined her hand. "Too rich for my blood," she announced as she reluctantly dropped her cards.

"Okay, Doctor," Jack chided, "are you serious about this hand or is your indignation going to get the best of you again?"

"Oh, no!" she vehemently protested, matching the stake. "You're not going to spook me again, Jack the Rip-Off."

"Now, now, now, Doctor," Jack jested. "Don't be bitter."

"I fold," Frank disgustingly proclaimed.

"Me too," Lucinda followed.

"All right, Jack," Susan insisted impatiently, "what have you got?"

"Well, my friends," he pretentiously declared, revealing his hand one card at a time, "here is one queen, and here is another queen; and here are three....big....bullets. So I'll just reach in and gather up all your credits."

Susan slammed down her cards and snarled incoherently.

"That beats me," Reggie remarked in soft resignation, aimlessly flicking away his two pair.

Jack snickered with delight. "You bet it does."

Everyone slouched listlessly as Jack gathered up the cards, all except for Susan who was lurching forward, cheeks flushed with rage as she glared scornfully at the group of marines and their officer beyond.

"Your deal, Doctor," Jack said as he offered her the deck.

"Count me out," she lethargically replied as she rose to her feet without so much as a fleeting glance in his direction. "I have to get something off my chest." Stepping away from the table, Susan Oliver ambled steadily towards Lieutenant Reynolds.

"Thank God we finally got rid of her," Reggie scoffed in relief.

Reynolds politely stood upon her approach and offered his hand until he recognized behind her glasses the fires of fury intensely burning within her raging eyes.

"Were you the one in charge of that disaster in Eastern Europe?" she angrily challenged.

"Only after casualties took out the major, two....."

"Are you the butcher responsible for the deaths of all those men?"

"Now just a minute, Doctor," he responded with rising tension. "I don't...."

"You bastard!" she bellowed offensively, her voice saturated with panged emotion. "My sister's son was killed in Romania!"

"I'm sorry to hear that," he replied in a more civil tone. "A lot of sons were lost in that war."

"And power hungry, glory seeking men like you were responsible for it all," she rambled contemptuously. "You callously and cowardly abandoned them. You killed them all!"

The soldiers and civilians scattered around the rec room looked at each other in stunned and astonished silence.

"No, Doctor," he calmly but staunchly retorted. "The Eastern European Socialist Confederation killed them. I remind you that there was something of a war going on. My duty as acting Commander was to the safe return of the remnants of the battalion. I don't expect you to understand the military...."

"You're right, Lieutenant," she interrupted scornfully, her intonations running at a feverish pitch, "I don't want to understand. From whatever side of the border you come from, men like you are all the same. The military establishment has gone completely bonkers, all the way."

"Whose military establishment is that?" he deftly answered, summoning all his will to control his indignation.

Susan shook her head impertinently. "Soldiers! You all think you're something special because you run around with your fancy guns and bombs like a bunch of street thugs. You're nothing! All of your kind are just goddamn useless, ignorant scum."

"That's enough, Doctor!" Reynolds angrily yelled. "You may ridicule me to your hearts content..." His hand stretched out and pointed towards the contingent of stupefied uniforms. "....but those men don't deserve that kind of condemnation. They are dedicated, decent human beings that may be asked to risk their lives at any moment. I will not tolerate your vocal and public contempt of them."

Matt was sitting dumbfounded, somewhat mesmerized by the extraordinary heated exchange, until he could idly watch no longer. Leaping to his feet, he briskly paced to the scene and roughly grabbed Susan by the shoulders just as she was launching another one of her belligerent tirades. "Settle down, Susan," he passionately roared, spinning her body so she was forced to look his way. "I won't put up with this kind of hysterical outburst aboard my ship. Just cool it and walk away."

"Let go of me!" she huffed as she shook free of his grasp, turning back to scowl at Reynolds disdainfully. "Your occupation entails killing and destroying. You must be very proud."

"Go on, Susan," Matt forcefully directed. "Give it a rest."

"Well, I'm a doctor," she mockingly proclaimed as she was about to move away. "My job is to save lives."

Reynolds returned her gaze and solemnly replied. "So is mine."

Susan had taken several steps away when she suddenly paused and glanced grievously over her shoulder at her antagonist. "Well, you didn't do a very good job in Romania, did you." The bitter words had barely rolled off her caustic tongue before she was darting insolently from the room. Sighs of relief filtered from every corner as the bystanders gradually returned to their evening diversions.

"I'm awfully sorry about that, Lieutenant," Matt consoled as Reynolds soberly returned to his seat. "It's usually me that she's beating on. Susan's a bit high-strung and a little wacky, but she's a very good doctor."

"I'm sure she is," the troubled officer lethargically replied as he aimlessly stared down at the counter top. "I get a lot of that."

"She's an idealist," Matt continued. "A bit naive to the realities of the world. She took the death of her nephew pretty hard. You can imagine her indignation when he enlisted."

A wry grin momentarily cracked across his remorseful daze.

Across the room, Jackson Shoals lazily reclined in his chair, rubbing his tiring eyes with his fingers as he yawned. "I guess that brings to a close the evenings festivities."

Reggie shook his head in disbelief. "I haven't seen anything like that since the streets of Patterson."

Lucinda, who had been clinging to Jack's arm, playfully tugged at his sleeve. "Let's go, Jack. I need to stretch my legs." She batted her eyelashes enchantingly. "Do you think you can help me with that?"

Jack turned to Reggie with a roguish smirk. "If you good people will excuse us," he said as he and Lucinda rose from their seats.

Lucinda hovered over Nichelle as they walked by and whispered softly to her roommate. "Don't hurry back to the room, okay."

Nichelle smiled and snickered. "Have a good time."

As they joyfully departed, Nichelle looked hopefully towards Reggie who was idly flipping through the deck of cards. "It looks like I've been exiled for awhile. Would you mind keeping me company?"

"Not at all, foxy lady," he cheerfully replied with a beaming grin. "Do you have something particular in mind?"

The rapidly increasing hefty thuds of combat boots heralded the approach of the corporal whose stories had so distracted everyone and a young, sandy-haired private by his side.

"Excuse me," the corporal began in a soft but assured tone. "Forgive the intrusion, but we couldn't help but notice a few empty seats at this table. Would you mind a couple of grunts joining in?"

Caroline's expression radiated her delight with the prospect of the corporal's company. There was something about his mannerisms, gentle but masculine and confident, that mysteriously intrigued her. Something deeper than just a physical infatuation. Qualities that she so cherished about her husband, she thought. "By all means, Corporal," she happily sang out. "Pull up a seat."

"Of course," Reggie added. "We'll take marines money as well as scientists."

"I'm Robert Cooke," the corporal introduced as they seated themselves around the table, "and my friend is Private John Walinski."

Once the formal introductions were hurriedly completed, Caroline leaned towards the newcomers sympathetically. "I'm sorry about that scene back there," she said, her eyes indicating the general direction of the verbal skirmish before focusing her attention on the corporal. "I hope that you don't take it personally."

Corporal Cooke dismissed the notion offhandedly with a perfunctory wave of his hand. "We occasionally get that, ma'am. Not everyone appreciates the uniform. But gee....zus! Remind me not to get sick on this trip."

Across the room, Matt and Lieutenant Reynolds were finally loosening the tension strings, laughing and swapping highly exaggerated stories of their experiences while gulping down generous amounts of non-alcoholic beer.

"Stop by my office one evening," Matt suggested as he fought off an urge to belch. "I keep the good stuff there."

"Why, Matt, I thought alcohol was forbidden on CAS spacecraft."

Matt shrugged insolently as a devious grin came over him. "Captains are entitled to a few privileges. Besides, do you think I would set foot aboard this tub, full of space marines, completely sober?"

The two men continued to trade amusing gibes until a quick glance at Vijay shook his recollection. "Oh, by the way, Tom, you were right about the chess game. I was dead in three."

Lieutenant Reynolds gleamed in satisfaction, folding his arms as he settled back. "It was obvious," he brazenly stated, his brow rising along his forehead.

Matt was momentarily perplexed, his expressionless guise slowly transposed into one of contrived indignation as he ultimately perceived the jocular carping of the Lieutenant's intellectual prowess. He let it drop.

"I've been meaning to ask you, Lieutenant," he continued, leaning forward as he clasped his hands together on the table top. "What's the story with those funny black hats you fellows were wearing when you boarded?"

Reynolds was surrounded with an air of pride as his thoughts were briefly engrossed in reflective contemplation. "We are known as the Iron Brigade."

"The what?"

"The Iron Brigade, named after a federal unit of the American Civil War. Those high crown black hats were a distinguishing accouterment that they wore. We like to wear them for ceremonial functions."

Matt grew inquisitive. He relished the study of history, especially the period of the Civil War. The name struck a sympathetic cord within his heart. "What made you adopt that moniker?"

Reynolds took a deep breath. "When B Company, First Regiment was formed a few years ago, it was discovered that a significant number had hailed from Midwestern states including Indiana, Michigan, and Wisconsin, just like their namesakes did two hundred years ago. Some of the boys with an historical flare decided to recreate that honored identity, so here we all. In fact, four or five from my platoon come from those areas. The Iron Brigade was chosen for their reputation of toughness and steadiness in battle, very redeeming qualities for a military unit, wouldn't you agree?"

Matt nodded in accord.

"We even have the name inscribed on our flag," Reynolds continued. "Their story is not widely acclaimed, but they began to earn their notoriety at Groveton, Virginia, where they were first bloodied in a tooth-and-nail confrontation with the venerable Stonewall Brigade of Jackson's Corps. After that action came...."

"South Mountain," Matt interrupted emphatically, "after which General McClellan labeled the unit his Iron Brigade."

Reynolds body snapped erect, his eyes bulging in amazement. Matt arrogantly returned his gaze and resumed his dissertation. "That was followed by Antietam, Fredricksburg, and culminating on that fateful summer day in 1863 when they were decimated in a gallant delaying action on the first day at Gettysburg. I think that you and I are a lot alike."

Stunned to silence by the depth of Matt's historical familiarity, Reynolds gradually fell back against the padded chair and unleashed a brief but boisterous laugh. "Maybe too much alike, I'm afraid," he chortled gleefully. "It pains me to say this but, Commander Matthew Maitland, sometimes you can be amazing."

Matt nearly choked on his beer as he tried to swallow while chuckling. "I am, I am indeed!" he mirthfully replied. Once their good-natured cackling had naturally abated, Matt spoke to Reynolds in a more tranquil tone. "Well, Lieutenant, I'd say that you have quite a legacy to uphold."

Reynolds grinned and nodded in agreement. "So do you." An unusual hush between them evoked in Reynolds some troubling reflections on the historical past. His head solemnly lowered as he softly uttered his thoughts. "You know, the price for those hats was paid in full on those fields west of Gettysburg. I pray to God that our bill won't be coming due."

Matt raised his drink towards Reynolds in a salute of respect. "Amen to that, my friend."

Practically the same account had been relayed by the two marines to the poker participants whose natural curiosity had long given way to polite indifference in the wake of uninspired details and the onset of fatigue. All except for Caroline.

"That's a fascinating tale!" she energetically proclaimed, losing herself infatuously in the corporal's soothing deep blue eyes. "I must confess my ignorance when it comes to history."

"Nonsense! You are a very engaging conversationalist, Mrs. Hart."

"Please," she lightly said, reaching over to tenderly touch the back of his hand, "call me Caroline."

The story wasn't the only thing that fascinated Caroline. Robert Cooke was obviously an intelligent man, his articulation, cool and confident bearing, and near chivalrous etiquette mesmerized her. He had graciously offered to retrieve her favorite apple cooler from the dining room, then gallantly insisted when she initially protested. She felt a thrilling comfort when he placed a firm but gentle hand upon her back as he laid the drink in front of her. The fact that he was a soldier reminded her of fond childhood fables of dashing knights in shinning armor - Sir Lancelot incarnate. He seemed so different than the scientist types that she was usually exposed too; more down-to-earth, realistic, courtly, not so self-absorbed. For the hour that he was at the table, Caroline had no thoughts of her lost husband for the first time since the inception of her traumatic ordeal. Bit this gradual realization soon fostered heightened feelings of shame and guilt, as if her subliminal, lascivious desires were somehow betraying her devotion to him.

How could her mind entertain such worldly pleasures when their reunion was virtually at hand? But her hunger was undeniable. It had been so long since she had felt a loving caress, or gave one in return. She yearned for the playful teasing and tickling, the tight warmth of an affectionate embrace.

After the last hand had been dealt, the two of them leisurely strolled alone towards the living quarters. Within her frenetic thoughts, confusion reined supreme. She was undecided from moment to moment what her next move would be. She savored the attention that this interesting young man was bestowing upon her. Sheri was on night watch, she would be alone in the room. It was perfect. Caroline backed against the wall outside her door, crossed her arms behind her and pushed out her breasts. His salivating stare aroused her. The temptation was great to invite him in, but the love for her David still burned brightly over the vastness of space and time. She could not be unfaithful, not now. Bit his eyes couldn't resist examining her enticing figure and his designs for her were apparent, though he maintained his distance in a dignified manner. Caroline was flattered, smiling responsively.

"I enjoyed sharing part of the evening with you, Caroline," he courteously proclaimed, fidgeting nervously.

"I had fun too," Caroline replied with a slight abashed blush. "I would invite you in but...." She raised her left hand upward and fingered her gold band. "....I am still very much married. I'm sorry."

"I understand," he replied reluctantly, his head drooping in obvious disappointment.

"I'd like to see you again, though," Caroline enthusiastically suggested with renewed vigor. "Meet me for breakfast tomorrow?"

"I can't," he replied, looking back at her sparkling face. "the Lieutenant has us drilling all morning. Maybe dinner?"

Caroline's face radiated her pleasure. "I will look forward to it. Good night, Bob." She gazed at him longingly for what seemed like hours, then slowly turned into the open doorway.

"Good night, ma'am."

Once inside the quiet blackness of the room, Caroline braced herself against the closed, cool door and inhaled deeply, collecting her chaotic thoughts and rampant emotions. After a few moments she angrily flung off her clothes and dove onto the mattress, her littered garments marking the trail to the bed. Rolling on her stomach, she pounded the pillow in frustration and tormentingly wondered what may have been.

Corporal Cooke, having just relieved himself of a copious amount of fluid that he had consumed that evening, bumped into his distraught roommate, John Walinski, as he was about to exit the communal lavatory.

"Bob, what the hell do you think you're doing?"

Robert Cooke glanced at him peculiarly. "What do you mean?"

"You know damn well what I mean!" John fretfully barked. "She's the wife of the Martian colony honcho, for God's sake! You can't get involved with her."

A crafty smirk crossed the corporal's face as he walked past his friend, firmly patting him on the shoulder. "I just happen to enjoy her company, John. She's a classy, intelligent and sensuous woman. A rare combination in my experience. Besides, I think she likes me."

"Let it go, Bob," John forthrightly advised. "You're asking to have your butt served up on a platter."

"I know that she's a married woman," Bob resolutely explained. "But there's no harm in being friends. My grandfather once told me that a wink from a pretty girl at a party rarely results in climax, but a man is a fool not to push a suggestion as far as it will go."

The two marines glared at each other for a moment before breaking out in unrestrained chuckles.

"Okay, Bob, enough said," John conceded once the revelry faded away. "I have to take a shit. Just watch your step."

Little did John Walinski know that as he satisfied his bodily needs, fate was plotting to embroil him in a similar though infinitely more sordid circumstance. Emerging from the lavatory, he literally walked into the voluptuous, succulent blond figure of Lucinda Desjardin, aimlessly lingering against the wall.

"Excuse me ma'am," he bashfully said, his attention immediately directed towards her exposed, cavernous cleavage.

Lucinda wet her lips sensually and wiggled close to him. "Hi, soldier! My date had to turn in early, but I'm still full of energy." Her tight, peach colored, soft knit top clung half opened to her substantial curves, leaving little for the imagination to ponder. She lewdly brushed against his chest and wrapped her long arms around his neck. John was befuddled and speechless, gulping in nervous anticipation.

"Suppose you and I sneak off to some dark, deserted corner," Lucinda suggestively remarked, "and have some fun." Her hips and breasts undulated provocatively against him as her fingers ran gingerly through his closely cropped scalp. "I just love young blond men in uniform....and out."

Not a very polished man, John Walinski wrapped his arms around this forward, desirous woman and whisked her off to private surroundings where they lustfully took their pleasure with each other. In contradiction to his fears for his good friend, John was the one who became enmeshed in a torrid affair that would carry him far beyond the most lavish carnal joys that his imagination had previously conceived. It would later prove to be the final few pleasures of his young life.

A potpourri of love and passion, of adventure and new experiences intertwined within the chaotic thoughts of Caroline Hart as she restlessly rolled to one side, hovering around the murky borders of awareness as she lazily lingered in her bed long after the affable digital voice of the preprogrammed computer alarm had awakened her from a deep, peaceful sleep. She was still cognizant of the residual tingling effects of some thrilling, amorous dream, but she couldn't recall a single detail. Her stimulating trance was interrupted by a low buzzing sound emanating from the room's door. Shaken to full consciousness, Caroline quickly scrambled from her sheets and threw a luxuriant, purple satin gown over her shoulders. "Just a minute!" she hurriedly called as she raced around the room scooping up her discarded clothing and tossing them into a corner, then hastily ran a brush through her tousled, shoulder length, brown curls. Closing her gown with the waist tie, she depressed the unlock button by the doorway. "Enter!"

"Forgive the intrusion, Caroline." Matthew Maitland said as he gingerly stepped into the room and worked his way towards Sheri's bed. "I wanted to leave a little something for Sheri." He reached across the navy and gold CAS standard issue bedspread and carefully placed a small, neatly wrapped package on the center of the pillow.

Genuinely touched by the simple gesture of affection directed towards her bunky, Caroline daintily shuffled towards him, taking a seat on the edge of her slovenly berth. "That is so sweet," she proclaimed, her face beaming with delight. "You are a very considerate man. You know, Matt, she is very fond of you."

Matt wryly grinned in a brief moment of embarrassment. "Believe me, the desire is mutual." His body language was very expressive, and then he continued with dry serenity. "It does seem to be difficult to keep one's personal interests a secret on board this ship." He motioned towards the pillow. "A surprise gift, an occasional embrace, a friendly kiss. That is about all I'm comfortable giving as captain of this vessel. The captain is not permitted the luxury of...."

"You two should be a couple," Caroline timidly interrupted, not feeling comfortable being this informal and personal with the ship's captain. "I can't believe I'm sitting here having this conversation with you." Her head shook on a dilemma. "I've grown very fond of Sheri over the last few days," she continued with a mounting tone of fervent sincerity as her eyes gazed pleadingly into Matt's, "and I want to see her happy. Don't waist this precious time that you have together. You both are very dear, compassionate people and deserve at least the chance to explore the possibilities of a relationship. Don't throw away nearly three years, like I have done, just because of professional protocol."

Matt's upper body bobbed nervously back and forth as he inched away from the bed. "I see that I have to be more discreet. That is the second time in the last twelve hours that I've received the same advice."

Caroline briskly followed him towards the door, bracing her arm against the portal frame. "To be perfectly honest," she said simpering sensually, "I've become kind of fond of you as well."

The top of her silky, rich robe strategically fell open and despite his valiant efforts at control, Matt's eyes inevitably lowered anxiously to behold the upper swells of her ample breasts. His leering expression couldn't cloak his desirous appreciation of her. A more secular man would not hesitate to pursue his lust, but Matt was a man of principle and moral character and Caroline was a married woman. Besides, his desires were usually governed by his heart, and its chambers had only room for one. He summoned all his strength of will to silently bury those deep, intimate cravings for this tantalizing woman.

"When you get some vacation time," Caroline finally continued, bailing Matt out of an awkward situation, "I hope that you and Sheri will visit Dave and me at Jamestown. We'd love to have the two of you stay with us for awhile. I'm sure that you and Dave would get along splendidly."

Matt contemplated the notion for a moment. The idea of vacationing on Mars had a certain appeal for him, never having been on the surface before. There were countless wondrous vistas that he wanted to see some day. Just like the Arizona Grand Canyon, print and picture didn't do it justice. One had to experience it first hand. It touched the adventurous explorer within him. Being in the company of Sheri and Caroline also had its allure. "That is very kind of you," he cordially replied. "Thank you. It's kind of compelling to have some good friends living on Mars." His internal licentious tensions were slowly replaced with a growing gratification from the realization that life's profound experiences transcend the purely physical pleasures. "When this is all over, I'll see what I can arrange," he remarked as the door slid open. "Have a nice day, Caroline."

Caroline pressed her back against the wall as the door automatically closed, sighing in constrained pleasure. She had been delightfully aware of his lecherous gaze and was flattered by all the attention she was receiving. It had been so long since she had felt so feminine and alive, seemingly eons since her primal urges beat so vehemently within her soul. Resisting the temptations to indulge her awakening passions was becoming increasingly difficult. Just a few more days, she thankfully thought.

"Captain on the bridge!" Sheri called out in an unusually formal manner as Matt entered C & C. The unexpected greeting caused him to do a double-take, ending with a grin of amusement.

"Good morning all!" Matt exclaimed as he moved towards the operations station, tossing Sheri a peculiar glance. "Military protocol on this ship?" he quipped. "You must be kidding!"

Sheri's eyes lit up, her face beaming with joy at the mere sight of his presence after a long, dull, and lonely night. "The guys were just telling me about the minor fracas last evening in the rec room. I always seem to miss the good stuff. I'm surprised that she hasn't started something with you by now."

"Yeah, be thankful for small miracles," Matt replied in relief. "I would have tossed her insolent ass in the brig....if we had a brig in which to toss her." Muffled snickers could be heard around the room. "All right, Sheri," he continued after taking a deep breath, "night watch report."

"All systems nominal, Matt. No problems at all. It was another very boring shift." With gaping mouth, she yawned in fatigue. "Excuse me," she muttered apologetically, covering her orifice with her hand. "All operational checks positive. No sensor contacts."

"Very well," Matt professionally acknowledged. "Prime crew is on station, you may stand down." Matt inched closer to her and placed a kindly hand upon her shoulder. "Get some sleep and relax a little," he softly suggested. "I'll see you tomorrow."

Sheri gasped in depressing surprise. "Oh! I forgot, you have the watch tonight." She frowned in profound disappointment, having hoped to spend some time with him

Matt shrugged in resignation. "You ought to know. You designed the duty rotation."

Sheri silently chastised herself over her own ineptitude for scheduling him for night watch immediately after her own turn. Accepting the inevitable, she reluctantly sighed and straightened in front of Matt, forcing a smile through her chagrin. "Okay, Matt. I stand relieved." She blew a fleeting, puckered kiss in his direction and wearily staggered into the elevator to return to her quarters for some much needed rest.

Matt turned to Reggie who was patiently waiting nearby to assume the operations station. "Reg, run the com net. See if we received any low priority NSCA or CAS messages over the last twelve hours."

Reggie confidently stepped forward. "Permission to first run some weapons tests in the forward turret, Matt?"

"Very well," Matt agreed, slowly making his way towards the navigation console. "Jack, review all updated celestial navigation data. Verify that there is no meteor or other rogue cosmic body poised to intersect our flight path."

"Yes, Matt," Jack chuckled. "That would blow my whole day and irreparably damage my illustrious reputation."

Meanwhile, Reggie Lewis was climbing down the twelve metal rungs of the access portal to the floor of the small, vertical lift tube that led to the weapons room. Depressing a large, oval button, Reggie was gradually lowered some forty feet through the tight transparent walls to the deck of the cramped forward turret, the very nose of the great vessel. Emerging from the tube in the back of the compartment, Reggie's entire forward view for nearly 180 degrees was open to the brilliant illumination of the heavens. From behind the ultra thick, heavily reinforced and shielded, molded plates of shatter-proof glass, he could savor the brightness of the stars unimpeded by atmospheric conditions or the venting of the ship's gases. He leaned against the chair situated behind the laser cannon mount and looked out in awe across the vastness of the cosmos. What earthbound astronomer wouldn't give his right arm for thirty minutes in his position, he pondered. The peace and serenity was very comforting to him. As he was about to take his seat, he noticed something peculiar dangling from the left hand grip of the laser cannon, small, black, and flimsy. Upon closer inspection, he discovered that it was a woman's satin, French cut bikini panty, slightly sullied. With a growing level of irritation, Reggie ripped the garment from its perch on the end of the gun mount and shouted at the top of his lungs. "Jack! You depraved bastard!"

Reggie's frantic cry of indignation could even be heard on the bridge as its power resonated through the deck. Matt directed a puzzling glare towards his navigator. With a wily leer and diabolical glint in his eye, Jack casually reclined in his chair in singular satisfaction. "Well, at least my other reputation is safely secured."

Sheri Alderman exhaustingly trudged into her chamber and headed directly for her bed, not even acknowledging Caroline who was dressing in the opposite corner. Upon observing the return of her roommate, Caroline gleefully strolled towards her, only partially clad in her lacy, white lingerie after returning from a quick shower. "Hi, Sheri! How did it go last night?"

"Lonely and boring as usual," she lethargically answered, slipping off her watch and gold necklace and placing them on the night stand.

"Matt stopped by earlier," Caroline spryly continued, sitting on the edge of the mattress. "He left something on the pillow for you."

Sheri quickly glanced at the pillow and noticed the glittering shine of the gold wrapping sparkling under the room light and adorned with a cute red bow. She cheerfully looked back at Caroline as a wide smile broke across her face. "Did he say anything?" she eagerly asked as she seated herself, picked up the package and read the attached tag with the simple embossed message *YOUR SPECIAL* followed by his signature. Immediately she began to carefully unwrap, a subconscious effort to prolong the pleasure.

"He said a lot of things," Caroline responded as she watched Sheri with elated interest, "but not without a little prodding. He seems to keep his thoughts to himself, but a little feminine charm can open him up."

Sheri's diligent fingers revealed two small boxes. One contained several varieties of milk chocolate candy, a weakness of hers, and the second contained a small, elegantly sculpted vile of perfume. "Passion of Eden," she happily announced as she held out the tiny bottle. "My favorite perfume....and very expensive. He must have bought it weeks ago back on Earth. That is so dear of him. Here...." She reached out and grabbed Caroline's hand, pulling it towards her. "What do you think?" Opening the bottle, Sheri dabbed a small drop onto Caroline's upturned wrist. Caroline raised her wrist to her nose and inhaled deeply, moaning in delight at the piquant fragrance.

"That should get'em in the mood," she candidly proclaimed. "Hell, it could get me in the mood. I'll have to remember that brand."

Sheri closed her eyes and sighed in bliss, holding the bottle tightly to her chest as her mind aimlessly wandered through her fantasy realm of love and passion.

"He seems very cavalier," Caroline noted, interrupting Sheri's affable tranquillity.

Sheri turned to Caroline, her face glowing with renewed vigor. "That is one of the things that intrigues me," she admitted. "He has kind of an old world charm. Sort of Victorian in many ways."

"I know one thing, Sheri," Caroline added as she placed a gentle hand upon her knee, "he definitely has the hots for you. Before you guys strand me on Mars, I want to see the two of you become a couple."

Sheri lowered her head bashfully as she grasped the extent of Caroline's perception of her more intimate designs. "I'm afraid that it will take a little longer than that with him," she mumbled in a tone of disappointment. Looking up, she scanned Caroline's scantily attired body "I'm afraid I'm not as alluring as you are, not enough to overcome his inhibitions because he's the ship's captain."

Caroline glared at her with surprise.

"Oh, yes," Sheri continued assuredly. "I've noticed the way he looks at you." Her head dipped bleakly. "Sometimes I think he would find it easier to justify an affair with you."

Extremely touched by both the compliment and Sheri's dilemma, Caroline slid over to Sheri's side and put a consoling arm around her shoulder, pulling her close. "Nonsense. You are a very attractive woman. I can tell that he finds you very desirable. Most men would."

Sheri shook her head reluctantly before looking up in admiration, wary strands of long black hair straying unfettered about her face. "But you have a way of projecting yourself so sensually that attracts men like magnets. I could never seem to do that. I guess I'm a little jealous."

Caroline rocked back with a chortle of amusement. "You're being ridiculous. You have nothing to feel jealous about." In a more serious though tender manner, she reached out with her free hand and leisurely ran her fingers through a few loose strands dangling around Sheri's shoulder. "The truth is, Sheri, if I had bisexual tendencies, I would find you very desirable."

Sheri's shocked expression slowly mutated to a wide grin as she burst out in laughter. "Oh, that makes me feel so much better. Caroline, you're nuts." Sheri playfully pushed Caroline back on the bed that precipitated a brief wrestling and tickling encounter before they sat up together, giggling like idle school girls.

"Speaking of bisexual," Sheri remarked, regaining her composure. "Don't dress like that near Lucinda. I hear she goes both ways."

"I know," Caroline nonchalantly replied. "She propositioned me in the shower this morning." Giving Sheri a frisky nudge in the ribs, Caroline rose to her feet. "Don't worry. I politely told her I wasn't interested. Now go to bed." She started moving towards her side of the room. "But I am meeting her for breakfast and then she wants to show me some kind of fantasy computer game in her room."

"Are you crazy!" Sheri bellowed as she slowly unzipped her flight suit. "Alone with her! Watch yourself, Caroline, she's a little weird."

Caroline sniggered softly, unconcerned with her roommate's apprehensions. "She may be hedonistic and without morals but she won't do anything that I don't consent too. She's just fun to be around. Helps me to keep my mind off things, you know."

Sheri nodded in understanding as her uniform dropped to the floor.

"Besides, Nichelle will probably be there." Caroline studiously examined Sheri as she searched for her sleep shirt, not understanding her apparent insecurity considering how feminine she appeared in her revealing white bra and bikini. Strange, animalistic urges wracked both mind and body as she reflected on exhilarating sensations of passionate nights ages ago. The convoluted, carnal feelings and thoughts were frustrating, confusing, and unnerving to her. She shook her head in disgust at herself. "Shit, Sheri! You guys have to get me to my husband, quick."

Unhooking her bra and slipping on her sleep shirt, Sheri was unaware of the erotic turmoil tormenting her friend. "Excuse me?" she indifferently said as she drew back her bed sheet.

"Never mind," Caroline replied as she turned away, sliding each leg in turn into a pair of deep yellow slacks. "I'll get out of here for the day and let you get some rest."

"Thanks." Sheri yawned as she climbed under her sheet.

Caroline proceeded to finish dressing. "I hope to run into Bob later."

Sheri peered out of her covers with curiosity. "Who?"

Caroline's countenance brightened like that of a girl on her first date. "Corporal Robert Coole, a dashing young soldier sent here to protect us. I'll tell you about it later. Go to sleep."

Matt and Vijay leisurely sat inside the captain's suite following an hour of test monitoring in the engineering compartment, taking a break from the tedious routine of the day. Each surrounded a tall glass of pure, deep purple grape juice, a supply of which Matt always kept in his personal refrigerator since his friend was not a man that had acquired the vice of alcohol. In deference to Vijay, he chose to abstain from the stronger brew and join him in the delectable, naturally sweet taste of the vineyard. Matt casually reclined in a thickly padded executive chair, propping his feet atop his desk as the two men nostalgically reminisced about their younger days.

"Do you remember the training school at Pensacola," Matt cackled boisterously , "where we were learning how to operate these contraptions?"

Vijay, relaxing comfortably on the cushioned though modest sofa of navy and gold and subtlety adorned with the CAS logo, nodded his head as a broad smile came over him.

"That intramural football league we were in," Matt drolly continued, "when you were trying to tackle me in one game and my legs kept pumping like a piston...." His hands flailed wildly in the air for emphasis. "....and you were being dragged on the ground clutching at anything you could grab until you caught hold of my waistband and ripped my pants right off!"

Both men erupted in unrestrained laughter.

"It did facilitate stopping your run," Vijay noted with a mischievous glint.

Matt's head twitched. "I have to admit that I was a bit embarrassed. Charlie Evans, the Flight Officer aboard the Bunker Hill still rags me about that one."

"But you paid me back later when you talked me into playing in that pick-up lacrosse game. I nearly got myself killed."

Matt bobbed gleefully with satisfaction. "Ah, yes, I remember it well. That was fun."

"Fun!" Vijay calmly exclaimed. "You were the one who nearly widowed my wife."

"See," Matt humorously chuckled. "that's what I mean."

"I could barely walk for the next week," Vijay continued with contrived irritation.

Matt scoffed in disappointment. looking lifelessly down at his drink. "I'm afraid that you and me both are getting too old for that kind of shit." His eyes suddenly lifted. "I guess we'll have to stick with tennis and chess."

Vijay grinned. "A lot more beneficial to life and limb."

Matt pressed back against the pliable padding and aimlessly stared at the ceiling, sighing with the peaceful contentment of those joyful memories of days gone by. "Yes, Vij, we had some good times together, my friend. I...."

"Captain to the bridge!" resonated forcefully over the ship's internal intercom, interrupting their pleasant trip down memory lane. "Captain to the bridge!" repeated the unruffled though stalwart voice of Reggie Lewis.

Matt abruptly lurched forward. looking over at Vijay in total consternation. That call could only mean that something unusual was happening that required the captain's immediate attention - and it was seldom good news. Pangs of anxiety pounded through every fiber of Matt's being as he reached for the communications button on his desk. "Captain here, what is it, Reg?"

"We have a sensor contact, Matt." Reggie announced in a cool, professional manner. "Thought you might want to take a look."

Matt's dark brow raised in surprise and curiosity as he glanced over at Vijay. "I'm on my way."

Matt and Vijay hustled up to the bridge where Reggie was holding vigil at the operations station, finely manipulating several control dials and buttons.

"What have you got?" Matt emphatically inquired as he briskly strode to his side.

"PAMIS is indicating something solid maintaining a parallel course just at the edge of our scanning range....look there." He pointed to the large, circular monitor embedded in the left fringe of the instrument console. Matt bent low to get a better view. The indicator was dark and transparent with an illumines quadrant grid superimposed over the surface. As the Phased Array Microwave Imaging System cycled through its automated spherical scanning program every ten seconds, electromagnetic waves that were reflected back would be amplified and transmitted back to the monitor as a brief pulse of white light in the appropriate location on the grid as it related to the relative position of the ship. For three cycles, Matt watched as the white blip appeared in the same location, near the five o'clock position at the very boundary of the dial.

"Coordinates?" Matt questioned.

Reggie worked a couple of buttons and almost instantaneously the computerized digital display directly above the circular monitor lit up with bright red numbers that indicated the contact's three dimensional position in relation to the lateral and vertical planes of the ship as they intersected its central axis.

"122 degrees X," Reggie read aloud, "negative 162 degrees Y, and negative 79 degrees Z. It's in our gamma quadrant just within the ten million mile range of our sensors."

Matt did some quick mental visualizing. "That would put it off our starboard side, behind our stern, far below us. Any natural celestial bodies in that region?"

Reggie stoically shook his head.

"No comets, meteors, asteroids?"

Again the same silent response.

Matt spun around to face the navigation station "Jack, are there any reports of traffic in our gamma quadrant?"

Jack quickly called up the downloaded telemetry from the NASA flight plan files. "Central Control has no record of any vessel anywhere near our flight path, Matt."

"I don't think that it could be natural," Reggie speculated. "I have been tracking the reading for nearly an hour. It maintains a steady position in relation to us within fractions of a degree. Sheri sure knows when to take a day off."

Matt grumbled and scratched his chin apprehensively. "Hmmm.... strange, very strange indeed."

"At our present speed," Reggie added, "it's about fourteen hours behind us. I've directed additional instruments at the contact. They're indicating unusual levels of electromagnetic energy, heat displacement, and gamma ray radiation, all at that very location."

Matt's eyes bulged as the disturbing revelation began to congregate within his mind. He slowly leaned into Reggie and spoke in a deliberate tone. "Energy levels that could be produced by a....nuclear reactor?"

Reggie winced reluctantly and carefully nodded.

"What are you saying, Reg?" Matt vivaciously inquired as he shifted his weight impatiently.

"I may be one hundred and eighty degrees out," he casually remarked with a touch of immodest elan, "but we just might have a bogey tailing us."

CHAPTER

4

It came like a thief in the night, a deceptive enigmatic stranger lurking ominously around the fringes of a sleeping suburban neighborhood, serene yet sinister. An elusive banshee whose wail foretells some unfortunate occurrence. A metallic substance of heat and radiation where none had a right to be, holding a steady course on the periphery of the scanning range of the numerous data gathering instrumentation that the Guilford Courthouse trained in that direction. Attempts at various communication signals went unanswered, evoking a serious rush of adrenaline on the bridge. Verbal sparks snapped and crackled as the debate heated over the mysterious specter. NASA authorities were just as dumbfounded and could offer no plausible explanation for the aberration, though they assured Commander Maitland that they would investigate further, including checking with their space faring friends on the Eastern European Continent, in as an elegantly diplomatic manner as possible. Matt was not reassured. For several hours the crew monitored and analyzed the sensor readings reflecting back from gamma quadrant, all but eliminating any natural cosmic event. Whatever it was, it was intentionally or unintentionally maintaining its distance, like a sleek, spotted jaguar silently stalking a herd of wild antelope, patiently waiting to pounce on the unsuspecting stragglers. And then it was gone! In a wink of an eye, the PAMIS system's haunting white blip disappeared from the dark, circular screen, and the other sensor scans dried up as well. All that remained was the normal background interstellar radiation. Casper had vanished!

Matt contemplatively sat by the command station, all alone in the silence of the deserted, dimly illuminated bridge, surrounded by the glimmer of a thousand colored points of light faintly glowing atop the gray and mauve instrumentation consoles that hugged the walls of the half-octagon room. The bright glare of the computer terminal lit up his worn, grizzled face as he halfheartedly studied the display of a chess board over which he and Vijay, who was pulling the night shift in engineering, were battling. It was approaching midnight, shipboard time, as Matt was unable to resist releasing a boisterous, gaping yawn of fatigue, his aching, tense arms straining to their limits. He worked them around vigorously, attempting to loosen his muscles and shake some life into his weary bones.

"Anything wrong, Matt?" Vijay's concerned voice calmly blared over the console intercom. "You're already down four points."

"I know, Vij," Matt replied with a reluctant smirk. "I guess I'm having a hard time concentrating. That contact has me a bit nervous."

"But that was over eight hours ago," Vijay pointed out. "And very far away."

"It's still out there," Matt decisively remarked, leaning back in the chair and clasping his hands behind his head. "I can feel it. I only wish we had the time and the fuel to double back and take a look." Matt sighed in resignation. "But we have an urgent date with the Red Planet."

It was very unusual for the captain of a CAS spacecraft to pull the graveyard shift, one of the few perks available for his discretion, but Matthew Maitland had always insisted in sharing any extra duty required of his crew. With only three others qualified to monitor C & C systems, his participation in the rotation considerably lessened the general burden overlong voyages. This empathy with his subordinates did not go unnoticed, and they loved him for it. His only requirement was that he be placed on the same rotation with Vijay so the two of them could entertain each other over the intercom during the long, monotonous nights.

After several more moves in which the pieces flickered and jumped on the display, Vijay excused himself from the game in order to conduct some routine engine maintenance checks.. Matt used the time to run the standard diagnostic programs on all the bridge systems, systematically hopping from station to station as each task was completed. Lingering at the operations console, he stared apprehensively at the dormant PAMIS display and diligently worked assorted scanners for some elusive clue that would bring the mysterious visitor out of the closet, all to no avail.

Matt's deliberate electronic search of the heavens was interrupted by the high-pitched drone of the elevator door. He swing around to behold the enchanting image of Sheri strutting onto the bridge, carrying a silver metallic tray containing two steaming and potently aromatic mugs of coffee and a few scrumptiously thick, soft chocolate chip cookies. He grew instantly aroused at the sight of her enticing figure wiggling towards him, seductively decked out in white as pure as the driven snow. Matt couldn't help but to look her over with a bug-eyed expression of lust, the fact of its obviousness making him feel somewhat embarrassed. Her outfit was a fashion of the time and definitely designed to showcase a woman's assets. The pullover crop shirt was a snug, cotton, tightly woven fishnet knit that was meant to be layered over top of a modest body bra, but for which Sheri had substituted a plunging, lingerie one, whose lacy cups were clearly visible through the tiny weave of the crop top. Several inches of flat, naked torso led to her nicely rounded hips and thighs, barely covered by the bouncing hem of a loosely flowing, pleated, leather mini skirt. Her smooth, sleek legs were encased in tall, white leather boots that reached above the knee. If the intent was to get a man's blood up, it was surely having that affect on Matt. His heart pounded heavily within his chest and he could feel his stomach acids nervously churning. Anxiously, he cleared his throat at her alluring approach.

"Sheri! What are you doing here?" he tensely exclaimed, fruitlessly trying to hide his explicit attraction for her. "You know that no one but the night officer is allowed on the bridge at this hour."

Sensing the lascivious strain in his voice, Sheri replied with light-hearted, fabricated irritation. "Now, Matt! Give it a rest. You can put your manual aside for a few minutes. Look, I brought you a snack."

Matt was overcome by a slow, methodical grin and together they playfully snickered as Matt motioned with his right arm for her to meet him at the double-seated command and navigation station. Carefully placing the magnetic-bottomed tray on an open, flat surface between the instrumentation of the two consoles, Sheri handed Matt one of the hot, shatter-resistant ceramic cups and gracefully lowered herself into Jack's chair. Daintily crossing her legs, she gingerly brought the second cup to her lips, blowing sensually at the steaming water vapor before lightly sipping. Matt's dreamy-eyed gaze continued to ogle her from head to toe, lecherously lingering on her more prominent geographical points of interest. After sampling the rich, Brazilian brew, Matt lowered the mug with satisfaction and braced his arm against the chair as he leaned towards Sheri with that look of admiration and desire. "If I didn't know any better," he casually remarked, "I'd say that you're trying to seduce me."

Matt noticed the twinkle of pleasure in her eye as a hedonistic, crooked smile crossed her face. Playing along with his jest, she retorted indignantly. "Now why would you say such a thing? I'm shocked! After all, Matthew Maitland, you're on duty for Pete's sake! Besides, you're the captain, above all those human frailties."

They lost themselves in each other's gaze for a fleeting moment before the room blossomed into cackles of glee. Once the laughter had subsided, Sheri enchantingly batted her lashes at Matt. "Maybe peak your interest a little," she candidly admitted.

Matt bashfully dropped his head, nodding in hesitant confirmation before timidly glancing over at the lovely face framed by the succulent waves of her long, lavish black hair. "Believe me, Sheri," he implored in earnest, "my interest is definitely peaked."

With coffee in one hand and a chewy cookie in the other, Matt moved around the console and nervously paced in front of the huge main viewing window, wistfully staring at the twinkling of a thousand lights so magnificently arrayed before him, afraid of where his primitive, worldly cravings might take him.

"Do you know why I wanted to serve aboard an Independence class cruiser?" he softly examined, still peering out into space before answering himself. "Not because of a desire for space travel. I was driven from Earth. I wanted to get as far away from the memories of my ex-wife as possible; from people in general. I was tired of all the selfishness and conceit; of all the lies and hypocrisy; of the constant assault on personal freedoms; and the rampant lack of simple courtesy and respect for one another." Matt scoffed, shaking his head in disgust. "It surprises me that our society hasn't come completely unraveled by now. Relationships became a chore for me, a game of cat and mouse, and I got sick of it. Where is God's design in all of this, I kept asking myself. Life out here in the great cosmic frontier is much less complicated. All you have to worry about is dying. I came out here to get away from the rat race for nine or ten months out of the year. To find some inner peace within this pristine wilderness of the heavens." Matt paused with a blank expression, almost in a trance-like state as if hypnotized by the expansive universe ahead of him. Unconsciously his hand lifted reverently towards the window. "Sometimes I feel that I can just reach out and touch the face of God. It should be easier to find Him out here."

After a few moments of reflection, Matt shook himself from his stupor and turned towards Sheri, trying unsuccessfully to suppress a cheery glow of affection. "Yes, life in space was tranquil enough. And then you came along, sweet, adorable Sheri Alderman, tugging at my heartstrings. And now I'm going to mess this up too."

As if on cue from the script of some passionate, romantic Gothic play, Sheri rose from her seat and cautiously approached Matt , gently wrested the half-empty coffee mug from his hand, balanced it carefully atop the console, and then delicately snuggled close to him. With fiery flames of desire raging within them, they instantly wrapped their arms around each other in a fervent embrace. Matt tightly squeezed her delicate frame as his right hand lightly stroked the soft, supple hair on the back of her head. Matt luxuriated in the sensations of her warm, feminine body pressed closely to his, nobly fighting to control his wanton desires, dutifully remembering who he was and where he was. Moments later they were taking in the view in wondrous awe, more to do with the kindling fire between them then the dazzling, winking field of stars. Matt's arms were coiled around Sheri's naked torso as she ralaxingly reclined against him, purring like a kitten.

"The universe is beautiful," she sighed. "For a long time I've dreamed of being held in your arms like this."

Silently Matt's hands were on the move, rubbing and caressing. A few feathery strokes along her ribs evoked a series of light giggles as she sensually twitched and turned responsively. A hand deftly slipped behind and under her floppy, leather skirt to gently graze a pantied cheek. Sheri could feel a familiar burning tingling building within her.

"I love your touch," she whimpered in delight. "You're making me horny."

Sheri enticingly wiggled her hips against Matt, raising her arms to clasp her fingers together around the back of his neck, tenderly toying with some small, isolated strands of his short, dark hair.

"Who's teasing who?" Matt whimsically asked as he felt the pangs of sexual tension in the pit of his stomach.

Her luscious breasts pushed out provocatively and attracted the attention of Matt's roaming digits as his hands cautiously slid under her mesh crop shirt to cup them lovingly over her lace bra. Sheri's head rolled back against Matt's shoulder, moaning in pleasure. She spun to face him, their bodies pressing firmly together as their lips slowly joined in a long, ardent kiss. As their fingers furiously clawed at each other's back, Matt was beginning to feel his emotional control slipping away. All of his pent-up feelings and cravings for Sheri were bubbling to the surface. He was on the verge of committing a serious breech of conduct and for the first time in his life it didn't seem to matter. He wanted her. His hand began to awkwardly fumble with the belt tie to her mini skirt when their amorous adventure was interrupted by the low, deep beeping sound of the PAMIS system set to automatic alert.

Their mouths abruptly parted as they glanced in sudden alarm towards the operations station, then back at the shocking, startled expression of the other, still clinging together like Siamese twins. After a flash of confused hesitation, Matt loosened his grip on Sheri and bolted for the console, with Sheri in hot pursuit. It took just one quick cycle of the imaging system to confirm the return of the enigmatic blip on the lower right edge of the display.

"Our shadow has returned," Matt effervescently noted as he frantically began to access the sensor computers.

"Application error," the soft, monotone digital voice announced.

"Damn!" Matt bellowed in frustration at his mistake.

A gentle hand touched his agitated wrist. "Let me do it," Sheri serenely suggested, her bright blue eyes imploring with empathy.

"Thanks," Matt acknowledged as Sheri slid into the console chair.

"The guys were talking about this all evening," she remarked as her fingers efficiently manipulated the sensor and computer controls. "I always seem to miss the excitement."

Matt placed an appreciative hand upon her shoulder as he observed her every movement. "I don't mind admitting that it woke me up."

"There!"

The computer display revealed the familiar coordinates.

"Gamma quadrant," Matt announced as he hovered over her to get a closer look. "That is within one degree of our earlier contact. Let's get all our sensors trained on that location."

Sheri complied, then looked up at him with apprehension. "Another NASA ship?" she surmised.

Matt shook off the suggestion. "NASA has no knowledge of any Earth ship within fifty million miles of our flight path. It seems to be paralleling us, following and maintaining its distance, closely matching our speed." Matt looked up in absorbed contemplation for a moment before turning back to Sheri with renewed vigor. "It's as if it knows the parameters of our sensor capabilities but occasionally gets a little careless."

Sheri winced in bewilderment. "Wait a minute. No knowledge? This is traveling too meticulously to be natural. It must be of intelligent origin." Her body shuddered uncontrollably in speculative fright as her imagination ran haunting circles within her mind. "If it's not a known Earth ship then...."

"It's either a clandestine vessel or probe," Matt soberly interjected, "or...."

"Or what?" Sheri questioned impatiently, her baby blues bulging in horror, not certain that she wanted to hear the answer.

Matt straightened and lifted his brows. "Or an extraterrestrial intelligence of unknown origin."

Sheri stared at him in disbelief as if he were a crazed fool ranting and raving on some crowded city street. "Oh, shit!" she exclaimed, turning away as she brought a trembling hand to her forehead as terrifying chills shot up her spine. "I just knew you were going to say that."

"We'll just have to keep monitoring it," Matt concluded. "If it should draw closer in the morning while I'm asleep, awaken me immediately."

Sheri raised her head and signaled her understanding. "Shall I stay and help you tonight?"

"No, thank you, dear friend," Matt replied as he clasped her arm and helped her to her feet. "At this point our ghost is not a threat."

His eyes began to salaciously wander over her sensuous curves once more, stimulated by her seductive white outfit and natural beauty, but the mysterious follower was a strong antitoxin. Firmly grasping her shoulders, he pulled her close, gazing longingly into her enchanting eyes. "Sheri, you look very enticing in that outfit and I desire you very much. But what almost happened here tonight was wrong. There will be a time and place for us, but this isn't it. Maybe once we get to Mars and...."

"I know," she fervently interrupted with reluctant awareness but profound disappointment, a soft hand brushing against his bristly, whiskered cheek as moisture welled up in her eyes. "I will anxiously await that day. Please don't make it too long." Nervously she bit her lower lip and pleadingly peered at Matt like a lost puppy before pressing against his chest.

Matt's arms ensnared her once more and he cuddled her fondly, placing gentle, moist pecks on the top of her head. Matt savored her sighs of contentment that reminded him of love's most treasured moments. But an all too familiar uneasiness still gnawed at him like a swarm of pesky gnats. Lingering doubts circled over him like ravenous vultures each time he considered an intimate relationship. Was this engaging woman really the answer to his prayers, or just another costly mistake, a demonic temptress of fate poised to rip out his heart.

Gravity exists in interplanetary space. The attraction of all matter for all other matter is prevalent throughout the cosmos. What is missing in space is the affects of weight. Weight is felt when the force of gravity is resisted in some way. The chemical and electrical forces in a chair resist the force of gravity acting on a sitting person. These forces, like the force the chair applies to a seated person to keep him from falling, can be directly sensed by the body. Such forces are missing in space. Since not only the traveler but his spacecraft and everything contained within are freely falling around a planetary body, a star, a galaxy, etc., rather than supported by some other forces, there is no sensation of weight. The idea of increasing weight by being held fast in a circular path is just the way to limit these weightless affects on a space faring human.

Notice the unsettling quivering within your stomach as you soar around the top of a sharp curve the next time you take a leisurely country drive along a serpentine road. Your guts, along with the rest of you, want to continue in a straight line. Consequently, your body applies a little less pressure to the seat, because it weighs less! If you rounded the curve fast enough, you literally would be thrown off the seat in a state of free fall as weightless as an astronaut in orbit, save for any air resistance.

But what about at the surface of the road? Here your whole body wants to keep moving in a straight line, but the car wants to follow the road, so you are pressed against the side of the car by a mysterious force out of your control. At that moment you weigh more than your normal weight. Therefore, spin a synthetic space home around its central axis and an artificial or pseudo gravity environment is created.

Sheri Alderman guided the vivacious, garrulous caravan of arms and legs into the long, tubular fuselage that led aft towards the mammoth cargo bay and the engineering compartment beyond, where Vijay had so graciously consented to impart a few minutes of his precious off duty time to grant a brief tour to some of the more curious passengers, many of whom had never before been aboard a ship as illustrious as an Independence class cruiser. The bristling excitement of the crew upon hearing the news of the midnight encounter had quickly dissipated into profound chagrin as they reported for duty that morning only to discover that the puzzling sensor contact had been lost again, hours before. in fact. Here one minute, gone the next. What had expected to be an interesting day returned to the normal, mundane routine and Sheri soon found herself acting as activity director and hostess instead of investigating the unknown, a turn of events that was not very pleasing to her psyche. Some of the more boisterous ones reveled in the peculiar affects of walking in this artificial, weight-inducing habitat. A hand stretched forward tends to be pushed towards the outer wall. Moving across the corridor towards the ship's axis caused the body to veer in a curved path. Lucinda Desjardin and John Walinski particularly enjoyed drooping her tiny, conical automated nail polisher and watching its motion appear to skew to the side, accompanied by a deluge of unabashed innuendoes of a sexual nature. Yet in the space of the solar system, the polisher shoots straight down. In rotating space, the floor and outer wall of the passageway intercepts it's short-lived trip through the cosmos.

Sheri, with a keen, perceptive ear, could discern individual exchanges. She snickered in delight at the soft, jovial bantering between Caroline and Robert Cooke. Doctor Susan Oliver and her assistant, Doctor Benjamin Caldwell, seemed to be having a spirited discussion concerning some medical procedure involving explosive decompression, however any discussion that involved Susan tended to become spirited, she whimsically thought. Nichelle Bennett and Garett Yamakawa were conversing on the feasibility for routine maintenance on the colony's communications tower to be performed by a robotics drone. Sheri was relieved that the passengers were coexisting well, not withstanding Susan Oliver and the marines.

Approaching the entrance to the cargo bay, Sheri led her entourage into the rectangular access vestibule and electronically sealed the doorway behind them. There she instructed everyone to slip on a pair of burnished gray, samarium and cobalt alloyed bottom magnetic gravity shoes from their steel storage bins, placing their own rubber-soled footwear in the same compartment. The presence of a half-dozen pair of black combat boots enlightened Sheri to the close proximity of space marines just beyond those walls. Once everyone was ready, Sheri converged on the colorfully illuminated, square control panel to the left of the large portal that led into the cargo bay, and turned to address the group.

"Once I press this," she announced as she pointed towards a sizable, circular red button, "this chamber will slowly stop rotating with the rest of the ship and come to a complete stop when this doorway mates with that of the cargo bay. At that moment we will be completely weightless. For any of you who may be uninitiated to zero-g, it will feel a little weird at first. Remember to take short, deliberate steps. If anyone should start to feel nauseous, there are bathrooms clearly labeled in both the cargo hold and the engineering compartment. But Lucinda, don't stop there to polish your make-up."

Sheri depressed the red button as muffled snickers filtered through the room. The .6g of the vestibule slowly ebbed away and within ten seconds the room was motionless, the echoing clang of a locking mechanism and the high-pitched gush of an air seal signifying the completion of the alignment. Sheri pushed an adjacent button and the heavy steel door of the foyer laboriously slid into the wall as the occupants excitedly spilled out into the cavernous storage dock. As they began to wander about, their metal-soled shoes clanking against the steel floor, and getting adjusted to the sensations of weightlessness, they instantly became aware of a small group of marines hovering overhead, maneuvering around the tall ceiling and in and out amongst the towering stacks of crates and plastic containers with their surprisingly compact, battleship gray thruster packs strapped to their backs, controlling their propulsion and attitude with the hand grips that reached around their flanks. Jets of quick, bright flashes of liquid hydrogen , heated by the electricity generated from a storage battery charged by embedded solar cells, moved them in the desired direction. Lieutenant Reynolds and Sergeant Douglas stood in the middle of the bay, shouting instructions to members of the second squad and offering not so subtle suggestions for operational improvements of the equipment. Cooke and Walinski exchanged farcical glances, the corporal's squad having endured the same exercise earlier in the day.

Moving by the officers, Susan Oliver couldn't resist stopping to offer an impertinent gibe. "Your turn to watch the children, Lieutenant?"

"Hardly that, ma'am," Reynolds dispassionately replied as he continued to look away. "Training. Getting familiar with the operational capabilities of the equipment. I'm sure that a medical professional can appreciate that."

"Of course," she scoffed superciliously. "It takes years of study and training to learn how to save life. How much training is needed to take it?"

Reynolds dolefully sighed, leisurely clasping his hands behind him as he turned to Susan with a glint of impatience in his eye. "Would you trust me to perform heart surgery on you, Doctor?" he calmly inquired.

Susan snickered derisively as she cast a look of contempt. "Absolutely not!"

"And why is that, Doctor?"

Susan straightened assuredly and replied with a pretentious flair. "Because you have no medical training and would undoubtedly kill me."

"Precisely," Reynolds energetically responded with a crack of a confident smile. "That's why we constantly train on military and security matters. So an amateur doesn't come along and get everyone killed."

Susan looked around the crowded cargo bay in puzzlement. "You all should be practicing moving these containers, Lieutenant. When we get to Jamestown, that will be all there is for your boys to do."

Despite feeling his muscles tense with anger, Reynolds casually dismissed the intended insult and returned his attention to his troops overhead. "I sincerely hope that you are right, Doctor," he quietly remarked.

Half expecting another raucous argument, Susan did a double-take, momentarily speechless. Shaking off her surprise, she proceeded to rejoin the others. "Have a nice day, Lieutenant," she called out as she departed.

Reynolds courteously tipped the bill of his cap. "Ma'am."

Sheri, feeling more and more like a chaperon with a bus load of unruly school children, led her charges to the left rear of the bay where an access tube reached back to connect with the engineering section. There attention was directed behind them by a flaunting cry from John Walinski.

"Hey, guys!" he shouted to his comrades. "I don't need one of those damn jet contraptions."

All heads spun around to watch John stepping about six feet up the back wall, his body dangling in midair at a perfect right angle to the wall and parallel to the floor as if resting on a soft, bouncy, queen-sized mattress.

Robert Cooke leered at his friend, shaking his head in embarrassment. "Come on, John, quit screwing around. Show some respect for our host, for Christ's sake!"

John's clowning around drew the attention and irritated sneer of Lieutenant Reynolds. "Private Walinski!" he calmly but firmly called out. "Are you bucking for double duty today?"

The private's bearing suddenly turned stoic. "Sir, no sir."

Throwing caution to the wind, John briskly and haphazardly strode back down the side of the wall and quickly rejoined his party as they entered the tubular channel. Moving through the claustrophobic passageway, some began to experience slight disorientation, sensations of being suspended upside down, a stuffy head feeling similar to that of a common cold. All very common symptoms of zero-g. Holding one's arms at rest actually took some effort, as the limbs tended to float upward. Somewhat preoccupied with Robert Cooke's engaging small talk, Caroline took some carelessly excitable strides that found her floating towards the ceiling. Bob promptly reached up to clutch her by the waist and gently pulled her back down to the magnetic attraction of the floor. Giggling friskily, Caroline experienced a familiar thrill with the firm grasp of the corporal's hands, gazing tenderly into his intriguing, piercing eyes, lightly brushing his cheek with her fingers before they continued on.

At the end of the access tube the group passed through a large, heavy, vacuum seal doorway and emerged into the very wide but limited in length engineering room. A series of seated and standing independent stations lined the far wall, each equipped with an assortment of lighted electronic dials, buttons, switches, computer screens, and brilliant graphic displays, resembling something like a morphed image of an aircraft cockpit and a Christmas tree. Behind the heavily reinforced and shielded lead wall, the reactor room and the huge, conical exhaust nozzles beyond occupied the bulk of the immense compartment's square footage. Large rooms to the right and left contained the storage battery cells and the huge propellant gas cylinder tanks respectively.

Vijay gave a brief explanation of the operational function of each of the stations and proceeded to introduce the other members of his team that were present. "For any of you who have not had the privilege of taking his money ," Vijay announced as he pointed to solitary, balding figure sitting on a wheeled chair that was anchored to a slotted track on the floor in front of the largest array of consoles in engineering, "that fretful-looking fellow is our reactor officer, Frank Sharp. Don't be concerned about his receding hairline. It has nothing to do with working around nuclear fission. I assure you that what's left of his hair is not falling out."

Frank acknowledged the snickering crowd with a lazy wave of the hand and a farcical, cynical glance tossed towards Vijay before wheeling himself to an adjoining control panel.

"The gracious Nubian princess to our right is our systems engineer officer, Tracy Lang," Vijay chivalrously continued, "and our electrical engineer officer, Miguel Rodriguez, is in the habitat wheel doing some routine maintenance."

He allowed the people to look around for a few moments before gathering everyone together in the middle of the room and began to explain the intricacies of the nuclear propulsion system. Innocently oblivious of his audience, Vijay spoke with the technical jargon of an engineer, quickly losing their ability to understand his confusing explanations, all except for his roommate, the robotics engineer Garett Yamakawa, who was riveted to every word.

"The gas core is cooled by neon gas that flows just inside the silica shell," he continued as if he were an instructor at MIT. "Surrounding the core is a reflector made of beryllium. It's purpose is to reflect escaping neutrons back into the core so the fission process continues. We can control the fission reaction by inserting or withdrawing neutron-absorbing cadmium rods. As more neutrons are absorbed, the fission reaction is slowed down and vice-versa. We can spike the reactor in an emergency by inserting shut-off rods made of boron. In the case of overheating, we have relief valves that can help bring the pressure down. A thermal shield around the reflector helps to absorb some of the heat and radiation but most is absorbed by the propellant hydrogen gas and flushed out the nozzle."

Nichelle Bennett, the demure communication technician, fidgeted nervously. Her family could trace their ancestry to the great Zulu empires of South Africa, but she was the first to leave the comforting confines of the Earth. But space travel was still a daunting adventure for her. Her only previous experience had been a couple of assignments to the Moon and back, traveling in outmoded liquid fuel shuttles.

"Excuse me, Mister Prophu," she hesitantly interrupted. "This is all kind of new to me and I didn't understand a word you said, but it all sounds kind of dangerous to be around here." She anxiously stuttered, biting her lip, not wanting to sound foolish. "I mean, I've never been on a nuclear powered ship before."

Vijay compassionately looked upon her and replied in a confidently soothing tone of reassurance. "Relax, young lady. I have."

Upon their return to the living domain, Sheri was stopped by Lucinda in the corridor and invited into her quarters for a moment.

"What is it, Lucinda?" she impatiently asked. "I have duties."

Lucinda turned to Sheri with a peculiar luster in her eyes. "Thanks for the tour. I wanted a private moment to say that I noticed you last night in that alluring outfit. You have a cute figure."

Sheri was momentarily stunned at the intimation, gasping in surprise at the compliment. "Why thank you, I guess."

"I have a couple like it myself," Lucinda continued as she slowly wiggled closer, fluttering her lashes and sensually moistening her lips with her tongue. "I was thinking...." She paused, wantonly scanning Sheri's body. "....maybe we could get together later. You know, have some fun with each other."

Sheri could feel her stomach tightening with disgusting anger, annoyed and disheartened by the day's events, but was feeling particularly mischievous at the moment. She decided to play along before lowering the boom on her hedonistic passenger. She hummed in delight. "That sounds very interesting," she tantalizingly replied. "What do you have in mind?"

Lucinda's left hand reached out to finger and twirl a few strands of Sheri's wavy black hair about her shoulders while her other hand slowly began to loosen the snaps to her own tight, yellow blouse. "There are things I can do to really arouse and excite you," she seductively remarked.

Devilishly grinning, Sheri watched with a touch of jealous admiration as Lucinda flung the garment from her shoulders and posed provocatively in her revealing, low-cut, yellow satin bra.

"Do you like?"

"Very much," Sheri teasingly lied.

Lucinda suggestively snuggled close to Sheri and hesitantly began to fumble with the zipper of her flight suit. "I have some toys to tease you with," she lustfully noted as she gradually worked the zipper down, "or you can take your pleasure with me."

"That sounds terrific," Sheri softly cooed. "The only problem though, sweetheart, is that boobs don't excite me." Lucinda suddenly paused. "And if you don't get your fingers off that zipper," Sheri continued indignantly, "I'm going to rip off that pretty blond head of yours and shit down your neck!"

Lucinda was rudely taken aback, leering at Sheri in a state of shock. "Please forgive me," she hastily apologized as she gathered up her blouse and clumsily slipped it over her shoulders, "but I had to find out if you might be interested."

"If you will excuse me," Sheri politely but staunchly dismissed herself as she spun and darted from the room, readjusting her flight suit in mid-stride. She couldn't contain the insidious smile that overcame her as her mind reflected on the brief but intriguing encounter. The way Lucinda had been flaunting herself in practically everyone's face, she deserved it.

Her voice erupted in laughter.

Lucinda, unruffled by the perverse rejection, immediately contemplated her next affair. John and Jack were both easy prospects and very desirable. Caroline was quite fascinating and would probably be an exhilarating experience, but that would take some skillful manipulation. And then there was the Commandeer. Matthew Maitland would be quite a prize, and a good way to get back at Sheri. But that would be a delicate scheme. Was he even approachable? Any of them could prove useful.

After a few minutes interlude in the lavatory, Sheri emerged to the sound of a distant but growing intermittent rumble, like a troop of Lippizaner stallions on parade. She had heard the loud thumping pass by while relieving herself but was clueless as to what it was. As she continued on her way, the heavy, clopping reverberation grew in intensity, and her feet began to sense the vibration of the floor. Emerging from above the slope of her ceiling horizon, a thin column of olive T-shirts and baggy pants moved briskly along the curvature of the floor towards her, their heavy, thick-soled boots striking the steel plating in unison. She immediately recognized Lieutenant Reynolds in the lead, breathing hard and steady but otherwise silently composed. Sergeant Douglas ran to the inside, midway down the line, occasionally barking a rather uncomplimentary motivational instruction. The platoon raced by as if she were invisible, solely intent on surviving the ordeal. Her amicable expression abruptly turned to one of astonishment when she noticed the haggard flesh and flushed cheeks of Matt, his orange University of Virginia T-shirt and navy shorts dripping with sweat, bringing up the rear.

"Matt!" she wildly exclaimed as he exhaustedly strode by. "What in hell do you think you're doing?"

Panting profusely, Matt's tortured face glanced back her way as he ran up the floor curvature to her rear and forced his painful response between gasps. "Dying!"

Lucinda Desjardin was on the prowl again. Sex was like a drug to her and she needed daily fixes, or so she had convinced herself. She required the amorous attentions of a man to make her feel special and fulfilled, or even those of a woman would do nicely. And the more kinkier and adventurous the better. By the middle of the 21st century, most of the nastier social diseases had been controlled, including the cure for the devastating AIDS virus, so sex once more became something of a recreational sport for many, devoid of all the vexatious baggage of emotional attachment, and Lucinda was one of its prime time players.

Contraceptives for both male and female became very inexpensive, easy to use, and readily available, and thus all but eliminated the need for controversial abortions, though they were still easily and legally obtained if one so desired. With virtually all the physical risks removed, the only inhibitions remaining were moralistic ones imposed by a civilized society, and in just like every other epoch, were subject to boundless gray areas and individual interpretation. Throughout the dawn of the new millennia as technological and productivity advances produced increasing amounts of comforts, more and more people relinquished the growth of the mind and spirit to pursue the gratification of more secular desires. In pursuit of life's pleasures, children tended to be weaned on the microchip, interactive video, and virtual reality, without personal guidance and philosophy, a firm hand to enforce right and wrong, a spiritual awareness that so embodies the values and mores that defined civilizations since the beginning of time. Decades before many recognized the decline in decency and spirit and resisted these hedonistic impulses, tirelessly imparting the virtues and wisdom of the ages to their friends and offspring. Now their descendants were raising the collective consciousness of society, shining the light on a more fulfilling way of life that personified courtesy and respect, self-reliance and charity, integrity and perseverance, an inner faith in something greater than oneself. It would take generations to unravel this Gordion Knot of conflicting attitudes, but a more congenial humanity was on the horizon. Matthew Maitland and Thomas Reynolds were products of this upbringing. Lucinda Desjardin, Jack Shoals, and John Walinski were not.

Lucinda anxiously awaited for John Walinski to be dismissed from drill, growing more tense and irritable by the second after her humbling rejection. She could feel her skin crawling as her blood boiled in restless anticipation. Her fingers impatiently teased her luscious blond curls as she considered approaching one of the other eligible civilians. She had astutely prodded Caroline but quickly discovered that her immediate interest was in preparing herself to join her new found friend for dinner. In any event, John was the one she craved, with his boyish good looks, youthful vitality, and powerful drive. It was strange for her to be drawn to a younger man, but she couldn't deny the growing attachment she felt for him, a fondness that could become an impediment. It seemed to her like an eternity since she last had those feelings, beyond simple lust and the desire for pleasure. But that love tragically ended when her own wandering eye and libidinous thirst drove him away. She was admittedly self-indulgent, a weakness in her character, perhaps, but one she never apologized for. So she resigned herself to live for the moment, and sought her adventure out amongst the stars. When the marines were finally discharged, she nearly shanghaied him right out of the shower and spirited him away towards the cargo bay.

"Lucinda!" he called out in bewilderment as she secured the vestibule door to the cargo bay behind them. "Where are we going?"

"I want you!" she lustfully proclaimed with the passion of a wild tiger in heat as she began to unravel his heavy, mustard crewneck shirt. "But I want to do it in zero-g."

They merged in a resolute embrace, squeezing tightly as their tongues explored the deep, wet recesses of the other's panting mouth, her nails clawing savagely into the fabric on his back. Upon parting, they scrambled frenetically to undress each other, laughing and joking with youthful silliness until they were left standing in their underwear.

"What about the engineering crew?" John apprehensively asked as he stuffed their garments into one of the gravity shoe compartments. "One of them could walk through here."

Lucinda chuckled in amusement as she took his hand. It was all just a game to her, the risky nature of it adding to the intoxicating allure. "I don't think so, John. The crew just went off duty. The only engineer left is the night duty officer. No one should be coming back here, so relax. This is going to be fun."

Lucinda exuberantly pulled him towards the doorway, pressed the red button. Within seconds they felt their bodies floating upward, instinctively clutching a nearby handrail to pull their feet back down to the floor. Giggling playfully, Lucinda opened the immense, electronic doorway and the two of them drifted effortlessly amongst the crates.

"If the Sarge catches me down here like this," John remarked uneasily as his arms flapped wildly in the state of freefall, "he'll put my burger in a bun and chow down."

Lucinda braced herself against a tall stack of anchored containers, grinning immodestly as she shook out her succulent, long blond hair so it floated unfettered across her comely face. "Come on, John," she cried with willful desire, "how about putting your burger into my bun." Using the cargo as a launching platform, Lucinda flew directly towards him, their hands catching and twisting each other to avoid a painful impact. The force of their motion sent them bouncing off the back wall and spiraling upward in an exhilarating dance of love. Lucinda's pulse raced, her breaths rapid and deep, as they struggled to remove their remaining clothes, kissing and fondling fervently as they floated facilely towards the towering ceiling. Sensual electricity shot through every fiber of her soul, thrilling and taunting as her heart pounded with excitement at his every stimulating touch. The final consummation of this grandiose ballet proved frustratingly elusive as the momentum of their drifting, tumbling bodies made the proper mating angles difficult. Pressed together in a fireball of blazing lust, the computer whiz and the soldier spun zealously towards the rear wall where the mounted hand and foot grips provided the necessary leverage for the two lovers to finally explode together in tumultuous ecstasy.

After a long, soothing hot shower brought some vigor back to his aching joints, Matt grabbed the book that Sheri had given him and jaunted off to the rec room where he planned to await her arrival from duty. Being the center of social activity for the support staff aboard his crowded ship, the noise saturating every crevice in the spacious chamber made concentrating arduous at best. Seeking some peace and solitude, he retired to the only space within the Guilford Courthouse where he knew no one would be - the captain's suite. As he leisurely settled into his padded executive recliner, his thoughts turned affectionately to his engaging Flight Officer. Those few libidinous minutes on the bridge were the only moments during the voyage that they had the opportunity to be truly alone, and the prospects for the rest of the journey were just as bleak. He sighed in frustration. In any event, what was the point, he thought. If he was going to get physically involved with her, this certainly wasn't the time. He must have masochistic tendencies, he silently mused, to constantly torment himself like this. But it would be nice to just hold her snugly in his arms.

Propping his feet atop the desk as he lazily reclined, Matt opened the book and immersed himself in the wondrous pages of English colonial history in America. Matt was captivated by the accounts, enthralled by the risk and adventure of the Age of Discovery. Those were the days, he thought. The smell of the sea, the howling, cool breeze brushing against your face, the brightness of the reflecting sun off the billowing water, boldly sailing to some distant, exotic, undiscovered shore. That was freedom! The energetic, driving force of Sir Walter Raleigh particularly intrigued him. How he organized and dispatched the first English expedition in 1584 to explore the coast of present day North Carolina between Pamlico and Albemarle sounds. That was followed in 1585 by a party that settled on Roanoke Island, but were soon compelled to return to England because of conflicts with native Indians and shortages of food and equipment. The trials and tribulations of the colonists in an untamed world fascinated him. Raleigh sent a third expedition in 1587 to settle on the same coastal island, and that began one of the great mysteries of the colonial period. Matt became absorbed in the compelling tale until his concentration was interrupted by a light buzzing sound emanating from his door.

"Come!"

"I hope I'm not intruding, Commander." Lieutenant Reynolds cautiously stepped into the room, politely removing his cap and briefly running his hand through his closely cropped scalp.

Matt quickly swung down his legs from the desk and straightened in his seat, casually flipping an idle hand his way. "Not at all, Lieutenant," he assured, reverently closing the book and gingerly setting it aside. "And by the way, the name is Matt." He motioned towards the sofa. "Please, have a seat." Matt rose from behind his desk as Reynolds accepted the offer and walked to his compact refrigeration unit and bar cabinet opposite the couch, opening the elegant cherry wood door and removing two short glasses and a fat, square, dark green bottle of Scotch whiskey. "Come for that drink I promised, Lieutenant?" Matt surmised as he began to fill the goblets.

"Just a small one, thank you. I'm not much of a drinking man."

Matt poured with the flash and flair of an English pub barkeep, whistling an indiscernible tune, before serving the golden spirits.

"I wanted to say how much I admired how you kept pace with those young boys today," Reynolds noted. "Not bad for an old man."

Matt shot a piercing dart of contrived resentment towards Reynolds before returning to his chair. "Where do you get that old crap?" he frivolously quipped. "I try to keep myself in some kind of shape."

Reynolds grimaced with caustic repugnance, scoffing acridly after taking a hasty gulp. "Aaaahhh....disgusting stuff."

Matt chuckled in amusement. "Yes, isn't it."

Reynolds cleared his throat and sat forward. "Actually, Matt, I wanted to ask your permission for something."

Matt leaned forward with attentive curiosity.

"I always try to have a unit social activity the night before we deploy on an assignment, give the boys a chance to blow off some steam," Reynolds serenely explained. "Since we will be arriving at Mars in a couple of days, I was wondering if you would permit me to serve each of my men one flask of beer, the real stuff. I managed to smuggle a case on board."

Matt's brows rose in astonishment.

"I know the regulations about serving alcohol on CAS spacecraft," Reynolds nervously continued. "But I was hoping that you would permit an exception in this case."

Matt sat motionless for a moment, his face frozen in disbelief. Finally he cracked a waggish smirk and settled back in his chair. "I don't see why not." He shrugged non-chalantly "I've been known to fracture a rule or two in my time. Just don't get anyone stoned."

Reynolds sighed in relief. "No, of course not." Reynolds smiled. "Thank you, Matt. The lads will appreciate this."

Matt bent forward, clasping his fingers together atop the desk. "You surprise me, Lieutenant. Smuggled beer on my ship!"

With a crooked smile, Reynolds simply rolled his shoulders.

"I see that I'm going to have to have a talk with my friend, Jose Alvarez, when I get back to the Constitution," Matt whimsically concluded. "It seems that dock security isn't up to snuff."

The two men shared a brief laugh as Matt rose to his feet and stood by the side of the desk as he poured himself another drink. Reynolds respectfully declined.

"I only drink socially...." Matt explained as he rested his weight against the sturdy furniture "....and to help me sleep. Deadens the mind, you know." Matt's expression went blank for a fleeting moment, lost in the subconscious world of jumbled recollections. "Sometimes I can't sleep without it," he continued frankly. "I think too much." He slowly proceeded behind the desk once more, his free hand talking in conjunction with his mouth as his voice turned more sprightly. "Never think, Lieutenant. Be a good soldier and never think." He paused again, dropping his head morosely. "You pay a penalty for thinking," he somberly added.

"Sometimes I have the opposite problem," Reynolds offered dolefully. "Nightmares. There are times I'm afraid to go to sleep. Visions of three years ago, the din and anguished cries of battle, the dazed looks of confusion, fear and horror, the dirty and bloodied faces of boys almost young enough to be my sons, the sickly-putrid smell of death. It's kind of a sobering stimulant."

Matt folded his arms and looked upon him with a sympathetic eye. "What do you do?"

Reynolds's mouth twitched insouciantly after downing the last drop of Scotch. "Grab hold of my wife," he honestly replied with a genuine smile of pleasure. "If she's not with me I look at her picture and train my thoughts on joyous times with my family. And pray to God." He reached into his back pocket and pulled out a compact, black, eel skin leather electronic card and video holder, eagerly pressing a button that activated a short, personalized video image of his wife and family and handed it across the desk to Matt. "The lovely woman there is my darling wife, Cindy," Reynolds proudly announced as Matt carefully gazed at the tiny display. "And my two wonderful daughters are Alicia, the older one, and Megan, who was born just a year before the Lunar Conflict." Matt enviously studied the images as a lump settled in the middle of his throat. The suppressed and abysmal emptiness of his own life suddenly oozed to the surface of his consciousness. He was contented enough, but never truly happy. To share a life with a woman he loved, and who would love him for who he was in return. To raise some children and to watch them grow and mature under their combined guidance and tutelage, to pass on to them the values and beliefs that he so cherished. That is what he yearned for, what he was missing from becoming totally fulfilled. That and faith. Faith in God, in man, in himself. All were waning.

"That is a lovely family, Tom," Matt commented as he returned the stylish leather displayer. "You're a lucky guy."

"I like to think so. It's a tough life for them, I mean me being a soldier. Cindy nearly became a basket case during the Lunar Conflict, with me gone and having to care for an infant. Fortunately the war didn't last very long. She was unusually apprehensive and fearful when I departed on this mission, I don't know why. I told her it was just another job, a milk run, just a far away one, that's all. How about you, Matt, any family?"

Matt dispiritedly shook his head, unable to meet the Lieutenant's eyes. "Mom and Dad," he softly replied. "One married sister, that's all."

"Never been married yourself?" Reynolds continued to pry.

Matt sat back and folded his hands in his lap, sullenly sighing in resignation to the fact that for some reason he felt compelled to recount those painful days, though he was determined to be succinct. "Once, for two years. Long ago it seems, almost like another lifetime."

Reynolds shifted his weight with inquisitive vigilance, anxiously wondering why such a seemingly absorbing and congenial fellow hadn't fallen under some enchanting woman's magical spell. The anguish of Matt's memory illuminated across his face like a neon sign.

"I was in training, learning how to fly those small lunar shuttles during my early days with CAS," Matt forthrightly recalled. "I returned to my home in Virginia a day early. I wanted to surprise my wife, you see, whom I simply adored." Matt looked waywardly at the ceiling and frowned, shaking his head in disgust before peering across the desk once more. "I surprised her all right!" His voice grew boisterous and agitated. "I found her in our bed with another man!"

Reynolds sat frozen, his eyes popping out in horrified shock. He couldn't begin to fathom how that must have felt. Such a betrayal of the most intimate trust was unconscionable to him, though he wasn't naive enough not to realize that such conduct was prevalent in many relationships, just one more reason why humanity was in such a mess.

"Needless to say," Matt solemnly continued, tossing up his hands in abject hopelessness, "I was devastated. I had no idea that anything was going on. She just got lonely, she claimed. A....how should I say it....heated discussion erupted that lasted well into the next morning. I gathered up every possession that I could pack in my car and never looked back again. The only time I've seen her since was in divorce court. Matt hesitated, staring vacantly across the room. "I never have fully recovered from that trauma," he quietly lamented. "I really loved her."

An uneasy silence encompassed the cabin, enhancing the cracking sound of the stress vibrations on the metal plates and conduits of the superstructure as Matt brooded and Reynolds could think of no comforting advice to offer. Finally, Matt snapped out of his lethargy, pressing his body forward as he laid his arms atop the desk. "Well, so much for my ill-fated marriage," he bellowed vivaciously. "To this day I have never been able to completely trust another woman to the point I'm comfortable committing my total soul and passion. I wish I could, because there is someone I think is very special."

"That is most unfortunate," Reynolds deplored sympathetically. "I've only known you a few days but you seem to be a decent, compassionate man." He lurched to the edge of his cushioned seat with the air of stoic resolution. "I sincerely hope that you can find that kind of happiness. It's what makes life worth living. I will pray for the healing of your broken heart and the restoration of your faith."

As the reflected illumination from the Martian world grew increasingly brilliant in the forward window, the mood of the passengers and crew sparkled with renewed excitement and anticipation as they gathered for their after dinner ritual in the recreation room. Flippant chatter, like the incessant chirping of sparrows during the warming thaw of spring, filled the air. Animated talk and laughter, upbeat and jovial, was everywhere. Desirous expressions of delight at the prospect of applying one's trade on another planet; of investigating the marvels of this scientific wonder; of possibly sight-seeing such magnificent geographical anomalies like the colossal shield volcano, Olympus Mons, of the massive and expansive canyon system of Valles Marineris; of renewing an old acquaintance. For many, this would be their first trip to this extraordinary, alien domain. For others, it would be a wondrous return to the colony they helped engineer or design. For some, it would be their final journey.

Sheri and Matt skulked off to the ship's tiny surround theater to watch a movie, but were quickly crowded in by others. Unlike the old days, when an affectionate couple could snuggle in the dark, back corner while all eyes were trained forward, modern cinematic entertainment put the viewer in the middle, while the movie developed all around them, necessitating turning your head in all directions. They enjoyed themselves, nevertheless, contented with the warm clasp of the other's hand. Only a brief shoving scuffle between Jack Shoals and John Walinski momentarily dampened the merriment, and they were quickly separated. The private objected to the navigator's wanton attentions directed towards the habitual seductively attired Lucinda Desjardin, but the flirting was more like the other way around. To the casual, astute observer, the smart money was placed on both men sharing her ample feminine charms before the dawn of a new day.

Nominal. Nominal. Nominal. The digital readouts, computer analysis, and visual displays all read like the society page of the New York Times ----boring. Or was it the financial page, he couldn't decide. Reggie Lewis diligently monitored all the sensor scans continuously sweeping across gamma quadrant for any clue to the whereabouts of their enigmatic specter. He fancied its actions to that of a dubious vagrant tailing him along the darkened city streets of Patterson, ominously lurking in the shadows and murky corners, sizing-up the most opportune time to mug his next victim. His hypnotic attention was gratefully diverted from the routine drudgery of the night shift by the high-pitched swish of the opening of the elevator door. He turned, grinning like a Cheshire cat as his eyes focused admiringly on the delectable, refined face and slender bodily frame of Nichelle Bennett, standing apprehensively within the confines of the lift.

"Excuse me, Reggie," she timidly called out, cowering as if standing on the precipice of a towering, rock-strewn cliff in the eerie black of night. "I hope that I'm not disturbing you."

"Shit, no," Reggie gleefully replied as he leaped to his feet and raced to greet her with open arms. She had been expected. "I was wondering when you were coming. I was beginning to think that you were going to stand me up."

Nichelle cautiously stepped onto the dimly illuminated bridge and fell into his arms in an affectionate embrace.

"Welcome to my home away from home," Reggie mirthfully roared, spreading his arms and viewing the surroundings.

Nichelle nervously clutched his arm as she surveyed in awe the vast array of steady and blinking lights arranged on the numerous consoles around her. "Are you sure it's okay for me to be here?"

Reggie sloughed and grumbled. "Not exactly. The captain would probably put his foot so far up my ass that I could chew on his soles with my teeth if he ever found out, but as they say back at Administration when we complain about hazard pay, 'risk is our business.'"

"Well, I'd hate for you to get slammed because of me," she reluctantly stated, still worried about the propriety of her presence.

"Now don't get flaky on me, Nichelle. It would take a lot more than a little indiscretion to cause Reggie Lewis to crash and burn." With a guiding arm around her waist, Reggie led her forward towards the large window. "I want to share a special sight with you, but it's not up here."

Passing the operations station, Reggie stopped to set the scanners on their automatic, preprogrammed search patterns. That done, he escorted Nichelle over to the main window where he opened the floor hatch that led to the forward turret below. "Down here," he urged, briefly grabbing her hand before proceeding down the steps to the lift. Reggie looked up and noticed her timidity, a frozen cast of dread etched across her face. He paused, motioning with his hand. "It's okay, Nichelle, follow me down."

Carefully and with baited breath, Nichelle descended the series of steps to press against him in the close confines of the lift tube. A push of a button began their plunge. The sudden drop startled Nichelle, causing her to firmly clutch his powerful shoulders. He took hold of her hips to steady her, enjoying every moment, particularly cognizant of the stimulating sensation of her modest breasts brushing against his chest. Squeezed together, he began to appreciate the subtle preparations she had made for their visit, much more elegant than the occasion warranted. She had applied generous amounts of eye shadow, lip gloss, and facial creme. Her perfume diffused a strong, alluring aroma. Her long, black hair laid in lavish waves behind her shoulders. She wore a loosely-fitting, glimmering, shoulder-snapped, magenta silk blouse that was tucked into a pair of dressy, creme colored, pleated cotton slacks. Feminine and classy, but not seductive. It made Reggie feel very special that this lady would go to such lengths for just a simple meeting and chat. Looking down at his own worn, dingy flight suit caused him some embarrassment. Off the ship, he considered himself a meticulous dresser.

Upon arrival, the couple stumbled out into the tall, cramped compartment of the forward turret. Nichelle gasped in awe at the spectacle arrayed before her. The light from a million distant suns winked at her from all around her forward view. Holding her hand, Reggie led her to a point by the side of the laser cannon mount, to the very bounds of the shielded, transparent nose. Looking out over the limitless expanse of the universe, she felt like a guardian angel from heaven, soaring effortlessly through the currents and eddies of space and time, keeping watchful vigil over the stuff of creation.

"What a marvelous sight!" she astonishingly proclaimed as she shook her head in disbelief, amazed at the clarity and enormity of her view. "It's greater than my wildest expectations. I thought the view from the observatory on the Caucasus Mountains on the Sea of Serenity was something special, but this dwarfs it by comparison."

"I love to come down here and just gaze out," Reggie remarked as his eyes admiringly scanned the heavens. "It's as if the universe is my private domain. I just have to reach out and touch it. Best damn view on this whole ship."

"It's almost spiritual," added Nichelle portentously. "As if this was the golden highway to meet God."

Reggie muttered and stammered uncomfortably. "I....I've never been much for religion. I simply see the beauty of nature out there. Look! Do you see that bright point of light to the top right?" His left arm extended towards the dot while his right gently wrapped around her shoulder. "About the size of an old currency dime."

Nichelle's eyes closely traced the line of his arm until they focused on the flickering orb, the most radiant object in the sky.

"That's where we're going, man," Reggie proudly announced. "That's the planet Mars. It is so close to us compared to all other bodies that the reflection of the sun's rays makes it the brightest object we see."

Reggie stepped back, reached for a control panel at the base of the turret, and pressed a tiny button. Instantly the compartment was filled with the melodious strains from the old 20th century Gustav Holst symphony, *'The Planets.'* Pushing the hand grips of the laser mount to the side, Reggie settled into the station's comfortably padded chair, slapping his thigh with his hand.

"Come on Nichelle, make me a happy man."

With a snigger of delight, Nichelle wiggled onto his lap, shifting her body until she found the most cozy position. Throwing her arms around his neck, she nestled her head against his chest, gazing longingly through the glass at the lucent, twinkling blackness of space. Reggie's head reclined back, his arm coiling snugly around her waist, as they watched the stars and savored the music.

"Funny," she quietly mumbled. "I took you for soul or city camp sounds. Classical is the last thing I would have guessed."

Reggie laughed. "Only if the mood is right. I can sit here for hours and listen to Bach, Tchaikovsky, Wagner. It's very soothing. However, the next movement coming up in a minute is very stirring. Appropriately enough, it's called *'Mars, the Bringer of War.'* I love it."

Sitting cuddled together in warm serenity, Nichelle and Reggie listened to the hauntingly inspiring, martial orchestration of their destination's namesake. The powerful masterpiece inspired an uneasy question within Nichelle's active mind.

"Reggie," she softly beckoned, "have you ever been in a war?"

"No," he dryly replied, tenderly brushing the side of her head, "except for a football game at Morgantown, West Virginia. Relax and listen to the music."

As one harmonious piece followed another, they silently lost themselves within the comfort of the other's embrace, as if riding on the lush, velvety fibers of the magic carpet of the cosmos. Nichelle closed her eyes and purred in pleasure as Reggie's gentle fingers brushed supplely through her fluffy tresses and along the back of her neck. The urge to loosen her blouse was compelling, but looking down at her sweet face pressed against his heaving chest was pleasure enough for the moment. He had forgotten how it felt to hold a woman in his arms under a starlit sky in the cool autumn breeze along the Jersey shore. This was better. His lips slowly and devoutly pressed lightly against the crown of her head. Nichelle was fast asleep. Reggie beamed in tranquil satisfaction as he burrowed deep into his seat, firmly grasping her lithe figure as the melodious chords continued to accompany the field of stars in exquisite harmony. Gradually he felt his lids grow heavy and his head sluggishly drooped to serenely unite with hers.

Did my grandmother leave the phone off the hook again? Reggie's mind envisioned her jovial, old gray head hovering over a simmering, aromatic pot of homemade vegetable stew, a tattered country-style apron clinging to her short, plump frame. With her eyesight and coordination failing, she seemed to always have trouble properly seating the antiquated receiver after a call. He heard it again, a distant, repeating, high-pitched beeping sound. Visions of a large aluminum trash can with accordion arms and legs and a fishbowl for a head invaded his subconscious. A century-old television show that his grandmother always enjoyed the reruns of. The trash can waved its retractable appendages and frenetically shouted out, "Danger! Danger!" His brows slowly raised. It was clearer now, coming from above. He stirred. His movement awakened Nichelle, who sleepily yawned, covering her mouth with her hand. He recognized it now, like the electronic signal from a pager. It was the automatic alarm. Something was not nominal.

"Oh, shit!" he bellowed. "Come on, Nichelle, wake up." He roughly shook her to full consciousness and swiftly jumped to his feet. "We have to go, now!"

"What....what's wrong?" she groggily questioned as Reggie pushed her along towards the lift tube. "What's happening?"

"It's the bridge alarm," he gravely replied. "Quickly, get in."

As the lift ascended, Reggie checked his watch. He had been asleep for over an hour. "Damn! My butt is going to fry for sure." The pulsating beeping tone increased in intensity the closer they approached to the deck of C & C. His first instinct was that their interplanetary shadow had returned. "It's probably just a sensor contact that we've been tracking," he reassured, more for Nichelle's consolation than his own. With his hands forced around her waist in the constricting tube, he yearningly stared into her dazed, confused eyes. "I'm sorry about this. I was hoping for a more personal and idyllic ending to this evening."

Nichelle reached up with her hand and affectionately touched his cheek. "Me too. I enjoyed our private rendezvous." Her voice was sweet and sensual. "Another time, perhaps."

Reggie lowered his head to kiss her when the lift came to a sudden stop. His secular desires would have to wait. Within microseconds he activated the hatch and charged up the ladder, immediately turning towards the operations station. But the flashing crimson image nipping at the corner of his sight was not emanating from there, but from the engineering console across the room. The distressing, high-pitched beeps were also blaring from there. Throngs of terror ripped at his heart as he raced to the post, where multiple indicators were brilliantly beaming their warnings of peril. His fingers frenetically called up the engineering systems analysis program.

"You had better leave the bridge," he firmly advised Nichelle as she emerged from below, remaining staunchly focused on the monitors. "Quickly."

Nichelle had the look of dread and panic, but apprehensively complied. "Yes, of course. I'll see you later." Casting a fearful glance in Reggie's direction, she briskly entered the elevator that would whisk her below.

The data being disclosed on the numerous engineering displays revealed an ominous shadow creeping-up on the safe operation of the ship, a Sword of Damocles dangling ever nearer over their collective heads. The nuclear reactor temperature was dangerously rising.

"Bridge to engineering!" he distraughtly called out upon reaching the communications console. There was no response. "Bridge to engineering!" Nothing but excruciating moments of ghostly silence. With steadily increasing tension and acute frustration pounding at his mind, Reggie desperately yelled into the speaker. "Bridge to engineering! Come on Frank, you shithead, wake up down there, man!" Not even a crackle of static could be discerned, only the stillness of the grave. Reggie angrily cursed, anxiously running his hand through his frizzy hair. Finally he took a deep breath and linked into the private quarters of Vijay Prophu. His tone was calm but vehement. "Vijay, we have a problem with the reactor."

It felt like the delicate paw of his childhood cat impatiently nudging his arm on a lazy Saturday morning, motivating him to awaken and start a new day, hopefully beginning with a generous feeding. Matt sleepily rolled over, senselessly lost in stage one of non-REM, somewhere in the twilight of awareness and sleep. He felt firm pressure on his shoulder, and then his torso began to rock. Wearily cracking his eyelids open, it took his pupils a few seconds to adjust to the darkness before he recognized the slanted eyes and thin face of his diminutive roommate, Yong Chang, hovering over him in trepidation, distressfully communicating something in a light Asian accent.

"Matt!" he called, tugging at his arm. "Commander! You're being paged!"

Matt glared peculiarly at the middle-aged planetary science engineer whose ancestors had immigrated from Taiwan a hundred years before, until he was roused to full alertness. Only then did he become fully conscious of Reggie's resolute alarm. "Captain Maitland to the bridge! Please respond!"

With a sudden surge of adrenaline, Matt swung upright and clumsily groped for the communications panel by the side of the bed. "This is Maitland. What is it, Reg?"

"Sir, we have a situation. Your presence is required on the bridge."

Matt was taken aback by his formality and obvious desire to avoid specifics, undoubtedly aware of the proximity of other ears. "Very well, Reggie, I'll be there presently." With the elasticity of a rubberband, Matt sprung from his bed and rashly slipped into his flight suit as Yong looked on in silent consternation.

"Don't worry," Matt nonchalantly remarked as he hurriedly zipped up his garment. "It's probably just some routine emergency. Happens all the time in space. Go back to bed."

Curious heads anxiously peered out from the safety of their rooms as Matt bolted past their quarters, apparently awakened by the stirring of other members of the crew. As he entered the main cylinder, his ears became cognizant of soft, rapid thuds receding towards the stern and upon turning, noticed the tiny, dark frame of Tracy Lang running towards the cargo bay. Something was terribly amiss. Uneasiness turned to nervous dread as he was struck by the realization that he wasn't the only one losing sleep this night. Sprinting the rest of the way, he rushed onto the bridge panting profusely, a cowlick crowning his disheveled hair. "What the hell is going on, Reg?" he irritably barked after taking a deep breath, joining him by the engineering console.

Reggie looked up with an uncharacteristic grimace of distress. "Reactor temperature is steadily climbing and I get no answer from Frank," he frenziedly replied. "I don't know where the hell he is, man!"

Matt gazed at Reggie with piercing fire before leaning over to check the indicators for himself.

"I've already informed Vijay," Reggie continued more assuredly. "He's on his way there now. I thought it best not to sound the general alarm with all these passengers on board."

"Perspicacious thinking, Reg," Matt replied as he straightened to face him. "The last thing we need is a ship load of panicked people."

"It's been about ten minutes since I killed the warning alarm, and the temperature continues to rise dangerously close to hazardous levels."

"I'm heading down there," Matt briskly announced. "Continue to monitor the board. We may have to scrap it completely"

"Aye, Captain."

Vijay recklessly dashed into the engineering compartment where the immediate sight confronting him caused his robust frame to pause hesitantly for a moment. The motionless, seated body of Frank Sharp was slumped over the control board at the reactor station, half-empty, sealed lid coffee mug on a magnetic tray by his side with a few minuscule crumbs from a recently devoured sandwich floating listlessly above his head. The reactor monitor panels were lit up like the Las Vegas Strip with multiple warning alarms beeping incessantly. Rushing to his side, Vijay pulled back the limp form and quickly checked the pulse. Slow and faint but definitely detectable. There was no sign of injury or any physical trauma. Carefully he lowered Frank's head to rest on the console and quickly began to assess the situation. Reactor temperature and pressure were both in the danger zone and continuing to rise. Coolant levels and gas flow were mysteriously well below optimum parameters. He had just begun to manually adjust the controls for the neon tanks when Tracy dashed into the room, soon followed by Miguel. Tracy hurried to Frank's aid but was harshly pulled aside by Vijay's powerful, determined grip.

"He's okay, for now. I need you to quickly get the cadmium rods inserted. We must slow down the reactions and relieve some of the pressure before we have a core breech."

As Tracy moved to the appropriate station, Vijay placed a firm hand upon Miguel's shoulder "Get on the relief valves and see if you can bring down the pressure."

As his staff diligently went about their tasks, Vijay returned his attention to the coolant controls. All indicators read nominal except for the fact that only about half of the required coolant gas was reaching the reactor chamber. "Not another defective sensor module," he silently scoffed at the possibility of an all too familiar problem. He resolutely accessed the computer diagnostic system for the reactor. Within seconds it reported in its soft, monotone, digital voice what he already knew. Rising temperature and pressure but no mechanical failure that could be detected. Vijay was perplexed as he scratched his chin nervously, chaotic thoughts wracking his brain. Suddenly, like a flash of divine inspiration, a single notion ascended above the jungle of mental suppositions. What if the problem wasn't within the reactor chamber at all? His fingers willfully pressed the voice interface button. "Diagnostic analysis, neon containment tanks."

The few brief seconds seemed like an eternity before the affable though passionless voice reported. "Mechanical failure, containment tank two."

Vijay's heart thumped within his chest, praying to his gods that he didn't have a ruptured coolant tank on his hands. "Specify failure."

"Outlet valve malfunction."

Vijay rashly darted to a nearby storage closet and hastily stepped into a bright orange, heavily shielded radiation suit that was designed to deflect the tissue damaging electromagnetic waves. "I'm going to have a look at those tanks."

Tracy turned to him with the look of desperation. "You had better make it fast. We've managed to slow the rate of increase, but I estimate we have less than fifteen minutes before core breech is imminent."

"Prepare the boron rods," Vijay irritably ordered. "If I can't fix this thing, we'll have to spike the reactor."

"What!" Matt's emphatic voice clamored out above the tumult as he scampered into the room. "Spike the reactor?"

"We'll have to shut it down, Matt, if coolant levels can't be restored," Vijay solemnly but sternly asserted as he finished dressing.

"How long will it take to reactivate?" Matt worriedly inquired as he bent over to check Frank's inert body.

"If there is no appreciable damage," Vijay replied as he grabbed the radiation helmet with its large faceshield and long, synthetic shoulder flaps, "thirty-six to forty-eight hours."

Matt frowned at him in annoyance. "Vij, we don't have that kind of time."

Vijay grimaced as he slipped on the helmet. "We don't have time to blow-up either!" his hollowed voice dryly proclaimed. "No point standing around chatting, I have work to do."

Matt gave an approving nod and a casual salute as Vijay moved to the left rear of the room and activated the vacuum seal hatch led to the reactor chamber. The next moment he was gone as a whirling gush of air heralded the closure of the door behind him.

"What happened to Frank?" Matt inquired as he turned to Tracy.

Tracy shrugged ignorantly. "We just found him like this. Shouldn't we get him to the infirmary?"

"Never mind, Tracy," Matt coldly replied, "keep your attention on that reactor."

Tracy despondently turned back to the console. "Aye, sir."

Matt scurried over to the communications panel and emphatically hailed Reggie on the bridge. "Reg, wake-up Doctor Oliver and get her ass down here right away. Frank is unconscious."

Vijay maneuvered outside the massive biological shield of the reactor containment chamber, constructed of feet thick reinforced concrete containing heavy iron, steel, and lead punchings. Under normal circumstances, the radiation suit was not necessary beyond the thermal and biological shields, but Vijay reasoned that caution was prudent at this point, remembering the words of Byron - *'All's to be fear'd where all is to be lost.'* However, in the event of an explosion, what difference would it make? He found where the two huge cylindrical ducts entered the reactor chamber overhead and followed them into another isolated room that housed twin towering vats of neon gas, each twenty feet in diameter and stories high. Even through the insulation of his suit, Vijay could feel the icy coolness of the air the closer he walked to the tanks. An unprotected hand touching one of the vessels would instantly freeze. Locating the control panel to tank number two along the near wall, he immediately checked the visual dials and discovered that no gas was flowing from the tank despite the computer controlled order for disbursement. Instantly he unlatched the front of the panel and swung open the door to expose all of the electrical switches, circuits, and modules. With the aid of a small spotlight from his utility belt, he was able to quickly locate the gas flow outlet switch. He winced back in shock and horror. To his chagrin, he discovered that the auto setting had been reset to the off position....manually! The outlet valve that regulated the release of the coolant neon gas from the storage tanks to the reactor chamber was permanently locked into the closed position. He reached out and slid the circuit switch to the auto setting. Anguished seconds of silence followed. Nothing happened. His mind raced through the possibilities once more. The automatic setting should have enabled the computer command to open the valve. He angrily flipped the switch to off and back to auto again. Only the low whooshing sound from the other tank could be heard. Anxiously he checked his watch. He had less than ten minutes before the reactor would have to be completely shut down and seriously jeopardize their mission. With the intuitiveness that twenty years of system design work could inspire, he set the selector to off and used the battery powered bolt remover taken from the compact tool satchel clinging to his belt to loosen the circuit board. Delicately pulling it away from its housing, he checked over the connections from behind, specifically the ones leading to the outlet switch. He noticed it immediately. It stood out among the myriad, twisted connections like a naked woman at a black tie party. One of the lead wires was severed. At closer inspection, a nice clean cut. Vijay grew enraged as he reached for his tool bag - this was no accident! Using a small, square magnet to anchor the board to the front panel in the zero-g environment, Vijay muttered a few choice curses from his ancestral Hindi dialect as he efficiently spliced the line and connectors together with a portable electrical repair kit. Once satisfied, he swiftly reassembled the board within its housing and tensely held his breath as his unusually shaky fingers flipped the selector switch back to automatic. He looked up hopefully at the huge, cylindrical conduit that stretched from the neon tank through the wall and waited in the relative, tortuous silence. The serene moments of pure agony were finally interrupted by a metallic clicking from deep within the bowels of the duct, followed by the glorious, uproarious swishing of air as the coolant gas whisked from the storage tank on its belated journey to the reactor chamber. With a thankful sigh of relief, Vijay closed the front panel and checked the indicator. Neon gas was flowing normally from tank number two. He had done it!

Wearily reemerging into the engineering compartment, Vijay noticed that Doctor Oliver had arrived, dressed in her standard issue light blue NASA work suit, assiduously hovering over Frank's motionless body, now reclined against the back of his chair, as she performed a methodical, preparatory exam. Matt was standing uneasily to the side while the other engineers dutifully continued to monitor the reactor systems.

"Is he going to be all right, Susan?" Matt impatiently questioned in a tone reflecting profound concern.

"I don't know, yet," she replied with a hint of annoyance as she continued her examination. "His vital signs are low, but steady and regular. I'll have to get him to the medical analyzer and run some tests. Doctor Caldwell is on his way with a gurney. Until then, I won't hazard a guess."

Matt huffed in frustration. "Very well, Doctor."

Noticing Vijay in the doorway, a reserved grin crossed his face as he slowly approached him. "Nice work, my friend. Temperature and pressure are gradually lowering to normal levels."

Vijay exasperatingly ripped off his protective helmet and indifferently tossed it aside, ignoring its floating trajectory towards the ceiling in the weightless environment. Matt could see the uncustomary distraught and angry scowl that was dominating his facial expression.

"Hey, Vij! What is it?"

Vijay folded his arms fretfully. "Would a turned off control switch and a severed connection interest you?" came his satirical response.

Matt's eyes bulged in disbelief. "What?"

Vijay restlessly shifted his feet as he recounted to Matt exactly what he had found. "Someone had to have gone back there." His expression was flushed with worry and concern as he softly whispered. "Matt, we have a problem."

Matt was stunned to silence, frozen like an icy stalagmite to the floor. Not wanting to believe his ears, he threw up his hands, tossing his head around in confusion. "Wait a minute. SOME....ONE....Frank?"

Vijay shook off the suggestion. "Someone."

Their debate was interrupted by the approaching low rumbling sound of magnetic wheels against the seams of the metal floor, drawing ever closer until Ben Caldwell appeared pushing the medical stretcher in front of him. It was easy for the two doctors to move Frank's weightless body from the chair, strapping him down on the litter so he too, like Vijay's helmet, didn't drift aimlessly away.

"We'll take him to the medical bay," Doctor Oliver said as she turned to Matt. "Don't worry, we won't lose him."

"Thank you, Susan," Matt politely replied.

"Would you mind saving that sandwich container and coffee mug?" she asked, glancing over towards the console at the magnetic tray holding the items. "We may need to analyze the contents."

"Of course," Matt agreed, nodding at Tracy to comply with the request.

The men watched with weighty concern as the two doctors ushered their stricken reactor officer out of engineering before soberly turning back to face each other.

Vijay smirked. "I don't mind telling you, Matt," he whimsically expressed, "that there were a few choice moments that I wished I was somewhere else. Anywhere else would have done."

Matt was not amused. "Come on. Vij, quit crapping around. Get to the point."

"The point, Captain, sir, is that there is suddenly someone on board that knows a whole damn lot about a ship's nuclear reactor."

"One of us?" Matt questioned in implausible disbelief. Vijay simply shrugged. "Who?"

Vijay sighed reluctantly. "There are all sorts of engineer types on board. Two or three of them may possess certain knowledge."

"What are you saying, Vij?" questioned Matt impetuously.

"What I am saying, Matt, is that I believe that we have a saboteur on board."

CHAPTER

Omniscient and Herculean, the Roman God of War stretched out his mighty hand and snared the feeble creature that was both servant and metallic monument to the perseverance and inventiveness of this strange, inquisitive species called humanity; these curious beings that had the arrogant audacity to invade his sphere of influence. Slowly and deliberately it was drawn closer, kicking and squirming with the tenacity of Caesar's legions as blasts of flame and gas resisted the pull, but this was his realm and his laws would rule. Little did this great deity realize just how much man had progressed over the centuries, and he too could now manipulate the forces of nature; that he was no logger constrained by the power of its bolts. Mars could no longer hold sway over man. In fact, Mars was now at man's beckoning call. Or was it?

Ever since the mishap in the reactor room, the Guilford Courthouse had been periodically firing its twin decelerator engines mounted on each flank of the bulky engineering section to slow her forward inertia in preparation for Martian orbit. The reduction in speed had to be painstakingly subtle in order to keep the fragile human inhabitants from smashing and mangling themselves against the forward walls. Still eighteen hours away, the glowing sphere, now filling the right-center of the forward window, was a glistening crimson silver dollar in a vast black vault of a million scattered white-hot pennies; but still too distant to make out any surface detail without the aid of a higher resolution setting of the magnifier screen. Nevertheless, even from a distance of more than 8 million miles, Mars power could be felt - its gravitational field pulling and accelerating

115

the ship which compelled the preprogrammed navigation computer to compensate for attitude and speed in order to keep the ship on its proper orbital approach.

The natural exhilaration of the crew at the imminent approach of their objective was severely tempered by the anxiety, distress, and fatigue brought about by the disturbing events of their previous sleepless night. The morning hours had ushered in an air of murkiness and gloom as a vigorous and boisterous round of heated conjectural debates erupted within the suddenly perilous walls of the great vessel. The possibility that there was someone on board who would intentionally damage the ship and endanger the lives of all was a very fearful and sobering notion for everyone. Matt regretfully felt obliged to order the implementation of a security level three alert which restricted access to the bridge and engineering sections to escorted invitation only and required all night duty personnel to carry loaded sidearms. As might be expected, wild speculation ran rampant amongst the passengers as a host of unsubstantiated rumors permeated the common areas of the central disk. Their frustrated attempts to pry some answers out of a passing crewmember were unceremoniously met with the generalities and evasiveness of the most cunning and astute of Washington politicians. This was a simmering pot of intrigue that Matt was adamantly determined to keep a tight lid on, at least for another 48 hours. The sooner he could get them off his ship the better.

As Jack fed some minor parameter adjustments regarding Martian orbit into the guidance computer, Matt instructed Sheri to run another comprehensive sensor sweep of gamma quadrant, searching for any sign of their shadowy ghost. With their gradual deceleration, he felt that Casper might tip his hand again, but alas, she found nothing but the background noise of the heavens. Frankly, Matt would have preferred finding it running up his tailpipe.

With his misgivings appeased, at least for the moment, Matt paid a visit to the medical bay, accompanied by Sheri and Vijay, where they found the spectacled Doctor Susan Oliver sitting studiously behind an austere, creme colored, aluminum alloy desk, examining some text on the medical monitor. Behind her on a narrow, high bed equipped with rising metal side rails laid the unfortunate, dormant body of Frank Sharp, clad in a navy CAS hospital gown.

"How's Frank doing?" Matt inquired with a tone of earnest concern as Vijay doggedly brushed past the doctor to stand by the reactor officer's side, firmly taking his limp hand into his own.

Doctor Oliver lifted the glasses from the bridge of her nose as she leaned back and swiveled to face her visitors, wearily wiping her forehead with the back of her hand. "He's in a coma," she forthrightly announced. "A coma induced by a metabolic abnormality."

"Abnormality!" Matt exclaimed with surprise as he braced his back against a steel cabinet and folded his arms. "Caused by what?"

Doctor Oliver sighed in despondent frustration. "We found traces of Chlordazide Five throughout his bloodstream. That's a Benzodiazepine drug that...."

"Wait a minute, Susan," Matt impatiently interrupted as he vexatiously stepped forward, shaking his head in confusion as his hands flailed aimlessly in the air. "Please speak in English for the benefit of us poor, dumb space cadets."

Susan briefly smirked at the remark as she ran a tiring hand through the curls of her frazzled, blond hair. "Okay, Matt, okay," she ruefully consented. "Chlordazide Five is like a barbiturate. It's a central nervous system depressant....strongest stuff you ever saw!" Her head jolted emphatically. "Well, let's just say that a few milligrams could topple an elephant."

Matt, Sheri, and Vijay nervously exchanged glances of alarm.

"It's primarily prescribed for severe cases of insomnia and hyperactivity," Susan continued, staring up at Matt with a glint of trepidation. "It's very dangerous stiff, Matt. A slightly heavier dose would have killed him."

Sheri gasped frightfully, holding a quivering hand to her chest. "Then you're saying that Frank is going to recover?" she anxiously asked.

Susan nodded solemnly. "He should be up and about in two to three days with one helluva headache."

The worry on Vijay's face had not dissipated with Susan's prognosis. "Can you awaken him, Doctor?"

Susan shrugged indecisively. "We could try some powerful stimulants to counteract the drug, but I'd advise against it. It would shoot his body chemistry to hell. It's better that we allow his body to cleanse itself naturally."

An annoying itch irritated Matt's upper left arm as he frenetically sorted through a hundred disquieting questions that darted through his imaginative mind. "Well, how did it get into his system in the first place?" he ponderously queried as he scratched.

Susan looked puzzled, blankly staring beyond her guests as her teeth mindlessly kneaded the plastic ear tip of her eyeglass frame. "We're not sure....yet!" Her bearing became more resolved as she refocused on Matt. "There are only two ways it could have got into his blood. It was either injected or ingested." Susan's body straightened, her hand flicking away a stray blond hair from her brow. "We checked him out thoroughly and could find no sign of a hypo dispenser mark or even a needle puncture."

Vijay, who had been training his attention on Frank, suddenly lifted a lifeless arm and pointed to a tiny circular area of discoloration above the elbow joint. "Were you examining him with your eyes shut, Doctor!" he angrily bellowed. "I can see a dispenser mark right here."

Susan became enraged, rashly flying off the chair to confront him. "I can't believe that you could consider me that incompetent, Mister Prophu," she furiously retorted in his face. "Those are my injections, you idiot! I've been adding nutrient and oxygen supplements to his bloodstream, helping to invigorate his metabolism. Maybe I should go down to engineering and look over your engines."

Growing intolerant of the pointless bickering, Matt irritably erupted. "That's enough, you two! Just put it on ice. We're all on the same side here. Everyone is a little strung out right now."

Ashamed of his callous outburst, Vijay lowered his head in embarrassment. "Please forgive me, Doctor. I didn't mean to chide you like that. I'm just worried about Frank."

Painfully aware of the emotional irrationality of her own ego, Susan calmed herself and placed a sympathetic hand upon Vijay's shoulder. "Yes, yes, I understand," she tenderly cajoled. "We're all a bit uptight over this incident."

Summoning back her professional demeanor, Susan turned to Matt once again. "As I was saying, it must have come from something he consumed. Doctor Caldwell is n the lab now analyzing the sandwich crumbs and the coffee residue. We should have something definitive shortly."

Matt was relieved with the encouraging prognosis, but his tension was far from eased. It was becoming apparent to him that someone had intentionally drugged his reactor officer to eliminate the only human obstacle from free access to the reactor chamber. It was a very sobering and unsettling situation that he found himself engulfed, one that was beyond his experience.

After politely thanking Doctor Oliver for her tireless efforts on Frank's behalf, Matt and his two close companions retired to the relative serenity of the captain's suite where Matt wasted little time braking in to his elegant cherry bar cabinet.

"Pick your poison," Matt called out as Sheri and Vijay settled comfortably into the couch, pausing in regret for an instant after realizing his unfortunate choice of words.

"The usual for me," Sheri casually announced.

Matt mixed together the orange juice and vodka combination before raising a bottle of grape juice towards his troubled engineer. "Vij?"

"No thanks, Matt, I'll have what you're having."

Matt's jaw dropped in astonishment. Vijay drinking whiskey, he thought, that was unheard of!

Vijay snickered in amusement at the sight of Matt's bafflement. "After these last twelve hours, I owe it to myself," he frivolously added.

Matt shrugged acquiescently and mixed together two scotch and soda's. Everyone was strangely silent as Matt delivered the refreshments, with Vijay draining his pilsner glass before Matt could turn around as if he were drinking water from the purest artesian well. With a guttural hum of satisfaction, Vijay used the back of a forefinger to wipe a drop of wayward liquid from his lower lip. Matt raised his brows in wonderment. "Another?"

"Please, large and straight," Vijay replied as naturally as if he were talking about the weather.

Matt retrieved the dwindling green bottle and refilled the empty glass. Before Matt could replace the cork, Vijay had downed part of the whiskey with the alacrity of the most adroit Joe Six-Pack. Matt leered at him with contrived indignation. "Please, feel free with my scotch."

Vijay looked up and smiled. "Thanks, I will."

Leaving what was left of the scotch on a nearby table, Matt slowly moved behind his desk, shaking his head in bewilderment. Much more than his friend's sudden affinity for alcohol was odd about this frightful situation. Matt could sense the tension from their wracked expressions and tremulous gazes of impending doom. Sheri gasped in exasperation as her body restlessly fidgeted against the pliant navy cushions, the sharpened nails of her trembling fingers nervously tingeing the sides of her glass.

"I don't mind telling you guys," she remarked, cradling the drink in her lap, "that I'm scared shitless!"

Matt took a hurried swallow and stammered. "You...and me both."

Sheri glanced warily at both men before wrenching forward, pressing into the desk with agitation. "Somebody tried to kill Frank!" she excitedly cried. "Shouldn't we be checking the beverage dispensers and food packs for contamination?"

Matt looked at her with disdain. "You'd be wasting your time," he scoffed acrimoniously. "That was no random incident, Sheri. Someone wanted Frank out of the way so they could get to the reactor. Get a grip."

Sheri gulped down the rest of her Screwdriver and slammed against the back of the sofa, folding her arms in a pouting huff over the admonishment. Regretting his brusqueness, Matt felt a sympathetic urge to comfort her with a passionate embrace, but more disconcerting thoughts regarding Frank dominated his attention. Something just didn't add up. "You know," he reflectively pondered aloud, "it seems to me that someone went out of their way not to kill him."

Matt noticed Sheri glaring at him peculiarly. "Come on, Matt. What kind of harebrained notion is that?"

"Yeah! Yeah!" he exclaimed with renewed vigor as he leaned towards her. "Listen, there would have been plenty of ways to kill him. That Chlor....Chlorda....whatever is pretty powerful stuff if Susan is correct. A slightly larger dose would have killed him. I don't think that whoever was responsible would have made that kind of mistake. I think that they just wanted Frank out of commission for a day or two."

Sheri smirked, her head bobbing in comprehension. "You may have a point there but why induced coma? Why not a mild sedative, or a blow to the head for that matter?"

Matt threw up his hands and twitched. "Do I look like Sherlock Holmes?"

Sheri bashfully lowered her eyes and devilishly grinned. "I'm rather partial to the racy space mysteries of the super-sleuth Fawna Lorelei."

Matt was shocked at the revelation, sitting silently flabbergasted as his mind recalled his second-hand knowledge of the stories noted for their keen and sometimes unusual sexual appetites of the siren detective. He wondered what other interesting personality tidbits his dearest friend had thus far hidden from him. Even when upset, she looked very enchanting and sensual to him. If he could only find the courage to fall in love again, he thought. "Sheri," he softly whispered as his torso hovered over the desk top, "we have to talk. Later."

Sheri quietly giggled, her cheeks blushing a rosy pink. Matt fondly gazed upon her as erotic thoughts crept into his head before abruptly becoming perturbed for momentarily allowing himself to be so distracted from the seriousness of the ship's business. It was so unlike him for his mind to salaciously wander this way. The emotional diversion only served to heighten his own doubts as to his ability to maintain an effective command should he become enmeshed in a more intimate relationship. Mentally berating his own weakness, Matt kicked his attention back to the pressing matter at hand. He noticed Vijay sitting quietly in a stupor, starring glassy-eyed across the room, his mind obviously lost in the contemplative wilderness of some obscure paradox.

"Vij!" Matt intensely called out. "What are you thinking?"

Leisurely crossing his legs as he set aside his near empty glass, Vijay turned to Matt but mesmerizingly focused beyond him as if beholding the apparition of the great deity Maya herself. Something was definitely bothering his friend. Matt tilted his head with curiosity at the zombie-like figure of his chief engineer until Vijay finally fluttered his lashes and rejoined the sentient world.

"Forgive me," he said with muffled breath as he clasped his fingers together. "I was just thinking that...."

The pensive pause made Matt impatient. "Yes, go on."

Vijay sighed heavily as he shifted his forearm against the padded armrest. "Well, while the two of you were fretting over Frank's condition and spicy detective stories, I was giving some thought to the actions of the intruder in the reactor room. Very odd."

Matt sneered facetiously at the initial chiding remark before sliding to the edge of his seat as his interest was peaked. "I'm listening."

"It occurred to me that the saboteur went to an awful lot of trouble to disable one neon tank."

Matt was confused. "I'm not following you, Vij."

Vijay lurched forward. "If the intent was to destroy or disable this vessel," he confidently surmised, "the person or person's had plenty of opportunity to do more serious damage. The sabotage to the neon tank control unit was difficult to isolate but easily repaired once found. Why not strike at a more critical system in a more destructive way? Rupture the hydrogen tanks, inhibit the exhaust flow or the recycling system, breech the gas core itself, or simply smash a few vital control panels for that matter. We could have very easily been crippled for good."

Matt and Sheri exchanged illuminated glances of surprise as if Vijay had simultaneously turned on the lighting grids to each of their dark, dusty attics. The emergency was serious enough, Matt thought, but Vijay was right. With apparent adequate understanding of the reactor system, why wasn't more critical, perhaps irreparable, damage done? Why the cloak-and-dagger stuff at all? Matt turned wishfully back to Vijay. "What's your assessment?"

Vijay rolled his eyes uncomfortably, choking on a lump in his throat. "If this wasn't so scary, I'd say it was a mischievous prank by one of my more colorful CAS engineering instructors at the training academy, seeing if I'm awake out here."

Matt chuckled amusingly.

"Look, Matt," Vijay continued in a more serious tone. "If you give me the parts, I'll build it. If it's supposed to flush, I'll keep it flushing. If it breaks, I'll fix it. But don't ask me about the workings of the mind. Psychology is totally alien to me. I don't have any specs on that."

Despite the gravity of the predicament that confronted them, Matt couldn't contain a mirthful grin at his engineer's manner. Turning to Sheri, whose anxiety inhibited her ability to see any humor in the situation, and light-heartily called for her input. "So, Sheri, what would Fawna Lorelei do in a case like this?"

Doctor Oliver's medical report confirmed their fearful suspicions. Frank Sharp had been intentionally drugged. Doctor Caldwell's chemical analysis had revealed trace amounts of Chlordazide Five in the residue of the coffee mug. Upon a more detailed examination, he discovered a tiny puncture hole in the polystyrene lid of the ceramic mug, the type of mark that could be made by an outdated hypodermic needle. In addition, the minuscule breech had been subsequently sealed by a drop of epoxy glue. The report concluded that the act could have been accomplished in a matter of seconds, most likely while Frank was briefly in one of the adjoining rooms performing a routine systems check or an innocent bathroom break.

The revelations did nothing to assuage the consternation of the Guilford Courthouse crew, but at least they knew what they were up against. Matt enlisted the cooperation of the two medical professionals in not disclosing the specifics of the incident to any of the passengers. Panic had to be avoided. Once he delivered his cargo to Jamestown, he would release all pertinent information to the appropriate authorities and let them worry about it. Assuming, of course, that they make it to Jamestown. Matt resisted the suggestion of periodic armed patrols as unduly alarmist and instead instructed Reggie to more closely scrutinize and record the corridor monitor images for any unusual movement. Constantly looming over them was always the danger of another attempt.

The crew became the center of attention that evening as individuals and small groups clamored around them in search of the latest scuttlebutt. All except for Caroline Hart, who after her initial inquiry into Frank's condition, sympathetically changed the direction of her conversations to her own excitement of nearing Mars; and the soldiers, who through their training and discipline, left the matter alone and devoted their time to the trivial pursuits of the night.

The incessant prying and interruptions finally compelled Matt and Sheri to excuse themselves from their colleagues in the rec room and they soon found themselves aimlessly meandering through the hollow corridors of the ship, lost in frivolous conversation. The journey culminated at the captain's suite, where they could finally steel that which had thus far so frustratingly eluded them - a few moments alone together. Battered and fatigued from the lack of sleep and the harrowing events of the past 24 hours, they hadn't even bothered to change out of their uniforms. Wearily collapsing together on the familiar couch, they took comfort in the warmth of each other's silent embrace. Matt cuddled her lithe form tightly, savoring the congenial pressure of her cheek against his chest, the softness of her thick, black hair lightly brushing against his chin. Her hip pressed solidly against his thigh as she snuggled closer, purring like a pampered kitten, flattering dark eyelashes slowly closing in peaceful repose as her delicate hand rooted itself more firmly around his waist. He fondly gazed upon this enchanting woman, his hand lovingly massaging her upper arm and shoulder blade. He had been fantasizing about an opportunity such as this, of slowly undressing her like a treasured gift at Christmas, relishing every prolonged moment; the stimulating sight of her feminine lingerie as it teasingly accentuated her womanly charms; the feel of her sultry, silky-smooth skin sliding blissfully under his gentle fingertips; the tantalizing sounds of her moans of pleasure in response to his arousing caress. He wondered if he could really be feeling genuine love for her, or was this just another primal urge that he so often had to contend with? Without a definitive answer, he was left once more to deal with his conscience and his fear, and he was just too worn out to fight that battle again. With Sheri nuzzled close to him, their bodies joined in a hundred places, Matt could feel the gnawing tension in the back of his neck slowly oozing away. Enveloped around her in the silent darkness, he found the perfect elixir for relaxation and he immersed himself in the soothing tranquillity that flooded his soul. It was a warm contentment that he hadn't experienced in years, not as forceful as physical sex but ultimately more fulfilling. Maybe he was falling in love after all, he surmised. His lips tenderly pressed against the crown of her head. He felt her fingers twitching against his ribs, a soft, delectable sigh escaping from deep within her throat. Carefully he inched his head to the side to get a better look. Sheri was fast asleep. Smiling with innocent delight, Matt reclined against the back of the sofa, taking solace in the knowledge that a woman as desirable as Sheri could feel such comfort within the grasp of his arms. He felt his own lids growing increasingly heavy as his head periodically drooped uncontrollably. This was not at all what he originally had in mind. Vijay would later gleefully boast that he caught the two of them sleeping together. Strict interpretation would support his assertion. He found them sound asleep.

Giant swirls of reddish-orange blossomed like the azaleas of spring against the blackened meadow of the forward view. Deeper, more rustic hues trickled across the dazzling sphere, intersected by spacious tracks of darker brownish-gray. Tiny puffs of unharvested cotton freckled the burnished face of the God of War, its northern and southern polar regions adorned with permanent caps of irregular layers of white and creme. Mars was less than 200,000 miles away and appeared to the bridge crew to be slightly larger than the Moon as seen from Earth orbit. As smiles erupted all around, they gazed in reverence and wonderment at the gleaming crimson ball in all its majestic shades and shadows. Unfortunately, it was a sight that only the four of them had the privilege to enjoy, the windows of the central disk still being oriented towards the vastness of space. The exuberance and pleasure that Matt was experiencing was obvious to all. It was his third trip to the Red Planet, and the view of the final approach never failed to entrance him, with its striking rustic coloration's and the general mystique that surrounds it that always seemed to produce a thrilling shiver that went careening wildly down the foaming rapids of his fleshy river.

"Isn't that beautiful!" he excitedly proclaimed for all to hear. "You know, I've never actually been down on the surface before. I'm really looking forward to this."

"I'm looking forward to getting some real food," roared Vijay's waggish voice as he whirled around from his engineering station. "I'm getting mighty sick of those dehydrated and irradiated CAS food packs. That is if you will allow me to go down to the surface." He swiveled back to face his console and mumbled softly but assertively. "And you will."

Also fearful of being relegated to the vacuous, austere corridors of the ship for the duration of the visit, Sheri interjected a subtle suggestion of her own. "I hear that their agri-dome produces a strand of corn and peas that have an unusually sweet flavor. I can't wait to sample some."

The desirous conversations of his crew were not lost on Matt's awareness. They were no different than he was when it came to the magnetic allure of an alien world. Since the mission profile called for a minimum three day stay even under the best of conditions, he had decided to rotate everyone down in shifts, if all went well. Jack would be the only member particularly busy, shuttling people and cargo back and forth in the planetary lander.

Flaming jets of hydrogen gas puffed from the nozzles of the decelerating engines, drawing its energy from the enormous power generated from the *'light bulb'* reactor, as the automatic guidance system increased the frequency rate of burns in preparation for Mars orbital insertion. They had now been periodically firing for 36 hours, gradually reducing the ship's maximum bullet-like momentum by ninety percent, still approaching the planet at 40,000 miles per hour. Even that pace would need to be halved in the next five hours or the craft would be in danger of overpowering the planet's gravitational field and either burning-up or recklessly skipping out into the vacuum of space.

It was less than two hours before MOI when Jack finally reported to the bridge, dragged from his abbreviated rest period to pilot the ship the rest of the way in. Matt wanted his experienced, flamboyant helmsman at the wheel during this critical time so he had personally relieved him from night duty a few hours early so he would be fresh for the job ahead.

"Well, Jack, nice of you to join us," Matt humorously chided. "I hope you didn't spend that time entertaining one of our female guests."

"Not this time," he replied with a sheepish grin. "Thanks."

Matt shrugged nonchalantly. "I can't have my navigator so fatigued that he does something unusually stupid, like crash my ship into Phobos."

The russet world was growing increasingly larger in the window as Reggie relinquished the navigation seat to Jack and joined Sheri at the operations console. The mosaic balloon of red's, orange's, brown's, and dabs of fluffy white slowly inflated before them, nearly filling the right third of their panorama. Jack diligently fed updated telemetry into the guidance computer, fine-tuning the approach.

"We'll still coming in a little too fast," he calmly announced. "I'm switching to manual and extending the next DE burn two minutes longer."

Solicitous eyes hastily glanced around the room at the unwavering self-assurance displayed by the young navigator. Jackson Shoals had a congenial swagger about him that nudged the borders of conceit, but this air of confidence, his boyish good looks and engaging charm had soothing affects on the people around him. He would need all those traits in the days ahead.

Entering the desired orbit was an act that required exact precision. Factors such as mass of the planet, that is its gravitational pull, the radius of the orbit to the planet's core, and the speed of the spacecraft all had to be calculated precisely. Exact velocity was the most difficult to control, so much so that circular orbits were almost impossible on initial insertion, elliptical orbits becoming the standard norm - with a circular path obtainable with a series of mid-course orbital corrections if one so desired. The Guilford Courthouse was freely falling along a linear trajectory tangent to the planet Mars, driven by the force of its own inertia. The speed had to be adjusted so the gravitational field of the planet deflected the ship into a curved path in such a way that it paralleled the curvature of the planet. In effect, Mars would be falling away from the ship just as fast as the ship fell towards the surface. Jack feverish worked the navigation systems   as the expanding reddish-brown horizon curved closer to the center of the window. "Twenty minutes to MOI," he excitedly reported as he punched some new data into the guidance computer. "We need one more DE burn of three minutes and twenty seconds."

Matt felt a surge of uneasiness at the series of last minute decelerating corrections that Jack was initiating. He turned to him with an expression of concern. "Did you verify your figures and get computer confirmation? We can't afford to miss this."

Jack responded with a piercing gaze that undoubtedly reflected his indignation on the notion that his proficiency would ever be questioned. Matt quickly acquiesced.

"Very well, Jack," he acknowledged as he held out his open palms. "Initiate when ready."

Matt could sense the vibration of the steel floor panels cascading through the soles of his shoes as the braking engines blazed one final time. A low, muted rumble emanated from the ceiling and outer walls in response to the stress applied to the superstructure. Jack's attention was concentrated on the score of monitors and digital displays as the seconds ticked by, methodically calling out status such as time and speed and distance. As their velocity progressively slowed, the ship's forward momentum was gradually pulled towards the planet by the forceful hand of its mass.

"Twenty seconds to DE cut-off." Jack confidently announced, beginning a numeric countdown over the final ten. "....five....four....three ....two....one....and....DECO!"

The computer controlled guidance system terminated the thrust of the engines exactly on cue. The crew anxiously settled back into their padded seats as Jack verified the navigation status.

"Speed at three point seven mules per second and trajectory looks good. We're in the pipe!"

Matt exuded a sigh of relief and nodded approvingly. "Now it's in the hands of Johannes Kepler and Sir Isaac Newton."

Imperceptible to the crew, the ship was indeed being influenced by the gravitational attraction of the Red Planet, gingerly cutting a new curved path above its surface. Jack had to rely on instrumentation to confirm their attitude and orientation in relation to the world below. Satisfied with the readings, he glanced across at Matt with a beaming smile of gratification. "Matt, we're in Martian orbit."

Cheers of joy swept across the bridge as all hands spontaneously exchanged congratulatory shakes and hugs. Matt fell back in his chair, cutting loose an exhilarating cry and haughtily proclaimed. "Now that is how we do things! Well done, Jack. Well done."

Matt allowed himself a few moments to vent-off some of the emotional stress that had been building within him, but quickly collected his composure. He fully realized that their mission was only partially complete. Now came the momentous task of ascertaining why the colony had suddenly severed all contact with Earth.

The elliptical orbit of the Guilford Courthouse took it from an apogee of nearly 1100 miles to a perigee of just under 500 miles, directly over the low latitude ridged plain of Lunae Planum, fifteen degrees north of the equator, whose western slopes sheltered the home of the permanent human inhabitants of Mars.

"Sheri, try to raise Jamestown," Matt ordered, hoping to establish contact before the planet's rotation carried them beyond the visible horizon.

Sheri eagerly activated the external communication system and set the transmitter to the colony frequency which she had scrupulously committed to memory. "Jamestown colony," her affably assertive voice beckoned into the console microphone, "this is the Continental American Spaceship cruiser Guilford Courthouse in Martian orbit. Come in, please."

All ears on the bridge strained to pick-up the first delightful words of acknowledgment from the colonists below. They waited in silent, nervous anticipation with only the subtle background noise from their own environment to accompany the mental din of their own convoluted thoughts. The ghostly stillness from below was deafening.

"Jamestown colony, please respond." Sheri's tone revealed a hint of trepidation. "This is the CAS cruiser Guilford Courthouse."

Matt dolefully slumped in command seat as their hails continued to be greeted with frustrating silence, as if they were the last living creatures in the entire universe. Matt quietly lamented, resigned to the inevitable. This eventuality wasn't exactly unexpected. He had always thought it unreasonable to expect that they would be able to establish a communication link when Earth could not, just because they were in orbit. Matt spiritedly spun towards Sheri as the others were looking around in dismay.

"Sheri, their relay satellite is in a 200 mile orbit above Lunae Planum, am I right?"

Sheri glanced back in puzzlement and nodded.

"Try bouncing a signal back to us off of their CRS. Let's see if their communications satellite is functioning properly."

Sheri quickly manipulated a few controls and attentively listened for the return signal. After a few brief moments she removed the private receiver from her ear and turned to Matt with raised eyebrows and an offhanded smirk. "CRS is nominal, Matt. It seems to be working perfectly."

Matt pondered judiciously for a moment. They had just eliminated one of the theories making its rounds - that the communication satellite was malfunctioning. The problem would have to be resolved on the surface.

"Very well," he coolly said as he rose smartly to his feet. "We'll have to do this the old-fashioned way. Staff meeting in the wardroom in one hour. Reggie, you have the con."

With resolved determination, Matt stalked energetically off the bridge and retired to the privacy of his quarters where he immediately began to study the support staff profiles once more along with personnel data on the colonists themselves. Some unusual events had been reported by the colony in the weeks preceding the emergency, as well as a series of rather heated discussions between the Jamestown Administration and the NSCA authorities. As he scanned a myriad of information on his terminal, a strange feeling of uneasiness slowly crept over him, a frosty chill of fear that nibbled at his spine. He piously scanned the list of families, the names of several dozen young children. His heart was filled with remorse as his mind wandered in tangents. Children, for God's sake! What if something disastrous had befallen them? What if their anguished cries for help could not be received? Or could it be something more secretive, more sinister? Could the very agency that contracted for their services be withholding vital information from him? Could his own company, CAS, be a willing accomplice in deception? And what of the marines? The platoon of young, gritty ground pounders that he was slowly growing attached too. Was there, in fact, some dark, clandestine purpose for their presence, despite the Lieutenant's innocent posturing? Only one thing was certain, Matt reasoned. He wouldn't find any answers sitting on his ass in this tin can. In order to bring this mission to a successful conclusion, he would have to do what he had so fondly dreamed of doing for so many years. Matt Maitland would have to sift the sands of Mars.

Effervescent and vociferous suppositions and opinions flew wildly back and forth across the oval, beige aluminum alloy table between Sheri, Reggie, and Vijay as they debated the current situation and alternatives for their next actions. The elongated table sat eight but only five seats were occupied - those three in the middle with Matt sitting quietly at one end and Lieutenant Reynolds, who was passively resting with folded arms, at the other, watching and listening like an eagle guarding its nest. The usefulness of their arguments was moot, for the next course of action was clear to Matt, but he felt that it was wise to allow his staff to express themselves and release some of their pent-up frustration. He brought the verbal melee to a close only after their testiness became apparent when Sheri responded to a light-hearted remark by Reggie concerning the colonists welfare with a robust punch to the upper arm.

"That's not very funny," she bitterly admonished. "We're talking about families here, good, decent people."

"Settle down, all of you!" Matt implored, holding out his open hands. He paused as the frolicking voices slowly ebbed away and all eyes were trained in his direction. "That's better. Now, I invited Lieutenant Reynolds to join this meeting because he has an integral part in the next phase of our mission." Matt's eyes shot a swift, dubious glance towards the officer. "Whatever that part may be."

Reynolds politely acknowledged him with a smart nod of the head. "Thank you, Commander."

"Obviously we're going to have to effect a landing and make personal contact," Matt forthrightly continued. "When tomorrow will our orbit bring us over Lunae Planum again?"

Sheri quickly accessed her electronic, leather-bound, computer pad. "In about fourteen hours, Matt. That's early morning local time."

"Will we be near perigee?"

Sheri silently confirmed with a delicate bow.

"Then we'll depart in the lander in fourteen hours," Matt decided, before looking up inquisitively at Reynolds. "Does that sound acceptable to you, Lieutenant?"

Reynolds shoulders casually twitched. "We're not in a combat situation. Daylight is fine."

Matt cleared his throat. "Well, I'm sure glad to hear that," he facetiously replied, followed by a brief hesitation as he gathered his thoughts. "Normally I wouldn't leave the ship under these conditions but since I am mission Commander, I'm obliged to accompany the first group to the surface. Reggie, you will be in command of the ship in my absence." Matt grimaced with a keen sense of trepidation as he reflected on their earlier adversities. "Keep a close watch on the scanners. That bogey may still be lurking out there somewhere."

"Understood. But it's been two days since our last contact. Do you really think that it's still shadowing us?"

"I do," Matt responded decisively. "We all know that something was out there. Where else would that course have taken it but to here. I somehow doubt that it would trail us to the middle of nowhere and simply turn around." His argument reflected worry and caution. "If you make any contact at all, I want to be informed immediately." Matt took a deep breath. "Now for the transport schedule. The PL can carry a maximum of eighteen people with limited equipment. It will take two trips to shuttle all the support personnel and God knows how many more to move all that cargo."

Reggie snickered softly. "Jack-boy is going to get in a lot of extra flying time. What about fuel? We certainly don't have enough for many midair Martian gymnastics, man."

Vijay leaned forward and replied with calm assurance. "The colony produces its own methane/oxygen propellant. We can refuel the PL at their spaceport. Which reminds me." Vijay glanced gravely at Matt. "All those extra DE burns has depleted our hydrogen reserves to the point that it endangers our ability to make it back home except for a free return trajectory. See if you can barter some from the colony." He relaxed against his chair and chuckled. "I'd hate to be forced to ask CASOC to send out some swaggering old tanker jockey to refuel our drifting carcass. That would be embarrassing."

Matt wholeheartedly agreed. Meanwhile, Sheri was eyeing her portable terminal with a reserved, sullen expression, like a lost puppy in search of its master. "I suppose you won't have room for an Ops Officer."

"I'm sorry, Sheri," Matt apologetically replied as he gazed at her affectionately. "Only personnel involving vital colony functions can go on the first flight....however." Matt straightened and briskly turned to leer at Vijay. "....I would like my Chief Engineer to accompany me to act as a general engineering consultant."

His husky frame swayed as his face sparkled with a wide grin of delight.

"What about a medical specialist," Sheri questioned, shaking off her obvious disappointment.

"Yes, that would be prudent," Matt concurred. "Doctor Oliver should go, and Jack, of course, to pilot." His right hand began to count off the roster using the fingers of his left. "We should take the nuclear engineer, the electrical systems engineer, one of the planetary science engineers, and that communications technician may be very necessary....what's her name?"

"Nichelle," Reggie softly replied with a vacant downward expression, already mourning her impending absence. "Nichelle Bennett."

Before Matt could continue, the suddenly somber, hawkish cast of Vijay drew his attention. "And the marines?" Vijay apprehensively queried.

Instantly Matt understood the stoic look. The mere fact that they were included in this enterprise was unnerving. It was a poignant reality check, a coastal beacon warning of the very real and imminent dangers that may await them on the shores of this magnificent rustic ocean. He remembered the time-honored adage, bred from a valiant tradition; marines don't start fights, they finish them! Matt couldn't shake the tremulous intuition that some would never leave the Red Planet. Solemnly his fingers clasped together as his head drooped. "Yes." A few reflective moments elapsed before a revitalized Matt called out to the far end of the table. "Lieutenant Reynolds! Get your men ready. But we only have room for ten."

"Yes, sir. I'll need to leave a few behind in any event to expedite the transport of our equipment."

"One other thing," Matt cautioned, his tone turning more doleful. "We must prepare ourselves for another eventuality that I'm sure none of us care to contemplate." Heart rates skyrocketed with tense anticipation as all attention was keenly directed to the head of the table. "I don't want any mention of this to leave this room, but there is a very real possibility that we will find everyone dead."

Heads turned and eyes bulged in horror as the latent fears of everyone in the room were forced to the surface. That very thought had occurred to each and every one of them at some point, but all had suppressed the possibility as too dreadful to consider and much too frightening to openly discuss. In that event, the support staff and the crew itself would have to filter through the wreckage of lifeless human debris to piece together the answers, a nightmare of unimaginable proportions.

"We must keep our wits about us," Matt soberly continued, his deep brown eyes piercing each person in turn. "We can't allow panic or hysteria to spread among the others. So whatever happens, just keep cool and get the job done. Maintain tight security and vigil over sensitive areas of the ship until we can transport everyone down. I'll feel a lot better when all have disembarked."

Upon adjournment of the meeting, the group slowly filed out one-by-one until Sheri hesitated in the doorway, finally stepping back inside and allowing the door to slide shut behind her. Mat instantly recognized the fearful imploring in her eyes.

"Matt, remember yesterday when I told you how scared I was? Now I'm petrified. Are you sure that you will be all right down there?"

"Hey, I have an army with me," Matt insouciantly consoled, rising to his feet and walking towards her with open arms. "What can possibly happen?" His head winced in conjunction with a broad smile. "How about some luck?"

Sheri looked bewildered. "What?"

Matt's arms lurched invitingly forward. "You know, a little kiss for luck."

Her soft, delicate face lit up with the brightness of the radiant sun as she raced into the clutches of his masculine grasp. Their lips pressed passionately together as their arms embraced in a vise-like grip. Matt's hands roamed firmly across her back, tightly compressing her breasts against his chest. Her hands vigorously clutched the back of his neck, fingers lithely dancing through the dark scalp at its base. Their breaths grew rough and deep as their tongues feverishly explored the other's warm, moist orifice. Matt felt the rumblings and stirrings of burning desire deep within his loins as his hands wantonly caressed her lower, fleshy cheeks. If he could only find a compromise between his feelings, his fears, and his devotion to duty, he pondered. Their pleading eyes exchanged longing gazes as their mouths reluctantly parted. Matt chuckled, bringing his hands around to glide through her wavy black hair and to gently touch the sides of her pure, lovely face. "I'm really getting to like you, you know."

Sheri replied with that sweet, enchanting grin and twinkle in her eyes that Matt so adored as she clasped his right arm, tenderly kissing the top of his hand before cradling it against her rosy cheek, softly purring in contentment. Slowly she guided it down to the base of her neck where her fingers deftly manipulated his so that together they held the zipper of her flight suit, languidly pulling it down several inches before coming to a gradual rest just below her exposed cleavage. Releasing her grasp of his hand, Sheri lustfully wrapped her arms around his waist and snuggled close, grinding her hips seductively against his.

"When this is all over," she immodestly assured, "you can finish it yourself."

Later that evening, Matt found himself roaming the tanned, hollow corridors of the central disk, feeling a bit lonely and detached, the burdens of his command weighing heavily on his mind. Sheri's company would have been a welcome diversion, but she was standing watch on the bridge for half the night before Reggie would relieve her. Nearing the recreation room, his attention was drawn to the sound of deep, melodious singing voices emanating from within. Moving closer, he recognized the familiar tune and words that he had so often heard as a kid while watching old war movies or historical documentaries. Curiously peering into the spacious room, he immediately noticed the entire platoon gathered together in a semi-circle in one isolated corner, all proudly proclaiming the chords of the Marine Corps Hymn. Matt inconspicuously slipped into a seat by a small round table near the doorway and respectfully observed the proceedings with a certain amount of admiration. Every soldier was wearing his prized tall-crowned black hat, the left brim raised and pinned to the side, completely adorned with the opulent black feather and powder blue hat cords. Their unit battle flag, the national flag with the words *The Iron Brigade*' embroidered in illustrious gold across its face, was exaltedly displayed to their front. Corporal Cooke was apparently orchestrating the festivities, standing by the flag as the others leaned against the lone nearby table or sat on the floor around him. Lieutenant Reynolds and Sergeant Douglas stood passively off to the side, allowing their men to run the show for a change. Each nursed and savored a smuggled flask of beer that Reynolds had sought permission to distribute. Between enthusiastic though badly performed renditions of various military ballads, Corporal Cooke relayed humorous tales and war stories from the Lunar Conflict and implored the others to recount some of their amusing experiences from their boot camp or advanced training days. The scene reminded Matt of an old campfire setting in the Army of the Potomac on the eve of Antietam or

Gettysburg, without the fires, of course. Matt became so absorbed by the marines that he failed to perceive the feminine form slipping into the seat beside him, until a gentle hand upon his upper arm startled him to awareness.

"I'm sorry, Matt," the soft, sensual voice of Caroline Hart apologized. "I though that t I was the only one on pins and needles this evening. May I join you?"

"Please do," Matt replied, shaking off his momentary fright.

"I'm surprised to see you alone. Where's Sheri?"

"On the bridge for part of the night," he responded disconsolately.

"In that case," Caroline decided, "if you don't mind, I think that I'll join you for awhile. I think your handsome, young navigator just rescued me from Lucinda. She was telling me about these extraordinary DNA bioprocessing chips and we were engaged in girl talk when she got in an ornery mood, asking me to undress and take a pleasure pill with her and playfully tickling me in the ribs." She leaned back in the chair, grabbing her wrists behind her.

Matt enviously leered at her. "Lucky girl," he mumbled to himself.

"Dave used to drive me crazy doing that," she candidly admitted before bowing in reflection. "Now I miss it."

Matt seized the moment to thoroughly examine Caroline for the first time. How her thick, brunette hair glistened under the artificial light; how it curled and laid sumptuously about her shoulders. The turmoil that he knew was wracking her soul was now well concealed by the charming gaze of her hazel eyes, the softness of her lashes, the silky smooth complexion of her rounded cheeks. He loved how her snug, thin white blouse with plunging neckline and garnished with thin strips of cherry red leather around the shoulders and sleeves clung alluringly to her ample curves, the tightness revealing the imprint of the cups and straps of an apparently very sexy lace bra beneath. Her deep yellow, elastic waist, cotton slacks tightly hugged her hips and firm thighs. The potent aroma of her perfume was intoxicating. Matt could feel the stirrings of primitive passions welling-up within him which caused him to feel a little uncomfortable, not the insatiable drive and uncontrollable desire that similar yearnings involving Sheri were able to induce. Curious, he thought. It was only then that he became embarrassingly aware that Caroline was observing his lecherous ogling of her protruding breasts. His eyes dipped shamefully. "I'm sorry."

A wry smile crossed her mouth as she teasingly thrust them forward even more. "Please, don't be. I'm flattered, I really am. But we both know that we have our own important love interests. But I appreciate the attention. It's been so long since...." Caroline paused in stoic reflection, her mood suddenly growing somber as a look of consternation slowly crept over her. "Matt, I'm frightened," she softly proclaimed as she leaned towards him and folded her arms on the table. "What could have happened to my husband?"

Genuinely touched by her tormenting ordeal, Matt sympathetically reached out and clasped her hand between his as his fingers lightly massaged the skin. "Everything will work out, Caroline. I'm betting it's simply a problem with their communication system. Try to relax. You'll be frolicking around in bed with Dave in no time."

Libidinous looks were exchanged between them before Caroline lowered her head and blushed. Within moments they were quietly chuckling together in amusement.

"That's better," Matt chortled. "Your husband is a very lucky man to have such a wonderful, enchanting woman who loves him."

Caroline's head shook and sagged once more as moisture glimmered within her eyes. "No, I'm afraid he's not," she distraughtly moaned. "I was the lucky one, just too foolish to recognize it." She sniffled, wiping a finger across her face. "I should have gone to Mars with Dave from the beginning. I thought a few years apart wouldn't change anything. That we could adapt to the lack of closeness. I was wrong. Now I'm afraid that I may have lost him forever; that our love may never be rekindled as fervently as before."

"I'm sure he'll be overjoyed," Matt remarked as he placed a consoling hand upon her shoulder, his fingers affectionately rubbing towards her neck, "busting his pants when he sees you again."

Caroline and Matt shared mischievous glances before erupting together in laughter. Regaining their composure, they sat back and leisurely returned their attention to the platoon of marines ahead. The others mingling in the room also watched and listened with fascination from afar, keeping their distance and respecting the unit's spacial privacy. The sad truth was, in fact, that most had kept their distance throughout the entire voyage.

As Matt couldn't resist the temptation to occasionally look over Caroline's alluring figure, he began to notice a bewildered and confused stare clouding her bright demeanor as they listened to Corporal Cooke leading the men in a series of marching and drill cheers set to that old familiar cadence of boot camp marches. Finally she turned to him with a puzzled expression. "What's this all about?" she asked, tossing up her hands cluelessly. "I don't understand."

Matt shrugged offhandedly. "It's just a soldier thing. Bonding together. Relieving the tension. Tomorrow they venture out into the unknown."

She nodded with complacency. "Weird."

Once the chanting had subsided. Lieutenant Reynolds stirred from his point of observation and moved to the front to address the group. Dashing and impeccably accoutered in his olive and mustard uniform adorned with that proud historical hat, Lieutenant Reynolds seemed to Matt to be misplaced in the current timeline. He fancied him in some far-off land, mounted on a sleek, muscular Arabian and dressed in a more glittering, opulent fashion, leading the last great cavalry charge.

"I'd like to begin by publicly thanking the captain of this great vessel of the stars for granting permission for this subtle breech of regulations for which your thirst buds now enjoy, Commander Matthew Maitland."

The marines as one turned towards the entranceway followed by a tumultuous chorus of cheers, their insulated plastic flasks raised in the traditional salute of the toast. Shying away from the attention, Matt melted in his seat, turning his head away and raising his hand to limply brush off the raucous adulation, nonchalantly acknowledging their gratitude. Giggling mirthfully, Caroline grabbed him roughly by the shoulder and shook him friskily. Placing a gentle hand upon her back, Matt began to ponder the urge to pursue her sudden playfulness until an anonymous voice in the crowd redirected his attention forward.

"Who are you quoting this time, Lieutenant? Patton? Napoleon?"

Lieutenant Reynolds grinned and shook his head, the men having grown accustomed to his philosophizing before major events. "No, my inspirational rendition for this evening is taken from Shakespeare."

The announcement was greeted with a tirade of moans and mutterings.

"Yes, yes, I know. You all look forward to Shakespeare about as much as you do for root canal. But it's time that you enhance your literary education. I will attempt to paraphrase a selection from the play, *Henry V*, when young King Henry of England addressed his badly outnumbered troops before the battle of Agincourt in 1415."

It only took a few lines before all within earshot were riveted to his stirring recitation that would have been applauded within the majestic walls of the British National Theater or the Lincoln Center. Matt was entranced by his clarity and zealous passion that would have rivaled the most accomplished Hollywood or stage actor. impressed with the difficulty of such a fervent presentation without the benefit of a single note or prompter. He thought that Reynolds had missed his true calling.

"If we are marked to die, we are not enough to do our country loss. And if to live, the fewer men the the greater share of honor. God's will I pray thee wish not for one man more.

Proclaim it throughout my host! That he which hath no stomach for this fight, let him depart. His passport shall be made and crowns for convoy put into his purse. We will not die in that man's company that fears his fellowship to die with us.

This day is called the Feast of Crispian. He that outlives this day and comes safe home will stand on tiptoe when this day is named. He that shall see this day and live old age will yearly on the vigil greet his neighbors and say 'tomorrow is Saint Crispin's. Then he will strip his sleeves and show the scars and say 'these wounds I had on Crispin's Day.'

Old men forget that all shall be forgot but he'll remember with advantages what feats he did that day. Then sound out our names, as familiar in their mouths as household words." (Substituting their own names to the delight of all assembled.) *"Reynolds, the Lieutenant, Douglas and Cooke, Benetiez and Walinski, Warwick and Anderson, be in their flowing cups freshly remembered. This story shall a good man teach his son and Crispin Crispian shall ne'er go by from this day to the ending of the world! But we in it shall be remembered. We few. We happy few. We band of brothers. For he*

today that sheds his blood with me shall be my brother.
Be he ne'er so vile, this day shall gentle his condition
and gentlemen in England now abed will think
themselves accursed that they were not here; and hold
their manhood's cheap while any speaks that fought
with us upon Saint Crispin's Day!
*   All things are ready if our minds be so. You*
know your places. God be with you all!"

The room exploded in wild applause and exhalations, the young marines slapping and tugging at each other in an excited frenzy. Matt was totally awed by the scene, and he discovered that he and Caroline had nudged closer together, her attention having also been consumed by the thrilling narration. Even as his fingers unconsciously traced congenial circles around her shoulder blade, Matt's thoughts were becoming disjointed. Intuitively he felt a disturbing uneasiness, and it had nothing to do with his seductive companion. The Lieutenant's motivational intensity seemed to him to be a bit much for the mission profile. After all, this wasn't Agincourt, or the Romanian mountains, or Copernicus crater.

"That feels nice."

Matt felt a tug at his sleeve that abruptly interrupted his internal deliberations. "Hmmm....," he mumbled, turning to Caroline.

"Your hand. I want to thank you for comforting me this evening. This illuminating diversion really helped to take my mind off things." Caroline noticed Matt's vacant expression. "You seem preoccupied. Is there something troubling you besides your normal, manly urges?"

"Oh!" Matt quietly exclaimed with a half-smile, being laggard in recognizing the meaning of her remark. "It's not that. I'm not sure what it is - exactly."

As the platoon meeting broke up, Matt observed Lieutenant Reynolds approaching the doorway. Excusing himself from his conversation with Caroline, Matt lurched towards the officer as he passed by, recalling another troubling line from that famous Shakespearean play. "If these men do not die well, it will be a black matter for the King that led them to it."

The comment caused Reynolds to suddenly pause, turning towards Matt sporting a crafty grin. "I see that your literary education is up to snuff. Are you projecting me in the role of the King?"

Matt couldn't hide his skeptical misgivings as he looked up at the man that he had grown to like and respect. "You tell me, Lieutenant."

"What do you mean?"

"It's as if you're preparing these men to hit the beaches of Normandy. Are you sure there isn't something that you're withholding from me?" He forcefully took hold of Caroline's shoulder and pulled her close. "I sincerely hope that these people are not going to be needlessly endangered." Releasing his suffocating grip, Matt tenderly took hold of her trembling hand when he became cognizant of her surprised and fearful gaze brought about by his disturbing line of questioning.

"I assure you, Matt," Reynolds replied with emphatic sincerity, "I have no additional intelligence on the condition of the colony. I would never willingly put the lives of these good people at risk. We are pledged to protect them, and you, from all danger. That's our job."

"What danger!" Matt decried.

Reynolds insouciantly rolled his shoulders. "Unknown. That's why we're here. Well, if you'll excuse me, I'll see you at assembly. Goodnight." He courteously looked at Caroline and tipped his hat. "Ma'am."

As the Lieutenant departed, Matt twisted to peer into Caroline's pleading eyes, his fingers tightly squeezing her hand. "I guess we'll know this time tomorrow."

CHAPTER

Terrifying jolts and heavy, rumbling vibrations shook and rocked Matt's chair as the Nathanael Greene rapidly descended towards the ruddy, ridged plain of Lunae Planum. Compressed molecules of carbon dioxide along with trace amounts of nitrogen, argon, and oxygen rattled and buffeted the planetary lander in the wake of its fall through the thin stratosphere, shooting trembling and shuddering shock waves through the fragile though exhilarated bones of the human occupants. Matt could sense the tremors of the steel floor panels penetrating the soles of his boots, the quivering of his seat through the heavy insulation of his environment suit, the uncontrolled jostling of his arms against the padded armrests; feeling like he was riding inside some gigantic skin massager and half-expecting the ship to fly apart at any moment. Tightly clenching his mouth, he could hear his teeth chattering. The sound of a faded roar, like the deep whine of a boiler room, could be heard rumbling outside the metal shell. From his vantage point in the copilot's seat, Matt could see the blazing orange-red glow that tinged the squared nose, as was the case beneath its thermal shielded belly - the build-up of heat caused by the constriction of the air that was being forced together faster than its ability to flow around the plunging transport. Matt found rather amusing the efforts of Lieutenant Reynolds to alleviate the fears of some of his raw and green charges who thought that the ship was on fire. They were so young, he thought, but what a treat as a military assignment for a young man, to be able to walk on the surface of another planet. As the lander drew closer, Matt could feel the force of gravity exert its power. The increasing pressure on his ribs made breathing

141

difficult and laborious. His torso was pushed firmly back against the chair, his vision becoming fuzzy, heart rate jumping. "We're really feeling that gravity now," he proclaimed with painful effort.

"We should be out of this chop in a minute," Jack assured him as he labored to keep the nose up as the PL continued to dive towards a thin smudge of white puff, periodically firing the vertical braking thrusters to slow down their rate of descent.

Plunging through the troposphere and emerging from the meager cloud ball, the whole exalted grandeur of the red tinted world was arrayed before them. With the reduction in speed and altitude, the tormenting vibrations from slicing through the atmosphere had settled down and the pressure of the g-forces stabilized to the point that the passengers could finally relax and enjoy the panorama that few earthlings ever had the privilege to witness. Those seated by the oval side windows could look out beyond the rear of the curved wings could instantly perceive the immense and massive depth of the many meandering, interconnected channeled canyon systems of Valles Marineris that lay behind them just below the equatorial line. Before them stretched the solidified crustal clays of the low-latitude plain of Lunae Planum, complete with its wrinkled ridges and freckled with widely scattered craters, some extending several miles in diameter. It was rather docile and boring terrain - for Mars! Those fortunate enough to be seated to the left could behold in the far distance the monstrous, towering caldera of Olympus Mons looming over the horizon, still more than 1100 miles to the west, its volcanic peak stretching so high that it could be recognized long before any of the surrounding countryside ever appeared along the horizon. Intoxicated gasps of joy and wonder freely bounced between the walls as heads swiveled and strained like marionettes on a string to savor as much of the scenery as possible as the strange and intriguing surface features rose ever larger in the windows.

The pinkish Martian sky had rarely played host to a soaring blue bird from the nest of an Independence class cruiser. The PL was bathed in a deep navy and extended some 120 feet from stem to stern. The nose was squared with rounded edges and formed in the shape of a half-octagon. A pair of elongated, cambered, triangular Delta wings were located amidships, made of stainless steel and titanium alloys. The 25-foot thick stressed-skin fuselage was of semimonocoque construction and consisted of sheet aluminum reinforced with steel longerons within the structural frame. The fuselage fed into a slightly larger, half-hexagon compartment that housed the liquid fuel methane/oxygen primary engine and solar battery storage cells that provided the electrical requirements of the ship. Small stabilizing wings extended from its flanks as well as a vertical fin that rose on top between a black set of solar panel cells. Evenly spaced along the bottom of the fuselage was a set of conical VTOL (Vertical Takeoff & Landing) thrusters. A broad band of lustrous gold cut through the navy coating along the center of each side of the fuselage for the entire length of the craft, broken only by the large, circular insignia of Continental American Spaceships directly above the wings, that encompassed the name, *Nathanael Greene*, in its design. Similar flaxen stripping adorned the middle of the wings as well as the tail fins.

Falling below 10,000 feet, the iron-rich landscape looked barren and harsh, a dry, barren wasteland without a hint of any human presence. A few saguaro and sagebrush, or maybe even a coyote or two would have looked right at home, Matt thought. The visitors could distinguish the albedo markings in the ejecta blanket of the largest craters, the seemingly infinite variety of tints of oranges and reds and browns that layered along the ridges, and the shading effects within the crater lips and around the many large boulders strewn about the plain. Off to the distant northwest, Matt caught a glimpse of the first sign of civilization - flashes of glimmering white light along the horizon. It was the rays of the sun reflecting off the glass domes of Jamestown. They were nearly there. Reaching for the communications console, Matt decided to try again.

"Jamestown colony, come in, please. This is planetary lander Nathanael Greene from CAS Guilford Courthouse now on final approach. Come in, Jamestown."

Once again the attempt proved futile. The hollow sound of silence was maddening. Matt turned upon hearing the staggering approach of Lieutenant Reynolds, ominously attired in his murky, dark bronze space suit sans helmet, carefully grasping anything available to maintain his balance.

"Still nothing," Matt announced as Reynolds braced himself against the back of Matt's blue padded chair. "That's it over there." His finger pointed to the direction of the flickering light reflections.

Reynolds nodded and leaned towards Jack. "Before landing, Mister Shoals, I'd like you to give me a slow and low complete three-sixty around the colony."

Jack sighed reluctantly. "Just like Copernicus," he mumbled softly with a pained grimace. "That's when the shit really hit the fan."

The Nathanael Greene descended under 2000 feet and at a range of fifteen miles the individual structures of the colony became discernible. Jamestown was laid out in an area of a little more than one square mile and was primarily an underground facility. The prominent surface features were five large geodesic domes made of flat, polygonal, reinforced and heavily shielded plate glass held together by steel alloy bracing's. Four of the domes were located at the geometric corners of the imaginary square. The fifth, a taller dome, was positioned precisely in the center between the other four. Low, light pinkish-gray concrete tunnel enclosures connected each perimeter dome to the larger central one like the spokes of a wheel. As Jack guided the craft closer, smaller surface constructions could be identified. A rectangular concrete warehouse building of the same unusual coloration was connected by a small tunnel to the dome to the northwest. A gigantic array of dust covered square solar panels blossomed like behemoth desert flowers to the west, splotches of black and silver peeking through the thin veil of russet particles. A rising, tubular gray and red communication tower stood due east of the central dome, the expansive black bowl upon its head searching up into the heavens. But Matt noticed something odd. The light reflections to the northeast were more subdued. That section of the perimeter seemed shaded, immersed in strange shadows. The PL slowed to a crawl as it crept up on the colony boundary.

"Good God!" Matt exclaimed in stunned alarm.

Everyone inside strained their heads forward to catch a better glimpse of the source of all the dismay in the cockpit. Flying at 600 feet along the eastern perimeter of the colony, they observed a jagged, gaping hole in the middle of the northeast dome. Thousands of shimmering fragments of glass saturated the wide pile of debris. Twisted and mangled frames of metal warped grotesquely inward. Fine grains of freshly cultivated Martian soil radiated out in all directions. Broken and craggy pieces of rock of varied sizes were strewn about everywhere, the largest chunk resting amidst the wreckage within the structure itself.

Disheartened looks were exchanged between soldiers and specialists alike as Matt activated the onboard data computer, toggling through a series of selection screens and cursing under his breath over the fact that CAS hadn't installed quicker voice input computer systems in PL's. Finally he located the structural plans for the Jamestown colony. "That dome housed factory and scientific research facilities," Matt announced to no one in particular. "They had recently opened an underground residential area, but not currently occupied."

Reynolds shook his head dejectedly. "Occupied or not, I'd hate to think of any pour souls who may have been working in there when that dome collapsed."

"They wouldn't have the time to pee in their pants," Jack offhandedly remarked.

Matt grimly reached for the transmitter control. "Guilford Courthouse, are you getting this?"

From the softly illuminated bridge of the Guilford Courthouse, Caroline Hart looked on in horrified silence as the first discernible images of the wreckage of the dome was relayed from the cockpit camera of the planetary lander to the communication monitor aboard the cruiser. Chilling shivers of fear and shock shot wildly through her spine as she stared helplessly at the distressing transmission, her body shuddering uncontrollably. She had spent a restless night in nervous anticipation of the day's events; had arisen in the wee hours of the morning to pack her clothes in preparation for her final transport to the Martian surface and the dawn of her second life with her husbands. Though her eyes showed the lines and weariness from the strain of her ordeal, she had taken great pains to make herself as beautiful as ever. Her succulent brunette hair was meticulously groomed, laying lushly about her shoulders. Her face was as smooth and silky as the finest chemise, made possible by the tedious and generous application of pore cleansers and facial creme. Rich lip gloss accentuated her pink, sensuous mouth. Technically on assignment from the NSCA, she was compelled to wear what she considered an unflattering standard issue light blue NASA flight suit while on duty, but she was most deliberate in her selection of enticing and seductive lingerie which she hoped to reveal at an opportune time son after her reunion with her husband. But suddenly her amorous desires and excitement were buried under a torrent of unrelenting premonitions of the worst kind as she was confronted with the reality that her love, as well as his life, may have been summarily extinguished on this arid, frozen wasteland.

Reggie's eyes were also trained over Sheri's shoulder with intense curiosity, as well as those of Corporal Rafael Benetiez who Reynolds had requested be allowed on the bridge in the event that emergency orders needed to be conveyed to the four marines remaining on board regarding the equipment and supplies. Sheri solemnly glanced up at the others before turning back to the console. "Roger that, Nathanael Greene," she replied in dismay. "We see it."

Lieutenant Reynolds reached out and lightly tapped Jack on the shoulder, pointing to the north indicating his desire to keep circling. With an acknowledging nod, Jack maneuvered the craft past the damage and continued to skirt the colony around the northern perimeter. Everyone scrambled to the port side windows to catch a glimpse of the layout and the rugged, reddish-brown landscape beyond. It occurred to Matt that even if the colony's communications had completely broken down, they must certainly be aware of their presence by now and someone would surely attempt to establish visual contact. But none was forthcoming. As the ship cruised around the western boundary near the rising, rock-strewn hills that nestled close to the outer perimeter, Matt could detect no sign, no flash, no signal of any kind. The rest of the surface structures appeared perfectly sound, not a hint of a scratch on any dome or tunnel. Jack and Reynolds scrupulously searched the surreal surroundings for any sign of life, to no avail. No people, no robotics, no rovers, not even an indentation of a meshed track imprint on the ground.

"Looks like an old mining ghost town," Jack flippantly remarked as he scanned the scene. "The only thing missing is an old grizzled-face prospector leading a heavily laden pack mule."

"This is very odd," added Matt's strained voice as he nervously scratched his chin. "I don't like this." His internal deliberations were precluded by a firm grasp upon his upper arm.

"I'd suggest that we get on the deck," Reynolds emphatically counseled.

With a heavy sigh of anxiety, Matt nodded in agreement. "Okay, Jack, let's get out to the SP."

Swinging around the southern end of the colony, Jack flew the PL in an easterly direction towards Jamestown's spaceport, situated two miles away. The wide black macadam road that led from the central dome to the air terminal served as a guide as Jack simply followed its straight, level course, fine reddish-orange grains of soil and dust lazily drifted across its darkened surface, giving it a somewhat dappled appearance. The elongated, pentagonal, three-story terminal building appeared in the distance almost immediately. A beacon of bright twinkling light on its roof revealed the location of the circular, glass enclosed control tower along the western edge as the rays of the sun beamed off its face. Upon closer approach, the windows lining the three floors came into view and housed the administrative offices as well as all the services for embarking and disembarking of passengers. The remaining two-thirds of the salmon-creme concrete building was a towering, single level structure, windowless except for the tall sky-light ceiling, and contained spacecraft maintenance and refueling facilities, storage tanks, and a small fleet of ground shuttle transports that ran to and from the colony. An above ground monorail system had been designed, but there was no visual evidence that construction had begun. Like Jamestown itself, the space terminal appeared deserted, no sign of even the most mundane activities. Attempts to contact the control tower failed. As Matt frustratingly continued his efforts with the radio, Jack carefully searched for the landing pad, it's bright blue and yellow lights mysteriously absent. The massive, square, pale gray tarmac was easy enough to spot, but the thin blanket of roving, rust-colored Martian dust helped to obscure the exact location of the landing grid. It took several slow, circuitous passes before Jack could identify enough portions of the large, white painted crossed lines with their unlit embedded lights to make an educated guess, not that precision really mattered in this instance. Shutting down the main engine and firing the VTOL's , Jack leveled the ship, extended the four large steel landing support struts, and cautiously lowered it towards the pad as if it were made of glass. Exhaust spewing from the nozzles kicked up heavy red clouds of feathery particles that swirled like cyclones around the lander, but cleared away the debris directly below that revealed that X really does mark the spot. Jack was right on target. Blinded by the whirling dust, the passengers inside were jolted in their seats as the landing gear settled softly on the hard tarmac, the legs absorbing most, but not all, of the shock of touchdown. The air inside was buzzing with the sounds of exhilarated chatter as Jack shut down the thrusters and the dust began to settle, slowly unveiling the sight of the terminal and the barren, rock-littered landscape. They had finally landed on the planet Mars!

As Jack continued his shutdown procedures, Matt unbuckled himself from his chair and switched the video feed from the external camera to that broadcasting from the inside of the cockpit. "Guilford Courthouse," he called out over the communication system, "the Nathanael Greene has successfully landed on the surface of Mars."

Matt fondly gazed at the smiling, pretty face of Sheri as she appeared on the tiny six inch monitor, her succulent, flowing black hair framing the pleasing picture.

"We saw it, Nathanael Greene," she sighed in relief.

Matt strained his neck to get the full view from the cockpit. "We'll be disembarking shortly, GC. There are no landing grid lights, no signal from the tower, no sign of activity of any kind. Very eerie."

"Understood," she acknowledged. "We'll be standing by. Matt, please be careful."

Matt cracked an appreciative grin and dipped his head. "We'll be fine, Sheri, don't worry. I'll leave my suit com link open so you can monitor my conversations." Rising from his seat. Matt placed a firm hand on the shoulder of his navigator. "Nice job, Jack, well done. You'll stand by here for the moment. Monitor our transmissions and stay alert, just in case."

Jack grimaced. "Great! First a bus driver, now a house sitter."

"Sorry, Jack, but I'm going to be too busy to keep you out of trouble."

"Just as well," Jack replied with a farcical twitch. "All those ground humpers make me nervous."

Matt gave Jack a brotherly slap to the upper arm before directing his attention towards Lieutenant Reynolds. "Well, Lieutenant, how do you want to proceed?"

"The airlock can only hold four men at a time, am I right?"

Matt silently confirmed the assertion.

"Then my men will go out first and secure the landing pad and terminal. Your people can follow, but don't let them wander off on their own or enter uncleared areas."

"Very well, Lieutenant," Matt acquiesced. "It's your show...." Matt paused, glaring sternly. "....for the moment."

Reynolds took a few steps back and motioned for Sergeant Douglas to meet him at the airlock. "Have Cooke and Walinski stay with the Commander," he quietly instructed. "I'll take three men from the second squad and secure the LZ. You follow me with the rest and secure the terminal building."

"Yes, sir."

"All right, Sergeant, get them on their feet."

"On your feet," Douglas shouted in his deep, gruff tone as he walked purposefully down the center aisle, a voice that drew the instant obedient attention of the rank-and-file and had an intimidating effect on the civilian specialists. "You mangy, mud rolling, bad ass men of iron! Get moving, people!"

The soldiers clamored into the aisle and hustled back to the cargo hold, ripping open their crates of military gear and life support packs.

"Move it!" he continued to badger. "Break out that equipment. They're not paying us by the hour. Let's go, marines!"

The entire ship's complement was treated to the clunking sounds of laser rifle stock against the steel floor; the sharp clicking of metal power clips slamming into their barrel magazines; the snapping and clinking of copper fasteners on utility belts; the rattling of tin, aluminum, and plastic objects in canvas satchels; the rustling of environment packs against the fabric of space suits as they were strapped and adjusted; the clanking of heavy steel helmets as they dangled from their packs before being firmly seated; the soft clicking of protective gloves as they were locked into wrist collar rings; the dull thud of insulated boots as they clopped across the floor. Within a few short minutes the entire troop was assembled in their dull deep bronze space suits, the only insignias displayed being that of a small American flag on the right shoulder and the triangular regimental patch of the 1st US Space Marines on the other.

Lieutenant Reynolds led the men forward, laser rifles in their right hands, space suit helmets in their left. He and Matt exchanged silent glances of respect before entering the airlock with his section. Matt didn't fail to notice how their compact, bronze environment packs were loaded down with extra equipment, their utility belts crammed and bloated, each man carrying a hand-held rocket tube strapped to the flat top of their packs. He still had difficulty fathoming the rationale behind such precautions, but those fellows were certainly loaded for bear, he thought.

Once inside, Reynolds secured the automated vacuum sealed pressure door behind them as the men opened their oxygen tanks, activated their heated, thermal controlled life-support systems, and finally twisted on their large, polystyrene composite helmets and locked them securely into the collar ring sleeves. A third of this oversized fish bowl consisted of a thick transparent shield that covered the face from the chin to the forehead and wrapped around to the temples. The rest was a solid, dull bronze that matched the non-reflective color of their suits. Small, tubular spotlights protruded out from each side of the helmet, and a dark night vision visor was fastened on top that could be swung down over the faceshield for use. A tiny oval camera lens was embedded in the front crown of the helmet but the monitoring equipment that would afford centralized viewing of the observations of all platoon members was still packed away in containers aboard the Guilford Courthouse. Three communication buttons projected from the lower right side of each helmet. The first was for general internal conversations that could be picked-up by other helmet receivers within a range of a few miles. The second was a private channel for helmets within a few yards. The third was a universal communication link that could be received by other systems many miles away. They stood in a tight circle, each man checking the connections and gauges of the life-support pack of the man in front of him. Reynolds tested their internal transmitters, receiving voice acknowledgment from the other three. Satisfied with the operating condition of their space suits, Reynolds pushed the last com button on his helmet.

"Nathanael Greene, this is a com check. Tango, Victor, Charlie."

"We read you loud and clear, Lieutenant," Matt's voice came resonating back through his helmet speaker.

"Section one ready to disembark," he continued. "Be advised that we are depressurizing the chamber now. I shall leave my com link on an open channel." Reynolds' gloved hand reached out and pushed the appropriate button on the airlock control panel. Through their external receivers, that allowed for the sounds of their environment to be heard inside their sealed helmets, the men could hear the high-pitched hissing whirl of the ship's atmosphere being evacuated from the room to be steadily replaced by the frigid, poisonous air from the outside world.

"Take up positions a hundred yards out," Reynolds instructed. "And keep your eyes opened. No firing without orders. There are supposed to be friendless in the area."

Once the depressurization was complete, Reynolds pressed a second button on the control panel and the chamber began a deliberate descent towards the surface. They could hear the low drone of the hydraulics slowly ebb away followed by a sharp clank and a sudden jolt that threw them slightly off balance. Quickly recovering, Reynolds hit a third button, the vacuum sealed outside door slid open, and the four soldiers spilled out onto the dust-littered tarmac, darting in four different directions like excited mice in a cheese factory. As Reynolds took a knee and surveyed the odd, rustic landscape to the west and the glittering of sunlight off the distant colony domes, he allowed himself a few moments of selfish exhilaration. He was actually standing on the surface of another planet, a much more potent emotional thrill than his first step on the Moon. But he would have to contain his elation, for there was so much work to do, and too many unknowns.

The engineers and scientists inside were buzzing with enthusiasm as they scurried to press against the port and starboard windows to get a better look at the soldiers as they cautiously wandered about the perimeter. Sergeant Douglas had moved his section forward by the airlock and joined Matt in the cockpit. Matt mindfully observed those men who could be seen from the forward windows, listening with heightened interest and curiosity at the internal conversations ringing within Reynolds' helmet. Even from that distance, he could occasionally see a marine touch the lower left side of his helmet, whose location contained the button that activated the faceshield's magnifier - sort of a full view binocular. Filtering through the idle though animated chatter and occasional dry and rank humor, Matt deduced that they could detect nothing but a barren, frigid wasteland. No sign of life, activity, or even a tiny scrap of crumpled metal or plastic garbage. The apparently vacant spaceport was the only evidence of any past human presence in the area.

"Commander Maitland, the perimeter is secured," Reynolds' voice reported over the communication console. "The place appears deserted. Send out section two."

Matt nudged Jack on the shoulder. "Bring her up."

From his seat, Jack was able to remotely raise the airlock chamber to its normal position within the body of the ship.

"You heard him, Sergeant," Matt proclaimed with a friendly pat on the back.

"Yes, sir."

Once the Martian air had been purged and replaced with breathable air from the ship, the Sergeant led his small troop into the chamber and repeated the process. Within a couple of minutes they were standing on the tarmac floor, hustling towards the pinkish walls of the terminal building.

Without waiting for the initial reports from Sergeant Douglas' team, Matt decided that his time for personal glory had arrived. Briskly strutting through the main cabin, he abruptly paused by Vijay's seat. "It's time, Vij. Care to accompany me to the surface?"

"Are you kidding?" he exclaimed, leaping to his feet. "You couldn't give me a year's pay to pass this up."

The two of them made their way to the cargo hold where the company's EVA environment suits and space helmets were stored in bolted cabinets. As they were strapping on their gear, Corporal Cooke and Private Walinski casually sauntered up, fully loaded like their comrades.

"We've been ordered to accompany you, sir," Cooke respectfully announced.

"Yes, I know," Matt coolly replied as he continued to concentrate on the proper adjustments of his equipment, finally looking up when he had finished. "Well, I hope you boys are ready for this."

"We're marines, sir," Cooke proudly said. "We're always ready."

Matt glanced at him peculiarly. "Huh...huh" he dubiously moaned, trying to recall if he had been that self-assured and foolish at that age. "All right then. Let's not dally around, gentlemen."

As they locked themselves in the chamber and checked each other's gear, the differences in the appearance of their suits became readily apparent. The standard issue NASA space suits that all civilian organizations adopted were a reflective, glimmering silver-gray that contrasted mightily with the subdued bronze of the military outfits. The life-support packs were nearly identical except the NASA ones were bathed in a clean snow white and not as laden with extra auxiliary equipment. The NASA helmets were similar in shape, size, and function but were of a deep yellow color and lacked both the camera lens and the night vision visor.

"All that gear looks heavy, Corporal," Matt observed. "How can you move so limberly?"

"You get used to it, sir."

Matt smiled. "Well, you'll be pleased to know that Martian gravity is just .38g. That should ease your burden a little."

The four men activated their environment packs and slipped on their protective helmets, locking them securely into the collar rings. Again, the room air was evacuated, to be equalized by the outside atmosphere. After several silent moments, Matt turned to the Corporal.

"Those were some interesting stories you told last night."

"Thank you, sir," Cooke bashfully replied as he bowed his head and shuffled his feet. "That's why I joined the Space Marines. To see the galaxy and tell tall tales, though this is as far from home as I have ever been." He returned Matt's look. "I'm afraid I was born a century too early. I've always fancied myself a Buck Rogers type."

"At least with the ladies," quipped Private Walinski. The two soldiers exchanged amusing glances and snickered quietly.

"You certainly play the part well," Matt noted, the corporal's demeanor and modest swagger reminding him of that fictional character.

"I may not be Buck Rogers, sir." Cooke continued, "but you're in good hands. John and I will watch your back."

Matt fidgeted restlessly. "That's fine, Corporal, but the question is who will be watching your back?"

The men frivolously grinned at each other.

"One other thing, sir," the Corporal added in a sober though casual tone. "Should something erupt out there. please keep real low. That shiny silver suit and bright yellow helmet would make an excellent target."

Matt smirked with contrived derisiveness. "Corporal, you're an awful lot of fun to be around, do you know that?"

It seemed to Matt that the airlock chamber took an eternity to descend to the tarmac. A rush of adrenaline tingled every fiber of his being as he anxiously anticipated the momentous moment. It felt better than sex. His heart rate jumped as the drop was brought to a gentle though shuddering stop. Thrilling chills of exhilaration shot through his spine as the chamber door opened and the strange. rocky, rust-hued world unfolded before him. With reverent strides, Matt and his companions emerged from the airlock and took their first gingerly steps on the face of another planet. The wild sensations bombarding him were too numerous and rapid for his brain to process fully. The fact that he was actually standing on manmade macadam and not Martian soil did nothing to lessen the effect or the experience. He noticed the fine russet grains of dust and soil leisurely drifting over his boots and across the gray tarmac in front of him, driven on by the Martian breeze. The low-lying ridges to the east and south were strewn with rocks and boulders of a thousand shapes and sizes. He could make-out the darkened shadows of the lips of large, distant craters, the lighter coloration's of the ejecta blankets around them. He could see the rising, rugged hills to the north and beyond the reflecting domes of the colony into the plain to the west. The pink sky was bright and clear save for an occasional high. fluffy puff of white. There was a peculiar reddish tint to everything. Matt extended his hand to Vijay who clasped it firmly, their left hands grabbing the other's shoulder, laughing joyfully with childhood glee like that first day at the ocean.

"We made it, Vij!" Matt passionately exclaimed. "We actually made it! You and I are standing on the planet Mars. Magnificent, isn't it?"

Vijay nodded in agreement as he scanned the horizon. "Remind me to gather a couple of rocks for my kids before we leave."

As they moved away from the shadow of the ship, Matt could hear the clusters of conversations sweeping over the general com link.

"Lieutenant Reynolds," Corporal Cooke beckoned. "Be advised that Commander Maitland is now on the surface."

"Roger that, Corporal."

Sergeant Douglas' section had disappeared inside the terminal building. All on the ground could hear their concise reports and the barking instructions from the Sergeant as they proceeded to clear each room and floor, one at a time. There was no casual levity now as the men methodically searched for signs of life as well as signs of danger. By the time Lieutenant Reynolds had rejoined Matt and his group, their sweep was nearly complete.

"What do you make of this, Commander?"

Matt twisted and turned in a quandary, not sure how to answer. "I....I don't understand this," he stuttered, the ecstasy of the last few minutes severely dampened by the reality of the situation. "This terminal employs over thirty people. Where the hell are they?"

"Maybe they're hiding?" Vijay suggested.

Matt quickly spun and tossed him a disgusted look. "That's crazy!"

"Not if they were afraid of something," Corporal Cooke added.

Matt glanced at the Corporal in bewilderment, then turned and clutched the upper arm of Lieutenant Reynolds. He was experiencing an uneasy feeling that was churning in the pit of his stomach, and he didn't like it. Once more a seed of doubt was planted concerning the Lieutenant's forthrightness. "Afraid of what?"

Reynolds was momentarily taken aback by Matt's zeal, shrugging his shoulders and stepping back that caused Matt's gloved fingers to release their grip. "How should I know. I've never been on this planet before." He took a few quick strides towards the terminal building before glancing back. "Do you know of any monsters on Mars?"

The rhetorical question spurred Matt's philosophical mind to action. Indeed, no evidence of indigenous life had ever been discovered ever existing on Mars, let alone monsters, but what would prevent human beings from bringing some of their own?

Matt and the others followed Reynolds as he approached the massive, closed hangar doors of the maintenance and storage facility, listening to the tempered, succinct accounts of the soldiers clearing the three floors of the main terminal. The place appeared deserted but little had been disturbed. Counters and desks were neat and orderly, files seemed to be full and organized, no damage to the facility could be detected. There was still power in the building as the solar cells on the roof had kept the electrical batteries charged. The only abnormality that appeared to the marines was that a few pieces of electronic equipment seemed to have been removed, along with a conspicuous absence of data storage and programming disks. Sergeant Douglas, now in the maintenance hangar, had a much more interesting report. Most of the large, heavy equipment seemed to be intact, but the vast array of small hand and robotics tools that the repair and refitting facility must have had was reduced to a pitiful scattering of an idle piece here and there.

They entered through a nearby access service door and emerged in a cavernous open bay, brightly lit, except for the darkened shadows in the corners, by the natural light that penetrated through the roof. There was an eeriness about it, like wandering the cobwebbed halls and climbing the creaky stairs of some old abandoned mansion. Matt could see overhead power conduits that had been pulled from their fittings, exposed cabling and wiring dangling in the air. Large, treaded, titanium and steel robotics assemblers and welders stood menacingly by their stations, their numerous metal framed, pointed and pincered appendages hanging limply by their sides, lifeless and dormant but somehow unsettling, like the haunting surreal figures in a wax museum. The gray concrete floor was scuffed and soiled from constant activity, small patches of red crust staining its painted surface. There was an absence of vehicles, no short range hover craft or passenger transports of any kind. Only two refueling tankers and a pair of two-man open-air rovers were neatly parked in the storage garage.

It was then that Matt observed Sergeant Douglas emerging from the long shadows cast by the vehicles, his powerful, composed voice beckoning from the helmet receiver. "They all seem to be intact, Lieutenant," he dutifully reported as he approached. "Out of juice though. The solar batteries are dry and need recharging. They will run on liquid methane/oxygen propellant and there seems to be plenty of that around."

"Thank you, Sergeant," Reynolds acknowledged. "I thought Private Warwick was with you?"

"He's in the adjoining room, sir, checking out the status of the containment tanks. Big suckers!"

"Excuse me, Sergeant," Matt politely interrupted, "but is that all the vehicles you found? My information indicates that more than a dozen ground transports and several hover craft were stored in here."

"Sorry, sir, but that is all there is."

Matt frowned at still another irregularity. It seemed very unusual for so many vehicles to be gone at one time, including all three of the pressurized shuttles whose sole function was to ferry passengers and staff from the spaceport to the colony and back again. He opened his transmission link to the PL. "Jack, have you been listening?"

"Yeah, it doesn't sound like they're throwing you guys a surprise party."

"Call up the terminal's last known motor pool inventory," Matt instructed. "Chime in when you find the information." Matt began to feel the pressure of time as he turned to Reynolds. "Lieutenant, I think we had better get to the colony, ASAP."

"I concur. We won't find anyone here."

Jack's research confirmed Matt's assumption; more than a dozen land vehicles and all the hover craft were missing. Jack discovered an interesting notation that indicated two of the rovers had been dispatched weeks ago to Coprates Chasm in Valles Marineris, a reference he remembered from his briefings which concerned mining operations, but there was no mention of any additional distant projects requiring their use. As they began to filter out of the building, Matt instructed Jack to send out the rest of their party.

"I was counting on some wheeled or treaded transport," Matt casually remarked to Reynolds.

"We'll just have to travel the old-fashioned way," Reynolds replied, then continuing upon noticing Matt's dubious look. "Boot leather."

Matt grinned in amusement, then pivoted to peer into Vijay's helmet. "Vij, why don't you and that nuclear engineer, Harold Donovan, put some gas into one of those terrain rovers and make your way to the colony's nuclear reactor that's buried under a hill a mile or so beyond it to the west and check it's status. I don't want any nasty surprises."

"Previsionist thinking, Commander," Reynolds offered after overhearing the comment on his receiver. "Sergeant Douglas and Private

Warwick will help you get both rovers running and accompany you to the site to provide security."

As Lieutenant Reynolds began to marshal his forces near the terminal, the remaining five members of the initial support team were being deposited on the tarmac packing as much diagnostic equipment and tools as they could carry, which was limited at best. Two had been here before, assisting with the initial design and construction of Jamestown. For the rest it was the first time on an alien planet, staggering about aimlessly as if in a daze, bombarded by visual and emotional stimuli as had everyone else who had first set foot on this unusual and intriguing place. Matt joined them as they slowly began to make their way towards the main terminal and immediately recognized the general physique and purposeful gait of Doctor Olivrer as she sprightly bounded up to him, a bulky black medical bag draped over her shoulder, her bulging utility belt lined with small, plastic supply pouches. "Matt, why the hell have we been loitering around here?" she agitatedly challenged. "We should be in route to the colony by now."

Even through the reinforced and tinted faceshield, Matt could see the all too familiar fireballs burning within her eyes. "Just settle down, Susan," he sternly admonished. "We have to first thoroughly check out the terminal, from top to bottom."

"Shit! It's obvious that no one is here," she adamantly returned. "We have to get to Jamestown immediately. Even a few minutes could be critical. People may be hurt."

"Before we go strolling down that road," Matt replied with a growing level of impatience, "the marines must make certain that the terminal is secure, that there is no sign of trouble."

Not being a person who easily contains one's frustrations, Susan Oliver brushed past Matt to unceremoniously stop Lieutenant Reynolds in mid stride as he walked by. "Lieutenant....Lieutenant! Let's get moving. We should have been on our way to the colony over a half-hour ago."

The Lieutenant paused, briefly looked up in dismay, then reluctantly turned to face his antagonist. "Well, Doctor," he facetiously remarked. "I didn't know you did your undergraduate work at West Point?"

"Don't be so condescending, Lieutenant. There may be people who need my attention."

"Listen, Doctor," he delicately but resolutely began to explain. "It is our job to make sure that you arrive at Jamestown on your own two feet, not a sliced and diced carcass stuffed into a body bag. Now, if you will excuse me."

As Reynolds moved away, Matt reached out to grab Susan by the arm. "Will you please put a lid on your insolence, Susan, and let the poor man do his job," he angrily pleaded. "There is no available transport so we have a two mile hike ahead of us. So you had better get yourself prepared."

"I know that," she haughtily scoffed. "We heard all the boring details in the lander. I may be unpleasant but I'm not feeble. I can keep up with the best of you."

The chorus of chattering ringing incessantly within the padded confines of Matt's helmet was being relayed to Jack's communication monitor on the PL who in turn transmitted the signal back to the attentive ears anxiously awaiting on the bridge of the Guilford Courthouse. Caroline Hart had been watching and listening with the stoic calm and poise of the most stalwart of troopers, but now her expression was betraying the tension and emotional stress from the ongoing developments on the planet below. Waves of unrelenting fears and doubts caused her body to tremble uncontrollably, her stomach churning and cramping sickeningly. She began to nervously chew on the fingernails of her right hand, withdrawing into the thoughts of her own little nightmare world. Within those ghostly, haunting corridors ran the frenzied speculations of her distressed mind. Where was her husband? Why would he allow an integral part of the colony, such as the space port, to be unattended? Even if their communication system had completely failed, why hadn't someone made an effort to greet the landing party? What in heaven's name was going on down there? The fact that no deaths or damage to the terminal facility had been discovered did nothing to alleviate her consternation. Caroline couldn't suppress the traumatic, grisly mental image of hundreds of lifeless bodies littering the floors of the geodesic domes as Matt and the others sifted through the decrepit corpses. She grimaced in torment, fidgeting restlessly. Sheri sensed her agitation and looked up with soothing eyes, reaching out to firmly clasp Caroline's left hand in support. Caroline forced an appreciative smile through the gloom of her countenance, dropping the right hand from her mouth to tightly sandwich Sheri's as if to use it as a conduit as if to sap the life-force of her inner strength. It worked for a few moments, but she was a physical woman, and what she really needed was a warm, consoling hug. All those with whom she had grown close over the past trying week were busy. Robert and Matt were on the surface below. Sheri's comforting arms would have felt very reassuring, but she had her own duties to perform. And Lucinda's brand of affection wasn't exactly what she was looking for. Sheri's offered hand was a most gracious and caring gesture and Caroline clung to it like a rope thrown to a drowning man. If she could only be actively employed right now, she reasoned, she could handle it better. But deep in her heart she realized that she'd probably just be a burden to those around her. She felt anger and frustration at her own emotional weakness. The more her thoughts rambled, the more light-headed she felt. An uncomfortable queasiness settled in her stomach.

"Excuse me," she frantically said, releasing her grip on Sheri's hand. "I have to go to the bathroom. I'll be back shortly."

Sheri rose to her feet to follow as Caroline dashed for the elevator.

"Stay at your post, Sheri," Reggie firmly ordered.

Sheri hesitated, pointing in Caroline's fleeing direction. "But she may need...."

"Your station, please!" he sternly commanded with a disapproving glare.

Reluctantly, Sheri settled back in her seat. "Yes, sir."

Caroline briskly jogged through the main fuselage and up the ramp that fed into the central disk, single strands of her intricately groomed, lush brunette hair rebelliously flying out in the draft caused by the rapid forward motion of her gait. She bolted into the lavatory and past the bent frame of Lucinda Desjardin, who was hovering over a sink in front of a mirror, applying liberal amounts of mascara to her already entrancing facial skin. Even in her present emotional and ailing state, Caroline immediately perceived the oddity of her appearance. Lucinda was wearing the regulation light blue NASA flight suit, not the usual provocative attire that she was accustomed to seeing her in. A fleeting glance at Lucinda's reflection in the mirror as she passed showed the zipper of her suit to be half opened, revealing generous amounts of deep cleavage for all to see. That figured - Caroline was not surprised.

"Hi, Caroline," Lucinda warmly greeted with a bright smile and brief backward glance before returning to her grooming. "What's the story? Are we going to be transported down soon?"

Ignoring Lucinda's question, Caroline charged into the nearest stall, gagging and hacking and spilling her guts into the bowl. Lucinda heard the unmistakable sounds, put aside her make-up, and rushed to

Caroline's aid, placing a supporting hand upon her slumping back, patting her gently until the nausea subsided.

"My God, Caroline!" Lucinda cried out. "Are you all right? Maybe you should go see Doctor Caldwell. He might be able to give you something for your stomach."

"No, no," Caroline protested as she straightened, wiping her mouth with a tissue before backing away from the toilet. "I'll be okay. Just a bit upset right now." She inhaled deeply. "There, I feel better already."

She staggered clumsily coming out of the stall, her body shuddering uncontrollably. Lucinda took a firm hold of her with both hands and guided her towards the basins. "You're trembling all over," Lucinda observed with some concern. "What's been happening?"

Caroline became nearly hysterical, swiftly rambling through the day's events in thirty seconds, her words and sentences running together almost incoherently.

"Okay, okay, Caroline," Lucinda interrupted. "I get the picture. Try to settle down. Here, I have a mild sedative in one of my pouches. Would you like one? It's non-prescription."

Caroline looked at her skeptically for a moment before nodding. Lucinda unzipped one of the pliant hip pockets of her suit and pulled out several small plastic vials. Caroline's brows raised in surprise. "Are you a pharmacist too?"

Lucinda snickered, holding up each tiny tube in turn. "Everything for a rainy day. These are the sedatives. This is a stimulant. These are vitamins; birth control pills - got to have those...." The two women leered mischievously at each other and giggled. "....and EPI's, erotic pleasure inducers, for those lonely nights."

As Lucinda returned the pills to her pouch save for the sedatives and filled a small recyclable cup with water, Caroline thought it odd, though not necessarily unusual, for Lucinda to be packing EPI's. After all, she couldn't conceive of Lucinda experiencing many lonely nights. She had on occasion experimented with the psychologically addictive drug before, but she found the human touch to be much more enjoyable....or was.

"Let me take you back to your room where you can lay down for awhile," Lucinda suggested as Caroline quickly downed the barbiturate.

Lucinda steadied Caroline's shaky, unbalanced body as she escorted her to the relative comfort of her room, gingerly easing her down to the mattress of the bed and lifting each leg in turn to remove her shoes.

"Let's make you more comfortable," she emphatically stated as she gripped her flight suit zipper and adroitly pulled it down, gently slipping it off her shoulders letting it drop to her waist in one swift motion. Still feeling weak and disoriented, Caroline laid back and submissively lifted her hips allowing Lucinda to pull the garment off her legs.

"I've occasionally fantasized about this," Lucinda candidly admitted. "But not under these conditions, of course."

Caroline couldn't tell if Lucinda was being facetious or not, but the way she was feeling she didn't really care. Left dressed in a slinky black lace bra and matching silk bikini, Caroline rolled onto her stomach and buried her head into the soft blue and gold cased pillow. She felt light pressure parting her thighs and the weight of Lucinda's body camping between them and moments later a smooth, delicate hand tenderly rubbing her shoulder blades and down the small of her back. The massaging fingers felt so relaxing that she soon found herself dozing off, oblivious of Lucinda's lecherous gaze or the movement of her kneading hand onto her pantied rump. Lingering for a few minutes, Lucinda resisted the temptation to be more daring, finally hovering over Caroline to kiss her on the back of her head as she began to rise to her feet. "I'll leave you to rest now."

Cognizant of the shifting weight, Caroline rose up and clutched Lucinda's arm, pulling her close in a tight embrace. "Thank you, Lucinda, that was very kind of you. You're not so depraved after all." They silently pressed together for several seconds before Lucinda pulled away and lifted herself from the side of the bed.

"Or maybe I am," she replied with a devilish grin, "now that I've gotten a good look at you. I tend to collect on my favors." With a licentious wink, Lucinda strolled towards the door, but paused and struck a provocative pose. "You know, I could really do some things for you besides a relaxing massage. Whatever you'd be comfortable with. Feel free to look me up anytime."

Caroline smiled and nodded, too unsteady and queasy to discern Lucinda's suggestive remarks. But she did feel gratefully indebted to her as she laid back down on the bed and closed her eyes, breathing steadily. The sedative and Lucinda's soothing hands had served to calm her fragile nerves and soon she was feeling much better, though weary and drained. She decided to rest for a few more minutes, but no longer. She had a compelling need to return to the bridge to hear firsthand the reports from those courageous souls down on the surface who were attempting to contact her missing husband.

Lying broad and straight, the black fabrication of man shown against the reds, oranges, and tans of the surrounding countryside like a beacon of light pointing the way home to Jamestown. The road was splotched with patches of compressed reddish-brown Martian soil, dragged from the landscape and encrusted by the weight of the wheels and treads of countless all-terrain and construction vehicles. Fine, granular rustic debris continued to sweep across the road in front of their feet, driven by the gentle breeze whose high-pitch whirl served as background noise filtering through their external helmet receivers. The ground between the terminal and the colony was low and flat, strewn with thousands of rubbled rocks and stones of infinite scope and potmarked with an occasional crater. The level ground, coupled with a gravitational force less than four tenths of that on Earth, made the hike leisurely and comfortable, even for those laboriously hauling extra equipment, not that this alien environment didn't present some peculiar problems. Sudden movements tended to throw one off balance. Several of the visitors could occasionally be seen stumbling around like drunken sailors at some exotic port-of-call. With weakened gravitational forces and low air pressure, body weight was lessened. The mass of the life-support packs and any auxiliary gear shifted a person's center of gravity towards the outside of the skin. It felt as though one had been hollowed-out inside. It took awhile to get used too. The few who had walked on the planet before took great amusement at the clumsy antics of the novices.

Matt looked up wondrously into the brightness of the distant sun, at the sporadic, wispy puff of a high rising cloud and was amazed at the pinkness of the sky. It was a very strange sight to see. Enormous amounts of minuscule dust particles, stirred by massive seasonal global dust storms and the smaller, more common local winds, are constantly suspended at great altitudes in the atmosphere. With the high angle of the daytime sun, these particles were most effective at reflecting the red light waves of the spectrum and, along with their natural rustic color, gave the sky its eerie and ominous appearance. The thin atmosphere, only one two-hundredth the pressure on Earth, provided little protection against the cell damaging ultraviolet and gamma radiation of the sun's powerful rays. Matt knew that their suits were heavily shielded, but prolonged exposure was not recommended. He could forget any notion of camping out on Mars; no oxygen to fuel the flames of a campfire in any event. The glistening glass domes loomed ever larger as they neared and Matt could make out the jagged peaks of the Echus Montes hovering over the far western horizon beyond the colony.

Lieutenant Reynolds had placed two men fifty yards ahead of the group as they briskly closed in on their objective. The communication link was permeated with jabber as it seemed that everyone felt compelled to verbally express their enthusiasm as they absorbed the images of their surroundings. The mental and emotional state of people in such a hostile place was a particular concern, especially for Matt and the Lieutenant, on whose shoulders fell the enormous responsibility for their safety. The talkative nature of the team was a good sign.

Lieutenant Reynolds dropped from his position at the head of the column and meandered back towards Matt, who was more than a little surprised when he approached Doctor Oliver instead, who was walking by his side. "Doctor Oliver, you're the medical professional amongst us," he said as he reached into one of his utility pouches and removed a handful of small, cylindrical hypo vials. "I think you should have these and administer them if necessary."

"What's this?" she exclaimed in puzzlement as he forced the vials into the palm of her hand.

"Heavy tranquilizers," he explained. "If someone loses it down here, they could snuff themselves out in a wink of an eye."

"Oh, that's just great," she replied with disgust as she reluctantly added the drugs to one of her medical kits.

"I'll keep a few with me," Reynolds audaciously added, "in case we have to sedate you."

Doctor Oliver smirked and shook her head derisively as he moved away. Overhearing the conversation, Matt found it difficult to suppress his chuckles as he slowly roamed towards the side of the road. It had just occurred to him that even though he had been on the surface for nearly an hour, he had yet to actually step on Martian soil. He moved cautiously along the edge, hesitating as if contemplating taking those first spring season strides into the cold, foaming surf of the Atlantic ocean. It was such a simple thing, but the fact that this world was foreign to human life and evolution carried with it a certain thrilling appeal. He raised a leg deliberately and stepped out. He could sense the red-orange ground crunching under his boot. His other leg carefully followed. It felt exhilarating. The soil was crystal-hard sand, like tiny grains of salt. It behaved mechanically like a wet, sandy beach, yet was extremely dry. The texture and characteristics reminded Matt of the soil in the deserts of Arizona and New Mexico called caliche, a type of clay that is solidified into a crust by the evaporation of water. His boots left small indentations in the duricrust which were surrounded by small radial cracks. Everywhere there were streaks and patches of even finer, powder-like, red-hued particles, brighter than the harder crust, that leisurely drifted across the irregular terrain. Even though his boots were outfitted with tiny heating elements that traversed the soles, Matt could still detect a distinct chill penetrating the material. The same held true for his thick-gloved fingers as he stooped to touch a small, craggy rock. Without the heating fibers, working outside would be nearly impossible. An exposed hand for only a few brief seconds could cost a man his fingers. Indeed, only the soil properties and the absence of moisture reminded Matt of a desert. Some of the civilians joined Matt in frolicking amongst the many scattered stones and boulders like school children at recess. After some time, Lieutenant Reynolds grew slightly annoyed and ordered everyone back on the road, ostensibly for their own safety, including Matt himself. This part of the mission had now divulged into a military operation and the Lieutenant now had the authority.

Even as he was enjoying himself in the Martian dirt, Matt had noticed that the Lieutenant had sort of slithered off by himself. Upon returning to the road, Matt jaunted up to Reynolds from behind. Looking over his shoulder he found the Lieutenant silently studying a small letter and picture on his electronic pocket photo and message book. Unable to get a clear view, it appeared to Matt to be the image of a young, robust, handsome African-American man in Marine Corps dress blues, his arm around an attractive woman of similar age wearing a knee-length, summer type floral dress. The Lieutenant seemed to be hypnotically absorbed by the photo and the contents of the message that he alternately continued to switch too. Curious, Matt moved along side the officer and nodded cordially. "Lieutenant, you seem to be preoccupied with that. Bad news from home?"

Reynolds dolefully shook his head. "No, nothing like that."

Matt glanced over at the picture, noticing the smiling faces and the sergeant's stripes on the uniform. "A friend of yours?"

Reynolds vacantly stared at the sky for several seconds before Matt could hear is heavy sigh. "No, Commander, he wasn't. I never knew him." With reverence and care, Reynolds turned off the compact PM holder and returned it to his thick chest pocket, safely zipping it shut. Sensing that he had accidentally intruded upon a deeply private matter, Matt pursued the subject no longer.

Just several hundred yards away the road became an intersection, the north-south trail branching off to facilely encircle the colony's perimeter only to rejoin again on the western side in a single road that led to the nuclear reactor plant. The east-west path continued on to the very walls of the central dome itself. By now Vijay had refueled the two open-air rovers, got them operational, and had caught up with the party, patiently creeping along at the rear of the column. Upon reaching the intersection, Matt instructed him to follow the southern road, circumvent the colony, and head west to the reactor site, keeping in regular contact. Sergeant Douglas led the way, followed by Vijay, who was casually relaxing while allowing his engineer companion to do the driving. Harold Donovan took the brunt of some good-natured harassing from his colleagues for riding all the way, bantering with them as he drove by.

Proceeding beyond the intersection, the visitors developed an appreciation for the enormity of this engineering feat. The domes were anchored on a thick concrete support base and stretched some 600 feet in diameter. The precision molded, inches thick sections of glass sloped sharply upward and narrowed to join at the pinnacle some 50 feet above the ground, its stress and shatter-proof properties enhanced with chemically treated compounds to protect against the harmful radiation from the sun. The central dome, with two above ground floors, rose some 65 feet into the sky. And this was only the construction that was visible from the surface. Each dome had two levels of subterranean space, and tunnels that connected the outer domes to each other. Twisted metal and the light reflections off the small, jagged slices of crushed glass from the damaged dome could be seen littering the ground in a compact section to the distant right. It seemed odd to Matt that the debris from a meteorite strike would not be scattered over a wider area. Cautiously the group followed the road to the primary outside airlock of the central dome, the structure housing the administrative, operational, and control functions for the entire colony. Suspicious of the ghostly silence and the absence of activity, the soldiers apprehensively shuffled up to the vacuum seal door, keeping a watchful vigil in all directions.

"What do we do now?" Corporal Cooke asked drolly. "Knock?"

Lieutenant Reynolds took a few short steps towards Matt with a resolute but questioning countenance, as if seeking sanction for a decision that he had already made. "Well, Commander, do we crash the party?"

Matt felt the pangs of nervous uneasiness doing cartwheels in the pit of his belly as he nodded emphatically. "I don't see where we have any choice, Lieutenant. Open her up."

Matt stood by Reynolds side and watched him reach out with a solitary gloved finger and press the large, square, green access button to the central dome airlock. They could hear the gush of air as the inside atmosphere was evacuated followed by the low rumbling of the door mechanism. Fortunately it was still operational as the heavy metal hatch slid ponderously into the framework to the right. Two privates cautiously poked their heads and laser rifle barrels around the darkened corners. After a brief frozen pause to take stock of their immediate surroundings, the two men disappeared inside, hugging the wall as they moved. They were soon followed by two others, Lieutenant Reynolds, then Matt and his private escort. The chamber was average room size and dimly lit, a yellow emergency lighting tube on the far wall being the only illumination, except for the splash of outside glare now filtering through the open hatch. Once declared safe, the remainder of the party joined them and sealed the airlock hatch. Instinctively the marines activated the twin spotlights on the sides of their helmets and, like sheep in a herd, the others conformed as well. Copious disks of light fleetingly danced off the obscure, barren walls and ceiling of the room as animated heads swiveled in all directions. Finding the control panel by the hatch that provided access to Jamestown, Matt asked the electrical systems engineer, Andre Fedorov, to join him, pointing to the emergency lighting and asking for confirmation of his suspicions.

"I'm afraid you're correct, Commander," he acknowledged. "With the ceiling grids out, the facility is operating on low consumption emergency battery power only."

Andre Fedorov was in his mid fifties, large streaks of gray throughout is closely cropped hair betraying his age. Of Lithuanian heritage, Andre had been a member of one of the original design teams that planned the Jamestown project and had participated in part of its electrical and power distribution construction. This was actually his third trip to the colony and he knew its systems and layout better than anyone. Matt asked him to stay close. He would lean heavily on his advice.

Lieutenant Reynolds ordered everyone to huddle against the walls on either side of the doorway, soldiers out in front, and upon his signal Matt pressed a button that sucked out the Martian air, equalized the pressure, and the now familiar mechanical whirl heralded the opening of the inner seal. In groups of two the marines spilled out into the murky corridor, prudently fanning-out in both directions, crouching low and taking a knee every few yards. The hallway was desolate, shadowy, and haunting. The ceiling rose ten feet high, its lighting grids black as night. The only illumination coming from the emergency fluorescent tubes spaced every 75 feet along the outer wall and, of course, their helmet spots. The corridor gradually bent around in a gentle arc, tracing the outer shell of the base of the dome. Not a sight or sound beyond their tiny foothold could be detected.

"Commander Maitland," Reynolds formally addressed over the local channel. "What are the chances that they have security robots?"

"My mission reports made no mention of that capability," Matt replied. "This is an open facility. There is nothing classified or secret about it. There's no reason for them to have any. I wouldn't worry, Lieutenant."

Reynolds frowned at Matt's naiveté. "That's why you're not a marine. I suggest we start with A and C."

Matt concurred with a slight nod of the head and turned to Andre. "What is the most expedient way to Administration and Control?"

"Second floor. Down the hall to the right is an elevator."

"Negative on that," Reynolds adamantly interrupted. "Elevators can make such lovely traps. We need a stairwell."

Andre looked on with trepidation. "Just beyond the elevator," he hypnotically replied before snapping with conviction. "Look, gentlemen, I'm no soldier, I'm an engineer. I grant you that this situation is peculiar. But I know these colonists. They aren't radicals or activists. They're decent, free-spirited people, many with families. Pioneers on the new frontier. They're not a threat to anybody."

"You may be right," Reynolds casually remarked as he brushed by. "But something may be."

The interior design of the domes were all similar and the same on each level, resembling the spokes of some gigantic wheel, except for slight modifications in the two northern domes that housed manufacturing facilities. The main corridor circled the inside of the outer shell along the concrete base. The inner walls of this passageway were lined with entrances to rooms of various sizes that gradually narrowed towards the center like slices of apple pie. The central spokes of these domes and their sub-surface extensions were open common areas accessible by two opposite hallways that linked them with the main corridor. They served divergent functions save for the one on the upper floor of the central dome. There entry was by permit only and contained the operating brains of the Jamestown colony. It was Administration and Control, where Matt and the others were heading.

"What atmospheric readings are we getting?" Matt queried to no one in particular.

Each marine carried on his belt a small, lightweight, rectangular black and silver instrument, resembling a compact tape recorder, designed to measure certain conditions or to scan for biological, chemical, or physical properties. Corporal Cooke paused and raised his device chest high, turning in all directions. "I'm reading unusually low amounts of nitrogen and oxygen, breathable though, if your not running around. Temperature is a chilly 42 degrees. Only trace amounts of CO2. Nothing to indicate that there is an internal rupture somewhere or that Martian air is seeping in from the damaged dome."

Matt perplexingly looked over at Andre.

"If the area around the ruptured dome hadn't been sealed off," he calmly reported, "Martian air would be mixing in here right now. The emergency power system is set on bare minimum. Just enough air to survive on and enough heat to prevent everything from freezing up."

Matt nodded. "We'll keep on our suits until we can boost the power supply. Is there sufficient power for computers? Communications?"

Andre shook his head and scoffed. "Not a chance."

They continued on, snaking against the inner wall a foot at a time as if negotiating the treacherous path through a minefield, passing opened doorways to working offices, data processing centers, and storage rooms. A marine disappear into each of these darkened suites only to reappear seconds later with the same account. Neat and orderly with no sign of disturbance, or recent occupancy for that matter.

It was at this time that Matt received a report from Vijay advising him of their arrival at the hillside entrance to the underground nuclear reactor a mile west of the colony and that they had not found a trace of any recent human activity. Matt recounted the conditions in the central dome and expressed his fears that the reactor would not be in satisfactory operating condition, considering that Jamestown appeared to be running on minimal battery power only. Matt was informed that Harold Donovan's initial investigation indicated no radiation leakage or unusual heat or gas displacement. Matt reiterated a cautious warning as Vijay and his party prepared to descend the reactor shaft and then returned his attention to his immediate surroundings as the first marines passed the elevator and turned into the vestibule that contained the stairwell.

Slowly and in single file they began to ascend the two flights of steps, Private Anderson on point, followed by Private Simmons, Lieutenant Reynolds, Matt, his escort, and the others. They rubbed their shoulders against the right wall, scrupulously checking each corner before rounding it. It was difficult to clearly see in the distance under the subdued light and the helmet spots weren't very effective beyond a few yards. The stairs ended in a small foyer that opened into the main second floor corridor. Privates Anderson and Simmons scurried to each of the front corners and peered into the deserted, though strangely bright hallway. Here the outer wall of the corridor was the glass plates of the dome itself, anchored into the concrete support base at floor height and extending down through the ground level. The men were mesmerized by the view of the reddish-brown, boulder-strewn ridged plain to the south. The natural light penetrating the dome was a comforting change from the dreariness of the first floor.

"The central corridor is about thirty feet to the left," Andre pointed out as everyone gathered near the opening.

Lieutenant Reynolds nodded to Private Anderson who cautiously proceeded out into the hall in that direction. The inner promenade wall on the second level was completely solid, no doorways or portals anywhere. That was because all the offices on this level were directly associated with the mechanical and planning operations of the colony and thus were faced towards the inner hub. The wall was painted in a light beige and liberally decorated with paintings, prints, and drawings, many of them depicting water scenes on Earth - sort of a casual reminder of home. Moments later they were entering the long, broad passageway that joined with the central hub and Jamestown Administration and Control. Private Anderson clung to the left wall as Private Simmons dashed across to squeeze his body tight against the right. Private Walinski left Matt's back to join his comrade on the other side. They silently crept forward like a prowling panther in the gradually narrowing corridor, able to identify more and more of the control center as it was bathed in the orange glow of the late morning sun. Corporal

Cooke placed a firm hand on Matt's shoulder as he moved past him to take up a close position in line behind Reynolds. Matt understood the silent gesture. His safety was the Corporal's job, and he would shield him from all harm. But deep in his heart and soul he realized that everyone's safety was ultimately the responsibility of Reynolds and himself, and they would be the one's to fry if things went wrong. At that moment he began to have an inkling of what Lieutenant Reynolds had been experiencing. What would be worse, he thought; to die with those you commanded or go on living with the knowledge that many of those that you had been responsible for had died? Matt wasn't sure what his choice would be. None of the above would be most preferable. They paused just before the archway, crouching low to ascertain the immediate situation. The left near quarter contained the entrances to a number of offices and a conference room. The remaining circumference of the central hub was lined with a broken series of black and gray consoles and electronic and computer stations, not unlike those aboard the Guilford Courthouse. All that were visible seemed to be dead and powerless, as dark as a starless night. The center of the hub was ringed with five identical Y-shaped cubicle stations, most equipped with various computer terminals or other electronic gadgetry. A couple of stations looked stripped or its components were never installed. One-by-one they deactivated their helmet lights, being useless at this point. Lieutenant Reynolds lightly tapped Anderson on the shoulder and pointed to the left. The private rose as if being played in slow motion and mindfully stepped along the wall towards the offices. Private Simmons copied the movement to the right.

"Wait a minute!" Private Walinski hollered in distress as he raised his scanner from his utility belt. "I'm picking up movement on the motion detector."

Within milliseconds their external helmet microphones picked-up a shrill, high-pitched buzzing sound emanating from the far side of the room immediately followed by a sudden burst of a blinding, narrow-focused flash of yellow-white light striking the wall slightly above Anderson's head, leaving a tiny, smoldering bore cavity in its wake.

"Son-of-a-bitch," he shouted in panic as he dove for sanctuary inside the opened doorway of the nearest office.

Instantaneously Private Simmons flattened himself behind the left side of a large console while the others cowered near the entrance with their faces to the floor.

"What the hell!" Simmons cried out.

"Someone's firing at us!" bellowed an alarmed anonymous voice from the rear.

"Everyone keep down," Reynolds ordered as he pressed forward for a better look, activating his external speaker. "We're US Space Marines, don't fire!"

Only agonized silence greeted the Lieutenant's call.

"I'm not picking up anything on infrared but us," Anderson distraughtly reported.

Cooke and Walinski slithered next to the Lieutenant. The other three marines burrowed against the corridor walls nearby. Nothing could be seen but the bottoms and legs on inanimate work stations.

"It's moving again," Walinski announced. "To our right, about two o'clock."

"I don't see shit!" Simmons frantically cried out.

Reynolds thought he heard a strange, external metallic rumble amidst all the frenzied chatter ringing in his ears. "Quiet!" he sternly admonished. "Listen." The low, faint sound became more discernible. "Like the motorized revolutions of an axle," he commented.

Corporal Cooke quickly digested the available information and decided to put himself in a better offensive position. "Cover me," he said to Walinski and in one swift motion he rose to his feet and recklessly dashed forward as low to the ground as he could scurry.

"Bob!" Walinski screamed in horror as another invisible bolt from the front right zinged past the side of the nearest Y-cubicle just as he plunged beneath its divider, a brilliant splotch striking the door frame of a nearby office.

"Damn!" Cooke bellowed. "That one nearly parted my hair!"

The marines all had their laser rifles leveled but no clear target on which to aim.

"It stopped again," Walinski proclaimed. "It's coming from somewhere behind that station to the far right."

Matt was terrified, creeping along the floor just behind the marines. He had been trained for spacecraft combat maneuvers and had served on a ship under combat conditions in the past, but CAS never prepared him for something like this. He was a spaceship captain, not a ground pounder. He could feel his heart pounding, his skin crawling with tension as he raised his head to look out over the Lieutenant's shoulder.

"Keep your head down, sir," Reynolds firmly warned.

Matt felt a certain measure of relief knowing that he had a man of Reynolds' experience and character to rely on in situations such as this.

Aware of the uneasiness and fear among the civilians, Reynolds crawled back to address them. "I want all non-combatants to hug the floor and withdraw very slowly down the corridor."

Doctor Oliver naively rose to her knees and was immediately grabbed by the arm and roughly pulled to the ground by Reynolds just as another yellow-white burst impacted near the bottom of the overhead archway, small bits of fuming, scorched plaster dripping down around Matt and Private Walinski.

"Christ!" she angrily swore.

"Eat the floor, Doctor," Reynolds hollered vehemently, "if you don't want to get your insolent ass toasted."

She glanced at him impudently. "You'd like that, wouldn't you?"

"Not at all," he replied as he started to crawl back. "I reserve that privilege for myself."

Meanwhile, Corporal Cooke was drawing fire each time he poked his head around the corner of the divider, specks of searing light burning peep-holes in the upper wall behind him. "I thought I saw some rubber wheels," he reported, panting heavily. "But I don't have time to line up a shot. We need to draw it out into the open space on our right flank."

"Roger that, Corporal," Lieutenant Reynolds concurred, hesitating for only a brief moment to think. "Simmons, use your cube. Toss it into the right corner. If it's tracking motion, it may follow."

"Yes, sir."

Private Simmons removed from one of his pouches a transparent, phosphorescent cube used to illuminate small darkened areas. Shaking the gelatinous contents to start the chemical reaction that produces the light, Simmons tossed it like a grenade towards the right side of the room. It hit the floor and skipped towards the curving row of perimeter consoles like a shooting star. Another laser burst passed well above it followed by that rumbling, high-pitched whine.

"It's on the move again," Walinski excitedly reported as he checked his motion detector. "Moving forward, but not towards us. Off to the right."

They would only have a second to identify the target and fire before all of them would be in imminent peril. In that open space to the right,

Corporal Cooke and Private Anderson would have the clearest field of fire. Suddenly that second was upon them as the thing emerged from behind the work station obstructions in pursuit of its phantom quarry. Matt only had the chance for a fleeting glimpse. Cold dark gray steel; a chassis of sloping plates that looked like that of a tank, with small, broad rubber wheels, but smaller than a desk; a fat, cylindrical neck rising about four feet from its center topped with a rotating, low but broad hexagonal shaped head embedded with a tiny infrared sensor eye on its front face and one finger-like sensing projection extending out from each of its forward sides; a lower rectangular projection in front on which was mounted a swiveling laser gun that resembled the shape of a 20th century soda bottle with squared-off flanks at its base; a metal encased, light bulb-like extension attached to the front angled plate that swung rapidly from side to side; a bulky black box mounted behind the central column that he suspected contained the power source and computerized controls for the beast. Then a blazing flash, a puff of smoke, and a spray of tiny glimmering fragments of shredded steel as the narrow, focused beams from the rifles of Cooke and Anderson struck the machine on its framework and control box. It listed lifelessly to the side, one of its wheels shattered, the power source perforated.

"It's a damn sentrybot!" Private Walinski exclaimed as everyone labored to their feet once the smoke had cleared away.

"Aren't those things programmed to give verbal warnings first?" questioned a wary Anderson as they cautiously approached the disabled robot.

"Apparently not this one," Cooke replied as he poked around the metal carcass with his rifle barrel.

"Lucky for us, huh, that it wasn't a better shot," Walinski frivolously commented as he contemptuously raised and lowered the limp and lifeless barrel of the sentry's gun.

"Yeah," Cooke agreed, pausing in thoughtful reflection. "I wonder why? Maybe that robotics engineer we played cards with can tell us later."

Matt exhaled a mountainous sigh of relief as Lieutenant Reynolds helped him to his feet, then felt the pull of a firm tug on his arm.

"Did you say something about not being concerned?" Reynolds whimsically remarked.

"Is this what you expected, Lieutenant?"

Reynolds scoffed. "Hell, this is nothing like I expected," he regretfully answered before turning to Doctor Oliver as she fretfully straightened the various disarrayed pouches hanging from her belt. "Are you all right, Doctor?"

"No, you idiot!" she irascibly screeched. "I was just scared shitless! I think I wet my pants!"

Reynolds grinned. "Aren't you glad we came along?"

Susan Oliver responded with a derisive sneer as Reynolds moved off to join his men.

Having regained his composure, Matt began to dutifully recount the events that had transpired for the benefit of Jack in the PL and the interested souls worried sick aboard the Guilford Courthouse. Meanwhile, Nichelle Bennett found the communications console while Andre Fedorov took a seat on the opposite side of the circular room by the expansive arrangement of operations stations. Both found their displays and controls completely powerless, though they appeared to be undamaged. Nichelle began to pull apart the electronic modules, examining the chips and connections. It was nearly impossible for her to work with such intricate, detailed circuitry wearing those thick-fingered gloves. She began to run the tests she could using the portable diagnostic analyzer that she had carried with her, but nothing could be activated until power was restored. Andre found that power could still be controlled and allocated to any desired systems, if only he had volts to allocate. The batteries were slowly draining, though surprisingly getting a minimal recharge from the reactor itself, but nothing was being produced by the normally dependable solar cells. That wasn't surprising. He saw it on the flight in. The solar panel array was covered with dust. If he could get the robotics scrubbers back in operation, or clean it manually for that matter, they could produce enough power to get by with until the reactor could be brought back to normal capacity. Until then, they were rather helpless. One thing seemed apparent to him. The colony had been neglected for quite some time.

By the time Matt had finished his communiqué, Corporal Cooke had rejoined him and pointed out the Chief Administrator's office. Matt headed for the open doorway but Cooke quickly grabbed him by the arm. "I'll check it out first, sir. Stay behind me."

Cooke cautiously peered around the corner, then took a few measured steps inside, eventually disappearing from view. After a few anxious seconds, Matt noticed Cooke's left hand extending out the doorway, motioning for him to enter. Matt turned into the spacious, gray carpeted office and was immediately cognizant of a peculiar claustrophobic feeling. It only took a moment to understand why. The second level was totally open to the Martian landscape, including the main corridor, except for the enclosed offices. That seemed very strange to him. On Earth it was usually just the opposite. The office was nicely furnished with a large, mahogany desk, cherry wood cabinet, plush mauve chairs and sofa, and matching lush drapes that gave the illusion that a window occupied the rear wall. But it still seemed Spartan and stoic. Matt leisurely browsed, examining every little detail. The walls were conspicuously devoid of all pictures or decorations, though he noticed that several hangar hooks were still nailed in place. The desk top was completely cleared off except for a solitary computer terminal situated at one corner. Deep in thought, Matt wandered behind the desk, lowering himself into the pliant, cushioned seat of the black reclining executive chair, his environment pack preventing him from leaning back. He opened the drawers and found them empty except for a broken pen and a few meaningless scraps of paper. The disk files still contained all the basic operational programs, but all of the reference, research, personnel, and personal files seemed to be missing. He could find nothing to indicate what became of the colonists. Something else odd occurred to him. Matt looked around in all directions, in the back of the drawers, under the desk. Surely there would be a picture of Caroline Hart in this office. But no picture could be found.

"Did they forget to pay the rent?" Cooke jokingly remarked.

"Hmmmm...." Matt pondered thoughtfully, in a flash his mind recalling tiny morsels of colony administrative reports that subtly indicated a festering, uncertain amount of dissatisfaction. "Or maybe somebody kept raising the rent?" he astutely replied.

Lieutenant Reynolds' head stuck through the doorway as Matt was climbing out from behind the desk. "Commander Maitland, A and C is dead." He suddenly paused and dropped his head, regretting his unfortunate cliché. "Sorry. This level is secured. With your permission I'd like to take my boys and clear the subterranean levels under this dome, though I'm doubtful that we'll find any sign of them."

"Very well, Lieutenant," Matt agreed with a lamentable nod. "I believe that the first underground level is commerce and the second contains the colony's recreational facilities."

"That's right, sir."

"Carry on."

Reynolds' voice resonated sharply inside all helmets. "All right marines, with me. We still have a job to do. Cooke, Walinski, remain here."

As Reynolds and his men were departing for their journey below, Matt received another transmission from his friend. This one was both reassuring and troubling at the same time.

"We're outside the reactor containment chamber now," Vijay tranquilly reported. "We've done a very preliminary and superficial examination of the reactor controls and physical plant and to be quite honest, Matt, we can't find anything wrong with it."

Matt's brows raised in disbelief. "What?"

"It's operating automatically at bare minimum capacity. I won't clutter my report with a lot of technical jargon, but the fission process has been intentionally retarded, manually. Just enough to provide power for this plant, produce a little heat, and a small recharge for the emergency batteries. The facility is completely on line and there is plenty of breathable atmosphere here. We can climb out of our suits to work."

Matt was completely dumbfounded by Vijay's findings. "Why would they do that?"

"I can't explain it, Matt. We should be able to enhance the fission reactions at any time."

A sudden, chilling fear wracked Matt's soul. There must have been some rational reason for the reactor to be nearly shut down. Cataclysmic visions of blazing infernos and mass destruction went careening wildly through his imaginative mind. "Now wait a minute, Vij," he forcefully cautioned. "What are the chances of something going tragically wrong if you start firing up that thing?"

"Plenty," came his frank response. "Harold would like time to thoroughly inspect all control systems, containment vessels, relay stations, and conduits that feed into the colony's main power grid. If all goes well, we may be able to restore adequate power to Jamestown in eight hours."

"Very well," Matt replied. "Take all the time you need, just be careful. I need you back on the ship."

"It's nice to be in demand," Vijay snickered. "Maybe this is a good time to talk about a raise."

"Don't push it," Matt drolly warned. "By the way, have you seen any evidence of recent activity?"

"None, Matt. It looks like it's been set on automatic for awhile."

"Understood. Be advised though, we had a little run-in with a very angry security robot. Keep up your guard."

"Relax, Matt, everything is under control here. Sergeant Douglas and Private Warwick are keeping constant vigil watching our backs. It's been very nice chatting with you, but I really have to start helping Harold. After all, that's why you brought me along in the first place."

"Very well, Vij. Take care, buddy. Keep me informed."

With his mood a little more brightened, Matt leisurely strolled out of the Administrator's office and checked with each member of the support team as they dutifully picked through papers and files and worked with the equipment that they had at their disposal in an effort to collect any clues as to the fate of the Jamestown inhabitants. Fruitless to this point, Matt took a moment to gaze wondrously out over the red-hued landscape to the south that opened up before him, the salmon colored space port terminal building looming in the distance and the macadam road leading to it being the only signs of previous human occupancy.

"Jack, have you been following all of this?" Matt called out over his long range link.

"I'm still awake," came his boyish tone. "I've been sitting here twiddling my thumbs while you guys have had all the fun."

Matt snickered. "I don't mind telling you that there were moments that I would have preferred sitting back there and twiddling my thumbs. Put me through to the Guilford Courthouse, then return to the ship. It doesn't appear that we'll be needing an emergency evac. Get some rest and be ready to transport the rest of the team at first light. We need their help."

"Understood, Matt. You're now in two-way communication with Sheri."

Caroline Hart stood frozen behind the others, like a finely sculptured marble statue that grace's the halls of any one of a thousand museums; silent, stalwart, and unmoving. A flesh and blood Venus de Milo. Part was due to the calming affects that the chemical reactions of the sedative were having. The rest was utter horror, as if glued to a seat during the scariest scene of a monster movie. Outwardly she was an iceberg drifting with the frigid wind-swept currents of the mutating Jamestown sea. Inwardly, she was a bubbling volcano, a pool of boiling emotional magma just simmering below the surface. She had returned in time to listen to the sounds that reverberated within the confines of Matt's helmet; his detailed visual narration; the cautious and concise reports of the young marines; the continuous jumbled chatter reflecting perplexity and anxiety, like the chirping of a flock of birds. Her eyes slowly widened in stark terror, glossed over in a mesmerized trance, as she listened to the descriptions of the deserted central dome, its neglected condition; the acute whizzing of laser shot; frenzied cries of panic, fear, distress. The emptiness of her husband's office hit her soul hard. Caroline trudged zombie-like to the command console and gingerly eased herself into the padded chair. She continued to hear Matt's report and instructions, but she really wasn't listening anymore. She was hopelessly lost in her own private nightmare of dismay and disillusionment.

"Be sure to include my account of our encounter with the sentrybot," Matt instructed, "and our projections for the restoration of partial power when you transmit our Sit Rep to NSCA Control. Oh, by the way, I think that Miss Bennett could use some help with this communication system. Why don't you join us for a day or two."

Sheri's somber face suddenly brightened with glee. "I will, Matt, I will. And thank you. Thank you very much."

"One final thing," Matt sullenly continued. "Conclude our initial report to NSCA by saying that we've only had time to check the central dome and it may be days before we can cover the entire colony. There is a chance that we may still find dead or living colonists huddled under one of the other domes, but I wouldn't even fathom a guess as to why that may be. Personally, I don't expect to find them. On initial inspection, it appears that Jamestown has been abandoned. I say again, I believe that Jamestown has been abandoned."

That last statement was too much for Caroline to bear. Tears welled-up in her eyes as she burrowed her reddish face into her folded arms atop the console. Her worst fears had not been realized. There were no bodies, no suffocated, frozen, or mangled corpses, no deaths. This disclosure may have been worse. The uncertainty of it all was ripping her spirit apart, and her agony would only continue. Everyone had simply vanished! Her body was torn with convulsions as she erupted in torrents of unrelenting tears of anguish and hopelessness. Sheri rushed to her side with a consoling embrace as Caroline buried her weeping head into her chest, her hands clutching at Sheri's shoulders like a wild kitten. Thoughts and images of her husband flooded her mind. In a few traumatic moments, her memory relived every past experience together, both joyous and sad, passionate and serene, stimulating and mundane. But her final conversation with him hauntingly lingered at the forefront of her thoughts. His last words to her had a suddenly profound and distressing connotation as the reality of the predicament was ingenuously thrust upon her. David Hart was gone!

CHAPTER

Long furrowed rows of once tall, green stalks and expansive carpets of leafy foliage mow sat drooping inertly towards the Martian sands or lay withering away against its hardened crust in a dying sea of drab combinations of yellows and browns under the massive glass canopy of the Agri Dome. Matt looked on from the concrete walkway near the entrance, shaking his head in pessimistic dejection as Sergeant Douglas and Private Anderson cautiously searched through the small sheds and storage tank rooms that dotted the perimeter of the enclosure. The scene reminded him of the video images of the terrible Midwestern drought of 2038; of the stories Sheri had told him of the hardships experienced by her parents and grandparents on their Kansas farms that nearly forced her family into bankruptcy. The normally moist soil was dry and arid, just like the clays outside. The ground was peppered with tiny silver nubs capped with flat, notched, rotating heads that were the dispensers for the life-giving water and nutrient solutions that now sat dormant. The Martian sands provided a solid foundation for plant roots to take hold but lacked the macronutrients of nitrogen, phosphorus, magnesium, and potassium that all plants need and are readily found in fertile Earth soil. The colonists had quickly discovered that by introducing these elements and providing an Earth type atmosphere, agriculture could flourish on this planet. When power was curtailed, the automated sprinkling system was terminated. Everything was dead or dying.

Matt curiously watched Tammy Jacobs, the forty year old robust, husky agronomist with short but thick dirty blond hair scurry irascibly among the plowed files of decaying plants, touching and probing with her

180

portable agricultural analyzer, finally strolling over to the large hydroponics pool located along the right side of the dome. They hadn't been there for fifteen minutes and already her shoes, work suit pant legs, and hands were caked with red-brown dirt stains. The hydroponics pool, also called the soilless culture, supported plant roots in a water solution. The necessary nutrients for growth were provided in the solution surrounding the roots. The pool was now three-quarters drained from evaporation and the absence of recycling and new water production. It contained lettuce, beans, carrots, peas, and tomatoes. Tammy knelt by the edge and dipped her hand inside, pulling out a dripping, shrunken head of lettuce, its outer skin shriveling and fraying away. She took several more readings, grimaced painfully, then stood and approached Matt wearing an aggrieved expression.

"It looks like these plants have been unattended for at least two weeks," she irritably reported. "Oh! It breaks the heart to see this farm in this condition. The vegetables in the HPP are in the best shape. They consumed the last of the nutrients in the solution days ago, but if I can quickly resupply the pool with the appropriate soup, I think I can save most of them. The storage tanks seem to contain an adequate supply." Tammy frowned and sighed reluctantly as she turned towards the furrowed ground. "However, the rest of it is too far gone. We'll have to dig it all up and begin from scratch."

"What are the chances of blight or some kind of airborne contaminate?" Matt worriedly inquired.

"There's no fungus or plant disease on Mars," she candidly replied, "Unless it was imported. But I'll run some chemical analysis on the plants and the soil. But I believe that what you see is simply the result of lack of water and nutrient elements. I could use the help of those bioengineers. There is an awful lot of work to do."

"I'll inform them."

"And I'm going to need water, Commander, lots of it."

"The water reclamation and production system is just coming on line," Matt attempted to explain. "It will take some time to produce all we need. There is still a small supply in the storage tanks, but we have to conserve. I'll try to allocate what I can to you, but it won't be much, at least for the next few days."

As good as advertised, Vijay and Harold Donovan had thoroughly inspected the physical plant of the nuclear reactor and were satisfied with its operating condition to the point that they were able to boost power production to normal levels. In the interim the marines had diligently searched the commerce level of the central dome and the recreational level beneath it. Again, they found no evidence of a human presence or any clue as to their whereabouts. The illumination of the lighting grids and the restoration of power to many of the instrument consoles in A & C was very comforting to Matt. It felt so good to finally be able to peel out of that bulky, confining space suit; to be able to twist and turn and bend limberly; to feel and to touch with his own fingers again. Andre Fedorov was able to bring the essential systems on line; atmosphere and heat, automated factories for water production and distribution, computer facilities and other electrical needs. Once Lieutenant Reynolds had declared the central dome secure, Matt had gathered everyone, with the exception of Vijay and Harold who remained at the reactor site, in the common area of the subterranean commerce level where they settled into benches and plastic chairs beside rounded tables that ringed a wonderfully exotic rock garden consisting of many natural and human sculpted pieces of Martian red stone arranged and formed on clay in an impressive exhibition of statues, arches, and bridges. Matt felt relief at his ability to clearly see again in the corridors and rooms below the surface dome without the ghostly shadows creeping nearby or the glare from helmet lights. There they ate a simple meal of cold field rations brought by the marines, a menu that made everyone very appreciative of the selection and quality of those tiresome irradiated food packs served aboard the Guilford Courthouse. Both physically and mentally exhausted from the day's trying events, Matt dispatched his team to the Jamestown Hilton for a few brief hours of rest, a group of 25 rooms that served as guest quarters for visitors and temporary research teams working at the colony and occupied about a third of the level's floor space. Lieutenant Reynolds assigned a rotating double guard to each end of the area, just in case. Many fell onto the soft beds and dozed almost instantly. Those light sleepers that were awakened by a strange creak or the heavy clomp of a combat boot outside had trouble falling back to sleep again. There was just a spooky feeling about staying in a place where nearly 400 souls had mysteriously vanished.

Though tired and weary, Matt slept restlessly that first night. He was both puzzled and confused. The environment system of the colony seemed to be operating efficiently. Water was able to be produced in sufficient, if not surplus, quantities by the factories that absorbed the water vapor from the air, from the melting of the permafrost, and primarily by the combining of hydrogen with the abundant Martian carbon dioxide in the atmosphere which produced methane and water. The methane was liquefied and stored for fuel. Oxygen was produced when part of the water was electrolyzed. The hydrogen was then recycled through the methnator process. The remaining oxygen requirements were fulfilled by the direct disassociation of Martian carbon dioxide. Heat was pumped into the colony from the enormous temperatures produced by the fission reactions of the nuclear power plant. A myriad of troubling questions flooded his mind. Why had the reactor been all but shut down? What compelled the colonists to leave in the first place, if in fact they had left at all? Was there trouble with the food supply? An unknown disease that Doctor Oliver had been unable to detect? Why not aliens from another solar system? The damage to the one dome must have been unnerving, but the possibility of additional meteorite strikes could not have been so threatening as to force the need for a general evacuation. He rolled and twisted sleeplessly, unable to clear his thoughts. The mission had now mutated from one of reestablishment of contact to one of search and possibly rescue. Something else to challenge his beliefs in man and God. It looked as if he was going to spend more time on the Red Planet than he had originally bargained for.

Under the rising brilliance of the early morning sun, the Nathanael Greene returned with the rest of the support team, including Sheri, along with all the equipment and supplies that they could carry. Lieutenant Reynolds had sent two marines to meet the newcomers and to escort them on the same two mile hike to the central dome. The initial team members who had been on planet for more than 24 hours and had suffered through a restive night grew rapidly impatient at the incessant though innocent chatter during their reunion within the glass enclosure of Administration and Control. After all, they hadn't broken into a lifeless dome where humans were supposed to have been, slithered like snakes along haunting, barren corridors in restrictive space suits, been shot at by a security robot, and scared to look around the next dark corner. The new arrivals hadn't been around long enough to appreciate the very real dangers that still existed in and around the colony's borders, and their job was just beginning.

Feeling more like a Caesar or Alexander the Great than a civilian mission commander, Matt marshaled his military and technical forces and divided them into three groups for his next campaign. He sent Lieutenant

Reynolds with four marines and a small party to checkout the Residential Dome to the southeast. He and Sergeant Douglas led four marines and several others to the Agri Dome to the southwest which also harbored the medical facilities and some science labs on the first underground level and additional living quarters on the second. The others remained in the central dome, working in A & C or the rooms below.

Matt stoically poked around the examination rooms of the Jamestown Medical Center while Doctors Oliver and Caldwell made a quick inspection of its functional status and supply inventory. At least Ben Caldwell had brought good news with him when he arrived. Frank Sharp was out of the chemically induced coma and recovering nicely. His prognosis was for a return to duty in a day or two with no adverse effects save for a mild headache. Matt was impressed with how neat and orderly the rooms looked; sheets tight and snug, cabinets neat and organized, everything spotlessly clean. Whatever happened here apparently didn't come upon them suddenly. They had time to prepare. Leaving one of the rooms, Matt clumsily bumped into the hulking frame of Sergeant Douglas.

"Excuse me, Sergeant," Matt apologized, clasping his arm before stepping back in surprise.

"No problem, sir," he replied with an effortless upturn of his left hand. "We've completed our sweep of this floor. If anything happened here, I think we missed it."

Matt's head dipped in consent. "No one has been treated in here for awhile. There's not even an old bandage in a trash receptacle."

"No, sir. With your permission I'd like to take my squad down to the second level now. Private Warwick will remain with you as security."

"Very well, Sergeant, carry on."

Soon after the marines departed Doctor Oliver distraughtly stormed into the curving hallway in search of Matt, closely pursued by her colleague. She found him inside one of the compact though homey patient rooms. Matt could easily perceive the distress in her facial contortions.

"Matt, we've got a problem."

A shivering chill shot up his spine as his imaginative and highly speculative mind began to envision people dropping dead in their tracks from some hostile microbe in the air. "Yes, Susan," he said with concern, "what is it?"

"There is a conspicuous absence of portable diagnostic equipment and supplies, including bandages, drugs, hand instruments, and emergency blood stocks."

Matt shook his head in bewilderment, partly in response to her excessive agitation over something not totally unexpected considering the circumstances. "Are you sure? How bad?"

"I've got the model inventory supply chart in my hand," she adamantly responded as she held up her black bound computerized data portfolio. "We estimate there is less than twenty percent of the normal consumable medical supplies on hand and even a smaller amount of hand tools. If we have to treat a rash of injuries or perform a major operation, we may not be able to handle it. I need the emergency medical supplies still on board your ship. All of them. Please have Mister Shoals transport them down on his next trip."

Matt moaned hesitantly. "I'm sorry, Susan. Military equipment has top priority. Lieutenant Reynolds was quite specific."

"Damnit, Matt!" Doctor Oliver exploded, stomping her feet angrily. "Don't give me any of that military bullshit! All those boys are going to do is put people into this hospital. Sorry is what you're going to be if I don't get those supplies. I need them, now!"

"Okay, Susan, okay," Matt consoled with a gentle pat on the shoulder as she petulantly ran her fingers through her frazzled blond hair. "I'll see what I can do for you."

As the doctors returned to the activity of evaluating the supplies and equipment that were available, Matt contacted Sheri at A and C with instructions to relay the request back to the Guilford Courthouse. Unfortunately, Sheri and Nichelle had been unable to get any of the colony's communication systems to transmit or receive external messages. She would have to await the Nathanael Greene's return to deliver the instructions on their own short range portable transmitter. Matt felt his stomach churning with anxiety once more. It was unnerving for him to be out of direct contact with his ship for this length of time. Too many things could happen - most of them bad.

The squad of deep olive and mustard uniforms carefully descended the wide, spiraling concrete ramp that led from the ground floor of the

Residential Dome to the living quarters of the first subterranean level, their laser rifles flanked at the ready. They had successfully cleared the park area above, another reminder of Earth constructed by the colonists that included a twenty foot waterfall, a meandering creek, infant evergreens, white pines, balsam firs, oaks, and meticulously sowed Kentucky bluegrass, all imported from home at great expense, now all tinged with withering shades of brown from lack of water circulation. With the restoration of power the water pumps would be active again and the congenial park would soon be sparkling once more with vibrant greens, a totally foreign coloration for the Martian world. Tiny twinkles of brightness from the ceiling lighting grids reflected off the marines combination binocular/night vision goggles that were strapped around the brim of their heavy steel olive drab helmets that ringed around their foreheads and dipped down to protect their ears and the back of their heads. Private Walinski led the way into the subtly bending corridor, followed closely by Lieutenant Reynolds, Corporal Cooke, and the others. Caroline Hart was also with them, having insisted on being permitted to go to her husband's room, as well as several other specialists. She had cried herself to sleep the night before, but once the initial shock of her husband's apparent disappearance had run its course, she had awakened more composed and emotionally ready to assume the duties that may be required of her. She had a renewed determination to not only search for clues as to the fate of David Hart, but also to ensure that Jamestown continue as a functioning colony so that his hard work and sacrifice over the last three years and their painful separation were not all in vain. She followed closely behind the five marines, growing a little annoyed and impatient at the snail-like pace but fully understanding the need for caution. She listened intently to the concise chatter between the soldiers as they scraped against the wall, checking each room as they passed. They hadn't progressed very far before the conversation ahead turned abruptly grave at the desperate cry of Corporal Cooke.

"Wait a minute! I'm picking up something on infrared."

"What!" exclaimed Reynolds. "Are you sure, Corporal?"

Cooke made a hasty manual adjustment to the instrument. "Yes, sir. Heat source about fifty yards ahead."

The marines crouched low, nervously fingering their rifles. A few indistinguishable deadened noises filtered through the air in the otherwise spooky silent hallway. They could discern a soft, high-pitched rustling, an occasional creaking sound, a few faint clomps like that of a horse hoof on soft carpet.

"I'm getting a reading on my motion detector," Private Walinski excitedly reported as he held up the rectangular device and pointed it down the passageway. "It's moving, down the hall and away from us." He took a few strides forward and frantically looked back at his comrades. "I see a moving shadow, Lieutenant. I'm going for a closer look."

"Get back here, Private!" Reynolds vainly shouted as Walinski dashed recklessly around the gentle bend of the corridor.

The men could hear the soft clomps become more rapid as the sound intermingled with the heavier thuds of Walinski's boots.

"Son-of-a-bitch!" impulsively cursed Corporal Cooke as he leaped to his feet and chased after his friend.

"Cooke!" Reynolds turned angrily to the others. "The rest of you freeze. Don't move until I return." In a flash, the Lieutenant also vanished around the ghostly curvature.

Almost immediately they heard a distant, low-pitch whine and then a hard thump. Within seconds, Cooke found Walinski's motionless body lying flat on his back. He rashly charged forward, hurdled his fallen comrade and took a frenetic look around. The hallway was empty. No sound, no shadows, nothing. He checked his infrared scanner. The reading was gone. He knelt beside his friend and checked his vitals, glancing warily in all directions.

"He's still alive, sir," Cooke announced as Reynolds approached. "Unconscious but alive. I see no sign of injury."

Reynolds immediately pulled out his pocket communicator and contacted Sheri who was at the main communication console in A and C. "Medical emergency, Residential Dome, sub level one. I have a man down. Send a medic immediately."

Caroline apprehensively stared at the others as she overheard the conversation down the hall, the words resonating off the concrete walls. She began to shudder in fright when the Lieutenant and Corporal came into view dragging by the arms the unmoving body.

"What happened to John?" Private Simmons fearfully inquired.

"We don't know yet," Cooke replied as he removed his helmet and powerlessly ran a hand through his closely cropped hair. "I didn't see a damn thing."

Caroline found herself instinctively cowering on the cool cement floor, pressing against the others as if to form a palisade of mutual protection with flesh and bone. She thought herself aimlessly spinning within one of her nightmare worlds, listening to Reynolds' imperturbable exertions to calm the panicked commotion coming from his young marines. It would take some time for medical help to arrive from nearly a mile away. The Lieutenant sent Simmons forward about 100 feet to act as sentry while the others timorously checked out the intervening rooms. By the time the doctors arrived, Caroline's anxiety had been abated, nothing of importance had been found. The infamous heat signature and the blip on the motion detector were long gone. All was back to normal for a deserted colony, except that one marine was down. Some of the soldiers lifted Walinski onto a stretcher attached to a flat trailer bed of the compact, egg-shaped, shuttle car that the physicians had arrived in. Doctor Oliver proceeded to examine him using her portable, shoulder-slung, hexagonal shaped electronic medical analyzer. She inserted various attachments into ports on the instrument and, working as a team, they used the sensor tips to touch or scan over various parts of his head and chest, the readings being instantaneously displayed on her machine, recorded and collated within the computer's memory files. Slowly Private Walinski began to regain consciousness.

"Wha....what happened?" he groggily asked as he turned his head. "I....I feel so tingly."

Doctor Oliver placed a firm hand on his shoulder. "Lay back and relax. You've experienced some trauma."

The other marines worriedly gathered around their stricken comrade.

"There's no visible surface injury or any internal bleeding," Doctor Oliver reported when she noticed Lieutenant Reynolds' stare of apprehension. "His body shows signs of being subjected to a heavy electrical charge or some kind of electromagnetic force. His entire nervous system was briefly paralyzed. Heart rate is steadily becoming stronger. There is no indication of exposure to any harmful radiation."

Lieutenant Reynolds solemnly moaned past the Doctor to the head of the cot and leaned close to Walinski's ear. "You're going to be all right, son," he said softly and serenely. "Can you remember what you saw? What hit you, Private?"

Private Walinski slowly rolled his head towards the Lieutenant. "I chased after....after this....shadow," he painfully mumbled as he struggled to express his muddled recollections. "I got close....It was tall....hulking, crinkled....the dark, dreary gray of death. That's all I remember, sir." He closed his eyes and breathed heavily.

"That's enough," Doctor Oliver insisted as she forced her way between Reynolds and her patient, rechecking the soldier's pupils and heart beat. "Can't you see that he's disoriented? Now if you're finished badgering my patient, I'd like to get him back to the hospital to run further tests."

"I'm okay," Walinski deliriously proclaimed as he tried to rise. "I have to get back to my post."

Doctor Oliver put a firm hand to his chest and nudged him back down again. "You are at your post, soldier!" she forcefully asserted.

Lieutenant Reynolds adamantly clasped the Doctor's arm as she was about to climb into the open cab of the transport. "Will he be all right?"

Susan Oliver nodded. "Yes, but if you ask me, if you all have chosen this line of work, none of you are rowing with both oars in the water." As Ben Caldwell backed up the tiny car to swing around in the corridor, Susan shot a fleeting glance back at Reynolds. "Aren't you glad now that I came along?"

The tiny band laggardly gathered themselves together and continued judiciously down the suddenly foreboding corridor of the first residential sub level. Moments after the marines renewed their search, Caroline noticed Corporal Cooke casually working his way back towards her and her colleagues, finally stopping by her side. She couldn't help but smile at the personal attention, especially with everything that must have been tugging at his mind and emotions. She somehow felt a comforting sense of security when he was around, as if he could prevent all harm from touching her.

"This situation is a little dicey to say the least," he calmly said as he peered at each person in turn. "I don't want anyone wandering off by themselves, is that clear?"

All heads quickly nodded their understanding. Caroline felt a surge of importance, a feeling of being special in some way, when his hand tenderly touched her shoulder and his eyes delved mystically into hers.

"Now Mrs. Hart, you mentioned something about your husband's room being down here. Do you know where?"

"Not exactly. I know the number is 1A. It shouldn't be too far."

The Corporal instantly reasoned that she was correct. There were fifty living units on this level that formed a circle around the central hub. Room 1A was between 2A and 50A. They were presently standing outside 46A. "Follow me," he directed. "I'll take you there."

Caroline kept close behind the gallant soldier as he rejoined the men ahead, one of them darting into each room as they approached.

"I've got 1A," he emphatically called out.

The unit numbers were clearly delineated in black against the pinkish-creme wall to the left of the broad door frame. Corporal Cooke stopped just outside of 1A and slammed his back against the wall. "This is it," he hastily commented with a quick glance towards her. "Wait here until I get the lights on."

Caroline's thoughts drifted. It was only during times like these that one appreciated the modern convenience of computer controlled, voice activated environment systems. Not exactly revolutionary at the time of Jamestown's construction, the audio controlled system was deemed to extravagant for budgetary parameters so the more standard manually activated computer monitored system was installed. The corporal would have to grope around for the light switch. But like for other endeavors, the marines were not exactly unarmed. He reached into one of his utility bags and removed his transparent plastic phosphorescent cube. Shaking its gelatinous contents to a brilliant glow, he leisurely tossed it into the middle of the room. Swinging his goggles over his eyes and setting them to night vision, Cooke gingerly peered around the door frame, rifle barrel leveled. The cube had bounded to a rest near a large arrangement of interlocking sectional square-cushioned seats that formed a gentle arc in mauve and gray. It's light illuminated several other small wood and metal furnishings as he slowly crept inside, but he relied on his night vision to see the large desk, computer console, and black leather chair to his left and some metal framed cabinets and display shelves to his right. As the room narrowed towards the back, he noticed the metal and stone shelved divider that separated the family room from the tiny kitchen and dining nook. Not as spacious as the Hilton but comfortable nevertheless. To the Corporal's great relief the room appeared to be deserted. The nearest environment control panel was on the wall to his right. He inched that way, keeping a sharp watch all around him. A press of a button activated the ceiling tile lighting grids and the room was immediately bathed in a sea of gentle, non-glaring brightness. The Corporal raised his goggles and seated them along the brim of his helmet, breathing steadily as he momentarily shielded his eyes until they adjusted. Then with an outstretched hand and a few steps towards the door he motioned for Caroline to enter.

Caroline tremulously passed through the doorway, taking small, calculated steps as if she were walking onto the rough, icy surface of a newly frozen lake. Her first impression was that of a furnished apartment waiting to be rented. It was clean, organized, unlived in. She carefully moved around the perimeter as the Corporal ducked into the bedroom to the right. She recognized his black leather chair from which he sat during their long distance conversations. His vidphone and computer terminal were still firmly seated atop the desk. But the desk itself was barren and empty. No papers, no electronic portfolios, no pictures. He possessed at least a dozen framed photographs of them together or her alone. He most certainly would have kept at least one on this desk, she reasoned, but none were present. Opening the drawers, she found none of his personal disk files, his logs and records, entertainment software, nothing. Exasperated and frustrated, Caroline searched the room more thoroughly. All of the large pieces of furniture, the sectional sofa, recliner, desk, floor lamps, shelving units and cabinets, all seemed to be there. But his audio component unit was gone. So was his surround movie projection equipment. She desperately opened every drawer and every cabinet door. There was no sign of his prized music disk collection or his film library. The home videos that she had made for him, including the erotic one, were also missing as well as the few hard bound books that he treasured. She had so looked forward to cuddling close to him on those soft, commodious cushions under the subdued pinpoint light of a simulated starry night listening to some contemporary light cosmic wind music or a classical symphonic performance. A tear formed in her eye. A gloomy despondency pervaded her spirit. She listlessly braced herself against the back of one of the sectionals until Corporal Cooke emerged from the now illuminated bedroom.

"The bedroom is clear," he adeptly announced. "Like in here, there's not much to examine."

Caroline raised her head abruptly and hurried past him as he reclined against the wall and lowered his rifle in repose. The sight of the spacious bed immediately greeted her, complete with its high mattress and elegantly sculptured cherry wood headboard embedded with mirrored panels, shelving, light tubes, and tiny cabinets with gold metal handles. The mattress was covered with a deep maroon spread trimmed in gold with a large, circular design in the center depicting an aerial view of the five glass domes ringed with the inscription *Jamestown: The First Permanent Human Settlement On Mars*. She had fantasized for what seemed like ages about this moment - entering his bedroom on the surface of Mars. She envisioned a warm, loving embrace, trembling hands slowly undressing each other, frolicking wildly on top of the spread, touching, kissing, and caressing, locked tenaciously in the fervent arms of passion, burning the sheets with exhilaration and desire. She had experienced insatiable yearnings to be teased, toyed and played with, to experiment, to have her emotions and senses erotically assailed. But without his presence, reality soon set in. The bed was cold, austere, lonely. She would sleep in it, but without his warmth beside her, it would just be another meaningless and dreary place to rest.

Lethargically Caroline moved over towards the walk-in closet. Except for a pitiful few colored plastic clothes hangars, the closet was bare. Not even that purple East Carolina T-shirt that she had recently sent to him remained as a reminder of the former occupant. She sullenly sauntered over to the simple chest-high oak veneer dresser, resigned to the inevitable, and remorsefully gazed into the vanity wall mirror. Frowning in sorrow, she thought she saw a few wrinkles forming under her eyes. A result of fatigue and stress, she hoped. She grew agitated at a slight touch of gray at the roots of her bangs, but it was just an illusion created by the glistening of light off her lavish brunette hair. Was she getting too old to start a new life, she wondered? She felt the pressure of a race against time, and time was creeping up on her. She opened the four drawers of the dresser, then looked around in all directions. There wasn't a personal item or memento in sight. Everything that defined David Hart, everything that had made him the man that she had fallen in love with, was gone. She somberly closed the drawers. As she was shutting the final, top drawer, her eye caught sight of a diminutive, flat black plastic object wedged tight against the back of the drawer. She reached in and carefully removed the pocket photo displayer that had been standing upright on its side. A torrent of emotions bubbled to the surface, staring hypnotically as her finger repeatedly pressed the button that cycled through a series of photographs. She gasped and sighed at the memories it elicited, clutching her chest as she delicately backed up to the edge of the bed and gingerly eased herself down. Tears began to flow like a raging river down her rosy cheeks as she reverently gazed at the pictures of Dave and herself, in T-shirts and shorts, several with their arms affectionately draped around each other. In a number of them, their smiles were infectious, standing by the side of a wooden cabin that overlooked the distant banks of Fontana Lake through a dense grove of heavily foliated trees. It was an extended weekend in the Smoky Mountains that would be remembered for all time. The days were filled with relaxing swims, boating, and adventurous hiking amongst the trees, peaks, and waterfalls. The romantic nights evolved into wild, passionate, and occasionally kinky love making that excited every fiber of her soul. It was the last time that they had taken a trip together. One month later Dave was on his way to Mars. Troubling and disturbing questions tormented her every thought. Why was he so adamant about accepting the Chief Administrator post here? Why hadn't she expressed her concerns more forcefully? Why did he have to be so adventurous and impulsive, to want to carve out a new existence in this God-forsaken place? What was wrong with what they had together on Earth? And why had she been so afraid to join him here? What made her think that they could be just as happy living separate lives millions of miles apart? Why was she so governed by familiarity, comfort, security, and the acceptance of friends while he was motivated by independence, risk, personal enlightenment, and a drive to savor the taste of the unknown? Why did she have to be so ambiguous, rolling with the tide, while he was so decisive, spitting defiantly into the wind? Their mutual stubbornness had led them to this. Their unbridled love, their past, present, and future ripped asunder by this untamed, barren wasteland. She pressed the cherished photos against her moistened face and sobbed uncontrollably. Aware of her frail emotions, Corporal Cooke hesitantly and nervously entered the room.

"Forgive me, ma'am," he bashfully said, looking down at the floor. "These quarters are secure. I have to get back to my squad. If there is anything I can do for you...."

Caroline nobly struggled to suppress her freely flowing tears, forcing a trifling smile through her aggrieved expression as she looked up and nodded while wiping the back of her hand across her eyes. Cooke stood fidgeting, feeling sympathy for her plight, unsure as to how to approach her.

"It's a tragedy, ma'am. I'm very sorry."

She bowed and swallowed hard. "Thank you." She quickly glanced up when she perceived him turning to step away. "Oh, Bob?"

Cooke froze in his tracks and spun around. "Ma'am?"

"I would really like it if you would start calling me Caroline."

A gratifying smile turned up the corners of the Corporal's mouth. "So would I, Caroline."

She noticed him twitching awkwardly again as he silently stood in the doorway, eventually pointing out towards the main entrance.

"I....I have to go," he nervously stammered. "I'll be right outside if you need...."

"Thanks, Bob," Caroline softly replied with another nod as she swept away an isolated tear. "You've been very kind. Please, get back to your duties."

Corporal Cooke tipped his helmet in respect and reluctantly backed out of the room, leaving Caroline to grovel over her lost dreams. She devoutly fingered the photo displayer and forlornly lamented. "Why can't I follow?"

Jamestown was once again bristling with activity. By the latter part of the afternoon of the second day, the marines had finished securing the rest of the colony, with the exception of the damaged dome whose subterranean ceilings had collapsed, making underground entry impossible through all the debris. With the frightening exception of the mysterious force that had knocked Private Walinski into next week, nothing unusual had been uncovered. The northwest dome, which harbored automated factories, science labs, and was the home for the water reclamation and power relay stations, appeared to be the least disturbed, with only smaller pieces of lab equipment conspicuously absent. The factories that processed raw materials, produced steel, glass, and concrete, framework and chassis for robotics haulers and land rovers, synthesized methane and hydrogen, all seemed to be perfectly functional, though only the mechanical engineer had a clue as to how to operate them. Fortunately the air and water miners and processors functioned at the touch of a button. The adjoining surface warehouse building, connected to the dome by a short tunnel, still contained a pair of excursion rovers and three short range exploratory models, though the bulk of their considerable all-terrain fleet was missing, no longer a surprising phenomenon to the newcomers. The building was fully stocked with a variety of neatly stored robotics cargo haulers, delivery platforms, and transports. Garett Yamakawa was joined by Vijay, who had left the nuclear reactor site and entered the Industrial Dome by way of the underground access conduit that linked them, and together they tirelessly labored to power the cargo haulers and program them to make the delivery run between the spaceport and the warehouse building. By that time Jack had made several resupply runs; the bulk of the marines equipment, Doctor Oliver's precious medical supplies, and an ample store of food packs now piled high inside the terminal building and guarded by two marines who had come down from the Guilford Courthouse to act as cargo expediters as well as sentries. The robots would pull their long trailers of crates and cartons all through the night to bring the supplies now sitting at the spaceport to the colony.

As the bluish tint of the receding sun dove for the horizon, Lieutenant Reynolds finally met up with Matt to hold a private counsel inside the Chief Administrator's office. The first order of business was billets for everyone. Matt decided to delegate that responsibility to Sheri and temporarily pulled her away from Nichelle's side and called her in . Jointly they decided it would be prudent to keep everyone together on sub level 1 of the Residential Dome. There were more than enough rooms there to accommodate everyone presently on the surface. Caroline Hart had already made it known that she wanted to stay in her husband's room. Reynolds was insistent that his marines be quartered together. With instructions in hand, Sheri left the room and proceeded to work on the assignment, systematically making the arrangements beginning with Caroline in 1A and reserving the last fourteen rooms for the marines. It was by no coincidence that Matt would find himself assigned to a room next to Sheri. Her amorous designs compelled her to avail herself as many opportunities to get close to him as possible, however long that took.

Despite the absence of any sign of activity or intrusion, Matt was extremely concerned about security and the safety of his people, still visibly shaken by the news of the attack on Private Walinski. All of the medical tests proved negative and he was soon back to his unrefined self. His recollections were still fuzzy and murky - everything had happened so fast. After being released from the hospital, he was relieved of any further duty for the rest of the evening. He wearily retired to the room assigned to him to rest, but he would not be alone for long. Lucinda Desjardin would soon be on the move, and he would spend the evening fielding a hundred questions and deriving blissful gratification in the partaking of her feminine charms.

Something had been there, they couldn't deny it. If it got in once and eluded them, it could do it again. Until they understood everything that had happened, no one was safe. The two men mutually agreed that a double guard would be posted around the living quarters at night, one at each end.

A third would continuously patrol the entire level. Matt was adamant in emphasizing that no one should travel alone to other parts of the colony and that all personnel carry portable pocket communicators so that they could be in contact with someone in a moment's notice.

With Jamestown slowly reviving from the diligent efforts of the support team, Matt could train his attention on the larger picture - what had become of the original colonists? A search of the surrounding area needed to proceed at the earliest possible moment. Lieutenant Reynolds had in his possession a large, highly detailed contour map of this region of the planet's surface which he unfolded and stapled to the wall. They agreed on a systematic, circular search pattern that progressively expanded outward from the colony until such time that a trail or other clues were uncovered that would encourage a concentrated effort in one direction. The exploration would primarily be conducted by the marines, who would refer all geological or physical anomalies to the appropriate scientists. The three exploratory rovers and the marine's jet packs would be the principle means of mobility for this endeavor.

With the logistics of resupply and security finalized and a rudimentary game plan for the next operational phase of their mission established, Matt left the office feeling more reassured of their ability to sustain a prolonged presence at Jamestown and to continue the investigation, at least until the NSCA made a decision as to the status and future of the facility. Cognizant of the need to reestablish a direct link with the ship and to Earth itself, Matt made his way towards the eastward facing periphery of the room that overlooked the macadam road and rustic plain leading to the distant spaceport where the series of communication consoles were located, complete with their vast array of multi-colored dials and buttons, digital displays, speakers, and video monitors. There he found who he was searching for - Nichelle Bennett, sprawled out on the floor by one of the gutted stations. He needed only a second to see the answer to his question regarding the system's status. There were neat, cavernous square holes in the bases of several consoles where protective metal plates used to be. The floor surrounding her was littered with thin circuit boards and rectangular electronic modular units replete with transistors, wires, and microchips. A couple of portable computerized data pads rested by her side, their screens displaying some complex schematic diagrams that she kept rising up to refer too as she regularly applied the sensor probes of her cereal box shaped system analyzer to various compartments of the modules.

"Son-of-a-bitch!" she bellowed aloud as she threw down the pen-like probe in frustration and forcefully slammed the module back into its housing within the console, unaware of the mission Commander's presence behind her.

"I won't ask you how it's going." Matt called out as he fought the urge to grin in amusement.

Nichelle's lithe body instinctively jolted and shuddered in fright as she rolled over sporting a wild-eyed, startled expression. "Damn! Don't do that," she shouted with heavy breaths, clutching her chest tightly. "You shouldn't be sneaking up on people like that."

Matt smirked and took a few backward steps, bracing himself against the corner of the nearest cubicle. "I can see that I won't be talking with my ship anytime soon."

Nichelle wiggled up to a seated position and wearily wiped the back of her hand across her sweaty brow. "I'll tell you, Commander, I've been at this all afternoon and I'll be damned if I can find anything wrong with it. I should be able to snap these components back in place and it should work perfectly. Bit I get nothing! No transmission, no reception. I sure could use Sheri's help again."

Matt nodded. "I'll have her report back here as soon as she's finished with the quartering arrangements. Why don't you take a break for awhile. It looks as though you could use it."

Nichelle shook her head emphatically. "Later, I want to finish this station. Sheri and I have tested every circuit, chip, and relay in most of these panels." She pointed to the stripped consoles behind her. "We're not nearly finished yet, but if there is a problem with this equipment, then I'm the Queen of England."

Matt was puzzled. "What then?"

"If I can't isolate the problem here, then it must be in the tower. I'll have to examine it tomorrow. I hope that you don't have plans for Sheri because I'll need her help for that. It's not a one woman job."

Matt kept his off-color thoughts private. He did indeed have plans for her, but not until much later. Leaving Nichelle to navigate through her electronic jungle, Matt proceeded to converse with Andre and the other specialists who were working in A and C. With Garett's help, Andre had been able to reactivate the diminutive, centipede-like automated scrubbers that softly skimmed across the sensitive panels of the solar array, sucking up accumulations of the ever present Martian fines that constantly blew across its surface. With most of the energy consuming production factories shut down, the bulk of Jamestown's electrical requirements could now be generated from the conversion of energy from the potent rays of solar radiation. During these discussions he kept noticing Lucinda energetically scampering like a bee in a hive between the computer stations along the southwest fringe of the dome and the mainframe and processing facilities on the level below. Even in the pervasive tense and business-like atmosphere that the preceding events had induced, her alluring femininity was magical. He marveled at how well her ample curves filled out her work suit, how her resplendent, long succulent blond hair curled and waved unfettered against her back like a wild filly running free across the Great Plains. She would be a great one-nighter, he pondered, if he was predisposed to that sort of behavior, but she had the pick of a host of younger, eager mates and it was his understanding that she had been doing just that. But it was still very intoxicating when she greeted his approach with a sensuous, moistened lip smile and the enchanting batting of her captivating green eyes.

"Well, Miss Desjardin, I see that you have the computers up and running. Nice going."

"It was no problem," she smugly replied from her seat with an immodest toss of her head. "Once the engineers restored power, it was just a matter of initiating the start-up program."

Matt supported his weight against the console as he folded his arms and leaned towards her with a hopeful countenance. "Have you been able to access any of the colony's data bases?"

"I'm scanning all department and official data bases now for the most recent log entries." Lucinda settled back in her chair and frowned with chagrin. "So far I've found only entries nearly four weeks old. The same stuff received by the NSCA and information that we've already been briefed about. Other files seem to be fractured or have mysterious gaps that I can't explain." She took a deep breath and enticingly shook out her luscious blond hair. "If any files were opened during the crisis, they may be shielded under some security code, pancaked, deleted, or somehow magnetically erased. This could take some time to unravel."

Matt stared vacuously, aimlessly tapping the metal console with his fingers. Lucinda shifted forward, reaching out to lightly touch the palm of his hand, a covetous twinkle in her eye. "If you're feeling a little lonely tonight, look me up later."

Matt grinned in delight as he bent close to her, not sure why he still felt gratified to receive an invitation that he knew had been offered to just about everyone else during the voyage. "If I understand your intimation correctly," he quietly answered, "it is a most tempting offer. But I'm afraid that I'm at the point that sex is constantly on my mind but rarely on my agenda." He stood erect and patted her on the shoulder. "Please inform me immediately if you uncover anything of value." With the exception of your clothes, Matt frivolously thought to himself. He playfully poked her in the ribs as he walked by, eliciting a sudden twitching spasm and a loud cackle.

Lucinda's conniving mind went to work, grinned impishly as she turned her attention back to the computer terminals. "So you're not all starch and polish after all, Commander," she quietly mumbled to herself. "I may be able to get to you yet."

As the orange glow of the morning sun slowly stretched upward from the horizon to brighten the reddish landscape, the early dawn mist still tenaciously clinging to the deep depressions and crater floors of the distant plain, Matt found himself rummaging through the mangled, twisted, and scattered debris of what remained of the northeast dome. His good friend Vijay was with him, as was his former roommate, Yong Chang, astro-physicist Karl Ziethen, and geologist Raymond Ponsonby. Corporal Cooke and Private Walinski, fully recovered from his traumatic ordeal, were once more acting as security for Matt and his party. They were soon joined by Lieutenant Reynolds who had just finished dispatching two teams in exploratory rovers to probe the rising hills to the north and west. There examination of the wreckage was briefly interrupted when their attention was drawn to a low, faint rumbling roar coming from the heavens to the east. Looking up into the rosy sky they noticed a tiny glimmer of light descending through a high, wispy cloud towards the spaceport, followed by short, regular bursts of smoke and flame. Matt couldn't suppress his smile of pride as the decelerator engines broke the fall of the Nathanael Greene to the surface. Jack was returning with the first of the day's resupply runs.

"What a mess," Reynolds groaned as he gingerly picked his way through mounds of scrap metal, concrete, rubber, and plastic and around irregular lumps of smashed and crushed machinery, half buried under broken glass and stone and dirt. "It doesn't look like anyone even tried to clean it up."

"At least there are no bodies," Cooke noted. "It probably struck late at night."

Yong Chang and Raymond Ponsonby carefully stepped down the edge of the shallow depression caused by the meteorite's impact to examine the rock as the others skirted along its rim.

"Be careful," Matt fearfully warned. "There are a lot of jagged edges there. Don't snag your suit."

The meteorite was a small fragment of something that must have been much larger, roughly fifteen feet by ten feet and reaching a height of about eight feet at its zenith, with chips, fractures, and deep gouges where large chunks had been stripped away, much of its remaining glassy mineral face fused and molded together as if subjected to a great amount of heat.

"It must weigh a couple of tons," Yong noted as he foolishly tested his strength against its mass.

"I can tell from just a rudimentary examination that it is not composed of an iron-nickel alloy," Raymond reported to all over the helmet transmitter. "I'll need to run some chemical tests and X-rays to positively identify it as a stony meteorite."

"You may be wasting your time, Ray," Karl interjected as he ponderously trudged to the lip of the crater from outside the boundary of the dome where he had been studying the clumps of dirt, glass, and concrete thrown out by the force of the impact. "I've been looking at the ejecta blanket. It only radiates out a few hundred feet from here. It would seem to me that a meteorite strike, even one this small, would have dislodged soil and debris over a much wider area."

Matt had been casually sifting through the remains of cabinets and desks in search of evidence, dispassionately listening to the conversations of the others; his scientific interest relegated to the physics and astronomy of traversing a spaceship through the dark, hallowed corridors of the cosmos. But that last remark sparked his attention. Briskly he strode over to the edge of the depression. "What?"

"That's right, Commander," Karl reaffirmed. "I think that debris from this strike would have dotted the entire boundary of the colony, if not periphery damage itself. This crater is much too shallow as well."

"I found that odd myself," Yong added skeptically.

"There's something else," continued the doubting physicist. "Most of this rock should have vaporized on impact, along with most of this other junk. If it did, then its original mass would have been sufficient to devastate the entire area."

Matt frowned in frustration, kicking anxiously at the loosed ground as he barked at Karl. "So exactly what are you insinuating?"

"I don't believe that this dome was hit by a meteorite,"

The sound of silence in the following seconds was deafening as the men exchanged prolonged stares of incredulous cynicism.

"That's crazy, Karl!" Raymond disdainfully scoffed with a subtle shake of his head. "What drugs have you been taking?" His hand pointed resolutely towards the broken roof. "Look up there. See how the steel support braces are bent inward. How most of the glass was driven down within the structure. And how did this rock get here? Telepathy? I'm sure they didn't intentionally build this dome around it. It's obvious that something crashed into it from the outside."

Karl sighed heavily. "You may be right, Ray, but the physical evidence just doesn't add up. If this rock struck the dome, then it originated from within the Martian atmosphere, not outer space."

Ray chuckled derisively. "What, flying rocks?"

Vijay turned to Matt and placed a gentle hand upon his arm. "Karl makes some valid points, Matt. We haven't encountered any plausible explanations since we landed on this planet. I wouldn't totally discount his conjecture."

Matt assentingly nodded at Vijay and spun around to face the scientists. "Okay, Karl, if not the meteorite, then what?"

Karl ignorantly tossed up his hands. "I don't know. An explosion, perhaps."

Yong glanced at him in bug-eyed shock. "Sabotage?" he distressfully queried. "Wait a minute." His helmet tossed wildly. "An explosion would have driven the framework and glass outward."

Karl stared up at the broken dome for a prolonged time. "I'm not so sure," he softly muttered before turning towards the marines. "Lieutenant, do you have an explosives expert in your platoon?"

Reynolds turned to Corporal Cooke who confidently stepped forward. "I had eight weeks of special demolition training about two years ago," the Corporal announced.

"So tell me, Corporal," Karl consulted, "is there an explosive that you're aware of that could be placed say....on the roof that could have caused this kind of damage?"

"Sure," he unwaveringly replied. "a shaped charge could do it."

Matt forcefully stepped forward. not at all enjoying the direction that this inquiry was taking. "A what?"

"A shaped charge, sir." Cooke began to talk with his hands. "It's an explosive designed to propel its force in one direction only. Such a charge positioned on the roof would have blown everything inward."

A chilling and sobering shiver of fright wracked Matt's senses as he agitatedly stared at Karl. "Are you suggesting that someone intentionally destroyed this dome?"

Karl immediately became defensive. "I'm not suggesting anything," he retorted pungently in a voice rippling with tension. "It's just another possibility that we might consider."

"But why?" Matt bellowed.

"Matt," Vijay interrupted after perceiving his growing irritation, "let's not dismiss one possible explanation simply because we don't happen to like it."

"Lieutenant," Karl called out with greater calm. "May I borrow the Corporal here for a couple of hours?"

"Certainly, if the Commander has no objections."

Karl turned to face Matt. "While Ray runs some tests on the rock, I'd like permission for Yong and the good Corporal to help me search for remnants in this wreckage."

Matt's head drooped as he reluctantly exhaled a heavy breath. "Sure, go ahead." He paused in reflection before vigorously glancing up in bewilderment. "Remnants of what?"

Karl responded with casual elan. "Why a bomb, of course."

Sheri reveled under the glare of the mid-morning sun as she diligently worked at the base of the tubular communication tower, its alternating wide bands of bright red and light gray spiraling towards the sky. Sheri methodically applied the sensor probe of her system analyzer to every circuit and microchip, the same sort of manual examination she had assisted with in A and C the day before. Nichelle was several feet above her, standing on a small, grated, white maintenance platform, tearing apart and reassembling electronic modules as if it were her ultimate calling in life. Sheri's attitude was a little more relaxed. After all, she was a spaceship Flight Officer, not a communication engineer. After nearly 24 hours of monotonous testing and probing, she was feeling a little bored. Her mind began to wander. She couldn't recall a sun this bright on any of those lazy summer afternoons during her teenage years as she scampered lazily across the freshly furrowed fields of her parents Kansas farm. If they could only see her now, she mused. She imagined sprawling out on a webbed chaise lounge in a skimpy bathing suit, soaking in the balmy, tepid rays. Within the confines of her pressurized and heated environment suit, it was hard to appreciate the harshness of her surroundings. How could a world so bright and arid be so cold? Temperatures this time of year could soar above 10 degrees Fahrenheit during an afternoon heat wave. At night they would plummet to well below minus 100 degrees. Even this far from the star, ultraviolet light waves were threatening and deadly. One would need a good sun block, the thin Martian atmosphere unable to provide nearly the protection from solar radiation as that of the closer Earth. The urge was strong to return to her days of youth on this untamed planet, to drop her tools and go prancing off across the dust swept plain and among the enormous multitude of fascinating reddish-brown stones and boulders that saturated the landscape. The call to explore the shores of the unknown was powerful, but there was important work to complete. A communication link with the Guilford Courthouse had to be established, and quickly. The sound of an affable, sprightly voice ringing within her helmet snapped her out of her mini-trance.

"How's it going down there," chimed a vivacious Nichelle. "You got awfully quiet."

"Sorry. Everything so far seems to be in perfect working order. My mind sort of drifted off on its own. This place is so intriguing."

Sheri could here Nichelle's delighted chuckle. "I know what you mean. Working out here has awakened my imagination as well. I occasionally find myself looking over my shoulder half-expecting to find some Martian monster creeping up on me. It's kind of spooky."

Sheri giggled in amusement. "Really, Nichelle, aliens?" she gibed. "Let me tell you something. I've been in the space service for over ten years and I've never encountered any kind of life that is indigenous to any planet other than Earth. I think that you can relax."

"You relax," Nichelle quickly replied. "I'll feel a whole lot better when we get back inside."

Sheri was beginning to feel that all their best efforts were futile, a waist of time. "You know, Nichelle, if we can't soon find this problem, we ought to just set up the auxiliary communication system that is still packed aboard the Guilford Courthouse."

"We'll find it," Nichelle stated with confidence. "There's got to be a reason." She paused briefly, her intonation changing to a softer, lighthearted pitch. "Tell me, Sheri, what do you know of Reggie Lewis? I find him kind of....interesting."

"Well, I know that he's been divorced for a few years. He has a little girl. He played football at Syracuse." Sheri snickered to herself. "He has kind of a wandering eye, sort of a ladies man. Actually, I think that he's a bit of a swaggering pirate at heart. But he does have his moments. He's more cultured and refined than his outward demeanor would lead you to believe. Why do you ask?"

She could hear a drawn out heave.

"Oh, I don't know," Nichelle flippantly replied. "I was with him a couple of times aboard your ship. He just fascinated me."

Sheri became delightfully excited at the revelation. "Why, Nichelle, do you have a crush?"

"Wow!" Nichelle suddenly exclaimed. "What do we have here?" She held up a small black electronic module within the tiny clawed grip of her pliers-like hand tool and carefully examined the circuitry. A number of relays and microchips appeared fused or severed and the board itself showed signs of scorching. "What do you make of that?" she said as she passed the module down to Sheri. "No wonder the damn thing wouldn't work. The electron surge of the carrier waves had no way to get from the antenna to the tuning circuits and vice versa."

Sheri studied the damaged module meticulously. "What could have caused this?" she pondered aloud as she handed the module back to Nichelle. "An electrical overload? Condensation build-up? The cold?"

Nichelle contemplatively shook her head. "I don't think so. It's too localized. Those scarring burns indicate a finely directed heat source, like a solder gun or electronic laser." She secured the access panel and stepped down the metal grid stairway to join Sheri at the base of the tower, holding out the component. "I can replace this with another module I brought along in my supplies," she continued before glancing up at the expansive black dish on top. "Then we'll see if this tune won't play."

Sheri pointed to the module. "We should show this to Matt....I mean the Commander."

Nichelle found the subtle slip amusing, as if Sheri still believed that no one was aware of her more than professional interest in her captain. "Damn right," she agreed, shaking it in front of her. "I think that it was damaged intentionally."

Matt had returned to the Administrator's office by early afternoon to begin recording the progress of the support team for his official log that would be transmitted later to NSCA Central Control. Jack was now disembarking the last of the marines equipment, including a large command rover and the missile defense system. His final delivery of the day would include personal baggage of the civilian personnel, a much heralded event that would allow everyone to feel a certain level of civility and comfort. All that remained on board were additional food packs, seed and fertilizers, hand tools, electronic and mechanical spare parts, and one two-man exploratory rover. In another day, Jack's shuttle missions would be over. Matt had requested that all project teams and individual specialists give him a preliminary report on the status of their work in the next few hours so he could include them in his communiqué. Sheri and Nichelle had found him earlier and summarized their disturbing conclusions before dashing off to the warehouse building to find the crate containing communication components. Garett Yamakawa had an even more interesting discovery. He had spent all morning powering and programming several of the colony robotics supply carts, sort of miniature versions of the cargo haulers that resembled those aboard space station Constitution. They followed the guidance sensor tracks embedded in the floors with their swiveling electronic eyes and according to their instructions delivered the appropriate supplies to either the Residential Dome or the Agri Dome and the medical and scientific facilities below. Once they had been put into service by early afternoon, Garett had a chance to take a look at the disabled sentry robot and whose metal carcass had been transported to the warehouse. What he found was surprising and unexplainable. The laser gun had been calibrated to fire eight feet high, well above the height of any human target. Neither Garett nor Matt could envision a situation where that would have been desirable. Good fortune was also something Matt couldn't explain. Several of the marines, not to mention the good Doctor Oliver, owed their continued existence to that anomaly, Matt silently concluded. Nothing new from any of the others had been unveiled, but some had yet to report. He hadn't even seen Lucinda, Caroline, or Susan Oliver all day. It was then that he overheard the frantic, distressed cry over the communication system originating from an outside helmet transmitter.

"Control, medical emergency! This is Private Anderson. Casualty en route to hospital dome. Please have medical personnel standing by."

Nichelle Bennett bounced enthusiastically up the spiral metal stairs leading to the maintenance platform of the communication tower with new module in hand, ignoring the unsteady shimmying construction in her excitement. She unlatched and swung open the access panel, snapping in place the new component with gleeful anticipation that often comes on the brink of successfully solving a complex dilemma.

"Module installed, Sheri," she announced over her helmet communicator. "Try it now."

Sheri, who had been anxiously watching in the distance from her perch near the communication station in A and C, eagerly rolled her chair a few feet to the right in order to manipulate the controls to the colony transmitter, tuning to the frequency of the ship. "CAS Guilford Courthouse, come in please," she professionally haled. "This is Jamestown colony back on the air."

She solicitously held her breath, nervously chewing on her nails during the few tormenting seconds of silence.

"Guilford Courthouse, acknowledge," resoundingly replied a familiar voice. "Sheri, is that you, man?"

Sheri flung back in her chair, flailing her arms through the air, cutting loose a whooping cheer of jubilation at the sharp sound of Reggie Lewis. "Of course it is you dumb shit," she jocularly remarked as she leaned forward once more. "Were you expecting someone else?"

"What do you mean?"

"Well, while we were working on the network, Nichelle expressed a certain amount of interest in you."

Reggie sounded pleased. "Yeah! What did she say about me?"

"Not much," Sheri answered happily. "It was more a matter of personal questions concerning you."

Reggie turned unusually quiet before he continued with an inflection laced with panic. "Damnit, Sheri! Please be a friend and don't tell her everything."

Sheri giggled, amused over his anxiety. "Relax, Reg, you could get lucky with her if you don't be a jerk. Stand by for a minute." Sheri switched over to Nichelle's helmet frequency. "Contact established with Guilford Courthouse," she exclaimed with unbridled cheerfulness. "Nice going." Sheri could hear Nichelle howling in celebration. "I've got your boyfriend on the link," she whimsically continued. "If you hurry your butt back in here, I'll keep him on the line so you two can talk dirty to each other."

Nichelle chuckled at the thought, though Sheri could sense that she was slightly embarrassed. "All right, Sheri, don't start trying to get me engaged, girl."

Nichelle reached out to close the rectangular panel, her thoughts so engrossed in the satisfaction of a job well done and some naughty amorous possibilities ahead that she was oblivious to a strange pulsating pinpoint of yellow light emanating from behind a large, irregular boulder at the concrete base of the central dome and a thin, blazing streak cutting across some of the anchoring bolts beneath her. Suddenly the platform took a downward jolt and listed to the west. Fright quickly overwhelmed her as she instinctively clutched the top of the panel with one hand to regain her balance while her other hand blindly groped for the handrail. Within moments the stairs fell away and her body began to drop. A pucker on her suit along the upper arm hooked on the ragged edge of the panel, leaving her dangling precariously for an instant before the sleeve ripped into a one inch gash under the stress of her weight and she went helplessly tumbling to the frozen surface below, violently crashing in pain beside the crumbled stairs, writhing and choking impotently as the atmospheric pressure of her suit slowly ebbed away and the poisonous Martian air filtered in.

By the time Matt had reached the medical clinic under the Agri Dome, Privates Anderson and Jones had already delivered Nichelle's still breathing body where the two doctors feverishly worked over her in one of the examination rooms. Sheri had beaten him there, pacing aimlessly in one corner of the reception area, a look of consternation etched in bold print across her drawn and haggard face. The two young marines were standing on the opposite side, still in their dusty, bronze environment suits and holding their helmets against their hips, being debriefed by Lieutenant Reynolds who had arrived only moments earlier. It was very fortunate that the marines had just returned from their excursion into the northern hills when Sheri's frantic cry for assistance on Nichelle's behalf came bellowing across the general communication channel. It was unlikely that anyone inside could have suited-up and reached her in time. The soldiers had raced at breakneck speed along the eastern road until parallel with the tower where they recklessly turned onto the plain and bounded and thumped over fretted ground and small stones to reach her quickly. Anderson had immediately applied a black, highly adhesive and bondable, airtight, elastic rupture patch to the tear on her sleeve, a piece of equipment every bit as important to a space marine as his environment pack or laser rifle. The rip was small enough that she still had an adequate supply of oxygen and the suit retained part of its heat. The greater danger was the steady loss of atmospheric pressure and the swift introduction of deadly carbon dioxide gas. After adjusting her pack to add more oxygen and to maximize the evacuation of CO2, the marines had carried her gagging, hacking, contorting body to their rover and sped off for the hospital. They had entered through the emergency airlock where the medical staff was waiting with a robotics diagnostic and stasis gurney to hustle her below. Now Matt silently waited by Sheri's side, his thoughts crowded with yet another unsettling event that had to be dealt with. They hadn't been on planet for three full days yet a handful of them had already stared death in the face. How much longer could they keep cheating the Grim Reaper? He had placed people in dangerous situations in the past, but had never lost a single life. As the tormenting minutes of helpless waiting ticked away, Matt found himself in private meditation of a kind that he realized he had been neglecting for quite some time. He was praying.

Twenty minutes later Matt's throat tightened when Doctor Oliver finally emerged from the examination room and slowly approached him. Nichelle was suffering from decompression sickness, the fast reduction of atmospheric pressure which causes the formation of nitrogen bubbles in the bloodstream and body tissues and cam lodge in the brain, lungs, or spinal cord, sometimes resulting in death. She was also afflicted with a mild case of CO2 poisoning but fortunately the two marines had reached her in time. She was coughing regularly and experiencing aching joints, nausea, and blurred vision, but no sign of partial paralysis. It appeared that Nichelle would live. Both Sheri and Matt breathed easier as Doctor Oliver continued her report, cautioning them on being overly optimistic.

"Nichelle is still in pretty bad shape. She has a broken ulna bone on her forearm. Her upper arm shows a bad case of expansion bruising where it was exposed to the cold air as well as a localized case of frost bite, but I think there are sufficient undamaged cells that she won't lose the use of her arm. I've seem much worse cases where the limb had to be amputated."

Matt and Sheri grimaced in an instinctive reaction.

"Don't worry too much," Doctor Oliver reassured with a gentle nudge to Matt's shoulder. "Ben Caldwell is an expert in these kinds of alien environment afflictions. She couldn't be in better hands." Doctor Oliver paused briefly, crossing her arms with a heavy sigh. "By the way, who got to her?"

Matt turned and pointed towards the two marines standing beside Lieutenant Reynolds, just out of earshot but looking on with a seemingly personal interest. Doctor Oliver seemed disappointed as she snarled and mumbled softly with facetious disdain. "You mean they actually saved a life for a change?"

As Doctor Oliver returned to her patient, Matt strolled over to the marines and enthusiastically shook their hands, thanking them for their life-saving efforts and relaying the prognosis. They appeared to be genuinely gratified that they were able to serve a useful purpose. But Matt could tell that something was troubling Reynolds as he pulled him aside.

"I find the timing of that accident a little unnerving," he soberly admitted.

"You ain't just whistling Dixie." Matt animatedly replied. "Sheri says that the platform seemed sturdy enough before. Kind of spooky."

Reynolds twitched. "Too damn spooky to be just coincidence."

Matt frowned as he scratched the back of his head. "I'll tell you, Lieutenant, I'm getting mighty tired of all this shit. It's time to find some answers. I'd send someone to check-out that platform as soon as possible."

"It's close to dusk now," Reynolds replied, checking his watch. "I don't want anyone poking around out there after dark. We'll have a look at it in the morning."

Raymond Ponsonby was eagerly waiting for Matt when he returned to the Administrator's office. The chemical analysis he performed on the rock sitting in the damaged dome confirmed his suspicions that it was neither composed of a metallic iron alloy or a stone rich in silicon, the characteristic fabric of meteorites. In fact, its chemical composition resembled that of the innumerable boulders scattered across the countryside. His conclusion left Matt speechless.

"I believe that the rock came from nearby, was manually subjected to intense heat and scouring and either hauled into the dome or dropped from the air to make it look like the dome was struck by a meteorite."

"Ray may be right, Commander."

Matt looked up to see Karl Ziethen standing in the doorway with Yong Chang and Corporal Cooke poised behind him, still in their environments minus headgear.

"After several hours of picking through dirt and rubble and smashed machinery, we found this." Karl held out a tiny fragment that looked like a pitiful remnant of a round, metallic cap with a couple of frayed and torn wires sticking out of one end.

Matt's eyes opened wide and strained to identify the object. "Now what the hell is that," he questioned with growing impatience and tension.

"It's what's left of a primer to a detonator, sir," Cooke responded.

"Someone set off an explosive device in there," Karl unwaveringly stated. "Maybe more."

Matt shuddered in horror. "Sabotage?"

Karl dropped his head and nervously shuffled his feet. "I'm not so sure."

"If sabotage," Ray said, glancing hastily around the room, "why bother with this meteorite deception?"

Matt lurched forward with a blank expression and softly responded as if the words were miraculously popping into his head as he spoke. "To make it appear to outsiders like a meteorite strike."

Dazed and confused looks were exchanged by all present. Matt gasped heavily and leaned back against his chair in quiet contemplation, his fingers clawing annoyingly at the padded armrests. "Gentlemen," he calmly surmised. "From what you are telling me, it would seem that the colonists blew up their own dome."

Later that evening Matt finally found some serenity and solitude in the privacy of his own quarters, having just put away his baggage recently delivered by the robotics transports. Everyone else was more or less engaged in similar activities and the marines were establishing their security outposts and patrol schedules for the night. His mind kept wandering over the events of the last few days, chewing on them over and over as he put away the last of his clothes in the roomy closet. The continuous rehashing nearly made him sick as he organized a few personal care products on a bathroom counter. This whole affair had taken a sharp turn into the Twilight Zone. He suddenly remembered the card that Sheri had left for him before their departure. He was very tired, but the warmth and softness of a woman's arms was a very appealing prospect right now. As he found homes for his entertainment software and surround movie player and disks, he tinkered with the notion of going next door and taking her up on that invitation. But reasoning won out over emotion as usual. Sheri was in dire need of rest as well, and Matt knew neither would get much of that if he found himself in her chambers. With a reluctant sigh of regret, Matt settled himself into the soft, deep burgundy cushion of a recliner, propped up his feet, and grabbed the book that Sheri had given him, placing it on his lap. A sudden recollection sent spine tingling shivers down his back. Something that he had read on the voyage out. He frantically leafed through the pages until he found the account. The irony of what he reread justified every fearful emotion. History was repeating itself on a planet half the size and millions of miles away. After establishing the English colony on Roanoke Island off the North Carolina coast in 1587, Governor John White returned to England where he spent the next three years procuring supplies. In 1591 he returned to Roanoke Island only to find the colony mysteriously deserted. To this day the fate of those early settlers has never been discovered.

"That's crazy!" Matt clamored as he exasperatingly tossed his hands into the air from his seat at the head of a large, oval oak veneer table in the spacious conference room next to the Administrator's office. "We still have nearly 400 missing people! We have a deserted colony where all evidence indicates that some of its facilities have been tampered with. We've been assaulted by sentry robots and unseen forces. And now the NSCA wants me to send out some science team to some far-off corner of this planet to search for some pot of gold at the end of the rainbow?"

"It would seem so," Sheri replied as she held out an audio disk. "Confirmation of the instructions and the response to your inquiry and objections just came through. I recorded it for you. NSCA is very adamant."

Matt groaned with frustration as he leaned back in his chair, running a hand through his frazzled black hair. "Tell me this isn't a government run operation."

Sheri and Vijay were seated near him, as were the two men whose duties were most affected by the NSCA directive, Yong Chang and Raymond Ponsonby.

"So much for independent command," Vijay commented forthrightly. "The decision's been taken out of your hands, Matt."

Matt lowered his head and grimaced in forlorn resignation. "When they control the purse strings, if they say fly to the sun, you're going to ....stock up on sun block." Matt bent forward and clasped his hands together, looking across the table at the faces of the two scientists. "Let me get this straight. The NSCA wants you two guys to go to some damnable place north of here to...."

"Vastitas Borealis," Sheri offered.

Matt tossed her an irritated glance. "Wherever. To go up there to search for signs of some thermal or magnetic field activity that you now say are no longer there."

"That's right, Commander," Yong asserted respectfully. "As you know, Jamestown reported some unusual energy displacement readings somewhere north of 55 degrees latitude and 50 degrees west not long before contact was lost." He took a darting peek of concern at his partner. "But we can find no trace of it now on the colony sensors."

"I asked Andre to check the instruments.," Ray hastily added, "and he assured me they are operating perfectly. Those signs no longer exist."

"The ship's scanners confirm that." Sheri added.

"And you know how those Earth-bound bureaucrats hate contradictory reports," Vijay quipped.

Matt smirked wryly and puffed in exasperation. "Could those readings have been natural phenomena?"

Yong sneered as he shrugged his shoulders. "The scientists making the report did not think so. But who can be sure of anything on this planet."

"We've been fully briefed on the situation, Commander," Ray confidently declared. "If you'll check your mission modus operandi, part of our original mission profile was to poke around up there."

"Don't worry too much, Matt," Yong pleaded with a voice stirred with excitement. "We want to go. It's a planetary scientist's dream."

Matt was once again beleaguered with those nagging scruples that always seemed to permeate his thoughts when trouble was 'afoot. Sending those men out in unfamiliar terrain and so far away from immediate support was a recipe for disaster. His historical mind likened it to a military general dividing his forces and sending part off into unscouted country without knowing his enemy's dispositions. But there was no enemy, at least in the classical sense. Or was there? In an enigmatic fashion, they had been fighting the entire planet ever since they had arrived. He could override the orders of the NSCA if he believed that lives would be put in imminent danger. But hard evidence would be needed to support such a position, but all he had to go on was a strange set of circumstances and an eerie premonition. And after all, as he was constantly reminded, risk was there business. Pounding the table lightly with his knuckles, Matt reluctantly grimaced in anguish and slammed back against the chair. "Very well, gentlemen, you'll leave at first light. Vij. help them get an excursion rover prepped for the journey. Be sure to pack plenty of food, water, and extra fuel in case your solar cells fail. There are no service stations out there. And each of you carry a sidearm, just in case."

The two scientists stood and exchanged smiles of satisfaction before silently acknowledging their understanding.

"We'll expect regular contact every eight hours," Matt firmly instructed as he approached to shake their hands. "I want to know where you're going and what you're doing at all times. And, of course, give us a holler if you run into anything unusual. Best of luck, gentlemen, I'll see you in....," his mind quickly did the calculation. "....about three weeks."

Caroline could perceive it immediately as the eastern slopes of the rising hills to the west slowly stretched into view across the horizon. The murky shadows cast by the large, dust-blasted boulders and weathered rock outcroppings could not cloak the distinctive contrast of the bluish-green patch of mottled ground against the expansive reds, oranges, browns, and grays of the rest of the visible terrain. The marines scouting the area had discovered it the previous day, a dozen miles to the northwest of Glow Hill, a name some affectionately gave to the rising ground that sheltered the nuclear reactor. The reports of its find was delayed by the grievous events of the previous day, so it was early afternoon before her tiny expedition could be approved and assembled. She was riding with her fellow bioengineer, Tegan McDowell, a tall, husky married man in his mid-forties whom she quickly learned had called in some favors and pestered some officials at the NSCA to get this assignment in order to get a few months away from his nagging wife. A vacation, he called it. Within the forty minutes it took to reach the site, she had taken the audio tour of his entire life, listening to him brazenly talk about himself at light speed. He was trying to impress her, she thought, but he seemed totally disinterested in what she had to say, so she kept quiet. The leering glint in his eye made her feel like a piece of raw meat in a skin market. She had seen that look before in roving-eyed scientists. He went so far as to tell her about his liaison aboard ship with Lucinda, but his bravado was noticeably subdued on the matter, and Caroline inferred that Lucinda had probably found him rather unexciting. She really hated men like him. She would have much preferred traveling in the exploratory rover that they were following. Corporal Cooke was leading the way along with Private Warwick, one of the marines who had found the garden the day before.

Caroline had been assisting the affable and industrious Tammy Jacobs in the Agri Dome when she heard the news about the test site. She was a botanist at heart with a passion for all types of plant life so she found the reformulation of the nutrient solution in the hydroponics pond and the preparation of the Martian fields for reseeding good therapy to take her mind off her aching heart. The work helped her to feel useful and needed again and to emotionally deal with the painful reality that she would probably never see Dave Hart again; to manage her disconsolate feelings of sadness, loss, and despair, but also a touch of anger and a sense of betrayal. How could he do this to her? Couldn't he have left some word for her? A note? An audio disk? A carving on the desk? Now she was energized with excitement that raced through her soul after Matt had asked her to investigate the strange growth on the distant slope. The notion that something could actually be living, perhaps even thriving on the frozen wasteland was exhilarating. As the rovers approached the base of the rocky knoll she had a peculiar sensation that she was embarking on a new adventure, that her life's journey was about to take a different fork in the road. Caroline had no idea how prophetic her impressions would be. She would never return to Earth again.

Locking their helmets and gloves into the neck and wrist collars, Caroline and Tegan entered the airlock of the rover and joined the two marines on the sandy, salt-hardened surface, analyzers and sample kits in hand. The plot was about a fifty-foot square parcel of land, bordered and sectioned off equally into six distinct segments by deep furrows filled with natural stone from the nearby ground. A small spike on which was attached a thin aluminum yellow plate tag numbered in black stood at the head of each division. Each plot was covered with a tiny carpet of bluish-green, darker blue-black, or all black clumped fuzz or stringy material. It was the site for specially engineered algae, fungus, and lichens that the Jamestown bioengineering researchers had established to test samples of plant life that may be adaptable to the harshness of the Martian climate. It was on rising, sloping ground to absorb the full effects of the midday sun and far enough off the beaten path to avoid unintentional contamination of the test results that may occur from human activity. Some resembled the type of algae that Caroline had been working with on the Ross Ice Shelf during the Antarctic summer over the past year's Christmas season. Initial analysis indicated that most samples were not doing very well, others showed some potential, though none were flourishing. She and her irritating colleague went to work clipping specimens of various strands of growth and sealing them in small, transparent plastic containers, scooping frozen soil samples with unique, cold climate heated diggers , and taking atmospheric readings. All would have to be returned to the biolabs for chemical testing and closer investigation. She hoped that the lab's data base still contained the reports on the colony's research, but with the state of other computer files in disarray, nothing was assured. It would certainly save a lot of time if she could get up to speed on their findings, but at least she had a purpose. The determination of the fate of her husband and the colonists was left in the hands of Matt and the marines, and in their resolve she had no doubts.

The two marines used the time to more thoroughly scout the surrounding countryside, nearly moving beyond visual range and violating their specific purpose - providing local security for the science team. As the dimming beams of the setting sun cast gradually lengthening shadows over the eastern slopes, Corporal Cooke hurried the scientists along , finally ordering them back to the rover for the return trip. They needed to reach Jamestown by nightfall or Sergeant Douglas would have their hides for dinner. Like the simmering summer streets of certain metropolitan neighborhoods, this was no place to be after dark. Heated words were exchanged. Caroline found herself breaking up an argument between the Corporal and Tegan after the latter made some disparaging remarks about the intelligence of grunts, finally physically shoving the burly man towards the rover.

"I'm sorry about that, Bob," she apologized upon returning to the Corporal's side. "He's just an obnoxious jerk. Be thankful that you don't have to work with him."

Cooke shrugged nonchalantly. "It don't mean nothing. We get that sometimes from civilian intellectual elitists who think that only they have all the answers. Come on, we have to get going."

"Maybe I'll see you later," she wistfully stated in a pleading tone.

Caroline could see through the sparkling light reflections off his faceshield a crack of a smile form on his lips as he nodded agreeably. Walking back to the rover she felt a sense of despondency in regards to Corporal Cooke and the marines for the way they had been treated or ignored by some of her associates as if they were somehow inferior. An inappropriate though historically not uncommon reaction to people whose job it was to protect them and their interests. After all, she couldn't recall many of her acquaintances that take the risks that these boys do.

The journey back was just as trying as the one out. Tegan had seeming mapped out their entire research program. Caroline staunchly insisted that Tammy be included in all planning, since she needed their help in reviving the once fruitful agricultural crop, an area to which he displayed only a rudimentary interest. She vehemently argued with him in a most uncharacteristic fashion over the direction they should pursue and reminded him that their mission profile emphasized that the three of them were a project team and not his private research staff; that they were to coordinate all activities together as equal partners. Once the fireworks had subsided and an air of calmness pervaded the cabin, Tegan apologized for his impetuousness, inviting Caroline to his room for coffee (having no luck finding any alcohol at the colony) to make-up for their disagreement. Cognizant of the ways of the world, she politely declined, then assertively professed that she found him offensive and their relationship would be kept on a strictly professional level. She would have preferred to spend the night with Lucinda, she thought. Finally subduing Tegan's motorized mouth, Caroline could relax in the privacy and stillness of her own whims. His suggestion did manage to rekindle some amorous notions that she had buried since the orbital insertion around Mars. Images of Bob Cooke and one or two others filtered through her imaginative mind. She seriously wondered if perhaps it was time to get on with her life, to sever the past, and to start building an intimate relationship once again.

Once safely back at Jamestown, the scientists took their samples back to the biolab that was adjacent to the medical facilities. There they stored them in a vacuum sealed vault that would preserve them under the conditions of the outside environment until such time they were needed for study. Tegan dismissed himself, retiring to the Residential Dome to start fresh the next day, but Caroline was too anxious. She hurriedly took a seat by one of the lab's computer stations. She was pleasantly surprised to find the files intact on the system's hard drive with no security code lockout. Accessing the file containing data on their plant engineering experiments, she discovered that the last entry was made about forty days ago and extended back many years. Caroline requested the summary subfile and began to hungrily digest its first entries and continued her study well into the evening. She discovered that her Jamestown peers were attempting to engineer an order of plant life that would be resistant to extreme cold, dehydration, and ultraviolet radiation. One that would require little water, have a tolerance for salt, could root itself to rock or the frozen clay soils, and could proliferate rapidly under these climatic conditions. And, of course, make use of the abundant Martian CO2 and exude oxygen. The use of a vast array of restriction and ligase enzyme tools for cutting and pasting desired sequences of DNA strands was impressive as was the intricate application of plasmid aggregations - mobile circles of desired DNA that replicate and travel independently of its biological host. The sophistication of their genetic engineering was more involved and complex than any project she had been involved with. Her effervescent mood briefly turned somber as she realized the depth of research that she had missed out on over the past thirty Earth months. Just one more entry to add to her list of regrets for not joining her husband from the beginning. Suddenly a horrific though chilled her bones and caused her flesh to shudder uncontrollably. What if they had accidentally created a toxic microorganism, a diminutive Martian Frankenstein, that had forced everyone to flee, taking their dead and dying with them? Of course, that was silly. From the moment that they arrived inside the confines of Jamestown, their analyzers and chemical tests revealed no harmful organisms in the air, water, cultivated soils, or the concrete floors and walls for that matter. Regaining her composure and reading on, Caroline came upon a report of an engineered strand that the researchers felt had the greatest opportunity for success. It was a dark blue-black crustose lichen, a fungus and algae living together and resembling a fuzzy crust that attached to a surface and was well suited for cold, arid conditions. Throughout the extensive text there was never a concise, precisely stated goal for the research, though many subtle inferences made the objective crystal clear. And it was an objective that crossed many scientific as well as philosophical disciplines; to make Mars more habitable for humans. The two major obstacles to that goal were water and atmosphere. Artificial heating of permafrost, part of the polar ice cap, and frozen underground reservoirs, if enough could be found, could not only supply their physical and mechanical needs but also add water vapor to the air and thicken the atmosphere. Surviving plant life would consume abundant carbon dioxide and release oxygen, as well as darken the surface that, along with a thickening atmosphere, would retain more heat from solar radiation. Additional heating of the surface would add more water vapor to the air, spur plant growth which, in turn, would add more oxygen and so on. Eventually over the course of a millennia, if not centuries, the planet could be altered to resemble Earth-type conditions, at least to the point where environment suits were unnecessary. Terraforming was the ultimate plan of the permanent inhabitants - if nothing went wrong.

By the end of the fourth day, marine patrols had uneventfully scouted in all directions, some extending out as far as 100 miles. At this time Matt decided to play a hunch and with the support and logistical assistance of Lieutenant Reynolds, they mapped out a two day mission to be launched at first light, a long range probe by two marines in an exploratory rover and equipped with jet packs. They would travel southeast along an old dirt road embedded in the terrain by the apparent passing of many wheeled and treaded vehicles and heavy construction equipment. The road itself was not a clue, it had been there for years. It led to the massive and exalted canyon system of Valles Marineris, so deep and vast that those in Arizona by comparison were like tiny cracks in a sidewalk. It was among those fluted and gouged steep walls, immense, abysmal gorges, and menacing, craggy precipices that much of the colony's recent mining operations had taken place. Just the logistics of moving the ore out of the canyons was a formidable task, so much so that they had constructed several basic and primarily automated processing facilities on the canyon floors themselves. The marines were to look for signs of recent activity along the road, stopping every two hours to scour the immediate area using their thruster equipment to hover and jump from point to point. The plan was to cover some 400 miles over relatively level terrain to Dittaino Valles and return by the end of the second day. Valles Marineris was still some distance beyond, but Matt reasoned that, depending on the initial survey, it may warrant further consideration as a candidate for exploration, as daunting a challenge as that would be.

And so Corporal Benetiez and Private Anderson were sent on their excursion, a journey that began with much eager anticipation but was quickly transformed into a sluggish, mundane assignment whose results ultimately proved to be indefinite. Their much ballyhooed return near sunset on the sixth day was celebrated like the return of the first heroes of Mercury and Vostok. But as they displayed their trifling findings on the great conference table in A and C, the men felt more like a pair of squalid old scavengers than courageous explorer-soldiers. Matt, Reynolds, Vijay, and

Sheri sat around one end of the large oval, closely examining and passing on each item as it was removed from a bulky, rectangular plastic storage container. Each object was tagged with the precise map coordinates from where it was found along with the distance from the road. Among the items were the top of a broken hammer, the metal handle bent obliquely and its rubber wrapping in shreds, the iron head stained in reddish-brown, some of its smooth edges chipped and dented; a fragment of a flat black and silver solar panel, its polished surface weathered, cracked, and lacerated; a small pocket transmitter with a missing selector dial, its internal circuitry now saturated with fine Martian dust; a dingy silver environment suit with a gaping rip along the shoulder seam and caked with rustic stains; a crumpled aluminum coated beer flask partially filled with sand, its skin and label scratched and scuffed but still rather glistening and distinctive. They even found a balled Hershey bar wrapper, ripped and soiled, that was pinned against the bottom of a large boulder nearly a mile from the road. Matt shook his head in amusing wonderment. An American tradition. Hershey chocolate bars on Mars! Who would have believed it at the turn of the century? Matt gazed across the table at the exhausted marines, seeking clarification. "And you say you couldn't find any off-road tracks?"

"Negative, sir," Corporal Beneticz responded with a weary sigh. "But those fines were drifting all over the place. They would probably obliterate any tracks in a couple of weeks."

"And no abandoned vehicles?"

"No, sir."

Matt lethargically picked up the hammer head once more, turned it in his hand, and disgruntledly laid it back down again. "These aren't that important. A lot of traffic went down that road." Matt dejectedly looked skyward and slumped back in his chair.

"But they can't be that old, Matt." Sheri noted. "In most cases the abrasion markings aren't that severe."

"Sheri makes a valid point," Vijay confidently added, his right hand reaching towards the assembled debris. "I would estimate from their condition that most of this could not have been lying out there for say.... longer than two months, if not a matter of weeks."

Lieutenant Reynolds sat quietly in deep contemplation, staring quietly at the junk as his fingers lightly massaged his chin. The refuse was found widely dispersed along the roadway, but seemed to have been concentrated over a ten mile stretch beginning about a hundred miles out.

Eventually he inquisitively turned to Corporal Benetiez. "You say you found this stuff randomly scattered near the road and not clumped together?"

"That's correct, sir. Something here and something there. Along that one stretch we'd find a couple items and then a couple more a mile or two later. Never a large grouping." He briefly chuckled. "They must not have any laws against littering on this planet."

The Lieutenant's face became flushed with the twinges of puzzlement. "I find that very strange. I would think that they would have discarded their garbage en masse." He quickly turned to the others to explain, his hands flailing the air above the table as he spoke. "I mean, it's not as if they could just crank down the window and toss the stuff out."

Matt's attention was immediately jolted, abruptly sitting forward and glancing profoundly at Sheri and Vijay. The Lieutenant's observation indeed seem quite significant and logical. but the two marines had an even bigger bomb to drop.

"We saved the best for last," Benetiez continued, instantly drawing everyone's concentration. "Both Anderson and I thought these last couple items were the most significant of all."

Sheri gasped in a combination of shock and dismay as the Corporal slowly removed each article from the container and passed them on to her. All who were gathered around the table recognized them immediately. The first was a shaggy, obviously well worn, light blue one-piece toddler sleeper adorned with tiny, fluffy rabbit feet, now bathed in the reds and oranges of Martian dust. An air of despondency filled the room as it was reverently passed around from hand to hand. The second was a transparent, insulated, tubular baby bottle with rubber nipple, complete with automated formula mixing compartments and internal heating elements, now idled by a malfunctioning dispenser unit. Matt morosely accepted the bottle from Sheri's trembling hand and studied it respectfully before holding it out in front of him. "This changes everything."

Later that evening Matt and Sheri found themselves casually lounging on the soft cushions of the spacious chocolate brown sectional pit sofa in Matt's quarters, tightly wrapped within the soothing warmth of the others embrace and encircled by the screens of the 3D video surround system that had been lowered from their ceiling compartments. They were encompassed by the graphic sights and vivacious sounds of some thundering, adventurous Hollywood space epic. They had shared a private microwave meal and Matt mixed each of them a couple of their favorite alcoholic drinks from his personal supply that he had transported down with the rest of his baggage. Sheri was wearing the same provocative outfit that had earlier so tantalized Matt on the bridge and once more he couldn't keep himself from ogling her. Not long after inserting the movie disk into the surround player and snuggling close together, Matt's anxious fingers began to roam. Soon the two of them were bouncing and rolling on the supple, velvety cushions, playfully wrestling, tickling and kissing as they giggled and moaned in delight. Articles of clothing began to fly leisurely through the air until the two of them were left stripped down to their white cotton underwear. After one particularly long, sensuous kiss, Sheri affectionately rubbed her cheek against Matt's and softly whispered into his ear.

"Matt, I think that I'm falling in love with you. You're the finest man I've ever known."

Matt reactively pulled back from his tight embrace and gazed into her pleading blue eyes and simpered with a slight snicker. "Boy! I sure have you fooled," he replied lightheartedly. "You haven't been talking with the right people."

Sheri suggestively pressed close with a lascivious expression, a hand delicately trailing along his upper thigh. "Don't you want me?"

Matt's heart raced with excitement and it was impossible to hide from her the extent of his interest. He found Sheri so very sexy, stimulating and sensual. His drive and hunger to caress and love her, lost for hours in the throngs of passion, was almost irresistible. His titillating fingers began to trace congenial circles across the soft cotton of her tiny bikini. Sheri moaned in pleasure, her legs ravenously widening. But he still hadn't sorted out his load of emotional baggage and the carnal desires he was feeling began to cause him some embarrassment, a ship's captain having such deviant designs on one of his crew. Quickly he raised his arousing hand and gently brushed her luscious, soft wavy hair against the side of her lovely face before coiling both arms tightly around her back, pulling her close so that the plunging, protruding cups of her dainty lace bra pressed against his naked chest. "Sheri, I'm really getting to like you. I desire you more than you could ever know and by the time this mission is over I may desire you even more. Bit if we consummate our relationship now, the mystery of our surroundings could become intoxicating. We may become blinded by our own ecstasy, the events of the day driving our erotic bliss. It would be terrific for awhile, but we may mistake our passion for love, become engaged, maybe even married. Then one day you will suddenly discover a darker side of me, annoying habits and interests, lewd fantasies, and decide that I'm a no good, self-centered, egotistical bastard and tell me that you never want to see me again." His hands released their grip and frivolously tossed palms up into the air and rolled his eyes in a facetiously disgusted way. "I'll be left emotionally scarred again and who needs all of that!"

Sheri found his performance amusing, chuckling lightly as she snuggled close to him again. She reached up and locked her hands around the back of his neck, tenderly kissing him on the tip of his nose. "Now you're being silly, and evasive. I've served with you for three years. You are so upright, principled, confident....except when it comes to relationships. There is no dark side to Matthew Maitland. I'm at least sure of that." She sensually wiggled her hips against him. "Tell me about your fantasies."

Matt smirked as his head drooped in embarrassment. He had never felt comfortable talking about his more aberrant sexual whims and now he regretted ever mentioning the word. There was always a painful danger of letting someone, especially a woman he had grown very fond of, too close to his drives, emotions, and motivations.

Widely grinning at his self-inflicted predicament, Sheri lowered one hand to playfully tug at his arm. "Come on, Matt, tell me."

Matt sat unmoving for a moment in emotional terror, such confessions normally being left for a time when a relationship was more firmly established. Finally he swallowed nervously, having reluctantly decided to acquiesce. Bending forward near her ear, he bashfully whispered a few stuttering but candidly explicit sentences regarding a few risqué activities that he'd like one day to explore with her, half expecting to get slapped at any moment. Sheri's shocked expression over his revelation caused his body to tremble in anxiety.

"Wow!" Sheri exclaimed with raised brows. "I would have never imagined that you would have kinky desires like that."

Matt felt unusually vulnerable, wary of her reaction and how it would affect her feelings towards him. He decided to boldly bluff it out. "Okay, okay, now you know," he bellowed in an upbeat, unabashed tone. "But you insisted. I guess you'll spare me all that emotional baggage of a love affair and walk out on me now."

Sheri looked at him peculiarly for a moment, then broke out in a short, boisterous laugh. "Matt, you may be more interesting and exciting than I had ever imagined." She affectionately draped her arms over his shoulders and they pressed together in another passionate, ardent kiss.

A surge of calming relief flooded Matt's soul coupled with a rejuvenated sense that perhaps he had found the right woman after all. As their entangled bodies slowly parted, her hand impishly sliding across his lap, Matt noticed the provocative, pouting gaze being tossed his way.

"So, Matt," she enticingly said as she moistened her lips and lowered her back onto the massive cushions, clasped her hands together above her head , and wantonly dangled her right leg on the floor while the left daringly draped over the back of the sofa, "I'd love to share one with you now. I bet that Lucinda has some great erotic toys we could borrow."

Matt grinned lasciviously, unable to keep from staring at the tiny junction of white between her legs. His hands began to caress her thighs as he felt the primal cravings for her stronger than ever. But those nagging doubts of the past, duty, and his own sense of morality still pestered him. He swallowed nervously. "I don't take intimacy lightly, as you know, not like some other people. I would like nothing more but I have to be sure. Sure that what I'm feeling is love and not lust." Matt reached out and offered his hand. With a slight frown of disappointment, Sheri swung her left leg to the floor and raised up to snuggle close to him again. His arms coiled around her and squeezed tightly with devotion. "Suppose I just give you a soothing massage for now," he softly suggested.

Sheri batted her lashes and burrowed her face against his sweaty chest, her congenial smile returning as she purred in contentment, savoring the simple closeness and the relaxing strokes of his fingers across her back.

Even through the sensual distractions of kissing and snuggling, even as his nimble fingers kneaded and rubbed her shoulder blades and spine, on occasion deviously and playfully dipping under an arm or between a thigh, Matt's attention was invariably intruded upon by the events that engulfed them all. As engaging and stimulating as Sheri's company was, thoughts of impending actions continued to meander through his mind. He and Reynolds had been planning the complicated logistics of a more deliberate search south, beyond the arc where children had apparently passed, striking down towards the great canyon system of Valles Marineris. That was until the winds began to roar.

Matt personally took the warning call from Reggie Lewis just after breakfast. Meteorological scanners aboard the Guilford Courthouse had detected a major disturbance building around the towering heights of the Tharsis Plateau to the west, the largest known plateau in the solar system - twice as high as the Tibetan plateau on Earth. High resolution infrared spectrometer readings indicated the development of a large temperature gradient in the atmosphere and anenomic sensors revealed powerful winds in excess of 150 miles per hour sweeping down the slopes towards the valleys and low level plains, some gusts approaching 200 miles per hour. Lunae Planum would be feeling its effects in a few hours. That could mean only one thing - dust storms!

Especially in areas near large scale topography, direct heating of the atmosphere by heat radiated from the surface, which doesn't absorb radiation very well, frequently causes local temperature differences as the lighter, warmer air rises, helped along by the pressing in on its flanks of the surrounding, heavier, colder air. This atmospheric mixing generates strong winds that lift huge amounts of micrograined dust particles from the surface and form thick clouds. The blanket of dust blocks much of the sunlight, gradually causing the atmospheric temperatures to even out and the winds to subside. Massive global dust storms that could last several months are not uncommon when the planet is near perihelion, but the orbital revolution had long past that point in the current Martian year. This was just a localized event, probably not lasting for more than a few days, but for the uninitiated, a terrifying experience.

Matt hastily called a briefing that included the members of his crew, Lieutenant Reynolds, and representatives from the major science and technical disciplines. Until the disturbance had safely passed, all outside investigative and scientific plans were immediately scrapped. No one was to travel outside the colony facility. All portable and fragile equipment currently employed on the surface would have to be brought inside or locked-down in place. Jackson Shoals, who had returned to the spaceport in the Nathanael Greene to draw a supply of methane and hydrogen from the terminal's storage tanks to replace the ship's fuel reserves, was ordered to travel to the colony to wait out the storm. The exploratory team of Yong Chang and Raymond Ponsonby had recently called in to report that they were grounded by the storm in a small valley northeast of Uranius Patera and southwest of Tempe Fossae with visibility at zero. Unsettled eyes warily strayed around the room in trepidation. No one quite knew what to expect.

"This sounds like a crisis to me," Doctor Oliver disconsolately remarked as she put her hand to her forehead before peering at the others around the room. "I mean we're talking about getting hit with greater than hurricane force winds. Can this place withstand that kind of power?" She paused, breathing deeply. "The only thing that scares me more than nature is...."she sneered across the table at Reynolds, "....soldiers carrying guns."

A wide grin spanned the calm, experienced face of the older Andre Fedorov as he leisurely reclined in the seat next to her and swiveled in her direction. "You amuse me, Doctor. I've seen these before and as Martian dust storms go, this one is mediocre at best. You must remember that because the atmosphere is so thin, a 200 mile an hour wind will only feel like a stiff winter gust on Earth. You'll be able to walk through it, just won't be able to see a thing. You can relax."

"Do you know how to operate any of Jamestown's meteorological equipment?" Matt asked of the engineer.

"Me?" he challenged, pointing at his chest. "Listen, Commander, I can put the stuff together and connect it to a power source, But I haven't a clue as to how to use it. Maybe Karl will know, but I doubt it."

Matt listlessly nodded in resignation. "If not, we'll have to continue to rely on the ship for weather reports. This situation would have sure been dicey if we hadn't been warned. I'd hate to be caught out there."

Andre chuckled and bellowed sprightly. "I knew we should have brought along a gorgeous weather babe."

Caroline listened quietly to the briefing and subsequent debate until a sudden realization caused her to tremble fearfully and abruptly spin towards Matt and fervently interject her thoughts concerning a colleague with whom she had dinner with the previous night. "What about Anthony Sabatini? He took a rover at dawn to go to mine N2 to examine the automated extraction equipment and to collect some ore samples. It's about fifteen miles northwest of here."

"Good thinking, Caroline," Matt gratefully replied, having forgotten about the unescorted sortie he approved. "Sheri, get Mister Sabatini on the rover transmitter and have him high-tail-it back here immediately."

"Yes, Commander," she officially replied with a covert, devilish leer aimed at Matt before typing some miles onto her portable terminal.

Matt returned her prurient gaze, recalling several suggestive images from the previous night before wrapping up the meeting. "Lieutenant Reynolds, please recall all of your scouting parties. Science teams may pursue what investigations they can in the labs and engineers can continue to work on and monitor internal colony systems. Otherwise, someone had better breakout a deck of cards."

Matt, Sheri, and Vijay stood anxiously behind the thick Plexiglas shell in the rounded nook of the ground floor observation lounge in the Residential Dome to watch the approach of the raging storm, the only point that afforded a clear, unobstructed view of the scabby crests and slopes of the rising hills on their western horizon. There the sky was an eerie darkness, a sharp contrast to the bright pink directly overhead. Soon the peaks on the horizon were obscured in turbulent, convective, viscous bronze haze that crept towards them like a sullied fog bank off the coast of Maine. Rising thousands of feet into the air, the colossal, oscillating cloud of dust rolled down the slopes towards the plain of Lunae like a giant tidal wave, whirling and surging towards the shore, its foaming pinnacles spraying out skinny streamers of lighter red and orange particles into the cloudless sky above. Small cyclonic funnels of sepia fines cut angular, surgical swaths through the steep, narrow gullies and hollows that sliced across the knobby ridges as the leading edge of the roaring gales poured over the summits. Suddenly the hills were goner and the eerie sky was blackened as if in the middle of a solar eclipse. Sheri pressed tremulously into Matt, his arm reflexively wrapping around her shoulder, pulling her close as the ominous, irresistible wall of burnt umber powder, now appearing much darker in the retarded light, rushed upon them.

"Holy shit!" Matt exclaimed in panic as the relentless wave threatened to overwhelm and bury them. "Look out!"

Instinctively their bodies recoiled, cowering in terror as their hands reached up to protect their burrowing heads as the powerful force of the storm crashed violently into the dome with a tumultuous boom followed by a loud and steady whooshing howl. Looking up cautiously, they could see the blanket of dust striking the curved glass panels and flying off overhead. The dome crackled and rattled as its thick panels quivered and shook while resisting the structural stresses inflicted upon it by the shrieking wind.

Through the din they could make out a regular, faint tinkling rapping against the glass, like a million sharpened fingernails tapping on elegant crystal. Though infinitesimal in size, the material being driven by the winds was still solidified, frozen, irregular. Ever since the last lava flows and massive floods millennia ago and without active plate tectonics, only minor geological transformations had occurred from temperature variations, meteorite impacts, and wind abrasion. Sandblasting rounded off and filled in craters, formed layered deposits of material, scarred and sculpted the walls of canyons and ravines, altered the face of slopes on mesas and mountains. It was fortunate that the plate glass panels were made of highly scratch-resistant properties. Naked skin would probably be ripped to shreds in minutes. Breaking from their intimate huddle, the three crewmates gingerly stepped forward in awe to the edge of the glass. Amidst the continuous pummeling of the Martian dust, brief dissipation's in the cloud thickness allowed periods of brightness to filter to the surface that permitted a fleeting view of the wind swept countryside before another compressed wave of whirling particles blinded them once more. Looking down at the floor, Matt noticed a fine luster accumulating at the foundation of the glass supports. Observing it as well, Vijay knelt on one knee and traced a finger through the thin powder, nodding with understanding.

"This dust must be less than micron size," he said rising to his feet and rubbing the material between thumb and forefinger. "Hard and rough, like salt. We had better find some vacuum cleaners, Matt. No hermetic seal will be able to keep this stuff out."

Though the storm had successfully idled the marine search teams and some of the scientists, such was not the case for Caroline Hart and her two colleagues. Tegan McDowell spent the day in the lab using an electron microscope and computer modeling programs to analyze the genetic composition of the samples of the engineered plants that they had retrieved from the test site. Caroline had donated her time to Tammy Jacobs in the Agri Dome, plowing the soil and reseeding a wide variety of crops with the aid of recently activated automated machinery. Tammy had been fortuitous in saving most of the vegetables in the hydroponics pond and Caroline actually enjoyed assisting her in the selection of the most mature for consumption. There menu would finally consist of a little fresh produce.

Not accustomed to such a physical work day, Caroline returned to her room dirty, sore, and exhausted. Peeling out of her soiled work suit, she wasted no time in jumping in to her tiny, private shower, the potent jets of warm spray soothing her aching muscles. Having nibbled on part of the day's hydroponics yield, Caroline had very little appetite left so she decided to forego a late dinner and Matt's invitation to join him and his crew in watching a 3D movie in favor of early retirement. Once her thick brunette hair was dry, she slipped into her purple silk chemise and sluggishly drew back her bedspread. Ashamed of the slovenly state of the rest of her bedding, she threw off the spread and began straightening out the sheets, sliding the mattress and dropping to her knees to tuck the sheets. Bending low to lift a troublesome bedskirt, she noticed a tiny, dim reflection under the bed near the headboard. A more focused observation revealed it to be small, flat, and square with a transparent top and black bottom, lying on the carpeted floor. She had torn the drawers and cabinets apart that first day but had never thought to look under the bed. Inquisitively she reached for it as she sprawled on the floor. It felt like plastic, smooth with edges, light but solid. Her fingers detected the grooves of a tiny metal hinge. Slowly pulling it out under the soft, non-glaring light of the ceiling grids, she identified it immediately. She had seen a thousand of these before. It was the clear polyethylene protective sleeve for a computer data disk, and more significantly, a small, circular chrome disk was lodged inside. Caroline's heart pounded. Could this be a personal log of her husband's? In a flash she leaped to her feet and bolted pell-mell to the terminal in her living room. She carelessly fumbled around in her haste removing the unmarked disk from its jacket and loading it into her processor, trying to contain her expectations. It may be only some mundane data base or entertainment software. Or perhaps simply a blank. Her body quivered nervously as the computer came on-line and the initial program screen was displayed. She recognized the standard format and shouted in joy. It was, in fact, an introductory page for a personal record. But her elation was quickly tempered. The subsequent entries were security coded. She needed a password, six to twenty characters. Caroline became frantic, unable to think clearly. She just had to access those recordings; find out who made them and what they were about. Her fingers ran frenetically through her wavy locks as a hundred disconcerted thoughts bombarded her brain. Her breaths became long and arduous in her anxiety. She couldn't wait, she needed to seek help now. Tossing on a matching silk robe and securing the waist tie,

Caroline hurriedly removed the disk from her computer and dashed from her quarters in slippers to those of Lucinda Desjardin, a few doors away. She was still panting heavily when Lucinda belatedly answered the persistent ringing of her door intercom.

"For God's sake, Caroline," Lucinda bellowed irritably as the door slid open. "What is so urgent?"

Caroline resolutely stepped into the doorway. Lucinda's scowl revealed a growing impatience. She had hastily thrown on a thin, cherry red satin robe with nothing but a skimpy panty on underneath as the protruding, pointed impressions under the luxurious material made apparent. Her long blond hair dangled loose and disheveled below her shoulders.

"Lucinda, I have to talk to you." Caroline's voice was excitable and demonstrative.

"Shit! Why didn't you first call me on the room com?"

Caroline could sense that Lucinda was still rather agitated over the interruption. In a mental daze, she feebly put her hand to her drooping forehead. "I don't know. I'm not thinking clearly." She raised her head to glare into Lucinda's eyes. "I just had to see you."

Lucinda stepped back with a waggish smirk as she admiringly studied Caroline's sleepwear attired body. "Caroline, you should have given me some notice that you wanted to spend the night with me."

Caroline was stunned for a moment before blushing in embarrassment, shaking her head vehemently. "No, you don't understand. It's not that. I just found this data...."

"Caroline!" Lucinda sternly interrupted as she lurched forward, firmly clasping her shoulders. "I have company." Her head tilted towards the bedroom.

Caroline turned to the right and instantly recognized the tall, handsome features of the young, sandy-hair navigator of the Guilford Courthouse , standing inside the doorway, naked from the waist up, hurriedly slipping a navy T-shirt over his head. She regretfully turned back to Lucinda. "I'm so sorry, Lucinda," she proclaimed with a voice teeming with genuine remorse. "Please forgive me. I didn't mean to interrupt your.."

"It's okay," Lucinda consoled, lightly shaking Caroline's shoulders. "It's okay. We had finished anyway."

Jack Shoals timidly stepped from the confines of the bedroom as he finished tucking in the tail of his shirt. "My shipmates are expecting me in the captain's quarters," he softly announced as he walked up and placed an arm around Lucinda. "I had better make an appearance."

The two embraced and exchanged a brief but poignant kiss.

"Thanks for the entertainment," Jack said with his enchanting boyish grin as they separated, casting Caroline a respectful glance as he past by. "Good evening, ma'am"

"I'll see you tomorrow, Jack," Lucinda called out as her eyes desirously followed him out before turning her attention to Caroline. "Now what has got you so excited to cause you to rush over to my room in your robe and nightie if it's not to play with me?"

Caroline offered her the flat plastic container. "I found this data disk under my bed. It's a personal log of some kind but it's security coded."

"Really!" Lucinda exclaimed with peaked interest as she carefully examined the disk.

Caroline eagerly looked on. "I thought you might be able to help."

Lucinda's face brightened. "Well, let's just see what we can see."

Caroline followed her to the desk containing the computer terminal like a puppy trailing its master. Hovering over her shoulder, Caroline held her breath as Lucinda sat down, activated the machine, and inserted the disk. The monitor brightened to display the same introductory page and request for a security code.

"I see what you mean," Lucinda commented. "Very interesting. This could take quite a few hours." She reached into the top desk drawer and removed another disk, loading the program into the system. "Fortunately I brought a RAPS software disk with me." She pressed the voice input button on her keypad. "Run program, drive B."

The computer began to apply the Random Access Password Selection program, arbitrarily selecting a potential line of characters to apply to the password field and filing to memory so as not to repeat the same sequence. The system shut down almost immediately.

"Error! Error!" the affable, feminine computer voice impassively proclaimed. "Password frequency violation. System terminated."

"Damnit!" Lucinda boisterously cursed, rapping her knuckles on the desk top, grimacing in frustration. "It's got a fracking PF inhibitor. Twenty password failures and the whole system shuts down." She sat quietly for a moment before removing the RAPS disk and restarting the computer. As the system came back on-line, Lucinda twisted around to look up at Caroline. "We have to try to do it the old-fashioned way. This may take a few weeks."

Caroline's spirit was yanked from her as she sighed in despair. She had such high hopes that her discovery contained a personal report from Dave, perhaps the unrealistic expectation that he had left a private message for her. But would he have cloaked those kinds of remarks in such secrecy? Tired and emotionally spent, Caroline silently staggered over to a nearby recliner and listlessly sank into its padded seat.

Both women sat unmoving for minutes, lost in their own thoughts, before an enlightened Lucinda turned to Caroline. "You say that you found this in your room, under what was your husband's bed?"

"That's correct."

"Hmmmm...."

Caroline's attention was reenergized as her body straightened. She could perceive that Lucinda was on to something.

"Password Jamestown," Lucinda spoke into the input microphone.

"Invalid Input."

"Password David Hart."

"Invalid Input."

"Password Administrator."

"Invalid Input."

As Lucinda futilely tossed words at the computer that she associated with the colony Administrator, Caroline was thoughtfully engaged in trying to remember her husband's favorite names, places, and numbers. As Lucinda was forced to restart the computer again, Caroline noticed Lucinda's puzzled expression turn to one of illumination as she casually looked her way. She caught a glimpse of a tiny upturn along the corners of Lucinda's mouth before she turned back to the terminal.

"Password Caroline."

"Invalid Input"

"Password Caroline Hart."

"Invalid input."

"Shit!" Lucinda screamed, slamming violently back against her chair. "I thought for sure that would be it."

A sound resonated deep within the dark recesses of Caroline's mind. Lucinda's last attempt had inspired a recollection from the past. It was familiar, from years ago, and very old. A melody, a tune, a single male voice. She had heard it a hundred times. She began to hum a few scattered chords, though the lyrics escaped her memory. David had played it for her while they were dating, adopting it as their song. He had stumbled across the ancient selection amongst his father's collection of Golden Oldies amongst soon became one of his favorites. He said that it always reminded him of her. It's rhythm was coming back to her now and soon she recalled the name of a twentieth century singer - Neil Diamond. Suddenly it burst upon her conscience like the blossoming rosebuds of spring.

"Lucinda, try Sweet Caroline."

Like magic, the processor faintly rumbled in response to the correct input and within moments the security shield was replaced with a bright blue playback selection menu screen.

"We've got it!" Lucinda happily exclaimed as she spun towards Caroline. "We're in."

Caroline ecstatically leaped to her feet and dashed to Lucinda's side, throwing her arms around her shoulders with cheerful delight, jumping up and down like a hyperactive kid. Lucinda giggled in amusement, looking up at Caroline with a mischievous smirk.

"Why, Caroline, are you coming on to me?"

Caroline responded to the query with a piercing, disapproving sneer as she unlocked her grasp and laid her hands on the back of the chair.

"Okay," Lucinda continued with disappointment as she shifted her focus towards the monitor. "Just checking. Maybe later. Look! There's just one file listed. According to the icon it's a visual recording."

"Come on then," Caroline urged impatiently with a gentle nudge to her shoulder blade. "Open it."

"Access file one," Lucinda instructed.

Caroline nervously nibbled at her nails as the selection menu display slowly turned black to be replaced with a rainbow collage of hundreds of tiny, multicolored pixels. Each of the diminutive squared images rapidly blinked in unison with only subtle changes in the splattering array of colors. The speech emanating from the speakers was garbled and incoherent. Anger swelled within Caroline's breast. "What the hell is this?"

"There's always something," Lucinda moaned as she dropped her head and shook it in disbelief, her succulent blond hair swishing against her back. Straightening, she swung around to explain. "This file's been scrambled. It's encrypted."

Caroline was shaken again. Her body shuddered. To be so close and yet so far. She lethargically moved to the side to sag against the end of the desk. "Is there anything you can do?" she imploringly asked as she brushed away a few wayward strands from her eyes.

"Well, I have some decoding equipment installed on the main terminal in A and C. I can work on it from there. But it's going to take time and there are great demands for my services. I'll start on it tomorrow."

Caroline sighed reluctantly, lethargically moving to warmly embrace Lucinda as she rose to her feet. "Thank you. It was impulsive of me to impose on you like this. I'm sorry for interrupting your evening." Breaking away, she crossed her arms behind her and slowly dragged her feet towards the door. "Please let me know the minute you find anything."

Lucinda briskly shuffled after her with her patented wiggle and enchanting guise. "I will. Caroline, please stay for awhile. Let me cheer you up." Her hand reached out and deftly loosened her waist cinch, yearningly staring at Caroline's plunging purple bodice as her satin robe fell open. Caroline squirmed and giggled as fingers from Lucinda's other hand wiggled across her ribs. "See what I mean."

After a few seconds Caroline backed away and promptly pulled her robe around her, sneering derisively. "Lucinda, you've been most kind to me, but I'm really not interested."

"No matter," Lucinda replied with a beaming grin. "I'm supposed to see John Walinski in a little while anyway."

Caroline rolled her eyes contemptuously. "I can't believe you," she chided. "You are some piece of work, a wanton seductress."

"And a damn good one too," Lucinda proudly proclaimed as she allowed her own sheer robe to slowly fall from her shoulders. "If you ever change your mind, you know where I am, even if you just let me look."

Caroline hesitated and tittered quietly. "All right, Lucinda. If you can uncover something meaningful to me, we'll see."

Caroline wasted little time in tracking down Matt and Sheri the next morning and effervescently reporting her discovery, making a general nuisance of herself for the rest of the day as she regularly pestered Lucinda about her progress, a complex and tedious operation that, along with other programming and maintenance projects requiring her attention, became an intermittent and painstakingly slow process. The news came as a welcome relief to Matt who made no attempt to contain his exhilaration of the possibility that the encrypted file might hold a vital clue to the fate of the colonists, since none of the other retrieved files had been of much use. It gave his spirit a resurgent shot of vigor, for he was burdened with yet another distressing event for which he felt powerless. Sheri had been unable to contact the geologist, Anthony Sabatini, who had failed to return from his excursion to the old mine shaft. Unless his transmitter had malfunctioned, he apparently was not in the rover. Since the mining facility was stocked with an emergency supply of rations and a small, portable pressurized chamber, Matt could only hope that the man had the good sense to stay where he was until the storm subsided. With all the blowing debris obstructing vision and blocking much of the sunlight, it was difficult to know what direction you were going let alone being able to see anything.

Matt attempted to take a brief diversion from the problems confronting him by meeting Lieutenant Reynolds in the common area park of the Residential Dome for lunch and a cordial though highly competitive game of chess. The park was becoming one of the social centers as groups of people would often prepare their meals in their rooms and bring them out under the dome to eat in the company of friends. And so the two men brought out their trays of chicken soup and cheese crackers and settled around one of the many circular, creme-colored polystyrene tables and arranged the battleground of chessmen between them. Matt could still hear the faded howl of the outside wind, an occasional rattle or shimmy of a reinforced glass panel. Looking up he could see alternating thick and thinner clouds of dark matter whisking rapidly across the top of the dome. It was necessary to employ artificial lighting to brighten the area since the storm effectively reduced the natural daytime illumination to about ten percent of normal. Even the ancillary lamps sprinkled sporadically amongst the grass and trees were lit assist in the regeneration of the greenery. The fingertips of Tammy Jacobs were everywhere. With ample water and nutrient supplements she had managed to revitalize the trees, the withering yellows and tans that had initially dappled the leaves were almost a distant memory. His nostrils even managed to catch a fleeting, modest whiff of pine and evergreen and an odor that reminded him of a freshly mowed lawn. The sensations made him reminisce about home. He missed the smell of flowering meadows, the trickle of a creek and the crash of the ocean. That and football. The two men ate and conversed on an assortment of trivial matters and made their deliberate and calculated moves in between. About twenty minutes into their contest, their attention was drawn to the solitary approach of Doctor Oliver, who was leisurely moving towards them along a gravel path that led from the banks of the tiny creek and snaked amongst an assortment of trees and merged with the concrete floor a few yards away.

"Why, Susan," Matt buoyantly greeted, "out for a stroll are we?"

She smiled and turned to look around at the forested park. "Yes, I like to walk for exercise." With hands resting inside the hip pockets of her pants, she rolled her shoulders with mellowness. "This is my favorite place to come. One of the few reminders of Earth."

Matt nodded. "I know what you mean."

"By the way," she continued with a vain twitch of her head, "Nichelle is feeling much better and her arm is mending well. She should be able to assume some light duties in a couple of days."

That was welcome news that brightened Matt's face. Any positive development at this point was a blessing from heaven. A closer inspection on the communication tower had uncovered evidence that several of the anchoring bolts that secured the platform had apparently been partially severed by a clean, razor-thin burn of a type made by a narrow-field industrial torch or even a laser gun. It was an act that could have been performed weeks ago, or by someone within their midst. Just one more acid pill to toss into his churning stomach. "Here, take a load off," Matt said as he motioned to the chair beside him with an open palm. "You have a unique opportunity to observe this action-packed thriller where three or four moves may be daringly made in ten minutes."

"No, thanks. I really should be getting back to the medical clinic. I never developed an interest for chess. It seems like a very cold and heartless game." Her piercing gaze was focusing on Lieutenant Reynolds. "It reminds me too much of war."

Susan always seemed to have a knack for getting under Matt's skin. He was amazed at how she could never simply walk away from a civil discourse without espousing one of her liberal hair-brained convictions. Consequently, since they rarely agreed on anything of importance, he couldn't resist the urge to throw a few facetious digs in her direction. "I suppose that you also hate football," Matt flippantly remarked with a comical swagger, "because it's a violent ground acquisition game that's a metaphor for world conquest."

Susan returned a crafty grin. "Exactly, a stupid, macho game."

With a wry smile Matt threw up his hands in resignation and returned his attention to the board. A couple of quick pawn exchanges was noticed by Susan as she was about to depart. She was ignorant of the strategy involved, but she could, at least, recognize the pieces. It compelled her to loom menacingly over Reynolds' shoulder.

"I've been meaning to ask you, Lieutenant, do all military officer types view the world as just a bunch of pawns in a global chess game?"

Reynolds was perplexed by the question. "Excuse me?" he said, twisting his neck and wincing over his shoulder.

"I mean civilians, ordinary people, stupid and naive youngsters who volunteer." Her tone was fervent and combative and her scowl could melt butter. "Are we all just pawns to be used and manipulated in a worldwide struggle for power, fame, and economic exploitation, brokered and engineered by rich multinational corporations?"

Reynolds' fingers angrily squeezed the piece that he had just removed, but his professional training enabled him to restrain his indignation. "Forgive me, Doctor, but where do you get these fanciful and ridiculous notions?" he adamantly but calmly replied, his contorted expression betraying his simmering rage.

"Is that what these colonists were too, and all of us as well?" Her hand motioned towards Matt and herself. "Expendable assets, disposable products to be used and discarded with the garbage, just like your boys."

Reynolds' face was burning with fire. He violently twisted his body around and shoved a pointed finger towards her chest. "My men are not expendable!" he roared with passion, his finger rapidly jabbing the air in front of her. "Never forget that."

"I wish I could believe you, Lieutenant," she replied with an incredulous glare over her shoulder as she pivoted to leave. "Too bad they weren't in Romania."

That night Lieutenant Reynolds found himself strolling alone down the long, dim corridor that connected the central dome to the northwest structure, fully accoutered with laser rifle, battle helmet, and detection gear as was required of all marines who traveled beyond the Residential dome. He had finished checking on his evening outposts guarding the group's living quarters and decided to take a walk, foregoing the use of a more speedier manually driven shuttle cart, several of which Andre and Vijay had recently re-powered and put into service. The exercise and solitude helped him to focus his troubled mind. The caustic remarks of Doctor Oliver had once more opened old wounds in his conscience. Convoluted memories of sights, sounds, and smells that only resided in the murkiness of haunting dreams burst upon his awareness like an over-inflated balloon. Those fateful events in the Romanian Alps tortured his soul. Sorrow and regret overwhelmed his spirit as he reflected upon the bloody pile of tarnished dog tags, the body bags, all those heart-wrenching letters to young devastated wives and grieving mothers. But with the support of a loving family and his stalwart faith in a compassionate, forgiving God, he was able to live with the outcome and move on. Except for the *incident*. That one agonizing moment that was frozen in time, those few terrifying seconds forever ingrained into his psyche. For a fleeting second he had stared squarely into the jaws of death, standing toe-to-roe within its grisly embrace as it surged upon him. But he was not consumed by its crushing arms that day. He owed his life to the inexplicable, crazed charge by a man seemingly possessed by demons impervious to danger. He survived when he should have died, another died when he could have lived. The gnawing guilt of that moment clung to his neck like a ball and chain, dragging him down, an oppressive debt that could never be repaid. And then there was the present. Like Matthew Maitland, he also had a private meeting with the Chief of Operations of the NSCA before departure from the Constitution. He emerged from that briefing with a little apprehension and a clearer understanding of why the government desired a military presence on this mission. The enigmatic events that they had encountered since their initial landing did nothing to alleviate his misgivings. His privileged insight grated acutely on his nerves. He had not intentionally misled anyone, but he was uncomfortable with sitting on covert material and at being anything but forthright in his relations with his colleagues.

Reynolds became so absorbed in his own self-reflection that he failed to recognize his arrival at the Industrial Dome until well inside. All was quiet except for the low murmuring hum of the water reclamation system and, as he moved along the perimeter corridor, the bass whine of the atmospheric processor and the rattle of aluminum and the soft whoosh of moving air through the ventilation conduits. Looking out through the glass shell into the inky blackness beyond, he could still see massive clumps of dark shadows whisking wildly around the dome, high-pitched howls penetrating the seals. Soon he was at the short, broad tubular tunnel that connected the dome to the rectangular concrete warehouse and turned inside. That was when his infrared scanner began to beep. Reynolds froze in his tracks, stunned by the sudden interruption. An ominous fear crept over him that caused his heart to race. A terrifying sensation for which he had some familiarity. He mentally kicked himself in the pants for his recklessness. What in hell was he doing out here by himself? He raised the scanner from his utility belt and checked the signal. A relatively weak heat signature was emanating from within the walls of the warehouse building. Leveling his rifle, Reynolds anchored the scanner atop its metal barrel and cautiously approached the wide portal. Swiveling his head from side to side, he set foot within the concrete enclosure. The infrared signal was coming from his left, close by. He activated his helmet lamps to illuminate the caliginous area and scrupulously stepped in that direction. A few faint, hollow sounds resonated from behind a fortress of nearby wood and plastic crates, a series of soft murmurs, groans, and titters. Then dead silence. Reattaching the scanner to his belt, Reynolds pointed his weapon and timorously moved between the outer row of containers. His auricular senses were immediately assaulted by the sounds of hasty, laborious shuffling on the floor and a few quick, heavy thuds of something solid against wood. His motion detector abruptly rang out with rapid pulsation's. Instinctively Reynolds jumped back into the aisle with alarm, his rifle and lights swinging in unison across his front, his anxious breaths short and deep. A quick glance at his instrument indicated air displacement just a few feet away. Collecting his nerves, he cautiously stepped between another section of crates. Creeping around a particularly towering mass of containers, his helmet spots suddenly flashed across a pale tan blob with several orifices that resembled a face, a human face. Startled out of his wits, he pointed the rifle and fingered the trigger.

"Don't shoot!" cried out a familiar voice as recognizable appendages raised up to shield the eyes from the bright glare.

Reynolds gaped in amazement. "Walinski?" he questioned in hesitant shock before dropping the head of his rifle and slumping back against a stack of cargo, emitting a big sigh of relief as he lifted the brim of his helmet.

"Yes, sir, Lieutenant Reynolds, sir," he shouted as he jumped to his feet and snapped smartly to attention.

Reynolds brows raised as he straightened himself, staring in bug-eyed shock, for Walinski was stark naked, standing erect before him and in more ways than one. "Private Walinski," he admonished with a tone of indignation, "what the hell do you think you're doing?"

The soldier hesitated, focusing directly ahead and swallowing nervously before forcing his stuttering response. "Ke....Keeping up.... relations with....the civilian pop....population, sir."

"Huh....huh," Reynolds mumbled skeptically, sliding to his side and gawkingly peering over his shoulder. The circular beam from his helmet light scanned the jumbled rows of freight beyond. The brightness soon captured the image of a laser rifle propped against a box, followed by a helmet, olive uniform, black combat boots, and assorted other garments littering the floor. The panning light soon enveloped a pair of naked long, smooth legs, and an extensive, thick mass of curly blond hair tightly wedged between some plastic containers. He immediately recognized the gorgeous facial features of Lucinda Desjardin cowering fearfully on the floor, tremulously clutching some clothing to her chest. Reynolds lecherously looked over the uncovered parts with a congenial smirk, nodding in admiration. His young charge may be rank and unprincipled, he thought, but at least he had a fine taste in women. A stern expression returned to his appearance as he stepped back to address the soldier. "You know you're not supposed to be here, Private."

"I'm sorry, sir." He gulped, quaking in his boots, or in this case, his feet. "Just upholding the honor of the Corps, sir."

"Oh!" Reynolds was puzzled but found the incident rather amusing. "How's that, Private?"

"Proving to the young lady that space marines make better lovers than fly boys, sir."

Reynolds' head dipped. "I see, Private." He could see the growing uneasiness and the panicked look of dread on Walinski's face, as if he envisioned himself scrubbing latrines for the rest of his life. "At ease, son, you're not on duty now."

Walinski's shoulders slumped as he exhaled heavily as Reynolds looked upon him scornfully like a disapproving father. Then gradually his face begun to shine like the blazing dawn of a desert sunrise and an ear-splitting grin turned up the corners of his mouth. Unable to contain his glee, Reynolds erupted in side-splitting laughter, much to the flabbergasted bafflement of his young subordinate. "I hope you're with me, Walinski," Reynolds exclaimed between cackles, "the next time I'm in battle. You know how to defend a hopeless position." Calmly, he wiped his hand across his mouth as he slowly regained his dignified composure. "But a good soldier must always be aware of his surroundings," he continued in his normal professional style as he inched forward. "Your impulsiveness will get you in trouble one day, son, but for now, carry on."

Reynolds proceeded towards the main portal while Walinski remained motionless, standing bewildered and confused. A devious, gratified smile gradually came over him, as if he had just stolen the crown jewels, and he eagerly went plunging back into the waiting, yearning arms of his insatiable lover. Taking a quick parting glance over his shoulder, Reynolds could hear a faint curse and a few soft, feminine giggles. "But I want the two of you dressed and out of here in ten minutes," he abruptly shouted.

"Sir, yes, sir," echoed Walinski's shaken though boisterous reply.

Reynolds entered the tunnel shaking his head in disillusionment. "Kids," he drolly mumbled to himself. He certainly didn't sanction frivolous, secular behavior, but he remembered his days of youth when he was a little on the wild side, lacking character, principles, and direction before he found a greater purpose for his life, one that transcended self-gratification and the trivial pursuits of the day. He hoped that he would have a positive influence in the growth of some of his men. He chuckled to himself. There was nothing like a whizzing bullet to get one's attention focused on the philosophical and spiritual matters of life.

Well into the third day of the storm there was no indication of abatement to the howling winds, though the Guilford Courthouse reported that local atmospheric air temperature differences around the Tharsis Bulge did show some encouraging though negligible signs of equalizing out. Since his search and exploratory teams were temporarily grounded, Matt decided to utilize a portion if them in a more meticulous search of all public facilities and laboratories for any written or data base information that may shed some light on the whereabouts of the colonists or the circumstances leading up to their disappearance. In that regard, marine patrols and other volunteers wormed their way through stores, restaurants, science labs, and recreational areas with a fine-toothed comb, examining every scrap of paper and accessing every program that was available, all seemingly concluding with the same frustrating results.

In the midst of this search and seizure operation, Corporal Cooke, along with Privates Walinski and Simmons, found themselves rummaging through the shelves, under the counters, and rifling through the stock and office areas of a small general store called James Mart, the Martian version of a discount variety store that was a fixture of every suburban shopping mall on Earth, still the preferred means of distribution over the innumerable on-line services. His initial reaction to what he saw struck him peculiarly. Shelves that had displayed a wide assortment of household goods, appliances, electronics, recreational gear, personal care products, and various sundry items were more than two-thirds empty with almost nothing remaining in the perimeter stockrooms. The corner department that had contained merchandise specifically targeted for the outside environment - pressure suits, rupture repair kits, heated hand tools, robotics dust scrubbers, environment pack spare parts, was completely stripped bare. It looked as if the store had been ransacked without the mess and destruction. Everything remaining was neat and orderly as if the store was still in business. Cooke moved behind the central register and accessed the James Mart data base. He studiously examined sales records, inventory files, and shipping records over the past half-year, that is Martian half-year (344 days). Curiously, the last transaction recorded occurred more than three weeks before the Guilford Courthouse had left the docking port of space station Constitution. His incipient analysis confirmed his suspicions. James Mart was missing inventory, a lot of it. Inquisitively he proceeded to examine sales and purchasing trends to see if there had been any unusual changes in the recent patterns of commercial behavior. The monotony of this task caused him to be easily distracted by the vivacious chatter of his two comrades who were surrounding a nearby glass counter. Slightly annoyed at the disturbance, he doggedly moved out from behind the central terminal station and irritably approached the two men. "What in hell do you two guys think you're doing?"

The two men had just removed from inside the display case two elegantly crafted wrist watches with gold bands, dust and cold resistant properties, and scratch and abrasive retarding crystal faces.

"Look, Bob, Martian watches!" Walinski called out with delight as he halted his attempt to slip it over his wrist and held up the unique and expensive item for his friend to see. "I've always wanted one of these."

"They're pretty cool," Simmons added with zeal. "You should take one for yourself."

Corporal Cooke had, of course, heard about the mystique of Martian time pieces. The rotational period around the central axis of Mars was 24 hours and 37 minutes. Early colony administrators had decided that since the Martian day was so similar to that of Earth, they would continue to use the same 60 minute per hour AM/PM cycle, with one small exception. Twice per day, when the hour, minute, and second merged at twelve on any hand or digital watch or clock, the entire timing mechanism would pause for exactly 18 minutes and 30 seconds before the seconds would resume ticking again. Consequently, 12:00 to 12:01 for both AM and PM would actually last eighteen-and-a-half minutes. These time pieces became a sort of collectors item back on Earth as well as a staple for the permanent colonial inhabitants. These untimed minutes soon began to be referred to frivolously as 'non-existence'. Some of the more secular members of the colony began to use the occasion , especially the midnight pause, to fashion a sort of rite during festive or other party nights. Their wild debauchery, drunkenness, and uninhibited carnal activities during those times became legendary and no doubt highly exaggerated as their escapades were recounted back on Earth. Those revelers who participated rationalized there behavior during that nearly twenty minute period with the argument that they could not possibly be held responsible for their actions at a time when they officially did not exist. The entire aura surrounding this carousing made for lively conversations in Terran coffee shops and bars and the sight of a Martian watch would often spawn one of these highly speculative discussions and generate mountains of prurient humor.

But the Corporal was not thinking about those amusing memories the watches inspired. He was distressed and disappointed over the actions of his friends. His cheeks turned red like Martian clay. "Put them back," he angrily ordered, his hawkish blue eyes piercing their hearts. "We're space marines, not galactic looters."

"Come on, Bob," Walinski protested with a cavalier sneer, holding out his hands indifferently, "lighten-up. It's not as if we're stealing from...."

"They don't belong to you," Cooke sternly interrupted with an emphatic thrust of his head. "And you are stealing. That's not what that uniform is all about."

Walinski's voice became combative. "Stealing from who? I don't see any shop keeper. This stuff is abandoned."

"You don't know that," Cooke staunchly retorted, using his hands to brace himself against the counter top as he leaned into the private's face, "and so what if it is. These people invested in this business, probably their life savings." His knuckles pounded against the glass as his body jerked animatedly with every word. "They risked everything to eke out a new life here, and now their decrepit bodies may be lying out there dead somewhere. You will not dishonor that life by cheating them. If they're dead, then this stuff belongs to their estate."

Walinski folded his arms in front of him, lowered his head shamefully and nodded. "Okay, Bob, you're the boss," he quietly acquiesced before looking up again. "But I think you're working overtime on that righteous soapbox of yours."

Cooke returned an aggravated stare, his hand reaching towards Walinski's face with a forefinger extended. "Are you finished?"

Walinski silently backed off, unmistakably realizing that his opinion was no longer welcome. "Sorry, Bob."

Cooke's rigid muscles relaxed from the tension as the watches were reluctantly returned to their display pedestals. "That's better. If you two hooligans still want those watches, I'll check with the Lieutenant about having your debit cards charged for them and the store's account credited. We don't take anything without paying for it. Clear?"

Meanwhile, Caroline Hart found herself aimlessly wandering alone amongst the sparsely merchandise circle and four-arm racks of Falanga's clothing store, fingering and examining the limited selection of colorful satin dresses, glimmering silk blouses, and revealing, tightly woven fishnet crop top and miniskirt sets, briefly forgetting the purpose of her visit. Her marine escort had made certain that the building was secure before moving on to the next unit, leaving her to perform the inspection. She had dutifully checked the office and counters for clues but her attention was quickly drawn to the rainbow assortment of styles and fabrics hanging from their polished chrome fixtures, imagining herself shopping there on a weekly basis. A disconsolate sadness touched her heart as she held up those garments that she found attractive. Caroline remembered the conversations she had with her husband , how he told her about the young, congenial owners who had left everything behind to open this shop less than a year ago. She recalled the excitement in his voice when he told her about the birth of their baby girl, one of the few upbeat moments of that last communiqué. What a tragedy this was for them. Caroline found herself inexplicably drawn to the infant department, a magnetic compulsion for which she was powerless to resist. A joyous warmth swept through her as she fumbled through the few remaining diaper sets, cute rompers, and furry sleepers. She desperately wanted to conceive a child of her own. How great it would be, she thought, to be a mother. To care for and nurture an infant, to cradle and comfort it, to shower her baby with all the love and affection brewing within her heart. She envisioned the feelings of pride and satisfaction that she would derive as her child grew and matured in both body and mind; how she would foster a foundation of principles and character, qualities that parenting had generally failed to develop over the last 100 years. She had always believed that she would make a good mother, if she would ever get the opportunity. With a reflective, forlorn sigh, Caroline put aside those items she had been handling and reluctantly pressed on, depressed by the fact that her time was passing by. Her spirits received a much needed lift when she came upon the women's sleepwear and intimate apparel section. She had always had a fondness for very feminine things for they made her feel attractive and desirable. And even though she was self-assured and an accomplished bioengineer researcher, she enjoyed those sensations. She gleefully sifted through the scanty selection of frilly, sheer negligees and chemises in rich, luxurious shades of purple, deep red, and majestic blue as well as a few pastel tints of mint, light yellow, and rose pink. Her fingers happily fondled the revealing, sensuous lace bras and tiny bikini panties of silk and cotton in basic colors sprinkled with a few fashion shades, though she preferred her lingerie in white or black anyway. Caroline's troubled mind continued to wander astray. She had an adequate supply of these sexy garments, of course, but she sadly reflected on the fact that there was no one in her life to wear them for - ever since Dave had gone off to this lousy planet. Her eyes caught sight of a prominent display along the back wall highlighting a small sampling of kaleidoscopic, highly erotic camisoles, corsets, and bra and panty sets, all minuscule, sheer, provocative, and several with tiny, strategic openings! The sight made her giggle. They were so carnal that they could be worn for only one occasion - party night during the time of 'non-existence'.

"Is everything all right?"

The beckoning hail made her jump. There was a terrifying glint in her eye as she quickly spun around with baited breath, her body trembling in fear as her hands tightly clenched a clump of cotton bikinis to her chest.

She released a giant sigh of relief once she recognized the thin brown mustache, handsome clean-shaven features, and purposeful gait of the dashing Corporal Cooke approaching from the direction of the entrance. "You startled me."

"I'm sorry, Caroline," he compassionately said as he stopped in front of her. "I didn't mean to frighten you. I just came from the store next door. Just checking on your progress." He reacted with a trifling smile as he focused on the handful of underwear pressed against her. "Doing some shopping are we?" he frivolously remarked.

Caroline dropped her head and blushed. She felt so silly being caught by a man playing with slinky lingerie, especially a man that so intrigued her. She shyly turned and placed the garments back into their bin.

"No matter," she heard the Corporal continue. "I'm sure that they would all look very sexy on you, if you don't mind me saying."

Within the deepest recesses of her passionate soul, the comment felt soothing and stimulating, though she was too reserved to ever publicly admit it. It sparked a brief flurry of vivid imaginations that caused her to blush even more and an unusual nervous queasiness to settle in her abdomen. "You may find out," she softly mumbled to herself.

"Excuse me, what did you say?"

Caroline shook her head, wiping-out the dreamy-eyed expression on her face and turned to him once she regained her poise. "Nothing, Bob, nothing at all." A broad glow of delight swept across her as she clasped her hands behind her back and swayed gently. "I'm afraid I've lost a lot of time daydreaming. I really should get back at it." Her hand reached out spontaneously and with the softness of a feather lightly touched Cooke on the side of his cheek. "Thank you for asking." Caroline strolled towards the office in the back but took an abbreviated glance over her shoulder sporting a sensuous smile. "And for your flattering observation."

Poking through the barren office, Caroline became annoyed at herself for being so distracted by feminine clothing and her growing attraction for the affable Corporal that it intruded on her purpose for being there. Seething at her own weakness, she began to browse the latest computerized mail files that had been transmitted to the store. Looking up from the terminal to rest her eyes, she caught a glimpse of something sitting atop the tall, aluminum storage cabinet on the other side of the room. It appeared to be a mound of brown fibers or fuzz of some sort. Curious, she moved out from behind the desk and walked over to the cabinet to investigate. Standing on her tip-toes, she daringly stretched up with all her might and blindly groped for the object until her fingers roamed across something soft, solid but pliant, squeezeable, like a beach ball covered with shaggy carpet. Gripping firmly, she pulled down the near weightless object from its lofty perch. It's rounded head, black beady eyes, pug nose, and splotches of white on its belly and under its chin reminded her of her own cuddly childhood friend. Seemingly every infant ever born had a lovable toy teddy bear to take comfort in, even when born on Mars. As Caroline's fingers gently kneaded the mushy fur, this one trivial toy seemed to bring to the forefront of her awareness every feeling of misery and despair that she had been amassing over the past five weeks, actually the last two-and-a-half years. Collectively they amalgamated into a surging torrent of grief that gushed to the surface and erupted like a boiling volcano. She mindlessly backed against the front of the desk as her emotions were overwhelmed with irrepressible sensations of despondency, fear, sorrow, loneliness, and hopelessness. Fragments of haunting images, thoughts, and feelings blended and fused like the ingredients of some steaming, macabre soup. Great pools of tears welled-up in her eyes as the agonies and frustrations of her separation and shattered marriage, her lost dreams, a childless life, and the loneliness and sexual unfulfillment of her existence, as well as a profound sorrow for the nearly 400 colonists flashed inescapably through the boundaries of her memory. And the children? What was it like for those poor children? Those innocent little ones who could not possibly understand or even be aware of those momentous events that had so engulfed them and sealed their inevitable fate. Like the opening of the locks of a dam, tears poured down her cheeks as she broke down and openly wept, sobbing loudly as she pressed the now damp fur of the toy bear against her watery cheeks. It was only seconds before she heard the steadily increasing thud of heavy boots drawing closer until her privacy was invaded.

"Caroline!" a concerned tone called out to her. "What's wrong?"

Naturally it was her Prince Charming, her Sir Lancelot and Sir Galahad, her courtly knight from the Round Table. He was like a magnet to her as he approached the desk. With tears raging like a flooding river, Caroline held out the toy imploringly, then threw herself into him, burying her lamenting head deep into his shoulders, wrapping her arms tightly around his back while still clutching the moistened bear. Caught completely off guard, Corporal Cooke hesitantly and gingerly placed a consoling left hand around her while his right searched for the edge of the desk against which he could prop his rifle. That done, Caroline felt the powerful grip of his arms as he firmly embraced her, a tender hand stroking the lush brown waves of her silky hair against the back of her head. The strength and warmness of his pressing grip felt comforting and satisfying to Caroline, whose fingers dug hard into his flesh, squeezing herself ever tighter against his chest. No words needed to be exchanged. She could feel an unusual glow of contentment flowing through like she hadn't experienced in what seemed like ages. Slowly her sobs and tears waned to a trickle. Caroline pulled her body back just enough so that she could longingly gaze into his mesmerizing blue eyes. His glare had a hypnotic quality on her unlike most men she had seen. It seemed to reflect not only strength, confidence, and passion, but also gentleness, decency, and respect. David had that look, but she found it very rare in recent years. Like the pull of the gravity well of a black hole, Caroline was compelled by unseen forces to draw ever closer to his mouth until their lips delicately mated in a gentle kiss. Swells of fervent yearnings surged through her and soon she was clawing at his back, their tongues locked blissfully in a prolonged, passionate dance of adoration as she sensed the tightening vise-like clamp of his ensnaring arms pressing her breasts into his chest. It was the most exhilarating and erotic expression of affection that she had ever experienced.

Disheartened by Lucinda's inability to solve the encrypted puzzle, Matt Maitland restlessly meandered by the store fronts along the winding corridors of the commerce level of the central dome, eliciting any sign of encouraging progress that he could find from the conglomerate search teams, to little avail. His journey took him past the religious hub of the colony, three comparatively small chambers separated from the rest of the business district on either side by twenty feet of meticulously sculpted Martian landscape save for several billowing fountains of cool, sprinkling water. Colorful murals painted on the three walls enclosing the depths of these mini geological gardens emphasizing cosmic and natural Martian scenery themes. Narrow stone pathways coiling around the red rock formations and past the spray of the fountains was obviously intended for moments of contemplation. Soft illumination emanating from inside the larger of the three rooms attracted Matt's attention. This was the multidenominational Christian chapel, larger than its darkened Islamic and

Jewish neighbors to accommodate the greater number of colonists practicing that faith. Curious as to why the chapel was exhuming a mystical glow, Matt cautiously stepped inside the open doorway. Off to his right in the tiny, darkened vestibule he noticed a laser rifle and steel helmet propped idly against the wall. The dimly lit chapel was arranged in amphitheater style. Five rows of black metal pews padded with soft burgundy cushions formed a gentle arc around the central alter with two tall walnut laminated lecterns standing on either side, all three draped with a luxurious white cloth trimmed in gold fringe and braid and adorned with various religious symbols. Extending out from the tall burgundy wall behind the alter was an impressive, towering, lustrous gold cross, glistening from the bright lighting elements embedded in the wall and shining down from spots perched on the ceiling. The three-sided extensions of the cross were like equal width, elongated pyramids, the light refraction's off the polished surface dappling tiny smudges of brightness on the ceiling and across the room. The side walls were lined with pointed arch stain-glass windows depicting various biblical events, gently gleaming from artificial illuminous fibers behind the glass. A small double-stack electronic lighting globe, a sort of surrogate candle in the shape of a vertical pair of transparent spheres, sat on each sill. Matt took a deep breath and looked around, admiring the pietistic and contemplative atmosphere the designers had created. Almost instantly his eyes centered on the solitary, somber image of Lieutenant Reynolds, sitting reverently with bowed head on the left-center of the front pew. Matt shuffled to the left and quietly approached him, mindfully sliding into the second row behind him. He noticed Reynolds holding within his quivering hands the same picture displayed on his electronic pocket photo book that he had been studying on the march in. Hearing the metallic creak of the bench as Matt settled his weight, Reynolds abruptly turned his head with a look of sudden alarm.

"Please forgive the intrusion," Matt dolefully beseeched, feeling somewhat guilty as he took a seat behind his left shoulder. "I didn't intend to disturb you."

"No need to apologize, Matt." Reynolds softly responded, wondrously looking around with open arms. "This place is God's house. It belongs to everyone."

Matt's head dipped as he felt a sudden awkwardness come over him. He perceived that the Lieutenant was troubled but was hesitant to pry into personal matters. Or could it be something that affected them all?

"Do you need me, Matt?" he earnestly questioned as if he felt he might be neglecting his duty. "Has something been found?"

"No, no," Matt replied, shaking his head emphatically, "nothing of importance." Matt paused and carefully considered the most delicate approach to assuage his curiosity regarding the Lieutenant's frame of mind. After several moments of clumsy silence, Matt finally leaned over his shoulder. "Are you all right, Tom?" he gently inquired with heartfelt concern. "You seem preoccupied. Is there anything I can do for you?"

Reynolds rolled his shoulders with a half smile, half grimace of anguish. "No, but thank you for asking." With a heavy sigh he turned away to gaze upon the glittering gold cross. "Sometimes I just need to be alone with my conscience for awhile. Occasionally the old nightmares return. It's hard to put the Romanian Alps behind me."

Matt gave Reynolds a consoling pat on the back before slumping against the pew. "I wouldn't be so pretentious to claim that I understand what you're going through," he candidly said. "I've never been under fire like that, never lost men under my command, but it wasn't your fault. Look, I read the Corps' official reports of the battle. You were completely exonerated of all culpability. Your unit had been taking heavy casualties long before command ever devolved on you. You were in dander of being completely overrun. You did what you had to do with the information available to save the men you could."

"I may have done everything I could," he soberly replied as a trembling hand wiped across a drooping brow, "but it still doesn't help. Sometimes the only peace I can find is in prayer."

Matt felt a growing amount of sympathy for the Lieutenant's plight but he knew the inner strength that this man possessed. He was one of the most capable, confident, and composed men he ever met, much of his vigor, no doubt, deriving from his faith. He wondered if there was more to the story. Leaning forward, he laid a hand firmly upon his upper arm. "There's something else, isn't there, Tom?"

Reynolds looked up into the heavens and nodded in abject resignation. With a wavering frown he blindly held aloft over his left shoulder the pocket photo displayer that he had been fingering. It was an unexpected reaction that caused Matt to freeze in his seat for a few seconds. With a peculiar glance and raised lashes, Matt humbly accepted the picture.

"His name was Sergeant First Class Jesse Carney," Reynolds calmly explained as Matt settled back and intently examined the photograph of the smiling couple, the handsome young man impeccably attired in marine dress blues. "He had reenlisted in the Corps just two months before the war with a promising career ahead of him. Like so many other young soldiers, Romania was his first pitched battle. I never knew anything about him....," Reynolds paused reflectively for a moment, "....until I submitted my recommendation that he be awarded the Congressional Medal of Honor....posthumously."

Matt straightened, his attention riveted as he carefully listened to the Lieutenant's grim account.

"It was a starlit night with a few thin clouds obscuring part of the sky, a brisk breeze whipping through the trees and a cool nip was in the air. My platoon was in a forward position along the perimeter, dug in on a rocky crest of sloping ground that was covered with foliage and timber. Carney's platoon was to our left." Reynolds' voice was low in tone but steady and forceful, almost reverent, as if conversing with God Himself. "Sometime after midnight our positions were probed by a reconnaissance in force. A sharp, desperate fire fight ensued and, as apt to happen in a skirmish, escalated out of control into a spirited engagement. I found myself in a foxhole near the left flank of my platoon line when a determined rush by EESC troops threatened to overwhelm us. They pressed close, in some instances just yards away. The men in the holes next to me were dead or wounded, leaving me in a very vulnerable position. I could hear the enemy soldiers as they rustled leaves and crunched twigs and loose stones as they closed in on my position. I emptied my cartridge magazine, the experimental L3 laser rifles were only being tested on the Moon, and was fumbling around my utility pouch to retrieve a fresh clip when I was rushed. At that very moment when death stared me in the face, this crazed lunatic came charging out into the open from about seventy feet to my left-rear, his automatic rifle blazing fire in all directions. He dropped three men not twenty feet from my foxhole and charged deranged across my platoon front and down the hill, screaming and yelling like a Visigoth barbarian possessed by demons, those bloodcurdling shrieks of anger and demented rage echoing fiendishly in the darkness. His actions that night saved my life and I dare say the lives of several others as well. We found his mangled body before we withdrew, about thirty yards down the slope." Reynolds paused with a heavy breath, his eyes lifting towards the ceiling beseechingly. "How can I ever repay that debt?" His shoulders abruptly twisted as he swiveled to look at Matt, an arm resting rigidly on the back of the pew. Matt could see the moisture building in his eyes as he valiantly struggled to contain his emotions, but his voice remained tranquil and unbroken. "What made him do it?" he questioned in bewilderment, his hands talking now. "A black man that I had never laid eyes on before. Why did he charge like that?" His head dropped in remorse once more. "He'd still be alive today if only...."

"If only what, Tom?" Matt sternly interrupted, unable to quietly sanction this self incrimination. "If he hadn't reenlisted? If there had never been a war? If your platoon had been sent somewhere else? If you had been an accountant instead of a soldier?" Matt pressed forward again, speaking more serenely. "I'm sure you're aware that there are things in life that just can't be explained or understood. You just have to have faith in whatever it is that you believe in that there is a reason and move on."

"I have faith," Reynolds proudly proclaimed as he nodded in understanding. "It is one of the few things that has helped me live with my war experiences." His tone became more melancholy. "All but this one. It lives in my dreams. That mad, reckless dash into the enemy and those diabolical screams seem to haunt my subconscious. I guess that I feel a certain amount of guilt knowing that I should have been lying dead out there while he goes back home to his wife." Reynolds devoutly took hold of the picture displayer that Matt respectfully returned, his finger pointing at the young woman as a tiny smile formed across his sullen lips. "His wife, Sonia, what a fine lady. She was very grateful for the letters I wrote to her about the bravery of her husband and a little something about the lives of the boys he saved that night. Keeping his memory alive is about all I can do. Even my wife has been corresponding with her."

The two men sat somberly for several moments before Reynolds shot Matt an inquisitive expression. "Tell me truthfully, Matt, do you pray?"

Matt slumped as he fidgeted restlessly, biting his lower lip, feeling a little embarrassed or ashamed if he was going to be forthright. He wasn't quite sure. "Honestly, Tom, not very much. I'm afraid. Unlike you, my faith has been waning lately. Probably ever since the betrayal of my wife." His eyes began to listlessly wander around the chapel. "Oh, I believe in God all right, but my devotion is lacking. Ever since my divorce I've seen misfortune, illness, and death befall the upright and decent while the unprincipled, the corrupt, and the devious seem to get wealth and fame and get away with all sorts of crime against law and morality. Respectful, hardy people trying to hack out a new life on an unforgiving world didn't deserve whatever affliction compelled them to abandon this place. Honorable men like yourself are tormented by past unfortunate events while others live prosperous, self-gratifying lives without the slightest concern for the welfare of another human being. Am I supposed to see God's design in all of this?"

Reynolds welcomed the opportunity to share some of his personal philosophy. "I'm afraid, Matt, that you may have a mistaken impression of faith," he said in his normal calm but decidedly more chipper voice. "Faith in God doesn't prevent bad things from happening to good people. It gives a person the strength and reassurance to endure and persevere over the misfortunes and obstacles of life as well as to develop an appreciation for the good things that happen. I believe that God uses people in crisis."

"I guess that we all have our crosses to bear, my friend," Matt remarked as he shifted his weight. "That struggle helps define who we are."

Their conversation was interrupted by the heightening sound of heavy thuds of leather boots that heralded the arrival of a third party. The attention of both was simultaneously directed to the back of the room where they had difficulty identifying the dark face obscured in the looming shadows of the subdued light.

"Excuse me, Lieutenant Reynolds, your presence is required in the common eatery, sir." His voice was powerful and gruff. "We have a little problem." The voice belonged to Sergeant Douglas. "Actually," he continued upon noticing that Matt was with him, " I need both you sirs."

Reynolds looked at him vaguely. "Oh! What's up, Sergeant?"

"Private Walinski and that civilian pilot, sir, that's what's up?"

Matt exchanged glances of annoyance with Reynolds before jumping to his feet, recalling the little wrestling entanglement aboard ship. "What have those idiots done now?" he mumbled to himself.

The dining court in the hub of the commerce level was much smaller in diameter than other communal centers due to the elongated wedge construction of the surrounding merchant units. It was a place where the workers in A and C as well as the business and their customers could eat lunch or dinner and get a snack. Several small take-out establishments were interspersed around the perimeter, all closed, of course. Not as elaborate as its counterpart in the Residential Dome, it had groups of round, creme tables separated by small geometrical garden plots of Earth-type flowers, now all withered, dried-up and decaying from lack of attention. One section was completely disrupted, with numerous tables and chairs upended and lying on their sides. Trays of half-eaten food packs and portions of their contents littered the concrete floor, tiny puddles of drink lying dormant by their fallen, empty cups. To his left, Matt saw a couple of marines and Doctor Oliver gathered around the seated, slumping frame of Private Walinski, the Doctor applying ointment to his battered face. To his right sat a weary Jackson Shoals, his usually meticulously groomed blond hair in total disarray, recoiling and grimacing from the sting from antiseptic spray as Caroline Hart hovered over him, dabbing at the blood trickling from the corners of his mouth.

"What happened here, Sergeant?" Reynolds disgustingly inquired.

"The two men became involved in a spirited disagreement, sir."

Matt rubbed his chin thoughtfully before facing the Sergeant. "Would this disagreement, by chance, be tall, blond, and have mountains of gold?"

Sergeant Douglas had great difficulty suppressing a grin of amusement. "I believe that it does, sir. It seems that the men discovered that the young lady had made arrangements with both of them this evening."

Matt and Reynolds shook their heads in dismay and frustration before approaching their respective subordinates. Jack became instantly defensive upon noticing his captain's approach.

"I know what you're going to say, Matt. Just let me say ...."

"I don't want to hear it now, Jack!" Matt angrily bellowed, his facial muscles straining with tension. "Get yourself cleaned up and report to me in A and C in twenty minutes. Understood, Mister?"

"Yes, sir."

Matt was fuming and cursing all the way to the Administrator's office. He wasn't so naive to think that interpersonal conflicts wouldn't erupt between such divergent groups of people thrust together in such extraordinary circumstances, but to have a one of his crew engage in brawling with a member of the support team, a passenger of the ship, was intolerable. He would have liked to have busted his butt, relieved him of duty, bit his flying talents, not to mention his optimistic self-confidence, were still very much in demand for the duration of this assignment. The closed-door meeting was boisterous and pointed with Matt launching into a tirade over his disappointment and outrage, lecturing his bruised navigator on proper ethical behavior and code of conduct while on a mission. Once he had finished with his verbal tongue-lashing, his face contorted and blistering red with fury, he ran his fingers aggravatingly through his thick black scalp and sat back in his executive chair. After a few moments respite to collect himself, Matt calmly looked at Jack's cut lip and swollen left eye and held out an open hand. "Okay, Jack, let's have it."

Jack sedately lowered his head and cleared his throat as he straightened himself before speaking in a low, chagrined tone. "First I want to apologize for my conduct and lack of discipline. I know my actions reflect badly on the crew of the Guilford Courthouse." His head lifted with renewed vigor and he continued more resolutely. "But, Captain, that byte-brained donkey shit was trying to move in on my night with Lucinda. You just can't sit around trading insults when the affections of a woman are involved. Sometimes the resolution requires a more direct approach."

Matt rolled his eyes in disgust. "You know, I have a sister back home with two boys, seven and five, and she keeps telling me what hellions they are, how I don't know what real stress and tension is until I have children of my own. But looking back on it I realize that I have you, and you're worse! Did it ever occur to that sex-crazed brain of yours that the woman might have some culpability for your predicament." Matt lurched forward, resting his elbows on the desk. "Listen to me, Jack. You can't go around punching-out passengers of our ship, whatever the provocation. And get a few things straight." Pounding the desk with his knuckles, Matt leaped to his feet. "One, that so-called byte-brain donkey shit is a soldier of the United States Space Marines and as such deserves to be referred to with honor and respect. You've had firsthand experience with them in action before, you should know better."

Jack abashedly looked away. "Yes, sir."

Matt's forefinger flew out to join his middle finger as he glared fiercely across the desk. "Two! Has your head been sniffing up your ass the last two weeks? Lucinda Desjardin is not your woman! From what I've been hearing she's slept with half the men on this mission and probably a couple of the women too. She's an out-of-control sexual inferno. You're bound to get burned if you play with her fire. You know how she is and the depth of her appetite. If you don't like playing by those rules, then get out of the game. Can't you see she's playing you guys for saps, disposable toys, have her fun and move on to another." Matt reached forward with his two extended fingers and lightly tapped Jack on the forehead. "Sound familiar? Start thinking with this head for a change instead of the other one."

Jack suppressed a muted chuckle. "Yes, sir."

Matt extended a third finger. "And three. I don't give a rat's turd how important you are to me. If you ever get involved in fisticuffs with anyone else again, I'll personally throw your unruly ass into the brig!"

Jack sat quietly with a puzzled look to his bruised face, finally remarking insouciantly. "We don't have a brig."

Matt irritably jolted forward, his hips digging into the edge of the desk as he thumped his chest with his fist. "I'll build one!" he hollered with contrived indignation.

Jack meekly slumped as Matt reseated himself. "Yes, sir."

Matt clasped his fingers together and mindlessly began to rock in the chair. "As a consequence for your actions, I'm restricting you to your quarters at night for the duration of the storm."

Jack's disappointment was apparent, casting the pout of a lost puppy. "Yes, sir. Does that mean I'm forbidden to see Lucinda?"

Matt snickered to himself in farcical disillusionment, amazed at how the charms of that woman had so captivated his psyche. "No, Jack, it means that you are forbidden to go to her quarters. Unfortunately, I have no cause to restrict her as well. There is nothing to prevent her from coming to your room. You're not under arrest....yet."

That clarification seemed to brighten Jack's attitude considerably. Matt understood that he could only demand a professional level of conduct while on duty and a certain level of civility while off, but an individual's interpersonal relations was his own business. As much as he would have liked to impress some sense into his navigator, Jack was free to mess-up his own life. "All right, Jack, drag that sorry carcass of yours out of here."

After dinner that evening, Matt and Vijay studiously sat across the oval, smoked glass dinette table in Matt's quarters hovering over a walnut chess board. Their concentration suffered minor distractions from the distant soft chatter and girlish giggles coming from Sheri and Caroline, casually lounging on the sectional sofa in the living room. Matt couldn't help but pickup bits and pieces of their lively conversation, the gist of which centered on the event involving Jack and Caroline's infatuating encounter with the gallant Corporal Cooke. Matt mused privately. It amazed him how women could expend so much energy, enthusiasm and words on such trivial matters of the day, yet often become lethargic and apathetic when the conversation involved more cosmic significance. But then again, he was forgetting about Susan Oliver. He whimsically pondered on why that was so. That alone would be enough to throw him off his game, but his mind was silently battling an even more inauspicious distraction. Those preoccupation's quickly had him down two pawns and a bishop.

"Once more your mind is not on the game," Vijay remarked with an air of disquietude as he held up a recently captured piece. "Are you still thinking about that little fracas involving Jack?"

Matt leisurely sat back with a desultory flick of his wrist. "Nahhh, that's done. What really has me worried is that geologist, uhhh....Sabatini. This storm has been raging for nearly three full days and we haven't heard a peep from him."

Vijay casually twitched his shoulders indifferently. "That is not necessarily bad, Matt. He would be unable to contact us if he has taken refuge in the mine. His suit transmitter cannot reach this far."

"And if he doesn't panic," Matt fretfully added. "We need to go out there and find him."

Vijay turned to petrified wood, glaring at Matt in disbelief. "You cannot send someone out there in this storm!" Vijay protested doggedly.

"Who send anything about sending someone?" Matt replied as he turned his head waywardly to the side. "You don't have to be a soldier or scientist to walk fifteen miles, you know."

Vijay staunchly held out his hand objectionably. "No, no, wait just one damn minute. You don't think that you are going after him?"

Matt leaned forward with a voice fraught with eagerness. "I can stay on the road by following the transponder poles. They're positioned only about 200 feet apart. I can walk directly from pole to pole all the way."

"That's suicide!" Vijay roared as his husky frame animatedly jerked in distress. "You cannot see five feet in front of you! I believe the colonists referred to it as red-out. You will tumble into a depression or stumble over a jagged rock and that would end your trip real quick."

"Well we just can't sit around here twiddling our thumbs when someone could be in trouble," Matt implored resolutely. "We have to do something!"

Matt had that rigid, intense look about him that Vijay had come to understand meant that his mind was determined and uncompromising. Overhearing fragments of the debate, Sheri anxiously stretched her head above the back of the padded sofa, her inflections reflecting heartfelt concern for his safety. "Matt, what are you planning on doing?"

"Jumping off the deep end," Vijay drolly replied as he vigorously flung back his wheeled chair and rose to his feet, pointing towards Matt with his right hand. "Talk to him, Sheri. See if you can pound some sense into that thick skull of his."

Matt looked at Vijay curiously. "Where are you going?"

"I need air," Vijay earnestly replied. "Listen, Matt, give me some time to think of something before you try to pull some crazy stunt. I'll talk to you in the morning." Vijay paused in thought, rubbing the tiny, scratchy nubs of the day's growth on his sturdy brown chin. "Let me talk to Garett. He may have some inspirational insights."

Matt checked his watch. "It's getting pretty late to be calling on folks, don't you think?"

Vijay glared at him scornfully with a resolve equal to his own. "I'll wake him!"

CHAPTER

The blistering gales howled and shrieked like demented sirens across the Martian countryside as the gargantuan robotics ore hauler crawled along the compressed, windswept dirt road that led to mine shaft N2, powerful gusts causing the newly installed aluminum roof to buckle and shimmy under its fury. The mining workhorse resembled a cabless dump truck, but more massive, long and rectangular, about the size of a railroad freight car. It was basically all open-air bulk ore hopper, chassis, and tread, its thick gray steel walls beveled, broad, and steep, wider at the top like an obese, stubby funnel. The nose of this hulk, lying directly above the front suspension, consisted of a six-foot square black metal box that contained the programming controls and electronic brain. It was capped by a three-foot diameter half-sphere with a thin two-foot projection reaching upward at an angle that ended in a light bulb shaped low frequency receiver. This instrument intercepted electronic signals sent by transponders, firmly cemented three-foot high metallic poles topped with thick, upright disks and painted either blue or yellow, and deciphered the message that guided the hauler safely along the road. The transponders were intermittently arrayed along both sides of the road and strategically placed to avoid all obstacles and hazards, positioned like the gates of an Olympic downhill course, telling the robot to keep to the left or right of each pole. On a clear day the path looked like a blossoming field of meandering lollipops in Candyland.

Deep within the cold, dingy belly of this beast sat Matthew Maitland, apprehensively listening through his external helmet receiver to the peppering, rasping roar of thousands of micron particles smashing against the outer steel skin like unrelenting waves of tiny unfettered hailstones dribbling off a tin roof. But he was not alone. Vijay and Garett, the architects of this resourceful endeavor, sat passively to his left, insisting on accompanying him in case of breakdown, most mechanical things having an aversion to dust buildup. Opposite them sat a marine escort consisting of Corporal Cooke, Private Walinski, and Private Warwick. And to his right was the indomitable Doctor Susan Oliver. He whimsically wondered how he managed to get himself into this fix.

Vijay and Garett had worked all night formulating the plan. It was Garett who conceived the idea of utilizing a robotics ore hauler as combination transport and Seeing-Eye dog. Together they powered and programmed the robot for the journey and spent several hours scavenging the warehouse and manufacturing facilities for additional materials. Once Matt had ecstatically approved the plan the next morning, they managed to enlist the aid of several marines and proceeded to make some modifications to the hauler. They ransacked rooms from the second subterranean level of the Residential Dome with almost perverse glee, ripping out mattresses and bedding to use as lining for the floor of the hopper in order to provide a more comfortable ride. Vijay managed to find a supply of aluminum sheet metal which they managed to cut into panels that roughly matched the dimensions of the open top of the hopper. Industriously they worked together through the morning, interlocking, bolting, and welding the panels together so as to construct a roof under which they could shelter. It was early afternoon by the time they loaded medical supplies, various miscellaneous equipment, emergency water and rations, and the bulky ore hauler crept out of the processing plant at a whopping ten miles per hour.

Barely a third of the way into their trip, the affects of the whipping dust was becoming a nuisance. The bright yellow helmets and silvery-gray of the civilian environment suits was tarnished by a thin film of rust colored powder. Looking up in the glow of the light cast by several small, square battery powered fluorescent lanterns, Matt could make-out a thin haze of fluttering, sprinkling particles permanently suspended in the air throughout the hopper. This micron-sized debris was just impossible to keep out. Matt gravely worried just how far the robot could travel before its mechanics and circuitry became to saturated to operate properly. Like the impulsive scratching induced by the itch of poison ivy, the rescuers constantly used their gloved fingers to brush away the settling dust from their suits. The grime wasn't as apparent on the dull, deep bronze of the marine outfits, but the reflective glistening of the particles in the subdued light made their presence undeniable. The mattresses were soiled with reddish-brown splotches and the floor already had a carpet several inches deep. The marines playfully scooped-up handfuls of the dust and leisurely tossed them over each other's boots.

"I haven't been in a sandbox since I was five," Walinski remarked with a cackle as he sieved a handful through his fingers.

"You mean it's been three years." Warwick sarcastically countered.

"Has anyone ever wondered what it would be like to be buried alive," Cooke rhetorically queried as he stared engrossingly at his partially engulfed boot. "We may find out today."

"My wife and kids once buried me in the sand during a vacation at Daytona Beach," Vijay freely admitted. "Everything but my head."

"And they dug you out?" Matt humorously questioned.

Vijay turned his head and nonchalantly shrugged his shoulders. "Well they really didn't have much choice. You see, I kept all our credit and debit cards in my shorts."

As everyone shared a brief chuckle, Matt noticed that Doctor Oliver had retracted into a more secluded world, assiduously scanning some text on her portable data terminal that she had propped on her lap. He could already see tiny russet freckles forming on the monitor screen and input pad. "Catching up on the latest medical papers, Susan?" Matt uneasily inquired as he gingerly leaned towards her.

"Just some personal correspondence," she indifferently replied without lifting her eyes from the screen.

"I wouldn't keep that thing open too long with all this dust flying around," Matt good-naturedly said. "You don't want to get it mucked-up."

"Thank you, but I'm about finished." Susan paused briefly while she finished reading the displayed note before sitting back and turning to Matt with some facetious advice. "I wouldn't be too concerned about it, Matt. It's just an exchange of ideas and philosophy with progressive, open-minded, liberal thinking friends. Not the cold-hearted, greedy, uncaring types that you're used to hanging around with."

Matt felt a sudden rush of rage nipping at the heels of his emotions but valiantly tried to temper his response with a little frivolity. "Ah, yes, of course," he replied with a nod. "Those same open-minded caring thinkers that sent most of Europe spiraling down the road of depression for half-a-century and nearly destroyed our country as well. Those same

Utopian ideas that propagated from the 1960's to well into this century that nearly bankrupted us and practically ripped apart the very social fabric of our society. Those self-anointed, high-browed intellectual elitists?"

Susan sneered derisively. "At least we support programs that help the poor and needy and unfortunate. Laws to protect the environment. Somebody has to do something to help the millions of downtrodden across the world. At least my colleagues care, which is more than I can say for you self-centered conservatives."

"There's nothing that the downtrodden face that can't be helped with freedom and a good dose of unbridled capitalism," Matt dogmatically argued, twisting his torso to face her. "Let's just examine, Susan, what nearly a hundred years of that philosophy has done. The more money that was thrown into welfare, the more people became dependent on a government handout. The more money that was put into poverty programs, increasing numbers of people went on poverty assistance. As the government engaged in increasing levels of wealth transfers, the tax burden on workers became enormous, pushing more working people into assistance programs. I calculated my total taxes last year to be about twenty percent, and I thought that was outrageous! I remember my grandfather telling me that at the turn of the century, the effective tax burden exceeded sixty percent. That's not only crazy, it's immoral! It surprises me that there wasn't a revolution right then. Despite all this revenue, government spending soared out of control, the debt ballooned to trillions of dollars. Excessive regulation and taxes stifled business, punished achievement, and discouraged the entrepreneurial spirit. Unemployment went up while productivity went down. At the same time, that progressive thinking was shredding the American culture. Multiculturalism crap Balkanized many urban areas where they ceased becoming a melting pot and nearly turned into their own little countries where English was almost a foreign language. Psycho babble bullshit from your elitist friends was offered to excuse every form of aberrant behavior, where personal responsibility was warped into blaming society. Criminals were coddled and pampered while the law abiding were taxed, regulated, disarmed, and terrorized by ever increasing levels of crime. Partial birth abortions were committed by the thousands while the same proponents decried as immoral the use of the death penalty for convicted murderers. It became a bigger crime to talk disparagingly about certain protected groups than murder and assaults. Permissive attitudes fostered rampant teenage pregnancy and drug use. There were greater outcries over smoking and fatty foods than illegal substance abuse. Government assistance programs simply encouraged and subsidized undesirable behavior. Parents, caught up in a materialistic world, pursued their own personal gratification while allowing strangers and the state to raise their kids. Marriage and family was vilified and ridiculed as quaint and old-fashioned except when it involved homosexuals. God and values were taken out of schools and condoms put in. A lack of standards and inhibiting competition dumbed-down students and failed to prepare them for the challenges of life. College graduates couldn't multiply or divide or even find Kansas on a map. Historical truths were twisted and distorted into politically correct garbage. Media bias intentionally misled the population and actively promoted the left wing agenda. Shall I go on?"

Susan scoffed in agitation, having long since ignored the substance of his dissertation. "No disrespect intended, Matt. You are a competent captain but sometimes you are so full of shit that it makes me nauseous."

Matt turned away, bobbing his head comically. "There you have it, a typical liberal reaction. When confronted with irrefutable facts they resort to name calling." Irascibly spinning back to face her, Matt forcefully continued. "The truth is, Susan, liberalism has been an abject failure wherever it's been tried. Forget good intentions, just look at the results. You can deny the truth until your cheeks turn blue but that is the legacy your utopian philosophy has left us all. I would think that liberals would have seen the errors of their ways by now but I keep forgetting, it's not really about people's well being, it's about power. The greatest threat to freedom, and I dare say the human spirit, is liberalism." Matt settled back against the padding and breathed deeply, looking vacantly ahead. "At least the Great Conservative Economic Movement took hold in the thirties and rolled back many of these government restrictions and redistribution programs. That and the newly born space colonization industry is the only thing that has revitalized our economy and given us our current prosperity. Unfortunately the social pendulum is just beginning to swing back to some semblance of sanity. It will take decades to undo the damage that's been done."

"I see that we hopelessly disagree on just about everything," Susan replied with unusual calm. "Most of those failures you cited were precisely because not enough was done, and some of the others I don't see as failures at all, just small steps towards a perfectly harmonious society. I'm for government helping people and providing a better life in every way it can. You sound like you don't want any democratic government at all."

"No, no," Matt chuckled with a shale of his head. "I'm for limited government, a less intrusive government. The record of the last hundred years doesn't indicate much help, does it? I believe that government can best help its citizens by getting out of the way. Taking the shackles off and allowing the individual to do and be the best he can be. That also means the freedom to make mistakes and to fail. The Founding Fathers never intended for the central government to be everyone's safety net. It's supposed to be an instrument that ensures that the people, both individual and collectively have the opportunity to pursue their own ambitions."

"And what happens to those who fail? Who need help?" Susan questioned somewhat cynically.

Matt reached over with a crooked grin and patted her affectionately above the knee. "That's when, Susan, the family, community organizations and you and your compassionate, caring friends come in. But that is not the role of the central government, that is, everyone who pays taxes. With the exception of our good friends over there," Matt motioned towards the marines, "and their brothers, the military, there is nothing much the federal government has done very well or efficiently. I think you'll find that people living with the blessing of unbridled freedom and liberty are the most generous, compassionate of all. If you ask me, it's liberals who don't care about other people, passing on that responsibility to the federal government so they don't need to be bothered and liberal politicians create a whole dependent class of voters." Matt checked his watch and brushed away an accumulation of dust from his suit before reclining back once more. "One day they'll be relegated to a natural history museum."

Susan folded her arms and scoffed incredulously. "Excrement! We've seen our greedy and insensitive individuals can be. Only a collective, centralized action can ensure equality and prosperity for all." Susan turned away, still fuming inside. She knew her philosophy was right, there just wasn't any evidence to support it.

The wide rubber treads continued to cautiously crunch and rumble along the frozen road, slashing a capacious path through the flying debris and gloomy murkiness of cloudy daylight like a Cossack wielding his razor-sharp blade. The robot reliably followed the circuitous course defined by the electronic transponders for the ninety minutes that it took to traverse the distance to the mine without incident, groping to a cumbersome halt just before the road banked sharply to the right to move around the side of the hill to the loading shaft. Garett's programming was impressive. Their destination was the main mine entrance, now situated some 200 yards directly ahead. With hyperaccurate topographical maps scaled to the yard, he was able to program the robot to travel the desired distance and to stop at the predetermined location. Garett punched some numbers into his remote control pad and checked the digital display.

"We're here, Commander," he proudly and vivaciously announced. "The mine entrance should be directly ahead of us."

"Then get us out of here, Mister Yamakawa," Matt instructed.

Punching some buttons on the remote, Garett was able to electronically lower the rear wall slowly as everyone struggled to their feet, shaking off the thin layer of dust that covered their suits and loosening their stiffened joints. The visible countryside from their rearward panorama was obscured in a profusion of dark, gloomy rustic shades, large clumps of reddish-brown material repeatedly whisking by, oscillating wildly in the stalwart flurry. Corporal Cooke tossed down a rope ladder with rubber sheathed rungs and one-by-one the travelers mindfully climbed out of the belly of the giant hopper and onto the compact, wind swept dirt road.

"John, take the point," Corporal Cooke ordered. "Andy, bring up the rear."

"Everyone please stay close to the person in front of you," Matt added as he stringently grabbed people by the arm and forced them together. "It will be easy to go astray out here. Let's get moving."

With Private Walinski leading the way, the human line gingerly crept towards the mine shaft, passing the right bend in the road onto a less compact one used by light rovers carrying personnel to the entrance. The high-pitched howl of the tumultuous gusts whistled and crackled in reverberating ripples through Matt's external helmet receiver but he found walking against these currents no more laborious than moving against a stiff autumn breeze back on Earth; the considerably weaker air pressure creating much less resistance. Cyclonic dust devils of infinitesimal sands and clays whirling high into the air and dense globs blasting into faceshields greatly impaired visibility. Staying focused on the point man was a challenge and only the largest of boulders along the roadside could be identified. At times it was like ruby starbursts exploding in front of them, not unlike the disconcerting, hypnotic affects of a snow blizzard, and one had to guard against the possibility of dust blindness. The entire world around them, from the frozen crustal clays to the heavens was bathed in eerie and murky reddish tints. They had traveled about a hundred yards when Walinski's excited voice rang out within everyone's helmet.

"I see a vehicle ahead!"

Like the tightly wrapped coils of a spring, each person in turn bounded forward after the one in front of them, briskly pacing towards the parked frame of an exploratory rover resting innocently in a widened plowed lot to the left constructed for that purpose. As the party inquisitively scattered around the transport, Corporal Cooke climbed the small metal stairs, opened the airlock, and stepped inside. Not noticing any apparent damage, Matt looked to the west where he could make out large portions of the looming, rugged, bald hills under which the mine was dug. He could barely discern through the lighter clumps of blowing fines an expansive darkened hole at the base, about eighty yards away, that must have sheltered the main entrance. His attention was suddenly diverted by a succinct, casual voice of Corporal Cooke as he reemerged from the bowels of the rover.

"No one inside, Commander," he reported during his descent and leap to the hardened surface. "In fact, it looks as if it's been uninhabited for days." With rifle leisurely grasped in his right hand, he sought out Matt. "The emergency rations and supplies are still stowed in place, sir."

"He must still be in the mine, God willing," Matt surmised. "Thank you, Corporal, let's move'em out."

"Yes, sir. John, checkout that depression along our right flank. Andy, get everyone back on the road."

As the small parade pressed on, Walinski cautiously crept along the edge of a steep ravine that fell away just a few feet from the shoulder.

"Watch your step, John," Cooke anxiously warned. "Don't get too close to the edge. There's loose rubble all over the place."

"I would, Bob," he jokingly replied, "if I could see my boots."

About midway between the parking lot and the mine entrance, Private Walinski noticed that a small piece of the embankment appeared to have recently broken away, looser, richer-looking red clay lying exposed to the frigid air, and finer particles being driven downwind by the breeze. Curious, the soldier inched closer to the precipice and gazed down into the narrow, scabby crevice. Through the raging dust, large patches of glistening silver grabbed his attention, lying inert on a rock outcropping about twenty feet below as mounds of ruddy particles drifted over top. As the howling winds constantly altered the visible scene, Walinski began to perceive a familiar form and finally caught a glimpse of something that looked like a yellow beach ball. "Over here, sir!" he frantically called out. "I found a body!"

Matt's head jerked to the right in alarm in conjunction with everyone else, just in time to watch the obscured, dusty form of Private Walinski perilously disappear below the ledge of the ravine.

"John!" Cooke screamed in panic as he raced ahead of the others to the bank. "What the hell are you doing?" The Corporal applied the brakes to his skidding feet on the loosened, hazardous ground barely in time to keep his unbalanced body from tumbling into the chasm below.

Matt followed close behind, firmly clasping the Corporal's shoulders to help steady him. They saw Walinski safely below, hovering over the limp figure and rolling it over on its back.

"It's the geologist, sir. I think he's dead."

The ravine itself dropped about seventy feet to the floor with sharply angled, fluted walls. But what made it treacherous was the icy slickness of the exposed rock and all the loose rubble and dust lying along the slopes. Numerous fat shelves and outcroppings would otherwise make scaling the sides relatively effortless.

"I've got to get down there," Susan Oliver brusquely declared as she impetuously brushed past Matt's shoulder and stepped to the rim. Before Matt could utter the first syllable of protest, her feet slipped on a glassy rock that sent her legs flying over the lip, her ass painfully bouncing off the rugged stone. She shrieked horrifyingly as her body twisted and went soaring into the Martian air, desperately clawing at the jagged edge with her left hand as she began to drop, reaching for Matt's lightning quick extended arm with her right. Matt's fingers clamped tightly around her wrist, breaking her short but tremulous fall. There was a solid landing just a few feet below, but the life-threatening danger was not in the fall but the possible damage to her life-support pack or suit.

"I've got you, Susan, just hang on." Matt strained on his knees to pull her upward. "Corporal," he grunted and groaned. "How's about a little help, please."

Cooke knelt beside Matt and lifted her other arm, but Susan bitterly protested, kicking her legs for leverage against the rock face.

"No! No, you fools! I want to go down. I have to get to Mister Sabatini. Please help me down to that ledge."

"I swear, Susan," Matt grumbled as he held her in place. "That obstinacy of yours is going to get you killed one day."

"John!" Cooke called out. "Work your way over here and give the Doctor a hand down."

Private Walinski used a couple of rock protrusions to climb to the ledge under Susan's dangling form, grabbed her legs and then her hips as he guided her down to solid footing. As Matt and Cooke reclined, breathing a momentary sigh of relief, the Corporal wryly glanced at Matt and mumbled dryly. "Yeah, like maybe by one of us."

Upon reaching the fallen geologist, it only took the Doctor a few seconds to certify that he was , in fact, quite dead, apparently for several days. All body heat was gone, frozen rigid like a popsickle. Saliva and frozen into tiny ice shavings in the corners of his mouth. His brows and forehead were speckled with white-gray crystals of frost as was the inside of his faceshield which displayed a wide, twisting crack. He had a gaping hole ripped out of his suit at the knee and his oxygen regulator had jammed. What happened could never be determined with certainty, but it was surmised that he had been caught in the mine when the storm erupted, panicked, tried to get back to the rover, became disoriented and stumbled off the edge of the ravine. His suit was snagged on a sharp edge and he bounced off a rock, cracking his helmet and damaging his environment pack. That or he was pushed! Even an autopsy required by the NSCA might not determine what killed him first. The fall? Lack of oxygen? CO_2 poisoning? Decompression? Frost bite? To Matt, it really didn't matter. The one thing certain was that the death was agonizing but probably mercifully swift. The only thing that mattered to the anguished souls that gathered around the rim was that the mission had suffered its first fatality.

Matt sunk back on his haunches in helpless dismay. A growing sickness churned within the tightening muscles of his stomach. He began to doubt himself. How could he have allowed someone to go off alone this far from the colony? He couldn't be a protective mother to everyone, of course, but should he have been more strict with the survey teams? He privately lamented, pounding his fist in his hand in frustration and remorse. Whether he could have done something different or not was a moot point now, it was too late for Mister Anthony Sabatini. "Gather up the body, Corporal," Matt ordered despondently as he staggered distraughtly to his feet. "Let's get back to the colony."

Later that evening Matt listlessly sat alone around one of the small tables that surrounded the common park of the Residential Dome, sluggishly picking at the stirred pasta of his half-eaten food pack. Upon his return to Jamestown he had skipped the communal dinner and retired to his quarters to accessed the personnel file of Anthony Sabatini in privacy. Vijay and Garett were also conspicuously absent, choosing instead to spend the evening cleaning out the excessive dust accumulations in the hauler and the retrieved rover, both of which remarkably survived the elements without difficulty. No one was in a particularly talkative mood to deal with the incessant questions invariably leveled by their inquisitive colleagues. Even Sheri's considerate and sympathetic efforts to console Matt's grief fell on deaf ears and he finally suggested that she spend the evening with Caroline so he could have the time to collect his thoughts and compose a letter to the family. He had never before felt like this - disconsolate, uncertain, and ineffectual.

"Buy you a drink?"

Matt shuddered, spinning around in shock, the potent yet serene voice jolting him out of his stupor. It belonged to Lieutenant Reynolds, invitingly holding out two flasks of genuine alcoholic beer.

"Please," Matt politely replied, extending his hand towards the opposite chair. "Where did you get these?" he curiously inquired as Reynolds leisurely took his seat and placed a cool, sweating insulated flask in front of him.

Reynolds lifted his shoulders and insouciantly replied with a smug intonation. "Some of the men found a case yesterday in the storeroom of one of the restaurants. I had to confiscate it, of course."

"Of course," Matt satirically mocked. "You're a pirate! I'll admit that I have an unopened bottle of Scotch in my quarters. It may not survive the night."

They each took a couple of measured swallows, looking aimlessly around in clumsy silence. Finally Matt lowered the flask to the table and peered directly across at Reynolds. "You're to be complimented, Lieutenant. Those boys with me today performed courageously and professionally."

Reynolds dipped his head in appreciation. "Thank you, Matt. I'm fortunate. They're good men, I would expect nothing less of them." He paused, taking another prodigious gulp. "Listen, Matt. I got the details from Corporal Cooke's report," he commented softly as he leaned forward, using a forefinger to wipe away a dribble of liquid from the corner of his mouth.

"When you're involved in space missions as much as you, something like this is bound to happen. Space colonization is a very risky business."

"I know, Tom, I know," Matt hastily replied, glancing to the side with sorrowful regret. "But understanding that doesn't help." A thousand little disturbing morsels of thoughts and perceptions tossed and blended within the synapses of his brain, his face growing vacant as he stared off into the void. "He was 43, had a wife and....three children." His monotone vice became more impassioned as he folded his arms across his chest and turned back to the Lieutenant. "I've been reviewing his file. Did you know that he was on the first survey team that landed on the asteroid Ceres?"

Reynolds cracked a half-smile as he shook his head. Matt drooped again, twisting his head as he ruefully grimaced in disgust with himself. "He was a member of my support team...." His hand pounded his chest. "My team! He was a passenger on my ship for a week and I barely knew anything about him. Not his interests, his hopes, or his experiences." His hands briefly flung into the air in exasperation. "Hell! I couldn't even remember his first name!" Matt quickly took another generous swallow from his flask. "Tell me, Tom," he gently implored as he bent over the table, "you've lost men before. How do you get over this?"

Reynolds sat back and turned to the side, taking several pronounced gulps before frowning and slamming the flask distraughtly on the table surface. "You don't."

Matt silently moaned in anguish as he slumped back, feeling confused and frustrated. Reynolds sensed his dilemma and understood all too well what he was experiencing. "In my business, an officer quickly discovers that when the first man dies you die too. If you stick around long enough one thing is certain - there will be others, you can count on it. About all you can do is use everything in your power to minimize the losses and carry on. Pickup the flag and move forward. You understand what I mean."

Matt still felt sick, bringing a hand to his throbbing forehead. "In other words, get used to it."

"No, no," Reynolds replied with a subtle twist, "you never get used to it."

Matt opened his hands beseechingly towards Reynolds. "What do I say to his wife? His children? How do I write them?"

Reynolds shrugged unwittingly. "I don't know. There's no magic formula." He pondered momentarily, thoughtfully rubbing his chin before a ray of wisdom brightened his expression. "Write to them the way you would want someone to write to your wife and kids." He pressed close with a tone of heartfelt sincerity. "Don't think too much. Just tell them what's in your heart and it will be fine. I'm sure they would appreciate that." Reynolds rose to his feet and moved past Matt, giving him a brotherly pat on the shoulder as he walked by. "Check the soul of Matthew Maitland. He's a pretty good guy."

Later that evening Matt found himself aimlessly reclining in the cushioned lounge chair in the darkened solitude of his quarters in an unshakable state of melancholy, surrounding a tall, tawny Scotch and soda. He had just finished composing the condolence letter and would include its contents with the next scheduled communiqué to NSCA headquarters. The tormenting soul-searching continued, making it impossible for him to rest. With the unyielding nature of the environment that engulfed them and the series of bizarre mishaps, it was a wonder that it hadn't happened earlier. But that hardly eased his pain. The haunting silence of his meditation was resoundingly broken by the steady, melodious beeping coming from his door speaker. Wearily Matt climbed out of the comfort of his chair and staggered to the control panel near the entrance, adjusting up to normal the brightness of the ceiling lighting grids and activating the external intercom. "Yes?"

"May I see you, Commander? It's Lucinda."

Matt leaned back against the wall and growled in exasperation, rubbing his hands over his eyes. "It's awfully late, Lucinda. Can't it wait till morning?"

"Maybe, but I have something I think you'll want to look at right away. It's important."

Matt sighed reluctantly. "Very well." He hurriedly tucked in the tail of his navy T-shirt with CAS Guilford Courthouse logo into his cotton denim trousers, rapidly ran a comb through his disordered black hair and automatically slid the door open into its wall compartment. His eyes were immediately entranced by the voluptuous beauty that sensually strutted through the doorway with long, extravagantly flowing, succulent golden locks. She was provocatively attired as always in a form-clinging, short sleeve, translucent, chiffon silk white blouse with the top snaps strategically undone to expose the upper recesses of deep cleavage. The lacy designs of her revealing white bra were easily seen protruding snugly against the thin material. A pleated, floppy-hem cherry red mini-skirt wrapped tightly around her hips and struggled to cover her creamy upper thighs. Fishnet stockings of the same color encased her long, smooth legs. She was sporting that come-on look that she was so good at projecting, those thin pouting lips with the heavy rose lipgloss, infectious girlish smile, those twinkling, mystical green eyes that pleaded and tugged at a man's soul.

"I hope I'm not intruding on anything," she apologized as she perched seductively against the wall, one foot raised and resting against it which alluringly lifted the short hem of her skirt, her arms locked behind her, erotically thrusting out her breasts.

Matt was suddenly feeling very awkward and uncomfortable as he tried to resist the compulsion to lecherously scan her, not to much success. "No, mot at all," he replied as he took a few steps towards the cushioned sectional before facing her once more. "Just doing some quiet thinking."

"That's a shame," she remarked with a crafty grin and an engaging tilt of her head. "A handsome, self-confident man like yourself shouldn't be spending his evenings alone. I have something for you."

Suppressing his lustful urges, Matt rolled his eyes in disgust and scoffed. "Some of us don't care to spend all our nights under the sheets. Permit me to be perfectly blunt, Lucinda. You have something for everybody." He snickered. "You know, some of the others are beginning to refer to you as gravity woman."

Lucinda glanced at him oddly.

Matt shrugged. "Because you seem to attract all matter. I was about to pour myself a drink, would you like one?"

Lucinda tossed back her head and laughed. "No, thank you. At least not now. I haven't heard that one before. Surely it must be because of my magnetic personality." Slowly she sauntered forward, swinging her shoulders and sucking in her lower lip. "I just enjoy the pleasures of the flesh. I've never experienced a ship's captain before."

Matt threw out his hands defensively. "And you're not going to now. Stop right there, Miss Desjardin. I'm a little tired of your...."

"But that's not why I'm here," she interrupted as a more serious countenance overtook her. "At about the time you were returning, I managed to unscramble the disk." From behind her back she produced the enigmatic software.

"What!" Matt exclaimed in astonishment as he grabbed the plastic sleeve from her hand. "Why didn't you inform me right away?"

"It took me some time to verify and then I was told not to disturb you. But I didn't think it should wait for morning. Besides, I thought you should see it before the others."

A sudden fear caused Matt to shudder as he looked at Lucinda apprehensively. "What's on it?"

She took a nervous, hard swallow. "It's from David Hart. But I think that you should just come with me to A and C and see for yourself."

Together they tore out of Matt's quarters and headed for the elevator, stopping briefly at the makeshift guardpost nearby. Private Anderson had the watch, sitting alertly behind a simple aluminum table, its top cluttered with an assortment of equipment and weaponry. His sandy-brown hair along the fringes of his olive helmet, youthful, beardless complexion, and boyish grin soon put them at ease as he stepped out from behind the table upon learning of their plans for the next hour, handing to Matt a set of scanners and a communicator.

"If your return is going to be delayed for any reason, sir, please notify this station at once. Also, if you run across anything unusual, call immediately and help will be dispatched."

"Thank you, Private," Matt restlessly replied as he slung the scanners over his shoulder.

"One last thing, sir," Anderson continued as he pick-up an automatic pistol, slammed in a clip of armor piercing rounds, and cocked a round into the chamber. "For close encounters." Gripping the barrel, he offered the weapon to Matt.

"What am I supposed to do with this?" Matt naively questioned as he hesitantly accepted the handle.

"Point it at the bad guys and pull the trigger, sir," he coolly replied with a straight face.

Matt grimly pondered the possibility, confronted again with the realization that their situation was still a very precarious one. "I hear you, Private. Back in an hour." Matt took a diverting note of Anderson's licentious trance directed towards his alluring partner. "That's okay, soldier," he muttered softly. "She has that affect on everyone."

The lift carried them to the ground floor where they proceeded to the tunnel that linked them to the Administrative Dome, boarded a four seat burgundy shuttle cart, and drove the roughly two-thirds mile. With a touch of enchantment, Matt curiously gazed at Lucinda's exposed thighs and her dressy attire. "Aren't you a bit overdressed for this?"

Lucinda smiled in delight and chuckled. "For this, perhaps. It gets me more attention than a work suit. I'll be glad to take it off if you like?"

Matt shook his head in bewilderment. "I'd like but never mind."

Upon arrival they raced on foot to the second level where Lucinda assumed her seat by the primary computer terminal. Moving in behind her, Matt noticed several ancillary pieces of unusual rectangular shaped equipment arrayed irregularly to the side and connected to I/O ports on the back of the processor.

"The encryption was affecting the data stream at one of three sources," Lucinda explained as the computer whined and hissed as it came on-line. "Either in the interpretation of the data from the disk drive, the processor's decompression of the video and audio to the appropriate control boards, or the accurate processing of that information from the V/A boards to the display. The latter is where the decoding equipment isolated the anomaly. It would seem that Mister Hart, or someone, inserted a spook into the program."

"Excuse me, a what?" Matt perplexingly asked.

Lucinda spun her chair a quarter turn, giving Matt a self-assured grin of expertise, like some renowned, high-browed scientist explaining his newly formulated theory to a class of college freshman. "It's an invisible, unidentified subroutine embedded within the body of the program that affects data interpretation at some point in the dissemination process until it is either decoded or deleted from the file. It's a bitch of a thing to isolate. This particular spook randomly scrambled the bitmapping imagery of the pixels within the video board before the data reaches the display, sort of like shuffling a deck of cards, so that each set of bits is assigned to the wrong pixel. It also softens the image resolution so all you get is a convoluted dotted matrix of distorted coloration's. The same scrambling jumbled the audio into noisy garble."

Lucinda turned back to the terminal and inserted the disk into the appropriate drive. Matt leaned over her, anchoring his hands atop her shoulder blades. He could only follow a portion of her dissertation which only served to compound the increasing distractions of her charming femininity. His mind wandered into the darker depths of his psyche. He could smell the sweet nectar of her perfume around her neck, the soft lushness of her long blond strands lightly swishing against his arm. His fingers unconsciously began to trace supple lines against the velvety silk across her shoulder.

Lucinda paused and glanced up at him with a libidinous grin. "Are you trying to befuddle me?"

Matt felt embarrassed, abruptly removing his hands and bracing himself against the back of the chair. "Sorry," he mumbled with a tone of chagrin. "That was not my intention." Matt was perplexed about his emotional reactions. He was on the verge of a potentially momentous event yet his thoughts were assailed by erotic fantasies involving a woman for which he had no personal affinity. He wondered if his sexual frustrations ran even deeper than he was ready to admit. His guilt kicked his concentration back to the matter at hand.

"Computer," Lucinda barked. "Run program, drive A."

The introductory screen appeared with the password input request.

"Password, Sweet Caroline."

With a light whine and rumble, the terminal soon displayed the playback selection screen.

"Access file one."

The same rainbow mosaic that displayed on her private monitor popped onto the screen.

"I've linked the computer to a decipher utility that will detect, hunt down, and disable spook subroutines. We call it the Ghostbuster." Her fingers optioned the voice command button once more. "Access auxiliary utility program G.B.1."

"Input file name," the feminine computer voice instructed.

"File name D.E.C dot G.B.1 slash Jamestown. Run."

Matt stared in awe as the color dot image on the monitor shimmied and coalesced like the focusing of a telephoto lens into the sharpened facial and shoulder picture of one David Hart. He was illuminated as if bathed in the glow of a high-intensity spot light but the surroundings behind him were dark and obscure. He was seated behind a desk on a richly padded black executive chair. He was wearing a deep purple T-shirt with an indistinguishable yellow design that extended well below the frame of the monitor. Recalling his photo from the colony personnel files, it appeared to Matt that he had grayed a little around the ears. His hair was longer and disheveled. His facial lines looked drawn and haggard, the glossy-eyed stare and drooping bags below betrayed the restless strain and uneasiness of authoritative responsibility of a colonial operation that had somehow gone gravely astray. The dark shadow of nubby growth around his chin indicated at least a couple days of grooming neglect. Matt carefully listened to the deep, somber voice, steady and forceful but with slight inflections of obvious anxiety mixed in.

"Personal log, Jamestown colony, Martian year 7, day 481 A.S."

Matt did some quick mental conversions. "That was about twelve days before we departed the Constitution."

The After Settlement Martian calendar was instituted 14 Earth years ago by the permanent inhabitants at the time Mars was at aphelion, the farthest point from its elliptical orbit from the sun, beginning with day one, year one. The Martian year consisted of 687 days, the time it takes the planet to make one complete revolution around the sun. There were wide seasonal temperature variations, but since they mainly consisted of cold and colder and there was no moisture fallout from the atmosphere, the colonists had yet to settle the debate on how to subdivide their calendar. At the time they were simply using a graduated numerical scale from 1 to 687 with no monthly delineation. They still referred to weeks when talking about 7 day time periods.

"Please forgive the encoding of this record but I'm afraid that all our computer files may be compromised. If this recording should survive me and you are not an NSCA representative, please get this disk to the appropriate authority on Earth." David Hart paused, breathing heavily, dubiously glancing around as if some dark, ominous presence was lurking nearby. "About 200 days ago we began to be plagued by a series of unusual or mysterious events which have been gradually intensifying. It began as annoying meteorite strikes, unexplained power outages, magnetic field surges, mysterious erasures in some of our computer files, a rash of damaged equipment, and a couple of minor laboratory explosions. Then the thermal and magnetic energy readings that we reported to the north were joined by intermittent electromagnetic displacement readings from the area around Arsia Mons to the southwest. Survey teams were dispatched to both locations. None returned." His fingers ran frustratingly through his uncombed dark hair tinged with streaks of silver before his arm flopped to the desk once more. "Several others have bizarrely disappeared, just vanished into thin air!" He emphasized the point by tossing his hands into the air in hopelessness. "There have been unconfirmed reports of strange sightings within the colony perimeter. Tall, murky gray figures that seemed to come and go within the shadowed corners of the night. Some of the colonists are pressing me to petition the NSCA for extraction or some form of assistance, but I can't sanction that. I've busted my butt the last two years in negotiations with those Earth-bound bureaucrats to grant us complete autonomy. If we want to be independent, we have to start dealing with our own problems. Most seriously, our communications with Earth were mysteriously severed seven days ago and our technicians have been unable to isolate the problem, but I don't rule out the possibility of sabotage. Everyone here may not be as they appear. The EESC research stations are all unmanned, the last team at Chryse Planitia having left for Earth several months ago, so there is no one else left on planet for us to contact. Panic is starting to set in and I'm uncertain how long I can keep this kettle from boiling over. It is my distinct fear that our situation may become untenable."

The display screen immediately faded to a bright shade of blue with the words *END OF MESSAGE* written boldly in white. Both Matt and Lucinda hypnotically stared at it in silent disbelief. Finally Matt exhumed a prolonged whistle of astonishment. "How about that," he mumbled.

"That's not all," Lucinda added vivaciously. "Look at this." She pressed the voice input button. "Display playback selection menu."

When the menu appeared, a second file selection was displayed.

"It's a pancake file," Lucinda confidently explained. "The first file must be played before the second file is offered for selection."

"Play it!" Matt excitedly beseeched.

Lucinda looked up and frowned in disappointment. "I can't. It's protected with a secondary password. I haven't had a chance to work on it."

Matt gave her upper arm a conciliatory pat. "What was he so afraid of that he went to all this trouble to protect his personal log?" he pondered.

Lucinda twisted her torso around, returning an inquisitive gaze. "Maybe he could no longer trust the people around him. Maybe he was afraid the disk would somehow fall into the wrong hands."

"What wrong hands?" Matt doggedly questioned.

Lucinda could only shrug unwittingly. "What do you make of all this, Commander?"

Matt guffawed facetiously. "I think we're all in a little trouble here, my dear. Something traumatic sure as hell went on, that's for certain. We've seen evidence that collaborates parts of his report." Matt wrenched his head and sneered skeptically. "But other aspects of his account lack a shred of proof."

Lucinda crossed her arms snugly and shuddered. "I don't mind admitting that I'm afraid. What are you going to do?"

Matt mindfully stared out through the dome at the blackened night and shook his head. "I haven't a clue." He stood unmoving for a time, immersed in thoughts, before perplexingly looking back at Lucinda. "Something puzzling strikes me though. This was a personal log, right?"

Lucinda straightened as her attention was peaked. "Yes."

"Funny that he made no comment or request regarding his wife."

Lucinda turned away in distress. "Shit! I think that I could use that drink now."

"I need a double," Matt cavalierly replied.

The pressures and tensions of their predicament coupled with the debilitating affects of several drinks were beginning to hold sway over Matt as he mindlessly passed around the perimeter of the sectional unit in his quarters, engaged in incessant chatter with seated Lucinda, their original professional conversation mutating more and more into silly trivialities, idle gossip, and jovial titters and snickers by the minute. The alcohol wasn't the only thing distilling its intoxicating influence. Matt's nervous movements had more to do with the seductive woman parked enchantingly on his sofa, taking every advantage to lecherously examine every angle and curve of her intriguing, enticingly attired landscape. When she moaned in discomfort and raised her arm to rub the back of her neck, Matt was quick to move behind her, tenderly kneading the tightened muscles, slowly moving his hands over the top of her shoulders. Lucinda threw back her head, eyes relaxingly closed, groaning in relief as the tenseness within her ebbed away. Matt was enjoying his vantage point as he loomed over her, instinctively peering down under the opened snaps of her tight blouse at the cavernous valley between her twin, protruding mountains.

"Your fingers feel so good," she whimpered with delight. "My whole back feels like a coiled spring."

Matt took the bait. "Would you like me to give you a back rub?"

Lucinda sighed in contentment as she raised her arms to clasp her fingers around the back of his neck. "That sounds terrific," she cooed. "Then you can work your way around front."

Matt grinned in amusement as his fingers trailed down her sides, watching her twist and squirm as she giggled, savoring her sensual movements before she released her clasp around his neck. Gathering their empty glasses, Matt deposited them in the kitchen and in the seconds it took for him to return, Lucinda was on her feet and had removed her blouse and skirt and was in the process of removing her stockings and garter. Matt petrified in mid-stride, partly in shock and part in lustful awe.

"Why are you doing that?" he timidly asked as he salaciously stared at her.

"Why aren't you stopping me?" she astutely replied.

Matt had no argument for that. "Good point."

Matt gulped hard as he moved into the pit. He had naively fallen into her web and he knew it. But her sensuality and sheer physical beauty were overpowering. He could understand how many men fell under her spell. It wasn't only her magnificent physical attributes but she also knew how to entice and play on a man's drives and ego. She was like an addictive drug for which a man could only crave for more.

Lucinda began to perform like a harem dancer as Matt approached, using her stockings like veils as she fluttered them freely through the air, raising her arms high overhead as she sensually wiggled and undulated. Stripped to her plunging white lace bra and matching French-cut bikini, her movements were extremely arousing. Matt gaped in awe, wondering how a human body could gyrate like that. Lucinda's hips could move faster than her mouth. She sensually backed her rear into him, her cheeks swaying methodically against his hip. He could feel the tightening and burning cramps of desire building within him as he reached out to gently rub the soft skin along her shoulder blades down to the small of her back. When he slid his roaming digits onto her rump she abruptly spun around and playfully flicked the stocking lightly across his face as a mischievous grin came over her. Still wiggling seductively, she continued to finger the stockings as she stretched her arms towards the ceiling and erotically shuffled close to him, grinding and pulsating against his groin, lewdly brushing her wobbling and protruding breasts against his chest. The carnal yearnings surging through his body were becoming overwhelming as he stared ravenously down at the rounded hills lewdly jiggling under his nose.

"Would you like to go to your bedroom?" Lucinda sensually urged.

It was a very attractive offer. He couldn't deny his lustful cravings to sample her ample charms. If they found themselves together on his bed, it wouldn't stop with an innocent massage.

"I....I don't think that would be a good idea," he timorously replied.

Lucinda gave him that enchanting pout and pressed even closer, her hips swaying more pronounced than ever as her legs suggestively widened. "Don't you trust me?"

Matt gulped nervously. "No, no I don't," he bashfully and honestly replied. "But more to the point, I don't trust myself."

Matt executed a deliberate retreat to the cushioned sofa followed closely by Lucinda who sat down beside him and sprawled across his lap.

"As you wish," she remarked as she moved a nearby brown pillow under her head. "My back is still tight."

After what he just witnessed, Matt found that hard to believe. As his fingers slowly kneaded and trailed their soothing magic across her shoulders and back, his thoughts once more centered on purely carnal fantasies regarding this mesmerizing vixen, listening to her melodious purring like that of a contented kitten. His hands moved lower, sliding onto sparsely-clad rump. He enjoyed the sight of the fleshy quivering of her cheeks under the skimpy white cotton. All those licentious images were making Matt mad. It was a purely physical attraction, he realized, but why was he spending his time in a potentially compromising situation with someone he was not particularly fond of when he could be contemplating the same erotic desires with Sheri? For fifteen minutes his fingers massaged her back , rear, and the back of her legs as Lucinda moaned and shuddered as her muscles were loosened and relaxed.

Once mollified, Lucinda rolled off the couch and with a leer of carnal hunger she moved in front of Matt and swished the stocking teasingly across his nose as she straddled his knees, spreading her thighs before crossing her arms behind her back, twirling the stocking around them. "Are you sure there is nothing more you want," she softly implored with an enticing sway. "I'll be yours tonight. I'll do whatever you like."

No, Matt was not at all sure. Having this extremely attractive and voluptuous young woman practically throw herself upon him made his sexual appetite nearly insatiable, not to mention a wonderful boost to his ego. Hypnotically staring at the tiny white triangle in front of his face and the conical mounds above pouring out of their skimpy protective shield, he could think of a hundred things he'd love to do with her. Her erotic oscillations and submissive posture caused his loins to burn with passion. Wild, uninhibited sex without consequence or responsibility certainly had its allure. The temptation was unbearable, almost. It would be marvelous and exhilarating, he was sure, but what about tomorrow? He realized that casual intimacy was great for the moment but ultimately unfulfilling, leaving a person desolate and empty until their next encounter. Lucinda didn't care about him. She didn't care for anything but her own gratification. He was just another man whom she hadn't experienced, an exciting diversion for the evening that somehow made her feel special and important. Many others had been swept up by her stimulating favors but he wanted something more. He had known others like her, none ever seemed truly happy. Then there were many like Vijay and Tom Reynolds who shared their time with their partner and then went off faithfully to their assignments, always seemingly able to keep their natural drives in check, drawing strength and satisfaction from the loving and caring moments that they fostered and nurtured over the years. Intimacy with a partner based on love, adoration, caring, and respect was what was ultimately fulfilling, not intimacy alone. Feeling a rash of guilt and anxiety that her continued presence could jeopardize a future possibility for that kind of relationship, Matt tenderly clasped Lucinda's hips and gently nudged her back, permitting him room to rise to his feet. "What I like is not the issue," he softly stated as he gazed into her eyes. "I'm sure, Lucinda, that you would be terrific and I appreciate your attention and desire as much as anyone. But I'm afraid that I'm not big on casual intimacy. I want a loving and caring relationship with it. I'm a one woman man and you aren't that woman. I think that we should just call it a night."

Lucinda frowned in disappointment but was soon back to her normal flirtatious and vivacious self. "I understand," she said as she began to gather her clothes and put herself back together. "You only promised a drink and a back rub. It was impertinent of me to expect more. But you'll never know what you missed."

"I know," Matt replied with a smile, still admiring her as she dressed. "But I did enjoy your company, your performance, and the view. You looked very sexy."

Lucinda beamed with delight as she tucked in her blouse, walking up to Matt and giving him a friendly peck on the cheek. "I had fun too, even if we didn't have sex. I'll work on that second message in the morning."

Matt's eyes followed the bouncing hem of her mini skirt to the door where she paused and tossed a devilish grin over her shoulder. "If you ever change your mind, the offer is always open. Whatever you like?"

Matt wished she hadn't said that, it just caused his imagination to run rampant again. As he settled himself into his pliant recliner, he thought about racing next door to Sheri and proposing engagement on the spot, then, of course, consummating their relationship and relieving his pangs o f passion. But he would have too much explaining to do. If nothing else, Lucinda's diverting temptation had awakened his dormant soul. His desire for Sheri was greater than ever. Powerful enough to overcome his fears of deceit, abandonment, and betrayal; strong enough to force him to accept the extra tensions and responsibilities accompanying a ship-board romance. The raging fire within him was for her and no other. He would ask her to be his woman at the first opportune time. Matt found himself chuckling. Wouldn't it be ironic, he thought, if they owed a future life together of love and marriage in no small measure to an evening of near indiscretion with a nymphomaniac on a frozen, desolate planet.

Imperceptible to the weary souls in the Residential Dome who sought comfort and security in the tranquil embrace of a dreaming sleep or the marine sentries who watched over them, the howling Martian winds outside began to relinquish their fury. Under the protective canopy of the reinforced glass shield, the whirling din of its power and the and the shaking and rattling of the panels slowly diminished as the vigorous force of the deadly atmospheric gales gradually softened like the shrinking power of the receding ocean tide. Thick clouds of reddish-brown Martian dust, driven by the roaring gusts, laggardly dissipated in the upper reaches of the sky and settled harmlessly to the surface like the gentle raindrops of spring. As the cold, dark night pressed on towards the glorious dawn of a new day, more and more twinkling stars became visible in the heavens above. By daybreak, the mighty storm had been reduced to a stiff winter breeze, the full brightness of the rising sun returning in all its splendor.

Immediately after breakfast, Matt and his small entourage gathered in the conference room where a lively debate ensued concerning the disturbing contents of the David Hart log. He had invited his trusted advisors, Sheri and Vijay, along with Lieutenant Reynolds and Caroline, and had Lucinda play the disk for them. There reactions were no different than his own; intrigued yet dubious, shedding light on some matters while submersing them further into the murky depths of others.

"It's obvious that something very unusual was going on here," Sheri commented as she scanned the room. "He seemed frightened to me."

"But we've seen very little evidence of the aberrations he mentioned," Vijay staunchly countered.

"I remind you," Reynolds disagreed, "there have been a few strange incidents."

"But nothing on the scale of what he alluded too," Vijay replied.

Lucinda lightly slapped the table with her palms in frustration. "Those strange forces he mentioned scare the shit out of me."

"Panicked, overzealous imagination," Vijay caustically remarked.

"Whatever happened here." Reynolds said as he glanced at each face. "I'm afraid we missed it."

Matt met Lucinda's searching eyes with a jaunty smirk that recalled their titillating encounter of the previous evening before seriously addressing her. "Lucinda, we need to see that second file."

"I understand, Commander." she soberly replied, returning a slight simper of her own. "I'll get on it right away."

Matt became curious at the surprising emotionless silence exhibited by Caroline throughout the whole discussion. Based on past experience, he half-expected her to suffer an emotional breakdown, but she had viewed the recording with stoic calm. When asked of her impressions of the condition of her husband, she responded with candor and composure.

"He looked more tired and stressed than the last time I talked with him." She quickly glanced at Sheri. "I'm not so sure if it was fear as much as general apprehension of facing an unknown future. He had definitely been neglecting his grooming, which was so unlike him. It was as if he didn't have time for it. He was always very meticulous about that. I noticed that his comments left out specifics, almost as if he were hiding something. That's not like him either." She briefly snickered. "He was always a good one for detail."

Matt gazed at her compassionately. "Please, Caroline, I don't mean to upset you or make any disparaging implications, but can you think of any reason why he didn't make any remarks concerning you in his private log?"

Caroline's head dropped in somber reflection before shaking negatively. "Maybe just too distracted by colony affairs," she softly replied, lifting her head again. "You'd think that if he wanted that record found, he would have included something for me."

"Maybe in the second file," Sheri encouraged, reaching out a consoling hand towards her. "Will you be all right?"

"I'll be fine," she replied as she valiantly tried to force a congenial smile that just wasn't there. "Nothing surprises me anymore. I've accepted the inevitable." She looked at Sheri with forlorn, glossy eyes. "He knew what he was doing. He abandoned me when he abandoned Jamestown." Her hand reached for Sheri's, her fingers clutching tightly as she bowed in sadness. "No, that's not quite true. Actually, I abandoned him, two- and- a-half years ago when I refused to come to Mars with him. I was so stupid. I'm getting what I deserve."

A buzzing sound on the room intercom interrupted the growing level of gloom surrounding the conference table. The call was from Nichelle who with wrist and lower arm wrapped in a protective cast gratefully assumed the duty station by the communication console.

"I'm sorry for the interruption, Commander, but Reggie, I mean Mister Lewis on your ship needs to speak with you."

Matt looked across the table at his two shipmates with a raised brow of fascination. "Thank you, Nichelle. Pipe it through here, please."

Within moments Reggie's mercurial though unusually serious voice crackled across the embedded speakers in the table. "Good to talk with you again, Captain. Now that the dust has settled down there, perhaps you would care to pay us a visit."

Matt settled back in his chair and laughed, thinking it was a rouse to get him back on the ship so Reggie could come down. "Now don't tell me, you old space dog, that you can't handle a simple orbit with half the crew?" he quipped.

"Not so simple anymore, sir." The comment and the 'sir' snapped Matt to diligent attention. "We've been tracking a sensor contact for twenty-four hours, slowing on an MOI approach trajectory. Five million miles and closing. Be here tomorrow. Our ghost has returned, and this time it doesn't look like it's going to vanish."

10

"Status report!" Matt rigidly demanded as he briskly bolted onto the bridge of the Guilford Courthouse, closely followed by Vijay and Jack who willfully scampered to their familiar stations.

Reggie Lewis, with the pallid eyes and drawn face of a man without sleep, looked up pensively from his seat by the brightly colored array of instrument displays, digital readouts, and computer terminals of the operations station. "Sensor contact now at three-point-two million miles and closing. Speed at ninety MPS and steadily decelerating for apparent MOI." His expression suddenly mutated into a warped combination of curiosity and amusement as he noticed the battered face of Jack as he settled into the navigator's chair. "Damn, Jack! What happened to you?"

Jack turned to his right with a tortuous grimace. "Marines. I hate those guys."

Reggie rolled his eyes incredulously and scoffed. "Shit, man! You mean a woman. I knew you'd get your ass in trouble on this trip."

"Stow it, guys," Matt impatiently interrupted as he stepped towards Reggie. "What other readings are you detecting?"

"Same as before," he replied as he examined the sensors again. "Unusual thermal displacement, increased gamma radiation and beta particle emissions, and electromagnetic impulses, all corresponding with the location of the contact."

"Have you tried communications?"

Reggie nodded. "Regularly for the last twelve hours. I've tried all the universal codes and even took a stab at the first contact binary and prime system mathematical protocols. Nothing. One more thing. We're also picking up trace elements of uranium gas."

A flash of insight suddenly blossomed onto Vijay's awareness, who had overheard Reggie's remarks from his engineering post. "That sounds like radiation from a nuclear power plant." he said with conviction. "In fact, it sounds like the aging Farnsworth coaxial-flow gas core engine. One of the problems with that design was the small leakage of uranium gas."

Whoever or whatever was approaching, Matt was concerned. Under the terms of the Space Colonization Accord of 2042, any colonial project and the world on which it stood declared under a state of emergency was off limits to all but rescue and investigative teams and outpost emergency resupply and transport vessels. And since the severed contact with Jamestown, Mars was so declared. With no other research facility currently manned, no human ship had any business being there. If it wasn't human, then they had a whole new problem. "Reggie, have the computer correlate the contact's movements from the time it reappeared and input the time and location from all the previous acquisitions and losses of sensor contacts from our journey. Question - is this the same ghost?"

Reggie accessed the appropriate data and verbally initiated the programming commands as Matt took his seat in front of the forward viewing window.

"Computer's chewing on it now. Matt," Reggie announced as soon as he had finished loading the parameters.

Matt felt good to be back in the captain's chair again. With all the magnetic appeal and thrilling exhilaration that working on the pristine Martian surface provided for his adventurous spirit, there was nothing like the satisfaction and contentment of commanding his own interplanetary ship. The stars were tranquilly arrayed before him like a fluffy, majestic carpet of twinkling, effulgent fibers. The vessel could carry him mystically across the heavens, respond faithfully to his every demand like a well trained horse, shield him within the protective atmosphere of its bosom. The ship was his. He could sometimes feel her quiver and vibrate around him like a passionate lover. It was almost as if it were an extension of his soul.

"Confirmed, Matt," Reggie dutifully announced, interrupting his mental meandering. "Target definitely originated from the same quadrant as the previous contacts."

"Okay, then," Matt reasoned, "using that flight data as a base, extrapolate its potential trajectory backwards. See if it could have originated from any known local point or did it come from outside the solar system?"

Reggie studied the schematic display of flight paths, gravitational fields, and orbital mechanics of planetary bodies . "It looks as if...." he said as he used his finger to trace the most probable course, "....it may have originated from...." He hesitated, spinning around with a wide-eye glare. "....the Earth."

Vijay stood with a puzzled expression and took a few deliberate strides towards Matt as he thoughtfully rubbed his chin. "Matt, I believe that some of the EESC warships still use the Farnsworth engine."

Matt was vivacious and decisive. "Reg, I want you to get hold of NSCA Central Control. I want to know the departure time and destination of every military, scientific, and civilian ship that has left the Earth or the Moon in the past month, clandestine or otherwise."

With the alacrity of a lynx, Matt swerved around to face Vijay with that air of single-minded purpose that everyone had grown accustomed too. "How soon can you give me full power on the reactor?"

"Tracy and Frank are transfer pumping the hydrogen that we brought back from the colony as we speak. We can be red-lining it in fifty minutes."

Matt nodded appreciatively. "Good. Jack, plot an intercept course. I don't want this thing getting too close. We need to encounter it while it still is out there."

Sheri Alderman, bleary-eyed and yawning, gently lowered herself into the comfortable executive chair in the Chief Administrator's office after a near sleepless night of restless tossing and turning. She had never felt so out of place in all her life. Before his departure the previous afternoon, Matt had officially appointed her Deputy Commander of the mission with complete authority to make all decisions and to take any action that she deemed necessary in his absence. He felt it important that a representative from the ship serve in that capacity and be present on the surface at all times, acting as a mitigating factor between civilian and military interests. Naturally, she wanted to be at his side as her ship sped through space to confront the unknown, but the confidence he displayed in her was gratifying. However, all through the night a subtle apprehension kept gnawing at her like an annoying gnat on a hot summer day. She always seemed to miss the consequential moments. She had spent the evening with Caroline and a few of the others playing cards and watching a movie, retiring early to her bed to hopefully lose herself in several lascivious chapters of the latest racy exploits of the sensual cosmic supersleuth Fawna Lorelei and upon sufficient arousal release her accumulating tension with an EPI which on occasion she had indulged in. But with all the distraction whirling around her, she quickly found the seductive story uninspiring and tossed the book aside, rendering pointless any use of the drug. She needed to feel Matt's gentle, stimulating touch, but his absence is what had thrust this responsibility upon her in the first place. Science teams and engineers were once more roaming around outside and the marines were planning an expansion of their search patterns. All of this she had to coordinate, evaluate, and approve.

And it didn't take long for things to really heat up. Nichelle reported a communiqué with Yong Chang and Raymond Ponsonby who were on their way north once more. They had encountered a disabled excursion rover near Gandzani crater about 100 miles south of Issedon Tholus within coordinate grid 34 degrees north and 93 degrees west and were requesting instructions. The engine was blown and completely dust saturated, though the men reported very little visible signs of weathering and concluded that it couldn't have been exposed to the Martian elements for too many weeks. All portable contents had been stripped from the inside and the serial number painted on the hull matched that of one of the colony's original inventory. Upon further investigation of colony records she discovered one small problem - there was no chronicle of any expedition into that area, as much as the tainted computer files could be trusted. She decided to have the men press on, more closely scrutinizing the surrounding countryside for further evidence.

That done, Sheri had precious little time to bask in the satisfaction of making her first important decision in her temporary assignment when Caroline came charging excitedly through the doorway followed seconds later by a worried Tammy Jacobs and the always unruffled, professional Lieutenant Reynolds.

"Sheri!" Caroline called out with distress. "We have a problem."

Sheri slouched back in the chair and sniggered sarcastically in frustration. "It looks like today is the day for it."

Caroline stared in trepidation. "Tegan McDowell is missing."

Sheri's jaw bone dropped in stunned silence, feeling a combination of fear and outrage as if a missing person was an affront to her for assuming command. "Missing!" she boisterously exclaimed. "What do you mean missing?"

Caroline motioned to the others. "We checked around. He's not in his room. No one saw him last night and he wasn't at breakfast this morning. He didn't report to the labs this morning or to the Agri Dome."

"Yesterday he said he was going to skip dinner in order to work late on some genetic splicing," Tammy added. "No one thought anything more about him. Hell! Most people don't care for the man anyway. It wasn't like he would be missed."

"There was no sign of disturbance in his room," Reynolds added. "My men are sweeping the Residential Dome now."

"Shit!" Sheri grumbled as she stood and began to nervously pace, holding her forehead as she felt the throb of an oncoming migraine.

Caroline frantically looked at the others, trembling in terror. "What are we going to do!" she cried. "He couldn't have just vanished into thin air."

"Caroline," Sheri said in a serene but robust tine as she walked beside her and placed a sturdy hand upon her shoulder. "Calm yourself."

"Why are you so disconcerted," Tammy half-mockingly asked of her colleague. "I thought you hated his guts."

"I do," she irritably responded, still quivering tensely. "What's that got to do with it?"

"I don't mean to alarm anyone," Tammy remarked, "but we could all be in jeopardy."

Sheri began to pace again, scratching an annoying itch on the back of her head. "Maybe, but let's not jump to any wild, unsubstantiated conclusions." She briefly froze in deep concentration, a million fragments of information and perception dancing wildly through her mind. "First, I don't want anyone traveling outside the Residential Dome alone." Sheri cast a grim look of determination as she glanced at each person in turn. "I mean **no one!** Lieutenant, I'm afraid that your men may be required to do a little escort duty."

"Yes, ma'am."

"What about Mister McDowell?" Caroline clamored in frustration.

Growing increasing perturbed, Sheri pointed an obstinate finger at Caroline's face. "Second, I want the two of you to go back to your work,

NOW!" Her wavy, black hair swished across her face as she abruptly pivoted towards the Lieutenant. "You will be in charge of the search. Do it systematically, however...." Her lifted hand wobbled aimlessly around her wrist. "....you military types search for people. Draft anyone you need, use whatever resources are available, but find him!" She paused, inhaling deeply as other ideas flooded her brain. "Question everyone. Find out who saw him last and when. And inventory the environment suits. See if any are missing."

Reynolds was impressed. "If he's on campus, we'll find him."

Sheri noticed the shocked, peaked faces of Caroline and Tammy as if they had just come out of some Saturday matinee horror show. "Thank you ladies," she bellowed with a stern but cordial tone. "The Lieutenant will inform you if your services are needed." As the women turned to leave, Sheri beckoned to them in a softer, more conciliatory tone. "Caroline, it's all right. I'll see you later."

Caroline affectionately grinned. "We both need to relax a little."

"You know, Miss Alderman," Reynolds suddenly spoke as he was about to follow the women out of the doorway, "Matt asked me to look out for you before he left. I see that he has no reason for concern."

Sheri felt a surge of relief flowing through her body like electricity as she sighed heavily, slumping back against the desk and running a hand through the thick strands atop her head. "Thanks," she said with an appreciative smile. "But I'm an emotional wreck. I don't know how much more of this I can take. Please, just find the man." A quizzical simper came over her. "What is that old saying? Never show fear or they'll eat you alive. I think that phrase was advice for grade school teachers."

Reynolds chuckled. "You'll do fine." Turning more solemn, Reynolds inched closer to her with a sympathetic smile. "He said one other thing that you may find useful. He told me that he would trust you, without reservation, with his very life. You can't say that about too many people. That's good enough for me."

Sheri felt a renewed sense of confidence and vigor as if she'd been dipped in magic waters, including a warm, symbiotic affinity for the man now on the bridge of the Guilford Courthouse, almost as if she could feel his strength and tenderness and passion sweeping over her , titillating her very soul. "Thank you, Lieutenant, for sharing that with me," she gracefully said with a joyful grin, brushing back a few wayward strands from her eye "I needed that. You're a fine man and I'm going to need your support."

Reynolds nodded as he backed towards the door. "With your permission, Deputy Commander? I'll keep you informed."

Sheri gingerly eased herself behind the desk once mire and returned to the computer study that had consumed her until the world around her began to unravel. She had been accessing every central colony computer file available, a task that would take months to complete, searching for any useful information at all. She ran across a file that someone labeled Earth Gossip Notepad that contained trivial messages from people on Earth to individual colonists of a general, non-personal nature. A subfile of this massive collection that caught her eye was entitled NSCA Gossip. She spent the next thirty minutes scanning the mundane, sometimes comical notes in order of entry, quickly discovering that a good percentage had been deleted or had erasure gaps. But as she wearily wiped her tiring eyes, a particular note popped onto her monitor that caused her heart to jump. Her head shook in disbelief as she read the note sent from someone on Earth to a colonist named John Osborne several weeks before the crisis who apparently then entered it into the communal file for future colony reference. The message included a smuggled copy of an internal NSCA memorandum referencing possible future directives that concerned Jamestown. "Matt is going to shit a brick when he sees this," she quietly mumbled in disillusionment. She instructed the computer to print the displayed file and settled back for a few fleeting moments to wonder what awaited Matt and her shipmates out there in the heavens.

The information received from NSCA Central Control was not very helpful. There were no flight plans filed that took a spacecraft anywhere near the orbital path of Mars. The EESC did report a research mission to the asteroid belt that mysteriously went astray several days after launch, but that was the only anomaly.

"Closing steadily on target," Reggie unwaveringly announced. "Range now under point three million miles. Contact is drastically slowing."

"Shit!" Jack cursed aloud. "They could be targeting us with a laser gun at any moment."

"If they have them," Matt quickly replied. "Remember, ours were just recently installed. Never been field tested."

"I have a funny feeling," Jack somberly commented, "that this might be that test. I had this same feeling at Copernicus."

Matt looked at him harshly. "We're not at war, Jack. Just mind your helm." Matt ponderously gazed out the forward window at the distant field of gleaming stars knowing that the secretive stranger was lurking out there, somewhere. "Okay buddy," he mumbled to himself, "let's see what's on your mind. Reg! Give me an open channel, universal frequency."

"Your com console is hot, Captain."

Matt pressed the transmit button, not at all certain that the recipient would be able to understand his message. "This is Captain Matthew Maitland of the Continental American Spaceships cruiser Guilford Courthouse currently engaged in search and rescue operations on the planet Mars. Your approach to this planet is in direct violation of the SCA agreement of 2042. Please break off your advance and respond immediately." Matt patiently waited for one minute before repeating his hail. Another anxious minute passed with only the eerie silence of space to greet them. "Any aspect change on target?" Matt fervently inquired.

"Negative," Reggie responded, still focusing on the scanner displays. "Maintaining current trajectory, speed now down to twenty-five MPS."

"I don't want him breaking one hundred thousand," Matt fearfully proclaimed, which happened to be the maximum targeting range of their own lasers. "Very well. Sound general quarters."

The high, whining siren of the alarm klaxon pulsated the battle stations alert throughout the ship in conjunction with the transformation of the normal soft white lighting into a flooding glow of throbbing red emanating from the ceiling grids. The three crewmembers in the engineering compartment scrambled into vibrant orange pressure suits, keeping their helmets nearby, in case ruptures or hull breeches needed repair, even though the outer hull had self-sealing skin against minor perforations. On the bridge, Vijay also hurriedly zipped into one of the suits stored there while Reggie scurried like a prairie dog down the floor hatch that led to the forward laser turret and missile fire control. Once seated behind the gun he began to charge the weapon while activating the deployment mechanism for the missile platform. With the low drone and hum of hydraulics, the whirling and clicking of gears, and the shrill, high screech of metal rubbing against metal, the large, rectangular platform painstakingly extended from either side of the ship from the bowels of the bay below the bridge, one-by-one exposing their 20-foot long fingers of death to the icy cold of space. The process lasted several minutes and culminated in a sharp, clanking reverberation below decks that signified the platform's lock-down in place. Once everyone was at their alert stations and securely buckled into their seats, Matt left his chair and assumed the operations station, a post which he had held on other types of vessels for several years before he was awarded his own command. Though he was very familiar with all the instrumentation, he would have felt more comfortable if he could have seen Sheri sitting on that chair. He could only allow his mind a fraction of a second to fondly consider her before his attention was riveted to the sensors. The PAMIS scanner detected the aspect change of the contact. It was to the ship's starboard, climbing and picking-up speed, running parallel to its original line before slightly arching to its front.

"Contact on new heading," Matt announced. "Giving us a wide berth. Speed up to thirty MPS and climbing." He looked up from the instruments as he instinctively perceived the action. "He's trying an end run!" he shouted as he peered at the others before turning back to feverishly some controls. "Jack, I'm transferring new trajectory data of target to your navigation computer. Plot a new intercept course to one hundred thousand miles, maintaining our position between him and the planet. Engage at maximum thrust when ready."

Matt could feel the g-forces pressing his chest back against the chair as the ship turned and gradually accelerated in an upward sloping curvilinear line in its attempt to cut off the extensive sweeping path of the intruder. As the angle of the pursuit slowly closed the distance between the two ships, Matt decided to give the transmitter one more try. "This is Captain Matthew Maitland of the CAS cruiser Guilford Courthouse to unidentified vessel. You have entered a restricted area in violation of international treaty. Turn around at once or we'll be compelled to force you back."

Vijay and Jack both shot worried glances towards Matt. He could only frown in abhorrence that force of arms might become necessary. Matt nervously awaited a reply as the range closed to 150,000 miles. Their laser targeting system would be able to acquire the contact in about ten minutes but he didn't want to get much closer. "Reggie, arm a missile," he ordered over the internal intercom as his hands continued to manipulate the ops controls. "I'm down-loading current navigation data of the target and us to your tactical computer. Program a missile to detonate five thousand miles in front of his nose. We have to show'em we're serious but leave plenty of margin for error."

Speed of the Guilford Courthouse, the speed, trajectory and attitude of the target, velocity of the missile, and the gravitational forces of Mars were just a few of the factors involved in programming the attack parameters for the weapon.

"Target solution programmed, Captain," Reggie calmly reported. "Ready to launch."

"Initiate firing sequence," Matt instructed.

"Tactical in control," Reggie responded. "Firing in five seconds."

Systematically he counted down from five to zero. Matt could feel a quivering vibration beneath his feet as the igniting engine rattled the weapons platform and a second later he imagined he heard a whooshing roar as the far left missile flamed off its support brackets. This, of course, was ridiculous since there are no sound waves in a vacuum. Trailing like a blazing torch in the blackened night. the rocket sped towards its predetermined coordinates at 500 miles per second.

"Missile away!" Reggie's animated voice beckoned. "Five minutes to detonation."

Matt assiduously studied the PAMIS scanner, curious as to the reaction of the mysterious craft. It wasn't long before it was engaged in evasive maneuvers, sharply turning and diving, eventually slowing down and backing away a few thousand miles upon realization that the ship itself was not targeted. At five minutes Matt looked out the main viewer to witness the eruption of a distant fireball. like the surging brilliance of a supernova then fade into oblivion with the same suddenness.

"That got his attention," Reggie was heard shouting mirthfully.

Matt noticed that the intruder had steadied-up across their path and was slowing to a near crawl. a sign that it wasn't going to take any belligerent action, at least for the moment. "Slow us down, Jack. I think he's having second thoughts."

Minute by minute ticked by as the two vessels limped along at a lazy pace on parallel courses, mirroring each other like two prizefighters circling the canvas, searching for weakness in the opponent. The bridge became strangely silent as Matt paced anxiously about as he debated over his next move, the others sedately immersed in cosmic thoughts of their own. The lull was becoming nerve-wracking and torturous when their heart rates were abruptly jolted from their lethargy by a beeping noise from the com system indicating an incoming transmission. All eyes exchanged expectant glances of apprehension as Matt reached for the receiver button.

"Here it comes," he said as he took a deep breath.

The small oval video monitor of the communication system flickered in brightness, focusing on the lean, imperious face of a middle-aged man wearing a dark green, black visor service cap encompassed by a small red band at the base and gold star insignia on front. Thin, graying strands poked out from under the bill of the cap around his forehead and his hair was closely cut above his ears. His penetrating, dark beady eyes, long, thin, hooking nose, protruding square jaw, and dimpled, fractured complexion gave him a stern and foreboding appearance. The tall hunter green collar piped with red and shoulder epaulettes of the same color indicated a uniform commonly worn by Eastern European Socialist Confederation military personnel. Speaking in Russian, his voice sounded resolute, though the mechanical masculine tone of the language translator tended to soften the emotional inflections.

"This is Major Alexei Zubov of the EESC light frigate Borodino demanding reason for unprovoked missile launch across our flight path."

Matt pointed to Jack and snapped his fingers, who perceptibly jumped into the command chair and accessed file data on EESC warships.

"Captain Matthew Maitland, CAS Guilford Courthouse. Major, we seem to be experiencing a problem in communication. You ignored our repeated hails and proceeded on an orbital insertion course to a planet that is under a state of emergency. Is it your intention to render assistance to those search and rescue efforts?"

"I apologize for the misunderstanding, Captain," Zubov replied rather passionlessly. "We are on our own humanitarian mission, delivery of emergency supplies and additional science personnel to our research station at Alba Patera in accordance with the articles of the SCA of 2042."

Matt briefly killed the sound and looked anticipatively at Jack.

"Light frigate Borodino," he summarized from the computer file. "Komarov class warship, Angelfish design. Recently replaced hypervelocity pulse gun with top fin mounted laser cannon, three hundred and sixty degree field of fire. Targeting range seventy-five thousand miles. Twin tubes mounted on lower fin can fire a maximum of ten dual-spreads of cobalt warhead torpedoes with maximum running speeds of three hundred miles per second. Farnsworth reactor capable of producing speeds up to two hundred and fifty MPS. Crew of six, capable of transporting up to fifty passengers and two hundred tons of cargo. Reported military uses include convoy escort, deep space reconnaissance, and small troop deployment."

A schematic drawing was displayed on the command monitor. The Komarov light frigate was much shorter than the Guilford Courthouse and only about two-thirds the mass and resembled two mated pyramids lying on their sides. The puffed main cylindrical fuselage narrowed sharply into a pointed nose, home of the bridge, and flattened in the rear. Two large, thick angular extensions, leaning back at about a 45 degree angle, protruded out from amidships on both top and bottom, giving the design the shape of an angelfish. A small dome mounted at the end of the top fin contained the new laser cannon and a bulky, rectangular rotating compartment at the tip of the bottom fin held the twin torpedo tubes, fire control, and magazine. A short but thick access tube connected the rear of the main fuselage to the second smaller, elongated, pyramid-like compartment which contained the main engine and reactor plant. Like the Guilford Courthouse, the entire main assembly rotated around a central axis while the engineering section was held in weightless non-rotating space.

"So our weapons have longer range," Matt concluded, "but they are better armed and are faster and more maneuverable."

"That's about the crux of it, Matt," Jack calmly replied.

Matt took a deep, measured breath, collected his thoughts, then reactivated the microphone. "Major Zubov, our information indicates that your research facility at Alba Patera has been unoccupied for nearly two Earth years. Economic considerations, I believe."

The crafty smirk from Zubov's reaction did not elude Matt's attention.

"I regret that our government's occasional lack of...." Zubov hesitated and stammered, unsure of a proper term "....precision sometimes puts us all in compromising positions. I therefore demand that you grant us free passage to our station on the planet surface."

Matt felt himself becoming increasing flustered. "I don't mean to be difficult, Major, but since when does the EESC make scientific transports using a Komarov class warship?"

Zubov shrugged ingenuously. "Economic necessity, Captain. All our serviceable civilian transports are on assignments."

"Huh....huh," Matt groaned with obvious skepticism. "I would love to comply with your request, Major Zubov, but first I need verifiable proof.

Now, if you would contact your government and ask them to contact my government, and if my government finds their explanation and documentation satisfactory, then my government will advise me in turn and then we can straighten out this whole mess. Then I would be more than happy to allow your vessel to proceed. Probably only take a few days."

Matt could see the rage building within the puffy, flushed cheeks of his contemporary as they turned beet red, his teeth clenching tightly in anger.

"Now, Captain, let me tell you just how wrong you are," he uttered delicately but inflexibly, grating his teeth annoyingly. "My orders are to deliver personnel and cargo on station at Alba Patera. Your civilian cruiser is an impressive ship but if you think that you can successfully challenge an EESC warship, then persist in your obstinacy."

Matt was fuming inside. He absolutely hated arrogance and conceit, not to mention that he didn't believe a word of the story. He would have liked nothing more than to eat this pompous Russian for lunch but in space confrontations, discretion was usually the better part of valor. He painstakingly battled to cork the bottle containing his foaming indignation. "I urge you to reconsider your position, Major," Matt cordially responded with resolve as he grimaced in anguish. "Wars, sir, have begun this way. The Lunar Conflict erupted over a minor, innocent incident not unlike this one. Let's not drag the world down that path again."

"I fought in that war and I know its scars," he said with conviction. "All you have to do, Captain, is back away and not impede my mission and we can prevent any further complications. As a courtesy I tell you this. I'm proceeding to the planet. If you try to intercede, I will be forced to push you aside. The choice, Captain, is yours."

Sheri's ears could immediately discern the raucous uproar coming from the common area of the Residential Dome as she ascended the elevator that led to the ground floor, carrying a plastic tray containing the steaming hot, freeze-dried chicken and vegetable food pack that she had just microwaved, and planned to join Caroline and some of the others for dinner. Entering the spacious park now bristling with much more vibrant greens and the soothing trickling of running water, she was instantly drawn to a large, standing jumble of people clustered together near some of the perimeter tables, hotly engaged in lively debate, untouched trays of food and fresh produce scattered about unattended. It seemed as if the entire staff was there, including a few of the marines, and it only took a few steps in that direction to realize that the discussions were anything but controlled. Gingerly she skirted around the group to set her tray aside, listening carefully to the excited ramblings, seemingly everyone talking at once. There had been no trace of the whereabouts of Tegan McDowell. That, along with the strange occurrences reported in the David Hart log and the news of the Guilford Courthouse's encounter with an unknown vessel dominated the arguments.

"What are we going to do about Tegan?" Tammy Jacobs tearfully asked. "How could he have just disappeared like this?"

"We've done all we can," Corporal Cooke distraughtly replied. "He's gone."

"None of us are safe," Lucinda distressfully added, looking with alarm at the others. "I mean he talked about mysterious forces and missing people." She turned to Caroline and placed a firm hand on her arm. "Caroline, was he ever more specific on those missing survey teams?"

Caroline looked haggard, dropping her head disheartenedly. "No."

"There could be spirits here," Tammy commented frightfully with serious candor. "Jamestown could be haunted."

Susan Oliver incredulously turned to her and scoffed. "Tammy, that's ridiculous!"

"I here rumors that the ship out there is some kind of alien contraption," Garett Yamakawa apprehensively added.

Andre Fedorov was baffled by his colleagues, smirking as he scratched the back of his graying head. "You people really should get a grip on your imaginations."

"Imagination hell!" Lucinda pugnaciously roared. "Have we imagined all the shit that's been going on around here? There may be aliens around this place right now!" She noticed Susan and Andre rolling their eyes disdainfully. "Don't look at me like that," she bellowed. "We have some pretty good evidence of some kind of malicious intelligence. They could even be noncorporeal entities."

Tammy glanced at the others with unabashed fear. "I don't want to die."

"Shit, Tammy," Susan tauntingly replied. "Do you know how lame that is? As if anyone here actually wants to die."

Garett was flushed with an expression of alarm. "We should call the ship and have them come back and pick us all up."

"One thing is certain," Andre continued. "If something happens to the Guilford Courthouse, we'll be stranded here unprotected."

"That's why we're here," Corporal Cooke nonchalantly remarked as he checked the energy level of his power clip to his laser rifle.

"No disrespect intended, son," Andre replied, "but you're just one platoon of dirt humpers."

"But not just any platoon, Gramps," he egotistically responded as he slammed the clip into the stock chamber and slung the rifle over his shoulder. "We're the Iron Brigade."

A few farcical derision's served to break the escalating tension, but only for a moment. As Sheri cautiously approached the argumentative group, they began to fire a series of blistering questions and suppositions directed at Caroline regarding past events and the contents of the log disk as if they believed that her final conversations with her husband had given her some unique cognitive insight into their predicament. Sheri noticed her tremulously backing away as their interrogating eyes bore down on her, visibly shaking as her speech became slurred and broken.

"Did you notice anything peculiar abut him," Garett insistently questioned. "Were his remarks natural? Was he under duress? Drugged? Irrational? Possessed?"

"How should I know!" she cried out in distress, wildly trembling as she shook her head.

"Come on, Caroline," Lucinda urged as she stepped forward and touched her arm. "He was your husband for God's sake. You must have noticed something."

Caroline shook free, wrenching backwards and clasping her hands around her ears. "Stop it!" she screamed hysterically. "Will you please just stop it! I can't tell you anything more."

Sheri rushed to Caroline's side, wrapping her arms around her trembling, quivering body. It was as if the whole weight of the responsibility for the colony's disappearance and their own precarious situation had crashed squarely upon her shoulders. And she was tormented by a groundless sense of guilt that she was unable to offer any aid to alleviate the festering fears of her peers.

"Leave me alone!" she yelled as she violently twisted within the vise-like grip of Sheri's embrace. "Just let me be! I don't know what happened here! I don't know what's happening now!" Caroline shuddered and broke down into torrential downpours of incoherent ranting and raving, fiercely convulsing until Susan dashed forward with a sedative hypo which she had carried in her waist cinch utility bag, one of those issued to her by Lieutenant Reynolds on the Martian road. Caroline relaxing collapsed unconscious into Sheri's and Susan's arms. Corporal Cooke was quickly at her side, lifting her gently from the ladies support.

"Take her to her room," Susan instructed. "I'll check on her later."

Corporal Cooke glanced disgustingly at the mortified faces of the huddle of humanity and shook his head as he passed by. "You people are some piece of work."

No sooner had Caroline been mercifully whisked away from the calamity, the agitated throng began to argue and bicker once more. Sheri could hardly contain her indignation, her blood boiling with anger as she contemptuously leered at the group with flaming arrows. "Will you assholes put a cork in it!" she barked churlishly. "Look what you did to that poor woman, not to mention ruining my appetite."

A dozen eyes looked at her oddly, then resumed their debates in just a slightly moderating tone.

"I heard someone speculate that the NSCA might order the ship home to avoid its destruction and leave us all here to fend for ourselves," Garett casually remarked to those around him.

The words managed to filter through to Sheri's ears and that was all she could stand. She furiously bolted towards Garett with a face teeming with rage , grabbed him roughly by the collar and forcefully drove him back, tipping over one of the light metal chairs in the process. "Do we have a hearing disability here, Mister?" she sarcastically roared. "What did I just say?"

Garett was stunned to inaction by the speed and tenacity of her assault. The others silently looked on in petrified shock.

"Let me tell you something you little weasel," she bitterly scolded as she tightened her grip around his neck. "You may be some hotshot robotics wizard and a good buddy of Vijay's, but those are all my friends out there and they would **never** abandon us here. Is that clear enough for you?"

Garett could only stutter with surprised timidity. "Su....sure, Sheri. Christ! Ta....take it easy."

"And that goes for the lot of you," she shouted loudly, releasing her strangulating grip around Garett's throat as she glared disdainfully at the others. "My ship has made contact with an EESC vessel, not some alien machine, and is in the process of investigating. When that is done, Commander Maitland will return. Meanwhile we will carry on our work."

"You mean until the next person disappears or has an accident," Lucinda rancorously commented. "Then what?"

"I've had it with your pessimistic whining!" Sheri screeched as she charged, deftly twisting Lucinda's arm behind her back while using her left arm to restrictively clamp around Lucinda's neck. "Did you think I was joking about ripping your head off aboard the ship?"

Lucinda struggled vainly. "Ouch! I hope for your sake that you're initiating a mating ritual."

Sheri twisted her arm tighter with a short guffaw. "You may enjoy this, honey, but I may not wait for your next sexual advance to use your headless stump as a toilet." Ill-tempered and infuriated, Sheri jostled with Lucinda before releasing her hold with a measured forward shove, following right behind the startled computer engineer with a warning finger pointed at her face. Lucinda spun to challenge her but froze, thinking twice about retaliation. With a scathing stare, Sheri then directed her chiding finger at each person in turn. "This is the last call for gripers and I mean last!" she boisterously hollered a the top of her lungs. Everyone recoiled humbly, partly in fear and partly in shame, not wishing to cross Sheri while she was so incensed. "Tomorrow we will resume our investigation, follow the marines security measures to the letter, and find some answers. The rumors, hysteria, and unsubstantiated speculations are over. Is that understood?"

With reluctant murmurs of agreement, the agitated mass dispersed into smaller groups and went about their business as Sheri wearily dispatched her now chilled dinner and listlessly strolled below to look in on Caroline. With Corporal Cooke keeping her company, she patiently waited in the living room for Caroline to awaken, engaged in stimulating conversation with the young though veteran marine, finding his stories both interesting and entertaining. After about thirty minutes they were alerted to Caroline's stirring by the restless rustling sound of legs against sheets and the soft creaking bouncing mattress coils.

"How are you feeling?" Sheri smiling asked as the two of them sat themselves on the foot of the bed.

"Very drained," Caroline mumbled rather groggily as she rubbed her eyes. "What happened?"

"Susan gave you a sedative," Sheri explained. "And Corporal Cooke here carried you back."

"Oh!" she exclaimed with a heightened level of interest and a charming grin of delight. "I wish I had been awake for that." Feeling an unusual lightness around her skin, she peered under her sheet and noticed that her work suit had been removed, leaving her in her white bra and panty. Feeling a little embarrassed, she instinctively clutched the sheet to her neck. "How did I get undressed?" she asked befuddled.

"We flipped a coin," Cooke humorously quipped, "but unfortunately I lost."

Caroline and Sheri both exchanged girlish giggles. "I thought you'd rest more comfortably without that dingy uniform."

"Thank you both. I seem to be saying that a lot lately." Caroline sighed regretfully as she relaxingly reclined against her puffy pillow. "I shouldn't let them get me so upset."

"They were pretty rough on you," Cooke observed as he rose to his feet. "It's perfectly understandable with all you've been through."

Caroline looked at him with disappointment. "Must you go, Bob?"

"I'm afraid so. I have guard duty soon. Just wanted to make sure you were all right."

"Then I'll see you tomorrow," she wishfully replied as both women watched him gather his helmet and rifle and slowly walked from her room.

"He's an interesting young man, that marine," Sheri confessed as she turned back to her friend. "We talked a good bit while you were asleep."

Caroline perked up, sitting upright and allowing the sheet to fall to her waist as she braced herself on her forearms. "Really? About what?"

"Oh, lots of things," Sheri replied with a pleasing smirk as she sensed a certain amorous interest. "Did you know that his dad left home when he was very young and his mother was an alcoholic?"

Caroline shook her head but her longing eyes betrayed her interest.

"He and a younger brother were raised by grandparents," Sheri continued. "Worked thirty hours a week at a grocery store all through high school to help support the family. Joined the Space Marines right after graduation. Was wounded in action. Never had a steady girlfriend. Never been in love."

Caroline's joyfully beaming mouth turned down morosely. "That's so sad," she moaned sorrowfully. "Such a hard life and never to experience the joys of love. What a tragedy. He's such a pleasant, considerate man. It's amazing that he turned out so well adjusted. Most women would kill to find a man like him."

"Yeah," Sheri concurred. "I hope he finds someone before something happens...." She paused in grim reflection, "....well, let's not think about that." Sheri grew silent, staring vacantly at the wall.

Caroline tossed back her sheet and slid forward, gently touching Sheri's hand. "You're worried about Matt, aren't you?"

Sheri lowered her troubled head and nodded. "I am. I'm worried about all of them. I should be with them." Her head lifted as she gazed at Caroline with concern. "You know, Andre was right. They could be in a lot of trouble out there."

"Two torpedoes forty thousand miles off the port bow and closing!" Matt shouted excitedly as he lurched up from the scanner. "Can we outrun their range?"

"Sure," Jack replied as the ship pulled and dove to the right, jolting everyone in the same direction, "except the acceleration needed would smear us against the walls like strawberry jam."

"Great!" Matt proclaimed facetiously. "Preparing decoy drones. Impact in two minutes."

"Jack! Swing us around." Reggie beckoned over the intercom. "Help me to lock-on."

The Guilford Courthouse continued its cumbersome, sweeping loop as it gave space, eventually presenting its starboard bow towards the targets.

"Can you get them, Reg?" Matt anxiously questioned. "Range now thirty thousand miles and closing."

"Imputing now." Reggie replied as he accessed and transferred the relevant current target data and navigational telemetry into his tactical computer. "Laser fire control has plotted a solution on first torpedo. Locking on target."

The laser gun mount encased behind its protective transparent shield whined like a softened generator motor and rotated to the right, the gun automatically elevating to the calculated firing position.

Matt studied the approaching threat on his sensor display with venomous adrenaline. "Fire!"

At a push of a button, the rounded fat cavity of the protruding black barrel of the forward laser turret glowed a brilliant yellow-orange for a succession of fleeting moments in conjunction with high-pitched buzzing pulses that echoed throughout the tactical compartment. An instant later the brightest star in the heavens burst forth only to fade inconspicuously away into the twinkling night.

"Torpedo one destroyed," Matt vigilantly announced. "Second torpedo impact in fifty seconds."

"Acquiring second target," Reggie reported. "LFC has locked-on."

Seconds later Reggie could see out the far right side of his turret another balloon fireball, blossoming like a rosebud, then just as quickly ebb away like the fading light of a dying sunset.

"Two for two!" Matt exhorted with glee. "Come on, Jack! Let's get after that socialist bastard."

Arching back to starboard and climbing, the Guilford Courthouse gradually accelerated towards the general location of the Borodino.

"I want to get within range of our laser targeting system," Matt advised Jack, "but stay out of his. Reg, prepare another missile for launch."

Combat in space was like war at sea by the middle of the twentieth century, the belligerent antagonists never coming within sight of each other, even with full magnification on their view screens. Targets of opportunity were electronically detected and weapon systems computer guided and controlled. Missiles, torpedoes, and self-guided mines used a whole host of detectable signals to isolate a potential target. Tracking a radar beam (painting the target), hydrogen gas emission, radiation discharge of various wavelengths, thermal signatures from power plants, and electromagnetic field intensity among others. Blind or proximity firing was almost never used except in defensive situations where the targeting system had insufficient time to assimilate enough data.

The PAMIS scanner indicated to Matt that the distance between them was rapidly closing, now at 110,000 miles.

"MGS has programmed targeting solution," Reggie's steady voice announced. "Ready to launch."

"Initiate launch sequence and fire," Matt ordered.

With the same blazing inferno as before, the far right finger leaped off the outstretched hand of the starboard platform and raced into the immense vastness of the void, seeking out one tiny, insignificant contrivance of man and send it back to the stars.

"Missile away!" Reggie called out. "Missile has acquired. Three-and-a-half minutes to target."

"Jack!" Matt shouted exuberantly. "Drop us Z minus five thousand but continue to close in. We'll use the missile for cover to get within laser targeting range."

"Somebody should be blowing a bugle," Jack mused with jocosity.

Matt recognized the signals from the array of scanners indicating that the Borodino was banking away sharply in evasive maneuvers. "Too late to hide now, my friend," he mumbled before his concentrated was summarily jolted by alert signals emanating from the Defensive Warning Net. "Two torpedoes ten o'clock high starboard bow!" Matt frantically shouted. "Jack! Full reverse!"

The roar inside the engineering compartment from the firing of the decelerator engines was deafening, its reverberations running along the metal plating all the way to the bridge. The swift slowing of forward momentum violently propelled everyone towards the front of the ship, Matt clinging tenaciously to monitor projections as the buckle of his chair dug painfully into his waist.

"You can't keep shaking the ship apart like this!" Vijay distraughtly cried out.

"Write to corporate headquarters." Matt sarcastically retorted. "We have to give Reggie a chance to target those torpedoes." Matt hastily scrambled to straighten himself by the DWN scanner. "Forty thousand and closing. Reg! Talk to me!"

"LFC targeting first torpedo now."

"Shit!" Matt screamed in terror. "Two more torpedoes one minute behind first spread. And that bastard has turned and is going for our flank! Our missile has been detonated seven thousand miles off target." He paused eerily for a flickering moment as he glanced at each one in turn and stared with unnatural serenity. "Gentlemen, we're running out of time."

"Torpedo one targeted," Reggie impatiently announced.

"Fire!" Matt bellowed. "Jack, get us out of here."

Another mushrooming puff of light bloomed in the distant heavens as the Guilford Courthouse applied forward thrust once more and arched abruptly to port.

"Switching LFC to top laser turret," Reggie informed as the changing attitude of the vessel oriented the nose turret away from the oncoming torpedoes, taking away his field of fire. Held in non-rotating space on the roof of the cargo bay, the smaller automated laser turret could acquire those targets unreachable by the primary nose gun.

"Copy that," Matt acknowledged. "Evasive maneuvers, quickly!"

The Guilford Courthouse rocked and pitched like a gigantic galactic roller coaster as it retreated and climbed and dove away from its menacing pursuers, flinging the crew in their chairs like limp rag dolls.

"This ship wasn't built for these space gymnastics," Vijay worriedly remarked.

"She wasn't built to be blown-up either," Matt sardonically replied.

"I can't get a target lock bucking around like this," Reggie angrily complained.

"Fire blind!" Matt clamored. "Paint the sky!"

Without a visual reference, it would be easier to hit an ant with a pea shooter. As Reggie proceeded to blast away, Matt did some quick mental calculating. The radiation and heat displacement from the proximity explosion of a detonated missile might disorient a homing torpedo, if not destroy it outright. The lead torpedo was within 25,000 miles. It would take nearly a minute to launch a missile. They had to act fast.

"Reg, disregard laser fire. Program a missile for proximity explosion, five thousand miles beyond launch point, in direction of incoming targets. Hurry! Don't wait for the command, launch when ready."

Beads of sweat dripped from Reggie's tense, dark brow as his trembling fingers nimbly entered the parameters into the tactical computer.

"Fifteen thousand miles and closing," Matt tersely called out.

"Programming complete," Reggie announced, wiping the perspiration from his brow. "Launching weapon."

Matt intensely examined the scanners for the next ten seconds until the sensitive instruments detected the surge of heat and radiation from the exploding warhead. He looked hard, holding his breath. "Torpedo still active," he shouted with an anguished grimace. An excruciating pause tormented the others. "Wait a minute...." His tone was hopeful. "Torpedo veering away. It's lost acquisition." A bright though discouragingly brief smile crossed his face. No one could relax yet. "Two active targets eighteen thousand miles and closing," he stoically proclaimed. "Preparing decoy drones for launch. Jack, get ready to climb the roof."

"Aye, Captain."

Matt had a few precious seconds before his next evasive tactic to ascertain the disposition of the Borodino. PAMIS indicated her movement in a circuitous route around their flank towards the planet but not, curiously, using the distraction of the torpedo attack to close within laser targeting range. However, at 95,000 miles, they were now within the targeting limits of the laser guns aboard the Guilford Courthouse, if they could ever shake free from those torpedoes long enough to line-up a shot. "Reggie, I'm transferring forward laser turret control to the command station. Concentrate top turret fire on those torpedoes. Jack, stand by."

Matt daringly waited until the torpedoes were thirty seconds from impact when he pushed the button that dropped three decoy drones from the belly of the ship. These large, barrel-shaped mechanisms with five interspersed antenna-like projections were electronic buoys teeming with equipment designed to emit every electromagnetic and light and heat wave signature known to space-faring vehicles in order to attract or confuse guided weapon systems. "Positive Z now!" Matt emphatically shouted.

The nose steadily lifted towards a forty-five degree angle as the Guilford Courthouse shuddered and shook on its climb of the cosmic stairway, slowly pitching to the right, the drones continuing to tumble in the direction of their forward momentum at the time of their ejection.

"Engines and reactor overheating, Matt," an excited Vijay reported between jolts and gyrations.

"Pit it in the red!" Matt roared back as his face contorted grotesquely. He could feel the air-sucking pressure crushing his chest as if being sat on by an overzealous circus elephant. It was neatly a minute before Jack leveled off the trajectory and eased off on the thrust which enabled Matt to pry himself from the back of his chair and check the scanners just in time to detect a cobalt warhead explosion. "Beautiful.... Damn! One torpedo still active!" he cried out in alarm. "I think it's got us. Eight thousand miles, starboard side. Reg, you have to nail it."

The coal black barrel of the laser cannon on the roof of the cargo bay pulsated inside with glowing yellow-orange reflections as Reggie rapidly squeezed off by remote control a steady stream of energy bursts in the direction of the approaching target. There was no time to input the necessary targeting information into the LFC system.

"Six thousand!" Matt shouted anxiously.

He could determine the general 3-dimensional direction and range from the tactical display but that was a vast parsec of space and that torpedo was mighty small.

"Five thousand!"

The laser flickered and hummed about once per second, Reggie continuously nudging subtle adjustments in rotation and elevation with his obese joystick control like he used to do with his childhood video games.

"Four thousand!" There was panic in Matt's voice, a tone and inflection rarely heard from the lips of the Captain. Jack had ceased evasive maneuvers since pulling out of the climb, giving Reggie a steady opportunity to center on the target. Too late for more dodging in any event. Reggie could see a fiery streamer closing from the distance, just along the right edge of the turret shell, reminding him of a burning meteorite plunging through the Earth's atmosphere.

"Three thousand!" They only had seconds left. It was coming on in a straight line now. Matt cursed the designers that the laser didn't have a wider beam. Reggie fired, made another minute adjustment, and fired again. If he could only fine-tune it in time.

"Two!"

A couple of quick bursts and suddenly the heavens erupted in a blinding splash of yellow-white light that completely engulfed the ship and flooded the forward turret as if bathed in a bank of stadium lights. Ferocious shock waves rippled against the hull, throwing the human inhabitants forcefully against the consoles or whipping wildly in their chairs, causing the vessel to list to port. Matt's head slammed violently against a monitor display, throbbing in pain as gushes of deep red blood poured from an ugly jagged gash across his forehead. He fell back limply against the chair as Jack regained control and righted her on course. A few electrical burnout's spread a thin fog throughout the bridge as Vijay scrambled to put out the flames with a hand extinguisher.

"Report damage." Matt struggled to command as he fought the biting ache in his head and a debilitating wooziness that sickened his stomach.

"Minor rupture on starboard side access conduit," Vijay reported as he stumbled back to his station, rubbing his sore left shoulder. "Automatic pressure seals in place. Reggie burned out the automated fire control energy coil to the top laser turret. The gun is now inoperative. Tracy is on her way now to make repairs. We still have optimum engine power, God alone knows how."

"Very well," Matt strenuously grunted as he laboriously pulled himself up to look at the sensors, wiping the dripping blood out of his right eye as he strained to find the location of the Borodino. He found it once more on an orbital approach to the planet, surprisingly away from them, and well beyond the targeting range of their forward laser. With quivering fingers he relayed the telemetry to Jack's guidance computer.

"Initiate pursuit, Jack," he weakly ordered as he unhooked himself and struggled to his feet. "We're going after that son-of-a-bitch." Matt gingerly tried to move his wobbling legs towards the command station as the ship began the pursuit of its quarry. Shaking and unsteady, he tumbled clumsily to his knees. Jack turned to him with surprise then gasped in appalling shock, noticing the ghastly cut and bloody face for the first time.

"Shit, Matt!" he exclaimed in horror as he rushed to the aid of his fallen captain and helped him into the command chair. "Let's get you taken care of."

"Mind your helm, Mister," Matt groggily said as he strenuously pushed himself up to the fire control tactical display on his console now operating the forward laser gun. He grew irritated when he noticed that Jack wasn't moving. "That's an order, Mister!"

"Yes, sir," he reluctantly replied as he slowly released his steadying grip around Matt's shoulder and resumed his post, periodically casting a worried glance to his right.

"That bastard is going down," Matt defiantly proclaimed as his battered, bloody face reflected an indomitable, determined force of will.

"He's out of targeting range, Captain," Jack respectfully reminded.

"I don't care!" Matt bitterly retorted. "We're taking our shots."

Using the PAMIS readings as a guide and with trickles of blood splotching the console, Matt randomly fired a succession of blind laser bursts in the general location of space he believed the Borodino was in. Vijay moved over to the operations station and studied the sensor readings in regard's to the target's reactions. To his surprise, after several minutes the vessel suddenly turned away from the planet and seemed to be increasing speed as it proceeded in the opposite direction.

"I don't believe it!" he exclaimed in awe. "I think they are breaking off! Moving away from us at our ten o'clock."

"Shall we pursue?" Jack eagerly inquired.

Matt wearily slumped in the chair and with a deep breath shook his head. "No, but we'll keep tracking...." He felt unusually weak as the smoggy bridge seemed to be spinning around him like a swirling top. He felt his mind blinking in and out as his head pounded like a hammer on an anvil until he found his body sprawling uncontrollably towards the metal floor.

They had tried to sneak their way in, but they were discovered. They had tried to bluff their way past, but they were not believed. They had tried to intimidate their way through, but their threats went unheeded. They had attempted to frighten them away, but though scared, the space between them was stubbornly held. They had launched a diversionary attack to keep them occupied and distracted while they slipped by, but their diversions were disposed of and their planetary approach challenged once more. Their mission could only be completed with a toe-to-toe confrontation, a duel to the death. But the EESC reluctantly concluded that this affair was not worth the risk of instigating another global war with the Western powers. Mars had evolved into a convoluted and sordid matter that was not worth the price in lives and resources, as the Lunar Conflict had so painfully reminded them just a few short years before. Their meager clandestine presence would not be reinforced; their urgently needed supplies would not be delivered; and that exasperating little covert rebellion of volatile separatists left unchecked, at least for now. So the Borodino and her assault troops were ordered home. Maybe one day a combined Earth force would seek to reestablish their authority and dominance once more on the Red Planet. Alexei Zubov was anxiously awaiting for that day.

Matt's initial waking sensation to go along with the pounding in his skull was an irritating scraping of his ripped flesh against a padded cloth, quickly followed by a biting, stinging pain invading the deep cut to his forehead. His eyes gingerly opened to the sight of Jack's anguished face hovering over him. "We're still alive," Matt groggily mumbled as he began to stir, piously crossing himself. "Jesus loves me." He winced in pain. "Ouch!" Matt hollered from the chair, grabbing Jack's wrist as the navigator pressed the antiseptic suture pad over the wound. "Take it easy. You have the gentle touch of sandpaper. How do you manage to arouse so many women with fingers like that?"

"I'm glad to see you back to your normal self, Captain," Jack chuckled as he dabbed a moistened cloth against Matt's bloody cheeks, now dried and streaky. "I injected you with a blood and oxygen supplement. That should hold you until the Docs can patch you up."

"Now, Matt," Vijay called out from his engineering station. "Are you through tossing this ship around with your space acrobatics? She could break apart at any moment and I'm the one that's going to have to fix her."

"Yes, Captain," Jack added with a devious grin. "I want to thank you for that thrilling experience. It was almost as exciting as sex."

Matt barely had enough energy for a pained snicker. "For now. I think that I've had as much fun as I can stand for one day. Anyone hurt?"

"I jammed my shoulder," Vijay replied as he massaged the limb. "Reggie pulled a rib muscle. Everyone has bumps and bruises, but nothing more serious. But you need to take it easy, Matt. You've lost a lot of blood."

Their attention was abruptly jarred with frightening alacrity by the sudden beeping sound coming from the communication console that was the signal indicating an incoming transmission. Startled and hesitant glances were exchanged before Vijay moved towards the station.

"No," Matt weakly protested, staggering to his feet. "I'll take it." Using Jack's shoulder to steady himself, Matt deliberately stepped over to the chair by the console, giving Jack an appreciative clasp to the arm as he reached for the controls. "Guilford Courthouse acknowledge, Captain Matthew Maitland here."

The image appearing on the communication monitor was that of a rather perturbed, grave-looking Major Alexei Zubov, his uniform slightly disheveled , the command center behind him encumbered with smoke.

"Why Major Zubov," Matt exhorted with a sly grin, concealing the burning rage festering within him, "we really must do this again sometime. Having a little trouble with your bridge?"

Zubov forced a contrived smile and shrugged nonchalantly. "Not at all, Captain, so kind of you to ask. Just a few minor short circuits from our invigorating exercise." Matt could see that he was perceiving the mustiness of his own bridge. "It looks, Captain, that you are engaging in that a.... American outdoor custom...." He struggled for an appropriate description. "....a....bar....barbecue, yes. That's it, a barbecue."

"Yeah," Matt replied facetiously, "we're grilling steaks. Russian bear meat."

Zubov's jaw clenched tightly as he glared at Matt disdainfully. "Don't be so impertinent, Captain. I didn't call you to exasperate matters but to settle them. My government does not wish to precipitate a general war over continuance of this tragic incident which can only result in your inevitable destruction. So against my personal nature, I've been ordered to withdraw."

"I see," Matt emotionlessly noted. although the phrase 'bite me' was flashing through his incensed mind.

"It's unfortunate that communication failures and computer errors caused the launching of weapons from both ships. It was an innocent accident."

"Yes, an accident," Matt replied. understanding the diplomatic complexities that revelations of the total truth to the rest of the world would entail. "We're a long way from home, Major."

He nodded solemnly. "We both are. Best wishes in your humanitarian efforts." His beady eyes bore into him. "Until we meet again."

A chilling shiver shot up Matt's spine as an unnerving premonition that this was but his opening act in the great Martian play came over him, wrought with foreboding feelings of apprehension and dread. He looked at Zubov with both respect and defiance. "Yes, until we meet again."

CHAPTER

11

It seemed to thrive under laboratory conditions. Cell division and reproduction appeared to be unaffected by the extremes of cold. It synthesized ultraviolet radiation and the abundant carbon dioxide into complex substances that sustained its metabolism in the harsh environment and eliminated into the air its waste product, oxygen. It required very little moisture, was excellent at absorbing and retaining the little heat energy available, and could root itself in frozen crustal clays and craggy rock outcroppings. Caroline Hart was ecstatic. It seemed almost perfect. Tegan McDowell had found the unmarked sample in a darkened corner of the containment vault and had begun the initial testing. As Caroline completed the work, fresh from her first sound night of sleep in what seemed like weeks, she found it perplexing that she could find no record of it in any of the bioresearch files. The intricate weaving of the composite DNA splicing was most impressive. It must have taken years for them to construct such an elaborate and ideal series of sequences, she surmised, a fact that made it even more remarkable that there was no evident record of the research on this particular strand of bluish-black lichen. Her avid enthusiasm grew as she allowed her mind to contemplate the magnificent possibilities. This organism could be the catalyst to breathing the first signs of life onto this barren, desolate planet. A chill of eager anticipation made her tingle all over. She hadn't felt this energized since before Mars had so altered the course of her existence. The engineered strand had to be field tested. She scurried in excitement over to the intercom panel embedded on the main desk in the lab. "A and C, this is Caroline Hart in the biolab."

"What can....for you....oline?"

The broken voice through the crackling noise was Nichelle's.

"I want permission to take a sample to the botanical test site. I need to speak to Commander Maitland right away. Do you know where he is?"

"He was....medi....getting his....jury tre....Susan. Now he's rest...."

"Nichelle, I can hardly understand you," Caroline said with some acerbic irritation. "What the devil is wrong with the intercom?"

"I don't ....but I've....jor....prob.... Can't....now, I'm....sy. Don't wait....me....proba....late....dinner."

Caroline sat back in bewilderment for a short spell before docilely resigning herself to the inevitable. She would be seeing Sheri and Matt around dinner time anyway. She could ask him for permission and an escort then. In the meantime, Caroline cleaned-up the lab and headed up to the ground floor in search of Tammy to discuss the promising prospects.

As the blazing reddish-orange glare of the shrinking sun gradually tinted the late day sky to illustrious hues of blue as the light was bent at increasingly lower angles over the central dome, all was not calm and serene within the protective glass panels of A and C. Nichelle angrily threw aside a portable electronic analyzer in frustration, unable to isolate any problem in her main communication console. She had been getting badgered all afternoon by complaints regarding internal communications. It suddenly seemed that all transmissions between the domes were subject to noise, interruption, and general interference, though communications within a single structure and external transmissions appeared to be unaffected. "Goddamnit!" she cursed as she slammed another panel shut. "What the hell is wrong with this piece of shit now!"

Finding nothing wrong with the primary station, Nichelle decided to go down to the ground floor where the main relay circuitry and conduits were located, not far from the electronic guts of the computer center and near the surface tube that led to the destroyed northeast dome. A visual inspection of the large but jumbled room filled with innumerable relay stations and several tiny corridors that provided access to wiring behind the walls revealed the problem instantly to her trained, astutely observant eye. Among the delicate circuit boards and interchangeable microchip modules of the main switching station of the network was a diminutive, disk-shaped foreign device bounded with a series of infinitesimal pulsating yellow lights. It was something she had seen before. All transmission signals between domes were processed through this junction and routed to their proper destinations. This device was a signal scrambler, designed to interfere of block specific frequencies or general transmissions in either an intermittent mode or continuous disruption. "What the shit is this doing here," she bitterly mumbled to herself as she popped out the module to which it was attached and began to use her miniature electronic tools with her one good hand to disconnect the device. Once removed she examined it with a combination of curiosity and contempt before nudging the module back in place within its housing.

"What did you find there?"

Nichelle jumped back against the wall in sheer bug-eyed terror, spilling her tools across the floor with the sharp rattle, clang, and hollow thump of metal skipping against hardened cement. She bent over, gasping for air when she recognized the familiar voice. "Holy shit!" she exclaimed, panting profusely. "You scared me half-to-death you peabrain. Don't do that shit to me! You and Commander Maitland must have the softest feet on the planet. Look at this." Nichelle handed over the device. "That's what was interfering with our communications," she explained as she turned her back to close the protective plate to the switching box and locked it in place with a grunt. "Someone had to deliberately install it there. What brings you in here anyway? Shouldn't you be at dinner?"

"Looking for you. I know about it. I put it there."

Nichelle turned around with an incredulous gasp. "Say what?"

The voice was calm but ominous and threatening. A sinister smirk unlike Nichelle had ever seen broke across the face like the possessed gaze of a homicidal lover in a horror movie just before the slashing of the glistening blade. "I needed to get you here, alone. I need your help, Nichelle. Help in perpetuating this charade."

Nichelle inched back against the wall as her heart fearfully pounded in timorous shock as she watched the short, stubby, pistol-like device with the pointed, thin wire tip being aimed at her chest. "So it's you!" she exclaimed in sudden revelation. "It's been you all along!"

The devilish sneer and nod caused her skin to crawl. "Sorry about the arm though. It was never the intent to injure you."

"What do you want from me!" Nichelle wailed in desperate panic.

The casual rolling of the shoulders was unnerving. "Just for you to take a little vacation, my dear. Tine to say good night."

Nichelle watched helplessly as a forefinger pressed back against the trigger. It felt as though she had just stepped out of the shower and had stuck her finger in an electrical socket. Searing currents running through her body jolted and paralyzed her and a second later Nichelle tumbled unconscious to the floor.

It was like a carnival atmosphere within the common park of the Residential Dome after dusk as individuals and pairs vivaciously trickled in from their labors throughout the complex and the surrounding countryside, seemingly revitalized and spirited at the return of Commander Maitland and his crew. Everyone wanted to offer their congratulations and, more importantly, to hear about all the details concerning the encounter with the mysterious Borodino. The incessant inquiries became a nuisance for Matt, his forehead bandaged and still throbbing after Doctor Oliver had attended him, interfering with his enjoyment of the bountiful harvest of fresh lettuce, carrots, tomatoes, peas, and beans that Tammy Jacobs had so thoughtfully provided for this occasion. But he politely and diplomatically addressed every entreaty, nibbling on his dinner between sentences. Fortunately for him, Jack was sitting at the other end of the table. Not one for shunning the limelight, Jack proceeded to hold court with highly expressive accounts of the adventure, adding touches of flair and dramatics that stretched the borders of truth and reality. For once Matt was grateful for the brashness and swagger of his navigator, for he wrested some of the unwanted attention away from himself. Lieutenant Reynolds sat across from him as eager as anyone to question him more thoroughly about the incident, but patiently chewed on his food and quietly listened until the enlivened throngs had drifted over to the more entertaining end of the table.

"Well, Matt," he finally spoke, "you're a hero now."

Matt turned his head and scoffed. "Shit! We came within a cat's whisker of leaving everyone stranded here." He slyly looked around to be sure no one was within earshot before whispering softly. "There were a few minutes when we were totally defensive. They could have closed in and gotten off a few good laser shots. We're very fortunate to be here right now. It doesn't seem like much cause for celebration to me."

A feeble smile crossed the Lieutenant's face as he took a swallow from his cup. "You prevented the intrusion and came back alive. That sounds like a cause for celebration to me."

Matt shrugged. "Maybe. I just can't figure out what in hell they were doing here."

Reynolds gazed at him with a puzzled expression. "Did you really make those sarcastic remarks to that Russian major?"

Matt smirked cantankerously, shaking his head at his own disbelief. "I'm afraid so. Pretty stupid, uh?"

Reynolds nodded as a bright glow of amusement swept over his face. "Very. You're fortunate the man didn't have a sudden change of heart and decide that it was a fine time to finish you off. God really must have been looking down on you." Reynolds settled back in his chair and folded his arms as his tone became more serious. "But I think that you were quite astute in your suspicions regarding their story. They wouldn't use military craft for civilian and cargo transport. They're up to something."

Matt sat frozen as a few unsettling notions gnawed at the fringes of his mind, slowly causing his blood to boil inside. He removed the crumbled piece of paper from his chest pocket that Sheri had given him earlier before looking up and sneering disdainfully. "And what are we up to?"

Reynolds glanced up in surprise. "What do you mean?"

Matt angrily leaped to his feet, causing his chair to tumble to the floor as he held out the wrinkled copy of the internal memo from the NSCA Advisory Council circulated among the highest agency officials and their central government overseers. "NSCA JC Seven dash Sixteen point Two. I have a copy in my hand!"

A sudden hush came over the frolicking throng surrounding Jack as everyone turned to see what had gotten the Commander so animated. Aware that his outburst had focused attention back his way, Matt timidly righted the chair and gingerly resumed his seat. "Sorry." As the crowd gradually returned their enthusiastic attention back to Jack and the fascinating incident in space, Matt continued his tirade in a softer but just as forceful manner. "Some of the recommendations and provisions in this document, to be implemented incrementally over the next few years, include denial of requests for representation in Congress or the NSCA Governing Council, rejection of petition permitting Chief Administrator position to be freely elected among the permanent residents, further restrictions on immigration in order to control growth and inhibit production capabilities of certain essentials, an increase in mining quotas and import taxes to help fund social programs on Earth, and a permanent military garrison to be stationed at Jamestown and I quote, 'to discourage radical separatist elements from organizing,' unquote." Matt irately tossed the paper towards Reynolds. "They don't intend to grant complete autonomy as originally chartered. They want a colonial possession!"

Reynolds was stunned as he picked up the crimped paper. "I don't understand this."

Matt lurched forward and bitterly retorted. "You were going to be sent here all along, weren't you?"

Reynolds frowned in dismay as he examined the document and shook his head in disbelief before dropping the page and looking back at Matt. "My platoon was slated for garrison duty here within the next year, yes, but to provide security for the colonists. not this."

Matt leaned back against the chair. folded his arms, and simpered. "So you were in training for Mars when this crisis erupted. So they decided to stick you aboard my ship now and move up the time table."

"We don't make policy, Matt. We go where we're told to go. But my only orders are to protect you and your party and provide security for the colony, nothing more."

Matt rose to his feet and shook his head in disillusionment as he refolded the paper and returned it to his pocket. "And I thought we were making progress. Government just can't stop growing and regulating people's lives. Some things never change. It's all about power."

It was two hours later when Matt found himself standing in weary but eager anticipation outside of Sheri's quarters after being invited over for what she termed a homecoming surprise. All he knew was that he couldn't bare many more surprises like had befallen him over the past couple of days. He was feeling rather weak and fatigued and just being close to her for a little while would do wonders for his emotional rejuvenation. Once the door electronically opened, he cautiously stepped into the darkened room with no sign of her. "Sheri, it's me. Where are you?"

"In here, Matt," came her sweet, sensual reply from the soft glowing luster emanating from her bedroom. "Come on in."

Deliberately stepping through the open doorway, Matt's senses were immediately bombarded by the provocative sight of scantily clad Sheri sprawled atop the bed wearing only a revealing, plunging white lace bra and a tiny white cotton bikini panty, her arms and legs stretching suggestively and invitingly towards the four corners of the bed. The far side of the mattress was littered with various implements, aids, restraints, and lotions intended for mature play, pleasure, and arousal.

"Don't just stand there ogling me," Sheri pleaded with that adorable grin. "Get out of that grungy flight suit and get your butt over here and play with me."

Matt was overwhelmed with desirous yearnings as he could hardly contain his lustful elation, nervously fumbling with his uniform zipper. "I like to look," he humbly offered as he finally managed to peel out of his garments, leaving him naked before her save for a tight pair of golden briefs trimmed in navy. "I can't tell you how sexy and appetizing you look to me right now," he admitted as he approached the near side of the bed, lecherously shifting his eyes from her rising breasts to the barely concealed junction between her widely spread thighs before pausing in hesitation. "I was just hoping for a more ideal, romantic situation to..."

"Matt," she gently interrupted as she stared at the growing bulge in his brief and grinned with delight, "can you forget about thinking for once and just allow yourself to feel for a change. I can see how desirous you are of me." She naughtily raised up and tenderly stoked him there for a moment that sent thrilling shudders rippling through him before laying back down and stretching her arms overhead once more. "I love you and I want you and it doesn't matter to me if you think that you're in love with me or not. I know in my heart how much you care for me. After these last few days, and nearly losing you, we owe it to ourselves. We may never get that perfect setting with a mountaintop picturesque sunset or that sandy beach with foaming ocean surf. So let's enjoy each other now before it's too late."

Matt could no longer contain or deny his lascivious cravings nor hide his amorous interests for her, whose rising heights she was quick to observe. The traumatic events of the last two days had also awakened him to the realization of just how much she meant to him and how precarious their situation had become. Either or both of them could have their lives unceremoniously ripped away at any moment. The battle in space had cemented his love for her. Sitting by her side, he leaned up and kissed her lovingly at the base of her neck. Sheri purred in contentment as his moistened lips sent titillating shivers careening like surging rapids through the chasms of her body.

"This may take three or four hours," Matt said with a crafty smile as he straightened and began to trace tender lines across her flat belly.

"At least," she replied with a radiant grin and a delightful giggle. "I asked Caroline to borrow some toys from Lucinda for me. Let's cut loose and have some erotic fun. You can have your way with me tonight."

Matt recalled the same offer from Lucinda. But this was different. Sheri was the woman of his dreams. She was the one that he so much adored. She was the object of all his fantasies and desires. There would be no more contradictions of duty and painful memories. It was right with Sheri and he was finally going to enjoy all of her affections and charms.

Sheri moaned and quivered in pleasure as his fingers caressed her upper breasts and over her dainty, rising lace cups. She whimpered and giggled as they trailed stimulating fibers of velvet across her stomach and ribs. Matt enjoyed the natural responsiveness that his touch induced, watching her skin ripple across her bones as she restlessly squirmed in bliss, listening to her sobs and cries of excitement as she kept herself stretched out and available. By the time his dancing fingers had lingered awhile on her undulating hips and trembling thighs, they were both worked up into a pretty good frenzy. Sheri roared in erotic passion, her hips thrashing from side to side as his electrifying fingers slid onto the softness of her bikini. Suddenly the irritating buzz of the room intercom snapped the libidinous mood like an arid twig. Matt abruptly stopped his exhilarating affections and looked up in surprise. Sheri angrily rolled over onto her side and simmered huffily as she scowled at the communication panel embedded on her night stand. She glanced over at Matt with imploring, despondent eyes and gently touched his cheek.

"I'm sorry, Matt. This should only take a minute." She lunged with her hand and irritably slammed the answering button. "Yes!"

"Sheri, it's Vijay."

She was incensed at the unwelcome interruption. "Damnit, Vijay! What the hell do you want at this hour?"

"I am very sorry, Sheri, but I am looking for Matt. I can't find him anywhere. Have you seen him?"

Sheri looked disconsolately at Matt and tumbled listlessly to the bed, her hands clawing in frustration through her wavy, luscious black hair. Matt disheartenedly slid up to the head of the bed and sighed in depression. "Yes, Vij, what is it?"

"Oh, good." His voice was more chipper. "I thought I might find you there. About time you two got together."

"Vij!" Matt bellowed vexatiously with soaring impatience. "This had better be damned important!"

"Unfortunately it is, Matt. Nichelle Bennett is missing. We can't find her anywhere in this dome and has not been seen since before dinner."

"Shit!" Matt grumbled as he agitatingly ran a hand through his scalp. Sheri shot upright in trepidation, gasping fright as she laid her hands on Matt's sturdy shoulders. "Inform Lieutenant Reynolds and have him shake out the marines. Then scrounge up some volunteers."

"For the morning?"

Matt scowled acrimoniously at the speaker. "Tonight! I'll join you outside in five minutes."

"Oh my God," Sheri wailed in despair. "Not again."

"You had better get dressed," Matt suggested as stood and began to gather his clothes. "I need your help too." Seeing the anxiety and disappointment written all across her face. Matt dropped his flight suit and grabbed her arms, pulling her to her feet and pressed her tightly to his sweating skin, an action that immediately triggered a long, intimate kiss as her breasts pushed firmly into his chest within his powerful grip, her fingers clawing wildly at his naked back. "We'll continue this at a later time," he softly insured as their lips reluctantly parted as he drifted adoringly into her bright blue eyes, his fingers softly running through her succulent black hair along the side of her head. "I promise you that."

The unusual point of glitter below the volcano summit to their distant west had drawn their attention for hours as the excursion rover crunched along the sharply defined tabular sheet lava flows at the northeastern base of Alba Patera. It twinkled like the sparkling of clear blue lake water under the brilliant rays of the Martian sun. To both Yong Chang and Raymond Ponsonby it was a baffling sight. Such natural reflectivity on the Martian surface was as foreign to it as a flowing river or humidity in the atmosphere. Not one of the more towering inactive volcanoes in the Tharsis Plateau region, Alba Patera was, nevertheless, easily the broadest, its base extending nearly 1,000 miles in diameter. Despite a height that barely reached three and one-half miles, its 60 mile wide caldera still dominated the distant skyline, its gentle slopes looming above the rising ridge-lined horizon like a diligent sentinel. When extreme magnification on the forward window failed to clarify the phenomenon, the two scientists decided to take a slight detour to have a closer look. For the next few hours the meshed wheels of the rover rumbled cross-country up a series of long, broad, sharply crested radial ridges , many whose pinnacles were gouged with channels several hundred yards wide that indicated the presence of hardened lava tubes. Maneuvering up these modest inclines proved tedious as the slopes were often fractured and striated, probably as a result of ancient overflows of lava from the main channels. Their deliberate ascent carried them past the series of shallow, pitted craters at Phlegethon Catena and near the southern approaches to the fissure system of Alba Fossae that ran northeast to southwest along the northeastern slopes of the volcano. From this vantage point they were still too distant to identify the source of the strange light reflections but Yong noticed something odd within the narrow, steep canyons to their right.

"Ray, take a look at Alba Fossae."

Raymond Ponsonby strained to get an unobstructed view out of the very far bounds of the window. "I don't see anything unusual."

"Pivot us forty-five degrees so we can use the magnifier."

From the sloping ground that overlooked part of the Alba Fossae fissure, the men could see an eerie haze settling around the northern extremities of the depression. At the highest magnification setting it appeared like a thin, dark cloud, rolling and undulating in shades of gray and black as it slowly dissipated into the atmosphere in long, slender streamers of fluffy filaments.

"It almost reminds me of old pictures of polluting mist hanging over city skylines," Ray casually remarked. "I think it was called smog."

"If I didn't know better," Yong added with fascination, "I'd say that something was burning out there. Look!" His finger pressed against a magnified image in the window within the body of the fog-like obscurity along the rubble, fractured floor. "Doesn't that look like a metal structural frame to you, all black and twisted?"

Ray glanced at him oddly. "You can't tell from here, Yong. You're imagining things. That whole channel is littered with rocks and mineral debris. That haze is probably just some odd atmospheric anomaly. Mars has a reputation for that. Large scale topography, you know."

"You may be right," Yong replied with obvious reservations. "But it's too late in the day for fog, and I've never seen haze that dark before, almost like soot."

"We're burning daylight," Ray noted. "We need to get much closer to the summit if we're going to identify that reflection. We can get a closer look at that fissure when we continue north."

"All right," Yong ambivalently agreed, uncertain as to which mystery intrigued him more, "but I want to inform Jamestown of our intentions and get further instructions. I've got a funny feeling about this."

Lucinda Desjardin wearily trudged back to her quarters from her mid-evening liaison with Private Walinski, slovenly pulling the tail of her snug, cable-stitching knit peach pullover from the waistband of her tight black leather shorts, her long, curly blond hair tattered and disheveled from her most recent hour of passion. She was too exhausted to brush it back to perfect symmetry after the past 48 hours and having gotten precious little sleep the night before, having magnanimously volunteered to participate in what she knew would be a futile and vain search for the unfortunate Nichelle. Still it was good to keep her finger on the pulse of all the major activities encompassing them. Her computer expertise was in constant demand, seemingly everyone had problems with their systems or software at one time or another. It was the perfect assignment for keeping tabs on the thoughts and progress of the other specialists. And it gave her the opportunity to apply her feminine charms on whoever she desired or thought would be advantageous to pursue. She had managed to create a few rifts, but more tension was needed. Distraction was her best ally. However, the command structure continued to elude her. She had taken her best shot at Commander Maitland and had barely come up short. But she was an accomplished temptress that didn't back off easily. She still had hope that he could be compromised. Reynolds was out of the question, unapproachable and pure as the driven snow. The ship's engineer, whose closeness to the Commander could provide an invaluable source of insight, avoided meaningful or flirtatious conversation with her like the plague. She wasn't about to try to entice Sheri again for she still valued her life. Caroline's gradual acceptance of her fate made her a viable and potentially fruitful candidate once again, especially due to her sensual vulnerability at this time, but she had noticed that Caroline was paying closer attention to that marine corporal, an affair with whom would certainly end any future amorous opportunity. But at this moment even lustful Lucinda was not much enamored with the idea of multiple partners. She was steadily growing weary of all the cloak-and-dagger stuff and though she thoroughly enjoyed the variety of her sexual experiences, for some strange reason she found herself inexplicably drawn to the affections of one Private John Walinski. Her heart and body were yearning for his attentions above all others, not a very covetous situation for someone in her predicament. Just wishing to feel the delicate softness of her silk chemise against her skin and jumping under her sheets, alone, for the first time in recent memory, Lucinda briskly strode into her bedroom and illuminated the darkness into a soft dim. As she was about to unsnap her shorts she suddenly felt the suffocating clamp of a warm, sweaty, brackish appendage pressing across her mouth along with vise-like grip of a powerful arm ensnaring her shoulders, pulling her tight against a solid though pliant object that she reasoned was an organic warm-blooded body. Frightened out of her mind, Lucinda twisted and writhed in a vain attempt to break free, her panicked cries for help muted and muffled into incoherent garbles.

"Keep quiet. I won't harm you," a firm but benign masculine voice in perfect English smoothly commanded.

Her frantic squirming only resulted in a tightening of his grasp like the constricting coils of a cobra.

"Calm down," he gently pleaded. "Are you Lucinda Desjardin?"

The sound of her name had a tranquilizing affect as Lucinda ended her struggles and calmly settled back against the warm frame, nodding her head in acknowledgment.

"Good," he sighed in relief. "My name is John. I've been sent by your people to contact you. Now, I'm going to take my hand from your mouth. Please don't call out. Okay?"

Lucinda nodded again. Slowly his hearty squeeze across her mouth relaxed and fell away to her arm as Lucinda panted heavily, still shaking from the tingling chills of terror, the stranger's arm still tightly locked around her.

"Is this room secure?" he asked with a tone of concern.

"Yes, we can talk freely," she gasped between laborious breaths. "No one will come in."

Lucinda began to regain her composure as his crushing hold slowly loosened. She had been expecting some kind of message or delivery, but nothing this dramatic. She spun around to behold the agreeable, whiskered face of a trim man in his early forties standing about six feet tall, his thick layer of long, soft brown hair slightly disordered above his brows and covered part of his ears' his engaging blue eyes disclosing both a measure of kindness and skepticism. He was dressed in a one-piece burgundy zippered work suit with an unidentifiable circular patch on the right shoulder.

"Shit!" she emotionally exclaimed, clutching at her chest. "You nearly gave me a heart attack. How did you get in here anywhere?"

John pointed up at the far wall near the ceiling where a large ventilation grate sat yawning freely in the air partially unhinged.

Lucinda turned to him in astonishment. "You mean you found my room crawling through that?"

"I can read a blueprint," John candidly replied. "Your last transmission told us which room was yours. You forget, I used to live here."

Lucinda smiled, folded her arms and began to pace. "I was beginning to wonder when I would be contacted. I haven't been able to get off a transmission since they got their communications back on-line. They may have been able to detect my signal, you know."

"Dave finally completed the last message," he continued as he unzipped the baggy chest pocket of his suit and removed the plastic sleeve containing a data disk.

Lucinda excitedly rushed up to accept the gift. "It's about time. I don't know how much longer I could have stalled them. I had been running out of excuses on why my fancy equipment had been unable to crack the second password. I'll load it first thing in the morning, very secretively."

John began to stray nervously within the room as Lucinda carefully placed the tiny disk in her top dresser drawer. "This is our last desperate attempt to scare them out of here," he ponderously remarked. "Or at least get them concentrating south. We could have used more time."

"They solved their reactor problem quicker than I expected," Lucinda explained as she approached her visitor. "They never even stopped. Even a little on-board intrigue barely slowed them down. They are a determined lot."

John shook his head in bewilderment. "We tried to tell your people that but would they listen? Noooo...of course not. They don't pay those people to quit. I always said that this was a scatterbrained plan from the outset. How can you hope to hide the existence of another settlement indefinitely? And now an open rebellion to boot."

"All great adventures are replete with risk," Lucinda noted as she placed a consoling hand upon his shoulder.

"Risk!" John bellowed in wide-eyed agitation. "Risk! Let me tell you about risk. My ass is grass if I get caught here. They landed here too early. I nearly got discovered planting evidence. I had to stun one of those soldiers. Fortunately I was still wearing one of your military space suits or I may have been identified. We only had the chance to assemble one of those sentry robots." He uneasily took a seat on the edge of the bed and anxiously ran his fingers through his frazzled scalp. "Hell! How did I ever let myself get talked into this? I'm a geologist, not James Bond."

Lucinda was perplexed. "Who?"

"A twentieth century male Fawna Lorelei. Never mind. You didn't give us enough time to prep the region that would lead them towards the Giant Crack and away from us. Are they buying any of this?"

Lucinda smirked. "Not much, though I believe that the clues they have gathered has convinced them to concentrate in that direction."

"Well, I hope you're right," John apprehensively replied. "But expecting them to pack-up and bugger off was a bit much to hope for, I think. After all, an entire colony of human beings disappeared from a multibillion dollar installation. You can't just sweep those carcasses under the carpet." He slapped his knees in annoyance. "And who anticipated them bringing space marines this soon. Our information must have been more accurate than we thought. With them here things could get dicey."

Lucinda clasped her hands behind her back and strolled in front of John. "I'm sorry that you all got caught up in our little revolution. We never intended to reveal ourselves."

John looked up assuredly. "It's your fault, you know. If that energy dampening field of yours hadn't broken down, we never would have detected those electromagnetic and thermal energy levels that sent me and my partner up that way in the first place. We never would have inadvertently stumbled across your experimental genetically engineered lichen field that compelled you to intercept us and has since kept everyone's candles burning late at night."

Lucinda shrugged, glancing at him with one of her patented crafty grins. "We just offered you the opportunity. It was your decision. We all want the same thing."

"Of course," John replied with a broad smile as he leaped to his feet with a congenial pat to her shoulders. "We were working on a diplomatic solution of our own when you came along and screwed everything up, changing our destiny forever. Frankly, with everything that has gone wrong, I'm surprised that this affair hasn't gotten completely out of hand. So continue to do whatever it is you do to cause disruption and confusion. Maybe we'll get lucky."

Lucinda nodded her consent. "The two disappearances and the stories of strange forces seem to be creating the most distress among the group. Perhaps we should feed that fear."

"Maybe," John answered dubiously as he began to aimlessly roam around the room once more, "but the more people that disappear, the riskier it becomes, not to mention the logistical problems. I checked on the hologram wall and your two guests before I stowed my environment suit and crawled over here. They're madder than a nest of angry hornets but behaving themselves."

Lucinda snickered. "Tegan deserved it. How can someone so full of himself be such a terrible lover." Her amusement quickly turned to a more solemn nature. "Tell me, how's it going up there?"

"Not bad, now that your screening equipment is functioning again. Loyalist forces are keeping a low profile. No one wants to risk detection in a major action. We think that their manpower and supplies are running low. Your people are just hoping that they can eradicate the problem before they try something desperate."

"Don't worry," Lucinda assured as she fondly touched his arm. "It's going to work out. We'll be able to build an unfettered, prosperous world here once this mess is behind us. But first we have to win."

John's face glistened with mild satisfaction. "I'll say one thing about that CAS ship, Lucinda. They did all of us and themselves a big favor, a really big favor, by driving away that EESC warship."

Lucinda quizzically tilted her head misapprehension.

"Your people intercepted some of their communications," John explained. "It was carrying military reinforcements and tons of equipment to the Loyalists. It looks like your little insurrection is not worth starting a war over back on Earth."

"At least not yet," Lucinda replied with a measure of foreboding. "I'll just feel much better when the Red Planet is peaceful again."

John scoffed. "With humans on it? Good luck. Anyway, the Loyalists should soon be forced to capitulate. Just yesterday there was a minor fracas in the northern chasms of Alba Fossae."

Lucinda stepped back in alarm. "Alba Fossae!" she cried out excitedly. "They have two scientists exploring near there."

John was overwhelmed with consternation. "Near Alba Fossae?"

"Somewhere on the slopes of Alba Patera," Lucinda added.

"Son-of-a-bitch!" he screamed as his body twisted distressfully in all directions. "The Loyalists are using an abandoned research station on Alba Patera as a base!" His inflections were laced with panic. "If those scientists run into them the shit is really going to hit the fan. I've got to get back to Perepelkin," he frantically declared as Lucinda reached out to calm him. "I've got to warn them."

"Settle down," Lucinda tersely implored as she firmly clutched his arm. "Just relax a minute. You're all worked up."

John took a few deep breaths until his muscles relaxed.

"That's better. Now, how are you going to get back?"

John paused for a moment as he collected his emotions. "Some of your aerodynamic geniuses came up with this tiny, egg-shaped, twin seat contraption that skims a dozen feet off the deck at a thousand miles per hour and is equipped with one of your energy cloaking devices that prevents electronic detection. It's programmed to go from point to point, avoiding all obstacles, using super detailed topographical mapping as a guide. It's a prototype. They thought this would make a good field test. It's hidden in a nearby ravine to the north. Love to take you for a spin around the world."

Lucinda grinned with delight. "When this is over you have a date."

John bobbed his head shyly and politely shook her hand. "I have to get moving. Thanks for everything. Best of luck. I hope to see you again."

Lucinda firmly held onto his hand as he was about to turn towards the ventilation shaft. "What's your name again?"

He hesitated, fondly gazing at her. "It's John, John Osborne."

Lucinda wiggled alluring in front of him, her lips moistening sensually as she temporarily forgot about her covetous attachment to the other John. "Well, John Osborne, are you sure you can't stay a little while longer?" Her hand reached for the tail of her knit top and ripped it over her head, her luscious breasts jostling seductively behind a revealing black lace bra as they were exposed to his ravenous stare. She enticingly slithered against his chest and coiled her arms around his neck. "Please stay. I've never made love to a Martian before."

CHAPTER

12

The atmosphere of apprehension and dismay within the glass enclosure of the central dome was as thick as a London fog bank rolling off the Thames as the huddled mass of forlorn faces listened in silent dread to the disconcerting words of David Hart's second message on the monitor of Lucinda's primary terminal, recorded five days after the first, according to the log. Anxious hands and feet fidgeted nervously where they stood, a seemingly epidemic of itchy scalps and crawling skin causing active fingers to scratch and claw as if their bodies were covered with an irritating rash. His voice was somber and composed as he related accounts of additional strange sightings, disappearances and sabotage. He told of the meteorite hit on the northeast dome that caused two fatalities and the culminating event that ultimately persuaded the colonists to abandon the site - some undefined malevolent tampering with the nuclear plant in which a core breech was barely averted and forced the reduction of power to the barest of minimums. As he intently listened to the report, Matt found David Hart's appearance as curious as his message. He was clean-shaven and well groomed, his brown hair with tinges of gray meticulously combed in place. His eyes had a certain lustrous sparkle, a lively spirit that was incompatible with the situation being narrated. It was a very peculiar contrast from his worn and haggard demeanor on his first log entry, considering the additional stress that he must have been under. The bombshell came near the end of the recording. Dave reported that no transmission or record of this activity had ever been made for fear of compromise or discovery, but for more than half a Martian year the Jamestown colonists had been covertly constructing, day

329

and night, another habitation somewhere deep within the depths of the scalloped walls of the immense canyon system of Valles Marineris. He declined to reveal the exact location for fear that the disk would fall into the possession of those forces working against them. The colonists believed that the vastness and ruggedness of the terrain's abounding fractured tributary channels would be the safest place to avoid detection. Actually it was an expansion of a project that they had been secretly working on anyway, a smaller settlement closer to their primary mining operations. But all normal colony functions had been scrapped until their safety and continued existence could be assured. His final comments contained an ominous warning but whose delivery revealed more empathy. emotion, and peppered with regret than his reserved manner had previously displayed.

"I would advise you to leave at once. Jamestown has been compromised by forces that we do not understand. Stay away from the northwestern latitudes. No party recently venturing there has ever returned. Please don't waste your precious resources looking for us. We have developed a sort of dampening field that hides all of our energy emissions. If the NSCA still has a presence on Mars when we feel secure in our position, we will contact you. Perhaps Hellas or Isidis would be feasible for colonization. I wish all my fine colleagues and associates peace and best wishes. Please tell my wife that I am sorry and that I hope she can find it in her heart to forgive me. She's the finest woman I have ever known but it's too late for her to follow me now. Our time has run out. This is Chief Administrator David Hart concluding the final message from Jamestown colony, bidding you all farewell."

An eerie silence resembling the cavernous emptiness of a deserted auditorium permeated A and C as the computer monitor returned to the playback selection screen. Sheri wrapped a comforting arm around a stunned Caroline, who could only lower her head and sniffle, raising a hand to cover her eyes. But there were no tears. She had no more grief to give. All the pain, despair, and sadness had been drained from her. She had resigned herself to the permanent nature of her separation for some time, but the sudden shock of its reality was still quite powerful. Hearing it from his own lips stamped an unequivocal finality to her ambiguous predicament. She was officially alone now, abandoned. She realized, however, that she had been that way for nearly three years. and that she only had herself to blame.

Matt sat petrified, lost in ponderous thoughts that did not involve fear, despondency, or nervousness. He replayed the entire recording in his head and dubiously twitched in a quandary. In regards to the damaged dome, David Hart was lying! They had uncovered convincing evidence that the dome was a victim of sabotage, and whether he was an active participant or not, the formidable efforts it took to make it appear to be a meteorite strike required a considerable amount of cooperation. The great question gnawing at him was just how much of the rest of the story was he equivocating? And why?

Lucinda's sudden spin in her chair to face the group shook Matt from his private deliberations. "We should make arrangements to leave as soon as possible," she fearfully offered as she warily glanced at the others.

Matt leered at her angrily. "Certainly not!" he adamantly exclaimed. "No command of mine is going to be run off with unsubstantiated fairy tales." He turned towards Reynolds who had been quietly standing behind him. "Do you concur, Lieutenant?"

Reynolds nodded decisively. "Absolutely, sir."

"Unsubstantiated!" Lucinda yelled excitedly. "Are you blind?"

Matt thrust a determined hand towards her face that gave her reason to pause. "I realize, of course, that something was here when we first arrived and that two of our associates are missing, but those are the only incidents that corroborate any part of his story." Matt looked into the troubled eyes of all those gathered around him. "In any event, I'm not about to leave before we ascertain the condition of Miss Bennett and Mister McDowell. Agreed?"

Reluctantly all heads somberly bobbed. Matt scanned the area behind him until he found Vijay leaning casually with folded arms against the wall of one of the triangular stations. "What about the reactor account?"

Vijay frowned, shifting his weight to his other foot as he skeptically shook his head. "I tell you, Matt, neither myself or Harold Donovan found any evidence of reactor problems. No radiation leakage, heat degradation, core damage, coolant problems, nothing. In fact, it's in remarkably good condition."

"Good," Matt said as he took a few resolute steps towards him, "but there is no better way to cripple this facility. I want either you, Harold, or Andre to be in there at all times. The reactor should never be left unattended. And I need a marine guard present as well." He looked back at Reynolds with a hopeful eye. "I assume you can handle that, Lieutenant?"

"Of course, Commander."

"Make sure you check all the access and service walkways throughout that facility, just in case."

"What about Ray and Yong?" Caroline worriedly inquired as she emerged from her stupor. "They're heading right for the area where Dave warned us about."

Matt was confounded. "Shit!" For a few brief moments he had completely forgotten about his exploration party on the slopes of Alba Patera. He briskly stepped over to Sheri in a tempered panic. "Quickly, get them on the horn. Have them abort their mission immediately and return to Jamestown. You must warn them!"

Yong Chang scrambled back into the rover, depressurized, and quickly took his seat behind the forward window and activated its magnifier to the highest setting. This was the closest view that they could get. The excursion rover was perched on the lip of one of the sharply crested radial ridges about 50 miles from the caldera's summit. Ray was still outside, collecting rock and soil samples from the quarter-mile wide lava channel winding before them. The oddity was still too far away for their helmet magnifiers to distinguish anything but the more powerful mag of the rover's window could delineate a little detail between bright flashes of glare. Yong estimated the location to be about 15 miles from the apex of the caldera and although their line of sight was completely unobstructed, it was still very difficult to identify. Nestled behind a jagged outcropping along the rippled slope appeared to be a long, low, rectangular gantry-like structural framework whose dark material resembled iron or steel. The rays of the sun ere bouncing off what looked like sheets of metal plating that encompassed much of the structure. Interspersed throughout were lighter cylindrical projections oriented at a slightly upward angle.

"Can you identify it from there?" Ray's voice beckoned over the communicator. "I can't see shit from here."

"No," Yong replied with an air of concern. "Bit whatever it is, that's got to be manmade."

"Could it be part of that old EESC research facility?" Ray guessed.

"I don't think so. I believe it's located at least fifty miles to the south. Hurry, Ray, I don't like this. I'm going to inform Jamestown."

Yong could hear the amusing chuckle coming from his partner. "Just a few minutes more. You need to relax. You're as jittery as my wife."

Sheri Alderman's voice sounded overly exuberant and slightly agitated after Yong established the transmission link. "Thank God!" she exclaimed. "I've been trying to reach you for thirty minutes."

"We've been outside collecting samples and doing a little exploring," Yong defensively explained. "Listen, there is something strange on Alba Patera. We still can't make a positive ID but...."

"Never mind that now," Sheri hastily interrupted. "Listen to me carefully. You boys have to get out of there and return to Jamestown immediately. We have reason to believe that you may be in some danger."

Outside, Ray was climbing out of the chiseled, shallow channel when he caught a glimpse of some subtle movement within the curving canal a half-mile or more to the south. The strongest magnification of his visor revealed several strange, murky figures sprinkled among the reds, oranges, and sienna tans of the rubble and boulders that encumbered the channel floor. The unusual contrast of color was the only characteristic that made their creeping, laggard progression noticeable at all. "Yong, there's something approaching from the south," he called out with inflections speckled with fright, "moving between the rocks in the channel."

Yong strained his eyes for a look, to no avail. "One moment, Jamestown. I'm getting an excited message from Ray." Switching to their private frequency, Yong sternly shouted to his colleague. "Ray! Get your butt back in here. NOW!!! We've been instructed to bug-out."

"On my way," Ray replied as he raced across the lava flow slope, dragging his cumbersome sample box by his side. "I've had enough of this skullduggery bullshit for one day."

"He'll be aboard in a minute," Yong reported to Sheri as he watched Ray scurry towards the rover airlock and out of sight of the forward window. An instant later he heard a loud, sharp groan and a heavy thump over the speaker. "Ray! What's your status, Ray?" Yong's plea was greeted with only silence. His voice became frantic. "Ray! Talk to me, Ray!"

"Excursion rover, report situation," a deeply intense, unyielding voice resonated over the long distance transmitter. It was Commander Maitland who, along with Lieutenant Reynolds, had rushed over to the colony communications station the minute Sheri had established the link.

"Ray doesn't answer," Yong anxiously replied. "I'm going after him. Wait a second!" His voice became hysterical. "There's something coming towards me from the summit. A great flaming arrow trailing...." The first few pitches of a horrifying scream were abruptly wiped away by a thunderous screech and crackle of electronic noise followed by the lonely, depressing snapping of static.

Matt furiously yelled into the microphone. "Yong, come in! Report status! Yong!"

Sheri touched his arm and looked up despondently. "He's gone."

"Goddamnit!" Matt wailed in distress and anger as he agitatingly stalked across the floor, arms aimlessly flailing in the air.

Lieutenant Reynolds, standing passively nearby, reached for his belt and removed his compact private military communicator. "Sergeant Douglas, assemble First Squad in the warehouse in thirty minutes. Full load, including thruster packs. Battle alert."

It took Matt a few moments to gather his turbulent emotions before storming up in aggravation to Reynolds. "What the hell are you doing?"

Reynolds returned a quizzical look. "What is the fastest way I can get up there?" he inquired, successfully evading the original question.

Matt scoffed. "Your jet packs, I suppose. Rovers would take days. Why?"

"I'm afraid their range is limited to one hundred miles. We could never carry enough propellant." He glanced at Matt peculiarly. "What about your PL?"

"Now wait right there," Matt bitterly protested as he held out his hands. "I hope you're not conceiving any crazy notion that's going to wreck my lander. You just can't set that ship down on any surface that happens to look level. So unless you brought some construction engineers to build a landing grid you can forget it."

Reynolds contemplatively scratched his chin. "Can it hover, maintain a stationary position above a fixed point, say, one hundred feet off the ground."

Matt rolled his shoulders, unable to follow the direction of his query. "I suppose so. There would be a lot of shimmying and bucking."

Reynolds smiled. "That doesn't matter. We can do it."

Matt was puzzled. "Do what?"

"The PL can fly us near the target area, hover, and my men can disembark by way of the airlock using their thruster packs to descend to the surface. That is, Commander, if you want to find out what happened to your scientists up there."

Matt's disposition was immediately brightened. "You bet I do, Lieutenant," he answered with a determined grin. "I'm sick of stumbling around in the dark." He turned to Sheri with renewed vigor. "Inform Jack that he's about to take out the Nathanael Greene on a little trip."

Sheri hesitated, glancing at Matt with concern. "He'll need a copilot to handle communications and monitor the instruments. I doubt if any of those marines are familiar with PL equipment."

Matt pondered briefly. "You're right. I guess I should go along."

Sheri objected. "But, Matt, I...."

"Forgive me, sir," Reynolds interrupted her complaint, "but both of us should not be away from this facility at the same time. Besides, your mission Commander. Your place is here."

Matt paused reflectively. He knew the Lieutenant was correct and he also knew what the logical choice would be. It wasn't a matter of competence or confidence. He didn't like the idea of exposing her to potential danger, not at all. He cast her way that adoring gaze that always made her body tingle, and this time was no exception. She understood the concern he had for her, but she wanted to go.

"You know that I'm a fully qualified PL pilot," she argued as her hips squirmed restlessly on the seat. "I know all the systems."

Matt wavered, quietly fidgeting on his feet.

"Damnit, Matt!" she hollered as she became quite disturbed. "Just about everyone else has put themselves at risk on this mission but me. I've just been doing odd jobs inside while the rest of you have been running around God's creation." Her face displayed a steadfast determination as her tone softened. "Let me do my share, Matt, or are you going to let your feelings for me affect the way you conduct your command? That's not the Matthew Maitland I know. If so, maybe your initial instincts were right. Maybe a relationship would be a bad idea."

Matt dropped his head and thought for a moment before swallowing hard and nodding in agreement. "Yes, Sheri, you're the most qualified to go. But you had better not wreck my lander."

Sheri beamed with joy, bouncing with excitement as she proceeded to notify Jack over the internal communication system.

Matt's mind suddenly focused on another terrifying notion that had been lingering within its depths since Yong's first report from Alba Patera but not forced to the forefront until now. He reached out a troubled hand, grabbing Reynolds' arm as he was about to walk away and gravely posed the question. "We are not alone on this planet, are we, Tom?"

Reynolds agonizingly vacillated for several seconds before he slowly bowed his head and smirked, shaking it from side to side. Matt was taken aback, astonished and dumbfounded that his friend would have held out on him. Carefully and with trepidation he pressed the issue. "Are we talking little green men here?"

Reynolds scoffed derisively. "Martians? You read too much fantasy. The Martians, my good friend, are us."

The National Security Agency had known about the existence of another settlement for three years but for political and security reasons had decided to keep that knowledge a secret. During the Lunar Conflict when the Space Colonization Accords were temporarily suspended, they had monitored an unusually large amount of shipping traffic originating from EESC member states, much more than could be justified by routine resupply missions to remote scientific research stations. Able to decipher only a small fraction of intercepted coded messages, analysts were, nevertheless, able to ascertain that cargo included construction and military equipment as well as personnel. Additionally, they had determined that over the past decade many more people had traveled to Mars than had apparently returned to Earth. Undercover operatives were dispatched to Jamestown but returned a year later with no evidence to refute the contention that the EESC had only temporary research outposts located on the planet. Still they knew that it was there; it's exact location, however, they could not be sure. What worried agency directors was the clandestine nature of its establishment. After all, Mars was not carved up into territorial possessions or spheres of influence; it was open for all. What was the purpose of keeping it a secret? Fearing that the Jamestown colonists may have fallen victim to some dark and sinister design, Reynolds and his platoon of space marines were dispatched at the last minute not only to provide some security for the rescue team but also to establish an initial military presence at Jamestown. Others were preparing to join them, if necessary.

After sending out his rescue team, Matt solicitously returned to the central dome, dug out one of those cold field ration packs brought by the marines, and somberly nestled around one of the circular tables that lined the natural russet rock garden in the hub of the commerce level. He didn't have much of an appetite and even a less desire for company. This phase of the operation was now completely out of his hands. Now the hard part began - the excruciating idle waiting. It would be over two hours before his team reached the Alba Patera region. One hundred and twenty minutes of churning stomach acids and a swollen, dried throat, unable to suppress the mangled, tormenting thoughts of everything that could go wrong. He was uneasily nibbling on a wafer when Vijay slowly strolled up and slid into the seat across the table.

"Harold, a couple of the marines, and I finished going through every passageway and service crawl space in the reactor plant. We found no sign of any intruder or any indication of equipment tampering."

Matt silently acknowledged the report.

"What are you doing?" Vijay asked with a touch of befuddlement.

The stress and anguish was written across his face in boldface type. "Vij, what if I'm wrong sending them up there?" His hands moved in a choreographic routine with his mouth. "Maybe I should have been more heedful of David Hart's warnings. If there is some mysterious and ominous danger lurking there, I could lose all of them at a snap of a finger."

Vijay clasped his fingers together on the table and pressed forward. "I had the impression that is why we are here. We can't find many answers hibernating under these domes." He sighed briefly. "You are worried about her, are you not, Matt?"

Matt crossed his arms and flung himself back against the chair in frustration, glancing off to the side in distraction. "Damnit, of course I'm worried about her," he softly groaned. "I'm worried about all of them."

Sympathetic to his friend's plight, Vijay attempted to divert Matt's attention, realizing just how intensely it tortured his soul to put others in jeopardy. "When we have finished here, what do you think the NSCA should do? Should we abandon our colonization efforts?"

Matt turned incredulously towards Vijay. "Absolutely not," he adamantly proclaimed with a piercing stare of admonishment, "as long as their are no enigmatic forces out there that we don't understand that are detrimental to human life. If there are others here, we have to find a way to coexist, or fight for our rightful foothold."

"To what end?" Vijay continued. "What would you like to see happen here?"

Matt's muscles relaxed. "Well, if the plant's Caroline showed me the other day are any indication, I'd like to see their terraforming efforts continue. Thicken the atmosphere, retain more heat, increase oxygen, slowly convert the planet so that human life could survive here naturally, without environment suits. That's what I'd like to see." Matt could feel some of his pent-up tension gradually alleviate as he was induced into discussing his aspirations for the Red Planet, which came as a great relief to Vijay who struggled to contain a satisfying grin as he listened to the vision. "Yes, indeed. Make Mars more Earth-like," Matt assuredly continued. "Who knows what can happen in a millennia, or even a few centuries. Breathable air, warm summer days, surface water, trees and shrubs."

Vijay chuckled. "Sounds like you would not mind being part of it."

Matt smiled. "The idea does have a certain appeal. I could get used to living here. But I'm afraid that I was born a little too early."

Vijay twitched and muttered fancifully. "Maybe not, Matt. What we do here may be the first step in kindling that dream."

Sheri felt an exhilarated sense of fascination and adventure thrill her soul as the Nathanael Greene rapidly skimmed a thousand feet above the rust-colored surface on its harrowing journey towards the unknown. Her wonder-stricken spirit still had plenty of room to hold the understandable fear and anxiety that accompanied any dangerous undertaking but her only regret was that Matt was not at her side to share the magnificent view of the Martian landscape. The drifting reddish-brown surface clouds of finely-grained powder leisurely glided sporadically across the craggy terrain like ruby crystals of snow blowing across the open Kansas farm lands during a blustery winter day as they flew over the Echus Chaos and turned north along the northeastern flank of the Tharsis Bulge, the highest known plateau in the solar system and encompassing an eighth of the planet. It's gently rising slopes ascended to their left-rear at a relatively steady two degree angle, eventually reaching nearly seven miles above the datum near the equatorial line and continuing to fall away to their right beyond Lunae Planum before leveling out a half-mile below the datum in the plain of Chryse. The Nathanael Greene soared past the right side of the conical-shaped rocky mountain volcano Ceraunius Tholus with its numerous grooved channels and large impact craters on its northern flank. Sheri strained her neck to get a look out the port-side windows as they cleared the natural obstruction and now had an open view to the southwest and the climbing ground all the way to their visible horizon. Sheri gasped in awe at the spectacular sight of the towering Olympus Mons caldera looming high into the cloudless sky well beyond the rising curvature of the planet. Reaching 17 miles into the atmosphere, its gargantuan size was emphasized by the fact that its 43 mile diameter summit caldera, outward-facing scarp and gentle flanks could be delineated from the ship, and it was still over 1500 miles away! Thirty minutes later they were passing over the long, narrow, gouged depression of Uranus Fossae and the large, shallow crater with complex scalloped edges of Uranus Patera.

"How much longer to target area," Lieutenant Reynolds impatiently inquired as he staggered forward, ominously decked-out in his crinkled dark bronze military environment suit minus helmet and gloves, checking his balance with his hands against the occasional shudder or dip of the speeding craft.

Sheri leaned towards Jack and reviewed the data in the guidance computer. "ETA in about forty minutes, Lieutenant."

"Thank you." Reynolds turned to Jack. "I want a slow, deliberate, circuitous approach to the TA. Let's have a good look around before we get too close."

"I hear you, sir," Jack apprehensively replied.

Reynolds spun aft. "Cooke! Walinski! Go to the cargo hold, break out the thruster packs and get them prepped."

Sheri warily glanced over at Jack whom she noticed had become peculiarly recluse. "You've been unusually somber on this trip," she noted.

Jack casually shrugged. "A little nervous, I guess. I've already been through one battle."

Aware of the brewing tension in the cockpit, Reynolds placed a consoling hand upon Jack's shoulder. "Steady, son. We can handle almost any contingency that may arise."

Jack frowned disparagingly. "Begging the Lieutenant's pardon, sir, but I ferried space marines down to Copernicus. It didn't help."

Reynolds nodded. "I understand, but at least you survived it."

Jack grimaced at anguished memories. "A lot of them didn't, sir."

Off to the northwest the ground steadily rose ever so slightly as far as the eye could see. Somewhere beyond the horizon was the 60 mile wide summit of Alba Patera, its gently descending slopes at less than half a degree and covering a total area extent of nearly a thousand miles. The Nathanael Greene banked in that direction and gradually climbed in conformation with the surface in order to maintain the desired altitude. From her forward seat, Sheri could clearly distinguish the various tabular lava sheets with well defined steep, chiseled flow fronts from numerous eruptions uncounted thousands of years before, all washed in the common Martian hues of reds and tans and irregularly stacked atop one another like stacks of offset pancakes. They passed over the line of scabrous craters and pits of Achernon Catena and then Phlegethon Catena. Jack decelerated as Sheri began to recognize the pattern of sharply-crested radial ridges described by the scientists. Her swelling anxiety as they approached their destination was tempered by the reassuring voice of Matt whom she had been in regular contact with throughout the flight. Moving west of the Catena's, the distant caldera of Alba Patera came into view along with that puzzling tiny speck of twinkling reflected light that had so engaged the curiosity of the two ill-fated explorers.

"We're approaching the point of last contact now," Sheri announced as Reynolds strode forward to hover behind her chair once more.

"Very good. Drop us a few hundred feet and approach cautiously."

Sheri relayed their position back to Jamestown.

"Understood, Nathanael Greene." Matt replied with concern. "Proceed at your discretion."

"Roger, Jamestown."

A small puff of grayish haze hung over the crest of one of the distant radial ridges. Below the lip along its rutted near slope sat a blackened mass strewn across the ground, still 50 miles away but standing-out like an oasis in the desert amidst the rustic coloration's of the countryside. Sheri activated the magnifier screen and focused on the obscured area.

"Oh my God!" Jacked gasped aloud.

A chorus of groans and huffs came from both Sheri and Reynolds as small mounds of burnt-out twisted and warped wreckage was arrayed before them. The blue paint of the metal plating was now charred and scorched, steel molding and structural supports all bent and contorted, broken fragments fused together by the heat of a blast furnace. There were pieces of plastic and upholstery scattered about for several hundred feet, trifling shreds of wire mesh from pulverized wheels littering the scene. A silver-gray form with deep yellow helmet lay motionless about 50 feet to the left of the bulk of debris. Disturbed mutterings came from the passenger compartment as the marines and Doctor Caldwell jockeyed for a look forward as those in the cockpit were stunned to silence.

"Are you getting this, Matt?" Sheri dolefully inquired as the forward picture was transmitted back to Jamestown. "We see one body and what appears to be the wreckage of an excursion rover."

"Roger that," Matt's melancholy voice confirmed. "Don't get too close. Deploy the marines to retrieve the body and examine the debris for..."

"Stand by one!" Sheri forcefully interrupted as a signal on the instrument panel caught her attention. Instantaneously her tone became frantic. "Incoming missile, seventy-five miles and closing. Jack! Get us out of here!"

The Nathanael Greene banked sharply starboard and dove, rapidly increasing in speed away from the blazing projectile fired from somewhere near the summit. Lieutenant Reynolds and the two marines in the cargo hold were violently thrown against the fuselage and pinned to the floor against compartment partitions by the crushing g-forces. All others were firmly pressed against their seats, Sheri using all her strength to move her head to read the instrument panel and her fingers to work the controls.

"Contact fifty miles and closing," she excitedly announced. "It's got a lock on us. Time to impact ninety seconds."

Jack's voice was hasty but composed. "The closest depression or mountain of any size are these fissures to the north, an I right?"

Sheri quickly accessed a navigation chart. "That's affirm. Alba Fossae and then Tantalus Fossae."

"Whatever," Jack sarcastically bellowed. "Who gives a shit! That's our best hope to lose this damn thing."

As the rate of acceleration declined, the three marines strewn about the deck were able to painfully crawl back to their seats and buckle themselves in. Jack guided the ship into the long, narrow depression of Alba Fossae, diving to within 20 feet of the ground in some places, skimming along the floor as fast as the limits of safety and physics would allow. He began to waggle the ship from wall to wall, heights of which never exceeded more than 75 feet, in an attempt to shake off the targeting track of the missile. The vigorous rocking and swaying tossed everyone's limbs and vitals limply in their chairs like puppets on a string, a couple of the marines becoming nauseous and spilling their guts onto the floor.

"Impact in forty seconds," Sheri desperately reported. "Come on Jack! Do some of that fancy pilot shit!"

Directly ahead lay the blistered and scorched debris of what appeared to be several vehicles and small flying craft scattered amongst the broken rubble of the fossae floor. Jack buzzed the ship within a few feet above the wreckage, abruptly pulling up the nose and flying out of the depression. Sheri was feeling fear like she had never known, her forehead dripping with sweat, but her senses were being ravaged by too many stimuli to dwell on her emotions. That must have been what Yong and Ray had seen from afar, she thought, but they had gone by too fast for any hope of identification. She surmised that Jack was trying to get the missile to lose its lock on the ship and redirect onto the debris. No such luck. "Missile has still acquired," she distraughtly announced. "Impact in thirty seconds."

"Damn!" Jack roared in anger. "Any chance of out-running it?"

"I don't think so," Sheri hastily replied, her voice cracking with tension. "We don't have the time. No weapons, no counter measures. We're in some pretty deep shit!"

"You still have me at the helm," Jack arrogantly proclaimed as he dipped the ship into the shallow fissure of Tantalus Fossae. Once more he flew the ship near the narrow, meandering channel floor, waggling wildly from side to side. Shudders of panic emanated from the passenger compartment as the jagged fissure walls rushed up precariously close to the fuselage windows, the wing tips missing scraping against the rocky precipices by only a few feet.

"Twenty-five seconds and continuing to close, Jack," Sheri said with agitation as she leered at him, eyes and mouth gnarled in desperation.

"Still too far away," Jack mumbled, his attention riveted forward. "I'll have to slow down a tad."

"What!" Sheri cried out incredulously. "Are you crazy!" Her protests were ignored as Jack's concentration was unshaken. Ahead in the distance the narrow channel bent sharply to the right.

"This one's going to take careful timing," he calmly declared.

Sheri activated the aft camera and watched on a monitor as the pointed cylinder trailing dense streamers of fire and smoke continually inched closer as it glided over the surface. "Fifteen seconds."

"This is going to be close," Jack shouted aloud as he straightened out the flight path and headed directly for the rustic, gouged cliff that seemed to be enlarging exponentially in the forward window. "Hang on to your lunch, fellows!"

With all his might Jack pulled back on the flight stick , raising the nose of the Nathanael Greene and climbing steeply out of the canyon as its belly scarcely missed nicking the top edge of the fracture. Faces contorted grotesquely as their bodies were crushed against their chairs due to the rapid ascent and acceleration against the pull of gravitational forces. The missile also climbed but its reaction was too late as it slammed into the upper reaches of the curving channel wall. Through the monitor, Sheri could see the ground and sky behind them engulfed in a brilliant, blinding yellow-orange glow. The reverberating clasp of booming thunder heralded the explosion of the warhead and its shock waves buffeted and jolted the ship as if caught in a blender, even though they were now miles away. Jack needed Sheri's help in steadying the bucking bronco until the terrifying vibrations subsided and the blazing flash faded into oblivion. Jack exhaled a gigantic sigh of relief as he banked the ship around to head back south. "I hope that I never have to do that again," he pensively proclaimed.

"Amen to that," Sheri replied as she slouched back in exhaustion. "That was some kind of flying, Jack. You're a master." With a radiant smile of appreciation she reached over and patted him fondly on the shoulder.

"Thanks," he answered with his usual bravado and boyish grin. "I am, aren't I. I wonder what I should do for my next trick."

Everyone was keenly aware just how fortunate they had been. The PL was still in good shape. Doctor Caldwell was attending to an ugly bump on the forehead of Corporal Cooke after issuing a few pills to relax a couple of upset stomachs and the rest had various muscle strains of one kind or another but nothing more serious.

"Nathanael Greene, come in! Please respond. Nathanael Greene, what's your status?" It was an agitated Matt, his hails having been ignored by Sheri for the past few minutes. The neglect was understandable for she had been rather preoccupied.

"Sorry, Jamestown," she finally answered once she had shaken herself from her little numbing trance. "Obviously we're still here. The missile impacted in Tantalus Fossae."

"Thank God," Matt proclaimed with a heavy sigh of relief. "Was anyone hurt?"

"Just bumps and bruises," Reynolds interrupted as he loomed behind Sheri rubbing a painful shoulder, "nothing serious. The rover was completely destroyed. No one on board could have survived. You can have your pilot deploy us at a safe distance and we can jet to the site, check it out and retrieve the bodies."

"We're skirting well south of the area now, Matt," Sheri informed. "What are your instructions?"

Matt wanted nothing more than to return to the scene of the crime with a little muscle, examine the area, collect the bodies and maybe extract a little payback, but the unknowns and the risk were both too great. "We have one confirmed dead and a second is probable," he authoritatively explained. "I don't wish to add to that number. There will be another time to send live bodies out after dead ones. Alba Patera is obviously too hot. Abort the mission and tell Jack well done. Come on home."

Matt solemnly turned to Vijay and Sergeant Douglas who were huddled behind the communications station and wearily rubbed his hand against his forehead. "What a mess."

"So there are other people on this planet," Vijay deduced. "Who are they? What do they want?"

"Apparently our EESC friends," Douglas flippantly remarked. "It would seem that they haven't been completely up front with us. And they want to remain anonymous."

"Sergeant, you had better put your men on alert," a disgruntled Matt instructed. "This thing could spin out of control and we'll be lucky to live through it."

"Yes, sir."

As Douglas left the floor of A and C, Vijay mumbled in disillusionment and took a few steps to follow before he suddenly paused and curiously glanced over his shoulder towards Matt. "Do you remember what you were saying about your dreams for human habitation on Mars? How you hoped that we could make this planet more Earth-like?"

Matt straightened in his chair and looked at Vijay with the broad, glossy eyes of heightened interest. "Yes, go on."

Vijay folded his arms and sighed disconsolately. "I submit that you have nothing to fear." He hesitated, taking another disheartened breath. "We've taken the first step. We've started to kill."

CHAPTER

13

"This sucks!" Jack detestably clamored upon hearing about the tension created at NSCA headquarters by the appalling account of the latest incident. "This could precipitate a world war on two planets!"

Sheri sneered at him incredulously. "No one is going to go to war over this."

"I wouldn't be so sure about that." he scrupulously replied with a skeptical flinch of his head. "One of the chapters of the Hundred Years War was incited by a box of tennis balls for God's sake!"

Matt passively sat amongst the small group clustered around some of the tables along the perimeter of the vibrant greenery of the Residential Dome park, sipping on a steaming cup of aromatic Brazilian coffee as he studiously listened to the jumble of vivacious voices bantering over idle speculations. He had just completed a lengthy communiqué with Earth in which he learned that the Bunker Hill was being dispatched to Mars with two platoons of space marines and a few additional colony support personnel. There would be no abandonment of Jamestown or of the search for her colonists. Estimated arrival time was in nine days. Everyone greeted the news with reserved relief, all except for Susan Oliver who stormed angrily out of the park after launching one of her bitter tirades against the military. It was well past the normal dinner hour but few had much of an appetite. Most nursed a mug of coffee or other colder beverage but no one was in a particularly jovial or sociable mood. However, no one cared to be alone either, preferring to share their misery and gloom together. Finally Matt spoke up to address no one in particular.

"Don't be too quick to disregard Jack's concerns. I could sense in the voices at Control that they were worried about the motivations of our European neighbors. We may have unwittingly pulled the trigger to some portentous interplanetary smoking gun. What we have to do now is remove the bullet before the hammer falls."

"Just for once," Sheri declared in frustration as she folded her arms across her torso, "you'd think we humans could come to this planet and leave the barbarity of war behind us."

"You must not be aware of the ominous words of Plato, Miss Alderman," Lieutenant Reynolds interjected from the neighboring table. "Only the dead have seen the end of war."

Matt turned his head and glanced at Reynolds peculiarly, who simply shrugged his shoulders and grinned with modesty.

"Well, I did minor in literature at Texas A&M."

"Well, professor," Matt soberly responded as he pulled himself away from the table, "you and I have some serious planning to do. Now that they've been discovered and blood has been shed, it would be reckless to assume that they would hesitate striking us here at Jamestown. Let's go over to A & C." Matt glanced over at Sheri with those amorous, yearning eyes that made her sensually tingle all over and spoke apologetically. "Don't wait up for me tonight. I have two more letters to write."

Once in the spacious conference room, Matt and Reynolds stoically hovered over a large topographical map of Jamestown and the surrounding countryside that they had spread across the oval oak veneer table.

"I don't mean to tell you your business," Matt remarked as he massaged his chin, assiduously examining the layout, "but I think it would be prudent to picket the hills to the northwest."

"That's right," Reynolds assuredly replied, having already made that determination. "Unfortunately the Echus Mountains are to the southwest and are quite useless to us in this situation." He leaned over the table and traced curving lines on the map with his finger. "We need to establish a couple of OP's on the highest hills we can find in the Echus Chaos to the north and northwest, say fifty to seventy-five miles out. Far enough to detect any approach hundreds of miles away but close enough to safely fall back to defensive positions. The ground to the northwest beyond the Chaos has a gentle rise but is otherwise relatively flat. It's at least another five hundred miles to the north before there is the next natural obstruction at Sacra Fossae." His finger lightly tapped a spot on the map as he straightened. "Yes, I think that electronic listening posts here will be able to provide us ample warning."

"One if by land, two if by air, eh," Matt flippantly remarked.

Reynolds looked at him strangely. "Something like that," he softly replied. "I'll survey the terrain in the morning. We need to find a series of defensive positions all along our northwestern perimeter where we can establish a skirmish line that a squad with thruster packs can quickly reach at a moment's notice."

"A skirmish line?" Matt questioned.

"The last defensive line will be just outside the colony boundary," Reynolds explained. "But we need to meet any hostile threat at least twenty-five miles out, before they can get within visual range. We'll set-up the OP's tomorrow and be operational by nightfall."

"Wait a minute." Matt questioned as he held out a dubious hand. "Two man? Lieutenant, you are only one platoon. Can't these posts be operated by one man?"

"Yes," he hastily replied with a slightly defensive tone, "but I don't want anyone left alone out there."

Matt nodded in understanding. Sullenly he strolled around to the far side of the table, rubbing the tormenting ache above his brows. The events of the day were mercilessly gnawing at his soul. His mind kept reflecting on the image of the panicked look of Yong Chang hovering over him as he was roused from his sleep the night of their reactor accident. He had been his roommate during the voyage and they had engaged in the usual small talk, but he never really took the time to get to know him.

Lieutenant Reynolds noticed the anguished, silent expression, immediately perceiving what was troubling him. "I'm sorry about your two scientists. It is a great tragedy."

Matt spun around and rushed heedlessly against the side of table with a wild-eyed, crazed look of rage and bitterness blistered across his face. "Damnit, Tom!" he screamed with fury, slamming his fist so hard on the table that it caused the sturdy legs to wobble. "Why didn't you warn me about those people before I sent them up there? You knew there could be danger!" His face was ablaze in fiery shades of red. "You knew and you didn't tell me! I would have never allowed them to go up there had I known about another rogue colony lurking about."

Reynolds hesitated, taking a nervous swallow. He had already been feeling a peculiar culpability regarding the affair and Matt's angry outburst had suddenly thrust his guilt to the surface. "I'm sorry, Matt," he quietly said with remorse. "I was under orders. We were not aware of their location, strength, or intentions. There was no evidence to indicate any hostility. The National Security Agency was simply fearful that they may have had something to do with Jamestown's predicament. I remind you that it was the head of the NSCA that issued those orders and he was fully aware of the situation. It wasn't your fault."

"That's not very comforting," Matt rancorously replied, shaking his head in disgust. "If you have anymore....orders, Lieutenant," Matt irritably continued as he rested his hands on the table and pressed forward, "requiring you to withhold information from me, please tell me now before any more of my people get killed."

Reynolds bowed morosely before looking up into Matt's incensed, piercing stare. "I assure you, Matt, there is nothing else."

Matt forcefully stretched out his hands towards the center of the dome, inferring all the others. "Assure them."

It took him hours to compose the condolence letters, trying to focus on the experiences of the men during their final journey and on what impressions he could remember. He wrote of their professionalism, their eagerness, and their courage in the desire to pursue their final adventure. He wrote as elegantly as he could but to Matt it seemed like a feeble and futile endeavor. How could any words do justice to their sacrifice?

Disconsolately he fixed himself a tall glass of Scotch and soda, quite intentionally adding many more parts of the whiskey than of the mixer, and settled into the soft cushion of the recliner that he had come to find so soothing and began to ponder on all the traumatic events that had befallen them. He wondered about the tribulations and thoughts that must have haunted the great adventurers and explorers like Sir Walter Raleigh and Columbus, Marco Polo and Magellan, Lewis and Clark, Amundsen and Armstrong. What were their reactions in times like these? Inevitably his reflections turned inward and mutated into a series of caviling questions of judgment and self-doubt. Why hadn't he buggered-out at the first sign of trouble? Was it personal glory and ego or a realistic assessment that they had a reasonable chance of accomplishing their assignments? Why had he allowed those men to make that hazardous journey? He could have told

NSCA headquarters that the trip was too dangerous. Was it because he was just blindly following instructions and didn't want to rock the boat, or was it a thoughtful and rational decision with a reasonable amount of risk? Why was he so adamant about hanging on here? He hadn't told the others that the NSCA had given grudging permission to withdraw everyone and leave the planet if he deemed the situation to be untenable and imminently life-threatening. Was it because he was afraid of the affects that abandoning the mission would have on his image and career or was it a justified, dogged determination to see the game through to its conclusion? Was he a reasonable man taking a reasonable chance or a foolish one in pursuit of some idealistic fantasy? And who was he to play God with the lives of so many precious people?

He remembered examples in antiquity of courage and tenacity of men facing daunting and fearful odds; the 300 Spartans at Thermopylae; the English at Agincourt, Rorke's Drift, and Arnhem Bridge; the RAF over the skies of Britain in 1940; the Canadians at Dieppe; the Alamo; Bataan and the Chosin Reservoir; Fort Wagner and Little Round Top. They all had something more strengthening their resolve than pride, duty, and the instinct for self-preservation. He wondrously recalled the stories of human character and courage in the face of adversity that so often go unnoticed but are occasionally showcased for all to see in the one spectacle that attracts the attention of the entire world - the Olympic Games. Stories of the undaunted human spirit like that of the aging Norwegian 50 kilometer cross-country skier in the 2026 Winter Games who, after qualifying for his team after three previous failures, insisted on running the race in the bitter cold despite suffering with the debilitating affects of pneumonia, refusing quit the race despite being dead last until he crossed the finish line and collapsed into the admiring arms of his competitors. And the Jamaican bobsled team in 1988 who painfully crawled out of their crashed sled, hoisted it over their shoulders, and carried it across the finish line so they would officially be credited with completing the race and proving to the world that they belonged among the best in spirit. He remembered watching archive videos of remarkable tales of faith such as that of gymnast Kerri Strug in the 1996 Summer Games. After falling on a vault and injuring her ankle, she prayed to God not for a miracle but for the strength to complete her last vault that would require landing on her injured foot and had to be successfully executed for the American team to win their first ever Gold Medal in the sport. Watching the grit and determination on her face as she courageously charged down the ramp and the agonized grimace that was the result of the price she had to pay for landing on her feet was one of the most uplifting sights he had ever seen. There was no doubt what had enabled Kerri Strug to persevere and endure. But the one Olympic moment that he was most fond of combined both character and faith. It was during the 1924 Paris Games and the man was sprinter Eric Liddell of England, considered nearly unbeatable. Upon learning that his qualifying heats were being run on Sunday, this deeply religious man refused to participate. Despite enormous political and national pressure and his own insatiable thirst to win a Gold Medal, he held on to his principles against running on the Sabbath. He would have sacrificed his dream of running in the Olympic Games if not for the selfless generosity of a teammate who offered him his slot in a longer race after winning a medal of his own. Despite being a longer distance than he was used too, Liddell ran like the wind that day to the utter awe and amazement of everyone present, winning the Gold Medal and proudly giving all praise and glory to the honor of God.

Remembering these sterling examples of inspiration caused Matt to angrily wonder what in hell was the matter with him? Many had a common theme; some belief in a benign power greater than oneself from which to draw strength to see the race through. And that power comes from within. It was faith. What had happened to his?"

With those inspirational memories fresh in his mind, Matt retired for the night, sprawling atop his bed and picking up the thick black book that had always adorned in night stand but which he had seldom opened. But now, in this alien place, it seemed to take on a special meaning, a magnetic compulsion. He had marked the pages of a dozen of his favorite passages and now he randomly opened the Bible to one of them. He could feel a comforting peace warming his soul and surging renewal of his confidence and strength of purpose as if he had been dipped in magic waters as he read Isaiah 40. His eyes grew heavy and before he could finish a restful sleep overtook him, the opened Bible lying limply upon his chest.

To secure the safety of Jamestown, Lieutenant Reynolds by midday had devised a defensive strategy which he whimsically termed MAD, Mobile Active Defense. He divided his meager little force into three four-man teams. It was a frightfully insufficient number for the job they were called upon to do, but that was the hand that had been dealt them. Each team would take an eight hour shift manning the outposts that were established on the highest ground in the desired area, about 75 miles to the north and northwest. One team would be available for duties around the colony while the third relaxed and slept. In case of a threat, the active colony team would be quickly assembled and fly out by thruster packs to one of nine previously scouted defensive sectors located about 30 to 50 miles away and could cover all possible hostile approaches from the north and west and which Reynolds deemed possessed adequate command of the sky and ground with sufficient cover. The team at rest would be mustered and assigned to defensive positions along the colony perimeter. The team manning the two outposts, situated more than 120 miles apart, would both be unable to support the defensive line unless an attack came between them. It was therefore decided that the outpost closest to the approaching threat would retire to the defensive sector designated for the initial stand while the other outpost would rapidly withdraw, firing thruster packs all the way, to help in the defense of the colony perimeter. It was a mild adaptation of the Daniel Morgan - Nathanael Greene strategy at Cowpens and Guilford Courthouse to whittle-down a superior foe. Reynolds and Sergeant Douglas would each take turns checking on the outposts during each shift, using combinations of rover and thruster pack to cover the considerable distance.

While this planning and organization was undertaken, some of the men were kept busy assembling the Defensive Missile Grid launch system and electronic fire control. The launcher was a large, square-frame rotating structure containing sixteen tubes, all mounted on a fat, cylindrical pedestal extending from the middle of a low riding, flat, treaded robotics platform, the entire assembly painted in a deep, nonreflective gray. The electronic fire control and targeting system was established on one of the triangular work stations in the center of A and C. In the adjoining cubicle the marines connected a bank of small closed-circuit monitors that received the video images from the miniature camera lenses implanted in the upper front of their space helmets, one monitor for each soldier. When functioning properly, the camera could transmit up to a range of 50 miles, not powerful enough to receive signals from the men on the picket line but capable of picking up transmissions from any of Reynolds' defensive sectors.

And so before the orange-yellow glare of the afternoon sun serenely tumbled from the sky, Reynolds and Douglas each crammed into a separate two-man rover with the initial outpost team, packed to the brim with electronic gadgetry, thruster packs, weapons, and extra propellant for their packs and oxygen for themselves, and proceeded to their respective rising, rocky locations that afforded a clear view to their horizon which unfortunately in this case was a lot closer than an Earth horizon because of the smaller circumference of the planet. Reynolds and Douglas helped the picket team establish the outposts well into the darkened night, setting up radar, thermal scanners that could detect the flame from a candle, motion sensors sensitive enough to detect the wiggle of a worm along the horizon, if Mars had any, and a seismometer that could register the rumble of a rover wheel several hundred miles away. Once the forward observation posts were established and their electronics operating properly, the two officers used their thruster packs to return to Jamestown, leaving the rovers to act as both shelter and home for the more sensitive monitoring equipment. Subsequent relief teams would make the 45 minute journey by flying 50 feet above the surface with the power of their thruster packs, using the homing beacon aboard each rover as an electronic road map to guide them in.

The distinctive, savory aroma of baking mozzarella and Parmesan cheese sprinkled with the marked redolence of tomato sauce and cooked ground beef along with the pungent odor of garlic bread saturated the air within the quarters of Caroline Hart. She had been slaving in her tiny kitchen for several hours in preparation for the eagerly anticipated arrival of Robert Cooke. From prior conversations she had learned of his fondness for Italian food and since lasagna was one of her favorite dishes she decided to give it a whirl. Caroline had considered herself an accomplished cook but, except for the rare family gathering, had been out of practice for nearly three years, not feeling motivated to go to such trouble and effort for only one. A soothing sensation of satisfaction and pleasure warmed her like a wool blanket on a cold winter's night as she prepared the pasta, drawing the ingredients from the ample supply of foodstuffs that she had brought with her among her personal baggage. It felt good to once again be doing something like this for a man with whom she had grown quite fond of. Corporal Cooke had returned from his first shift on the picket line, slept awhile, and resumed his menial duties within the colony. He would have a few precious hours before he had to return to the hillside outposts in the Echus Chaos and she wanted to make it special. He seemed very excited when he accepted her invitation the night before which only served to heighten her expectations. As the lasagna neared its baking completion, Caroline chopped up into a salad bowl a bountiful harvest of lettuce, carrots, tomatoes, onions, and celery that she had procured clandestinely. Helping out in the Agri Dome had its advantages. Tammy Jacobs had worked miracles as the crop yields were already showing drastic improvements, no doubt aided by the experimental AGR nutrient (Accelerated Growth Rate) which she had lobbied for inclusion with the agricultural supplies. As she prepared the succulent salad, she toyed with the notion of inviting Sheri and Matt over to join them. There would certainly be plenty of food. The thought had an enjoyable appeal but she quickly nixed the idea. She wanted this evening to be a private time between the two of them. There was precious little time to be alone and with the events of the last few days, who could tell what tragedy would strike next. When all was nearly ready Caroline retired to her bedroom where she peeled out of her T-shirt and shorts and put on a snug, short sleeve deep fuchsia soft ribbed knit pullover top and a pair of black pleated cotton slacks. Staring into the closet door mirror she carefully combed and curled her shoulder length brunette hair into perfect symmetry, delicately applied subtle amounts of eye shadow, facial creme, lip gloss, and concluded with a few generous dabs of her favorite perfume. As she provocatively posed in the mirror, satisfied with her feminine appearance, a sudden ominous and terrifying premonition swept over her that sent shivering chills ricocheting through her bones. She distraughtly remembered what happened the last time she was this meticulous with her appearance in preparation for seeing a man. After a moment's hesitation she sneered angrily at herself and, feeling a little childish and stupid, shook off the sensation and returned to the kitchen. She finished placing the settings on the cozy, square oak veneer table and was in the process of pouring some prized red Bordeaux wine from one of the few bottles that she had brought from Earth into a pair of elegant, thin crystal glasses when her preparations were interrupted by the buzz of her door intercom announcing the arrival of her evening companion. Caroline felt her heart race like it did on the brink of her first high school date. With the excitement of a giddy teenager she rushed to the door and enthusiastically ushered in Robert Cooke by the arm.

"Wow!" he exclaimed as he delightfully sniffed the air. "This smells great. It reminds me of this little Italian place I used to go to as a teenager back in Racine."

Caroline noticed his eyes scanning over her that induced a licentious smile that caused her abdomen to do thrilling cartwheels of nervous expectations.

Bob looked down in embarrassment at his long sleeve mustard knit turtleneck and baggy olive fatigues. "I must apologize for my appearance," he humbly said as his fingers lamely flicked at his shirt. "You look so nice and I'm dressed like this. I'm afraid that the Corps doesn't allow us to pack many amenities when deployed on missions."

"You look wonderful to me," Caroline replied with a longing gaze as she playfully squeezed his arm, admiring the sturdiness of his muscular shoulders and trim physique. She felt the warming blanket of joy sweep over her that she hadn't experienced in ages as she watched that engaging air of passion and gentleness slowly return to his oft solitary and introspective expression.

"While I was out there on watch last night in the cold darkness," he casually remarked, "I wanted to pick you some flowers, but I guess it's not the growing season. Somehow I thought a red rock wouldn't be appropriate."

Their eyes met in a deeply penetrating gaze before they both erupted in a series of loud, impulsive giggles.

"Come on, silly," Caroline chortled as she gave him a tender nudge on the back and pulled on his arm. "Enough of this nonsense. I'm hungry."

Caroline was immediately stunned by the ravenous scope of his appetite, as if he had been lost in a desert without provisions for a week. She watched in both amusement and amazement as he built a mountain of a salad out of the greens and assorted vegetables that she had prepared, smothering it with both types of dressing that were available. She took great satisfaction in listening to the moans and mutterings of palatable delight that escaped from his chewing mouth as he wolfed-down three mammoth portions of the tasty lasagna. All throughout they talked and they laughed and each finished several glasses of wine. Caroline was so intrigued by her guest that more than an hour slipped by in what seemed to her like a wink of an eye. Stuffed to bursting, both sat back and rubbed their bloated bellies.

"It's been so long since I've eaten like this," Caroline remarked.

Bob sighed as he took a delectable sip of wine. "Hell, I've never eaten like this. Caroline, you are fantastic! This meal was delicious."

Caroline bowed shyly but couldn't contain the wide grin that exploded across her face. Being appreciated was one of the simplest and greatest pleasures that she could derive from a relationship. After a few seconds of reflection she looked up in a quizzical manner. "Never?"

"Almost never," he replied. "I don't even remember my mom's cooking. My parents split when I was very young. Social Services gave my grandparents custody when my mom was unable to care for me. To be honest, my grandmother, as sweet and dear as she is, isn't a very good cook. We were rather poor, one of the reasons why I had to work so much while in school. We didn't have meat very often and rarely anything fancy. But, Caroline, you know what they say about soldiers. The best way to a soldier's heart is through his stomach. I think that you just merged from the on ramp and are speeding down the highway to my heart."

Caroline was touched as she bashfully dipped her head, snickering happily to herself. She rose to her feet and carried her dishes to the counter by the automatic washer, quickly followed by her companion. "No, Bob," she protested, wrenching the plates from his hand. "I'll do these later. You just relax. Let's go into the living room."

"Now wait a second, Caroline," he argued as he reached around her and opened the machine's door. "It was very kind of you to invite me over for this magnificent feast. The least I can do is help you clean up the mess." Gently taking back the dinnerware, he began to load them into the compartmentalized trays.

Together they loaded all of the dirty plates, glasses, and cookware and activated the cleaning cycle. While the dishes were washing, they cleaned the dinning table, acting like playful newlyweds as they jabbed and pinched and flicked damp rags against butt cheeks, joking and giggling incessantly.

"I used to hate that, then I kind of enjoyed it," Caroline admitted after wildly jumping and cackling in response to a prolonged poke in the ribs as they waited for the drying cycle to suck out all the moisture from the dishes. "Do it again." Caroline laughed and twisted once more before lazily falling back into Bob's chest, compelling his encircling arms to wrap snugly around her waist to support her. Caroline purred in contentment for a moment before spinning within his comforting grasp to face him, yearningly gazing into his deep blue eyes. As if on cue their lips slowly drew together and they embraced in a long and passionate kiss. Caroline could feel the pressure of his arms squeezing against her back, compressing her body into his as she clasped her arms around his neck, her fingers kneading the lower strands of his short brown hair. As their mouth's slowly parted, their eyes wondrously dancing within those of the other, Bob swallowed nervously, his hands still firmly locked around her lower back.

"This could get complicated," he timidly remarked.

Caroline gently shook her head and raised a finger to press it against his lips to quiet him. Silently she stepped back and took his hand, leading him into the softly lit living room where she turned on some contemporary music on the built-in audio sound system and then over to the pliant mauve and gray stripe sectional sofa on which they leisurely tumbled, intimately entwined within each other's clutching arms. Caroline rested her head upon his shoulder as her right hand reached across his chest to fondly caress his muscular upper arm as she listened to the music and worriedly contemplated her next words. She was convinced that her decision was the right one in order to get on with her life. but in the back of her troubled mind it still made her feel a little ashamed. Finally she turned her head and looked up into his slightly confused expression. "Bob, since Dave has officially been declared missing off-world and the inferences of his final message, I requested that my marriage be annulled. Otherwise, I just wouldn't have felt right being this close to another man." Caroline hesitated, her roaming fingers grinding to a halt as she noticed his look of surprise. "It's no different for the wives of your married marine friends if any of them, heaven forbid, be declared missing in action. So you don't need to be concerned."

Bob's head twitched uneasily. "He could still turn up, you know."

"It's over." Caroline resolutely replied with a shake of her head. "Too much has happened. I'll deal with that situation if it happens. He abandoned me." Caroline thoughtfully paused, finding herself instinctively pressing closer to his warm, comforting body as she vacantly stared-off across the room. "Or maybe I abandoned him," she remorsefully continued. "I should have never allowed him to come to this planet alone. I should have been with him. But I was too consumed with my own work and aspirations that I never realized that I was slowly losing him." She looked up at Bob with hopeful eyes. "I won't make that mistake again."

Caroline closed her eyes and buried her head against his chest as she luxuriated in the pleasurable sensations that were induced by the tender and affectionate strokes of his hand through her succulent hair on the back of her head and across her shoulder blades. Eventually her own hands were on the move again, reaching under his now disheveled shirt to massage his belly. As her fingers slid around his side. she felt the bump of a wartime scar. "Oh!" she called out as she curiously raised up and lifted the tail of his shirt to expose the mark. She gazed appallingly at the three inch jagged, pink ridge that crisscrossed his ribcage, her fingers tracing along the contour of its length. "That looks like it was bad."

"Shrapnel wound during the Lunar Conflict," he casually explained. "Actually it wasn't bad at all. It missed all the organs, luckily. Got two months recuperative leave though."

Caroline saw him smile at her. She was entranced with how cavalier he could be. With a joyous gasp she cuddled tightly around him once more. "What's it like in the space marines?" She felt a supple, moistened peck on the top of her head before Bob rested his neck against the back of the couch.

"With the exception of the occasional war, it's not too bad," he light-heartily replied. "It's a decent life for someone like me who didn't get to do much as a kid and have no attachments. I mean I not only have the opportunity to see the world, but the solar system too! That's pretty exciting, don't you agree? The only worry you have is dying, and if that happens than you won't have anymore problems, so what the hell! Actually, most of the time is rather dull. You occasionally have some interesting training experiences, especially with all the new equipment."

Caroline's fingers squeezed forcefully into his flesh as she relaxed against him, listening impassionedly to his stories, clinging to every word.

"I can remember training exercises not too long ago in the Taurus Mountains on the Moon," he told with a snicker. "Learning to fly with those thruster packs and bumping into cliffs. Earlier versions of our LR5 laser rifles were a real treat. Their barrels had a tendency to soften and sag from the high temperatures until they were made with some titanium alloy. The power clips to our current rifles drain very quickly, especially in severe cold, and have been known to overheat the thermal coils and causing them to fuse."

Caroline shuddered at the prospect of such problems but was amazed at how Bob seemed so nonchalant about it all.

"And our hand-held SAR's," he continued with another mirthful giggle. "Sometimes the rocket fails to ignite and never leaves the tube. Occasionally the laser guidance program fails and the rocket flies off on its own without direction. It's kind of amusing during training exercises but I imagine it wouldn't be too funny during actual combat. But I guess the soldier has been dealing with those kinds of problems ever since the first spear point fell off its shaft."

"Did you ever think about doing something else?" Caroline engrossingly inquired. "You seem to be very rational and intelligent."

Bob shrugged. "Well, I used to dream about going to college."

"Oh, really!" she said with eagerness as she sat upright and affectionately brushed his cheek with her hand. "When was that?"

He gave her that charming, roguish grin. "When I fell asleep in high school."

Caroline laughed. How she enjoyed his entertaining dry sense of humor! As her chuckles subsided she began to feel the pangs of an unsatisfied hunger steadily creeping upon her, and it had nothing to do with food. She stared lasciviously into his eyes as her hands worked under his deep yellow knit shirt once more, caressing and rubbing up to his chest. Without a thought and to her own astonishment she brazenly lifted the shirt over his head and tossed it aside. Normally she was never this aggressive. For his part, Bob offered no resistance. Caroline cravingly studied his powerful shoulders and chest but was immediately taken aback by the number of tiny healed cuts and scrapes that covered the flesh of his upper torso. Here was a man whose body had seen some mileage. She felt a sense of sorrow as her fingers traced loving lines along the old wounds. "Oh, my!" she softly moaned in dismay as she carefully examined the marks. "Such a hard, difficult life. So many scars." Her eyes sympathetically lifted to dive deliriously into his. "And never to have experienced the love of a woman."

Bob bashfully lowered his head in silent acknowledgment.

Caroline gently clasped his cheeks, lifted his face, and lightly pressed her lips to his mouth. "You're such a warm, kind, courageous person," she said between affectionate nibbles. "Most women would kill to have a man like you." She pulled slightly away from him, reached for her top, and slowly pulled it over her head. She enjoyed the sight of his lustful gaze as her breasts jostled seductively beneath her dainty, revealing black lace bra, the same one she had intended for her now ex-husband on that first day. With feminine guile she sensually wiggled up to him, thrusting her protruding breasts against his naked chest. "I want you, Corporal Robert Cooke." With animalistic passion they fell to the velvety cushions, arms and legs intertwined in an amorous embrace as their mouths and tongues joined in a series of long, fervent kisses, their fingers clawing and squeezing along bare backs. Caroline, her emotions aflame, took his hand and guided him into the bedroom where they gleefully removed the others pants and proceeded to erotically tease, caress, and excite each other into glorious ecstasy. Caroline whimpered in bliss as he took his time stroking and fondling her most sensitive spots. She relished and luxuriated in the arousing reaction that was produced by her desirous touch against the rising bulge under his tight olive briefs but it was difficult for her to resist the temptation to just lay back and savor the thrilling tingles of passion that his tender, fiery caress induced. She was inflamed with rapture by the time he finally removed her bra and black silk bikini and she his brief as they slowly and loving explored and stimulated each other's centers of pleasure, savoring like refined connoisseurs their sexual charms. By the time their zealous love-making had concluded, Caroline lay exhausted and sweaty, her body quivering from the tumultuous explosion of thrilling ecstasy that had wracked her flesh. It had been so long since she had felt such exhilaration. Her skin quivered responsively to his every touch as his fingers and lips lovingly roamed over her as they lay side-by-side, titillating her most erogenous parts. Bob was as tender and intensely exciting as his outward appearance attested. The evening had lasted only a few brief hours but it had been ages since she had experienced one that rivaled this. As Bob dressed to report for his shift out on the dark picket line, Caroline could not control the tears that suddenly flowed down her cheeks as he left her side. She wanted him to stay forever; it was hard for her to watch him leave the room to go off into the void. Her passions had been awakened again, her sensual fire rekindled. She once more felt like a desirable, feminine woman worthy of love and she didn't want that feeling of satisfaction and joy to be lost again. He would return to her, of course, that is if he returned at all. Those nagging and tormenting premonitions badgered her once more. Little voices in the back of her imaginative mind grating at her. She couldn't shake off the thought. At least she could say that Robert Cooke experienced the love of an adoring woman before he died. She felt loved and contented again but those disquieting notions made for a restless sleep. She had already lost her husband to this mysterious though unforgiving planet, she couldn't bare to lose Bob to it as well.

Matt was insistent and determined. "I want another search."

Lieutenant Reynolds rolled his eyes disgruntledly. "Commander, we've scoured every inch of this place. They're not here."

Matt leered with anger and irritation across the desk in the Administrator's office. "Then what happened to them, Lieutenant? I don't believe for a moment that someone could be made to vanish into thin air. You double-checked, there are no environment suits missing?"

"That's an affirmative," he replied with a steadfast nod. "All pressure suits are accounted for."

"What about transports?" Matt questioned with a more congenial tone. "Rovers? Scooters? Interdome carts? Robotics haulers? Skateboards?"

Reynolds suppressed a tiny snicker as he vehemently shook his head. "No, Commander. We physically counted every vehicle. Every machine and robot that could possibly be used for transportation has been matched with our initial colony inventory. Everything is accounted for, minus the one destroyed rover. Nothing is missing, except two people."

"And you found no bodies or signs of bodies outside?" reiterated Matt from an earlier discussion as the air was so thick with frustration that it could be cut with a knife.

Reynolds restlessly shifted his weight in the chair, aggravatingly running his fingers through the top of his hair. "My men swept every square foot of the surface within the colony perimeter....nothing."

Matt flinched anxiously. His logical mind was having trouble accepting the peculiar aspects of the mystery. "Well, Tom, they either have to be inside Jamestown or outside of it. Don't tell me that they slipped into another dimension. I'm sick of this shit! I want them found!"

Reynolds fidgeted nervously. "I don't know what more we can do, Matt," he defensively asserted. "We've checked every possible place."

"That's not good enough!" Matt bellowed defiantly. "I want the impossible checked too."

Reynolds glared at him in disbelief as if he were insane. "The impossible checked?" He suddenly paused as a singular, speculative thought touched his bran. His face lit-up like a light bulb. "The collapsed dome?"

Matt leaned forward with a cold bug-eyed stare and nodded.

"Nahhh....," Reynolds groaned with a disparaging flick of the wrist as he pressed back in his seat. "We've been through the rubble on the surface. There's nothing much left of the rooms. And the subterranean levels are completely caved in."

Matt straightened and folded his arms. "Looks caved in," he sternly suggested. "I want a more thorough examination."

Reynolds winced. "I don't mean to be difficult, Commander, but my men are spread thinner than a baby's hair with all their duties."

"I know, Tom. I know," Matt sympathetically acknowledged with an understanding nod. "Just let me borrow a couple of them for the day. My people will take care of this one."

Lucinda felt the arid dryness well-up in her throat as she could almost literally sense the chafing coils of the noose tighten around her neck. She had understandably grown increasingly worried and nervous ever since she had caught a whiff of the plan to undertake a more comprehensive search of the lower levels of the collapsed dome. If her guests would happen to be discovered, the gig was up. Ever since the news had jolted her attention she had been scrambling. Her clandestine plan to gain access to the nuclear reactor under the pretense of making computer repairs by inserting a viral program that would inhibit some of its files had to be suspended. She was compelled to find a safe haven to which she could retire should the need arise. She quickly decided on one of the many potential candidates within the expansive Jamestown complex and secretively supplied it with provisions and stowed her long range transmitter. Now she needed an edge, a sort of security blanket should the worst happen. She could simply fade away and become another missing statistic but that would end her usefulness there. She wanted to continue her disruptive work and the only way to keep tabs on the progress under the northeast dome was to hang around the Residential Dome or A and C.

And so she found herself where she had often fantasized but under much different circumstances; in the quarters of Caroline Hart, stripped to her vibrant flaming red silk lingerie as she studiously examined Jamestown's schematic construction plans, committing to memory the location and destination of conduits and crawlways while the room was permeated with the softened spattering sound of thousands of tiny watery droplets striking a basin floor that were emanating from Caroline's shower. Caroline had just finished giving her a soothing and relaxing back massage, the sweet strawberry aroma of the lotion that covered her skin pleasingly flirting with her nostrils like the honeyed nectar of a spring floral garden.

Her work suit had been discarded by the bed along with her small canvas utility bag that contained some personal effects, a few miniature electronic gadgets and computer components, some erotic toys, and her stun gun and automatic pistol. She had thoroughly enjoyed the experience but it did little to ease the heavy tension that burdened her mind. With all the surrounding dangers, her normal lustful instincts were greatly inhibited. Anything she did with Caroline would be strictly business, a tactical diversion. If she needed to get out of a tight jam, Caroline would make a suitable hostage. It had been easy for her to convince Caroline to spend a few hours with her, ostensibly to apologize for some earlier upsetting remarks and to trade some insouciant male talk. Besides, Caroline still owed her a favor or two and Lucinda used that sense of indebtedness for past kindness' to her advantage. After massaging the tension from Lucinda's aching back, Caroline was feeling rather clammy after a day splitting time between the bioengineering lab and the Agri Dome and insisted on grabbing a quick shower before she continued the favor. Lucinda didn't mind at all. It gave her the excuse to get into Caroline's computer and scan the needed plans. She was grateful that her compatriots hadn't tampered with those files before their arrival. To Lucinda, Caroline seemed much more invigorated, frisky, and uninhibited. Her relationship with Corporal Cooke really must have stirred her blood, she jovially thought.

Not long after the pattering of water spray trickled away and the low whine of a powered hairdryer roared forth only to fade away a couple of minutes later, a refreshed and peppery Caroline strolled into the living room, wearing a simple, tight white cotton T-shirt with an embossed designer logo and a pair of tan, baggy walking shorts. "What are you doing?" she asked as Lucinda felt a gentle hand wiggle through her long, succulent blond locks and tenderly rest upon her shoulder. "And why aren't you dressed, young lady?"

Lucinda grew a little uneasy as Caroline hovered over her and looked at the screen. "Oh, its nothing," she hastily replied. "Computer, main menu. Terminate program." She glanced up at Caroline as the monitor went blank. "Just looking at the plans for computer cabling ducts. I'm thinking about installing a couple more terminals." Lucinda knew that she was good at deception but thought that she had better quickly change the subject. "And I'm not dressed because I haven't finished with you yet." With a devilish leer she leaped from the chair and grabbed Caroline around the waist. The two women playfully jostled with each other like a pair of

Greco-Roman wrestlers before Lucinda pinned Caroline's arms behind her back and spun her around to face her amidst a torrent of gasps and giggles. Lucida used her free hand to brush away some wayward strands from the front of Caroline's eyes.

"I guess I'm yours now," Caroline cooed as she enticingly wiggled her shoulders, her breasts protruding provocatively.

Lucinda lecherously gazed at Caroline, her unbridled sensuality reminding her of why she found woman almost as desirable as men. She had to remind herself that Caroline was only offering a little innocent playful fun, that she was not interested in any carnal activity, and after all, she was just stalling for time. Lucinda needed to act like her normal, libidinous self, but it was imperative that she remained focused on the menacing circumstances swirling around her. "Have you heard anything from the collapsed dome?"

Caroline sighed in disappointment. "No, not a peep. I hope they get back soon. I'm supposed to see Bob for a couple of hours before he goes back on outpost duty again."

Lucinda grinned slyly. "Them I'll just have to entertain you until then." Her hand reached out to lightly brush against Caroline's cheek, trailing tantalizingly slow down the side of her breast, and gently danced across her ribs, causing Caroline to giggle and squirm responsively. "You know, Caroline," she said with a devious smirk as she moistened her lips with her tongue and traced a few tickling fingers across her belly, "I have some interesting things in my bag in the bedroom. If you will lose your shirt and shorts, we can have some innocent fun and get you all hot and ready for Bob's visit at the same time."

As Lucinda backed away she noticed a wide, ornery grin cross Caroline's face as the notion seemed to have an appealing quality for her. To Lucinda's utter surprise, the normally reserved Caroline reached for the tail of her T-shirt and alluring lifted it over her head.

The low whine of the electric motor of the robotics digger reverberated through the tunnel like the echoing rumble of a distant train through a mountain pass. It resembled a farm tractor on raised steel supports, frontal dual deep graters and scoops that dug into the loosened mound of red clay and pink cement and fed the debris to the mouth of a broad, oval vacuum tube that sucked the dirt over the top of the power train and programming compartment and down a long, cylindrical enclosed channel with a resounding whoosh and deposited the rubble into large, rectangular, beveled hoppers, smaller versions of the mining transports, which carried the debris out of the passageway. Garett Yamakawa, with Vijay's welcome assistance, was able to get the escavating robot and auxiliary hoppers powered and programmed for the effort at the northeast dome. Matt had also enlisted the help of Karl Ziethan and, along with his impressed crewmates, Sheri and Jack, as well as Corporal Cooke and Private Tomlinson, painstakingly tore at the tons of rubbish with picks and shovels along the flanks of the great digger. Matt held out the hope that parts of the main corridor were still intact. The portal leading into the first subterranean level was only partially obstructed and easily penetrated. The main hallway itself was darker than night, portable spot lights confirming the level of destruction. It appeared that the inner walls and parts of the ceiling had buckled and collapsed; dirt, cement, and bits and pieces of ceiling grids and steel supports piled high like massive earthworks where the inner wall and room entrances would have been. The mangled mountain of debris sloped sharply downward as it reached across the broad hall, so much so that only about a six inch layer covered the floor at the base of the outer wall which remarkably appeared to be quite stable. There was ample space along this left side of the corridor for a person to carefully squeeze through, but the portable spots showed that the narrow opening only extended back about 25 feet before the corridor was completely blocked from floor to ceiling. Matt made certain that they dug very deliberately, mindful not to risk a cave-in. The group dug and moved debris like a troop of World War One sappers burrowing a mine shaft towards an enemy trench, clearing a traversible pathway and inhibiting gravity slides by boarding-up the newly crafted slope of the mountain with fiberglass sheeting scavenged from warehouse stocks in the Industrial Dome. Matt became aware of the disgruntled murmuring coming from the others as the work dragged on. He understood their attitude but if they believed that the marines should do all the dirty wok, he irritably thought to himself, than he had an unpleasant surprise in store for them.

Jack paused, wiping the sweat from his brow as he leaned on the handle of his spade. "Hot-shot pilot to ditch digger in one fell swoop."

"At least no one is shooting at you, Jack," Vijay frivolously reminded him with a straight face as he walked by.

Jack returned a fleeting scowl before calling out. "That's only because there's nothing down here worth shooting someone for!"

Karl Ziethan leaned towards him after discarding a shovel load into a nearby robotics hauler. "I have a PHD in Astro-Physics from Cornell for Christ's sake! I haven't done this since I outgrew my sandbox."

The two marines stayed pretty much to themselves, unhappy, but efficiently doing what was asked of them.

"Does this remind you of home, Zack?" Cooke facetiously inquired of his red-haired, freckled face companion serving on his first mission.

"What you talking shit for," Tomlinson grumpily replied as if the Corporal should have known better. "I'm from the wheat fields of Nebraska, not the coal mines of western Pennsylvania."

"This is why you joined the space marines - new experiences."

"See other worlds, the recruiter said," Tomlinson mockingly added. "Well, I think I've seen enough."

The rustic clay stains on Sheri's flight suit caught Jack's eye as she approached. "At least we have equality of the sexes here," he mumbled to Karl. "Hey, Sheri! How did you get stuck on this detail? Not hot enough in bed for him?" He had just turned to Karl, cackling uncontrollably, when the backside of a heavy metal shovel came crashing into his rump with a muffled thud. "Ouch!" Jack cried out as he angrily spun around, his hand rubbing the soreness on his cheek. He could see the enraged storm of disgust burning across her face as she pressed close.

"One more obnoxious crack like that, Jack," she roared with fury, "and you'll be looking for your dick with a microscope."

"Okay, Sheri, okay," he pleaded as he innocently held out his hands. "I didn't mean anything by it. Cool your afterburners."

Karl's head dipped, shaking in disbelief as Sheri stepped away. "Be careful, Jack. I saw her in action the other night. It wasn't pretty."

Matt, who had momentarily been detained by Garett and Vijay behind the robotics transport hoppers, returned to the side of the forward inching digger just in time to see Sheri slipping down the narrow pathway ahead of them, using her hands to brace herself against the left wall as her feet stumbled unsoundly on the uneven footing. "Sheri, be careful down there," he called out with concern. "That pile could start sliding down on you. I want you out of there."

As Sheri twisted her head to shuffle out her eye caught a glimpse of a strange shadow on the wall. Her curiosity tempted, she slid along the wall towards it and upon closer inspection found a small, circular indentation embedded about shoulder high only a few feet from where the corridor was completely blocked. It was difficult to discern but she was able to detect the rapid pulsation's of some mysterious black light being emitted by the lens-like object. As she passed a finger in front she was startled by a shimmering of the debris mound directly next to her as if it had, within a wink of an eye, faded out and in.

"What is it?" Matt called out upon hearing her quick squeal.

"Somebody bring a light," came her resolute reply. "There's something in the wall."

Setting aside his shovel, Corporal Cooke strapped on his steel helmet with its twin side-mounted cylindrical lamps, picked up his rifle and squirmed down the fissure to join her. The additional illumination clearly defined the image. It was mechanical, built into the plaster, and definitely manmade. Sheri passed her hand again in front of the subtlely throbbing beam. The pile of dirt and cement opposite the device flickered and faded into a canvas of faint and distorted waves of coloration's as if looking at an impressionistic painting from under water.

"Look at that!" Sheri gasped as she pointed with her finger.

"I'll be damned!" Cooke exclaimed with a stare of astonishment. "I've heard of these."

"What's happening?" Matt bellowed impatiently.

"Stand back, ma'am," Cooke calmly warned as he gently took Sheri's arm and nudged her back towards the others. Cautiously returning down the constrictive path, Cooke leveled his rifle at the embedded lens. Before Matt could utter a word of protest he pulled the trigger. The indentation briefly glowed bright yellow and immediately popped loudly with in a smoking puff of singed plaster, glass, and sporadic sparks of severed electrical circuitry. As if commanded by mystical sorcerers, nearly a ten foot length of the mound of debris that was opposite the lens blinked and vanished, leaving a gaping hole beyond which the glow of artificial light could be seen.

"It's a fricking hologram!" Cooke excitedly proclaimed. "Sir, I think that you had better come down here."

Matt glanced at the others apprehensively, grabbed a portable spot light and gingerly pressed against the wall to join the Corporal. Matt directed his light into the newly created opening. The beam struck the solid plaster and cement of a perfectly intact inner wall. Just a few feet away was an automatic door to a room, just like those in the Residential Dome. Matt cautiously stepped towards the wall. The corridor to his right was indeed flooded and cluttered with the remnants of some major catastrophe. But to his left, with the exception of a thin barrier of dirt that had previously sealed off the hallway completely, the slightly curving walls of the corridor fell away as if nothing had ever happened above. The floor was free of litter, the walls firm, and the inner one potmarked with numbered doors at regular intervals. In addition to that, the ceiling grids were emanating a soft, non-glaring light. This section of the dome was still receiving power! One-by-one the searchers abandoned their tools and nervously crept into the open passageway.

"This place looks brand-spanking new," Jack proclaimed as he gawked at the walls and ceiling in awe. "Not a damn scratch on it."

"Corporal," Matt quietly ordered. "check these rooms."

Matt took a few steps down the winding corridor when a sudden pressure on his shoulder scared him senseless, freezing him in his tracks. It took a few moments for him to realize that it was only the firm grasp of his friend offering a congratulatory pat. "Shit. Vij! Do you want to give me a heart attack?"

"It looks like you were right," he serenely stated in his strong but benign tone as he inquisitively scanned the surroundings. "I think that someone has been having far too much fun at our expense."

By the time Cooke had checked the first three rooms, Private Tomlinson had joined him with their scanning equipment. "Nicely furnished rooms," Cooke commented as he activated the machines, "but no sign of occupancy." Instantly the motion detector began beeping like a pager. "Oh, fart!" he cried out. "I've got movement. Multiple signals....about fifty feet, around the bend."

Matt was petrified as shivers of terror crawled up his spine. Except for the two marines, no one was armed. and he had no idea what lay ahead. He silently directed everyone forward with his hand, the two marines leading the way, their backs scraping against the inner wall as they slithered down the corridor, one prudent step after another. As they closed on the strengthening signal their thermal scanner began pinging too, but the curving passageway ahead was empty.

"Must be in the next rooms," Cooke softly whispered as he looked back at Matt. With extreme caution the Corporal inched up to the red metallic door and pointed his scanner. With an emphatic nod that confirmed his suspicion, he leveled his rifle and backed off as he directed Tomlinson to pass his hand across the amber glowing electronic eye that would open the door. It didn't budge.

"It must be locked or security coded," Cooke quietly surmised.

"Blast the controls," Matt instructed, realizing that the automatic doors were designed to fly open in the event of electrical shorts or circuit malfunctions.

Suddenly a frantic, high-pitched voice cried out from within the enclosed room, followed by a series of hard, rapid thumping that resonated through the door. "Who's out there! Can anyone here me?"

"That sounds like Nichelle!" Sheri exclaimed as she bolted past the marines. "Nichelle, is that you? It's Sheri."

"Sheri?" she wailed in disbelief with a voice rippling in anguish and relief. "Is that really you? Thank God! Get me out of here!"

"Stand back from the door, Nichelle," Matt instructed as he placed a hand on Sheri's shoulder and exchanged smiles of satisfaction. "We're going to get you out."

A laser burst from the rifle of Corporal Cooke fried the tiny, square control panel in a brief eruption of fiery sparks and musty smoke. An emotionally frazzled Nichelle came bounding out of the room as the door slid open and upon seeing Sheri's beaming face rushed to embrace her. "I didn't think that anyone was going to find me," she shakily cried. "Tegan is in the next room."

Matt motioned to the marines to release him as well as his deep, husky voice could be heard hollering and cursing vehemently from down the hall. Sheri hugged her warmly before pushing her back at arms length. "Are you all right? You look well."

Nichelle rolled her shoulders. "The room was stocked with plenty of food, music and video disks, reading material, working plumbing." She snickered for a moment before turning somber. "It was actually rather comfortable except for the terrifying confinement and not knowing what was going on." With a combination of both irritation and distress, she forcefully clamped onto Sheri's upper arms like a vise. "Listen to me, Sheri. It was that bitch Lucinda. She imprisoned us here. And she has help!"

Caroline's incessant giggles, whimpering, and squirming came to an abrupt halt as she frantically scrambled to slip a silk robe over her sweaty, clammy body as the annoying buzz of the door intercom bellowed out in regular, irritating intervals. If it wasn't Bob Cooke, it was an unwelcome intrusion. As she watched Lucinda hastily slip into her NSCA work suit, she became amusingly curious at how she reacted to the initial sound at the doorway. She had never seen such a leering expression of diabolical delight turn in an instant to one of petrified alarm and fright. She had found their playful interlude a little uncomfortable and unusual but strangely invigorating. Lucinda had made her feel sensual and alive but she had been growing increasingly wary and uneasy at Lucinda's ravenous gaze as she seemed to take a perverse pleasure in the methodical application of her assortment of toys and powders to her stretched, lingerie clad body. But Lucinda had behaved herself. As she tightened her robe and strolled from the bedroom, she was praying that it was Bob at the door being so insistent. She really needed him now. Lucinda was right, she had gotten her ready for his visit. With the glowing embers of desire doing a slow burn inside her, she would be filled with unbridled passion tonight. With eager anticipation she approached the door and activated the speaker. "Yes, who is it?"

"Caroline, thank God. It's Sheri. I thought something might have happened to you. We're looking for Lucinda, have you seen her?"

Caroline was perplexed and confused by the urgency in Sheri's voice. "Why, yes," she replied with a hesitant stammer. "She's in here with me."

"Quick! Open the door and let us in!" Sheri was adamant and excitable. "She's the one behind the disappearances! Hurry!"

Caroline slammed her back against the wall and clutched her chest, her face wracked in terrifying horror as paralyzing chills shot up her spine, her heart pounding wildly as she shuddered uncontrollably. Finally she summoned the strength to reach out and depress the unlock button. Corporal Benetiez rushed in followed closely by Sheri, inauspiciously armed with an automatic pistol.

"Where is she?" Sheri impatiently questioned.

Caroline was too traumatized to speak. She simply pointed in the direction of the bedroom. Corporal Benetiez was already heading there. Moments later they heard his disheartened voice.

"There's no one here."

Caroline turned to Sheri with the look of shock. "I....I don't understand. She....she was right...."

Benetiez wearily staggered out, his rifle slumped lazily towards the floor. "She must have crawled out through the ventilation shaft. It's the only explanation. I'll inform the others."

Sheri soberly acknowledged his efforts. "Thank you, Corporal." As Benetiez left the room, Sheri took a firm hold of Caroline's arm who was still shivering in panic and confusion. "Listen to me," she demonstratively explained as she tried to shake Caroline's body to attention. "We found Nichelle and Tegan locked in rooms under the northeast dome. They seem fine. Doctor Oliver is checking them over now. It was Lucinda who did it. She stunned them and hid them away. She's very dangerous."

Caroline was incredulous. "What? But why?"

Sheri shook her head. "We don't know. Create confusion, maybe. We think that she might be working for the EESC. We suspect that it was she who sabotaged our ship and caused Nichelle's accident. We found a red stained environment suit in her quarters."

Caroline was puzzled and flustered, unable to follow the logic. "So what? All of our suits are soiled."

Sheri cast a chafing look. "Since we first arrived, when did her duties ever take her outside?"

Caroline felt a sickening pain in the pit of her stomach to go along with the erotic titillation that continued to taunt her. "Oh my God," she softly moaned as she staggered over to the sofa and collapsed upon its pliant cushions, covering her eyes with her hands as she buried her head upon her knees. Sheri trailed her over, sitting by her side and taking her trembling body comfortingly into her arms. Caroline was seething with emotions that she couldn't explain and at the moment wasn't feeling very good about herself. "I don't know if I'm more angry, frightened, or disillusioned," she quietly mumbled, pulling her hands away from her eyes to rest them on her lap, fingers clasped tightly together.

Sheri glanced at her peculiarly as she gently brushed a few strands of hair away from Caroline's eyes. "How do you mean?"

"I'm feeling rather stupid right now." Caroline became fervently emphatic as she turned to Sheri. "She used me!"

Sheri scoffed. "She used everybody, Caroline. I knew she was a little bit strange the day she boarded but I would have never suspected anything like this. Don't feel so bad."

But Caroline was tormented by a deeper consternation. "No, that's not what I mean. I knew that she was a self-indulgent, morally depraved person but I generally liked her. It didn't matter how she acted around others, she was usually very kind to me. I considered her a friend, a friend I could trust. I shared things with her, confided in her. She was the closest person I knew....next to you and Bob." Caroline quietly reflected on her past experiences with Lucinda before her head abruptly shot up and bitterly lamented. "And now you tell me that she's the damn enemy!" She put her hand to her forehead in frustration. "I can't believe it!" she despondently moaned. "She was right here. She could have kidnapped me, killed me, done anything she wanted too." Her anguished guise changed to one of befuddlement. "I wonder why she decided to split instead of...."

Sheri shrugged unknowingly. "Who can tell. But you're one lucky woman that she didn't take advantage of you."

As her disquieting emotions gradually settled, Caroline began to wonder what became of her anticipated male companionship. "Have you seen Bob?"

"Oh!" Sheri blurted, suddenly remembering a previous message. "I almost forgot. Corporal Cooke asked me to tell you that he's very sorry but he won't be able to see you tonight. He's been on the search detail all day and wanted to try to get a couple hours of sleep before he has to go back out to the outposts. He'll try to see you sometime tomorrow."

"Shit!" Caroline irritably cried out as she fretfully leaped to her feet and began to aimlessly pace the floor in front of Sheri, pounding her fist in her hand. "That's just great! I really needed him tonight."

"Caroline!" Sheri called out in bewilderment and concern. "What's wrong? Is there anything I can do to help?"

The dark, libidinous corridors of her psyche was tantalized for an instant before her conscious soul cast a disapproving scowl of disgust her way as she paused near Sheri's feet and frivolously replied . "Sure you could. But neither of us are into women, so just forget it."

Sheri looked dumbfounded. "I don't understand."

Caroline took a deep breath as she crossed her arms behind her, looking vacantly up to the ceiling. "You see, I was expecting to see Bob tonight so I allowed Lucinda to rub on some....how should I say it...." Caroline dipped her head in embarrassment as her hips swayed nervously. "....some powder that stimulates desire, if you know what I mean." Caroline watched the astonished gasp on Sheri's face slowly mutate to a waggish grin, eventually erupting in spasmodic laughter.

"I'm sorry," Sheri struggled to say as she tried to contain her chuckles after noticing the exasperated gawk she was receiving. "I don't mean to diminish your plight. It just strikes me as sort of funny right now. You do have a knack for getting yourself into bizarre predicaments."

Caroline was not amused but tried to lighten-up. "Well, right now I'm feeling rather desirous."

Sheri rose to her feet and placed a tender hand upon her hip. "Listen, if it's really that bad I have a couple of EPI's lying around somewhere. Would you like one?"

Caroline stepped back and held out her arms defensively. "No, I don't think so. That's a very nice gesture but I think I've had enough unusual entertainment for one night." Caroline reached out for Sheri's arms and ushered her towards the door. "You're a wonderful friend, Sheri, but I think that you had better go."

Sheri pressed close and gave Caroline an affectionate peck on the cheek. "As you wish. If you change your mind, just ...."

Caroline nodded her appreciation. "Thanks, Sheri. But I think I'll just use that time-honored, tried-and-true remedy."

Sheri lifted her brow quizzically.

"I'm going to take a long, cold shower."

Tom Reynolds cried out in horror as his torso jolted upright with fright in the darkness, the flimsy sheet limply falling to his waist, his heart racing as he gasped for air. He wiped his hand across his naked chest. His skin felt clammy and sticky, beads of perspiration liberally sprinkled all over him. It had been another haunting nightmare, but the images were so real. The charred and mangled bodies lying grotesquely amidst the smoldering, twisted wreckage of the rover. Miniature frozen deep red ponds where the flowing blood had collected and solidified in the frigid Martian air. It was as if he could actually smell the sickly-sweet odor, the acerbic stench of burning flesh. And it was all his fault. He could have prevented it all. Tom frustratingly ran his fingers through his disheveled hair. That was ridiculous, he had his orders. Besides, there was no real proof of danger, only surmise, conjecture, rumor, probability. It was bad enough that he continued to dream about those traumatic, harrowing events in the Romanian mountains. Now he had a new sense of guilt to occupy his subconscious at night. It was well after midnight by the time he had returned from checking on his outposts and received a report on the events that had transpired under the northeast dome. No one was getting much sleep anymore, least of all himself, but he was so weary that he could doze right off, if he could only stay asleep. Seemingly always those demons returned to interrupt his rest. With a gaping yawn of fatigue he settled his head back down on the pillow and closed his heavy eyelids. Just a few hours respite would be a welcome development. If only he could find Cindy out there somewhere in that fantasy world of dreams.

He found himself standing in his camouflaged fatigues on an open knoll richly carpeted with the vibrant green of meticulously manicured grass. His olfactory lobes detected something he hadn't sensed in quite awhile, the smell of the wild. Pure unfiltered air laced with the sweet, fresh fragrance of honeysuckle and pine. There was just a slight chill in the air as a gentle, serene breeze nipped tenderly at his face. The night stars twinkled overhead in all their majesty and brilliance in the cloudless sky like the flickering glow of a million campfires in the distant cosmic fields. Stretching out to his right for what seemed like infinity was the barren, rustic, freckled plain of Lunae Planum, tiny mists of red clay granules sweeping across the Martian landscape. He could see the jagged hills and rock-strewn valleys of the Echus Chaos. He could recognize the sharp-crested wrinkled ridges and gentle rising lava slopes of Alba Patera, littered with boulders and stones of innumerable shades of red, orange, gray, and tan, and cut by narrow meandering channels; desolate save for an acre of flowering plants blossoming in a mosaic of pinks, lilacs, yellows, and whites where death and destruction once stood. Towering towards the heavens well beyond the distant horizon was the signature landmark of Mars, the massive peak of Olympus Mons, as if the planet was raising its hand to touch the face of God. Situated prominently to his left rose the crest and thickly wooded slopes of the Romanian Alps, complete with large, craggy rock outcroppings and deep, rugged gorges. A pristine wilderness carved up by the irregular scars of trench lines and rifle pits. The peaceful rustle of leaves on the trees, the trickle of clear, cool water lazily flowing over the stones and dips of a nearby creek, and the melodious chirping serenade of nested sparrows brought a certain serenity to this hauntingly familiar place. Several hundred small, vibrantly colorful floral plots like those on Alba Patera marked the spots of the fallen and it seemed that he could reach out to touch a petal and instantly recall the name. He roamed freely around this strange world as if time and distance had no meaning, though his feet never really moved.

After what seemed like days but was merely fractions of a second, he found himself standing in the middle of the grassy meadow between the two divergent realms. As if conjured up by sorcerers, a large fog-like opaque cloud mystically formed in front of him whose sudden appearance nearly frightened him senseless. He watched in benumbed awe as the white borders randomly oscillated as a translucent, viscous material within the heart of the cloud churned and undulated, steadily thickening at each passing moment. His feet were frozen to the ground, he couldn't run away even if he wanted too. But there was a peculiarly soothing quality emanating from the mist, a sense of tranquillity and magnanimity that swarmed over him like he had never known. Slowly the gelatinous, palpitating mass solidified into a familiar, specter-like form, standing casually in the midst of a thin, filmy haze with sharply defined, fluctuating whitish-gray fringes, as if floating in the middle of a soap bubble. He instantly recognized the serene dark face and the immaculate Marine Corps dress blues from the picture he carried in his pocket. The supernatural apparition sent chilling shudders careening through his startled body. It was Sergeant First Class Jesse Carney! The star field brightly shining above the horizon behind the ghostly image gave it an enigmatic quality that approached omniscience. Jesse Carney's smiling face looked around the vista with what appeared to Tom as wondrous delight.

"This is strange." The monotone voice was calm and had a deep, hollow, reverberating quality as if speaking from the depths of a subterranean well.

Tom was bewildered and flabbergasted, able only to stammer facetiously. "You....you bet it is." He began to feel increasingly uncomfortable as those wandering, piercing eyes finally trained their unnerving gaze upon him.

"I am Jesse Carney."

Tom tremulously stood firm and returned the look with a courtly nod. "Thomas Reynolds." A sudden silent awkwardness came over him as he looked to the ground and nervously shuffled his feet, feeling compelled to ask a delicate question that was gnawing at his brain. Finally summoning the nerve, he swallowed hard and apprehensively lifted his head. "I don't mean to be offensive, but you're dead."

Jesse twitched nonchalantly and rolled his shoulders, much to Tom's relief. "That's all right. I am, in one form of reality. And I'm not."

Tom's expression was wrought with confusion but he began to feel a little more secure in his position. "Why are you here?" He found Jesse's ambiguous expression with his warily darting eyes rather perplexing.

"I'm not sure," he forthrightly replied in a tone that reflected genuine uncertainty. "I think, perhaps...." He hesitated, glancing back at Tom. "....for redemption."

"Redemption!" Tom skeptically exclaimed. "Mine?"

Jesse briefly glanced to the heavens and sighed. "I think....mine."

Tom's face went blank as he tossed his head. "I don't understand."

"I've been allowed to make this contact with you."

Tom could feel the tingling of unnerving chills creeping over him once more. "Allowed....why? Allowed....by who?"

Jesse began to leisurely pace within the boundaries of the translucent, fluctuating cloud, his sheepish grin doing nothing to alleviate Tom's anxiety. "When a young life is ended with no purpose, the soul is forever drifting through infinity in torment." He stopped and stared directly back at Tom. "I've been permitted this opportunity to meet the white man who gave a young black man's death meaning."

The swelling dryness in Tom's throat made swallowing the accumulation of saliva in his mouth difficult as he listened in awe. "How?"

"Trust in your faith, Thomas. It does you credit," Jesse responded in an authoritative though congenial manner, motioning with his hands in the appropriate direction. "There is a cosmic plan, for the Earth, for Mars, for the trillions of stars above. Each of us are born to a destiny. Some good, some bad, some historically momentous, most intangibly subtle though no less important, all intricately interwoven like the lavish fibers of an elegant Oriental carpet. We constantly alter the minor details with the choices we make in our lives but have faith that the universe will unfold as it should. There is a plan. Most of us never realize what that destiny is until it's upon us, if ever. My destiny laid on the slopes of the Romanian mountains." His head reverently turned to Tom's left. "To enable another man to meet his destiny. I never understood what that meant until you landed on this planet." Jesse pivoted and glanced to Tom's right, out into the image of Lunae Planum. "The others have drawn from your integrity, strength, and courage. They will need it for the trial ahead. For if they don't survive, Mars won't survive. There lies your destiny, Thomas Reynolds, to lead and protect these men and women so they may take the first infant steps towards mankind's future greatness on this planet. It's a mighty powerful destiny you have, mighty powerful."

Tom twitched restlessly in disquieting bewilderment and confusion, unable to fully appreciate the magnitude of the prediction. Being candidly honest with himself, his mind was troubled with another concern that caused his thoughts to drift. It was a singular and unique opportunity to clear his conscience. Humbly his head bent towards the ground. "There is something I have to get off my chest. It's been ripping at my heart ever since that night." Slowly he lifted his face, moisture welling-up in his eyes as he spoke in a voice choked with impassioned emotion, inflections spiked with anguished feeling. "Why did you go charging out in the open that way? Why did you sacrifice yourself like that?" His body tightened like a coil, his fingers clenched forcefully, the nails digging painfully into his palms. "Why didn't you just call out to me? Cover me from your hole? Toss a few grenades?"

Tom was surprised at the droll sneer and unwitting twitch that was directed his way.

"Man! I never knew that you were there!" Jesse replied with his first intonations of fervent emotion.

Tom's jaw dropped in astonishment and shock as if he had just been hit with a thousand volts. His whole perception of the incident that night had been wrong.

"I rushed out like that because I was scared," he calmly explained as Tom inertly listened in amazement. "I was scared senseless and panicked. Bullets and shells were whizzing overhead like angry hornets, the dead and wounded strewn all around me. I lost my head and foolishly charged down that slope, my rifle blazing away at anything that moved. There was nothing courageous about it."

Tom pondered on the revelation for a moment but its accidental nature did nothing to alter the result, or it's lasting affects. "No matter," he solemnly replied. "I feel an indebtedness that I will never be able to repay." He looked away, wiping a solitary tear from his cheek. His voice cracked at the release of his pent-up, bewildered, guilt-ridden emotions. "I've kept in touch with your wife, retold the story, remembered. It all seemed so feeble." Tom glanced up to meet Jesse's sympathetic and peaceful gaze. "I should have been lying dead out there, not you. Words are woefully inadequate to express the depth of my gratitude. I've been desperately needing to, somehow, to thank you ever since that battle. Thank you, Jesse Carney, for my life."

Tom felt a warm, consoling, loving embrace even though Jesse was still beyond his reach. It was as if the weight of a thousand anchors had been lifted from his heart as a contentment and serenity like he had never known swept over him like a surging tidal wave. It felt as if he was being smothered in the soothing and benign hand of God. While basking in this rejuvenating glow, he noticed the appreciative smile on Jesse's face as the misty, vacillating cloud moved forward.

"No, Tom, thank YOU. Because of you I did not die in vain."

CHAPTER

14

"Surely the nations are like a drop in the bucket;
they are regarded as dust on the scales....
He brings princes to naught and reduces the
rulers of this world to nothing.
Do you not know? Have you not heard?
The Lord is the everlasting God, the Creator of
the ends of the earth.
He will not grow tired or weary, and his
understanding no one can fathom.
He gives strength to the weary and to the weak
he increases might.
Even youths grow tired and weary, and young
men stumble and fall.
But those who hope in the Lord will
renew their strength.
They will soar on wings like eagles;
they will run and not grow weary,
they will walk and not be faint."

-ISAIAH 40: 15, 23, 28-31

The crash of the cascading water into the tiny pool below and the cooling tingle of the breaking ripples as the foam fizzed between her toes reminded Caroline of peaceful strolls through creek infested forests. She sat hand-in-hand with Robert Cooke by the 12-foot artificial rocky waterfall that was the showcase feature of the miniature wooded park under the glass of the Residential Dome. The spray from the tumbling stream blew a refreshing fine mist into their faces and formed tiny droplets of glistening moisture through their hair as their bare feet dangled over the small brick ledge and lazily flailed at the soothing swells as they approached the bank. Tammy Jacobs was inside the rock cliff facade intensifying the recycling water flow. With the water reclamation system operating at full capacity, they could afford a few amenities. With the onset of night, the stars radiated gloriously in the cloudless sky through the clear dome. It made the little park seem quite cozy and romantic. Caroline firmly grasped Bob's upper arm and snuggled close, nesting her head against his shoulder. Looking up she was still intrigued with how much more brilliant the stars glowed in the thinner Martian atmosphere. At night, Mars could have such a tantalizing and amorous affect.

The day had been uneventful. Lucinda was no where to be found and Matt was quick to suspend any more fruitless searches for lack of manpower, deciding instead to guard the sensitive areas such as the reactor plant, environment control system, A and C, and the computer network below. He even assigned himself and the members of his crew to some of those duties, relieving the meager marine force of some pressure.

Caroline was just getting comfortable, luxuriating in the gentle caresses that Bob's fingers were applying to her back when Tammy came bounding out from behind the mound of fake rock.

"How's that?" she sprightly called out as she skipped up to Caroline's side to observe her handiwork.

"It's magnificent!" Caroline exclaimed as she straightened her slouching frame and gazes at the sparkling, tumbling water with delight.

Tammy smiled proudly. "I figured a little water use for recreation won't hurt. The sound and mist will be very calming on everyone's nerves."

"You're working late tonight." Caroline observed after nodding in agreement.

Tammy, bubbling cheerfully, casually rolled her shoulders. "It's about the only time I have a chance to work on something like this. Besides, I'm meeting one of your buddies later tonight." Her eyes were glancing past

Caroline towards Bob. "Private Anderson is on outpost duty right now." Caroline noticed the tiny, salacious grin that crossed her face. "I thought that this might be a nice place for a midnight stroll." Tammy turned to Caroline with an amusing chuckle. "But I see that you have figured that out for yourself. You know, it's good to see you happy again." Tammy bent over and gave Caroline a sisterly peck on the cheek. "And to you too," she merrily added with a friendly pat to Bob's shoulder. "I'll leave you two to enjoy each other. Good night."

"Good night, Tammy," Caroline replied with a grateful gleam.

Tammy took a quick backward glance as she faded away along the compressed dirt trail. "You be careful out there, soldier."

"Thank you, ma'am."

Caroline moaned in contentment as she wiggled into a more comfortable position against Bob's chest. "She's such a hard worker....and so very sweet. I hope that she finds someone. Listen, I got permission from Matt, I mean Commander Maitland, to go out to the botanical test field tomorrow to check on our specimen lichen splicings. I need a marine escort." Caroline felt the squeeze of his fingers around her upper arm as he pulled her tight against him.

"Of course," he happily grinned. "But can you wait till the afternoon. Let me get a little sleep first once I return from the picket line."

Significant concerns regarding the future abstrusely crept into the deeper corners of her mind as she brought her arm across his chest. "Bob, when this is all over, what do you plan to do? Have you ever considered leaving the space marines and maybe settling down somewhere?"

Bob fidgeted nervously as he hesitantly stammered. "I....I never really gave it much thought. The Corps has been very good to me. It's the only life I've really known."

"Where do you think you will go next?"

Bob shrugged with uncertainty as he affectionately stroked the side of her head. "Who knows, wherever they send me. How about you?"

Caroline rubbed her cheek against his shoulder and kneaded his chest with her fingertips. "Well, after I had accepted the fact that Dave was gone, I thought I might stay here and re-colonize Jamestown. Keep the dream alive. But now I'm not so sure." Caroline lifted her head and gazed longingly into his radiant blue eyes. "That depends on where you go."

Adoration and passion overwhelmed both of them as their arms became entangled in a suffocating embrace, their lips and tongues pressing together in a long and fervent display of affection, their fingers roaming and clawing like tigers against the other's back. Caroline blissfully tossed back her head, panting heavily, her breasts erotically brushing against his chest as his titillating lips suckled sensually along her neck.

"It's late," she moaned between sobs of joy. "Let's go back. Make love to me, Bob....while we still have time."

It was quiet, very quiet. Robert Cooke clicked on his helmet and gloves after transferring reception of the rover's long range communicator to his internal receiver and stepped out onto the dark, frozen Martian surface. The million glimmering points of light that adorned and glorified the heavens were in sharp contrast to the dreary, dim black and gray images of scabrous boulders and shallow craters, nearly indiscernible from each other in the eerie darkness. The tiny potato-shaped moon of Phobos, affectionately termed Mister Potato Head, only slightly more than 13 miles in diameter and orbiting overhead at a mere 6 miles distance, looked more like a bright golf ball than a conventional moon, reflecting precious little light to the surface. The ground and any obstructions ahead were illuminated by the twin cylindrical lights mounted on the sides of his helmet. The crystal-like microscopic sandy granules crunched like brittle crackers under the weight of his boots as he moved towards the bent form of Private Walinski, hovering over the hexagonal-shaped detection scanners. The external light from his helmet briefly reflected off the Corporal's faceplate as he turned upon Cooke's approach.

"Anything from Simmons or the base?"

"No, not a peep," Cooke replied, twisting his head backward. "That thing is too claustrophobic. I'd rather be out under the stars."

Walinski wondrously scanned the sky. "It is peaceful, if you can get over the creepy landscape. You haven't said much about your little fling with Caroline Hart. Something's going on, you're spending an awful lot of time with her. She must be pretty hot stuff, a real ball-breaker."

Cooke grew slightly agitated. "You know that I don't kiss and tell, John. Let it drop. She's a very fine woman and I'm beginning to fall for her." Cooke sighed with the pleasant memory of their latest encounter. "And I think that she is falling for me, why I can't imagine. It could turn into something special." A sly grin brightened his face. "And yes, John, she's rather passionate and that's all I'm going to say."

"Okay, Bob." Walinski relented with a snicker. "You can keep the juicy parts to yourself. I guess I don't take relationships as seriously as you."

"Yeah, and look what happened to you," Cooke contemptuously remarked. "It must have been a real shock to learn that your lover was working for the other side!"

The two friends rechecked their equipment in awkward silence and observed the valley below the bluff on which they stood with the aid of their night vision visors, but it was difficult to recognize anything of significance. A thin, gray filmy mist began to form in the deepest depressions and gullies along the valley floor that gave a ghostly, gothic quality to the entire panoramic scene. Walinski froze in his tracks, searching the heavens again.

"Bob!" he contemplatively called. "Do you believe in God?"

Cooke stuttered maladroitly, never comfortable with religious subjects, as an unsettling twinge accompanied his ambiguous uncertainty. "Yes....No....I don't know."

"I mean," Walinski continued in an unusually pensive manner, "what do you think happens when you die?"

Cooke rolled his shoulders uneasily. "I don't know, John. Never gave it much thought.... Something. I guess we'll find out in time."

Walinski seemed a little uneasy as he propped a boot upon a small stone. "Being out here these last few nights on this strange world, as if we're the only two living things in the whole universe, has got me thinking about things. I can't say that I'm proud of some of the things I've done in my life. I've always been an agnostic, but sometimes I get the feeling that just maybe there is some divine intelligence out there, and if so, how will I atone for my actions."

All too familiar with the workings of the human mind under such conditions, Cooke casually stepped to his side. "I've been with the Corps for six years, John," he said as he placed a pacifying hand upon his shoulder. "I've seen and experienced my share of terrifying and unusual things. All I can tell you, my friend, is that there are no atheists in a foxhole."

Walinski grunted ponderously as Cooke moved away. "Perhaps I should start hedging my bets, just in case that...."

Cooke abruptly halted in mid-stride as the sound of panicked voices rang out over his long range receiver, stalwartly holding up an open right hand to silence his talkative companion.

"Multiple contacts altitude eighteen hundred to twenty-two hundred feet, bearing three....two....zero degrees. Estimated speed one hundred ninety knots. Range....four hundred miles and closing!"

With a peculiar grimace Walinski straightened and trampled heavy-footed along the grinding clay to join his friend. "Bob, what is it?"

The focused beam from the helmet light revealed Cooke's obvious troubled and pained expression. "It's Simmons and Jones," he soberly reported. "They've got radar contacts. John, make sure our thruster packs are fully fueled. I think it may be game time."

Thomas Reynolds had never known such happiness like the seeming eternity he spent with Cindy and his two daughters, sharing hundreds of exhilarating and special moments in magnificent, rainbow-like vistas, all cruelly brought to a dramatic and abrupt conclusion by the intense voice of Sergeant Douglas calling out over the intercom. Groggily he turned to the side and reached for the reply activation button. "Yes, Sergeant."

"Sir, our outposts are reporting contacts approaching from the northwest. Their present course will put them here in less than two hours."

Reynolds lurched upright and wiped the sleep from his dreary eyes. "Very well, Sergeant," he replied with a reluctant sigh, "assemble the men, full load. Inform Commander Maitland. I'll be there presently."

Reynolds rashly leaped from his bed and hurriedly dressed. He felt strangely invigorated, rested, composed, and at peace. He checked the clock - it was shortly after one in the morning. He had barely been in bed for three hours but felt like he had slept for a week. The dream had been so vivid, as if he had actually lived them only yesterday. It was like he had been mysteriously transported to some far-off exotic world. His encounter with the apparition of Jesse Carney the night before had been so profoundly inspiring that it relieved his soul and rekindled his spirit to the point that he felt reborn. And tonight there was Cindy, reliving with him there first date, the night he proposed on his knees, romantic sunset walks on the beach, shooting the Cheat River rapids, making blissful love, the birth of their children. And new experiences too. Amorous moments in wild, exotic, scenic locales such as the Grand Canyon, a luxury cruise in the Caribbean, overlooking the spewing and flaming lava flows of Kilauea in Hawaii Volcanoes National Park. And priceless moments with his daughters as well. Romping through green, freshly scented meadows with Megan and Alicia, family picnics along the banks of the Allegheny, trips to the zoo, birthday parties, all recalled as if he had just lived them, like they had been with him all along. He snickered to himself with pleasure. Of course they were, he thought, they would always be with him. Gathering up his gear he remembered one very important thing as he was about to leave. He had always made a vid disk for Cindy and the girls, updating it as circumstances required, before he went off on a potentially perilous mission, that would be delivered to his family in the event of his death. He rushed over to the desk and retrieved the disk and carried it into the bedroom where he devoutly placed it on the top of his dresser unit that contained clothes and other personal effects where he was sure that it would be found. Placing a photo displayer of his family inside his chest pocket, Reynolds picked up his laser rifle and bolted out the door.

Matt recklessly scampered up the stairs that led to A and C, blindly skipping most of them, after mindlessly crashing his shuttle cart into the tunnel wall outside the entrance portal. Panting profusely, he irritably jogged into the control room. "It's the middle of the night for God's sake!" he grumbled aloud. "Why can't crisises happen between eight and five?"

Sheri was already there, standing behind a soldier seated at the triangular work station containing the marine's electronic hardware.

"What have you got?" Matt brusquely inquired as he stepped up to the station located near the center of the domed enclosure.

"Well, sir," the short, spectacled, dark skinned marine replied without so much as a twitch of distraction as he continued to press buttons on the control panel of one of the various computer monitors, "one of our outposts has confirmed multiple radar and thermal displacement contacts flying this way, now three hundred and fifty miles and closing. Bearing and speed remain constant. I'm programming the robotics SAM platform to move to the predetermined position along our northern perimeter."

The low-riding missile platform slowly rumbled on its wide rubber treads from its position east of the collapsed dome along its directed course.

"Where is Lieutenant Reynolds? And who are you anyway?"

"Why, I'm Private Alonso Jamison, sir," he replied glancing over his shoulder with a look of self-assurance.

Sheri snickered. "Private Jamison has two years at Princeton."

Mat was surprised. "Princeton! How did you get mixed up with this bunch?"

Jamison leisurely flinched. "I just decided college wasn't for me," he explained with upturned palms. "The corporate and research world didn't excite me. I'm the unit's Tech Specialist. When the guys have problems with their equipment they come to me. They call me Mister Techno Sage." His voice exuded unabashed pride. "The Lieutenant is there." His finger pointed to the image on a monitor whose screen was labeled with the Lieutenant's name. It was a view from the driver's seat of a rover, looking out the forward window into the blackened night, the only visible terrain being the ground directly ahead that was illuminated by the rover's bank of spot lights. "The video from the helmet cams is transmitted and displayed on the appropriate monitor. We can see what each man sees on his individual screen, in living color. Right now Lieutenant Reynolds and Private Tomlinson are in our CR heading for defensive quadrant four, about forty miles away. Benetiez, Anderson, and Warwick are flying ahead with their thruster packs to secure the position." He indicated the applicable monitors that only showed a passing shadow of rock or depression below or a distant side view of a companion brought about by a twisting head, thin, fluffy, milky ribbons trailing behind the exhaust ports of their packs.

"What about these?" Matt questioned as he pointed to the four monitors that were consumed with flickering static lines.

"Those belong to our guys at the outposts. They won't be in transmission range until they return to quadrant four. Simmons and Jones are en route now. Cooke and Walinski will be retiring shortly to join our outer perimeter defense."

Matt did a quick mental calculation. "They don't have much time."

"No, sir."

Matt noticed a blank monitor in the bottom right corner of the array. "And that?"

"That's mine, sir," he offhandedly replied with a flippant glance over his shoulder. "As you may have noticed, I'm not wearing my helmet."

Matt grinned and gave the man a friendly slap on the back. "Thank you for that most enlightening tour, Mister Techno Sage."

"Yes, sir," he skeptically acknowledged, unsure as how to take the light-hearted compliment.

It was then that Vijay came storming in, followed closely by Andre and Nichelle, all gasping for air.

"It's becoming difficult to get any sleep around here!" Vijay whimsically called out.

"Vij! I'm glad you're here," Matt bellowed as he briskly met him and grabbed his arm. "I have a feeling that we could be in some trouble."

Vijay grimaced in distress. "Ouch! Insurance companies go broke when you get feelings like that."

"Listen, I want you and Andre to form damage control parties. Consolidate equipment where it can easily be reached. And draw sidearms."

"Okay, Matt," he calmly replied despite the fear etched on his face.

"And you had better distribute environment suits. Bring some up here as well, in case we're breached."

Matt felt his head spinning in all directions, caught in a traumatic and frightening whirling vortex of unbridled emotion and thought, swirling out of control. He valiantly fought to maintain his dignified composure, realizing that other terrified faces were looking to him for reassurance and strength. "Sheri, monitor the colony scanners," he firmly though serenely ordered. "The intruders should be registering now. Inform me of any aspect change." Swiftly turning to Nichelle, Matt placed a rigid hand upon her back and guided her towards the communication station. "We can use your help, Nichelle. Get on the transmitter and try to raise them." His voice rose in determination and intensity. "Find out who they are and warn them off."

"I'll try," she meekly replied as her trembling body took a seat.

"And get me Jack Shoals."

The large military command rover rumbled to a crunching halt within the narrow gully channel carved into the southern slope of the gently rising hill that was the forward position of DQ4 in Reynolds' active defense plan. There was every indication that the unidentified contacts would pass through this sector but they had to be prepared at a moment's notice to move to another defensive quadrant should the need arise. He had chosen the best available commanding ground to cover the entire area. The hill stood a half mile to the front of a low, extensive, undulating ridge speckled with a series of rugged, rocky knolls that rose up from the crest like conical warts on a witch's cheek. He selected two of these to defend, roughly a mile from the central hill, one to each side, so that it formed sort of a shallow triangle that provided interlocking fields of fire. Any intrusion into the quadrant could draw fire from at least two of the positions.

Private Warwick, who had reached the hill earlier, came bounding carefully down the frozen, dusty slope as Reynolds and Tomlinson emerged from the rover's airlock. "There's some concentrations of nice-size boulders and a few crater holes on the other side near the crest that will make excellent firing positions, sir," he diligently reported. "You'll find a shallow depression about twenty yards under the lip that would make a good pit for the eighty millimeter. Benetiez and Anderson are occupying that large bluff to our left rear."

"Thank you, Private. I want you to run a supply of SAR rockets over to them." Reynolds opened the hatch of a cargo storage compartment near the rear of the rover and handed him a heavy canvas bag containing the ammunition. Warwick slung the bag over his arm and shoulder and moments later was soaring into the night sky, his path marked by a rapidly dissipating smoky trail. He instructed Tomlinson to set up the mortar tube with its ammunition crates of small, rounded, shrapnel spreading shells ironically termed grapeshot after the nineteenth century cannon shell that scattered hundreds of iron mini-balls. In ground combat in a hostile planetary environment, a ripped space suit was often just as deadly as a precision laser burst to the head.

Once their tiny hill positions were secured, the most difficult part of the whole ordeal began - the excruciating waiting. Reynolds strapped on his thruster pack and a small supply of extra rockets and power clips and scooted over to the eastern knoll where he met Simmons and Jones as they came in from their outpost withdraw. He found them bristling with energetic excitement, anxiety, and fear, all perfectly normal reactions. A good dose of adrenaline could keep a soldier going when his other faculties began to fail him. Exuding his calming influence, he helped them establish the best positions for sweeping the valley and air space before them.

He found the mood on the left flank much more tranquil and relaxed as he could overhear on his helmet receiver the frivolous bantering between Corporal Benetiez and Private Anderson as he descended upon their location. Their joking and digging remarks concerning their previous scavenger hunt to the south came to an abrupt halt when they observed the Lieutenant's running landing along the summit. Reynolds found Benetiez in a diminutive crater pit about forty yards below the crest, aiming his shoulder launched SAR tube, checking the accuracy of the laser guided sighting scope mounted atop the cylinder. Reynolds motioned for him to relax as the Corporal snapped to attention.

"Nice of you to drop in, sir."

"How's it going here, Corporal?"

"Wonderful, sir. Just waiting for the opening of skiing season." Benetiez facetiously pointed to the array of rockets and power clips stacked on the crater floor. "As you can see, sir, I just moved in. You're just in time to help me shingle the roof."

Reynolds chuckled amusingly.

"Are they really coming, sir?" Benetiez somberly questioned in a sudden change of demeanor.

"I'm afraid so, Corporal. They're about a hundred miles away and closing. Be here in thirty or forty minutes. Where's Anderson?"

"About fifty yards that way, sir," he responded, pointing to his left.

Trudging along the rubble, icy slope he came across the soldier behind a group of boulders, digging into the frozen ground with his collapsible heated shovel in an effort to improve his natural breastwork. The steel head of the shovel was laced with an embedded intersecting web of thermal filaments powered by a battery in the handle. A few seconds of pressure against the dirt softened it enough to permit excavation but it was a tediously slow process. Of course, the digger had to be extremely careful not to press a leg or foot against the blade which would immediately burn a hole through his clothing or boot.

"It's a solid position, soldier," Reynolds commented as he came to rest, "but remember that you can only fire two or three rockets before they can lock-on to your vapor trail. You'll have to keep moving."

"I'll remember, sir. Actually, I'm looking forward to some action."

"He's not a well man, sir," Benetiez's droll voice came chiming over the helmet speakers. "He's suffering from delusions of glory."

Reynolds smirked. "You can't find an enemy behind every rock, Anderson."

"Personally, sir," he remarked dryly, "I'd prefer finding them in front of rocks."

Relieved that his men appeared to be in good spirits, Reynolds returned to his central hill position amusingly recalling his Henry V performance that he gave aboard ship. He was feeling rather like the ancient English King, moving inconspicuously among his camp on the eve of

Agincourt, gauging the morale of his men. As he landed near the rover and ascended the rugged mound he began to overhear the conversation between Warwick and Tomlinson over the local channel in his helmet.

"I want you to keep this for me." Tomlinson pleaded as he opened a gold case pocket watch with an elegant knotted chain attached, the inside lid displaying a picture of a beautiful young woman, "in case something happens and I have to be left behind. My girlfriend gave it to me after I graduated from SMTS. That's her. She knows of my fondness for antiques."

Warwick held out his palms in protest. "No, Zack, I don't want it."

"Come on, Jason," he implored as he leaned into him. "I want to make sure that it gets home. I still have a picture of her in my pocket."

Warwick backed away, still holding up his hands objectionably. "You're space happy!" he cried out. "Just put the damn watch away and relax, okay? Nothing's going to happen."

Tomlinson persisted, forcefully grabbing his hand. "Jason, I insist," he said as he thrust the watch and chain into it, folding the gloved fingers over the burnished gold. "There. I feel better already."

"All right, damnit," Warwick reluctantly mumbled as he dropped the memento into a chest pocket and zipped it shut. "If it will shut you up."

"Thanks, buddy," Tomlinson appreciatively replied with a slap to the arm before both men were startled to attention by the glaring beams from Reynolds' helmet lights as he carefully descended upon them.

"Expecting to die?" Reynolds disquietly asked of the pessimistic young soldier. "I don't like those thoughts. Having them....," he wavered, turning disconsolately to the side, "....sometimes....makes them come true." His inflection became more unyielding as he lifted his head. "Get your watch back," he commanded. "Scout the terrain along the hillside. This will be an active defense, not a static one. Keep busy."

"Yes, sir."

"Still no response," Nichelle called out in frustration.

Matt irritably looked up from behind the military cubicle. "Are you washing your transmission through the universal translator?"

"Yes, Commander, they're just not answering."

"Matt!" Sheri frenetically shouted from her outward facing console. "If I'm reading these instruments correctly, targets have slowed dramatically, about thirty miles per hour. Range seventy-five miles, maintaining original heading."

Matt turned to Sergeant Douglas who had recently stepped forward to the other side of Private Jamison. "Well Sergeant, what do you think?"

"Undoubtedly assessing the situation, looking us over, sir."

Matt was openly hopeful. "Maybe they'll change their minds, not wanting to risk a confrontation and further bloodshed."

Douglas lowered his head with an inauspicious shake. "After the other day, I don't think so, sir. They want something, and they'll roll over anyone who gets in their way. But we may still have a surprise or two."

Matt disheartenedly leaned into the microphone in front of the marine's communication unit. "Are you getting all this, Lieutenant?"

"Affirmative," came his hollow-sounding reply, the affect of sound vibrations reverberating inside his helmet. Matt looked at the image on the Lieutenant's monitor. He was standing on rising ground looking out over a lower valley but couldn't see any detail. "Even with magnification and night vision I can't see a thing. They must be behind the range of hills to our northwest. We'll get a better look when they cross over. Any idea of the number?"

Matt quizzically peered over the cubicle top towards Sheri. She was diligent and thorough in examining all of the scanners before swiveling around with an uneasy smirk to her otherwise adorable face. "Difficult to say, Matt. About a dozen small craft I think, maybe more."

"Okay," came Reynolds' restrained reply. "We'll take care of it. We can see them a lot better than they can see us."

"Don't start anything until we've exhausted all efforts to contact them," Matt warned.

"Don't let them get on top of us," Reynolds gravely replied.

"I understand," Matt assured before calling out to Nichelle. "Keep trying to raise them. Inform them that they are entering a restricted area under the jurisdiction of the National Space Colony Administration. If they break fifty miles, they will be considered hostile."

They cautiously rose into the star-freckled night, menacingly loomed over the jagged precipices like a pack of voracious buzzards waiting for the final spasmodic twitches of life from a dying carcass. Moving deliberately with renewed purpose, the metallic vultures crossed over the last of a series of craggy, bald-faced slopes and drifted above the valley floor beyond. Passing the crest of a couple more ridge lines would bring the glowing lights of Jamestown into view. It would become their new nest, one way or another.

The compact reconnaissance and war machines resembled flying ice cream cones lying on their sides atop thick, horizontal, rotating oval platforms. The main fuselage of these single seat craft was not much larger than an automobile, with the tip of the cone as the bow which housed a laser cannon turret. The main conical fuselage contained the cockpit behind which was the ice cream scoop, a revolving half-sphere with a short, stubby nozzle that mixed air and combustible propellant to provide forward thrust. The spinning oval disk on the bottom sucked in and compressed the surrounding air, creating a kind of mini cyclonic vortex beneath the ship that produced lift and provided a controlled cushion of air on which the vehicle was suspended. A long and narrow inclined cambered wing extended from each side of the main compartment.

From his observation point, Lieutenant Reynolds could see through his night vision visor the ghostly fluorescent images of metal frame silhouettes glittering in the distance like gigantic prehistoric fireflies. His external receiver could barely discern the faint, high-pitched humming sound produced by the ships electrothermal engines. "Look alive boys, they're on their way," he calmly advised over the local channel. "Helmet lights off, night visors down. Don't anyone get trigger happy. Wait for the command. I know that you are all scared and uncertain. But there are a lot of people depending on us; decent, honorable men and women trusting us to keep them safe. That's what the Space Marines are all about. Just keep your wits about you, do your jobs, and leave the rest in the hands of God. With luck this mess will soon be over and we can return home to our families. No matter what happens, remember that you are the Iron Brigade."

News of the impending confrontation spread through Jamestown like a devastating plague. Those not employed by Vijay in damage control preparations tended to cluster together in the common area of the Residential Dome, most aimlessly wandering about the park in a trance-like state, frequently taking precarious glances out the transparent panels towards the rising black landscape to the north and west. No one slept. A few lingered just outside the entrance to A and C but Matt forbade entrance to anyone who did not have specific functional responsibilities. That, of course, did nothing to deter Susan Oliver from rantingly storming in.

"Matt! You've got to stop this insanity!"

"I'm open to suggestions, Doctor," Matt calmly replied with a sharpened inflection that betrayed his displeasure as he continued to concentrate on the camera monitors. "Now will you kindly leave the room."

Susan stepped forward emphatically. "You've got to talk to them!"

Matt spun around angrily. "We're trying, Doctor. They refuse to respond. Now will you please leave. I don't have time for this."

Their policy disagreement was interrupted by the anxious plea of Lieutenant Reynolds resonating over the transmitter. "Targets now within optimum range. What are your orders, Commander?"

Matt perplexingly scratched his head. "Standby, Lieutenant." Matt's imploring eyes glanced over towards Sergeant Douglas.

"If those ships get within thirty miles," he candidly observed, "than we might as well open the doors and let them in, sir."

"Matt!" Sheri cried out in distress. "I'm reading a large craft and a few more smaller ones about twenty miles behind the first flight."

Matt shook his drooping head in hopeless despair.

"Probably a bomber, missile platform, or troop transport," Douglas professionally surmised.

Matt felt like a cornered tiger in a pit, and like a trapped animal there was only one thing left to do. "Nichelle!"

Her fist slammed against the console panel as she turned around in anguish. "They just won't answer!" she cried.

"Just let them come in, Matt," Doctor Oliver assuredly urged. "Show them we're peaceful."

"I don't think they care if we are or not," Matt bitterly replied.

Doctor Oliver noticed the contemptible leer that the Sergeant was tossing her way as he stepped forward. "Yes, Sergeant?" she cynically said.

"Just making sure whose side you're on."

Matt exasperatingly stepped between them. "That's enough! Ignoring hails and warnings and violating our air space doesn't seem like the actions of peaceful intentions to me. Our time is up."

"But, Matt! We can't...."

Matt furiously held up a silencing finger to the Doctor's nose. "Susan, you can leave the room now or I'll grab you by the seat of your pants and personally carry out your obstinate ass."

"All right, I'm going," she derisively replied as she moved towards the exit before briefly pausing. "You reactionaries fight your little war. Just don't expect me to heal all the pain and misery you cause."

Matt disgustingly returned to the military communicator as the Doctor stalked out in a huff. "Very well. Lieutenant," he reluctantly said. "Proceed at your own discretion."

With a prolonged whiz and pronounced woosh the rocket shot out of the shoulder-held tube like a Roman Candle, trailing smoke and fire along its laser-guided track, striking the unsuspecting intruder amidships in a thunderous fiery inferno that lit up the night sky like a miniature supernova, tumbling unceremoniously in a hundred flaming mangled fragments to the frozen valley floor where the blazes were quickly reduced to gray smoldering puffs in the oxygen deprived atmosphere. Within moments the air was filled with the sight of soaring, fiery streamers streaking into the blackness, ending in brilliant fireballs and plunging scraps of metal as they struck the fragile targets or continued harmlessly into the void. The excited chatter from the marines was incessant.

"Look at those mothers break apart!" Simmons could be heard to exclaim over the local frequency.

"That first one was Zack's," Warwick commented with glee.

"How about that, Raffy," Anderson called out to his nearby colleague. "His first mission and he gets a kill on his first shot."

The flying cones broke off in confusion, unable to detect the location of their antagonists, weaving and darting adroitly to avoid the rampaging rockets. Their instruments could not identify the presence of the marines, the military suits designed to retard the radiation of body heat, but the next salvo would most certainly betray their position.

"We flamed four!" Warwick proudly proclaimed as the ships regrouped above the distant hills for another approach.

"That's what I counted," Benetiez confirmed from his crater hole.

"Don't stay in one place for long," Reynolds warned his exhilarated troop. "Next time they're going to be all over our butts."

Next time came very quickly and with a vengeance. They approached the meandering hill-studded ridge line much faster and in staggered pairs. The hand-held SAR's had proven very effective at downing these craft - the narrow beam of the laser rifle would require multiple hits on a critical area on a fast moving target - but the supply of rockets was limited and their flight left a visible trail. As a pair of intruders flew obliquely in front of the right bluff, Private Jones sighted his glowing target and launched another rocket. Immediately the second ship tracked the burning propellant and opened fire with its laser cannon. Jones bolted wildly from behind his clump of boulders as the first burst struck the ground in front of him in a brief splash of glistening hot light and uprooted regolith. Unable to continue to paint the target with his laser sight, the rocket drifted astray and disappeared into the night. Laser bursts caused the ground to puff and spew behind him in rapid succession until a strike on a nearby massive rock caused it to shatter into several large, jagged pieces. Jones tumbled to the ground in agony, his life-support pack shredded and the back of his suit punctured with grievously large rips. A second later the deadly craft was sent spiraling to the surface in a ball of flame by a rocket from Private Simmons, but he had been too heavily engaged to be aware of the death of his comrade.

Corporal Benetiez and Private Anderson on the left knoll were madly scampering from point to point, firing and dodging as several of the flying cones buzzed around them like pesky mosquitoes, taking their shots and circling back across the valley to reform and make another run. They had difficulty tracking the fleet little insects as several rockets whizzed inoffensively by. Supporting crossfire from the central hill also had similar trouble. On the next attack run, Benetiez was able to maintain a solid tracking lock on the first incoming craft, the tumultuous explosion tearing off the nose and causing it to pinwheel downward and smash on the ground in a smoldering heap of twisted and fused metal.

"Ha....Hahhhh....!" he erupted in unbridled jubilation. "That's how the US Space Marines kicks ass you sons-of-bitches!"

About fifty yards away, Anderson was clumsily fumbling in his haste to load another rocket when he noticed a second ship angling towards the Corporal's position from a different direction. "Raffy, watch out!" he shouted at the top of his lungs, helpless to assist. "Get out of there!" He saw Benetiez turn to his left and look up and watched in horror as several bright flashes of yellow-orange struck around the crater, dust and frozen clay sprouting into the air like dwarf geysers, peppering the pit as if struck by pellets from a shotgun. "Raffy, no!" he screamed in panic as he saw his body limply collapse under the rim. As the attacker flew by and circled away, Anderson dropped his tube and used his thruster pack to quickly skim over to the shallow crater. "No, Raffy, don't do this!" he distressfully cried as he bent over the motionless body laying face down and contorted along the fluted slope. Anderson could hear the animated and concerned voice of Lieutenant Reynolds ringing in his helmet.

"Anderson, report. What's your sit rep?"

Anderson fearfully grabbed a shoulder and rolled the body over. The sight sickened him, causing him to gasp in horror. The helmet shield was completely shattered and the front half of his head was seared away into an oozing, bloody pulp that quickly solidified like a mass of frozen cherry jelly. "My God! He has no face!"

"Anderson!" Reynolds pleaded. "Respond immediately."

Anderson fought the churning rumblings in his stomach to keep from vomiting into his helmet. "It's Raffy, sir," he somberly replied in a state of shock. "He has no face!"

"Rock-up, Private!" Reynolds shouted agitatedly despite his own feelings of sickening grief. "You're going to be next if you don't get back to your post and start whipping some ass!"

Lieutenant Reynolds was experiencing terrifying flashbacks, feeling sick, aggrieved, and disheartened every bit as grave as those he encountered three years before. But he had to remain poised and stoic if the men were to maintain their composure. After the last attack run the surviving ships banked and headed away across the valley.

"Look, sir!" he heard Private Tomlinson merrily shout as he watched him leap from behind his stone-sheltered pit and pointed into the sky towards their adversaries. "We beat them back! They're running away!"

"Tomlinson!" Reynolds screamed in alarmed panic. "Get back down you fool!"

As Tomlinson turned in surprise the ground erupted in winking, luminous flashes and clamorous percussions followed by showers of dirt and splintered rock - laser fire from the final banking intruder several miles away. He instinctively covered his face from the raining debris and then slowly dropped to the ground. Within seconds Reynolds was by his side. He was semi-conscious, moaning, breathing erratically. The front of his suit had three small ruptures out of which tiny filaments of steam leisurely rose into the air as the warmth inside slowly leaked out to mix with the frigid Martian carbon dioxide. A small seepage of blood trickled from one of the wounds and froze into tiny ice shavings. Reynolds could see blood staining the corners of his mouth. Internal injury was likely, and it wasn't good. Immediately Reynolds took out his emergency medical kit that every soldier carried. With the patching tape he quickly vacuum-sealed the rips to prevent any further loss of life-support.

"Warwick, get a stretcher," he ordered over the communicator. "Hang in there, son," his soothing but broken voice urged, cracking with emotion that betrayed his dire concern. "You're going to make it, soldier." Tomlinson was dazed and incoherent as Reynolds injected the contents of two hypos into his arm. The solutions contained an oxygen supplement, a clotting agent, a generic blood supplement that could combine with all types, an anti-inflammatory drug, a metabolic stabilizer, and a painkiller. "You get to go home," he continued to talk as he sealed the puncture holes from the hypo. "Just stay with us."

Warwick soon arrived with a portable litter. "Let's get him into the command rover," Reynolds instructed. "Before our friends return."

"No, no goddamnit!" Private Jamison irritably hollered as he angrily pounded the top of the Benetiez monitor that had recently gone blank. "Shit!" Jones' monitor was dark as well, simply transmitting a static close-up of the blackened ground at night. Tomlinson's camera was showing smudges of pinpoint light in the heavens and an occasional piece of a bronze helmet or arm hovering over him. All the others seemed to be scanning normally. Matt fretfully paced behind the military cubicle, his hands nervously alternating between digging into his hips and running with futility through his tousled hair. He hated the feeling of being so powerless, watching idly as others put their lives at risk. His private fuming and frustrations were interrupted by Sheri's desperate and beleaguered cry.

"Scanners detect that the attacking craft have rendezvoused with the second flight behind the hills and are beginning to advance again."

With a deep, reluctant sigh he turned to Sergeant Douglas. "They could be here at any time. You had better get out there and see to your men. Cooke and Walinski should be back at any moment."

"Yes, sir. Don't worry, Commander, we'll keep them away."

Matt had to force a contrived smile through his pessimism. "I'm sure you will, Sergeant," he quietly said with a hearty pat to the shoulder. Matt rushed up to the military transmitter beside the array of monitors. "Tom! You've got bad company approaching again," he hastily called out. "You've done all you can there. Get your men out."

The bronze helmet and shielded face of Lieutenant Reynolds appeared on the tiny view screen of the communication console. He was inside the CR now after having moved the gravely wounded Tomlinson within its walls. Forgoing the timely process of pressurizing and depressurizing, the Lieutenant was still in his environment suit.

"Can't do that, Commander. Besides, I have a wounded man here."

Matt felt a surging mixture of surprise and aggravation. "What do you mean you can't!" he roared incredulously. "Fire-up your thruster packs and fly back to the colony perimeter. We'll get medical help to your man as quickly as possible."

Reynolds shook his head defiantly. "I can't leave a wounded man behind, not again. Besides, we can't fight while in flight and we'll never outrun those assault ships."

"Leave right away and you might be able to beat them back here," Matt hastily and vigorously suggested.

"No, Commander." Reynolds sounded cool, confident, and determined. "I have two dead and one wounded but I still have an effective fighting force. Even with their reinforced strength, if we can take out a few more of their ships, they may not be able to overwhelm your defenses."

Matt was quickly becoming frantic and enraged as he slapped the counter top with his hands in a resounding thump and audaciously leaned into the camera lens so that Reynolds could see the unmistakable rage that burned across his face. "Lieutenant! I am ordering you back, NOW!!"

Reynolds fidgeted anxiously for a brief moment before replying in a soft but resolute voice. "Please, Matt, don't make my last act one of insubordination. Send me out with your blessing."

Matt felt his heart sink, every nerve and fiber of his being quaking in torrents of anguish as he was compelled to confront the inevitability of the situation. His head darted aimlessly, his mouth grimacing in pain as he grappled with his swelling emotions. He couldn't be angry with the man he had grown to respect so highly. He should have expected a reaction like this from Tom Reynolds. He was annoyed by a tightening lump in his throat as he looked across the room with watery, grief-stricken eyes towards Sheri.

Her melancholic expression and sympathetic, glossy gaze revealed her shared remorse and it looked to Matt that she was fighting the urge to rush to his side with a consoling embrace. He knew that she understood how he felt and gave her a short, silent appreciative nod. Summoning all his will and strength to control his raging feelings, Matt suppressed the tears that were staining to flow down his cheeks. It was all so clear to him now as he settled himself in front of the camera. The man was going to die. "My prayers go with you....," he began in a tone choked with emotion, nearly breaking down before he could finish, "....and all those who serve you."

"Thank you, Matt," he acknowledged in a serene and grateful tone. "That means more to me than you could ever know. I guess the bill for those hats has come due."

Matt could barely speak, his voice cracking as tears welled-up in his eyes. "I guess it has," he labored to mumble. "You've worn them well." Matt clearly understood Tom's nod of gratitude and respect.

"Goodbye, my friend."

Matt's gloomy sadness as Reynolds signed off was abruptly shaken by the boisterous curse of horrified distress that Sheri exhorted as she turned in panic from her station. "Matt! I'm now picking up a third flight of low altitude ships twenty minutes behind the others and closing fast!"

"Son-of-a-bitch!" Matt furiously bellowed as he stormed towards the exit in a fuming rage. "People have been dying all around me! I just can't stand here and do nothing!"

"Matt!" Sheri cried out in trepidation. "What are you doing?"

"Whatever I can," his fading voice hurriedly replied as he scampered down the corridor.

Fearful of Matt's rashness, Sheri bolted over to the colony communications station, wrestled the controls away from Nichelle, and quickly contacted Vijay whom she knew was in the Residential Dome. "Vijay, it's Matt again," she excitedly barked. "He's going to do something stupid. I think that he might be heading outside. You're his best friend." Her inflection became animated and frantic. "You've got to stop him!"

They had difficulty delineating the murky, rugged, and pitted terrain that rushed past them fifty feet below as they whisked and sliced through the frosty Martian air at nearly 100 miles per hour, the pale gray streamers of exhausted propellant quickly dissipating behind them. The lighter albedo markings from ejecta blankets and subtle reflections from small surface clouds of drifting fines helped the two marines gauge their altitude as they headed towards the tiny, soft luminous speck glowing just beyond their horizon, the artificial lights of Jamestown that acted as a beacon in the darkness of the arid wilderness. Climbing to clear the bald slopes of intervening hills as they drew closer to Jamestown, Corporal Cooke began to pickup the long range transmission between the Lieutenant and the colony and immediately perceived the gravity of the situation.

"There must be one hell of a firefight going on over there, John," he remarked after overhearing part of the conversation. "It doesn't sound good. We had better hustle."

"Yeah, you're right. The Sarge is...." His attention was drawn to the approach of a large, ominous shadow ahead of them and descending. "Bob! Do you see that?" Cooke's attention was instantly captured by John's distressful pitch. "A couple of miles out or so and several hundred feet above us. I can see some blinking lights now."

"I see it," Cooke replied as he caught a glimpse of what appeared to be running lights. "I don't like it."

Walinski grew apprehensive. "Maybe one of those assault ships. Let's get out of here."

"How could that be," Cooke calmly replied. "It's coming from the south. But let's not take any chances. Head for the beach."

As the two marines began to reduce thrust and drop towards the surface, a familiar haughty voice came ringing over their short range frequency. "Hey, I thought you boys weren't afraid of anything."

As the object slowly sank closer and began to hover, Cooke recognized the sleek silhouette and moments later the illuminated insignia. It was Jack Shoals piloting the Nathanael Greene.

"Scoot on up here, the airlock is open," Jack jocularly entreated. "Compliments of Commander Maitland and the Guilford Courthouse crew."

The marines breathed a sigh of relief as the rapid pulsation's within their chests returned to normal as they fired a few short bursts to climb towards the lander. Cooke gingerly drifted safely inside but Walinski slightly misjudged his approach and violently crashed his right side into the fuselage with a heavy, dull thud. He tumbled downward, arms and legs flailing wildly to within forty feet of the surface before he regained control with a rush of adrenaline and shot up once more, inching tortoise-like the last few feet, finally diving into the airlock with the aid of Cooke's welcome helping hand.

"Shit!" he exclaimed as he regained his balance on the solid deck. "Don't ever make me do that again."

"Did one of you guys just bump into my ship?" Jack frivolously questioned over their com system as the airlock door sealed behind them and the craft began to execute a gentle bank.

"Never mind, Flyboy," Cooke responded with a slight tint of embarrassment. "Just get us out of here."

As the chamber began to slowly pressurize with the low, dull gush of filtering air, Cooke intercepted Reynolds' final transmission with Jamestown. "Hell, John!" he vexatiously exclaimed. "The Lieutenant isn't falling back as planned. They're standing their ground, trying to take out a few more of them. We've got to try to help them."

"Wait a minute, Bob," Walinski harshly protested as he took a firm grasp of his arm. "We have orders to fall in along the colony perimeter."

"Those are our friends over there!" Cooke adamantly clamored as he wrenched his arm free. "I just can't fly on back and let them die!" Without waiting for his companion's reaction, Cooke called up to the cockpit. "Hey, Jack! How long will it take to fly over to the fighting?"

"Just a few minutes," he replied in befuddlement. "Why?"

"Then take us over there," Cooke doggedly barked.

Jack found the notion unpalatable. "Now hold it right there," he boisterously objected. "Who do you mud-rollers think you are? My orders are to bring you back to the colony. And by the way, so are yours."

"Screw those orders!" Cooke shouted in anger. "Those are our buddies and they need our help. Now turn this lump of shit to the west and get us over there!"

"I can't take this ship into a combat zone," Jack vehemently argued. "It's our only link with the Guilford Courthouse. Besides, if I bring it back riddled with holes I'll never fly again. My captain will see to that."

"I'll shoot it down myself!" Cooke passionately hollered as he pointed his rifle towards the deck before taking a prodigious calming breath. "Look, Jack," he implored in a softer manner, "just take us within ten or fifteen miles. We'll fly the rest of the way ourselves."

Jack hesitated while he contemplated the consequences of his actions before finally banking the Nathanael Greene westward. "I must be out of my fricking mind to let you guys talk me into pulling this kind of stunt. We're all going to get our asses shot off."

Within a matter of minutes Cooke and Walinski once more found themselves suspended like soaring hawks above the Martian surface. As they descended from the southeast towards the right flank of the battle line they could clearly see the fiery trail of speeding rockets, fragments of darting, normally invisible, orange-red beams as the laser light reflected off the surface of suspended dust particles, the peppering succession of brilliant yellow flashes as the laser fire churned and singed the frozen ground, and the occasional puff of a tumbling fireball as if someone had struck a match and dropped it from the heavens. Taking shelter in a flattened depression in the distance beyond the defended hill on the right they could identify the soft blinking landing lights of what they assumed to be some kind of transport shuttle, depositing troops to root-out their elusive quarry. Their suspicions were confirmed when they overheard Private Simmons' frantic report. Ground troops were closing in on his position.

"Stay loose, Eddie," Cooke called out as they plunged towards the pitted, rock-strewn hill. "The cavalry is on the way."

"Cooke! Is that you? What the hell are you doing here? You and Walinski have been ordered to the Jamestown perimeter!" The brusque and aggravated voice belonged to Lieutenant Reynolds.

Cooke's beleaguered mind went blank for a moment. "I'm sorry, sir, your transmission is breaking up."

"Damnit Corporal!" Reynolds shouted furiously. "You heard me!"

"Sorry, sir, your transmission is breaking up."

Corporal Cooke was gratefully relieved when the Lieutenant finally acquiesced and accepted their presence.

"You don't follow orders very well but you're still a good marine," he said in a more auspicious tone. "Support the right flank. I'll deal with you later."

"Thank you, sir. We didn't mean to disobey, sir. Just the old military axiom, you see - march to the sound of the guns."

Ever since the first research facilities began to spring up across the Martian landscape like desert blossoms, the policy makers governing the Eastern European Socialist Confederation had cast a covetous eye towards the untapped mineral riches and the scientific and military potential that the Red Planet provided. Even as the heated blade of the first interplanetary dozer dug into the frozen regolith that would become the sight of Jamestown, EESC construction engineers were burrowing into the precipitous and scalloped walls of Perepelkin crater, home for the largest scientific station. Despite their public posturing and disdain for a colonial settlement, the EESC proceeded to covertly construct a subterranean base from which they could wield their power and influence as they saw fit. Their progress was slow and tortuous, disguising construction transports as scientific resupply missions, frugally controlling energy expenditures so as not to draw any undo attention. The perfection of the energy dampening field by some of their German physicists enabled them to accelerate the construction in anonymity, rendering their increased activity undetectable. Keeping the project a secret was a masterful stroke involving a complicated series of deceptions, disinformation campaigns, and clandestine communication codes. By the time the first settlers unpacked their bags under the Jamestown domes, Perepelkin had been inhabited and operational for several years. It took the EESC many more years to relocate an adequate amount of scientists, engineers, technicians, service and military personnel to Perepelkin - a dozen at a time crammed aboard scheduled and publicly announced resupply missions to their various research outposts. The clandestine nature of the settlement and the accompanying military build-up was in direct violation of the Space Colonization Accords of 2042, which attempted to prevent the carving-up of planetary bodies and their satellites into military spheres of influence as had happened on the Moon in the 2020's. The EESC had hoped to gain a dominating foothold on the Martian world from which such a commanding position they could exercise considerable strength and influence on two planets. The brief but traumatic Lunar Conflict three-and-a-half years before had given them the opportunity to strengthen the garrison at Perepelkin while the world's attention was riveted closer to home.

But the EESC planners made one critical miscalculation - the people they recruited to transfer their entire lives to another planet, including the permanent military personnel, were no different in desires and spirit than their Jamestown counterparts. All shared the unquenchable yearning to be free of government interference and control. Free of the stifling affects of over-regulation that inhibits productivity. Free of burdensome over-taxation that punishes achievement and thwarts initiative.

Free of confiscatory wealth transfer programs that restrain economic growth and subsidize undesired behavior. Free of costly and destructive social engineering and centralized economic planning that only served to stunt growth, cripple their economies, and create social upheaval. Free to be the best they could be unfettered by the shackles of a regulatory, restrictive bureaucracy. Free to enjoy all the fruits of their labors, without working half the year to support an ever-expanding state. Free to succeed and free to fail. To live and work and love, knowing that what you create is yours, good or bad. Free to establish a system that only uses public funds to provide for a common defense, ensure domestic tranquillity, and support those services that benefit all the people, not selected segments of the population. Many thought Mars would provide that kind of opportunity, so far removed from bureaucratic control. They were wrong.

The heightened military presence allowed many eyes to catch a glimpse of the true intentions of the Confederation. And so the seeds of discord were sown. In groups that seemed to expand exponentially by the month, they planned and schemed, mustered resources, and covertly negotiated business contracts with suppliers and buyers on Earth that circumvented their own government channels. When the settlement had become for the most part self-sufficient and the support of the bulk of the military was assured, the decision was made. It was simply a matter of time. And like so many monumental moments in time, their hand was prematurely forced by an unpredictable accident of circumstance. A mechanical failure in their energy dampening system that lasted three weeks and caused their detection and eventual contact with the Jamestown inhabitants when they stumbled across their botanical bioengineer test site. Once word of the Perepelkin colony reached Earth, all hell was going to break loose. The protests and political squabbling would go on for years while they were put under the constant tight scrutiny of an electron microscope, the kind of regulatory anal exam that they were trying to escape. So they decided to act. It was still possible to keep their rogue colony a mystery through the turmoil ahead, if they enlisted the aid of a potential ally, a people with whom they shared a peculiar kindred of the soul - the inhabitants of Jamestown. Then they rebelled, declaring formally but secretively to the EESC their independence from the Confederation. Needless to say, the EESC was not amused. Rebel forces quickly seized Perepelkin and the surrounding countryside, including their water harvesting facility near the northerly ice dunes on Vastitas Borealis.

Loyalist forces and their civilian sympathizers retired to the research station at Alba Patera which they converted into a base of operations from where they fought fiercely but were badly outnumbered. The EESC was in a difficult bind. They couldn't dispatch a fleet of warships to suppress the insurrection because of the unwelcome and potentially volatile reaction such a move would bring from the West. Even an increase in normal shipping would bring unwanted attention. They could smuggle in a few shipments of personnel and supplies, but for better or worse, the loyalists were mostly on their own. The EESC leadership envisioned the irony of their presence on Mars, once thought to be nearly dominating, now could be completely extinguished without the world having ever known that they were there.

Deep within the hollow, sculpted cliffs of Perepelkin, hundreds of interconnecting and layered chambers of various dimensions honeycombed like the hive of bees beneath the surface to form the immense, magnificent complex. A tall, husky woman in her late forties sat on a throne-like, burgundy upholstered chair in the middle of one of the larger rooms. She wore a forlorn expression on her face as she stared helplessly at the images broadcast on the 96-inch screen anchored to the front wall, her chin resting despondently in the palm of her hand. The vast patches of silvery streaks that permeated throughout her short blond hair glittered under the subdued, evenly distributed glow from the soft illumination of the ceiling grids. The darkened chamber was ringed by a rich palette of solid and flickering dots that marked the locations of dozens of functional stations in this operational nerve center of the settlement. To the left the wall was lined with nearly a hundred small monitors that received camera images from every public corner of the complex and all approachable avenues from the outside. A handful of men and women were sprinkled amongst the electronic posts and several others stood anxiously behind the troubled woman. There was a commanding aura about her but despite her stern and restrained manner, her clean complexion and gentle hazel eyes put those around her at ease. Sitting like the distraught captain on the bridge of a beleaguered ship, she watched as the camera aboard one of her approaching vessels captured the sight of blazing rocket trails and bright, billowing puffs flash across the blackness of night above the distant horizon. All ears harrowingly listened as their sophisticated communications monitoring system intercepted the garbled sounds of the frenzied and terrified cries from attacker and defender alike. Bringing her right hand to wearily rub her eyes, the robust woman shook her head in despair.

"It's all my fault," she lamented in Colloquial German laced with a distinctive Hanoverian dialect. "I should have foreseen this."

Everyone present who did not speak German heard the comment in their own language through the miniature universal translator plug that each person had hooked around their ear lobe.

A younger, smaller wire-rim spectacled man turned to her from his station by the enormous bank of closed circuit monitors and spoke in Belorussian. "I don't understand how, Ingrid? There was nothing we could have done."

Ingrid Zeschwentz glanced up with a disdainful frown. "Nonsense, Vlad. I should have anticipated this move once we drove them off Alba Patera. They required another base. What better place than supposedly abandoned Jamestown. Now we have lost all hope to retain our anonymity."

Vlad turned back towards the large main viewer as the obscure silhouettes of knobby, fractured hills slowly drew closer, briefly illuminated below the fiery streamers and flames of battle that periodically sliced across the night. "They sacrifice themselves like samurai, these Americans."

"They are a noble breed," another Slavic accent added from behind Ingrid's chair. "The past three hundred years should have taught you that."

Ingrid drooped and brought her hand up to massage her throbbing forehead as she moaned woefully. "I never intended for this to happen, drawing others into our affairs. We should have committed all our resources to finish this, no matter the cost. Now others must pay for our audacity."

Another tall, lean fellow bent over her shoulder and spoke in perfect English with a slight northeastern slur. "Can you help them?"

Ingrid took a worried, backward glance before concentrating once more on the picture of the fierce battle drawing closer on the big screen. "I don't know, John," she dejectedly replied. "I really don't know if we can get there in time. You had best inform the others."

Dressed in the glimmering silver of an environment suit, Matt feverishly struggled into the warehouse building that housed the surface rovers, clumsily weighted down by the gloves, helmet, and unwieldy life-support pack that he dragged against his hips. His deliberate pace towards one of the terrain vehicles was halted in his tracks when he was startled by the appearance of Vijay, Garett, and Andre bent over near the area, putting the finishing touches on zipping tight their own suits, the clicking of glove collars against metal sleeves most noticeable.

Upon hearing the laborious, heavy thump of approaching boots, Vijay glanced up indifferently and dryly remarked. "It's about time you got down here. What kept you?"

Matt looked flabbergasted, not sure of their intentions. "Vij! What in hell are you guys doing here?"

"What does it look like we're doing?" Vijay rhetorically replied as he locked his second glove in place. "Waiting for you, of course. I heard that you were about to make another foolish sojourn so I drafted some friends and thought we might keep you company."

Matt felt slightly incredulous but wasn't sure why, only that he hadn't intended to put anyone else at risk. "Don't you know that there is a war going on out there!" he adamantly barked.

"Sure," Vijay nonchalantly said, "and I'd prefer keeping it there."

While Matt finished suiting-up, Garett casually lifted to examine one of the pair of laser rifles that the marines could spare and which Sergeant Douglas had given a crash course in its operation before going outside. Garett haphazardly handled it like a child in a toy store, his finger unwittingly pressing against the trigger. Everyone instinctively cowered as a yellow-orange pinhole was singed into the side of a nearby half-empty plastic supply crate, catching a whiff of the caustic odor of the smoldering container. Vijay irritably ripped the weapon out of Garett's quivering hands.

"Give me that, you idiot!" he brusquely hollered. "Where did you drift off to when the Sergeant was talking?" Vijay pushed the safety lever on the stock and yanked out the power clip from under the thick barrel casing. "There, it's safe now," he said as he handed the rifle back. "Don't insert that clip until you're ready to use it, which I pray is never."

As Matt's heart rate slowly recovered from the sudden jolt of excitement he finished testing his environment pack at which time Vijay casually tossed him the other laser rifle.

"You take this one. I don't like guns."

As the weapon rattled against Matt's outstretched hands, a concerned Andre stepped over to Vijay. "What the hell are we supposed to use, fowl language?"

"I have an uneasy feeling," Vijay flippantly replied, "there will be rifles available by the time we get to wherever we are going." His face displayed a stern frown of impatience as he looked over at a hesitant Matt. "Are we going out or just standing around all day shooting the bull?"

Matt stared at him skeptically for several seconds before a sly grin broke across his face. "All right you crazy bastard, come along then. But don't make me carry your sorry ass back here."

As they were about to lock their helmets in place, they were interrupted by the soft, muted pounding of jogging feet and a haggard-looking Doctor Oliver, partially clad in her environment suit but laboriously dragging along her helmet, pack, and bulky shoulder medical bag came trudging wearily into the warehouse, panting profusely. "Wait a minute, guys. I'm going with you."

The four men exchanged puzzled looks. "This is not some college debating society, Susan," Matt sarcastically proclaimed as he staunchly stepped forward, pointing to the pressurized chamber that led outside. "There's a war going on! Men are dying out there!"

Susan grimaced disdainfully as she hastily struggled to strap on her life-support pack. "Well, maybe some won't if I can get out there."

Matt was briefly taken aback, forced to admire her dedication if not her attitudes. "You know you're likely to get your ass shot off," he warned.

Susan paused as she completed connecting her pack and peered at Matt with a droll, sly smirk. "I know. The question is from which side?"

Matt chuckled lightly as he moved behind her to double-checked her connections. "Okay, Susan. I'd surely hate to be the one to try and stop you. Now if you will please hustle along, we're kind of pressed for time."

"You realize, Matt," Vijay commented as the group headed for two fully charged, open-cab short range rovers. "if they break through to here, we are finished."

Matt stopped and faced his friend with a profound, mystical glint in his eye. "We're all in God's hands now, Vij," he said in a tranquil, almost spiritual tone. "Not in theirs."

The far side of the hill erupted in a series of geyser-like explosions as the two marines descended towards the craggy, pitted southern slope, spewing small clumps of crustal clay and regolith high into the air, each blast heralded by the blinding flash of yellow-white phosphorescence. The rounds from the mortar tube were being delivered by Lieutenant Reynolds from the central hill against advancing ground troops approaching the crest, the fire being directed by a besieged Private Simmons somewhere near the western apex. They could hear the thunderous reverberations that accompanied each impact. Just before dipping below the summit, Cooke and Walinski noticed an undetermined number of dark, ominous, murky figures creeping towards the crest like hooded demons in a haunted house, their progress hindered by the destruction raining down on them. They hit the rocky slope at a run and had their laser rifles unslung before they broke stride. Climbing the gentle rise towards the western edge of the flattened summit, they had barely moved a dozen paces before the charcoal silhouettes began to pop up along the top against the star field backdrop of the heavens. They dove for the cover of pit and boulder, their antagonists apparently unaware of their presence. Dropping their night visors, the marines could see the specter-like glow of a half dozen space-suited soldiers armed with laser rifles carefully moving westward from one depression or rock to another. Taking time to line-up potential targets in the crosshairs of their night scope sights, the two marines isolated high probability targets , their rifles emitting a low, whining hum as they pulled the triggers. Bright specks of dotted light marked the impact of each burst. Three figures tumbled limply to the ground before the survivors fled for refuge below the northern crest. Walinski chortled with glee. "We caught'em napping!"

Corporal Cooke knew that this was no time for a celebration. "Quickly, towards Eddie," he harshly cried. The suppressing fire along the northern slopes had abated as the marines covered each other from one shelter to another as they moved towards the western edge of the crest. Distant blinking yellow-orange pinpoint flashes and the occasional splintering of fragments from a nearby rock alerted them to the fact that they were drawing hostile fire. Thirty yards away they could see the ghostly image of Eddie Simmons, hunkering down under the lip of a small crater that had been entrenched with shoveled dirt and rock. Sighting targets and returning fire, Cooke and Walinski worked their way over to the hole that would afford a nice view of the valley to the north when morning broke.

"Hold your fire, Eddie," Cooke called out. "We're coming in."

Walinski, followed a few seconds later by Cooke, slid into the depression and crawled over to the eastern flank. "Hey, Eddie!" Walinski chimed as he scooted next to him, "Who are the unfriendly neighbors?" When no answer came he reached out and nudged his shoulder. "Eddie, are you having trouble with your transmitter?" His head limply dropped to the right as his rifle fell from his hands and skidded down to the base of the pit. Walinski became frantic. "Eddie!" he screamed as he rolled over the motionless body. Immediately he saw the four tiny laser burn holes that had bored through his chest, globs of blood frozen like pellets of dark red ice over each puncture. Cooke was already hugging the ground on the other side of the lifeless body, popping up to quickly squeeze off a few aimed bursts before ducking again. "Eddie!" Walinski wailed again in a state of shocked disbelief as he tried to shake life back into the feeble frame.

"He's dead, John!" Cooke agitatedly shouted as he roughly shoved his shoulder to snap him from his daze. "And so are we if you don't start kicking some butt! Now get on your weapon and start firing, soldier!"

Both men could see several haunting, crinkled, charcoal-suited figures inching closer, bolting from one hole or boulder to another. There were not many of them, the high-explosive shrapnel rounds having done their deadly work on the reverse slope. Like some perverse ritual of death, they aimed, fired, and cowered below the lip of the pit in rapid succession.

"I think they have us triangulated," Cooke animatedly proclaimed. "I smell a bomb." His voice turned loud and distressful. "Move! Get out of the hole!"

The two marines rashly scrambled out of each side moments before the pit erupted in a thunderous volcanic blast of orange flame, spewing clay and stone everywhere.

"Son-of-a-bitch!" Cooke torridly cursed as he scooted low to the ground like a frightened quail and dove into an adjoining fracture. "I'm getting too old for this shit, John! Are you all right? LS pack undamaged?"

Walinski's voice was shaky. "Yeah, I think so."

Cooke was caustic and emphatic. "You think or you are?"

"I AM," he aggravatedly replied with emphasis. "But that one nearly singed my crotch hairs. These stinken' turds just won't flush!"

Corporal Cooke spotted a charcoal gray figure cautiously creeping out from behind a collection of rocks about thirty feet to his right, apparently unaware of his close proximity. "Well, I have one that's about to become a Martian fossil," Cooke whimsically remarked as he targeted the solitary figure in his scope. His finger slowly pressed against the trigger but to his heart-wrenching chagrin nothing happened. In a reflexive reaction of frenzy, Cooke straightened and fired again. The laser failed to discharge. "Goddamnit!" he cried out in panic, ripping out the power clip. The thermal coils had overheated and fused, inhibiting a sufficiently intense light flash from exciting enough chromium atoms within the synthetic ruby cylindrical chamber inside the barrel to produce enough red light energy to formulate the laser beam. Frantically he fumbled for another clip in his utility pouch but his target had spotted him by then. The two men hesitated for several seconds, staring in fear like marble battlefield monuments. Without the glare of light reflections off the radiation treated faceshield, Cooke could almost make out the shocked and terrified expression of his young, inexperienced opponent, just as confused and afraid as he was, the fearful, dazed glint in the eyes. It was an eerie sensation to stare death in the face and have it stare back in such an apprehensive, almost involuntary and remorseful manner, as if being controlled and manipulated by unseen demonic forces. Cooke slammed the new clip into its chamber but before he could level his weapon he saw a quick reddish-orange glowing pulsation inside the barrel of the soldier's rifle followed instantly by a searing pain that bore like a drill bit through his torso. The smiling face and sensuous gaze of Caroline Hart was the last conscious image of Corporal Robert Cooke as he collapsed helplessly to the frozen ground.

"Bob! No!" Walinski cried out in anguish as he heedlessly dashed out across the furrowed clay, wildly firing his rifle as he awkwardly rumbled over the uneven terrain. The young EESC soldier, who never really understood the interplanetary debacle amidst which he had suddenly found himself embroiled, dropped lifeless to the alien world with several laser burns to the chest. Walinski dashed to the aid of his fallen comrade, oblivious to the sporadic laser shots that peppered around him. "Good God, Bob!" he cried, almost in tears, as he quickly looked around, firing a few random bursts before turning back in dread. "Don't do this to me. Please don't die." He hastily opened his medical kit as he took another quick look around his surroundings. Two small holes in Cooke's suit around the stomach and abdomen were leaking thin filaments of steam like the boiling water of a tea kettle, his heat slowly oozing away. He could faintly hear the soft, high-pitched hiss of air escaping from the punctures. Tearing open the packaging to the repair tape with fury, Walinski quickly sealed the perforations with the airtight patches. "Hang on, man, you're going to make it," he said in a pleading tone as he used the medical hypo to inject the life-stabilizing solutions into his arm. "I'm going to get you back, Bob," he continued to say between deep, heavy breaths as he sealed the injection hole, not at all certain if the Corporal was even still alive. "Come on, man, stay with me," he wailed as he gently shook his shoulders but Cooke's head simply fell limply to the side. Walinski became hysterical. "Damnit, Bob, you can't die on me!" The crunching sound of crystallized granules and minuscule stones crushed under the weight of boot soles shook him to attention. Gently lowering Cooke's head to rest easily on the ground, he grabbed his rifle just in time to see a shadowy figure move out from a nearby crevice. "You'll pay for this you fricking abortions!" he screamed in rage as he leaped from the depression and recklessly charged forward, flushed with anger and crazed vengeance. his laser rifle pouring deadly fire in all directions. Two murky gray forms dropped motionless before the deranged onslaught until a series of scorching bursts riddled his body as if he had been impaled on a bed of spikes and Private John Walinski fell dead, joining the others on their next great journey into the unknown.

Two weary, musty. dirt covered. crinkle-suited figures somberly wandered along the crest, taking stock of the enormous cost of taking this hill. They trudged tiresomely into the pit where Corporal Cooke lay inert and began to prod the body with their rifles. A shudder of intense fear and a series of sharp. loud popping sounds were the last sensations they would experience as metallic projectiles ripped through their suits and flesh and the last of the loyalist ground troops crashed to the Martian surface. Seconds later the crackle of heavy steps halted and a single pair of silvery boots. tainted and stained reddish-orange by the Martian dust and soil, came to a somber rest by the crooked. bronze-helmeted head of Robert Cooke.

"Cooke! Walinski! What's your sit rep?" The snapping and cracking background noise of an open but unanswered frequency was the only response that greeted the frantic imploring of Lieutenant Reynolds. Unable to contact anyone on the right flank, he began to feel the shuddering. debilitating fear and abject hopelessness that he had felt only once before on a hilltop and a night not unlike this one. As near as he could tell, he, Warwick, and the grievously wounded Tomlinson were the only ones left alive. From the crest he could see several glowing conical shapes moving unimpeded around his right flank in the distance, their distinctive designs blocking out fractions of the star field that brightened the heavens. There were only a handful of the vessels remaining but when the fast approaching third wave joined them it was unlikely that the defenses around Jamestown would be able to stop them. The facility would be leveled or forcibly occupied, its occupants captured or killed. His plan had failed! Half his men were dead! He had once again played an intricate part in another human disaster. His instant of self-deprecation was abruptly ended by the harrowing call of Warwick. Their SAR rockets had been exhausted.

"Concentrate laser fire on the lead ship," Reynolds calmly ordered. "We might get lucky." The target looked like a tiny firefly through their night vision visor. The only indication that the vessel was being struck was the minuscule pinpoint flashes of yellow light as the beams bore through the metal fuselage and the evasive maneuvering that the ship employed. Continuing to concentrate fire on a single target, they witnessed several more speckled sunbursts before the ship began to fly erratically, finally spinning out of control and plunging from the sky, exploding in a giant, blazing fireball as it impacted on the surface. Immediately Reynolds noticed one of the other ship's circling to approach from the southeast. "Warwick! Move your butt!" he desperately shouted just before he saw reddish-orange pulsation's blinking from its nose an instant before the ground in front of him disgorged into the air in small concentric cyclonic circles of clay, dust and stone in brilliant phosphorescence that steadily advanced towards him like a bouncing ball until...."

The two short range rovers careened and bounced wildly over the rutty, debris-littered terrain as Matt recklessly led his small party to the northwest at a feverish, breakneck pace that tested the strength and endurance of man and machine alike, their direct course lighted only by the flood lamps mounted on the front of each vehicle.

"Remind me to stop on the way back and pickup my stomach," Vijay whimsically remarked after one particularly hefty jolt over a rather large stone that nearly sent them all flying from their seats.

Fearfully clenching the back of Matt's seat, Susan Oliver leaned over his shoulder. "If we go any faster, Matt, we'll be traveling back in time. I bet you're a lot of fun on the highways."

But Matt was not in a jocular mood. He could only think of the conflagration ahead and his dogged determination to reach the scene and do something about it. It was then when his internal communicator received the news from Sheri. Immediately he slammed on the brakes, painfully throwing everyone forward as the safety belts cut into their flesh, the trailing rover barely avoiding ramming into their rear. "They've broken through," he soberly announced. "Be passing near here any minute." His voice became noticeably more excitable as adrenaline pumped through his bloodstream, cracking and raspy with a keen sense of urgency. "Everyone out of the rovers, hurry! Take cover wherever you can find it." As Matt scrambled out of the rover towards a clump of good-size boulders, he took a fleeting glance at the trailing Doctor. "Susan, you may want to stay clear of those of us who are armed. We'll likely draw some hot attention."

"Not a chance," she replied as she hunkered down beside him. "I haven't had this much excitement since my sorority days."

"For someone who abhors war," he commented as his eyes strained towards the horizon which exhibited a strange, glowing quality in the otherwise gloomy darkness, "you are sure anxious to get yourself into one."

"I told you before," she firmly admonished, "I'm a healer. There may be someone left I can save. As for the rest, you can all be damned."

"That may be," Matt scoffed as his attention was directed to the approach of some scattered shadowy images along the skyline. "Aim for the closest one," he instructed to Garett as it appeared that the intruders would pass them several miles to their right. Without night vision equipment, it would be difficult to identify the nimble craft, let alone target them through the scope. Matt aimed his weapon and attempted to track the nearest ship. Briefly looking away, he could see the running lights of the third flight above the horizon, rapidly gaining on their comrades. "Oh shit!" Matt bellowed, almost resigned to the inevitability of their deaths.

Suddenly a series of bright orange flashes winked rapidly at them from the distant vessels and within fractions of a second the sky to their right blossomed into bright daylight, deafening reverberations rippling through the thin atmosphere as the heavens were set ablaze in a mosaic of dazzling fireworks, hundreds of fiery fragments raining to the surface like the showers of an Oregon spring. Matt and the others instinctively cowered behind their feeble protection, only rising after the last of the burning embers had fallen like meteorites onto the plain beyond, the brightness of the sky slowly fading into eerie darkness save for the twinkling serenity of the canvas of the stars. Rushing to the highest point in the immediate area, the five stunned spectators exchanged flabbergasted looks of disbelief as the remote glimmering speckles hovered briefly over the horizon before leisurely receding into the night. Spread over several square miles on the level plain to the east were various masses of mangled, twisted, smoldering wreckage, the burning flames quickly extinguished in the oxygen-free air as tall, billowing gray plumes rose upward to be slowly splintered into razor-thin filaments and dispersed by the Martian breeze.

"What the hell just happened?" a bewildered Garett questioned.

"Every ship just got blasted out of existence," Vijay noted in awe.

"Yes," Andre vacuously added. "But blasted by who?"

Susan turned to Matt in a highly perplexed state. "I don't understand any of this."

"I don't either," Matt replied with astonishment. "But divine providence is also something you don't understand. I think that we just got ourselves a reprieve. Saddle up. There still might be someone left alive."

He found himself rising above the dusty, desolate world as if riding on the opulent, velvety fibers of some mystical flying carpet. He saw his lifeless body sprawled on the frozen ground, a ghastly looking wound that had ripped and burned a hole through his chest, red shavings and small puddles of blood that had already frozen staining much of the dull bronze of his suit. It must have been a very painful injury, but he had no recollection. In fact, he was feeling no pain at all, just a general sensation of comfort, warmth and serenity that permeated his whole being. Of course, he instantly recognized that he had no being in the traditional sense, no form at all. A noncorporeal entity, he believed it was termed. He could sense the presence of others, almost as if he shared their thoughts and feelings, but could only visualize the receding planet below him. He understood it all now, the whole thing. It caused him to chuckle in amazement. Who would have ever thought? The extent that some will go to satisfy that yearning to be free and independent, unfettered by the shackles of a restrictive bureaucracy. He saw Matt Maitland brazenly racing across the rugged countryside to come to his aid. That fool, he amusingly thought, he's just going to get himself killed. But in the same instant he realized that was not true. Matt's journey had just begun. His destiny awaited him somewhere in the future. It felt strangely satisfying and compelling to see him through these initial, tiny steps. He soared above the farthest reaches of the Martian atmosphere as if on the wings of eagles and he could see, rather conceptualize, the entire Red Planet. He could see the past, present, and future. And it would be glorious. He was amazed beyond belief. How could so many human mistakes, blunders, misunderstandings, and countless acts of callous self-interest coalesce to produce something that would be so magnificent. He already knew the answer, of course - he had always known. A momentary feeling of regret as Mars faded into the vastness of space was replaced with the joy and contentment in the knowledge that he and his charges would be remembered; that their deaths were not in vain; that their compatriots and unknown benefactors who survived this first trial would use the chance they gave them to build a new beginning, the next great hope for humanity.

Tom Reynolds felt himself drifting among the stars, driven by the currents and eddies of unseen cosmic forces. He felt a touch of sorrow for his beloved, grieving Cindy and his two anguished daughters but took solace in the fact that they would go on to live happy, fruitful lives; that they would one day come to the place where he had given his last full measure of devotion, and that he would forever remain in a special, hallowed place in their hearts. They would be together again at their journey's end.

His soul had traveled billions of miles in the wink of an eye where the wonders of the universe were displayed before him. Great worlds bathed in every conceivable color of the spectrum. Massive gaseous clouds of dust and matter - the cradle of the stars. Lustrous, vibrant, oscillating nebulae moving between the stars like giant crabs. There were brilliant white dwarfs, blinking pulsars, supernovas shedding their coronas and matter in their final dying gasps to be reborn again across the galaxy. Civilizations too, past and present. The universe was teeming with life, so strange and exotic in all forms that no mortal mind could ever conceive such an intricate tapestry. Tom understood why such life had been spread so far removed from each other. Mankind had enough trouble understanding itself; other intelligence of such complexity would be impossible. The differences between these worlds were too abundant to calculate, save for one profound characteristic that he wished he could share, somehow, with all the people of the Earth. Regardless of how the reference was made, God was with them all.

"You see, Tom, there is a grand design." The voice, or more likely telepathic communication, belonged to Jesse Carney. He was now with him, guiding him along. "Each of us are an important fiber in the grand tapestry of the universe, finely woven into a complex pattern but all interrelated. I've come to lead you home."

"Where are we going?"

"Salvation. Your life and death has affected others in ways that you are only beginning to understand, as mine had done three-and-a-half years before. We can both rest now."

They floated together through the cosmos at hundreds of times the speed of light. Tom's perceptions gathered and processed millions of bits of fact and thought, much greater than the combined power of all the computers ever built. How wrong human science and understanding had been. The universe was much too complex and abstruse for mere mortal comprehension. He had witnessed eternity's in a matter of moments and then his soul was suddenly encompassed by a radiant shroud of dazzling white light streaked with glittering filaments of lustrous gold. A peace and tranquillity settled over him that was much greater than the serenity that he first experienced upon waking from his dream encounter. He felt the presence of a powerful entity that surrounded him, omnipotent and benign, that caused a soothing, consoling warmth to permeate his being. The burdensome weight of his earthly troubles, both significant and trifling, were lifted from his conscience. All remaining guilt was vanquished from his spirit. He was like the old soldier who crossed the river. Reborn again to enter the Kingdom of the Ages. Tom sensed a serene, fatherly, compassionate communication, like a voice, originating from within the center of his being. *"Welcome home, my son, you have done well."*

"He's dead, sir."

Private Warwick was cradling the motionless body of Lieutenant Reynolds as Matt swiftly dashed up the slope to the side of his fallen friend. "Dear God, no," Matt lamented as he dropped to his knees and wrested the bloodied body from the soldier's grasp, pressing the Lieutenant's inert head against his chest. Matt had prepared himself for the worst, but there was nothing like actually witnessing the mangled frame of his comrade to bring the reality home. Several isolated tears inched slowly down his cheek as he sobbed in grief, rocking uncontrollably.

"Why, sir? What was it for?"

Matt gathered his emotions and looked up into the shocked, vacant gaze of Private Warwick. "I don't know, son," he replied with a confused shake of his head, retarding a final tear with a sniffle. "I'll be damned if I can tell you why."

By that time Doctor Oliver had moved alongside the perplexed marine and was flashing a hand light into his face. "Are you injured?"

"I'm....okay....I guess." he stuttered, seeming a little shell-shocked.

The Doctor quickly flashed the light across his body and examined his life-support pack. "He's in fair shape, Matt. Just slightly disoriented."

"If you ask me, Doctor," Vijay casually remarked as he strolled by, "none of us here are firing on all thrusters."

Matt dismissed the farcical remark as he placed a firm hand on the soldier's arm. "Are you the only one left?"

Warwick dropped his head. "I think so. Tomlinson is in the CR but he's wounded pretty bad."

Matt looked over at the Doctor and twitched his head southward but Susan had a firm grasp of her medical bag and was already several running strides on her way to the command rover. Matt reverently eased Reynolds' head to the cold, hard surface and rose gingerly to his feet and carefully stepped over to Vijay's side, gazing around at the outlines of faint, dusky shadows dotting the countryside under the dim glow of the star-lit night. The tiny mounds of flame had long been doused, billowing columns of blackened smoke still rising like chimney exhaust in many parts. An eerie murky gray haze settled like a thin cotton sheet above them. The light, high-pitched whirl of the Martian breeze could be heard through their external receivers as clumps of microscopic rustic dust powder continued to be driven across their feet. Before long all evidence of the human conflict would fade away except for the isolated piles of wreckage and fragments of debris that littered the plain, and given enough time, these too would be withered away and buried by the sifting sands. Matt gloomily scanned the aftermath and remorsefully sighed. "Here was a royal fellowship of death."

"It would be worse if they had company."

Matt looked at him disdainfully. "How can you joke about this?"

"I'm not," Vijay defensively replied. "We're all still in danger."

Matt's irritation was mitigated as he realized the error of his misinterpretation. "I know, Vij. This thing may not be over."

"Do you think the NSCA will abandon Jamestown?"

Matt found the notion repugnant. "Not if I have anything to say about it," he adamantly replied as his hand swept from side to side. "For their sakes, if for no other reason. These men will not have died in vain."

A few minutes later Doctor Oliver trudged dejectedly up to them. "Private Tomlinson is dead. I'm sorry, Matt, his injuries were too severe."

"Son-of-a-bitch!" Matt bitterly cried out, twitching in anguish while slapping the palms of his hands together. He began to pace nervously, kicking at the loosened crust and stone in frustration. If anything could have given the tragic death of Reynolds some meaning it would have been saving that boy's life. Now that too was gone. He should have come back like he wanted him too. But if they hadn't bought the extra time, maybe they would all now be dead. The conflicting possibilities ripped at his heart until everyone's attention was yanked to the west where a sharp shuffling and low crunching noise coupled with a steady, dull scraping sound was approaching in the darkness. Apprehensions grew until their helmet lights caught a glimmer of a solitary bronze suit, caked with red and tan dirt stains, staggering and stumbling towards them, the stock of a laser rifle lazily dragging the ground. Silent, mystified looks were exchanged before Doctor Oliver raced to meet him, shinning that bright light into his haggard and dazed eyes. It was Private Anderson, making the trek from the left hill.

"Are you hurt?" Susan questioned as she leered through his musty faceshield. "Do you need attention? Do you feel all right?" He remained speechless, standing starry-eyed in a zombie-like state, wobbling unsteadily with fatigue. A resounding dull thump was heard as her hand roughly slapped the side of his helmet. "Do you hear me, soldier?" she screamed, snapping him from his trance. He slowly brought a gloved finger to his mouth, tapped his helmet and shook his head as his hand swung back and forth. His microphone had malfunctioned. Susan checked him over from head to toe, declaring him fit but exhausted, although a large chunk of his thruster pack was torn away. Matt felt the first sensations of relief that he experienced all day. He recalled shared moments, as he would each time he read the name of one of the dead. The young man who had been fired upon by the sentry robot; who had helped to distribute those paltry rations that first, frightening night; who had rescued Nichelle and brought her to safety; who had bravely gone on that long reconnaissance to the south; and who had briefly bantered with him the night he listened to the numbing David Hart tape - had survived.

Warwick solemnly moved to greet his comrade as the Doctor completed her superficial exam. The two soldiers stood opposite each other like angular Martian rock, staring in silence. No words needed to be said. They had faced the same terror and din of battle, and they were the only two left standing. The emotions that were running rampant soon consumed them both as their rifles slipped harmlessly to the ground and they fell weeping into the tight embrace of the other. Matt and the others could only stand in quiet respect for the two warriors and their fallen comrades until the fast approaching radiance of a bank of bright white lights alerted them to the oncoming charge of a mechanized land vehicle from the southwest. Frightened to the bone as the hum of an engine and the rumble of meshed wheels against compressing stone grew louder, the marines grabbed their rifles as everyone scampered like rabbits to find some cover until Matt recognized the egg-like shape. It was the small, twin seat emergency rover always carried aboard the Nathanael Greene. It bounded onto the crest and skidded to a dust-flying halt as Matt raced up to meet it. To his astonishment, Jackson Shoals emerged from behind the wheel and moved to loosen the restraints of his unconscious, obviously injured passenger, Corporal Robert Cooke.

"Jack!" Matt called out in surprise. "What the hell are you doing here? Are you out of your damn mind?"

"I think I must be, Captain. I let those two ground pounders talk me into ferrying them to the battle zone. I was just leaving when I monitored their local channel and it sounded like they were in trouble. I just couldn't fly off and leave them, sir. I didn't want to risk the PL so I found a flat piece of ground behind a steep ravine a few miles away and used the rover to drive to that hill. I shot two of those charcoal bastards but found everyone dead, except for him, and he won't last much longer, I'm afraid."

Doctor Oliver was hovering over him by then, attaching probes of her computerized analyzer into various biological sensor ports embedded in the blood and clay stained environment suit.

Matt was very upset with the audacity of his navigator but found it impossible to lash out at such a selfless act. "Jack, you're incorrigible," he remarked in a stern though tempered manner. "First you disobey your instructions by bringing them here. Then you risk my lander by flying it into a combat zone, not to mention your own life. And finally you make a dangerous landing in the dead of the night to go to the aid of men that just a week ago you had been brawling with. Have I missed anything?"

Jack nonchalantly shrugged. "That's about it, sir."

Matt reluctantly sighed. "Just count your blessings that I'm a lenient man." His tone became much more intense. "But if you ever try to pull another stunt like this...."

Jack humbly nodded in understanding. "Yes, Captain."

Matt anxiously looked past Jack at Susan who was vigorously working her hand-held equipment.

"He's still alive," she reported, hastily ripping the attachments from their sockets, "but won't be for long if we don't get him immediately back to Jamestown." She spoke in a resolute, demanding manner that unveiled the need for urgency. "Help me get him inside the marine rover. If I can get at him, I might be able to stabilize his condition until we get back, but we must hurry."

Matt was emphatic. "Jack, drive him to the rover. The rest of us will follow shortly. Then get my lander safely back to the space port."

"Right away, Captain," Jack replied as he scurried back to the driver's seat. "If I can remember where I parked it."

As Jack raced down the slope closely pursued by the Doctor, Matt turned to the others who had gathered nearby. "I will accompany the Doctor. There are still three of us lying in the cold on the hill to our southeast. Private Warwick, take one of our rovers and gather them up. Vij, go with him. Anderson, take the other and bring back your corporal. The rest will come with me."

Matt paused in reflection, visualizing each face that was no longer with them. Edward Simmons, who had battled the sentry robot. Nathan Jones, who had helped rescue Nichelle from the poisonous Martian atmosphere. Zack Tomlinson, the boyish greenhorn from Nebraska who had participated in the discovery of the missing specialists. Rafael Benetiez, who led the exploratory mission towards Valles Marineris. John Walinski, who had escorted Matt on that first day on Mars, was assaulted on the second, helped investigate the collapsed dome, fell under Lucinda's addictive spell, and participated in countless other activities. And, of course, Thomas Reynolds.

"We'll take the Lieutenant with us," Matt somberly said as he bent to lift the body.

"No, sir," Warwick interjected as he and Anderson stepped forward, lightly clasping his arm. "We'll carry him to the CR, sir."

Matt respectfully dipped his head and shuffled aside. They were a family, that platoon of Space Marines. A family that he could never join. "Come on boys," he exhaustingly and sorrowfully grumbled. "Let's take them home."

CHAPTER

15

A torrential flood of hysterical tears poured down the cheeks of Caroline Hart as the robotics litter bearing the broken body of Robert Cooke arrived on the main floor of the medical facility, speedily pushed along its self-guided course by the low hum of its battery powered drive train, Doctors Oliver and Caldwell briskly jogging by its side, its small metal wheels clicking rapidly as they ran over the seams of the speckled tile floor. "No! Please God, no!" she tremulously cried, rushing up to touch the top of his head as if she possessed some magical healing power. His body was enclosed in a stasis shield, a semi-tubular electronic device painted with numerous lights, dials and digital displays that draped over the patient from neck to knees and aided the maintenance and monitoring of vital biological functions and pumped his system with fresh plasma and oxygen supplements. A pair of sensor patches ran from its flanks and were attached to the temples of his head.

"Get out of the way!" Doctor Oliver curtly snapped, her face musty, and haggard, her silvery blond hair tattered and mangy.

"How bad is he?" Caroline emotionally beseeched as she impulsively ran alongside. "Will he be all right?"

Doctor Oliver grew increasingly annoyed with the distraction. "Caroline, please....!"

"Heart rate weakening," Doctor Caldwell interrupted with concern as he examined the readouts from his side of the medial transport.

"Shit!" Doctor Oliver muttered. "I thought I had that stabilized." Her instructions became more emphatic. "Cardiac stimulator, quickly."

Caroline was nearing a nervous breakdown as the pangs of anguished panic ripped harrowing lines across her face. "Susan?"

The Doctor was absorbed in the pressures of the moment and had little patience for advisory pleasantries. "Get the hell out of here, Caroline," she harshly barked, "before we lose this boy!"

Sheri, who had been waiting with Caroline at the medical center, rushed up and pulled her aside as the doctors flew from the lounge and through the portal that led to the nearest operating room. Caroline collapsed into quivering convulsions within the grasp of Sheri's tight embrace, weeping profusely.

"It's all my fault, Sheri," she wailed in grief. "It's all my fault."

"That's nonsense," Sheri tenderly replied as she hugged her firmly.

"No, it's not," Caroline bellowed between distressful sobs. "God must be punishing me. First Dave leaves me. Now Bob may die." Her damp face buried into Sheri's shoulder as she felt the soothing warmth of Sheri's fingers pressing sympathetically against her back. "What have I done that was so bad to deserve this?" she cried amidst the flow of unrelenting tears.

Sheri silently cradled her, allowing Caroline to purge the misery from her system before pushing her back at arms length. "You're being ridiculous," she softly said with a gentle shake. "Listen to me, Caroline. You are a kind and decent woman. You brought a ray of sunshine into his life. You've been an inspiration and a joy to everyone around you. So get that crazy notion out of your head. We'll get through this together."

Within a few minutes Matt came trudging exhaustingly into the waiting room still wearing his silver environment suit minus helmet and gloves, now musty and laced with red and brown stains of dust and dirt, his whiskered face ragged and jaded, resembling more a wandering drunk than a spaceship captain. "Stomach and intestinal wounds," he announced as he hobbled up to them.

Still with a tight grasp around Caroline, Sheri surged forward to greet him with a kiss to the cheek and an affectionate embrace with her other hand, pressing her breasts against the side of his chest. For a few seconds the three of them were wrapped around each other in a great, sobbing triangular hug.

"Caroline, you know how sorry I am," Matt said as their faces parted, their arms still clinging around the other two.

"What are his chances, you think?" Caroline meekly wondered as she dipped her dripping eyes.

"Susan was rather nonspecific." Matt replied with a shrug of uncertainty. "She rates it no better than a push." His hand tightly squeezed her hip. "But he's going to make it. A man like that doesn't give up."

"And how are you. Matt?" Sheri gently asked as she cast a worried gaze and raised her hand to lovingly pass it across his frazzled cheek. "You look like shit."

Matt casually twitched his head. "I feel worse. I tell you, Sheri, I've been in some tough scraps and seen some heroic acts, but I have never, ever, witnessed anything like this." His eyes aimlessly roamed upward as he took a deep breath before looking back at her. "I ought to ground Jack's ass for good, but Cooke would now be dead if he hadn't found him." Slowly he released his grip around the two women and backed away. "Caroline, maybe you should go back to your quarters and try and get some rest. The operation is going to take awhile."

"No," she emphatically replied between sniffles. "I'm waiting here for Bob, no matter how long it takes."

"I understand." Matt soberly replied with a respectful nod before turning to Sheri and extending his hand towards the exit. "I'm going back to take a shower," he humbly said. "Put on a fresh uniform, shave."

"Maybe you should lie down and sleep for awhile," Sheri suggested adoringly. "You look exhausted."

Matt leisurely shook his head. "Yes. I'm tired. But after tonight, I won't be able to sleep for awhile. I'll be back shortly. Stay with her." He motioned towards Caroline before disappearing through the doorway.

As Matt emerged from the refreshingly warm shower, the dismal and foreboding blackness of night slowly gave way to the bright blue that quickly mutated into the pinkish-red of the morning dawn as the radiant beams of the ascending sun heralded a resplendent new day around Jamestown. When Matt returned an hour later, feeling cleaner but no less apprehensive, he found that the population in the waiting room had grown. Dilapidated and stunned looking privates Anderson and Warwick, along with a third marine, were sedately sitting together opposite Caroline and Sheri. Vijay was there as well, considerately delivering mugs of steaming, aromatic coffee to all present.

"How you guys doing?" Matt politely inquired as he passed by the group of dingy marines.

"Fine, sir," Anderson stoically replied. "Just waiting for news on Bob and feeling kind of numb right now."

"I know," Matt sympathetically said. "Sometimes it hits you that way." Accepting a hot mug from Vijay with a grateful pat to the back and an advisement to retire for a few hours, Matt took a seat on a padded blue chair beside Sheri, who was firmly clenching both of Caroline's trembling hands. Caroline's emotional outburst had exhausted all her energy to the point that she now contained all her anxiety within her, visibly shaking and attentive to all sound but otherwise quiet and reserved. Every snap and crackle was magnified in the strangely quiescent room, no one being in very buoyant or energetic spirits. Only the third marine spoke with any regularity, questioning the other two about their battle experience, but neither were in a garrulous mood. Matt found himself nodding off, the back of his head lightly bumping against the wall to rouse him back to attention. His embattled mind drifted, fondly visualizing the Corporal's boisterous though respectful antics in the ship's rec room; his courteous though frivolous bantering as they prepared to step onto the Martian surface; his cool and professional manner under fire from the robot; his calming and proficient presence during the dust storm excursion; his cordial, confident, and determined personality. He reminded Matt of himself in his younger days - brash but courteous, daring but reserved, and a little foolhardy with a certain flawed attitude of invincibility. He had worked closely with Cooke ever since they had landed on Mars. His death would be like losing one of his own. He grew even more restless overhearing Caroline's occasional tremulous whispers to Sheri and her increasing jittery fidgeting in her seat.

"I can't stand this waiting....I wonder how he's doing....I don't think I could bear to lose him."

Unable to contain his own uneasiness and thirst for some news, Matt bolted from his chair and doggedly stormed through the electronic sliding doors that led to the operating rooms of the medical center. Standing outside of the first OR, he timidly peered through the small square window whose curtains were only partially drawn. He could only see the bottom half of the surgical table but instantly recognized both doctors hovering over their patient, draped in light blue surgical gowns that covered everything except their eyes, their arms feverishly moving around as they tirelessly performed unseen delicate and intricate procedures. He was hesitant to interrupt but felt an overwhelming compulsion to find out something, pushing the intercom button situated by the window. "Please forgive the interruption, but I have a room full of concerned people chewing off their fingernails. Is there anything you can tell us?"

Doctor Oliver continued to concentrate on her work, ignoring Matt's call for nearly a minute before glancing up at him with a piercing, infuriated leer as if she was ready to chew razor blades. "Are you crazy!" she roared through her mask as Doctor Caldwell activated the com system on his instrument table. "We're in the middle of an operation for God's sake!"

"Please forgive me, Susan," Matt regretfully apologized as Susan refocused her attention on her patient. "Can you tell us anything at all?"

"Don't know yet," she responded more serenely. "We'll be awhile. I'll inform you as soon as possible. Now will you get the hell out of here!"

Matt was a little embarrassed. "Yes, of course, Susan. Sorry. You're quite right. Thank you."

All eyes anxiously trained on Matt as he meekly shuffled back into the lounge. Sergeant Douglas had now joined the group, everyone sitting on pins and needles. Matt simply rolled his shoulders and held out his hands in uncertainty. "Too soon to tell," were the only words he spoke as he wearily slid into the seat beside Sheri and sluggishly rubbed his heavy eyes. "The good Doctor kicked me out." All was silent as disappointed heads slumped towards the floor. Matt felt the warm clasp of Sheri's gentle fingers as her left hand reached out to hold his, her comely though fatigued face gazing both despondently and longingly into his. He knew that she understood the depth of his concern, and was just as worried herself. "I know, Sheri."

Across the room Sergeant Douglas breathed a large sigh and sprung to his feet, turning to the three lethargic marines. "All right, you ball breakers," he loudly chimed, "Time to sack-out for a few hours. You can't help him sitting here. Let's move it!"

"But Sergeant.....," Anderson protested.

"You heard the order, Private!" he barked. "You men are spent. I need you guys fresh and alert. We're marines and we still have a job to do. You can best help Cooke by guarding his butt. Now to your quarters!"

With great reluctance the soldiers gingerly rose to their feet and exhaustingly staggered out of the facility. Before the Sergeant could depart, Matt felt obligated to offer a few words, bounding from Sheri's comforting grasp to extend an appreciative hand. "You trained those boys well, Sergeant, my compliments. You should be very proud."

"Thank you, sir," Douglas unemotionally but politely replied as they exchanged a firm shake. "I am, but I have no cause for satisfaction, sir. Six of my people were killed, that's all that happened tonight."

"I understand," Matt replied with a somber nod. "Your loss....our loss is deeply regrettable. Just concern yourself with external security. The rest of us will assume your other duties and take some of the load off your shoulders."

Matt remained restive once the marines had left, unable to sit quietly with the others. He paced the floor uneasily, pausing now and then to arch his aching back or stretch his tightened muscles. Hours passed as he found himself dozing again in his seat as fatigue overtook him. The women beside him were winking in and out of awareness as well, stirred by any unusual sound. His mind wandered again. this time reflecting on the heart-breaking loss of Tom Reynolds. They had been through a lifetime of turmoil together in a matter of weeks and his death tore at Matt's soul like an open wound, a wound that would never heal. Finally everyone's attentions were aroused by the sound of steadily advancing footsteps coming from the surgical unit until a pallid looking Doctor Oliver emerged from the sliding doors. Everyone leaped to their feet in unison and anxiously moved to surround her as she stopped and flung back her surgical mask and hood, shaking out her stringy blondish-gray hair.

"Boy!" she gasped. "That was a bitch of an operation, I don't mind telling you. I haven't had a cut and sew job like that in ages."

Matt tapped his foot impatiently. "Come on, Susan," he beseeched, "how's he doing?"

A refined grin of satisfaction slowly caused the corners of her mouth to turn upward. "He's out of danger now. Baring infection or unforeseen complications, he's going to make it."

Susan's announcement spawned a boisterous chorus of cheers and whoops that would rival any Martian 'time of non-existence' party. Caroline broke down in tears of joy, wrapping her arms tightly around Sheri in a suffocating embrace of blissful relief. Susan was also the recipient of an indebted hug, to everyone's surprise, from non other than Matt himself. He had no problem putting aside his deep-rooted differences to express his appreciation for her lifesaving efforts. It was several minutes before the revelry subdued enough for the Doctor to continue her report.

"He suffered major damage to his gastrointestinal tract. What a mess! We had to clean out his system of leaking pepsin enzymes and hydrochloric acids before they were absorbed by and contaminated the surrounding tissue and organs. Then we had to close the tiny perforations in his small intestine. He won't be eating any of those putrid food packs or those buzzard-barfing marine rations for awhile. He'll be limited over the next few weeks to liquids, soups and a few cooked vegetables, nothing raw. I'll have Doctor Caldwell work up a dietary menu."

"Give it to me, Susan," Caroline resolutely urged as she wiped away the last of her happy sniffles. "I'll see that he gets whatever he needs from the Agri Dome and the food stores. I'll prepare it myself. When can I see him?"

"He's still in recovery. Let him rest a few hours. Why don't you come back tonight. But don't go bouncing him around, okay. I know how physical you can be."

"Okay, Susan," Caroline demurely replied as she bashfully lowered her head with a subtle grin. "I promise to control myself."

"You look like you could use a drink," Matt casually remarked as he scanned Susan's frazzled form.

"No, thanks," she graciously replied as she unleashed a gaping yawn. "Maybe when things calm down around here. Ben has kindly offered to monitor the patient so I can grab a few hours sleep. Right now I just want to go back to my room and collapse before you guys plan our next crisis." Susan took a few fatiguing steps towards the doorway before she suddenly paused and hesitantly turned back to Matt with a confounded cast. "You may find this difficult to believe, Matt, but I am truly sorry about Lieutenant Reynolds. I regret that I may have grievously misjudged him."

Matt was genuinely touched by her magnanimous gesture and definitive nod of her head. "Thank you, Susan, that means a lot to me."

Matt filed a preliminary report on the evening's tragic events with the NSCA and laid down to try and catch a few hours sleep. But as exhausted as he was, there was little rest for him. His mind kept visualizing all the enthusiastic, confident faces that were no longer with them. He had never before lost a life under his command; now he was sending home nine vacuum-sealed body tubes. It gnawed at him like a malignant cancer as he restlessly tossed about, an endless procession of what ifs invading every tormenting thought. He was therefore very grateful for Sheri's company when she arrived shortly after noon local time baring brunch, two trays containing steaming coffee, bacon and eggs food packs, and a meager sample of fresh produce that Tammy had harvested from the hydroponics pool. The mood between them was somber and reserved as they sluggishly picked at their trays, neither having much of an appetite. Once finished they quietly retired to the sectional sofa where there was much more silence than talk. Both were grappling with their own tortured feelings. To Matt, it was comforting just to have a few peaceful minutes with his arm around her shoulder, to feel her silky smooth cheek resting against his chest, her torso and hips warmly snuggled against his. "You know, Sheri," he finally remarked softly, "I've never felt this way before; useless, impotent. I no longer feel that I control events. They control me." Matt appreciated her respectful and understanding gaze and how she patiently listened to every word. Here was a woman who understood and appreciated the deeper machinations of his soul, and he would cherish her forever. He dipped, lovingly kissing her on the crown of her head. "In every situation I thought I took the correct and prudent steps, yet nine people have died and there is still no sign of the colonists!" As he laid back his head, Matt could feel an affectionate squeeze of fingers against his thigh.

"Stop chastising yourself," she sympathetically advised. "You did everything you could, short of abandoning the mission. And I know you won't ever consider that."

"Did I?" Matt questioned skeptically with a strange, undefined sense of guilt. "Did I indeed. Tell that to Tom Reynolds." Just the mere mention of the name caused his throat to tighten as his unrelenting grief and sorrow surged to the forefront. The others had been, unfortunately, relative strangers, but it was as if he had a road map through Reynolds' soul and he had taken the scenic parkway from end to end. "At least his nightmares are over now," he tearfully lamented in a voice cracking with emotion, a comment that Sheri could not understand. "Such a decent and honorable man didn't deserve this." Unable to contain the moisture dripping down his cheeks, Matt buried his face against Sheri's chest and openly sobbed. "It's just not right! Why did he have to die?" Matt could feel the loving caress of Sheri's hand through the hair on the back of his head as he slowly regained his composure.

"No, it's not right," she said as she locked her arms around his shoulders. "But he will always be with us as long as we remember."

Feeling slightly ashamed, Matt straightened to sit on his own weight as he wiped away a final tear. "I'm sorry, Sheri. I guess I'm not acting much like a spaceship captain."

Sheri smiled affectionately and daintily ran her hand down the side of his moist face. "No, you're not, just a human being."

Matt grinned and lightly took hold of her hand as it passed from his face, pulling it towards his mouth so he could kiss it tenderly. "Thank you, Sheri, for being here for me. I don't know about you, but I could use a drink." Matt delicately rose from the couch and strolled over to the bar cabinet where he fixed them each a tall, frosty glass. Their private moment was interrupted by the buzzing sound of the door intercom as Matt delivered the refreshment. They swapped glances of alarm before Matt, with a reluctant sigh and jingling drink in hand, moved to answer the door.

"Forgive the intrusion, sir," Sergeant Douglas said as he stepped smartly into the room upon Matt's invitation.

"Not at all, Sergeant," Matt replied as he headed back towards the sectional. "I just fixed some drinks, would you like one?"

"No, thank you, sir." Douglas courteously declined as he came to a standing rest. "I just wanted to report that I have spoken with USSM Command and we have been given our marching orders. When replacements arrive in two days, my platoon will be evaced by the Bunker Hill. I understand that you have decided to keep the Guilford Courthouse on station and remain here."

Matt leisurely shrugged as he took a seat by Sheri's side, who tossed him a look of surprise. "Well, I still have unfinished business here."

"Yes, sir. I gathered all of the Lieutenant's personal effects and will be taking the bodies back with us. I'll shortly be transmitting a letter back to his wife. He had told her of your friendship, she might appreciate a note from you."

Matt could feel the pangs of despondency begin to overwhelm him once more as his eyes glistened with moisture. His head flinched downward as he swallowed hard. "I'll send it," he struggled to answer.

Douglas turned and took a few strides towards the door before coming to an abrupt halt and spinning around. He had noticed how distraught Matt appeared. "You know, sir, people get hurt in this business."

Matt felt slightly offended as his body jolted forward. "Come on, Sergeant!" he bitterly roared. "You're not going to stand there and tell me he died for God, country, or the United States Space Marines!"

"No, sir," Douglas defensively protested. "I wouldn't say that shit to anybody. Tom Reynolds didn't leave his guts on some damn frozen wasteland millions of miles from Earth for hometown, cherry pie, medals, or any of that other bullshit. He charged his laser rifle and took it out for you, these people, and for First Platoon. Don't you give him anything less."

Matt was mollified by a sense of humility and esteem garnered from the indirect though highly profound compliment that erased his prior vexation. "Thank you, Sergeant," he modestly replied as he slumped in repose. As the Sergeant was about to leave, Matt was disturbed again by the beeping ring of the room com system. Matt irritably wiggled to his feet and walked over to the desk to answer. "Maitland here."

Nichelle's excited voice came blaring over the speaker. "There's an external transmission coming in for you, Commander."

Matt was annoyed. Those damn bureaucrats back at NSCA headquarters were always badgering and bugging him about something. "Tell those vacuum-headed paper pushers that I'll call them with a full report before the day is up."

"You don't understand, Commander," she advised with utmost vigor. "It's not from Earth. It's from here. I mean Mars. They claim the transmission point is from Perepelkin."

Everyone exchanged flabbergasted looks of astonishment.

"Shall I pipe it down there?"

Matt hesitated in confusion for a moment. "No," he decided, twitching nervously. "I'm on my way up now."

"A rather interesting development," Vijay frivolously remarked as Matt raced into A and C followed closely by Sheri and Sergeant Douglas. He had been working in the control center when the transmission was received and stood hovering behind Nichelle who relinquished her seat as Matt scurried up to the console. He was greeted by the commanding image of a middle-age woman's stoic though pleasantly contoured face in the vid monitor of the unit, capped with short trimmed but thick silver-blond hair, her engaging though despondent hazel eyes betraying the anguish of some internal strife. Her words were spoken in surprisingly good English, embellished with a heavy Germanic accent.

"Matthew Maitland, it is an honor to speak with you. I wish it could be under more pleasant circumstances. I believe it is time we talk."

Matt was noticeably tense as he stiffened in the chair. "You have me at a disadvantage, ma'am."

"Forgive me. My name is Ingrid Zeschwentz, recently elected First Consul of the newly formed and independent Colonial Martian Republic. I am sorry, Commander, that your people were unwittingly drawn into our revolution. I deeply regret any loss of life that you sustained."

Matt became enraged. "You regret!" he shouted as his body assertively lurched forward. "You regret!" Bitterness and animosity were etched all across his face. "You have killed innocent civilians, anyone who happened to be wandering around. You have killed boys barely old enough to carry a gun. You have killed people I care about who were doing their best to protect their fellow countrymen."

Matt could see the seemingly heartfelt sorrow and genuine distress that pervaded throughout her imploring gaze, but then again, she could just be performing a Clinton. "No, of course we didn't," she passionately replied. "Please believe me when I tell you I would have done anything to keep your people from becoming involved. It was EESC loyalists that killed your science team, that assaulted your facility, not us. It was our ships that destroyed the remaining attackers or this dialogue might not be occurring."

Matt was momentarily stuck in a quandary. He couldn't refute that.

"How bad were your losses?"

Matt dejectedly bowed and replied in a somber tone. "Very bad." He looked up to see her eyes droop in remorse.

"I grieve with thee. Their names shall be remembered with our own honored dead. They died as much on our behalf as they did on yours."

Matt was becoming more confused. "I don't follow you."

"Perhaps I should explain. You understand, Commander, that we have been living and growing under the slopes of Perepelkin years before the first dome of Jamestown graced the Lunae Planum landscape."

Matt's mouth was gaping in both astonishment and dismay.

"I know," she continued as if reading his mind, "in direct violation of the SCA agreement of 2042. At that time Perepelkin was well under construction and the initial inhabitants implementing the plans for the infrastructure. So we are all brigands, at least in part. But it soon became apparent that the goals and objectives of the Confederation were much different than the majority of those they convinced to settle here. Praetorian designs, dark and sinister. They wanted a clandestine base from which to study and control. The development of the ED field enabled us to accelerate the construction of our base by rendering the increased power expenditures undetectable to your monitoring instruments. Once fully functional, our government decided on a gradual military buildup in order to convert Perepelkin into primarily a military base from which they could dominate the planet when the need arose. We did not come to Mars for that purpose. The EESC was determined to keep its presence a secret until the revelation would yield the greatest political or economic advantage. The covert nature of the colony served our needs as well so there were no objections. But we were lied too, deceived, and our concerns and desires ignored."

Matt scoffed. "Even on Mars some things never change."

"Precisely. So we planned, plotted, and schemed. And when our intentions were discovered we were forced to act. We informed the EESC of our declaration to be independent and free of Earth control and rebellion ensued between us and those who still supported the Confederation. Your unfortunate exploratory team stumbled across loyalist forces on Alba Patera. You may not be aware, Commander, but you unknowingly became involved in our fight when your ship turned back the Borodino."

Matt's brows lifted in surprise. "What?"

Ingrid nodded. "The Borodino was transporting reinforcements and supplies for the Loyalist forces on Alba Patera. Your action rendered us a great favor and I thank you. The EESC could not announce what was happening or send a relief convoy for fear of exposing their clandestine operations. We also shared that desire to remain anonymous, undetected, and undisturbed until our predicament was stabilized. Without reinforcements or fresh supplies and pressed by our forces, the Loyalist position on Alba Patera became untenable. They therefore looked for the most advantageous place from which to continue the fight against us - the supposedly abandoned colony at Jamestown. I doubt that they were aware of your presence until they encountered your research team. And the rest, as your people say, is history. I must admit a certain culpability for the tragic events that befell you. We failed to stop them in time. I am deeply sorry."

Matt didn't perceive her final remark as he was intrigued by something she had previously said. "First Consul, you mentioned that Jamestown was abandoned." He had become skeptical of her forthrightness. "You wouldn't, by any chance, have any knowledge of their whereabouts?"

Matt watched with single-minded curiosity as Ingrid breathed a heavy, adverse sigh and slumped back in her plush burgundy chair, folding her arms across her stomach. "We had reports that Loyalist operatives had been subversively working within the colony for some time, creating disruption and confusion, feeding their natural fears of living on an alien world. They were trying to frighten them enough to request extraction or, at least, relocate to a more distant site. It apparently worked. The few transmissions that we were able to monitor seemed to indicate that they were preparing to move to a smaller facility that they had secretly been constructing somewhere in Valles Marineris, but we can't be sure."

"Huh....huh," Matt dubiously groaned, suspecting something else.

"But that is about all," Ingrid continued. "I'm truly sorry. We have been preoccupied with our own problems." Ingrid paused, taking note of Matt's puzzled and inquisitive look. "Yes, Commander, as you have discovered by now, Lucinda Desjardin is a stealth operative, but she's not EESC. She works for us."

Matt was incensed but managed to restrain himself from shouting. "For you! Do you realize what she put us through?"

Ingrid woefully acknowledged her awareness with a sullen nod. "I do, and I must apologize for the difficulty we caused you as well." Her tone became more assured. "Our principle objective was to keep our existence a secret. She was responsible for the sabotage of your reactor in order to delay your arrival if not encourage you to abort your mission."

Matt was fuming inside like a vat of boiling lava. "You put forty people in jeopardy!" he irascibly roared. "What gives you the right to...."

"Not true," Ingrid interrupted with a dissenting twitch of her head. "We took great pains to make sure that the damage was repairable and that no one as seriously hurt. At worst you would have been forced to shut-down the reactor. Once on the planet she employed her considerable talents to disrupt your computer and communication systems, to create distraction, tension, and discord, and to utilize your own fears of the unknown to our advantage. Anything to divert your attention away from the north."

Matt shook his head facetiously, feeling like he had been used and manipulated. "And the assault on our soldier, Nichelle's accident, the hologram?"

A crafty smirk parted her lips. "Quite correct, Commander. Upon learning of your approach we decided to establish what you might term a.... listening post, beneath the collapsed dome and installed holographic imagery to make the subterranean levels appear to be impassable. One of our people was nearly discovered when you arrived and forced to stun your man. The technician's misfortune was a regrettable mistake. She climbed the ladder before Lucinda could finish severing the supports with a laser gun."

Matt leered at her in wide-eyed astonishment.

"Yes, Commander, we have been watching you. But we never wanted to see harm come to any of your people. The Loyalist forced have been destroyed. The danger to both of us, for the moment, is over. The Confederation will no doubt react badly. If they attempt to return, we will be ready for them. I wish you success in your future endeavors but be warned, Commander, we intend to maintain our position and security. We desire no further contact until our situation is more firmly established. Do not venture beyond forty degrees north and twenty-five degrees west. We would consider such an intrusion an act of war and react accordingly. Only interaction of an emergency nature will be tolerated. I do not think that I need to remind you of our capacity to defend ourselves. When we feel the time is right, we will initiate contact if you still maintain a presence here. But for now we demand seclusion and privacy."

Matt reluctantly sighed. He certainly understood that he was in no position to challenge their wishes. "First Consul, we will abide by your restrictions. I trust that if you acquire any information regarding the Jamestown inhabitants, you will inform us."

Ingrid batted her lashes and dipped her head. "Of course, Commander. We do have one final request. You permit us to make arrangements to extricate Lucinda by hover transport from your spaceport and that you agree not to apprehend or confront her."

"She may withdraw in peace."

"Thank you, Commander. I believe that I owed you this courtesy call and an explanation of our position. This will conclude our business." Ingrid leaned forward as she stared earnestly into the transmitter camera. "It is my most treasured hope that one day your people and mine can share a common dream on this pristine world, creating a living monument to the perseverance and ingenuity of the human race."

Matt bobbed in agreement. "Let us both take steps to insure that day comes to pass."

"It would be nice, Matthew Maitland, in some future reality to be able to reach out, shake your hand, and call you friend."

"I will look forward to that day, Ingrid."

"Farewell, Matthew, take care."

"Likewise, Ingrid."

Vijay whistled in confounded amazement as the communications viewer went blank. "I've heard it all now."

Sheri looked over at Matt with a puzzled expression. "What do you make of her?"

Matt thoughtfully rubbed his chin, vacuously gazing into the air, before slumping leisurely into the chair. "I think she's genuinely sincere in the remorse she expressed and her statement of their intentions, but she's hiding something."

Caroline stood nervously by the side of the open air rover anxiously awaiting the arrival of her chameleon-like passenger, fully encased in her silver environment suit, her yellow helmet casually dangling from her left hand. She couldn't understand why her stomach was churning and tumbling like she was awaiting a blind date, but Lucinda always seemed to have a disquieting affect on her. She wasn't quite sure why but she had volunteered to escort her out to the spaceport. A hundred conflicting emotions were cascading and colliding within her mind and she had no idea what she was going to say to her. The memory of the entire sordid experience with her made Caroline feel irate, bitter, and gullible, yet strangely entranced and intrigued, like a moth attracted to the flame. She didn't have long to wait as the muffled clomp of boots and a whining rumble trumpeted Lucinda's arrival through the warehouse portal, her long, succulent blond hair wildly flowing down her shoulders and along the back of her space suit, carrying her helmet, gloves, and baggy shoulder pouch closely followed by a robotics cargo hauler containing the rest of her personal baggage. The gaping, bug-eyed stare of surprise that lit up her face upon seeing who was waiting for her was priceless to Caroline.

"Caroline!" she exclaimed with that charming smile of hers. "You're driving me out? How delightful. I expected to find Commander Maitland and a couple of heavily armed marines."

"I don't think he trusts any of the marines around you," Caroline flippantly replied. "And Matt is not too thrilled with you right now. In fact he told me to 'just get her the hell out of here.'"

Lucinda chuckled in amusement. "I really can't blame him. I tinkered with his ship, obstructed investigations, caused dissension and turmoil, and tried to seduce him."

Caroline found the final disclosure mind-boggling.

"Oh, yes," Lucinda continued when she perceived her shock. "Unfortunately, one of my few passes that fell incomplete. Very disheartening to the ego."

Caroline snickered, running a finger across her mouth before mustering the nerve to ask a more delicate question that had been nagging her. "Tell me, Lucinda. All that licentious behavior, was that just an act or are you really that depraved?"

Lucinda tossed back her head and with a short titter shook out her locks. "Well, I'm not quite that obsessed with sex. I use it like any other tool, one of my best." Her hand reached out and affectionately patted Caroline on the cheek. "But I do crave hedonistic pleasures, with men and women. I love playing those parts."

Caroline swallowed apprehensively when she noticed that familiar ravenous gaze that caused her body to shudder in both discomfort and pleasure, debating whether to continue this embarrassing line of inquiry. "And the other night...." She blushed. "....was that just part of the job?"

"At first, but I did enjoy your company. I have always found you.... interesting. I wish you would have allowed me to get more intimate."

"I almost did," Caroline shamefully replied as she turned away. "That's what bothers me."

"You now have your marine friend to look forward too"

The comment sparked another tormenting thought in Caroline's mind. "No bullshit, Lucinda. What do you really know of Dave?"

Lucinda frowned dispiritedly before leaning forward and kissing her cheek. "It's over, Caroline. Let him go. I'm sure he would want you to get on with your life." The conversation reminded Lucinda of another man. "Have you seen John Walinski? I was hoping to see him before I leave."

Caroline regretfully lowered her eyes and sadly gave her the news. "I'm sorry, Lucinda, he didn't make it back."

For the first time Caroline could see a touch of humanity in Lucinda's face as a few stray droplets wandered uncontrollably down her contorted cheek. "I really liked him," she mumbled between sniffles as she wiped away the moisture. "Shit! Story of my life. Come on, it's time to go."

Three days after the confrontation at the Echus Chaos the spaceport at Jamestown was bristling with activity as the Bunker Hill joined the Guilford Courthouse in orbit and began shuttling cargo and personnel to the surface. Matt spent the better part of the day familiarizing the newcomers with the colony layout and a synopsis of the events that had transpired since their initial arrival. He had just concluded a briefing with the leader of the fresh marine platoon when Nichelle informed him that his presence was requested in the warehouse building. First Platoon, B Company was preparing to depart. All except for Corporal Cooke, who would complete his recovery under Susan Oliver's care at Jamestown. Wanting to see them off, he hurriedly excused himself from the meeting, grabbed Sheri's hand, and together they boarded an interdome shuttle cart and headed for the Industrial Dome and the attached warehouse building.

Upon entering the expansive storage facility, Matt instantly observed a smartly dressed line of seven marines, attired in their olive jackets and pants and high-neck mustard turtlenecks, those peculiar though esteemed high crown, wide brim, black Hardee hats and their lavish adornments perched atop their heads. Private Jamison stood on the far right of the line proudly holding erect their battle flag. Behind them near their transport rovers neatly hung their deep bronze space suits on a portable garment rack, impeccably spotlessly clean and tidy, all grime, soiled blotches, and rustic stains steamed and air brushed into oblivion. Sergeant Douglas, standing to the left, stepped two paces forward and neatly pivoted to address his men. "First Platoon. Atten....tion!"

As if one being, six pairs of boots clicked together and laser rifles snapped to their sides, the ends of the stocks settling on the floor with a light, metallic thud. Matt was briefly taken aback by the formality as he approached the formation while Sheri respectfully stood off to the side. "Well, Sergeant, you fellows ready to bug out of here?"

The Sergeant stood rigid. "First Platoon, B Company requests permission to depart, sir."

Matt felt a sudden sadness come over him. "Permission granted," he dispiritedly replied. "And thank you. Thanks for everything."

"Before we leave, sir," Douglas announced, "we request permission to make an official proclamation to be entered into the company records."

Matt's brows rose in curiosity. "Very well, Sergeant."

Douglas cleared his throat as he removed a folded piece of paper from his pocket and studied the scribbled notes as Matt stood near him.

"For conspicuous gallantry in the face of multiple crisis and for intrepid, faithful, and selfless support of all operations of the platoon, the officers and men of First Platoon, B Company, First Regiment, United States Space Marines, do hereby proclaim Matthew Maitland, Captain, CAS Guilford Courthouse, an honorary member of the Iron Brigade and as a result do bestow upon him the revered symbol of our unit, our black hat."

Private Anderson stepped out from his place in line and approached Matt holding out in offering one of the historical head pieces. "Please accept this, sir, in honor of our fallen comrades."

Matt was dumbfounded and numb, feeling woefully inadequate and unworthy of such a gift. Every fiber of his existence tingled with the anxiety of the turbulent emotions surrounding the tremendous homage and respect they paid him and his humility in his belief that he did nothing deserving. He could barely utter a response. "I....I can't accept this," he stuttered as he held out a declining hand. "I don't deserve to...."

"Oh yes you do," Douglas boldly asserted, "if you'll pardon me saying, sir. You were willing to come to our aid in the heat of battle. From the outset you displayed leadership and courage. You treated every member of this platoon with dignity and respect. The men appreciated that, sir."

Anderson shoved the brim against Matt's hand. "Please, sir."

Matt's throat tightened like a noose as he modestly opened his palms and clasped the hat, gingerly pulling it to his body as Anderson returned to his place in line. Fingering the crown reverently he turned to glance at Sheri, beaming with pride as she sucked in her lower lip and brushed away a poignant tear, equally affected by the moving gesture. Still stupefied, Matt devoutly turned the hat in his hands and replied in a cracking voice. "Thank you, Sergeant. I will treasure this for the rest of my life." Unsure of what he would say, Matt stepped in front of the tiny assembly as his entire experience with them flashed by in a wink. He pictured Cooke on the surface, Reynolds' Henry V speech, slithering down darkened corridors, the battle with the robot, Nichelle's rescue, the harrowing journey in the dust storm, the collapsed dome, the mangled bodies strewn across the Martian hillside. That's what the hat meant to him. He could feel his sentimental emotions swelling, threatening to overwhelm him. But these were US Space Marines, and weakness was something he dare not show. Summoning all his strength to keep from breaking down, Matt passionately addressed the platoon with one simple, heartfelt phrase. "Gentlemen, it has been an honor....to serve with you." Snapping to attention, Matt raised his right hand to his forehead and gave his best rendition of a formal salute. The marines immediately returned the gesture.

"Good luck." Matt moved back to Douglas and offered his hand with a respectful nod. "All the best, Geroy."

Later that evening Matt and Sheri found themselves leisurely lounging on the cushions of his sofa in T-shirts and pants after the first hearty meal they had eaten in days. Matt still had the Hardee hat in his hand, caressing it respectfully like a priceless ancient artifact. "You know, Sheri." he said, pointing to the sacred item. "I never knew much about most of those guys." He shook his head dejectedly. "Never again. We should remember as much as we can about those we lost." His hand dropped aimlessly to the side as he scoffed in disgust. "I can't believe how some of the others ostracized them like the plague."

Sheri alluring slid and wiggled beside him, salaciously brushing a protruding breast against his arm. "I think that you may find a change in some of them after these last three weeks. Maybe even Susan Oliver."

Matt glared at her repugnantly. "That'll be the damn day!"

"You know, Matt," she said as she twirled a finger through his lengthening black hair, "some of the crew weren't pleased with your decision to remain here another three or four weeks."

Matt shrugged without concern as he put a hand to her waist. "I know. I suppose they are anxious to get back to Earth. This is not exactly your ideal vacation spot. But I just couldn't leave yet. I want to make sure we hang on to this little piece of Mars, more than anything in my life."

Sheri tossed him a quizzical look.

"Sounds crazy, doesn't it," he continued with a grin. "This barren, arid, popsickle scab on a carbon dioxide planet. You can't have all your oars in the water to want to live here. But the values change somewhere, somehow." He peered at her pensively. "Maybe when the first man died." After a reflective pause Matt dismissed the remark with a flick of his wrist. "Hell, Sheri, I don't know how to explain it. It just kind of grows on you."

Sheri pressed close and pecked him lovingly on the cheek. "You're a good man, Matt, and I think I know what you mean. A person can't put a higher value on something than to die for it, and if that's the case, then Jamestown is more valuable than all the precious metals mined here."

Matt smiled at her adoringly as their arms coiled around each other in an affectionate embrace, their lips fervently locking together. Just as their desirous hands began to intimately roam. they were shaken by the irritating buzz of the door com.

"I hate it when this happens," Sheri resentfully snapped as they abruptly straightened themselves on the couch.

With a friendly tickle to her ribs, Matt reached for the nearby electronic remote. opened the door and in stepped Lieutenant Sean McTavish, Third Platoon, A Company, First Regiment, United States Space Marines, as per previous invitation.

"Did you wish to see me. sir?" the young officer with fiery red hair and a slight Scottish accent politely inquired.

"Yes, Lieutenant. come in. Myself and a couple of my associates will be leaving in the morning for four or five days to take a look at Valles Marineris. Sort of a working vacation, you understand. I would like you to assemble your men in the warehouse building at zero-eight hundred. I would like a few words with each one of them."

"As you wish. sir." he consented with a perplexed look.

"Would you like a drink, Lieutenant?"

"Don't mind if I do, sir."

"Good. good," Matt remarked as he stood and walked towards the bar cabinet. "Have a seat, Lieutenant, and tell us about yourself. And by the way, the name is Matt."

The shadows crept steadily up the steep, scalloped walls of Candor Chasm, slowly masking the distinctive layered hues of red, orange, and tan as the receding sun fell towards the horizon. To Matt, Sheri, Caroline, and Vijay it was an awe inspiring sight. They stood atop the rugged precipice of Ferguson Peak, named after the first man to set foot upon it, a huge finger-like escarpment, and looked out over the great canyon system of Valles Marineris that majestically opened before them across their entire field of view and well beyond. The vista was made all the more wondrous and mystical by the sight of the blue sun dipping below the fractured landscape, the unusual sunset made possible because the microscopic dust particles constantly suspended in the atmosphere were more affective at bending blue light at small angles than red. Candor was one of the northern tributaries in the central part of this massive series of interconnected canyons that cut a huge 3,000 mile swath across the equatorial region.

Eddies and backwashes of smaller tributary chasms branched off from the major systems in all directions. Beyond their horizon to the southeast, Valles Marineris opened into a gaping hole over 300 miles wide and in some places four miles deep. In the fading light of dusk they were mesmerized by the steeply gullied canyon walls, the spurs between them sharply fluted with branching spines. In some places the sides of the walls had collapsed to form landslides and fan-shaped tongues of debris along the floor. They saw thick layered deposits that formed flat-topped mesas displaying a distinctively different fine vertical fluting than the pattern of corrosion on the canyon walls. The topographical immensity was numbing.

Caroline sighed in contentment. "I would have never believed that such beauty and peace could exist on this barren place."

Sheri perceived the emotional conflict racing through her mind. "You still think about him, don't you? We may yet find him out there?"

"Perhaps," she acknowledged with a nod. "I truly pray that he is well but I've made peace with my decision. I lost Dave years ago and I have only myself to blame. Now I have a new life, and maybe a new love. That's all I want now. I won't make the same mistake again."

Matt was captivated by the natural beauty, the finely sculpted cliffs and richly combined hues and tints that no human artist could ever hope to rival. "Look at that! Tell me there is no divine inspiration at work."

Sheri sauntered close to him and adoringly took hold of his hand. "Do you remember what you told me on the bridge that night? Do you really think that God is out there somewhere?"

Matt twitched. "No, no. He's not out there." He turned to gaze into her faceshield and tapped her helmet with his gloved knuckles. "He's in here. I finally saw the evidence for myself. I guess I've always known."

Sheri looked at him in puzzlement. "What do you mean?"

"I saw God at work in the life and death of Tom Reynolds. I saw Him in the compassionate heart of Caroline; in the thoughtfulness and support of my good friend Vijay; in the selfless and courageous actions of a group of young, undaunted marines." His hands reached out and tightly clutched her shoulders. "And especially within the soul of my esteemed Flight Officer, who stood by my side with love, invaluable counsel, and who was a great source of strength and comfort. Yes, God is a part of all of us. We just have to let Him in."

"That's a nice way to think about it," Sheri replied as she clasped his hand once more and together they scanned the dimming countryside.

"I discovered something else too." Matt casually added.

"Oh!" Sheri looked at him curiously. "What's that?"

Matt gingerly turned and took both her hands, gazing at her in silent reverence as his fingers tenderly squeezed. "I love you, Sheri. I love and adore you more than life itself, and I want you to be in my life forever."

Even in the subdued light Matt could see the radiant joy spreading across her velvety face. "Matt!" she cried. "Are you proposing to me?"

Matt shuffled his feet in the dust as a sudden bashfulness came over him. "I believe that was the general idea I was trying to convey."

Sheri leaped into the air and fell into his arms, embracing as affectionately as possible within the confines of their silvery environment suits. "Yes, Matt, yes, yes. I love you so much."

"We can pick out a diamond and wedding bands when we get back to Earth," Matt remarked as they separated but continued to keep an arm around the other's waist. "I've been kind of preoccupied lately."

Sheri laughed as Caroline and Vijay, overhearing the conversation, rushed to congratulate them. Sheri left Matt to accept an emphatic hug from an exuberant Caroline who nearly crushed her life-support pack in her enthusiasm. "I'm so happy for you," she cried in joy as she smothered Sheri in a swinging cradle. "Perhaps this signifies a new beginning for all of us."

Matt and Vijay were shaking hands and exchanging brotherly slaps on the shoulder, Vijay lacing his congratulations with crafty, comedic quips. When the elation of the moment had subsided they all stood together, hand-in-hand, and once again admired the darkening view of the etched and carved world before them.

"I hope that you're right, Caroline," Matt commented wistfully. "Perhaps we are on the verge of a new harmony, a brave new world."

"Matt," Sheri's solemn voice beckoned, "do you think Lieutenant Reynolds ever understood what he had done?"

"Yes, Sheri," Matt confidently replied with a gentle squeeze of her hand. "I'm sure that he does. They all do. Now it's up to us. Us and our mysterious friends to the north - to make something good out of the opportunity they have given us."

Vijay pivoted towards Matt with a peculiar look of uncertainty. "I can hear that familiar contemplative tone in your voice, Matt. Are you, perhaps, considering staking a claim here?"

A wily grin turned up Matt's lips as he casually rolled his shoulders, stammering briefly before uttering his response. "I would be lying if I said that I didn't find that particular notion strangely compelling, but that is a story for another time."

"Well, I don't mean to break up this sentimental party," Vijay continued as his feet nervously scuffed the ground, "but it's getting late. We will have to wait until tomorrow to set up the seismic and thermal detectors that those investigators from the Space Affairs Department want us to plant. Even with sophisticated equipment, it could take years to find the location of the colonists if they have no desire to be discovered. That is an awfully big hole out there."

"It'll take a lot longer than that, Vij," Matt mindfully proclaimed. "We can look all we want, but it will be a waste of time." All eyes stared mystified at him as he continued to observe the tantalizing landscape.

"What are you talking about?" Vijay unknowingly asked.

"They're not out there, Vij," Matt reluctantly responded as he motioned northward with a flick of his head. "They're up there, with them!"

Deep within the softly illuminated honeycombed chambers of Perepelkin, Ingrid Zeschwentz soberly watched the image of Jamestown on the central viewer of the settlement's control center, transmitted from a secret camera positioned in the distant hills. She observed the heightened activity between the spaceport and the domes, but all appeared peaceful enough, a pleasant change from the events of a few nights ago. Her private deliberations were interrupted by a call from her Slavic associate sitting at the monitoring station. "He has returned."

"Thank you, Vlad. Have him report here, please." She pondered the situation for awhile before she began to think aloud. "I detest being deceitful. I wish I could have been more honest with them."

"Our situation is too precarious right now," Vlad replied, spinning in his chair to face her. "It is best they know as little as possible."

"You are right, of course. Our survival here is perched atop a delicate balance. No need to risk tipping the scales at this point."

Their attention was directed to the doorway where a tall, husky, middle-aged man strolled into the room wearing a plain green one-piece work suit. His shortly cropped hair was graying on the sides and his face was sporting the nubs of a five o'clock shadow that had arrived a little early and the wrinkled, forlorn expression of some recent stress.

"Welcome back," Ingrid happily greeted as she rose from her chair and met her compatriot with a friendly peck on the cheek. "How was your sojourn north?"

"Just fine," he replied in perfect English with a slight southern twang. "Our water extraction station above the Hyperboreus aquifer is now operational at full capacity. You can rescind the rationing program. And the production from the northern permafrost is exceeding initial estimates. Aren't you glad you invited me along?"

"Very," Ingrid replied with a smile as she returned to her chair. "You missed all the excitement."

"So I heard," the man replied as he moved to her side and somberly stared at the screen with a worried frown. "Any news of her?"

"Don't worry, she's fine," Ingrid encouragingly assured with a gentle pat to his hand. "Lucinda's back. I'm sure that she will have scores of interesting stories to tell you."

He grinned briefly. "I bet. How long do you think you can keep this bottled up? When do you think you can announce the truth? They are bound to suspect."

Ingrid shrugged. "They do or they don't, it does not matter. Just so they stay clear of our area. Hopefully soon, but we must first insure our own self-sufficiency and security. There are still many problems to solve and we are not prepared for an international or interplanetary incident. The continued mystery will be advantageous for us, for now. You must start thinking like a Martian, my friend."

The man gazed nostalgically at the image of the place he knew so well and felt a single tear roll serenely down his cheek.

"I feel sorry for you," Ingrid consoled. "You still miss her."

He lowered his head and nodded morosely. "I do. I try to forget, but I can't." His head jolted up upon containing his sadness. "But no regrets. This is what I always wanted ever since I first set foot here."

"Welcome to the New World, Dave."

David Hart took one final sentimental glance at the distant geodesic domes glistening and flickering under the burnished solar rays. "I'm sorry, Caroline," he quietly mumbled under his breath. "Please forgive me, my love. You came too late for us, for I am Martian now."